Equinoxes

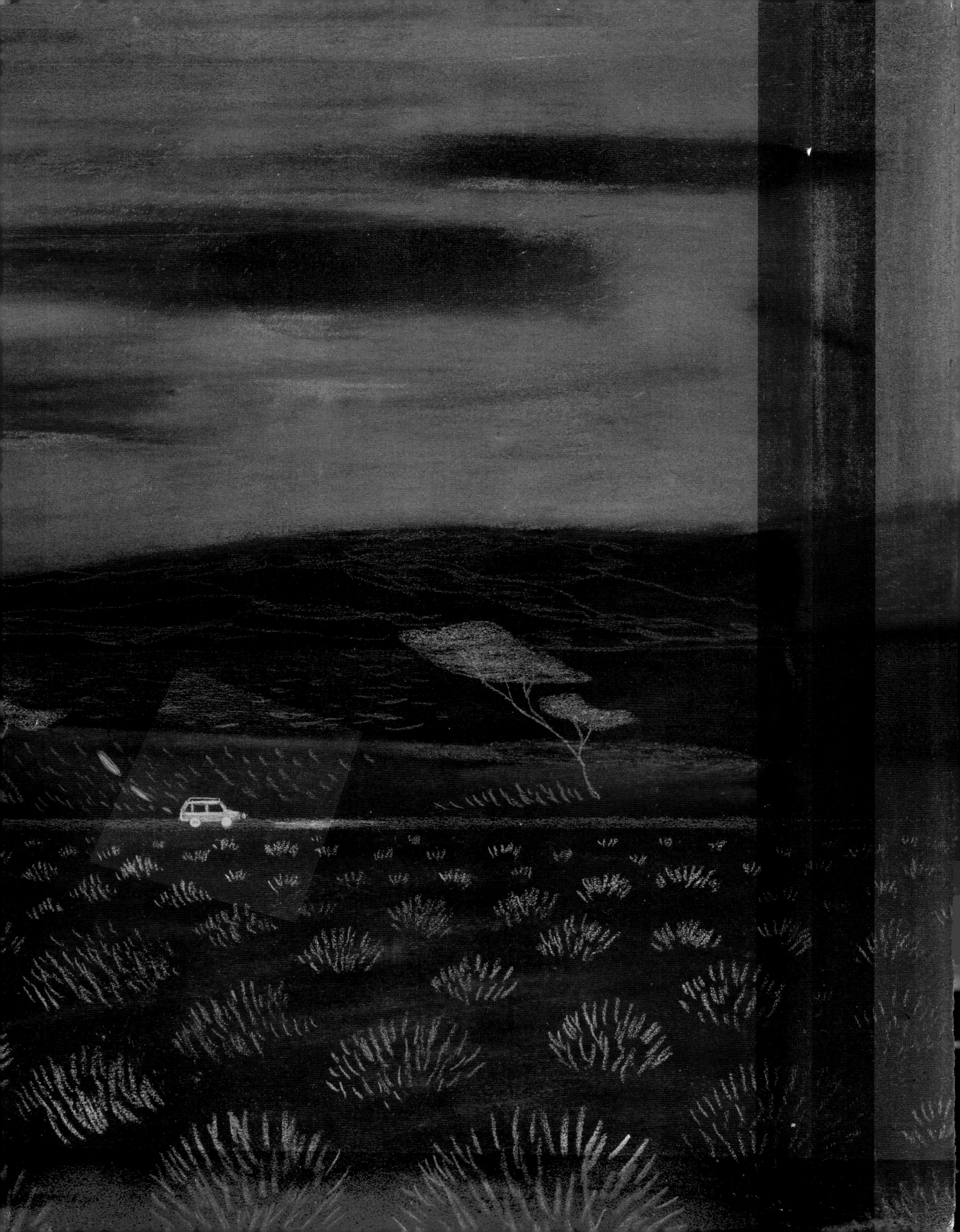

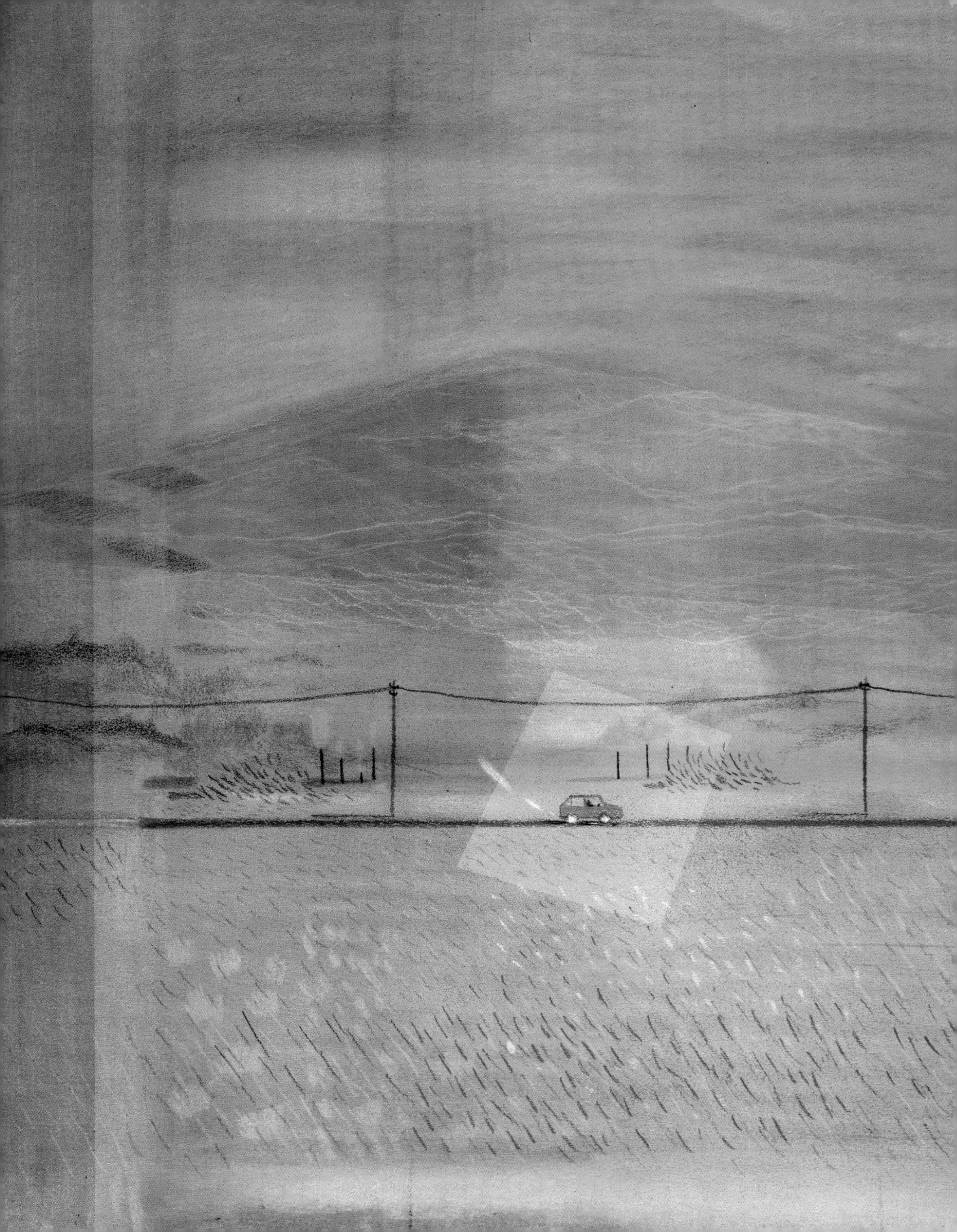

ISBN: 978-1-68112-080-5
Library of Congress Control Number: 2016908279
Originally published in French as Les Equinoxes
© Dupuis 2015, by Pedrosa
www.dupuis.com, all rights reserved.
© NBM 2016 for the English translation
Translation by Joe Johnson
Lettering by Ortho
Book Design by Philippe Ghielmetti

Distributed by IPG

1st printing September 2016 in China

Equinoxes

PEDROSA

nbm GRAPHIC NOVELS
Nantier · Beall · Minoustchine
NEW YORK

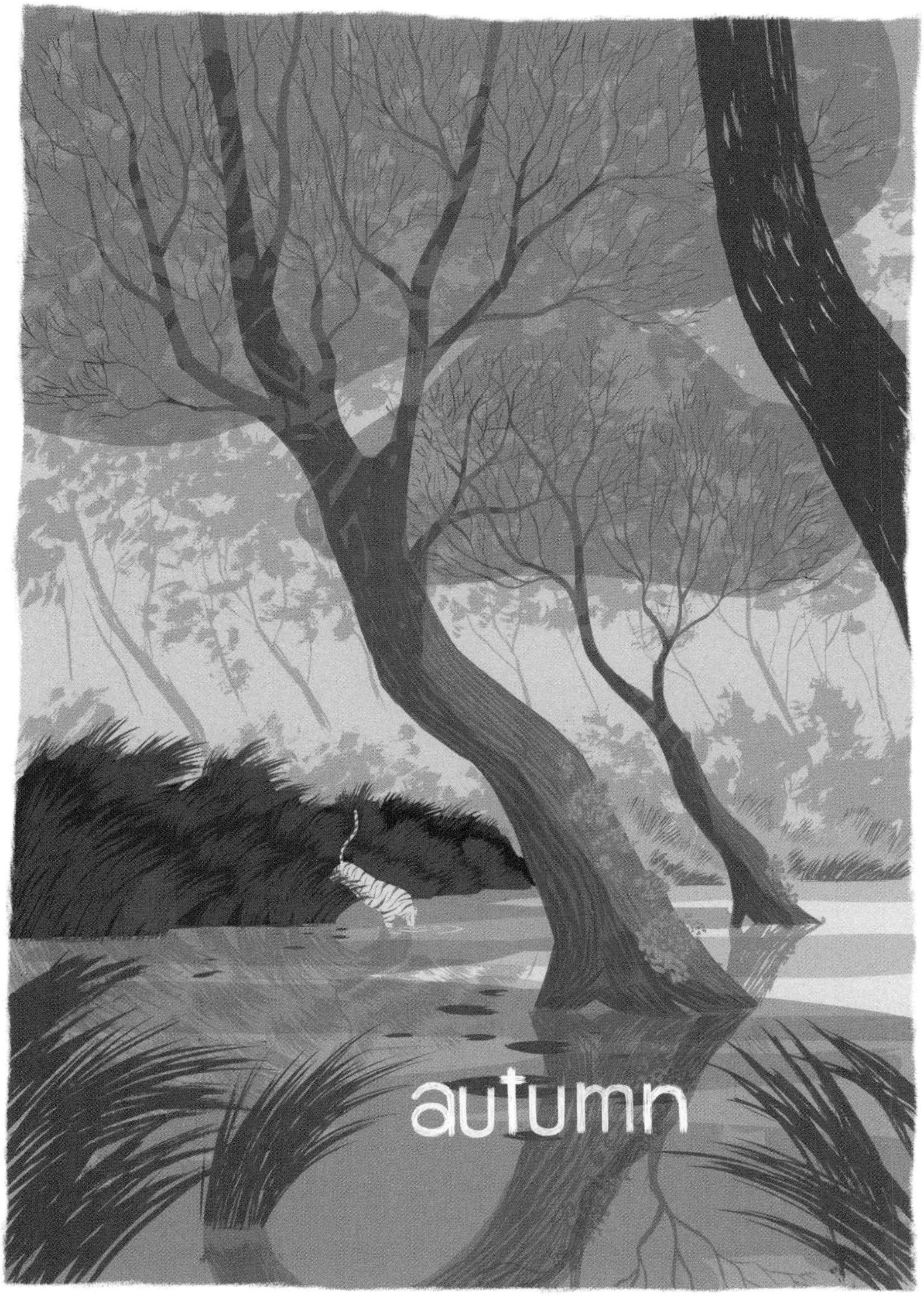
autumn

13

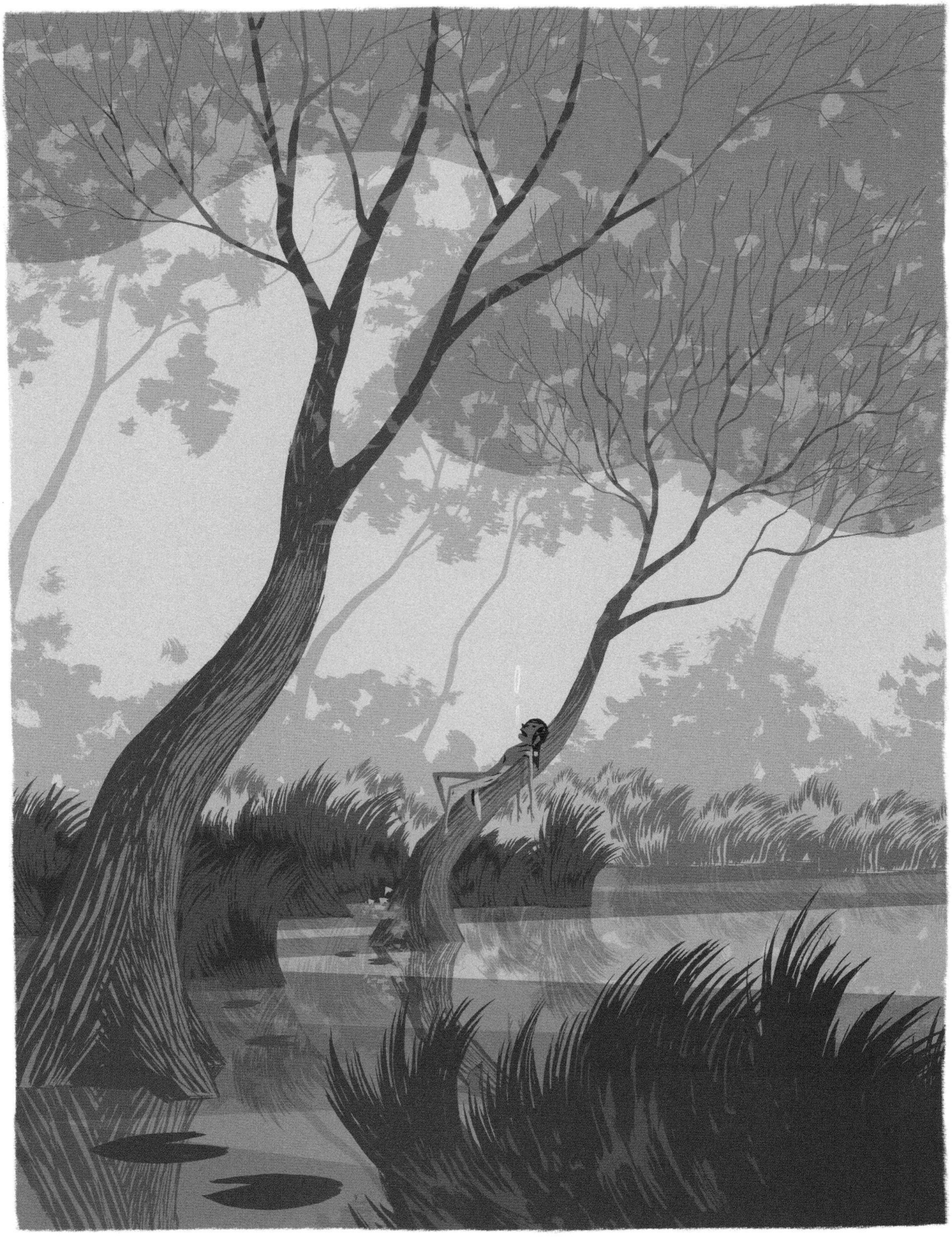

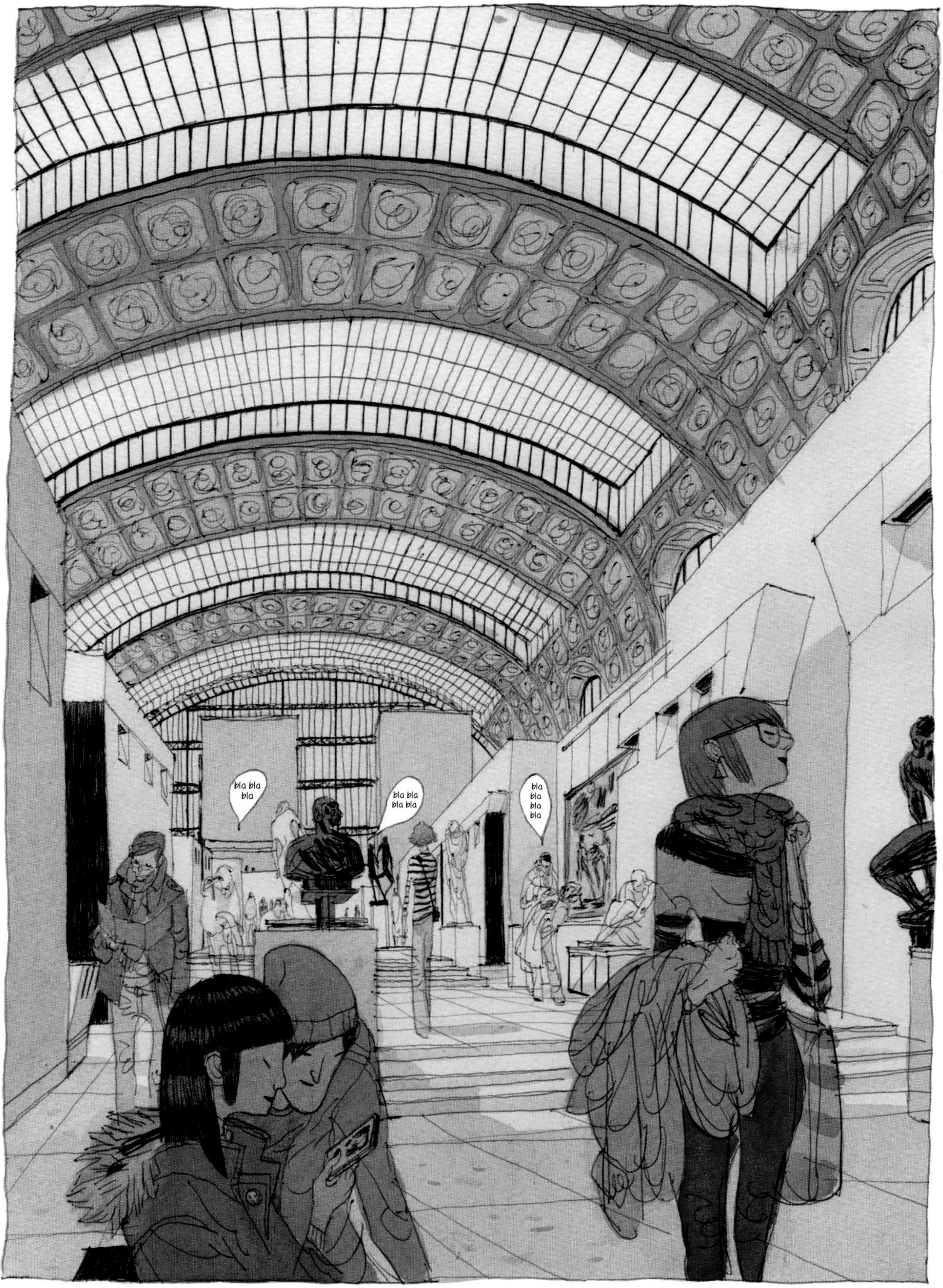
bla bla
bla
bla bla
bla bla
bla
bla
bla
bla

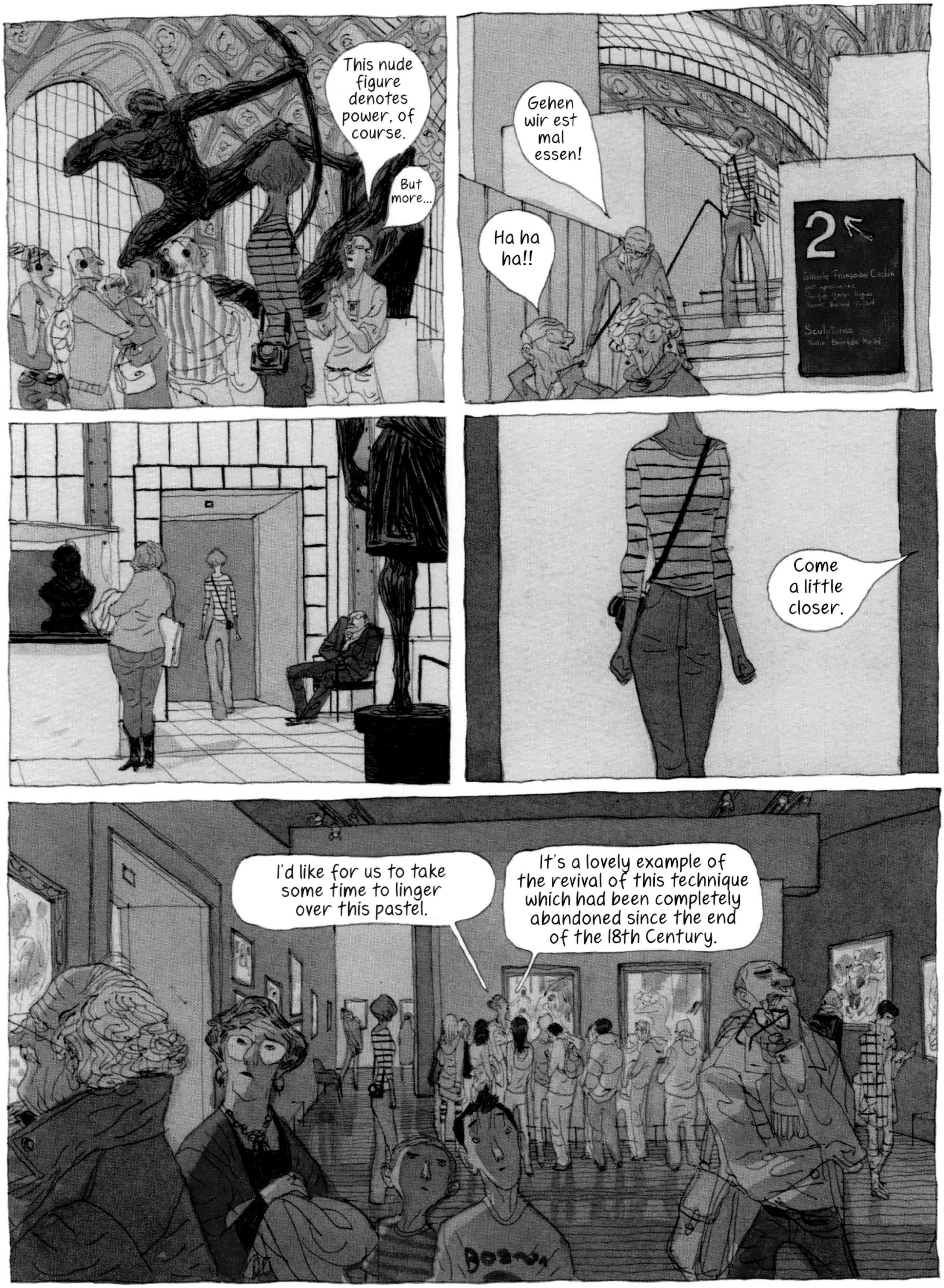
This nude figure denotes power, of course.
But more...
Gehen wir est mal essen!
Ha ha ha!!
2
Galerie Françoise Cachin
Sculptures
Come a little closer.
I'd like for us to take some time to linger over this pastel.
It's a lovely example of the revival of this technique which had been completely abandoned since the end of the 18th Century.

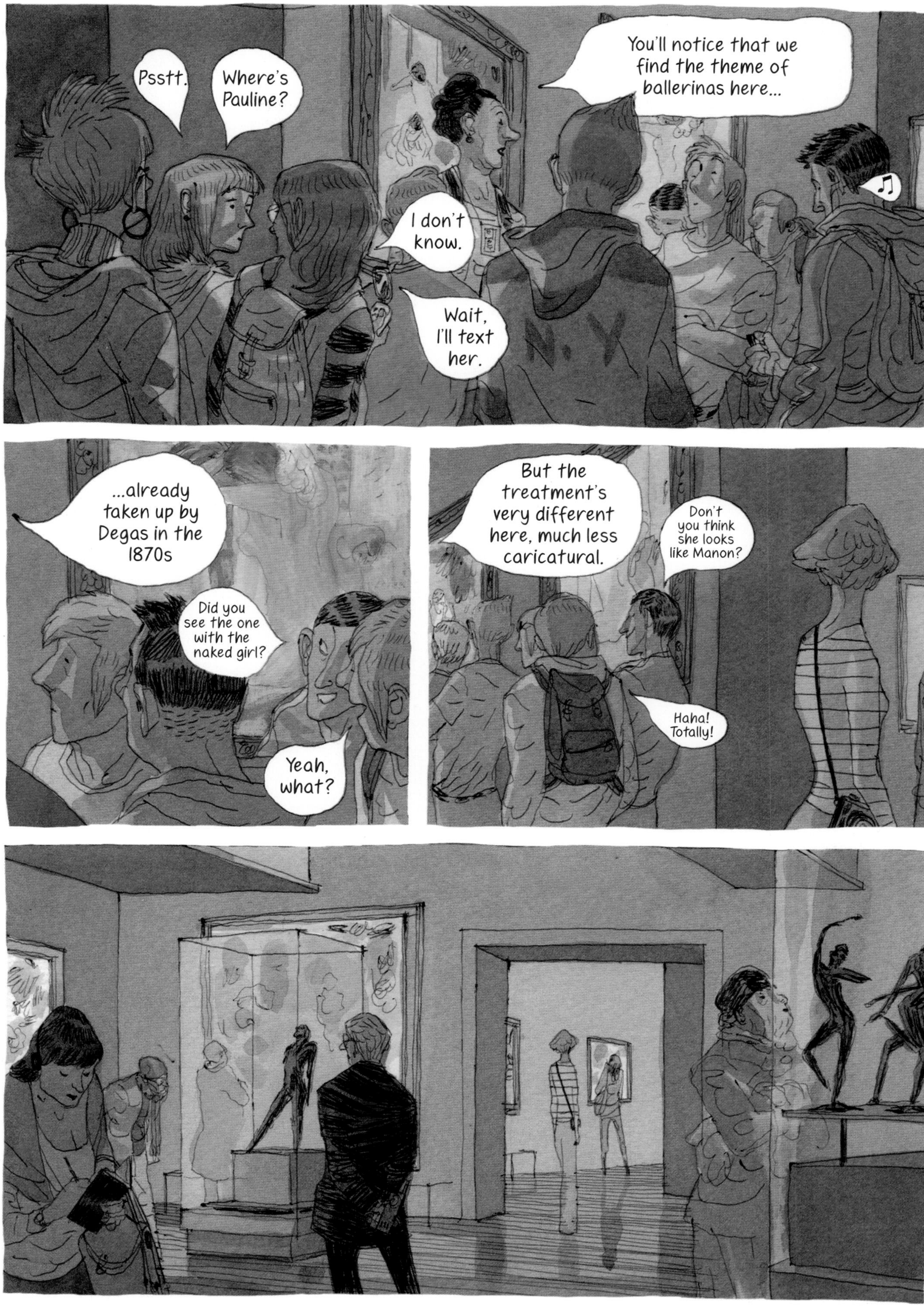
Psstt.
Where's Pauline?
You'll notice that we find the theme of ballerinas here...
I don't know.
Wait, I'll text her.
...already taken up by Degas in the 1870s
Did you see the one with the naked girl?
Yeah, what?
But the treatment's very different here, much less caricatural.
Don't you think she looks like Manon?
Haha! Totally!

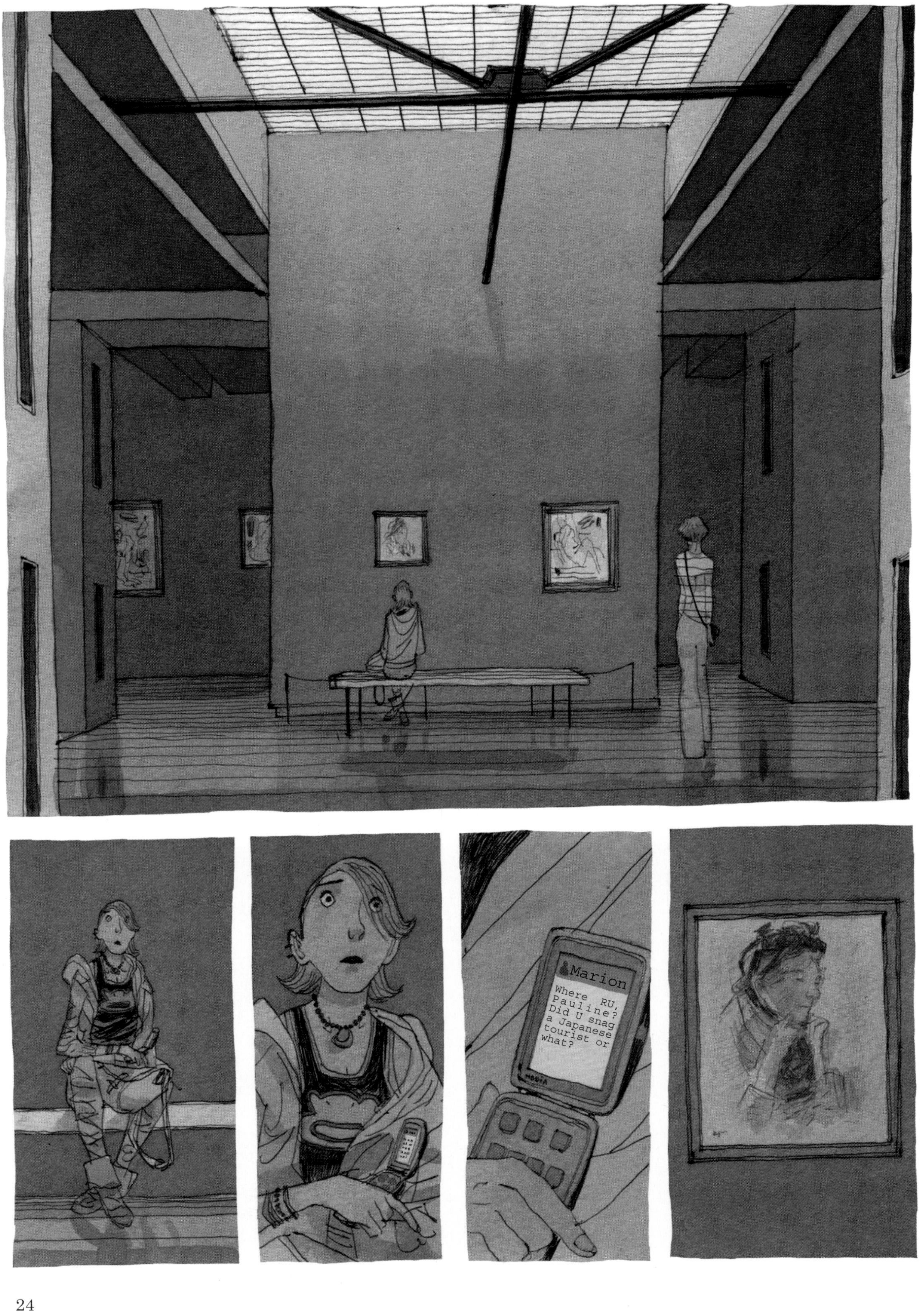
Marion
Where RU, Pauline? Did U snag a Japanese tourist or what?

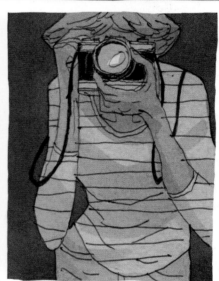

click

She was learning
without the desire to.

Like someone trudging up arid mountains with a robotic step...

Short of breath and her legs raw, in a place where others seemed to prance lightheartedly.

The visit had slowly dragged on since the beginning of the afternoon,
long hours of a familiar boredom.

Sitting on this bench, here or elsewhere, it didn't really matter very much, basically.

But it had been relaxing to keep apart from the group for a short while.

After a respite of a few minutes, she slowly raised her head and was getting ready to rejoin the other students from the Aristide Briand High School, but something held her back.

Midway up the wall she was facing, on a sheet of gray paper, scarcely bigger than an 11x17' sheet unfolded vertically, the charcoal portrait, enhanced with white, of a young woman tying up her hat.

An unexpected disquiet had been going through her since she began observing that image which summoned her entire attention. There, inside it, she seemed to see emerging within her some unknown place.

An immense lake.

The water seems a little cold still to her, but she'd like to go swimming in it one day. It must be good to just dive right in. To extricate yourself from the ground without hesitating, with taut muscles. To savor that brief second suspended between sky and earth, when your body no longer exists, before immersing yourself completely.
But she doesn't know how to swim, not yet.

For the moment, she stretches out on the shore, enviously watching the swimmers enjoying themselves and the waves sparkling in the light wind. Maybe tomorrow she'll try to walk around it.

It's a very beautiful lake.

AIRPORT NO!!!

AIRPO NO

Antoine?

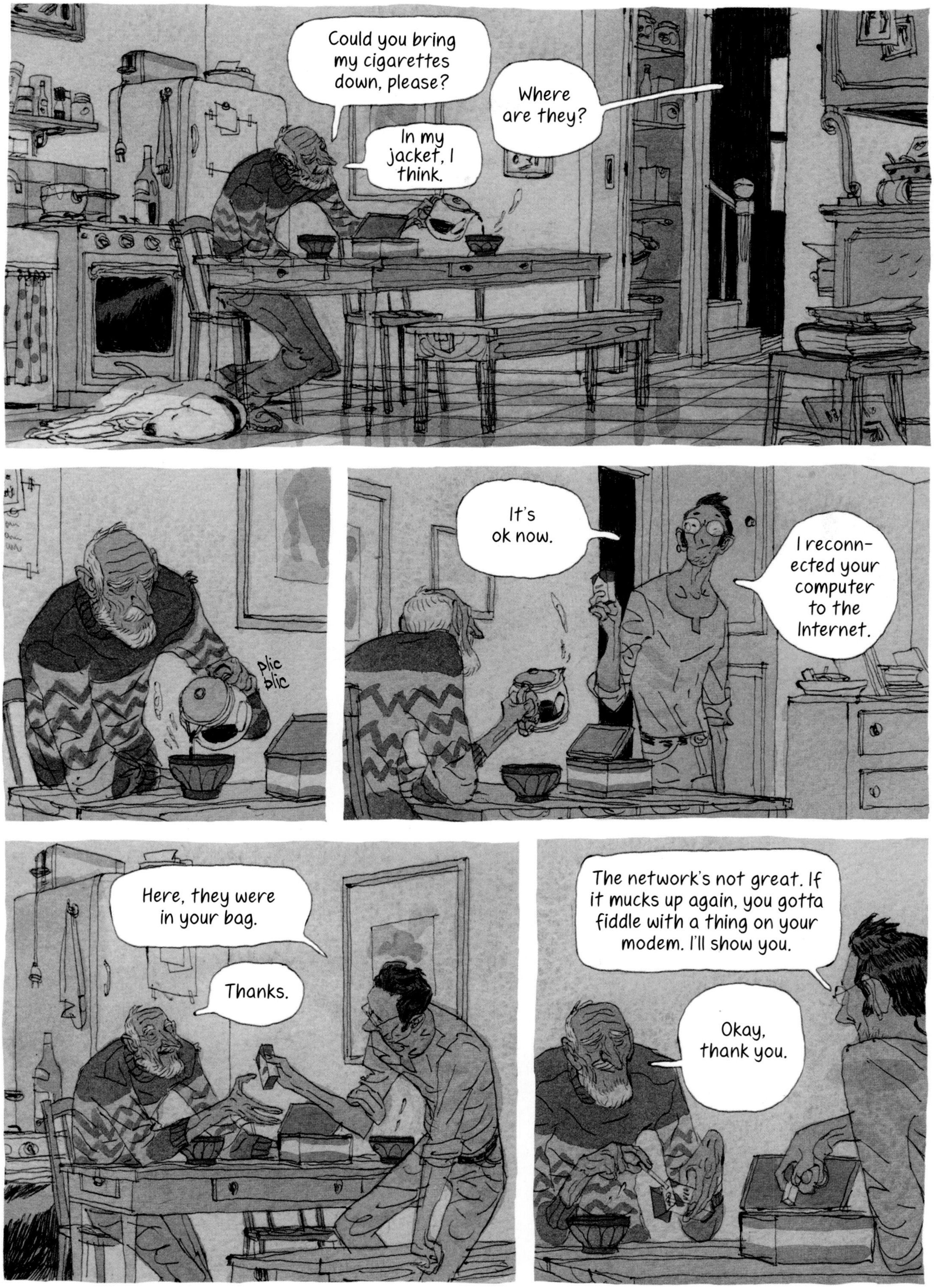
Could you bring my cigarettes down, please?
Where are they?
In my jacket, I think.
plic plic
It's ok now.
I reconn-ected your computer to the Internet.
Here, they were in your bag.
Thanks.
The network's not great. If it mucks up again, you gotta fiddle with a thing on your modem. I'll show you.
Okay, thank you.

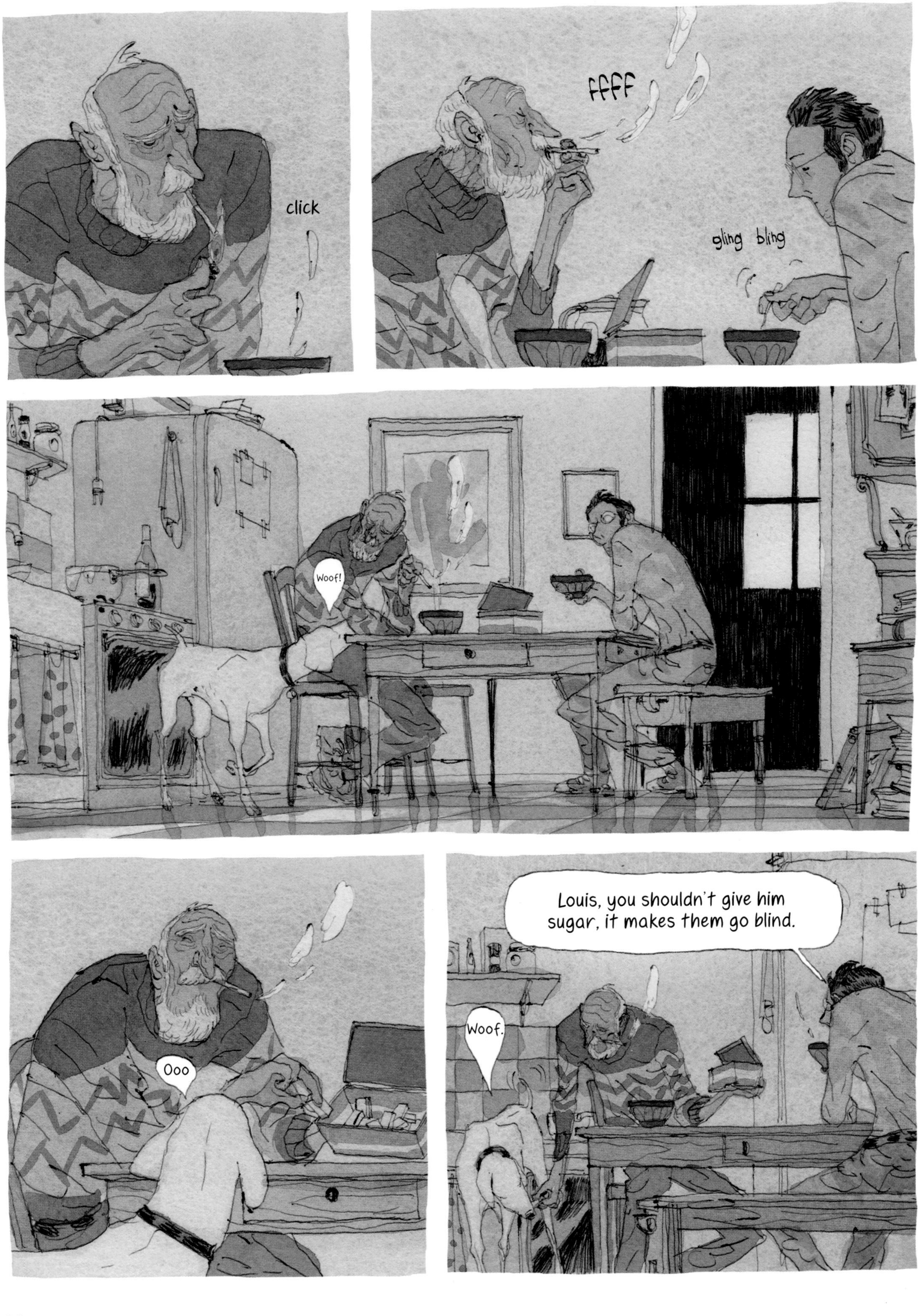
click
ffff
gling bling
Woof!
Ooo
Louis, you shouldn't give him sugar, it makes them go blind.
Woof.

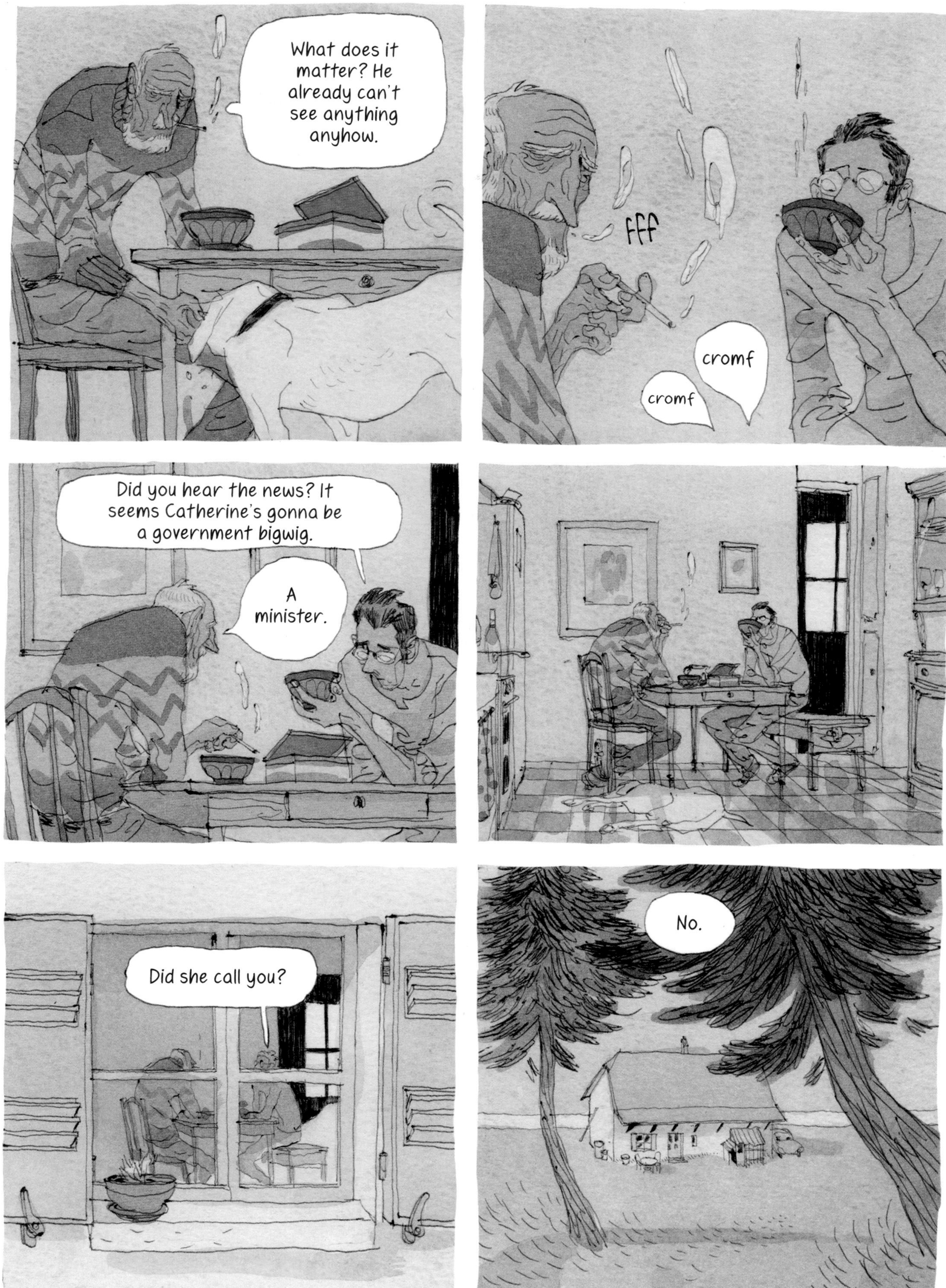
What does it matter? He already can't see anything anyhow.
fff
cromf
cromf
Did you hear the news? It seems Catherine's gonna be a government bigwig.
A minister.
Did she call you?
No.

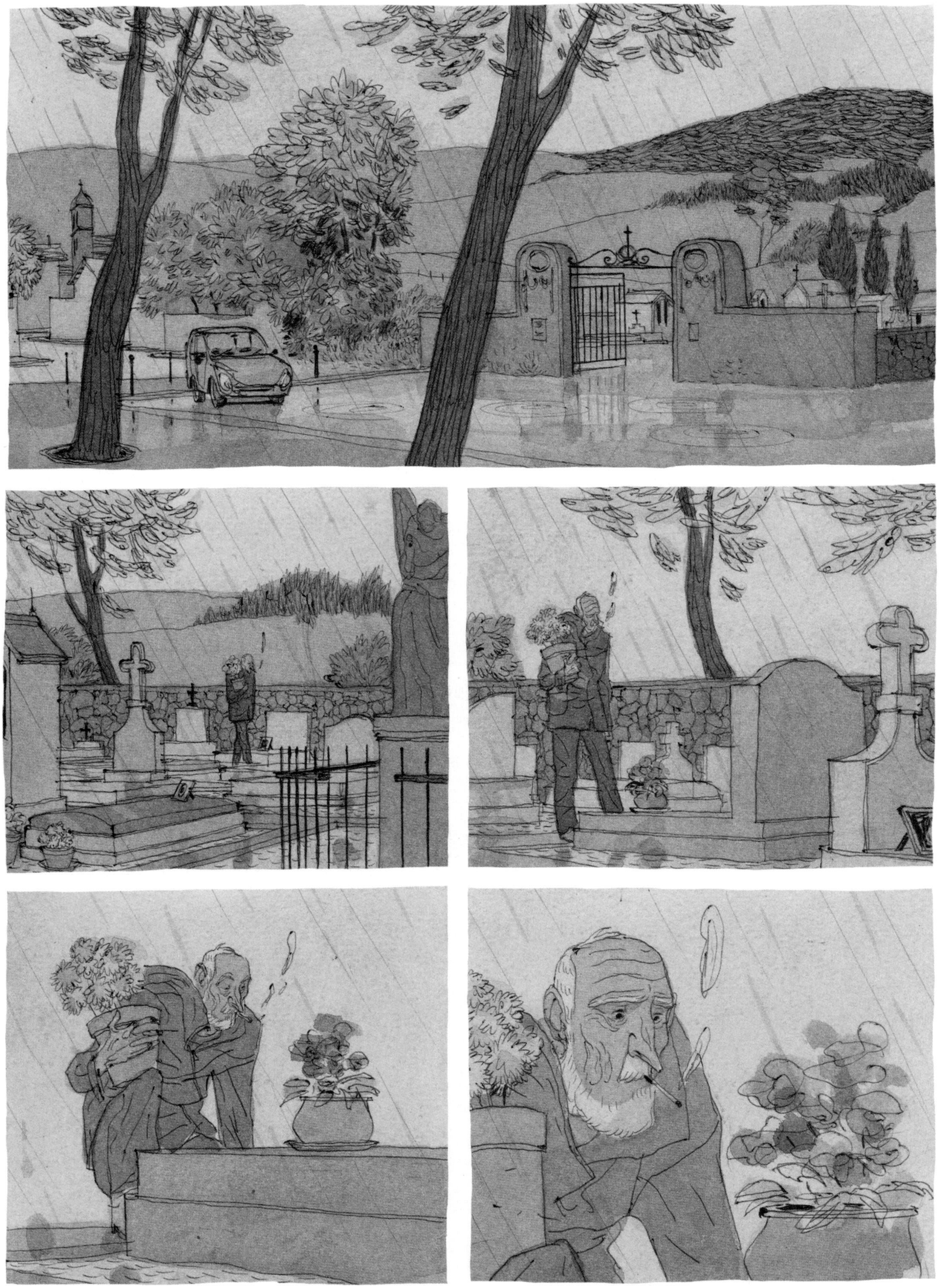

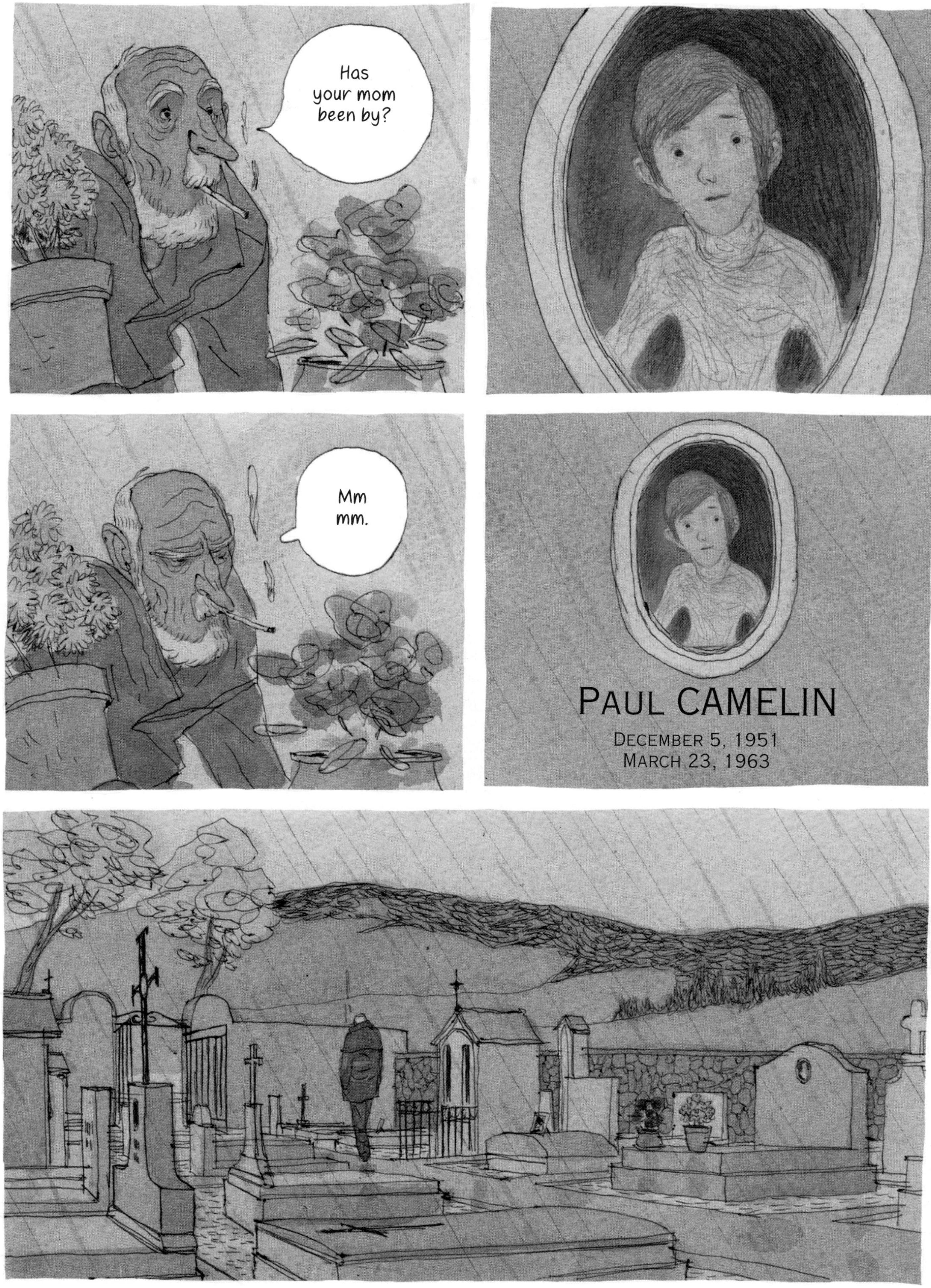
Has your mom been by?
Mm mm.
PAUL CAMELIN
DECEMBER 5, 1951
MARCH 23, 1963

Hh.
Hhh
Uh, Vincent?
Hh hh!
I think he's trying to say something.
Hhh!
Who is?
Hh!! Hh!!
Oh.
Yeah.
Hhh.
Two more minutes.
I'm almost done.

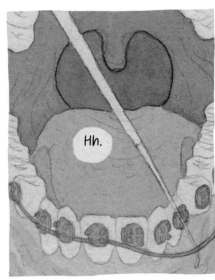

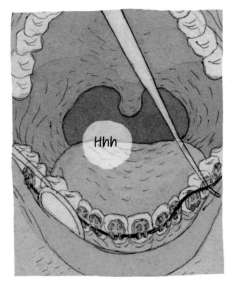

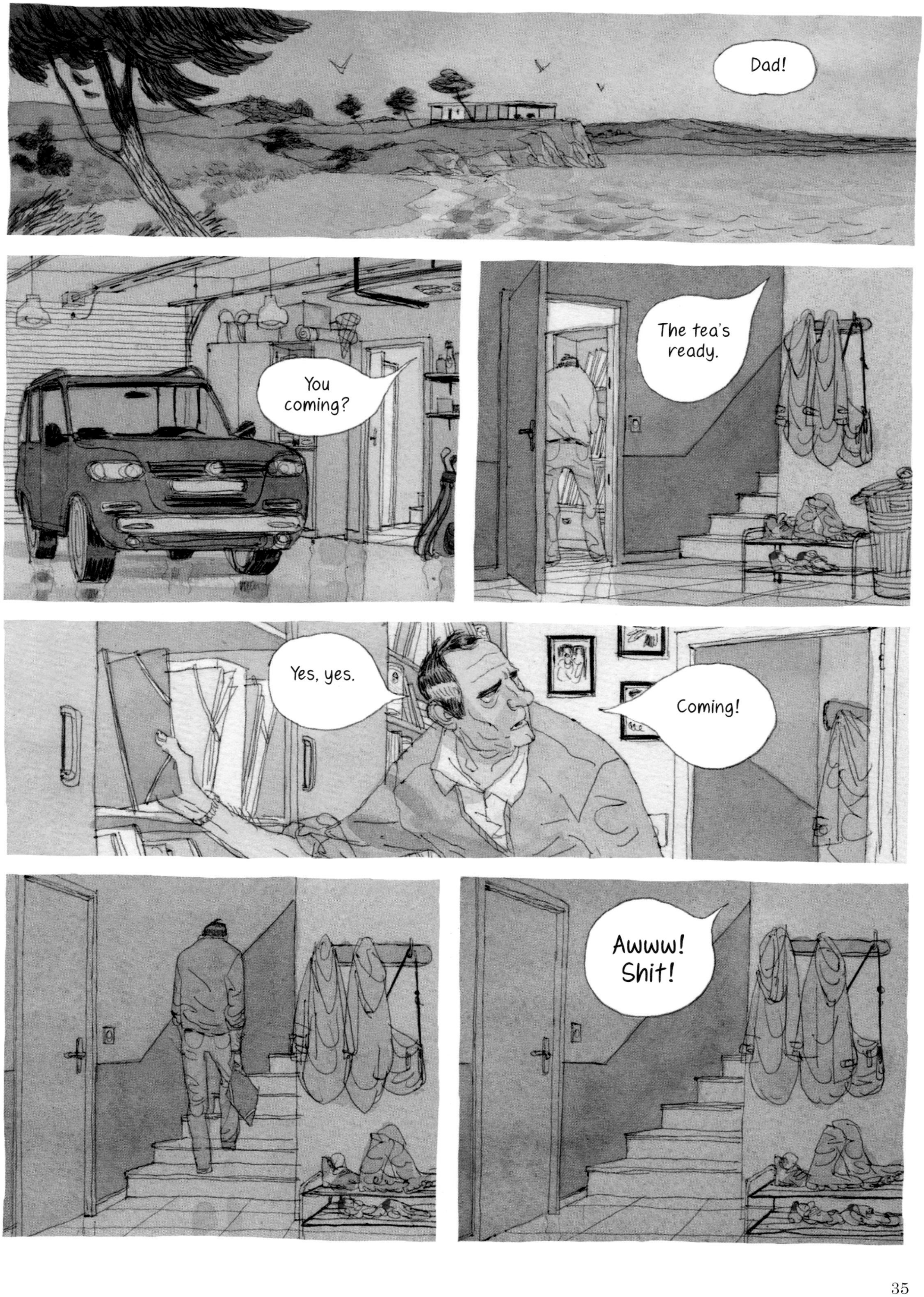
Dad!
You coming?
The tea's ready.
Yes, yes.
Coming!
Awww! Shit!

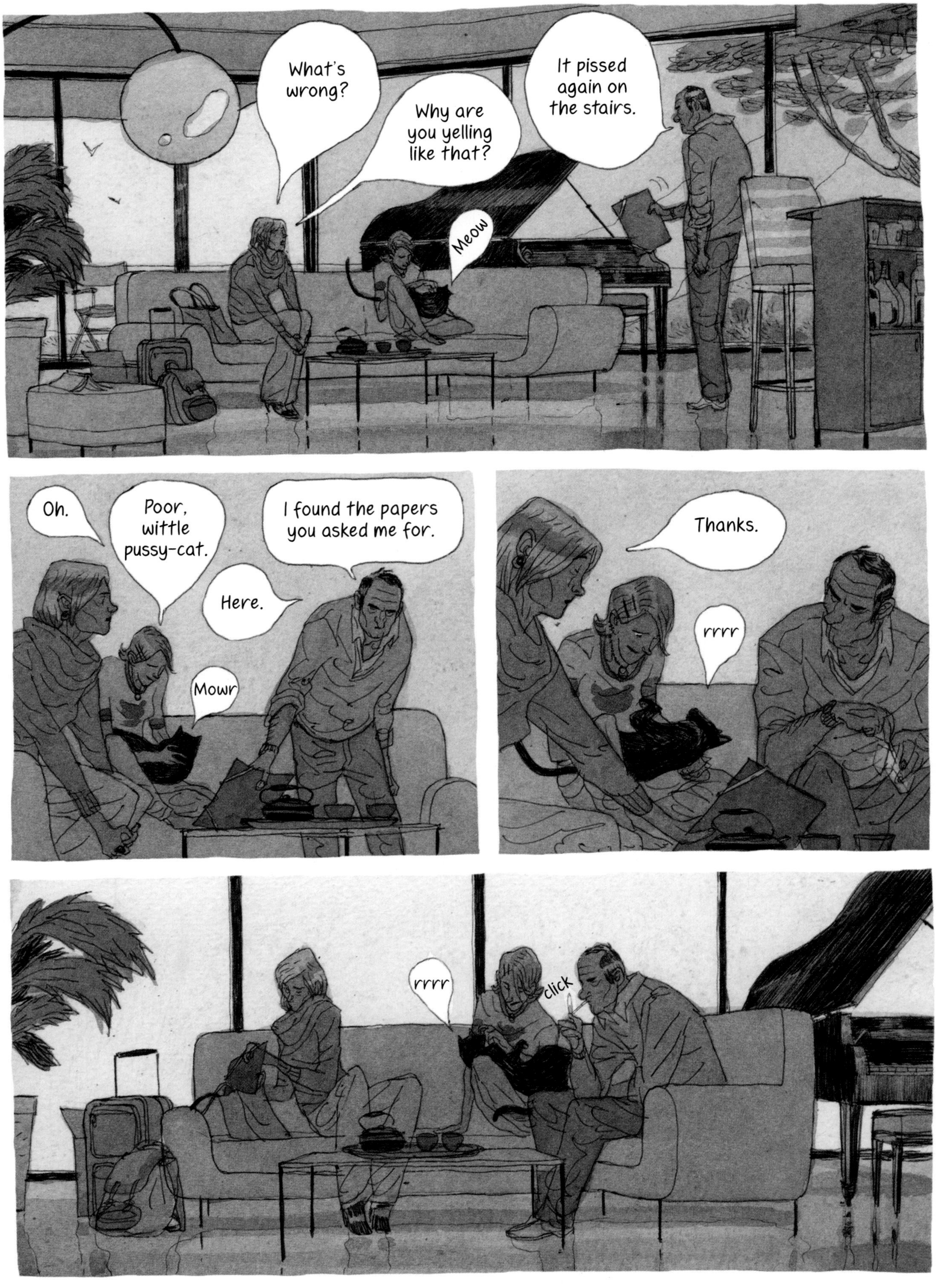
What's wrong?
Why are you yelling like that?
It pissed again on the stairs.
Meow
Oh.
Poor, wittle pussy-cat.
I found the papers you asked me for.
Here.
Mowr
Thanks.
rrrr
rrrr
click

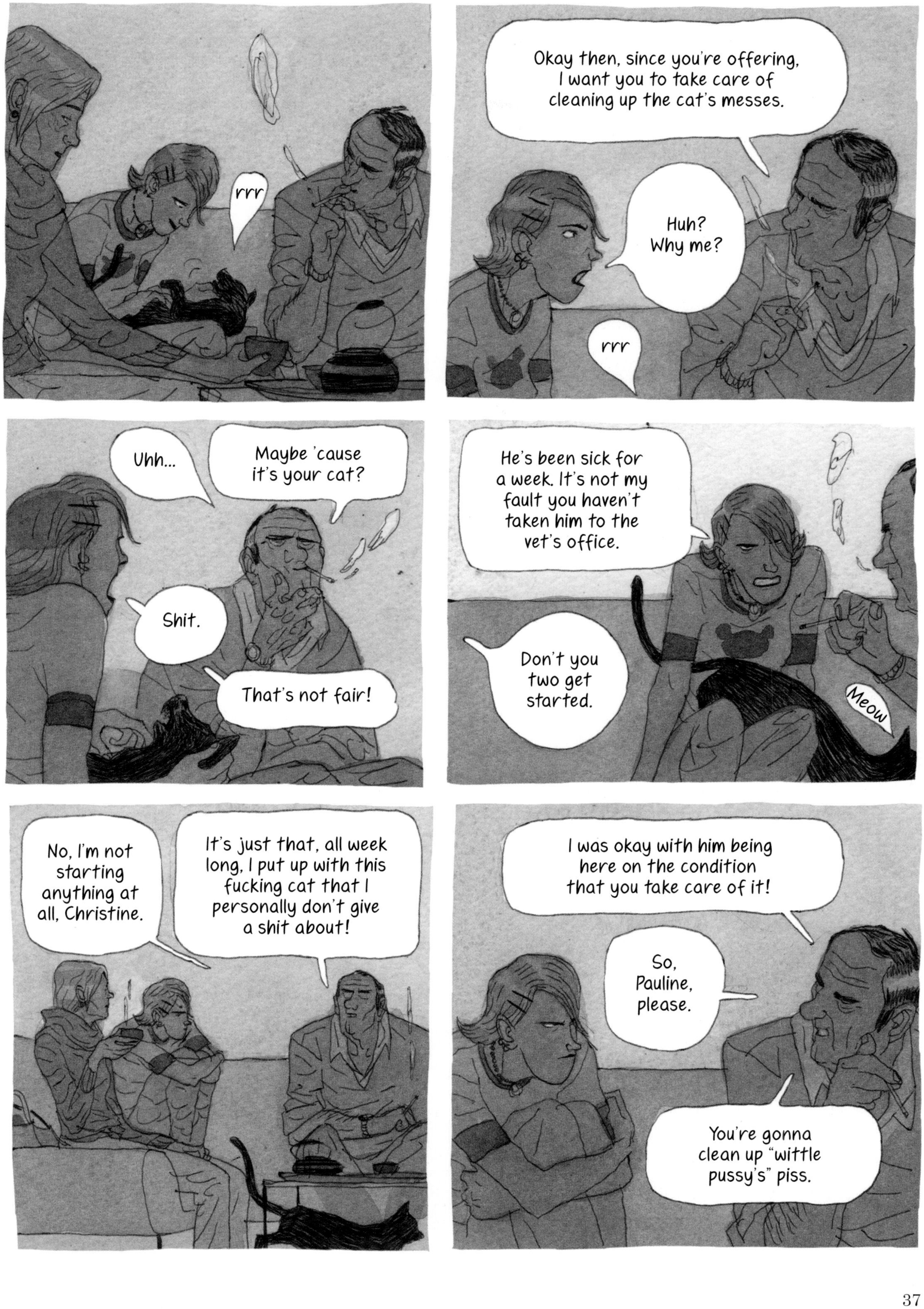
rrr
Okay then, since you're offering, I want you to take care of cleaning up the cat's messes.
Huh? Why me?
rrr
Uhh...
Maybe 'cause it's your cat?
Shit.
That's not fair!
He's been sick for a week. It's not my fault you haven't taken him to the vet's office.
Don't you two get started.
Meow
No, I'm not starting anything at all, Christine.
It's just that, all week long, I put up with this fucking cat that I personally don't give a shit about!
I was okay with him being here on the condition that you take care of it!
So, Pauline, please.
You're gonna clean up "wittle pussy's" piss.

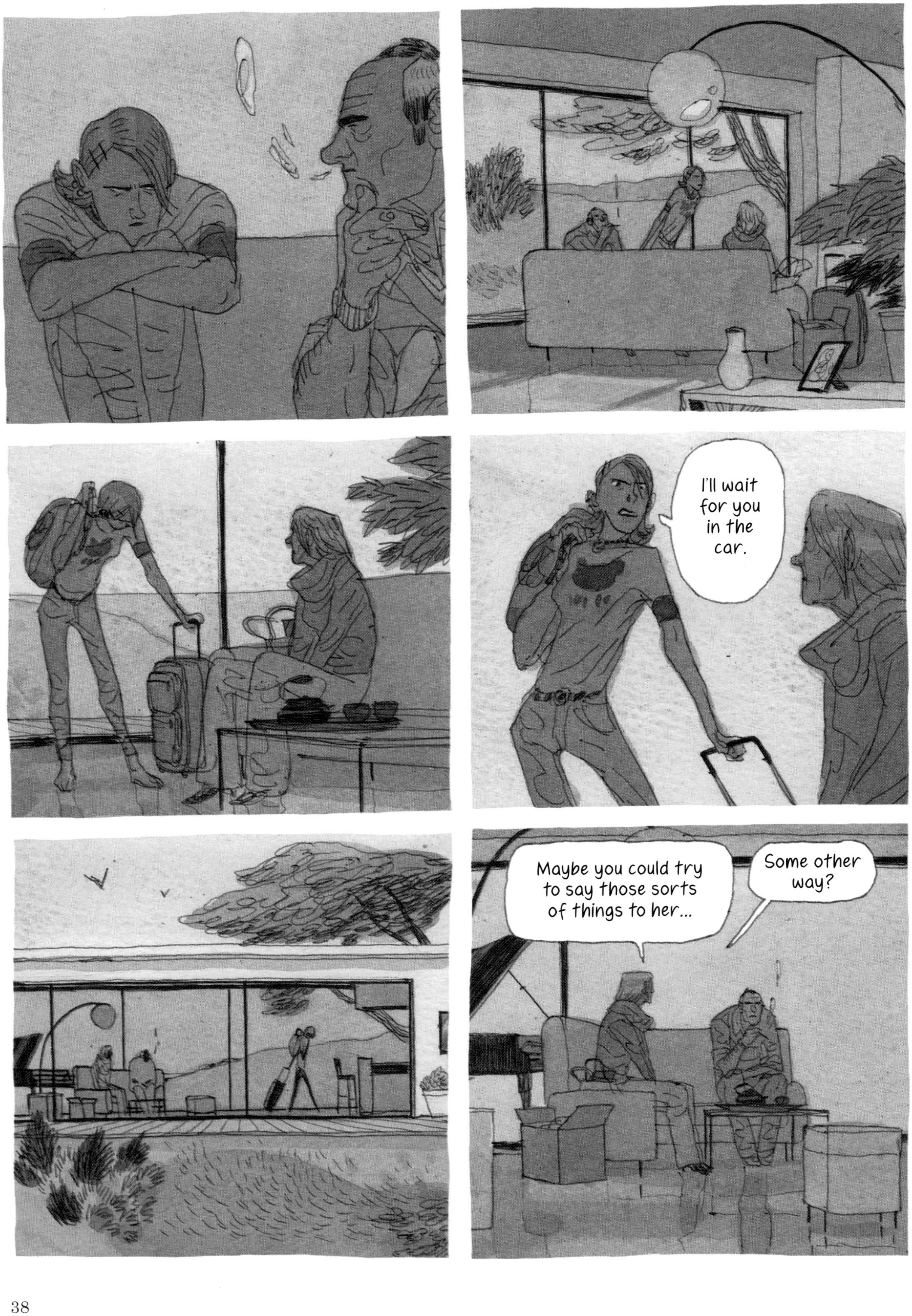
I'll wait for you in the car.
Maybe you could try to say those sorts of things to her...
Some other way?

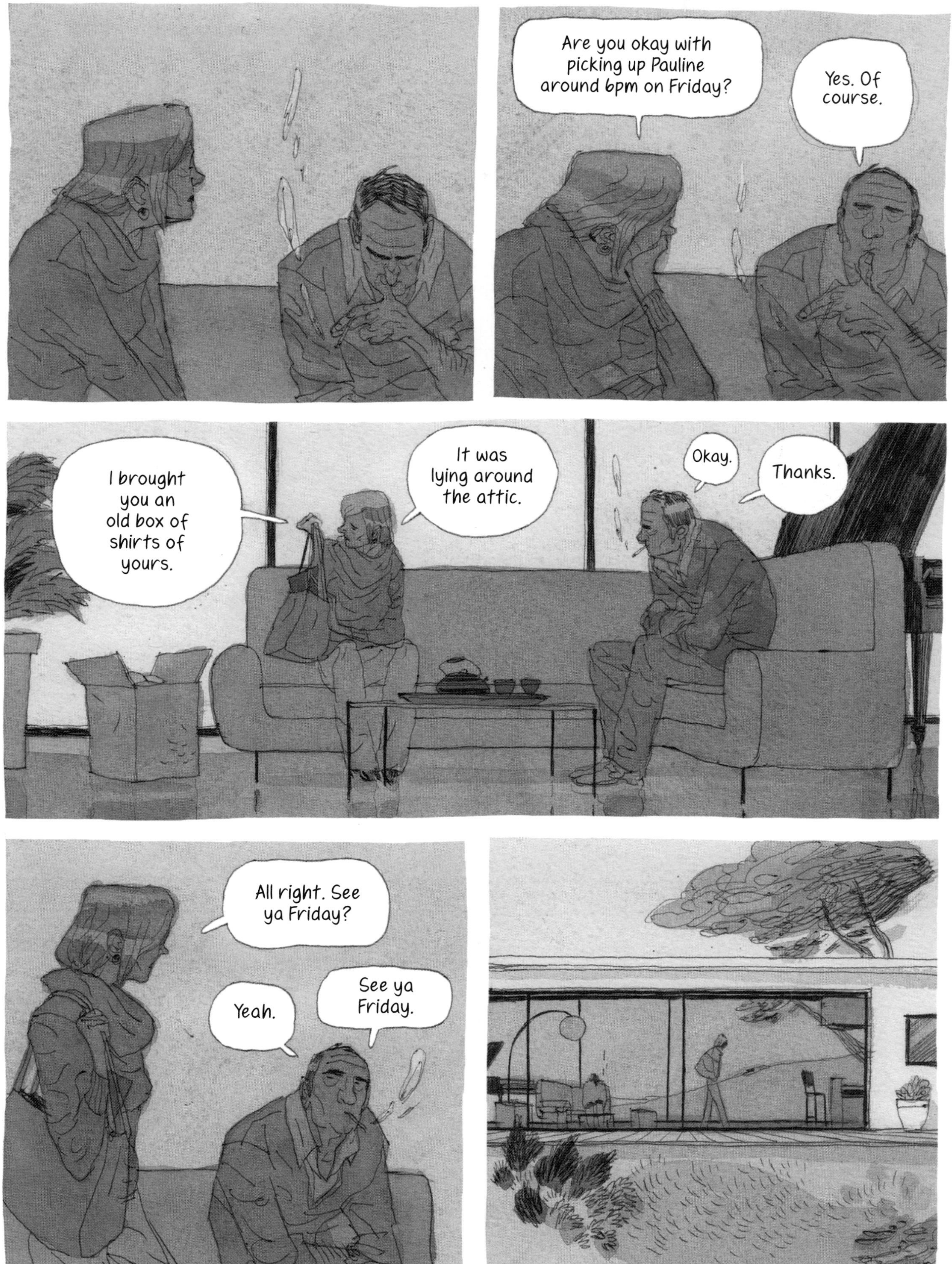
Are you okay with picking up Pauline around 6pm on Friday?
Yes. Of course.
I brought you an old box of shirts of yours.
It was lying around the attic.
Okay.
Thanks.
All right. See ya Friday?
Yeah.
See ya Friday.

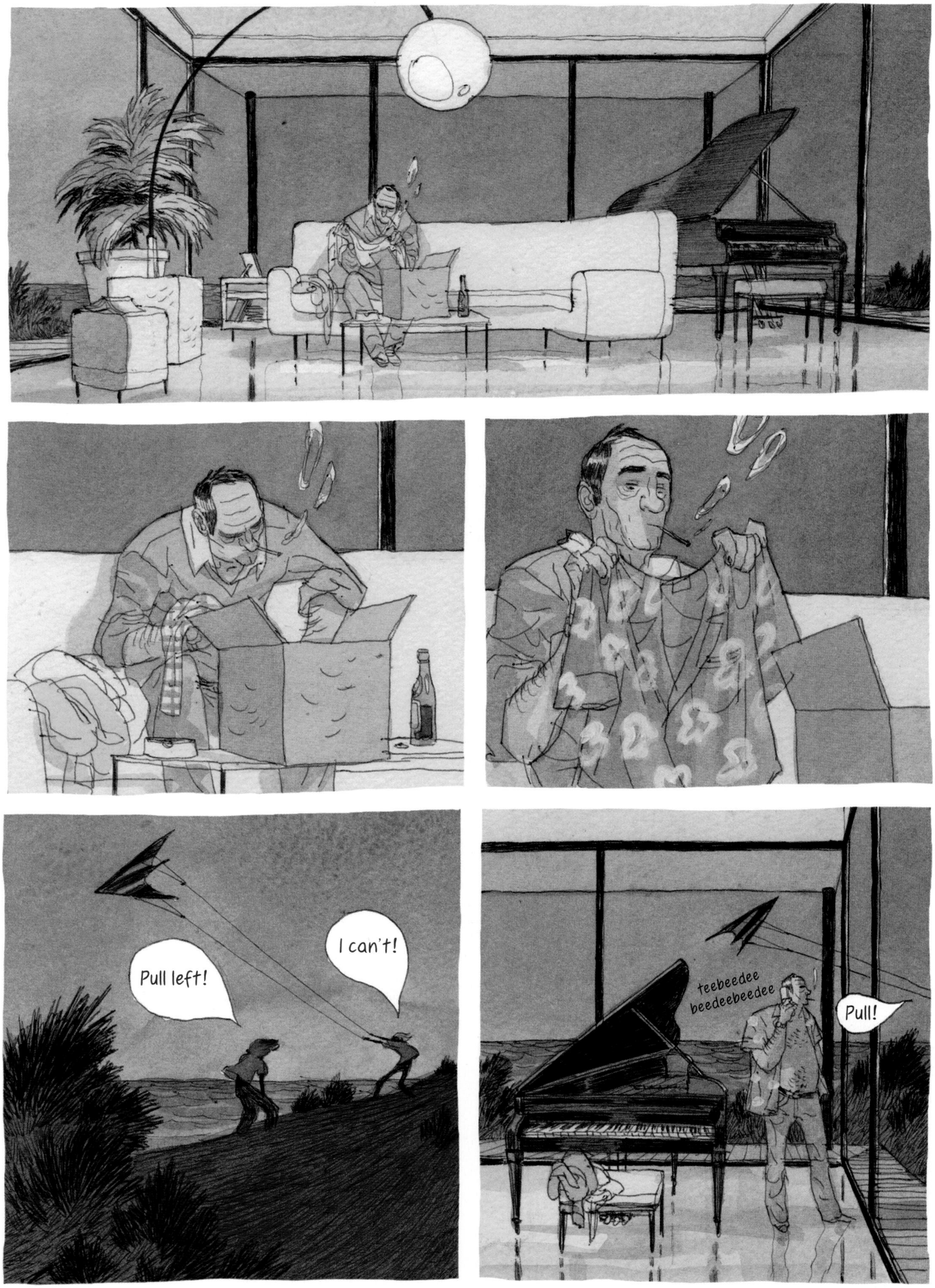
Pull left!
I can't!
teebeedee
beedeebeedee
Pull!

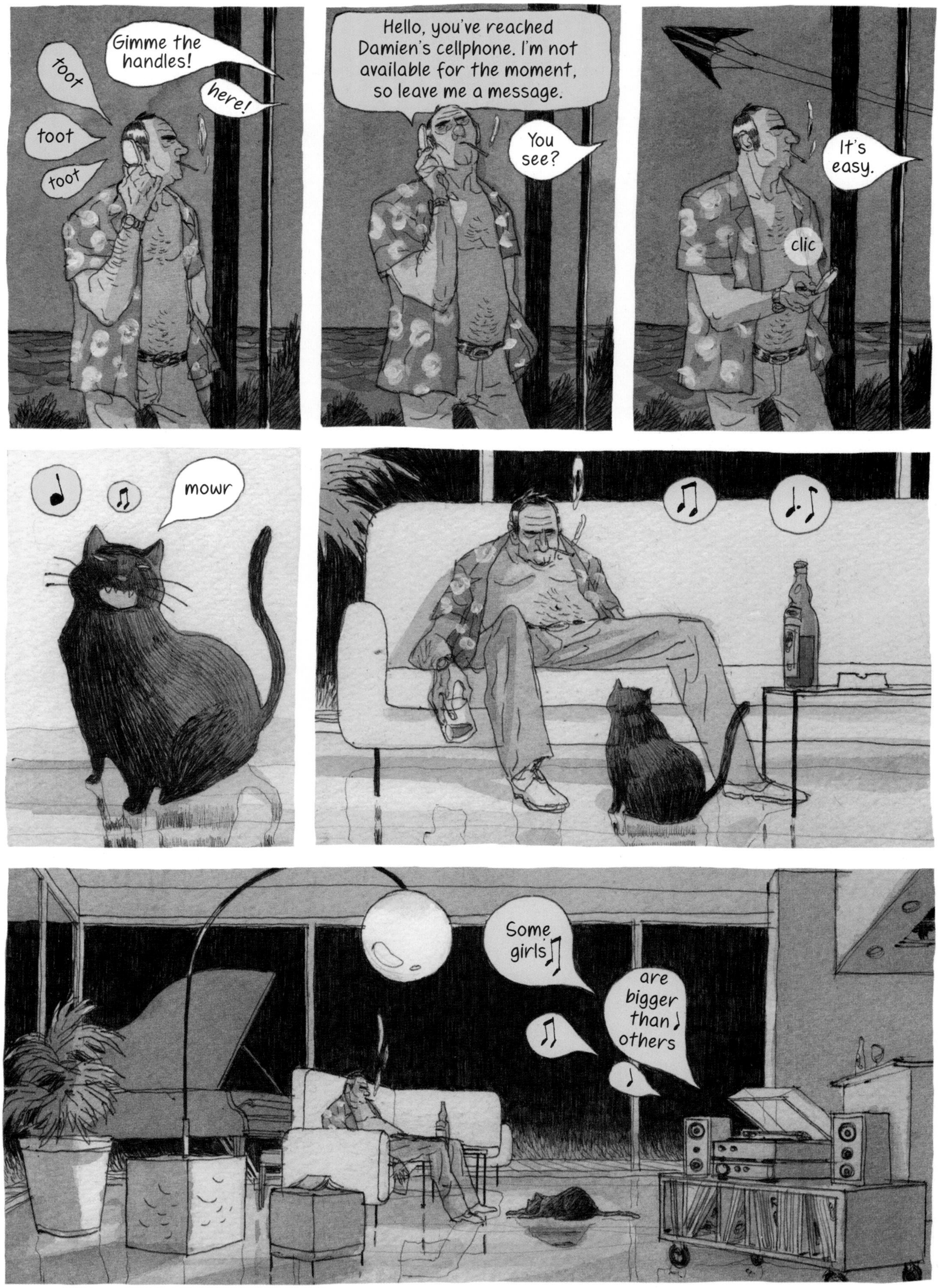
Gimme the handles!
toot
toot
toot
here!
Hello, you've reached Damien's cellphone. I'm not available for the moment, so leave me a message.
You see?
It's easy.
clic
mowr
Some girls
are bigger than others

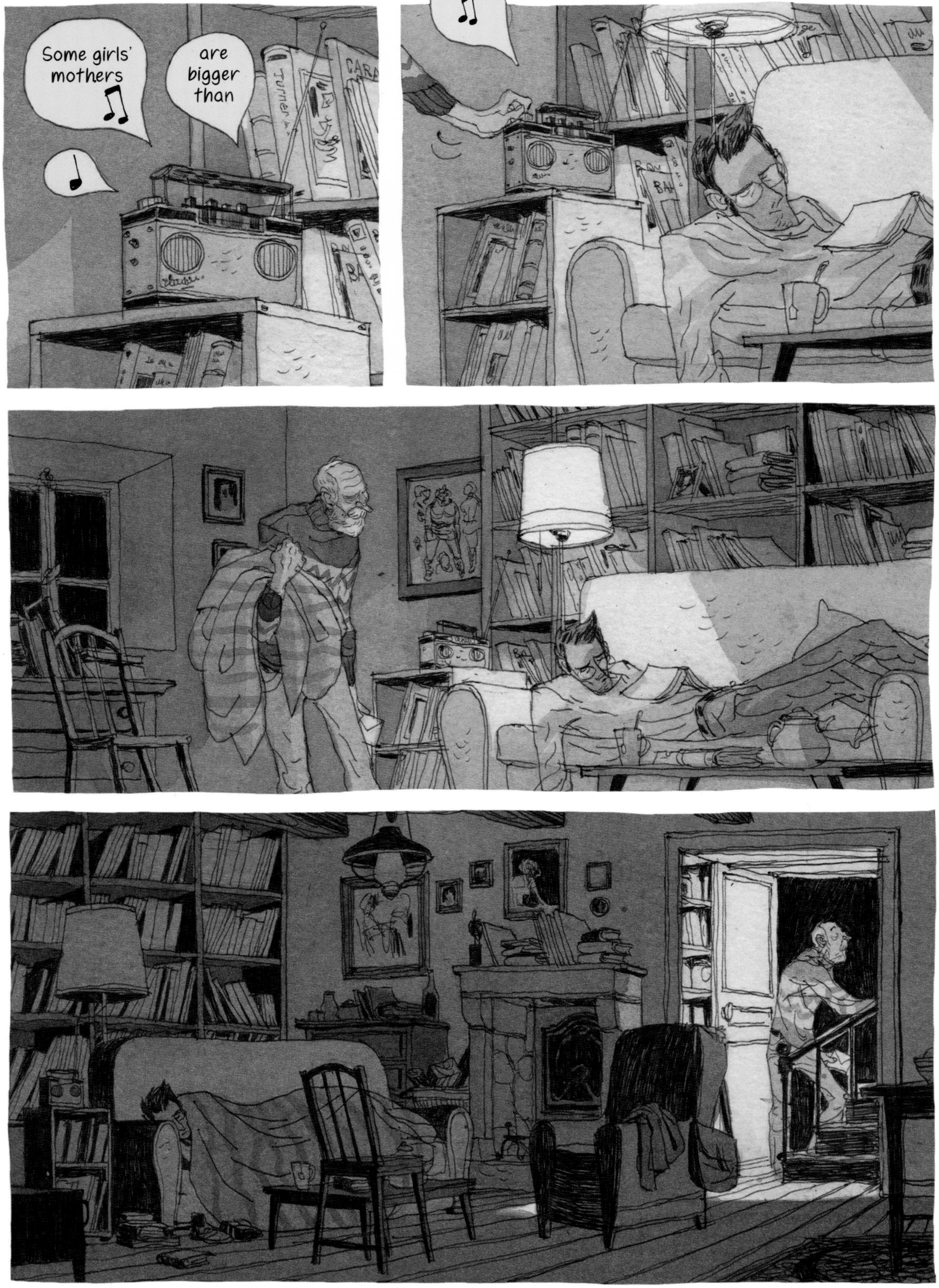
Some girls' mothers
are bigger than

Liberty-Equality-Fraternity
The French Republic

Mrs. Catherine Vallet

Minister of Sustainable Development and the Environment.

Is honored to invite you to attend the reception she is hosting at the Hôtel de Roquelaure, boulevard St-Germain 296, 75007 Paris, on the occasion of her taking office.

September 12, 2002, at 8:30pm.

Non-transferable invitation.

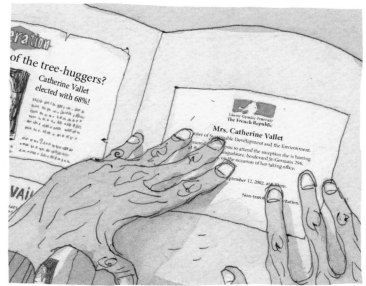

of the tree-huggers?
Catherine Vallet
elected with 68%!

Liberty-Equality-Fraternity
The French Republic

Mrs. Catherine Vallet

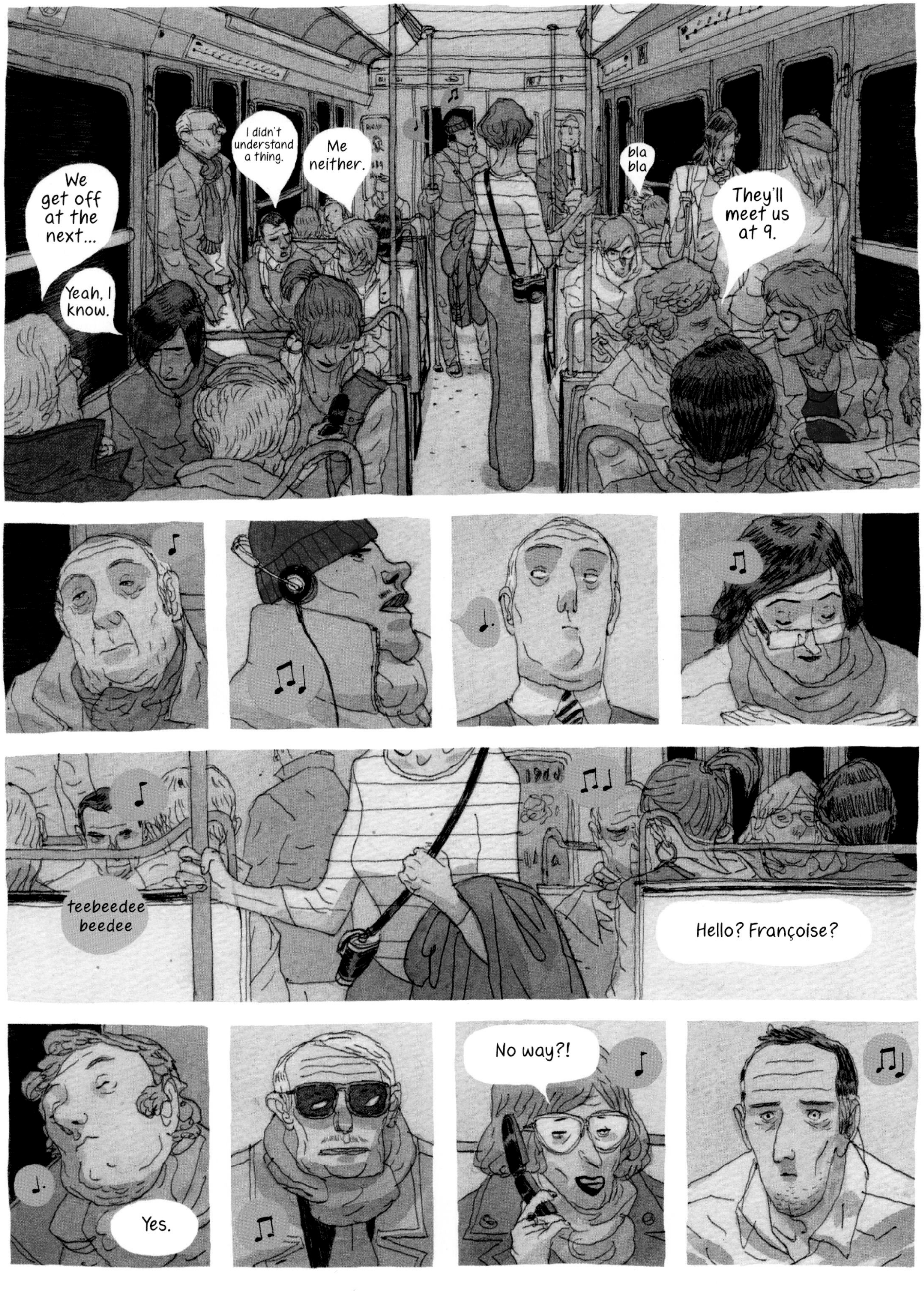
We get off at the next...
Yeah, I know.
I didn't understand a thing.
Me neither.
bla bla
They'll meet us at 9.
teebeedee beedee
Hello? Françoise?
Yes.
No way?!

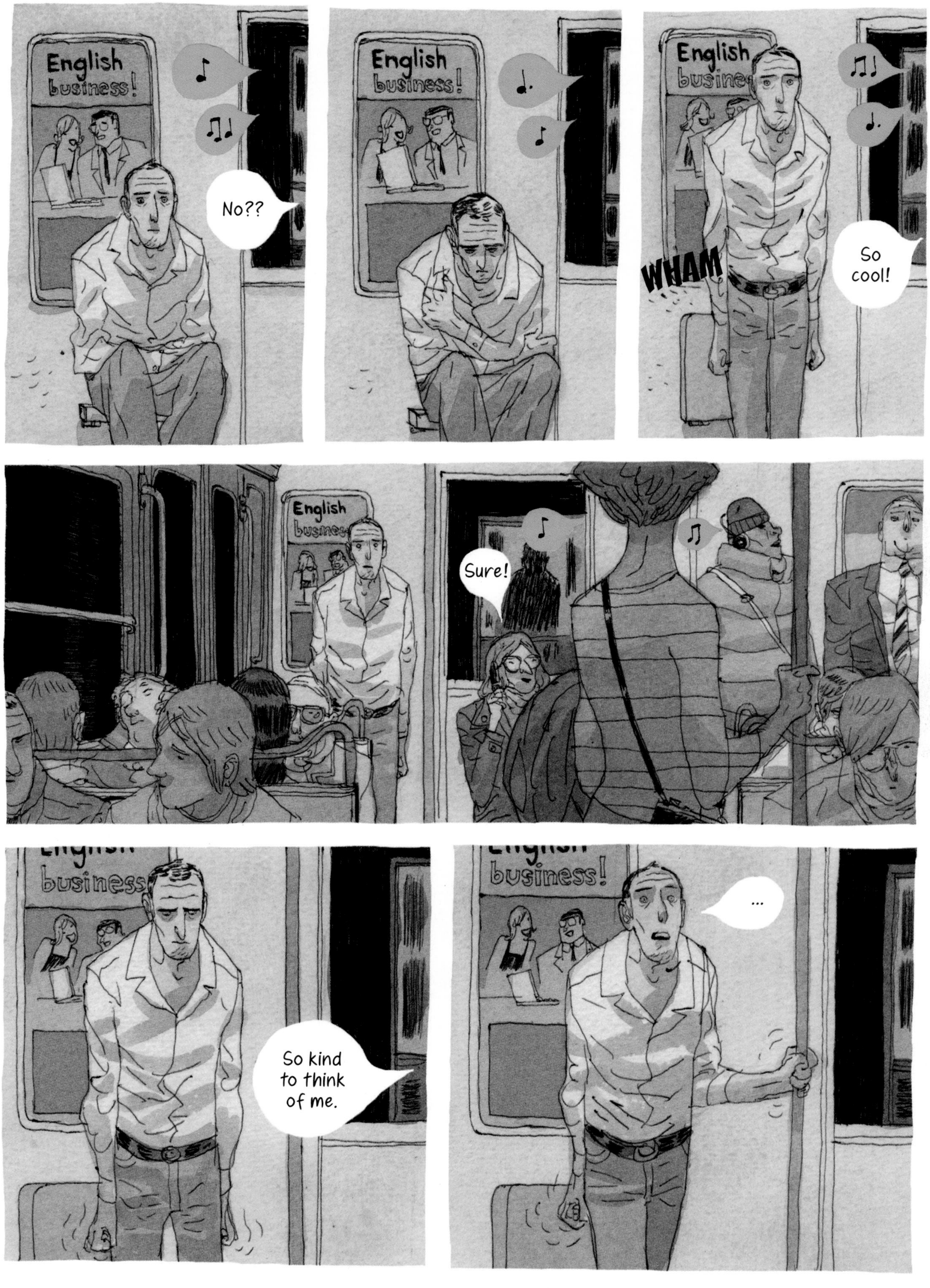
English business!
No??
So cool!
WHAM
English
Sure!
So kind to think of me.
...

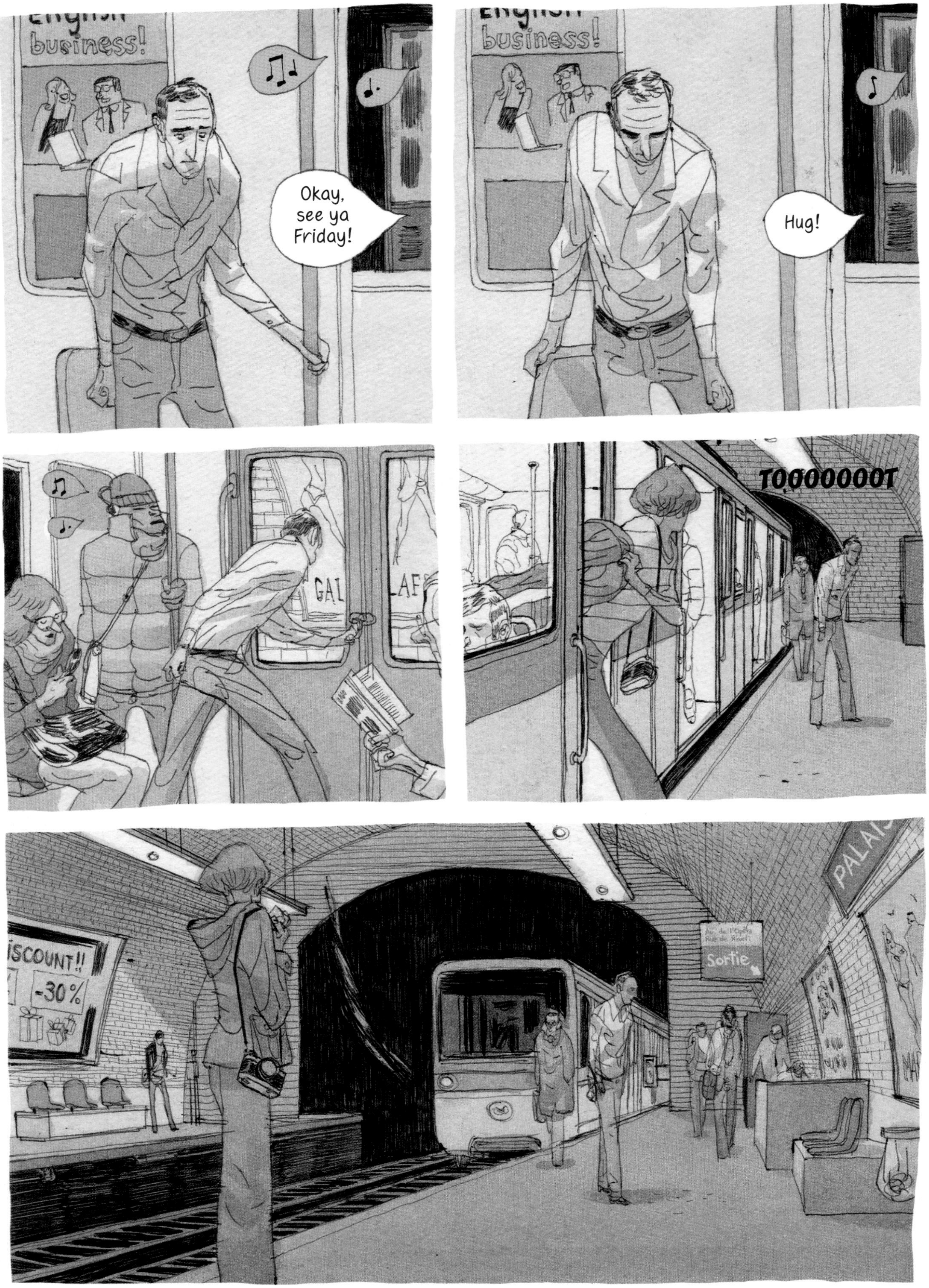
English business!
Okay, see ya Friday!
Hug!
TOOOOOOOT
DISCOUNT!!
-30%
Sortie
PALAIS

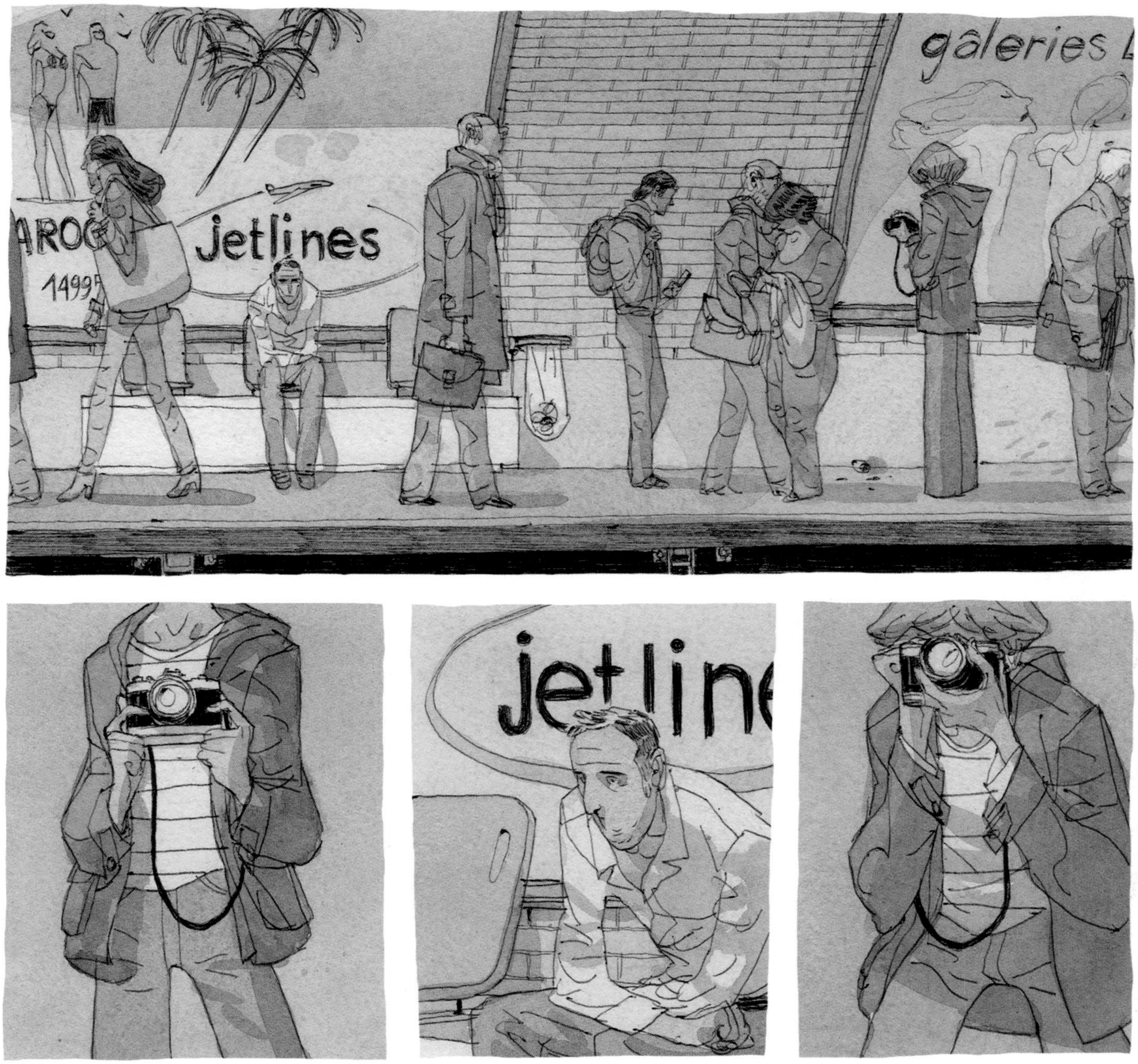
jetlines
gâleries
jetline

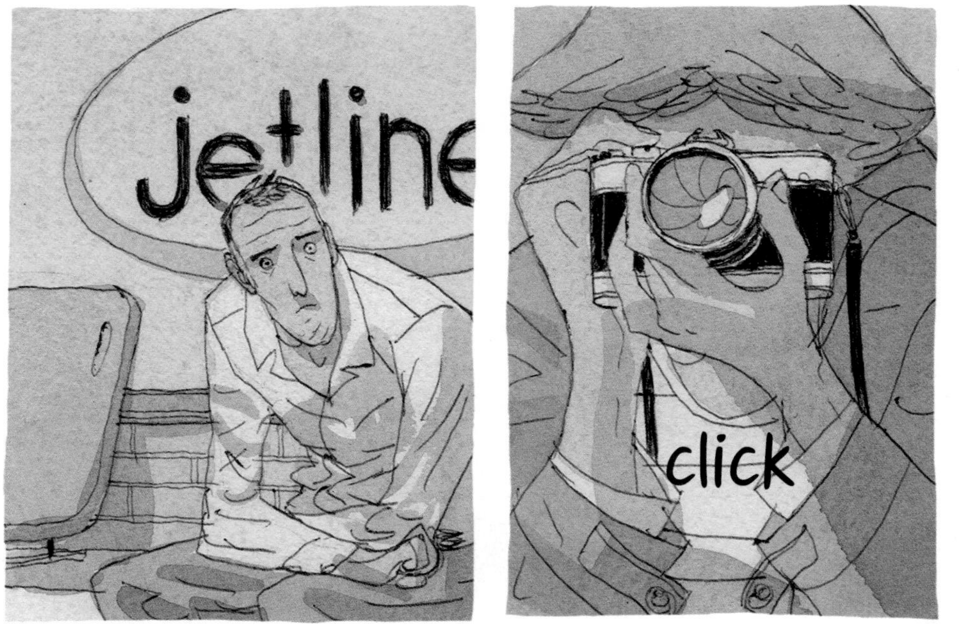
jetline
click

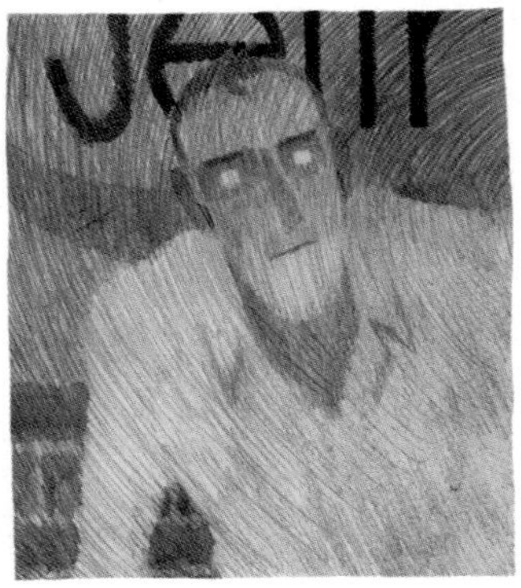

He'd run as fast as possible.

To the latrines lined up in the covered area in the school's courtyard, holding in, as best he could, the violent throbs of his guts.

With the door barely shut behind him, he had literally emptied himself on the spot before he'd even dropped his trousers,

a hot, stinky wave trickling down his legs, soiling the floor.

The new teacher, Mister Bollet, had found him there in tears, despondent amid the putrid puddle.

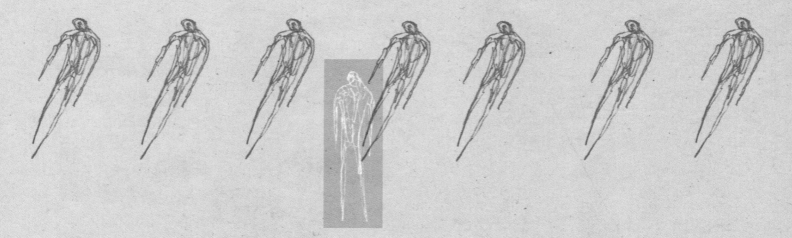

The subway trains pass before his eyes every three minutes.

The platforms fill, empty, and then fill again in regular waves. He observes this fluid back-and-forth of morning passengers, that of people with things to do. They all seem carried along by the reassuring illusion of being connected to one another, protected by an unwavering law of physics. Like atoms inside the same molecule, each with its place, its role. Yesterday still, he, too, had had his role, he remembers it. Today he must content himself with observing their ballet.

At the small, enamel sink in the workroom, stuck between the ditto machine, the herbariums, and jars of acrylic paint, Mr. Bollet had patiently washed him off, then had carefully cleaned his clothing. He remembers going back to the classroom. Whispers and laughs, a curt remark from the teacher, followed by a long silence. His damp clothes set near the heater. Naked, sitting on his chair among the other students, he observed them, and the most humiliating part was seeing them concentrating on their task as if he weren't there. As if he simply didn't exist.

They come and go in front of him. He'd have to reach out his hand, to pass definitively over to the other side, to feel guilty and ashamed for seeking to survive. He can't quite resign himself to that.

They come and go. He observes them, like a ghost would watch the living trotting about.

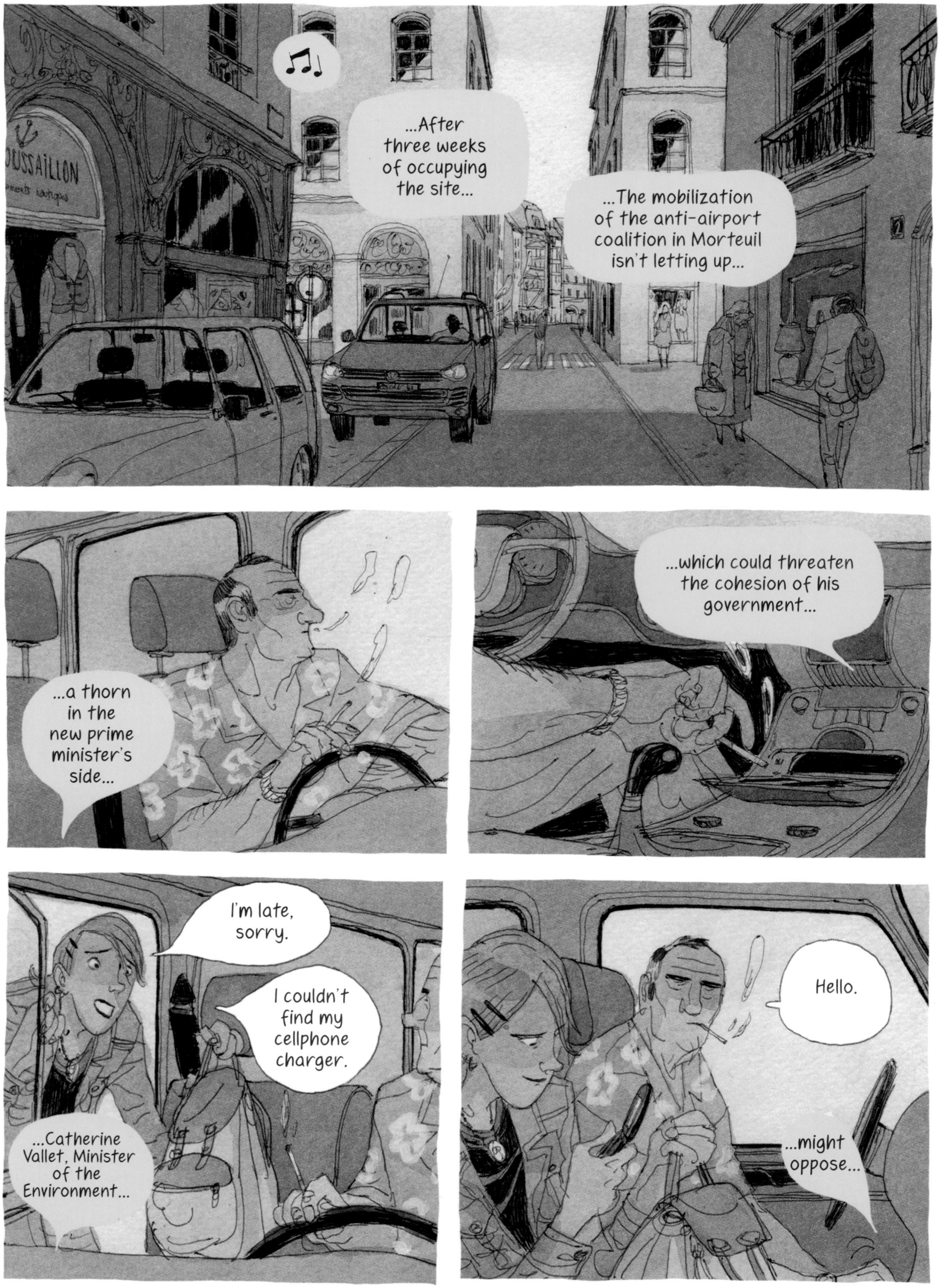
♫♩
...After three weeks of occupying the site...
...The mobilization of the anti-airport coalition in Morteuil isn't letting up...
...a thorn in the new prime minister's side...
...which could threaten the cohesion of his government...
I'm late, sorry.
I couldn't find my cellphone charger.
...Catherine Vallet, Minister of the Environment...
Hello.
...might oppose...

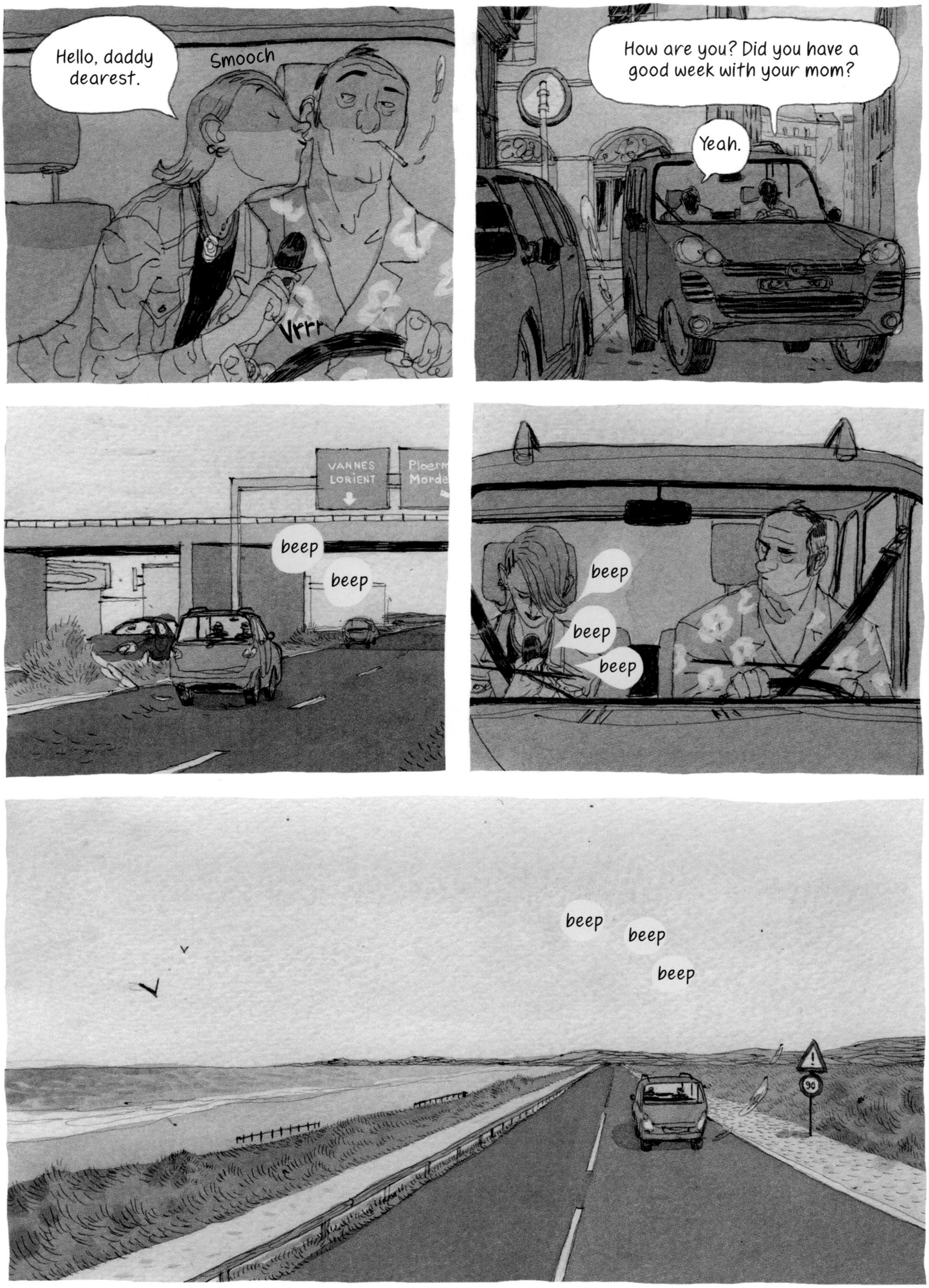
Hello, daddy dearest.
Smooch
Vrrr
How are you? Did you have a good week with your mom?
Yeah.
VANNES
LORIENT
beep
beep
beep
beep
beep
beep
beep
beep
90

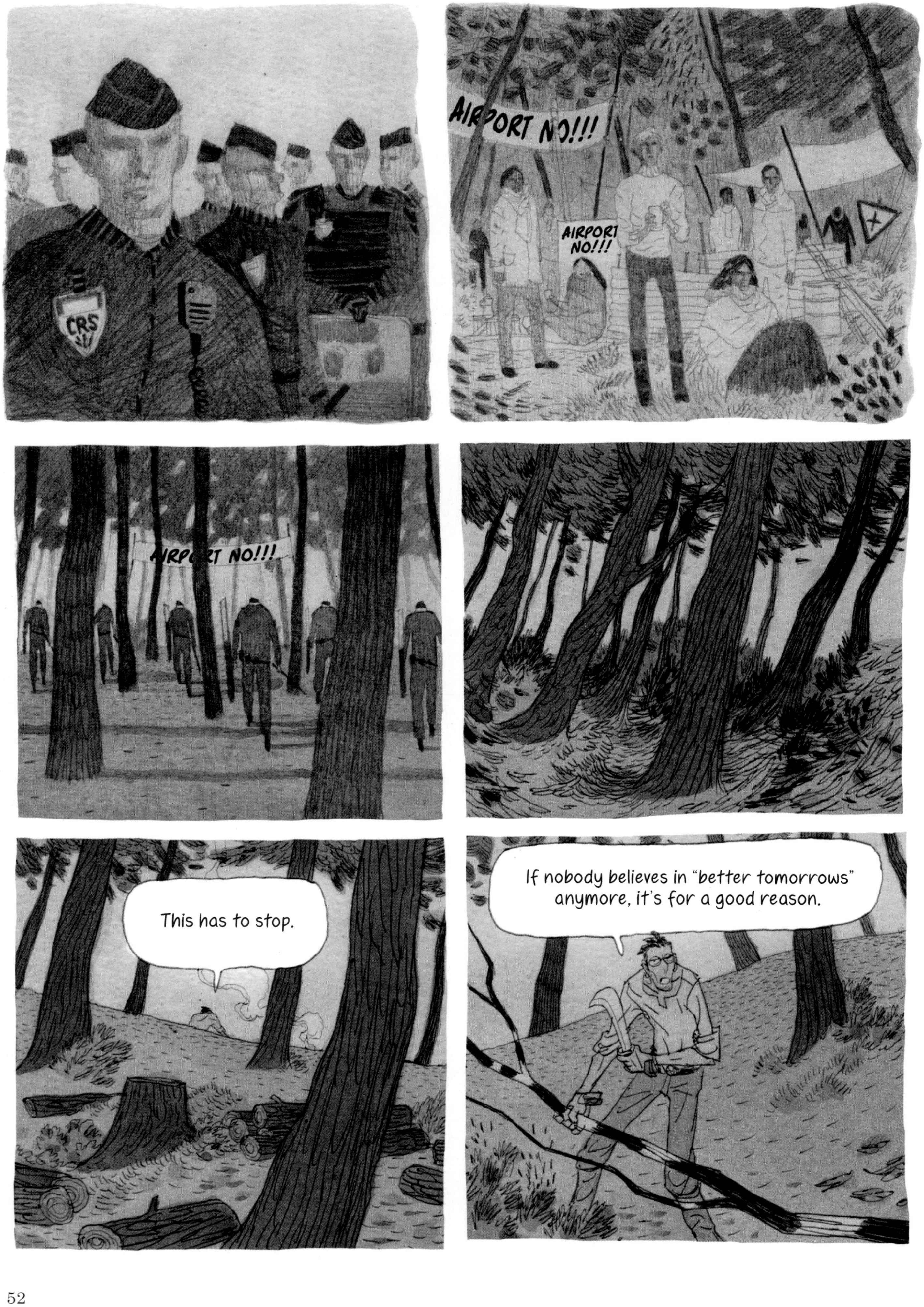
CRS
AIRPORT NO!!!
AIRPORT NO!!!
AIRPORT NO!!!
This has to stop.
If nobody believes in "better tomorrows" anymore, it's for a good reason.

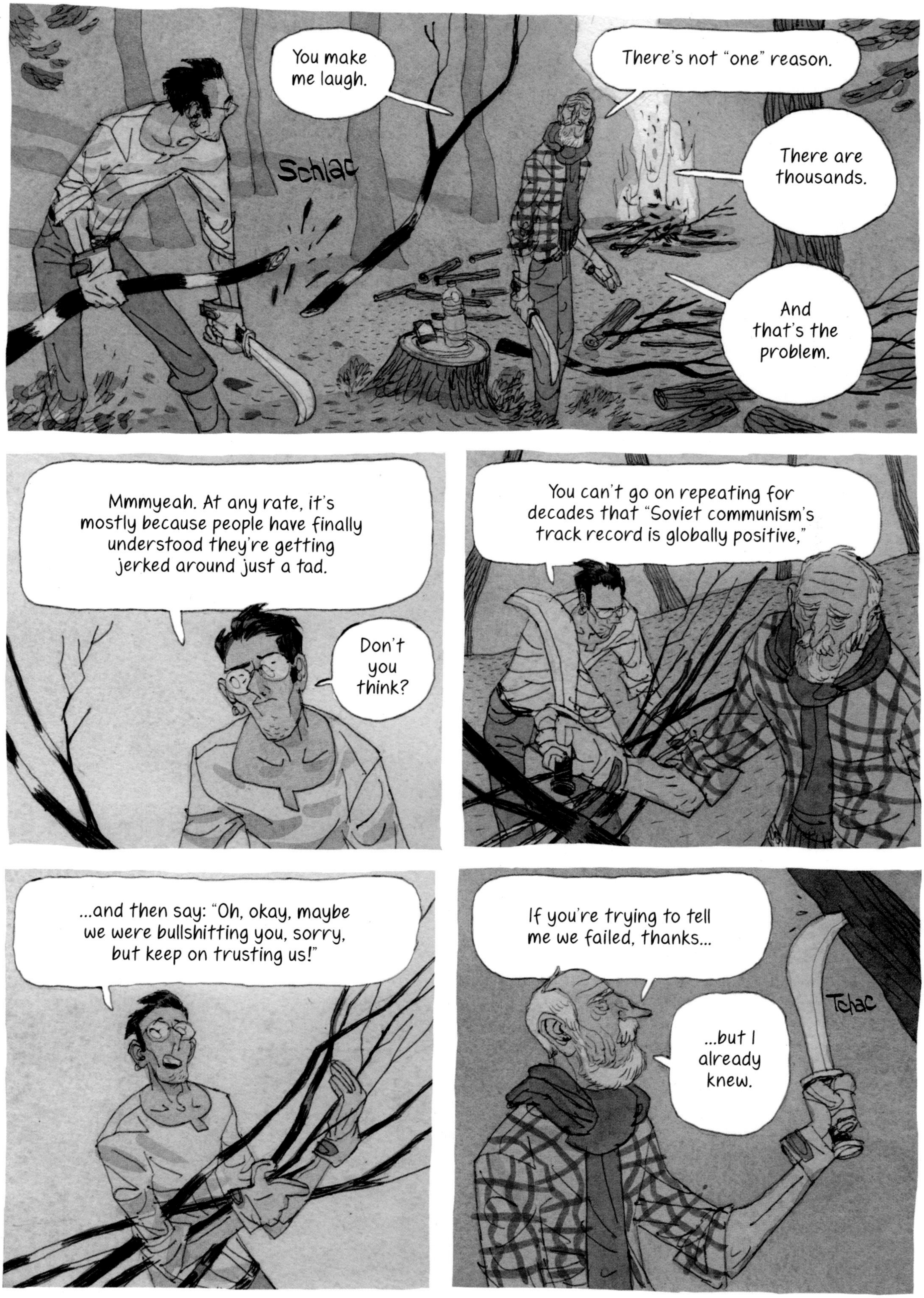
You make me laugh.
SCHLAC
There's not "one" reason.
There are thousands.
And that's the problem.
Mmmyeah. At any rate, it's mostly because people have finally understood they're getting jerked around just a tad.
Don't you think?
You can't go on repeating for decades that "Soviet communism's track record is globally positive,"
...and then say: "Oh, okay, maybe we were bullshitting you, sorry, but keep on trusting us!"
If you're trying to tell me we failed, thanks...
TCHAC
...but I already knew.

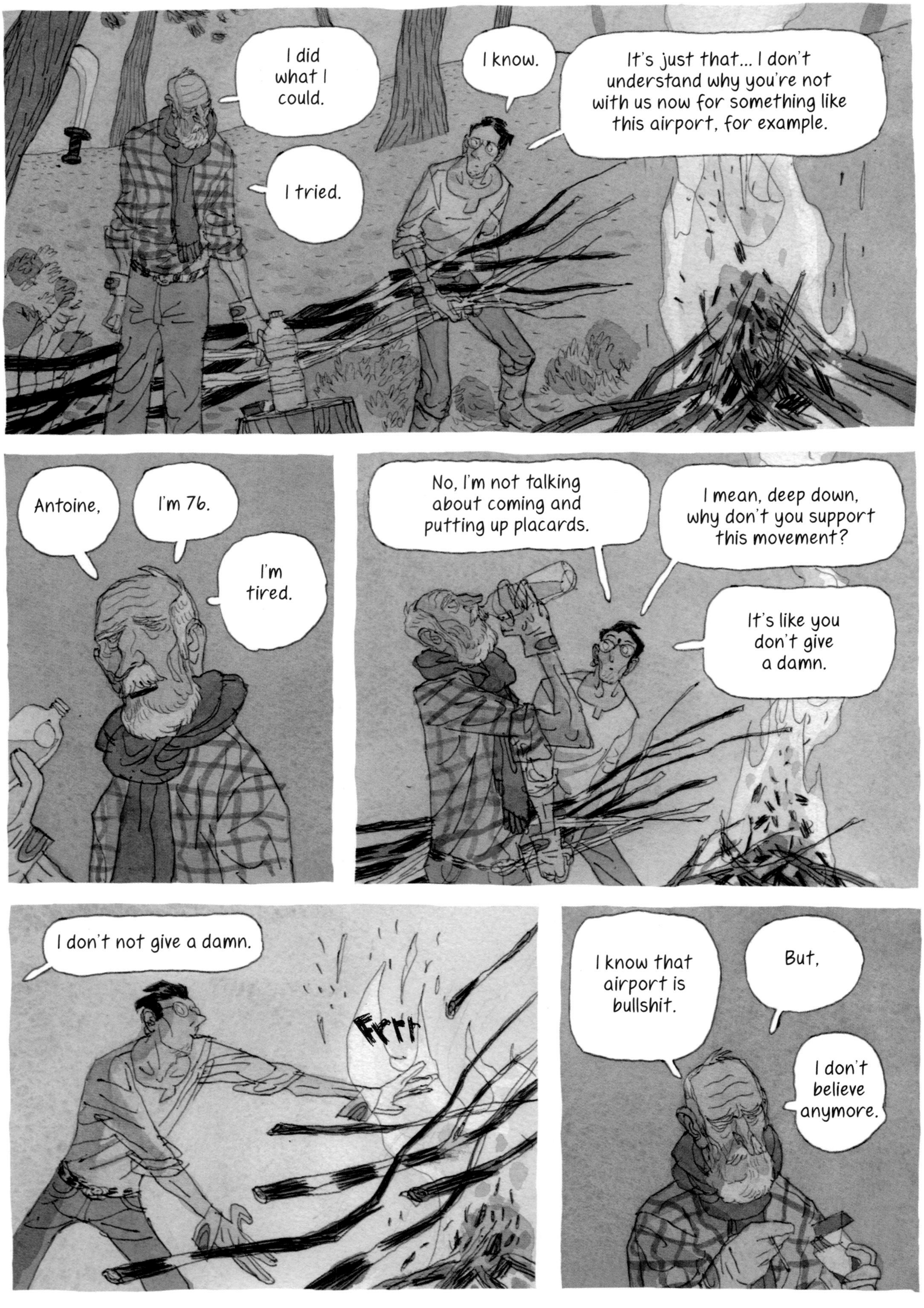
I did what I could.
I tried.
I know.
It's just that... I don't understand why you're not with us now for something like this airport, for example.
Antoine,
I'm 76.
I'm tired.
No, I'm not talking about coming and putting up placards.
I mean, deep down, why don't you support this movement?
It's like you don't give a damn.
I don't not give a damn.
Frrr
I know that airport is bullshit.
But,
I don't believe anymore.

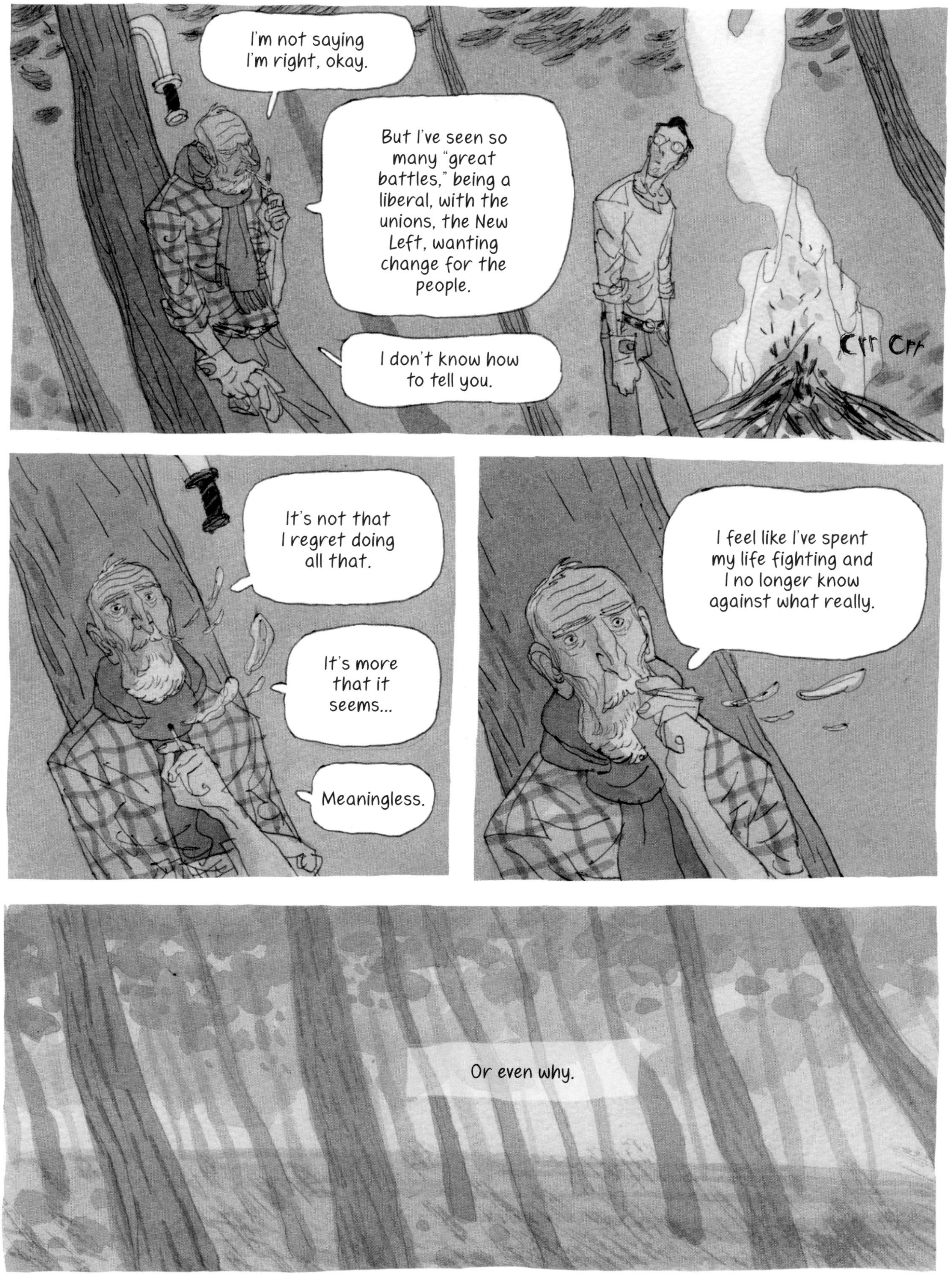
I'm not saying I'm right, okay.
But I've seen so many "great battles," being a liberal, with the unions, the New Left, wanting change for the people.
I don't know how to tell you.
Crr Crr
It's not that I regret doing all that.
It's more that it seems...
Meaningless.
I feel like I've spent my life fighting and I no longer know against what really.
Or even why.

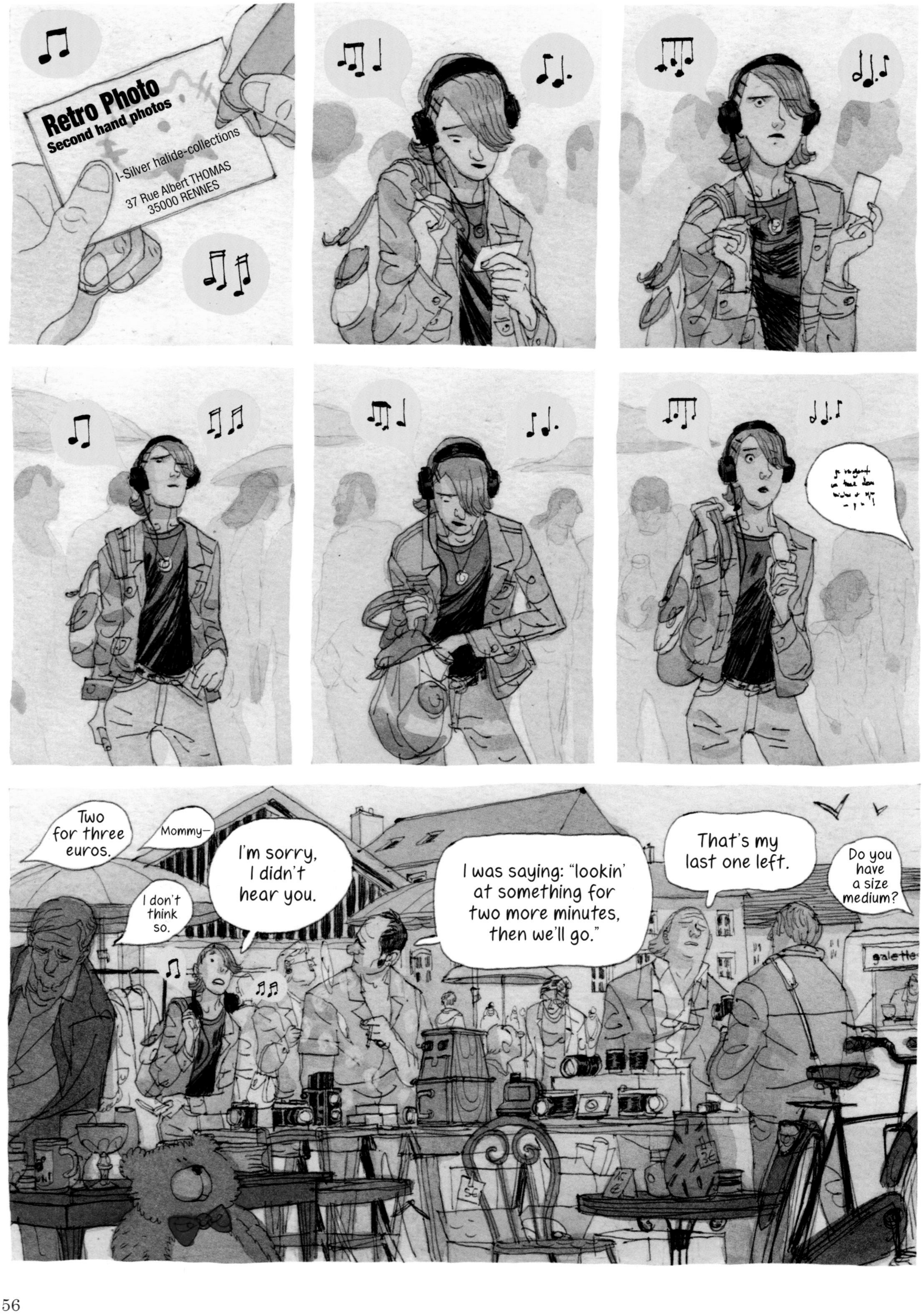
Retro Photo
Second hand photos
I-Silver halide-collections
37 Rue Albert THOMAS
35000 RENNES
Two for three euros.
Mommy—
I don't think so.
I'm sorry, I didn't hear you.
I was saying: "lookin' at something for two more minutes, then we'll go."
That's my last one left.
Do you have a size medium?

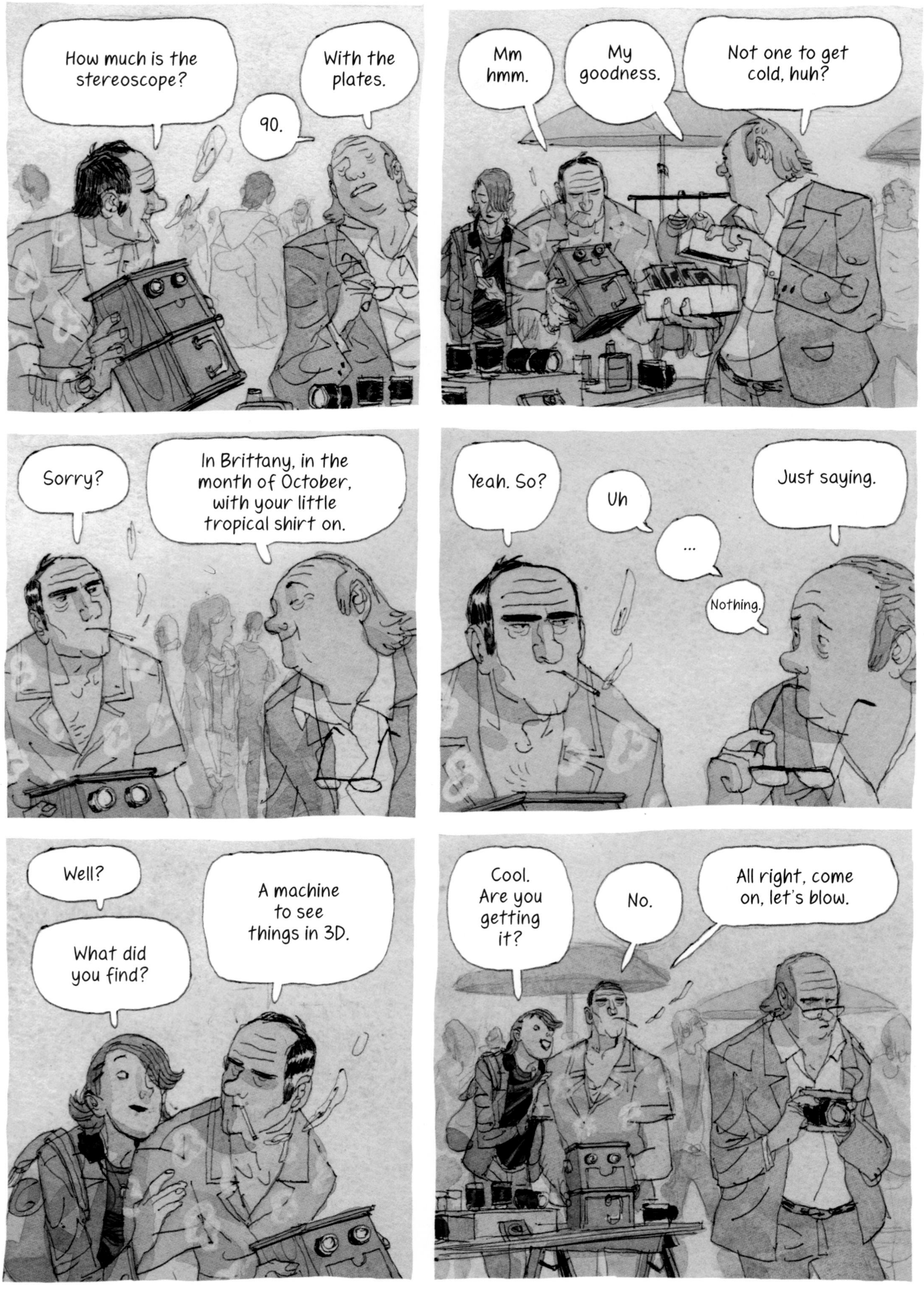
How much is the stereoscope?
90.
With the plates.
Mm hmm.
My goodness.
Not one to get cold, huh?
Sorry?
In Brittany, in the month of October, with your little tropical shirt on.
Yeah. So?
Uh
...
Nothing.
Just saying.
Well?
What did you find?
A machine to see things in 3D.
Cool. Are you getting it?
No.
All right, come on, let's blow.

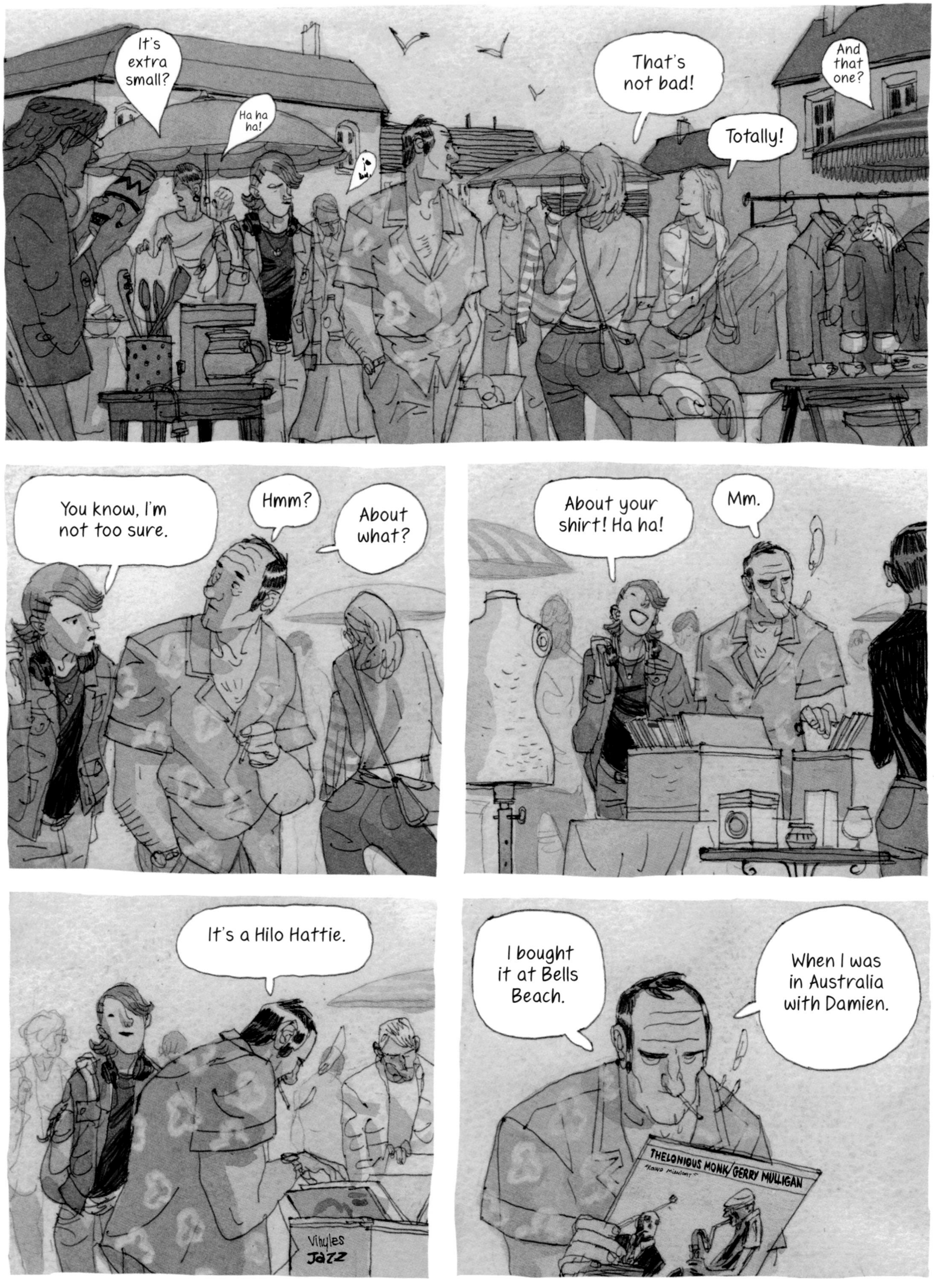
It's extra small?
Ha ha ha!
That's not bad!
Totally!
And that one?
You know, I'm not too sure.
Hmm?
About what?
About your shirt! Ha ha!
Mm.
It's a Hilo Hattie.
Vinyles Jazz
I bought it at Bells Beach.
When I was in Australia with Damien.
THELONIOUS MONK/GERRY MULLIGAN

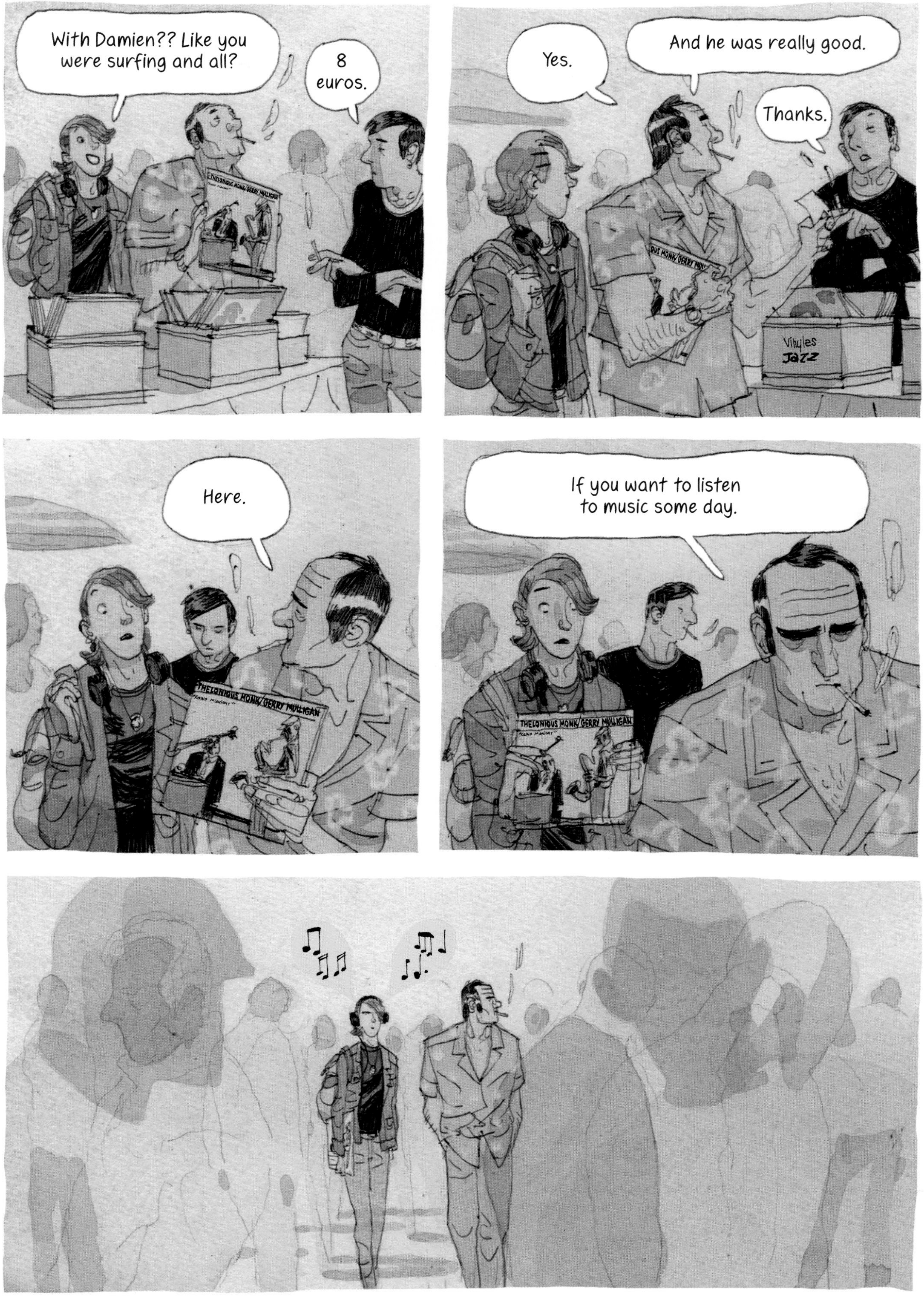
With Damien?? Like you were surfing and all?
8 euros.
THELONIOUS MONK/GERRY MULLIGAN
Yes.
And he was really good.
Thanks.
Vinyles
JAZZ
Here.
THELONIOUS MONK/GERRY MULLIGAN
If you want to listen to music some day.
THELONIOUS MONK/GERRY MULLIGAN

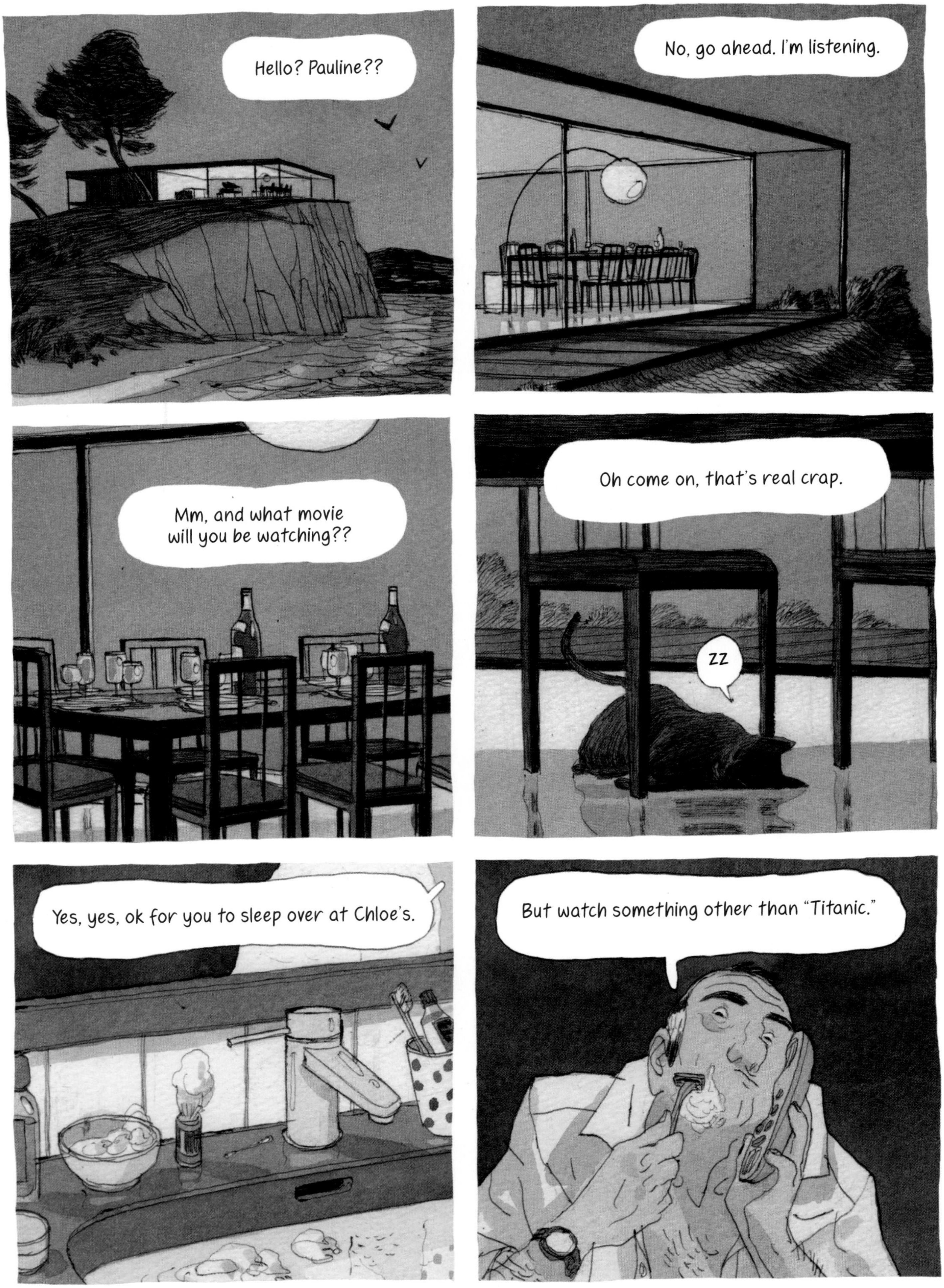
Hello? Pauline??
No, go ahead. I'm listening.
Mm, and what movie will you be watching??
Oh come on, that's real crap.
ZZ
Yes, yes, ok for you to sleep over at Chloe's.
But watch something other than "Titanic."

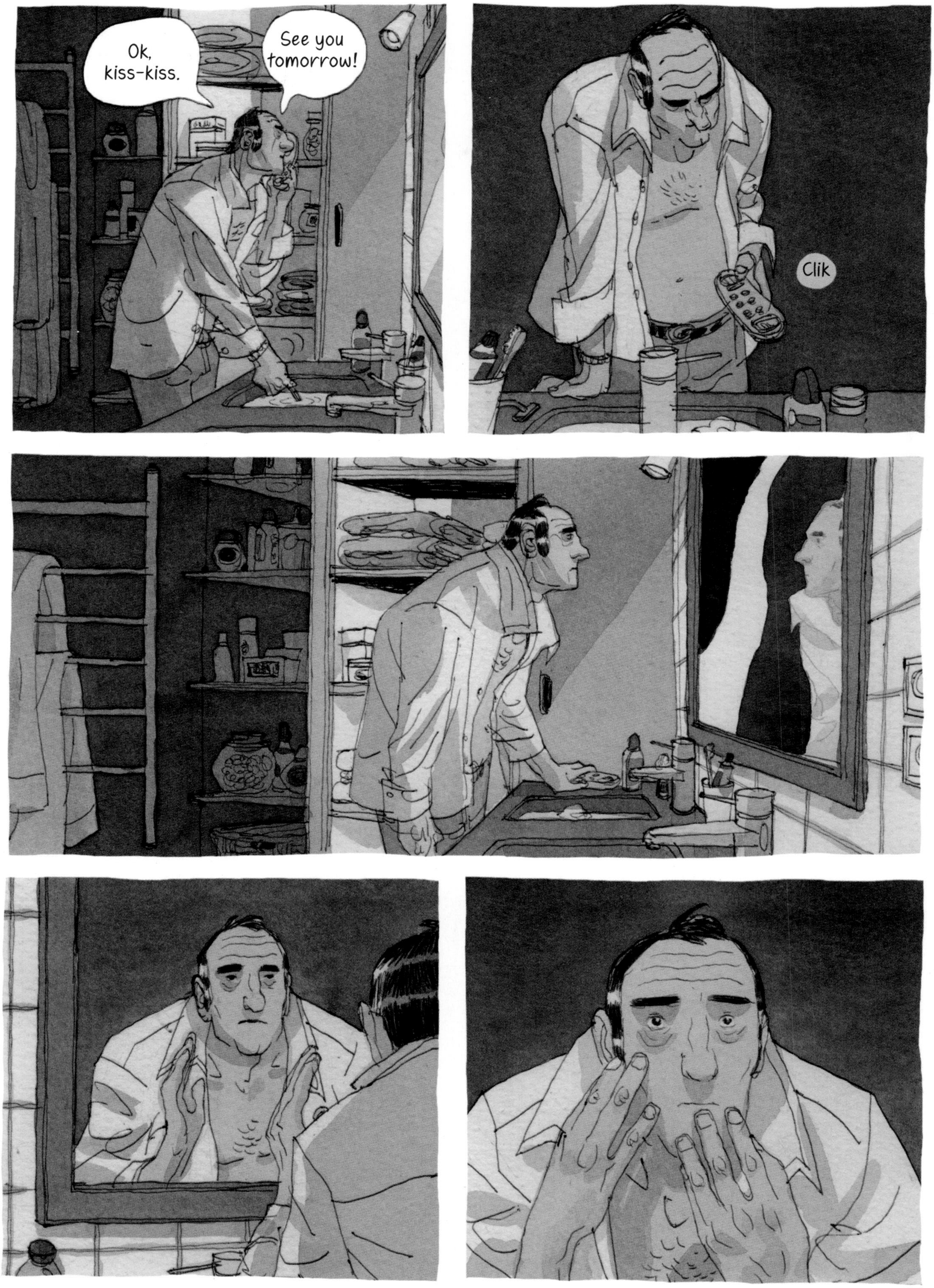
Ok,
kiss-kiss.
See you
tomorrow!
Clik

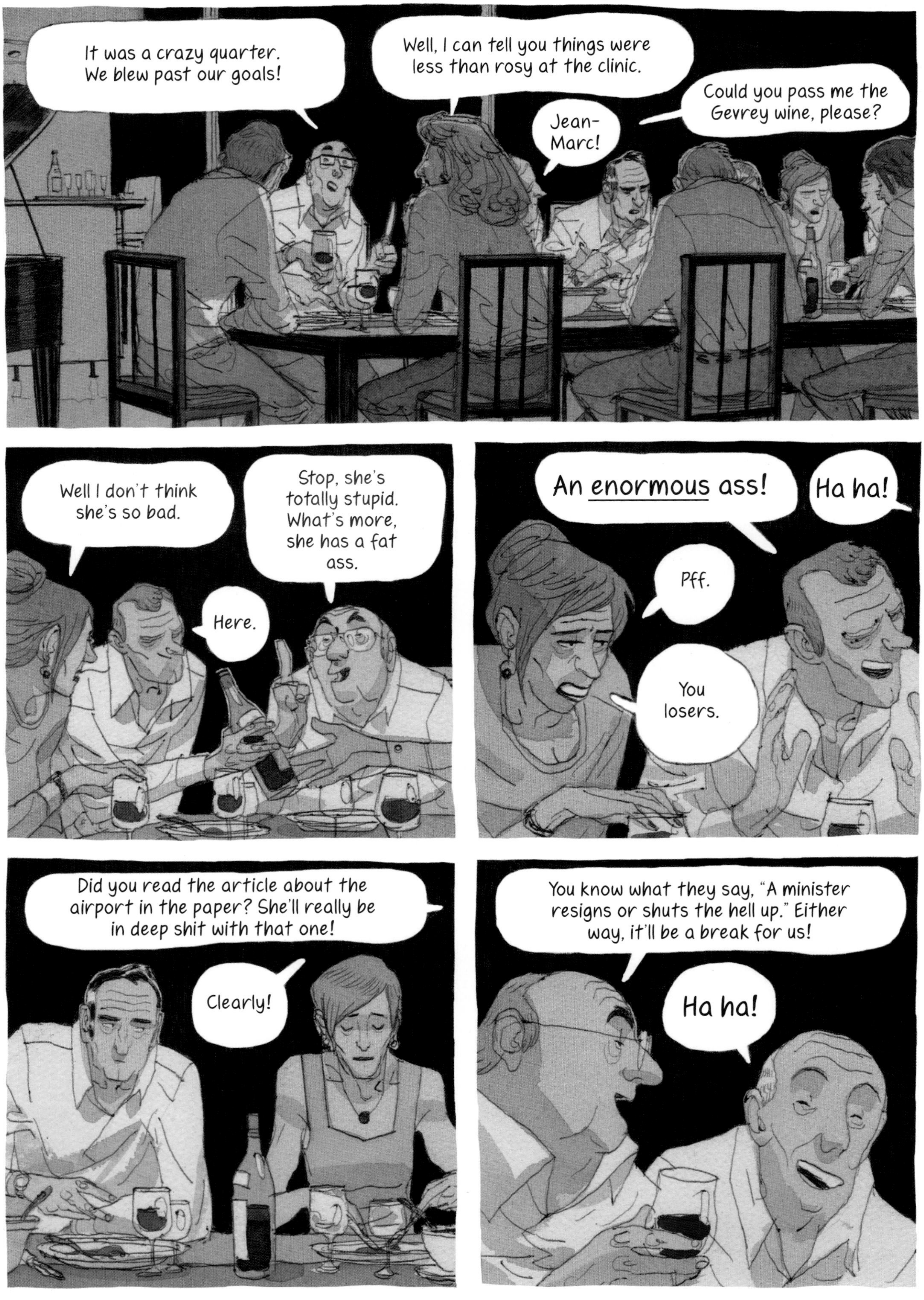
It was a crazy quarter. We blew past our goals!
Well, I can tell you things were less than rosy at the clinic.
Jean-Marc!
Could you pass me the Gevrey wine, please?
Well I don't think she's so bad.
Stop, she's totally stupid. What's more, she has a fat ass.
Here.
An enormous ass!
Ha ha!
Pff.
You losers.
Did you read the article about the airport in the paper? She'll really be in deep shit with that one!
Clearly!
You know what they say, "A minister resigns or shuts the hell up." Either way, it'll be a break for us!
Ha ha!

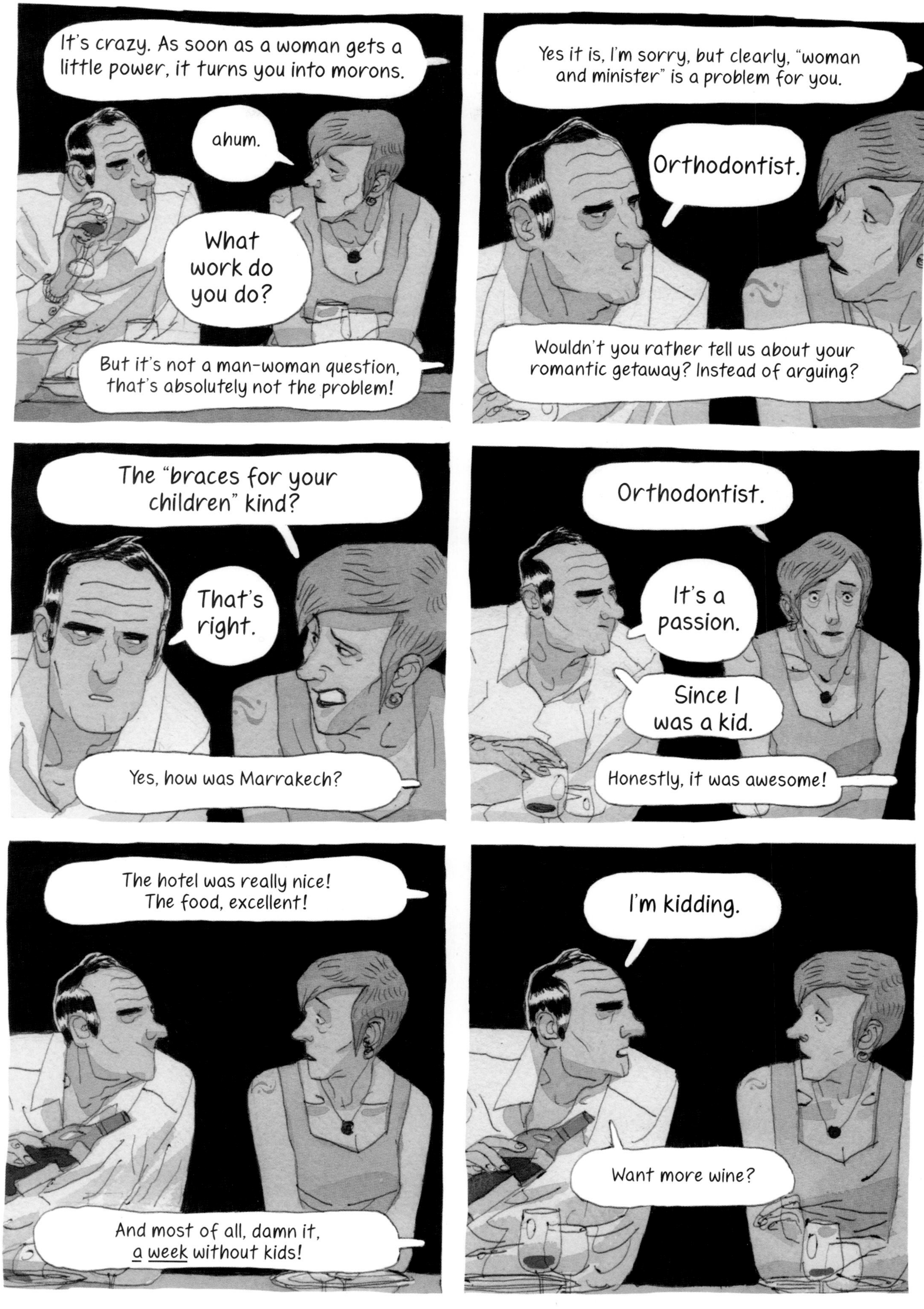
It's crazy. As soon as a woman gets a little power, it turns you into morons.
ahum.
What work do you do?
But it's not a man-woman question, that's absolutely not the problem!
Yes it is, I'm sorry, but clearly, "woman and minister" is a problem for you.
Orthodontist.
Wouldn't you rather tell us about your romantic getaway? Instead of arguing?
The "braces for your children" kind?
That's right.
Yes, how was Marrakech?
Orthodontist.
It's a passion.
Since I was a kid.
Honestly, it was awesome!
The hotel was really nice! The food, excellent!
And most of all, damn it, a week without kids!
I'm kidding.
Want more wine?

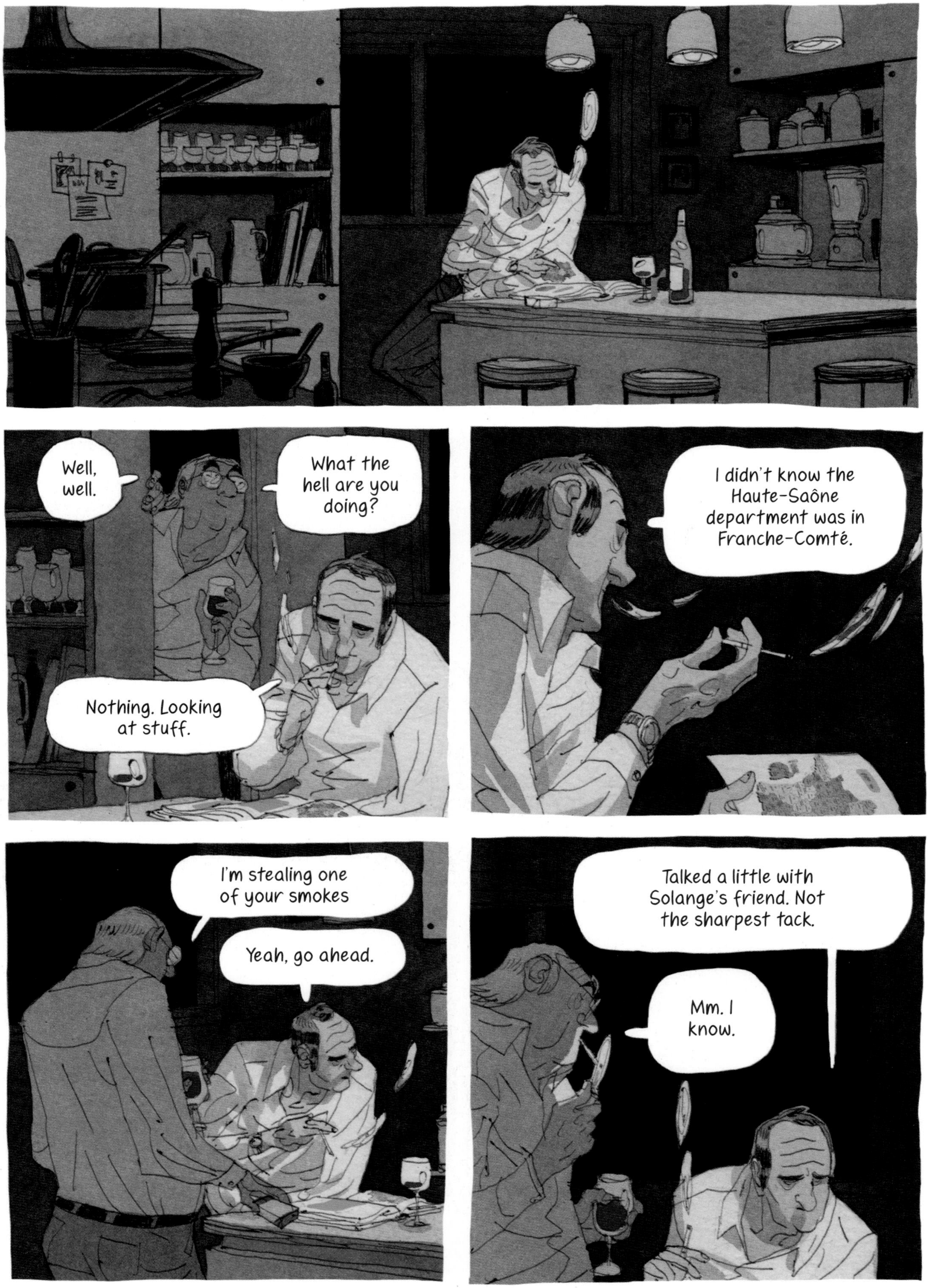
Well, well.
What the hell are you doing?
Nothing. Looking at stuff.
I didn't know the Haute-Saône department was in Franche-Comté.
I'm stealing one of your smokes
Yeah, go ahead.
Talked a little with Solange's friend. Not the sharpest tack.
Mm. I know.

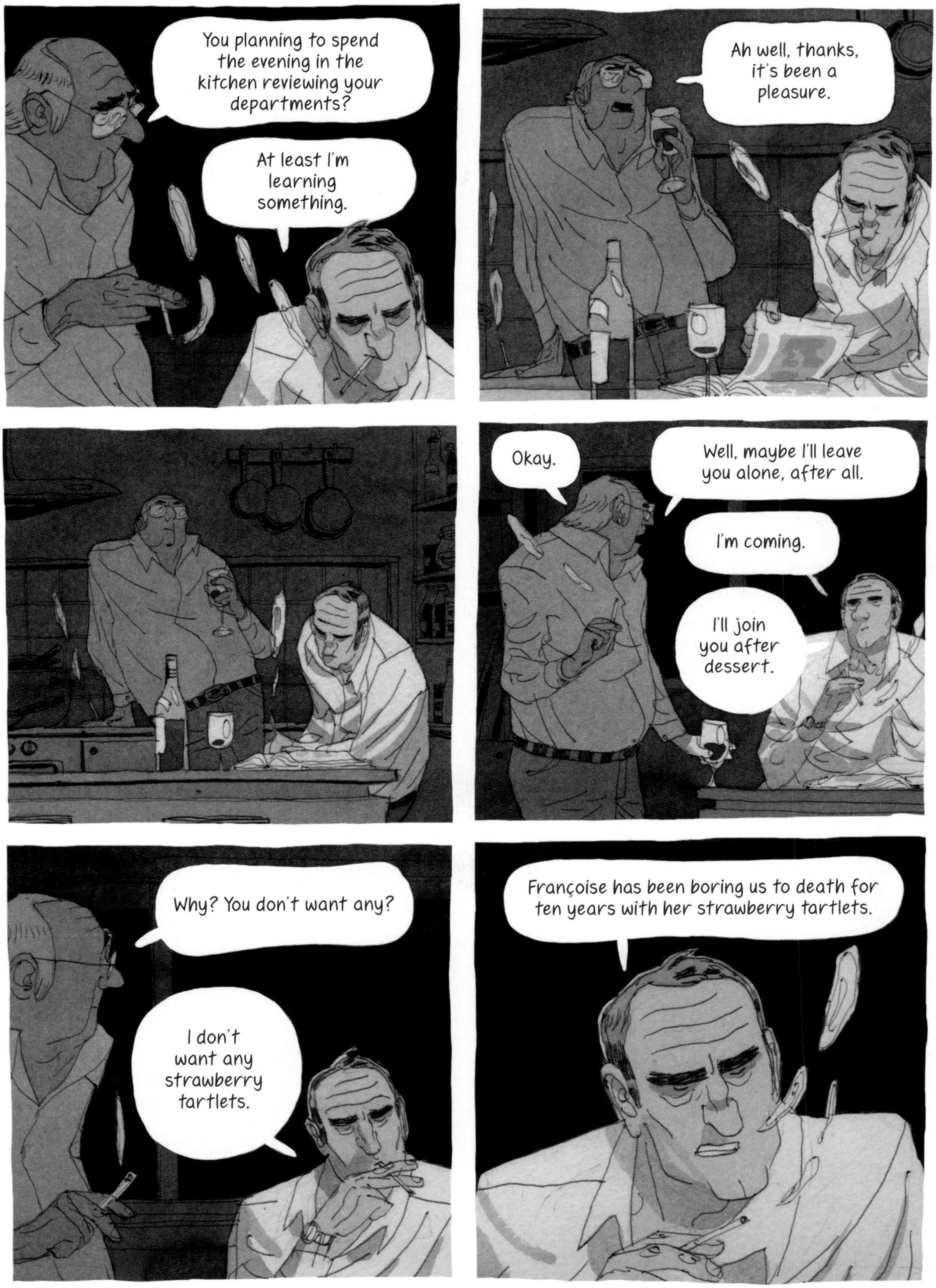

You planning to spend the evening in the kitchen reviewing your departments?
At least I'm learning something.
Ah well, thanks, it's been a pleasure.
Okay.
Well, maybe I'll leave you alone, after all.
I'm coming.
I'll join you after dessert.
Why? You don't want any?
I don't want any strawberry tartlets.
Françoise has been boring us to death for ten years with her strawberry tartlets.

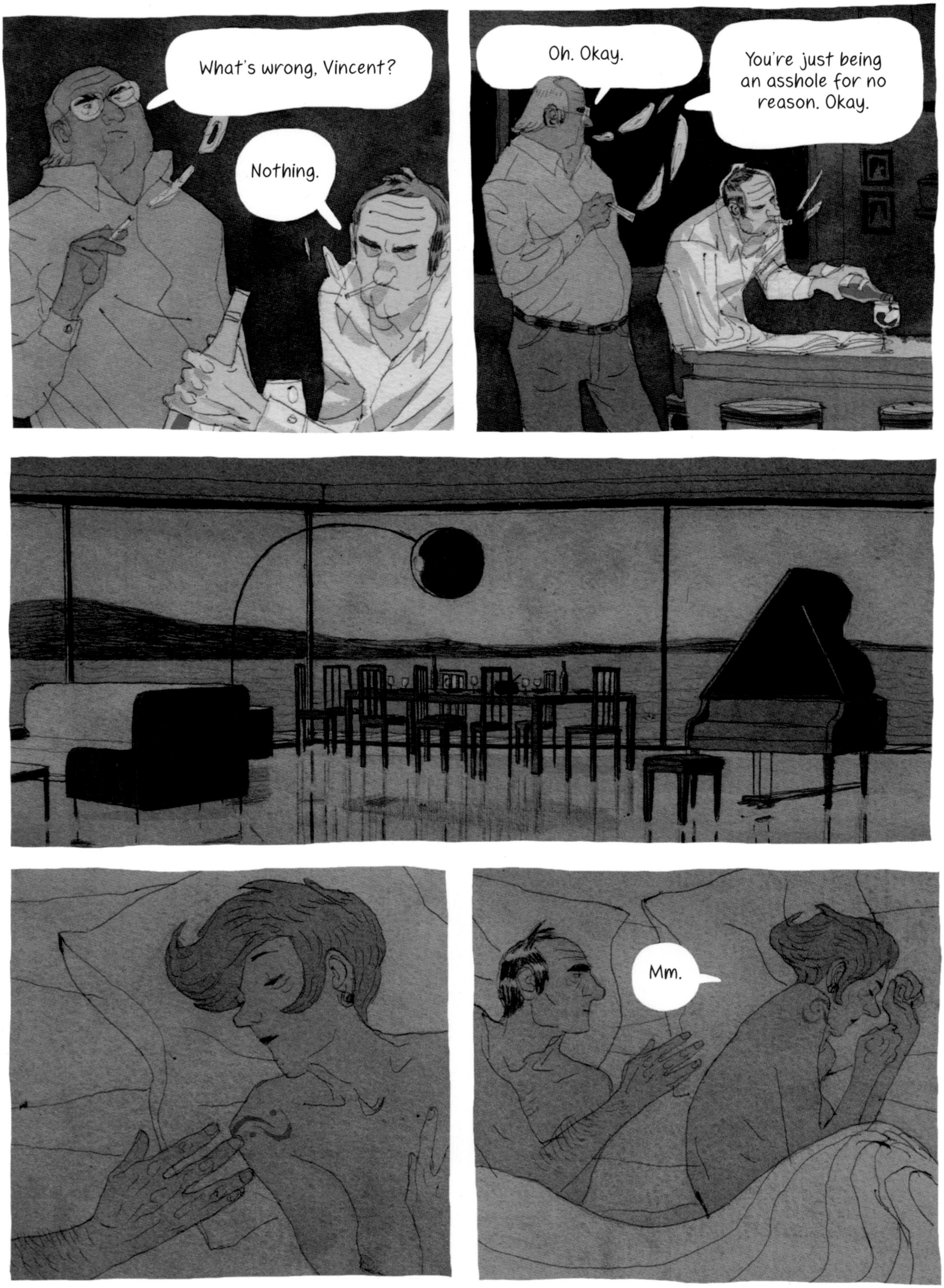
What's wrong, Vincent?
Nothing.
Oh. Okay.
You're just being an asshole for no reason. Okay.
Mm.

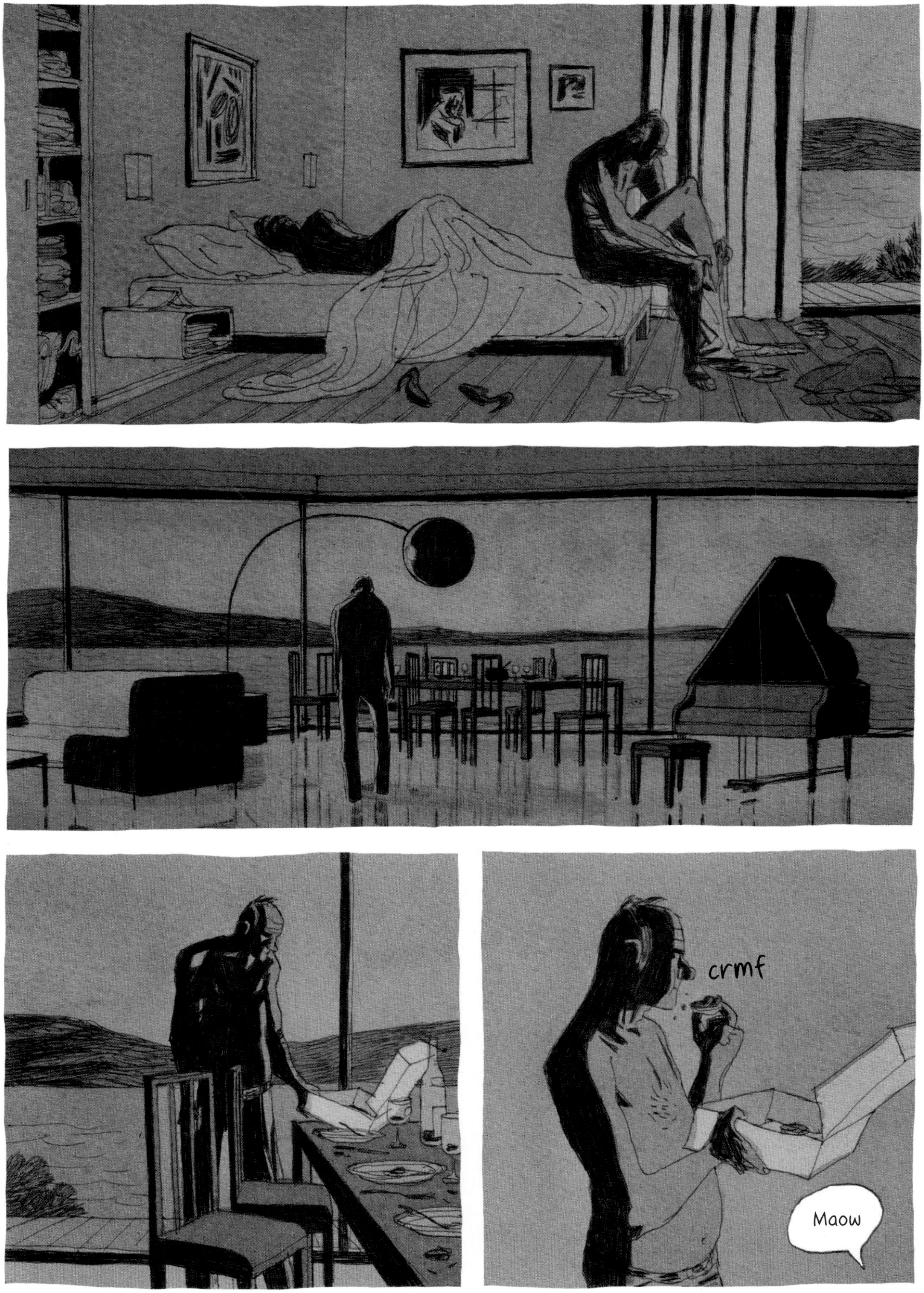
crmf
Maow

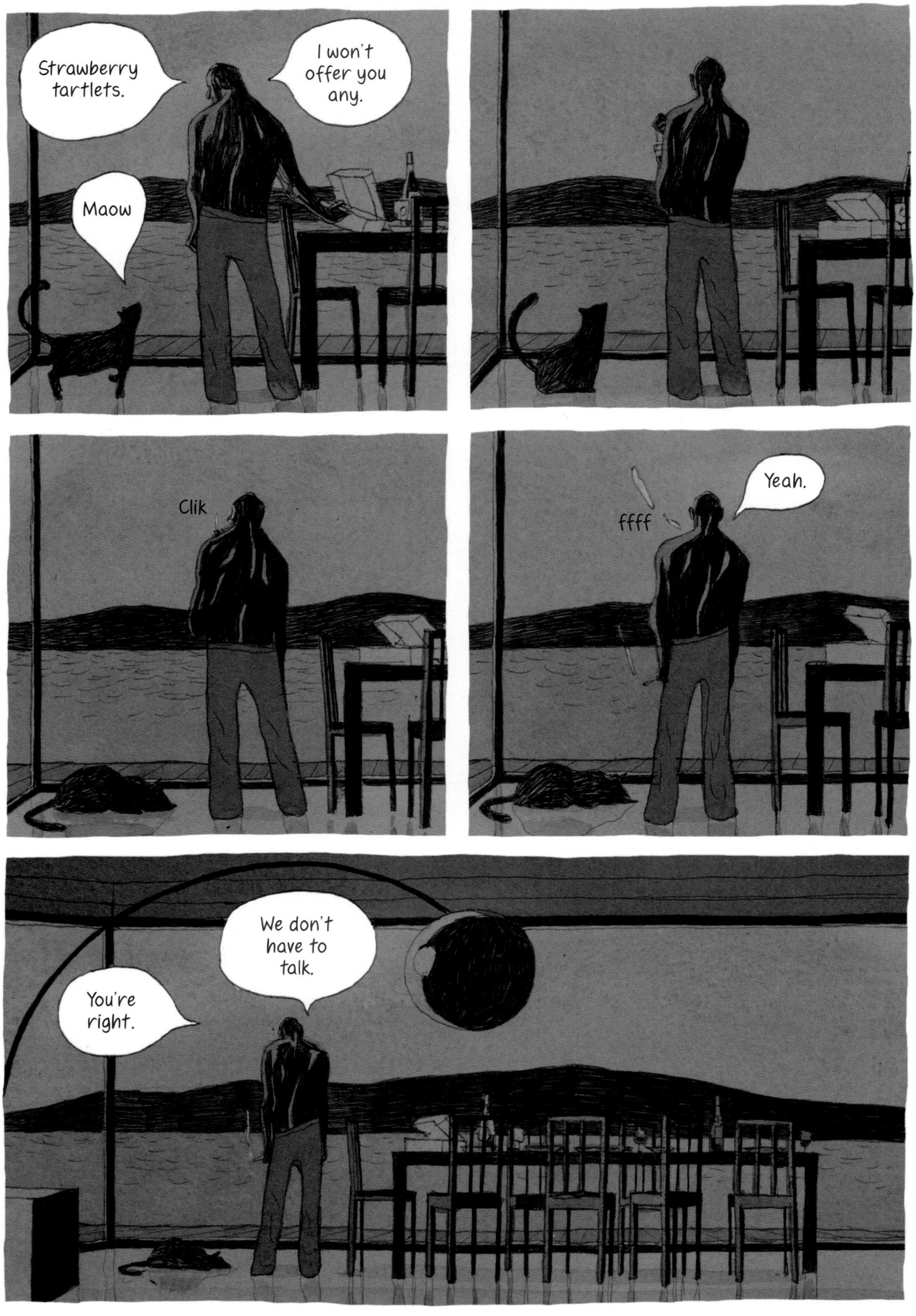
Strawberry tartlets.
I won't offer you any.
Maow
Clik
ffff
Yeah.
We don't have to talk.
You're right.

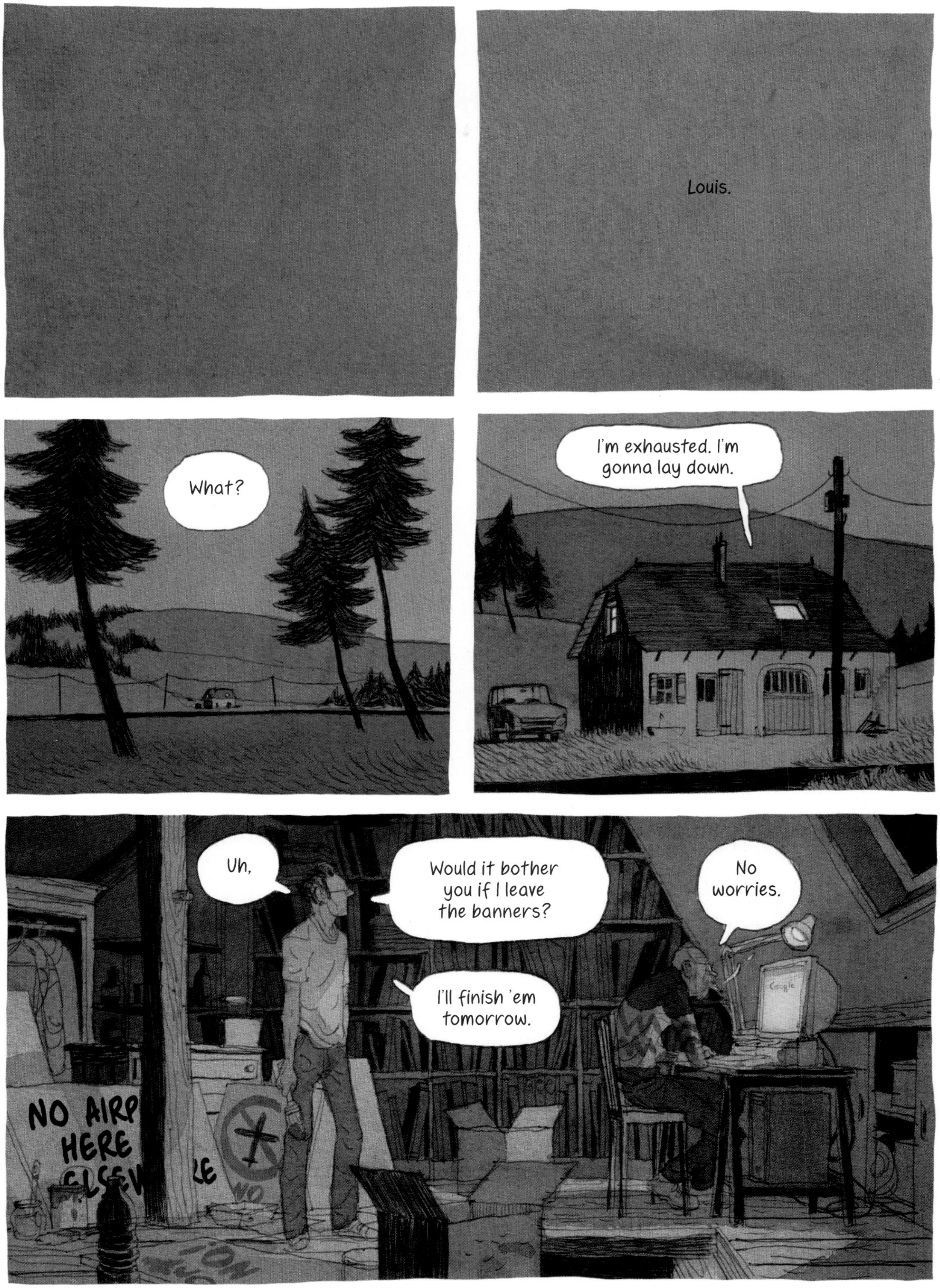
Louis.
What?
I'm exhausted. I'm gonna lay down.
Uh,
Would it bother you if I leave the banners?
I'll finish 'em tomorrow.
No worries.

See you tomorrow. Good night!
Yeah, 'night..
jacques perthus
Google Search
I'm Feeling Lucky
Clik Clik Clik
jacques perthus
Google Search
I'm Feeling
Clik Clik
Galle y Briac Kernoden
Jacques Perthus
Oil on canvas (12"x17")

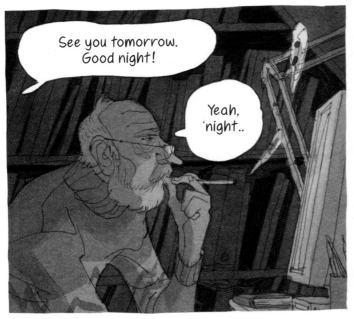

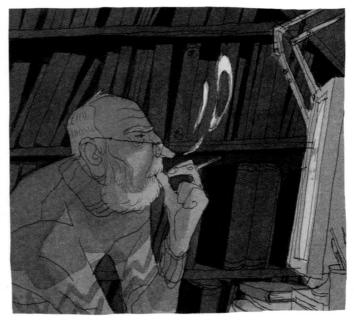

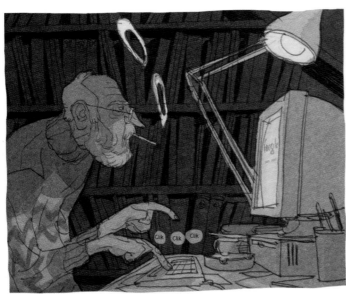

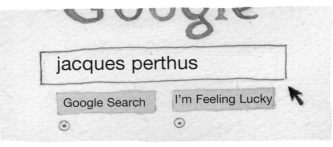

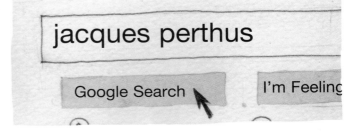

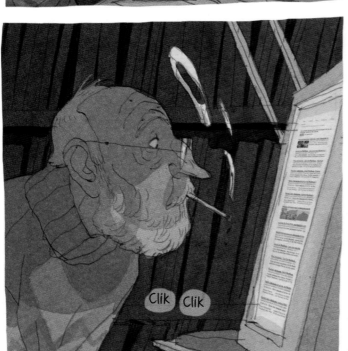

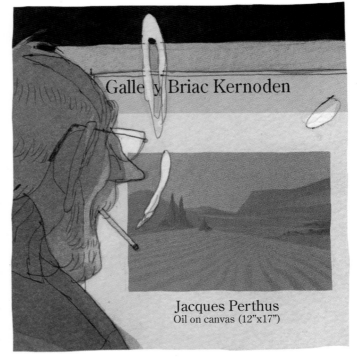

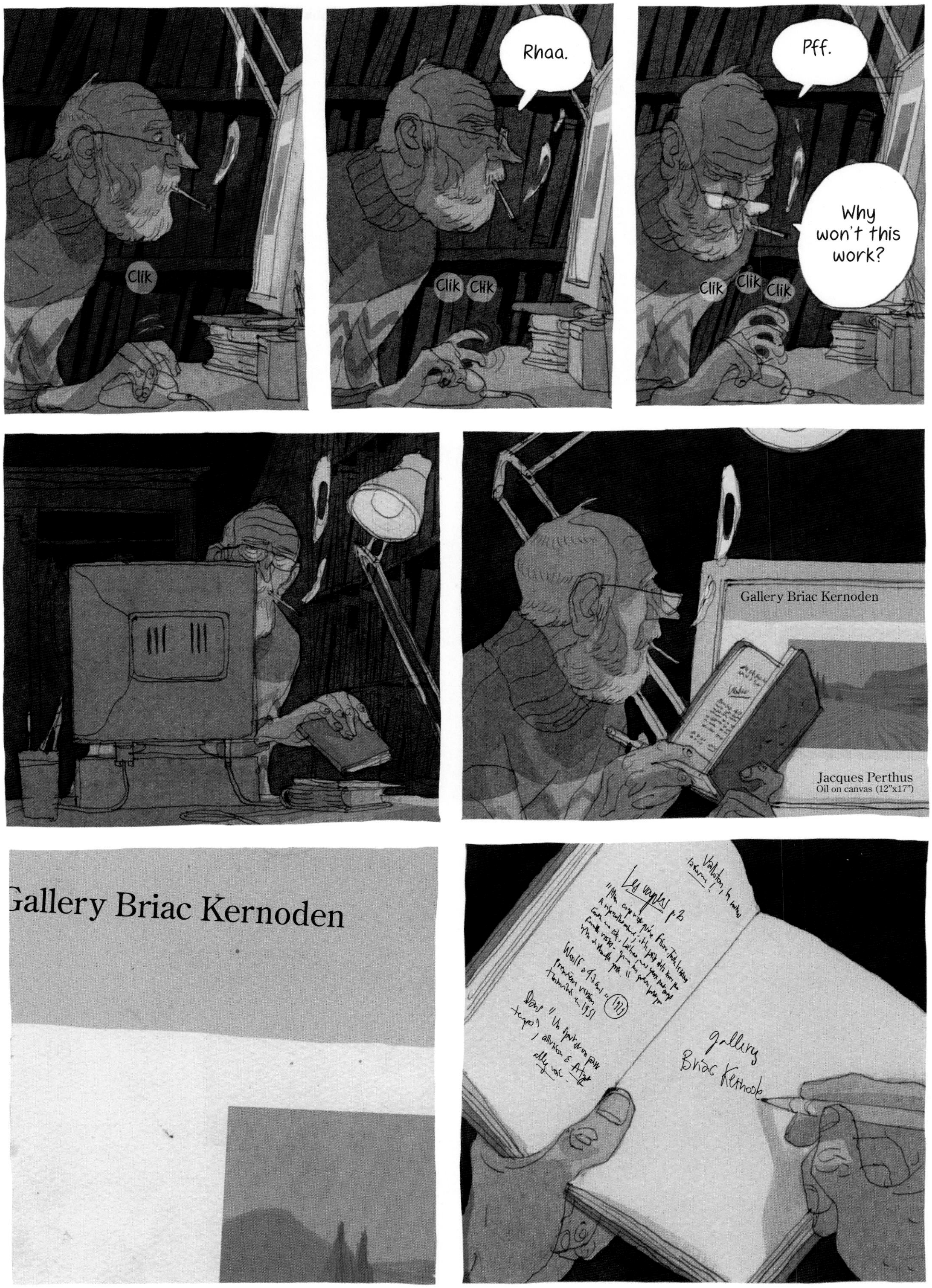
Clik
Rhaa.
Clik Clik
Pff.
Why won't this work?
Clik Clik Clik
Gallery Briac Kernoden
Jacques Perthus
Oil on canvas (12"x17")
Gallery Briac Kernoden

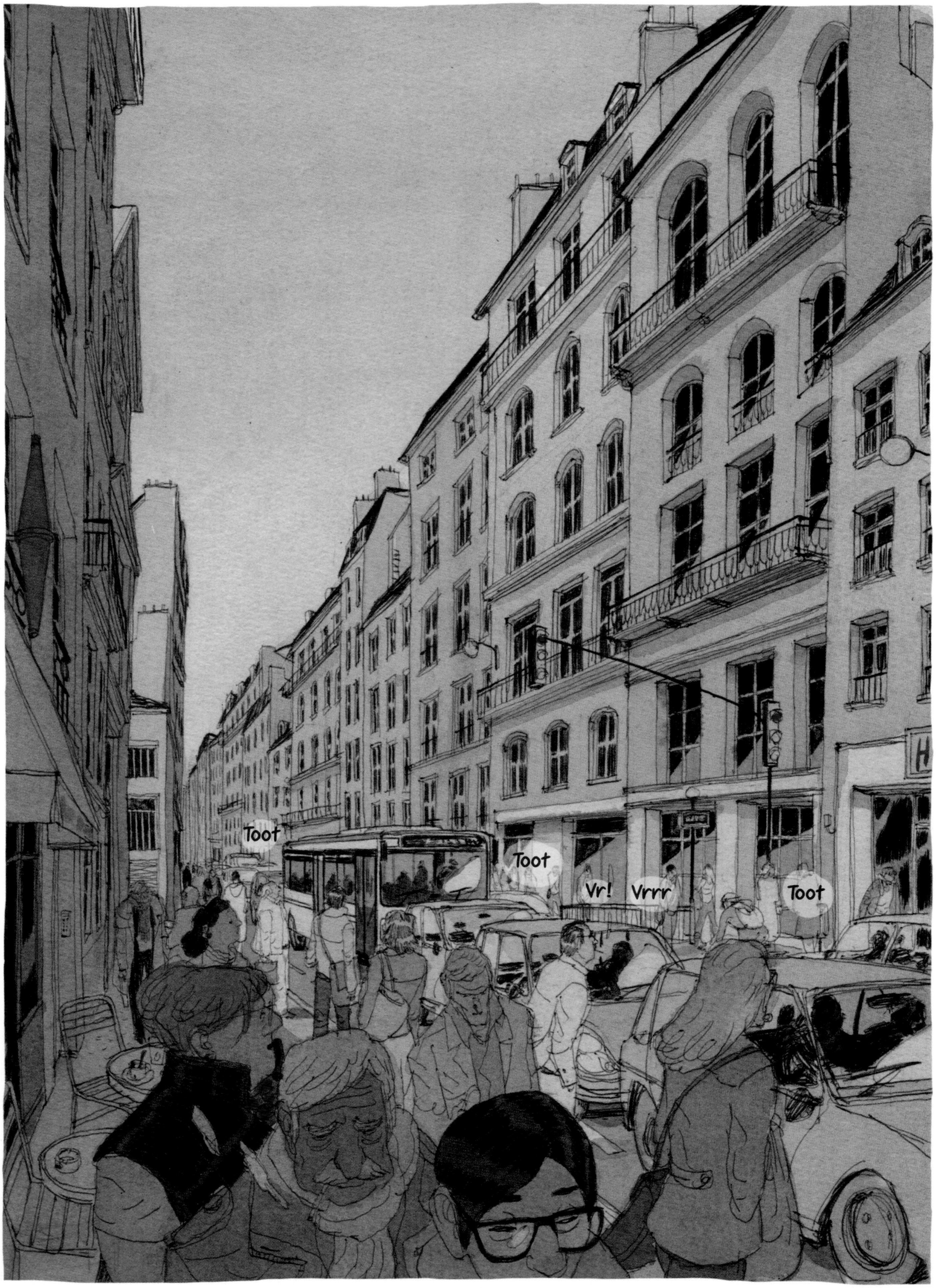
Toot
Toot
Vr!
Vrrr
Toot

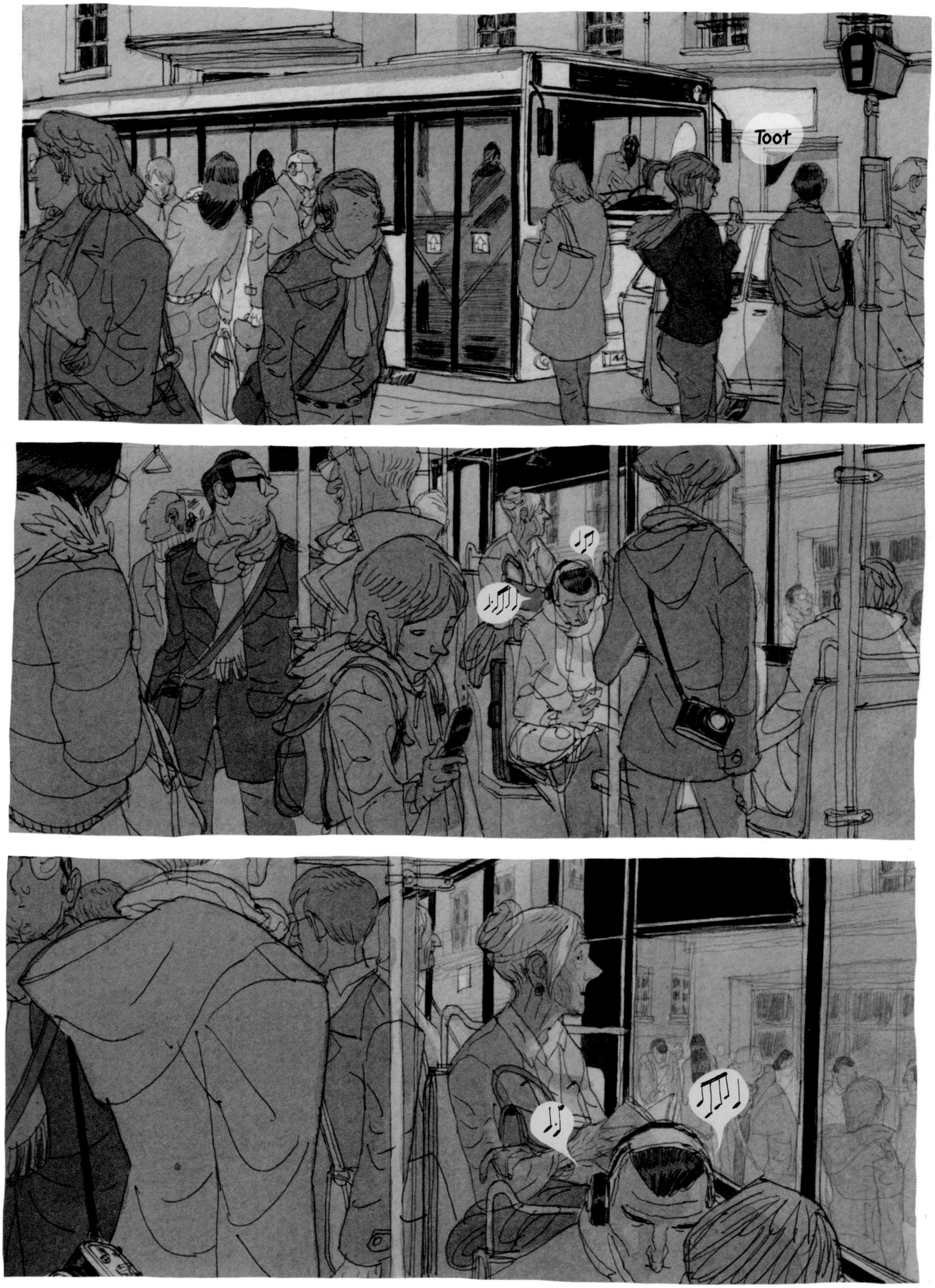
Toot

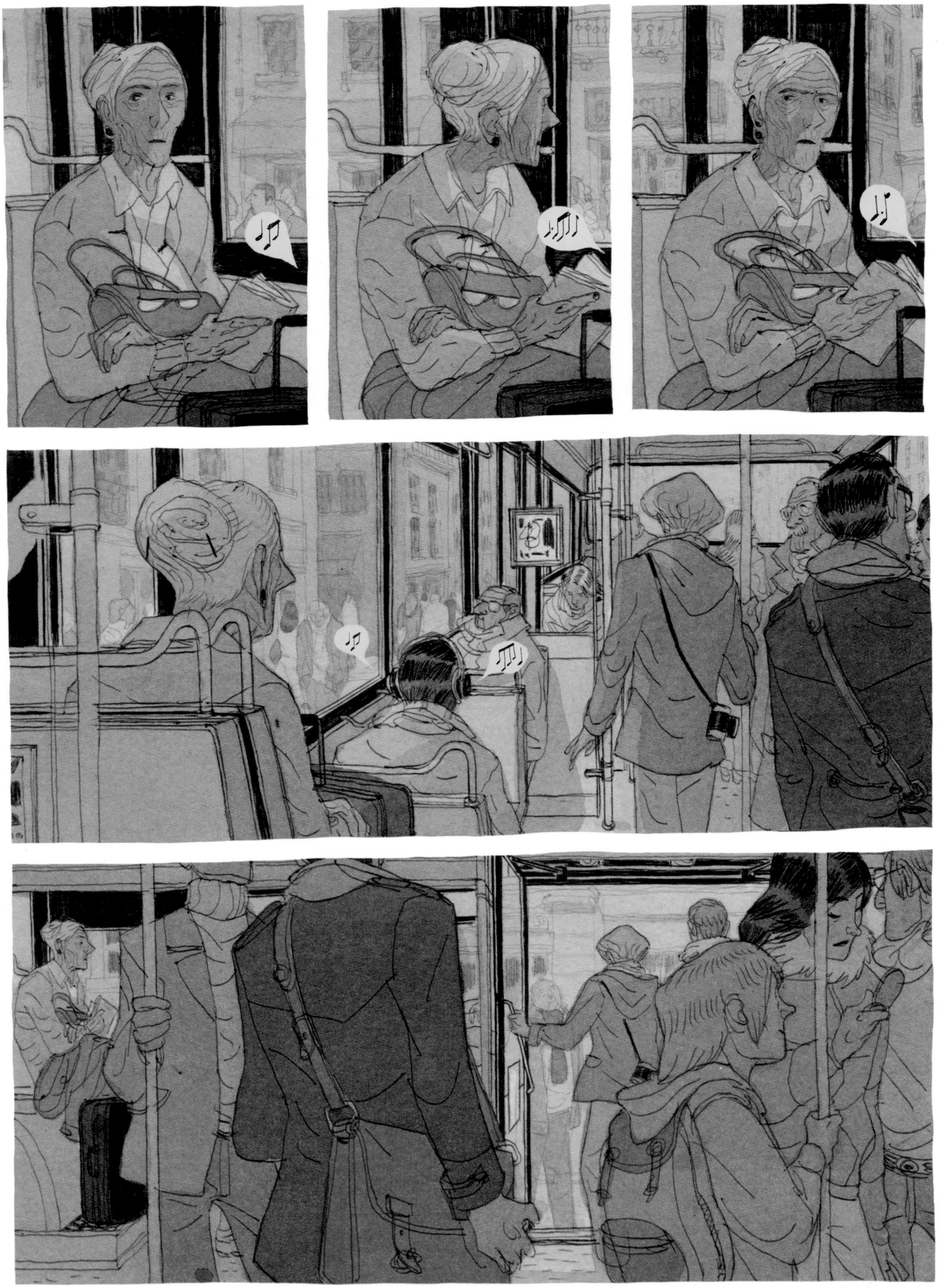

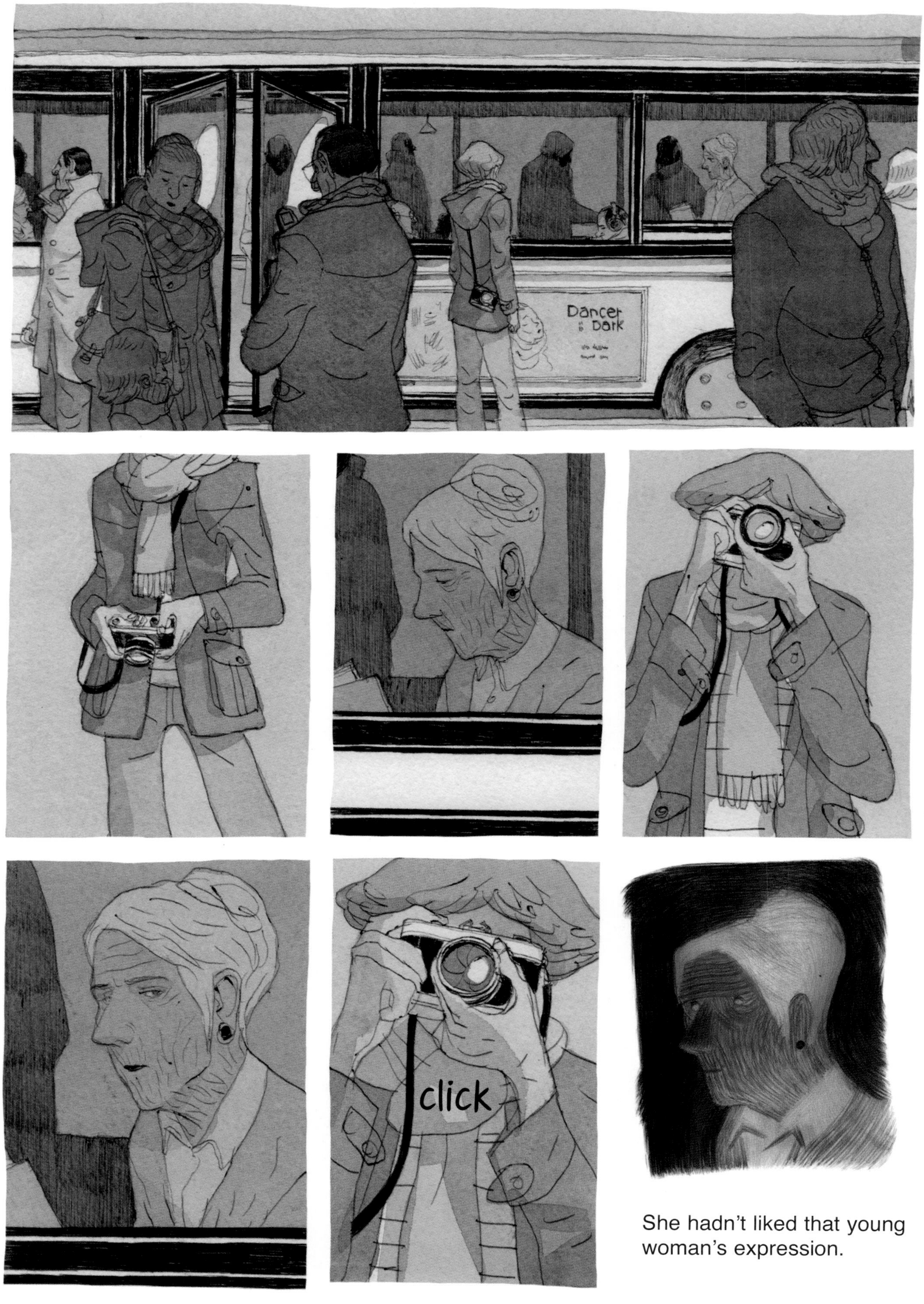
Dancer
Dark
click
She hadn't liked that young woman's expression.

But that's how everyone saw her nowadays.

The driver was driving roughly, in a herky-jerky way.

Despite all her efforts, her immense efforts for it not to happen,

for a very short instant, she'd lost her balance.

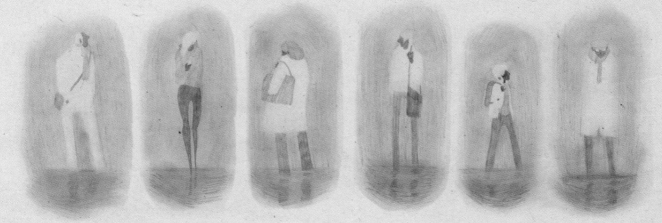

Not enough to fall. Just enough to tip a little bit and be forced to grab the vertical bar too fast, with a clumsy gesture betraying her weakness. The young woman had then risen from her seat, smiling, inviting her to take her place. Nothing serious. Nothing worse than usual. Just that look, always the same. She'd quietly thanked her and sat down, resigned. What good did it do to resist? What good would it do to tell her she was just as alive as she was?

She's trying, without success, to remember the name of that boulevard. The one going all the way to the Place de la Nation. Her Paris map is at home, in Claudine's china cabinet drawer, there where the family picture albums are stored. She still opens them sometimes at night, when she can't get any sleep. It's likely that'll happen tonight. Paradoxically, the fatigue of these trips to and from Dole only accentuates her insomnia. Some pictures in those albums have become family mysteries. Distant uncles, faces with forgotten names, big bellies, laughing eyes, hats, black cars, gardens. Immobile. For forever. Lives transformed into abstract figures on paper. It seems almost impossible to her to imagine those bodies animated with desires, hopes, and suffering. The country outing. The pouting child on the tricycle, the man with a pipe leaning against the cherry tree, the white tablecloth, and the flowery bouquets on the big table all seemed unreal to her to the extent of making their disappearance unimportant.
She, too, in turn, right before everyone's eyes, was slowly becoming an image in the album of the past. An irreversible mutation, difficult to accept, but that was just how the young woman had seen her. Solidly locked behind the mask of her old age.

She wished she could have told her about Louis, about the trip to Biarritz the year she started grad school, about the wine during evenings on the terraces, about the little blue window overlooking the port, about the softness of his sex against hers, then inside her, the strength with which he would hold her in his arms, how she loved it, having an orgasm with him, smoking cigarettes on summer evenings in Madeleine's garden, the smile of Paul, who'd never be coming back, whom she was so afraid of forgetting, the exhaustion of that last night spent with Louis, cuddling together, all those billions of seconds full of life. Why can't people remember that? Why do you have to carry your life with you like some performance that's ephemeral and invisible to others?

The familiar storefront of the florist on Rue Picpus. She'd have to get off soon. Grab her bag. Stand up slowly. Not let herself be surprised once again by the driver hitting the brakes. The next commuter train for Lognes is in twenty minutes, there's no use hurrying. There's no use being afraid.

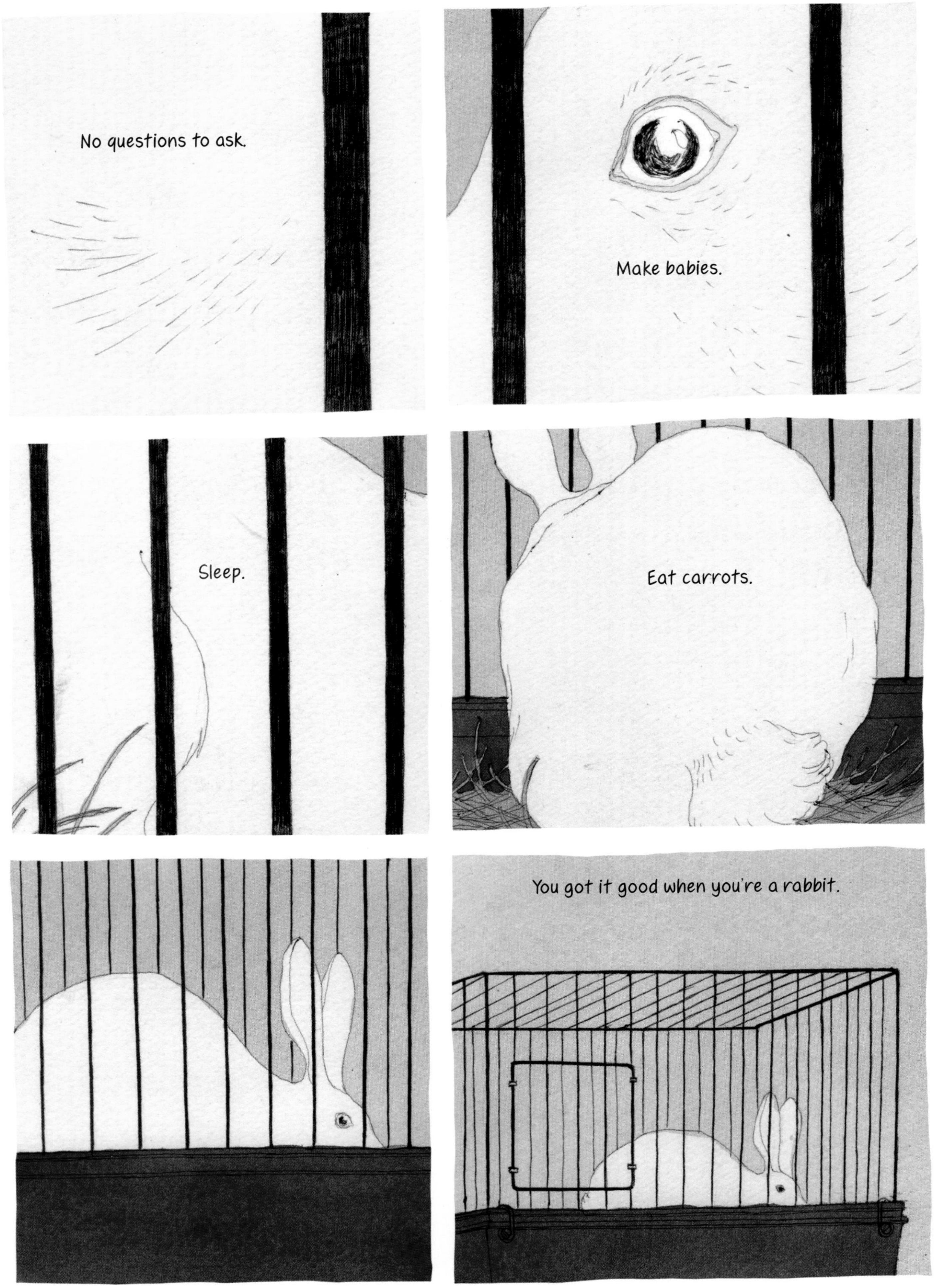
No questions to ask.
Make babies.
Sleep.
Eat carrots.
You got it good when you're a rabbit.

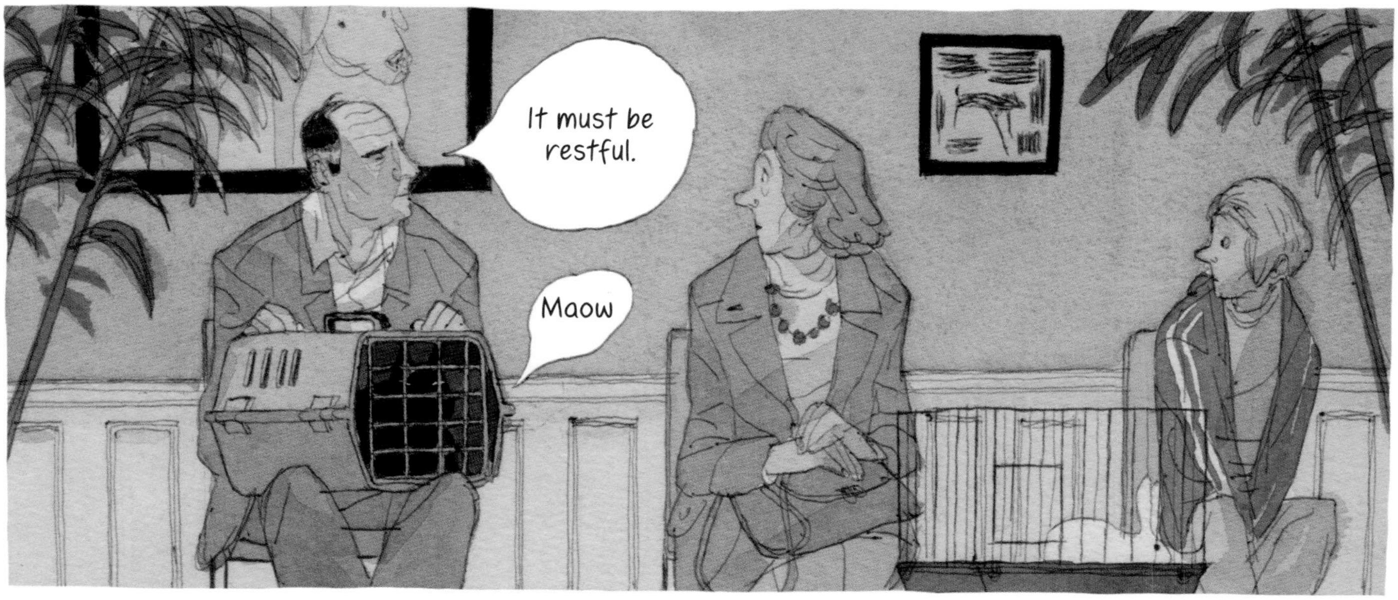
It must be restful.
Maow

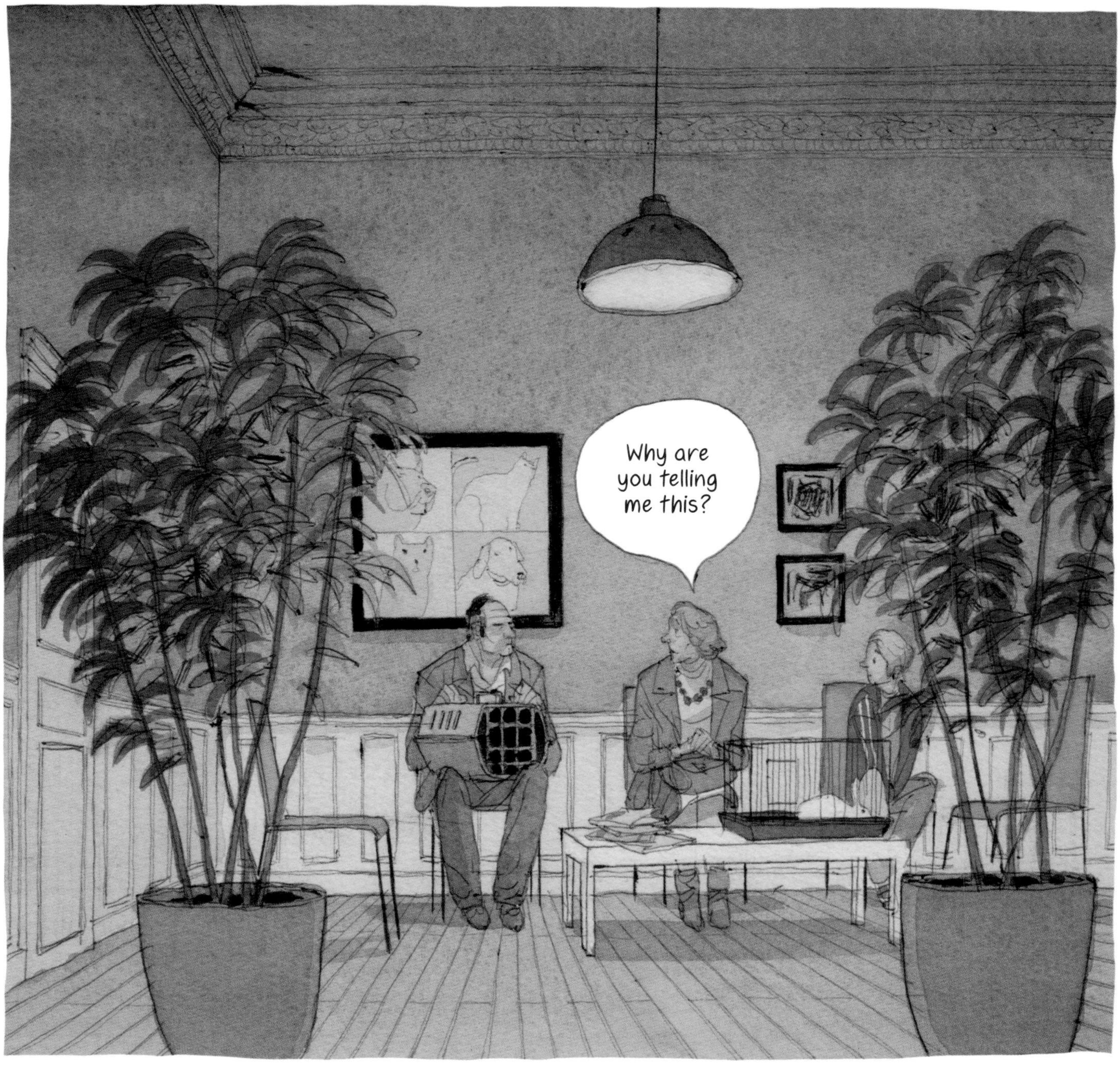
Why are you telling me this?

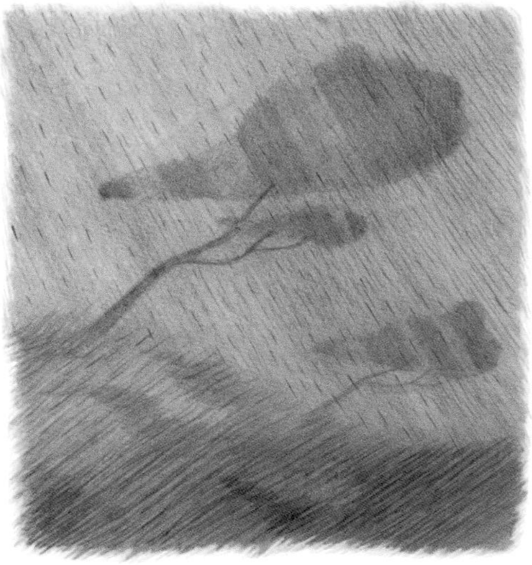

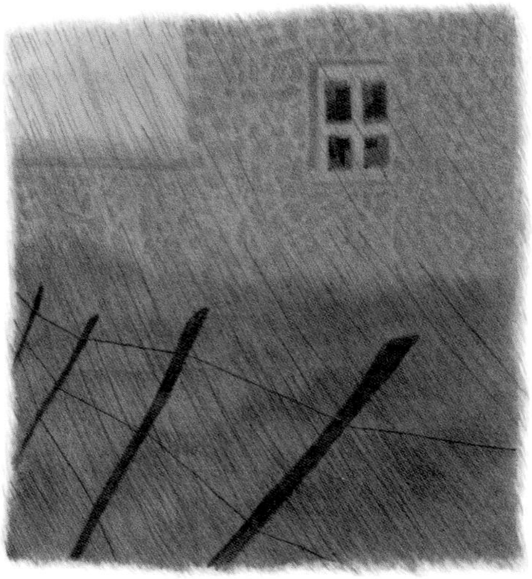

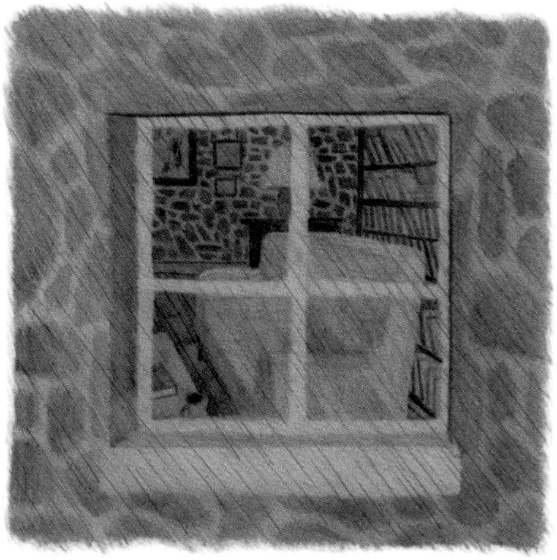

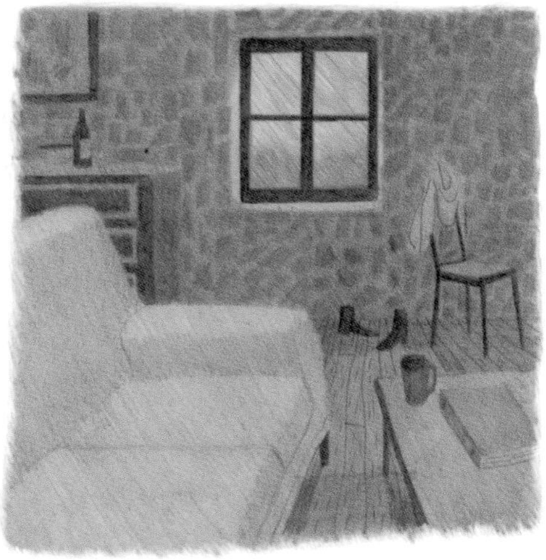

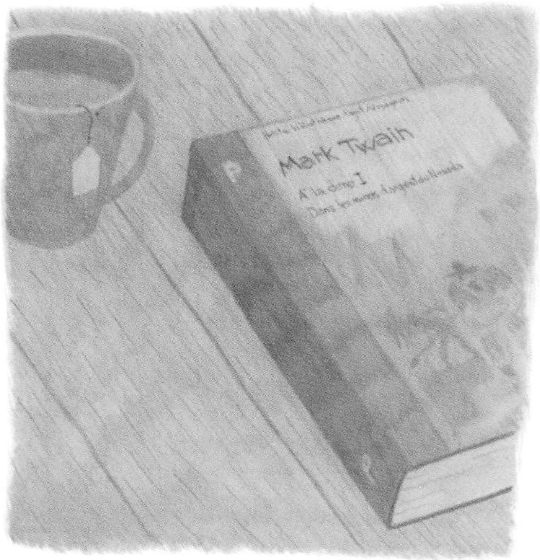
Mark Twain

I know this house well.

Sylvie had often invited us there, back when we all thought we couldn't do without one another. Back then, none of us could have imagined not being part of one of those weekends in Brittany. Sometimes, though, I'd have rather stayed alone in Paris. The fear of excluding myself from their circle, of losing a little of their friendship always won out and prompted me to follow along despite that need for solitude. I'd go, forcing myself a bit, troubled by that disagreeable feeling of obligation. We'd meet up at the Montparnasse station, and the few hours on the train to Redon would end up convincing me it was good to be with them. I'd made the right choice, I just had to let myself be carried along for two days by that collective enthusiasm, in which it was comfortable to forget yourself.

Little by little, I got used to the couch's indifferent color, somewhere between beige pink and sick salmon. I remember trying to kiss Sylvie there, one night when we'd all drunk too much. She'd quickly pushed me away with the back of her hand and couldn't keep herself from a fleeting, rather humiliating sneer of disgust. Not because I was a girl, but because it was me. I capped off the evening by puking in the garden after finishing my last bottle of mead with Fred. Soon I'll have been here for three weeks, I have my habits. A cup of coffee by the fireside, I eat, I read, I smoke, I sleep, all of it on the salmon-colored couch. There are lots of rooms upstairs, but it's way too cold up there. While handing the house keys to me, Olivier had a big smile on his face. But that kindly signal wasn't addressed to me, he was smiling at the kind, good person he considered himself to be. With all my strength, I'd held back from hitting him, from really hurting him, and then I thanked him, once again. Sylvie and he have been together since our college years. I'd run into them by chance, while dawdling towards the Bastille. "Oh wow, this is great, it's such a pleasure to see you!" I always wonder where these phrases come from, despite oneself. Uttered so naturally, without thinking a single word of it. Yet, I remembered perfectly my contortions to have and keep my place within the banal, little group of students we once formed.

Our forced happiness. Our little friendships. The tiny, useless dramas tolerated for lack of anything better, to not be alone. I'd played the game, like the others, neither better nor less well, but it was unpleasant to remember it after all these years by running into Sylvie and Olivier again. Maybe it was a bit true, after all. Maybe I truly had been happy to see them again, after having run away from them for so long. Olivier had never left college, now teaching public law, still just as implacably kind, brilliant, charming, his face smooth, not a shadow. Sylvie hasn't changed much either. I rediscovered her large blue eyes and the small, very black beauty spot on her neck, under her right ear. They'd invited me for dinner at their home, in the 20th arrondissement. Olivier had listened attentively to me, his head angled to the side, while gently swirling some sort of Bordeaux in an immense glass. Sylvie had laid her head on his shoulder and squinted a little at certain parts of my story. It could be summed up rather easily. I'd left college to meet up with a very handsome guy in Spain, whom I'd dumped two months later. For ten years, I'd been stringing together shitty little jobs here and there, when there were any. That's all. At the moment, I was almost out of money, so I was crashing at a girlfriend's place in Montrouge, but I was fine, I was managing. Yes, I'd like a little more wine. I didn't feel like telling them about the last three weeks at a chicken factory in La Roche-sur-Yon, how they'd paralyzed me. That's when I gave up. I didn't think I could go on much longer being a empty-minded robot eight hours a day. Eight hours thinking of nothing else but that instant when the factory whistle announces day's end. Eight hours before I could get on my bicycle, go to my parents' home, for lack of the means to pay for my own apartment. Trying to get rid of the nasty meat odor with two, three showers sometimes, and collapsing till the next morning, till the next eight-hour day. One morning, I didn't get up, it didn't mean anything anymore. I don't want to ever do that again, never ever.

I don't know why they offered me the house, as long as I needed it, if that'd help me out. It happened all at once. They'd looked at each other furtively, Sylvie poured me another glass, and Olivier made that proposal to me. I was a little drunk. I didn't feel obliged to pretend to hesitate, or to look grateful or touched by their gesture. At the moment, I was a little mad at myself. Olivier's smile when he handed me the keys had removed all my scruples. They needed to feel generous, I needed shelter. It was a simple compromise disguised as a gesture of reciprocal friendship.

It's a comfort being here. I don't have much, but it's not a struggle for me anymore. Before leaving Paris, I bought an old reflex camera near Place Clichy. That was stupid. I'll have to eat noodles for a month. I don't know what got into me. It'd been years since I took pictures. I was walking down the street, the keys to the house in my backpack. In the clear. Yet I had the feeling I was sinking. Around me, the passersby seemed like they were guided by a precise roadmap whose instructions simply had to be followed. Take bus 69 to go to Père Lachaise. Buy bread for lunch. Go get perfume samples at Sephora's. Deposit my check in the bank. Call Lyon for the November order. Everyone seemed to have no doubt as to what had to be done, and I needed, as well, to be able to cling to something, right away. I saw the Nikon in the window, I didn't think. Coming out of the shop, I loaded the camera right away, and I walked from Clichy to Montparnasse taking photos. With the last film roll, I almost attained "disappearance," that moment where all your vital energy is there, available, in your gaze, in your hands twisting the adapter rings without hesitating. You're nothing more than an eye. You don't think anymore. You don't exist anymore but you're completely in the moment at the same time.

I'd stopped after college and thrown it all away, except for a few negatives from Spain. What good was it wasting your time trying to catch invisible, impossible-to-name particles with your bare hands?

I needed time to realize I'd been feeling that since forever. That "thing" that resonates. I wanted to bring it out of me, to understand, do something with it, but what?

I sometimes wonder if I truly had so little need of others, or if I kept myself apart for lack of being able to be myself while with them. Our discussions seemed like parallel monologues. We shared nothing other than our mutual incomprehension. However, from time to time, I'd run into them. I'd see a body, a face and, for a short instant, I'd hear their music. I'd have liked to have taken them into my arms and say to them: "Did you sense that, too? Did you hear how beautiful it was? I was reaching towards you, and I saw something right and true. Something happened, here and now, which won't ever happen again." It was impossible to do that, I was incapable of it. I couldn't speak to them. They scared me, and I'd have scared them. So I took photos of them, without really knowing why. And then I stopped, to do useful, concrete things. To find a direction. A reason. I went along so for years, like a sleepwalker. When I awake, I don't know where I am, where I'm going, or how I got there, in pajamas on a salmon-pink couch.

If they're not too difficult over at welfare, I can hold out for a while. I just want to be left in peace. I want to be alone, with nothing else to prove to anybody.

The fire's dying down, but I really don't feel up to going out to look for wood. With all the rain coming down, it must be completely soaked, too. I'll try to fall asleep now, while it's still warm. I'll start up with Mark Twain again tomorrow morning. I stretch out under three thick covers made of heavy, blue wool that's a little itchy. My legs still hurt from having run around too much yesterday. The regular song of the rain on the roof reminds me I'm in a safe place.

I should get the Paris negatives developed.

I should have done some stretches, but it's the back of my thighs.

I don't know how you stretch those muscles.

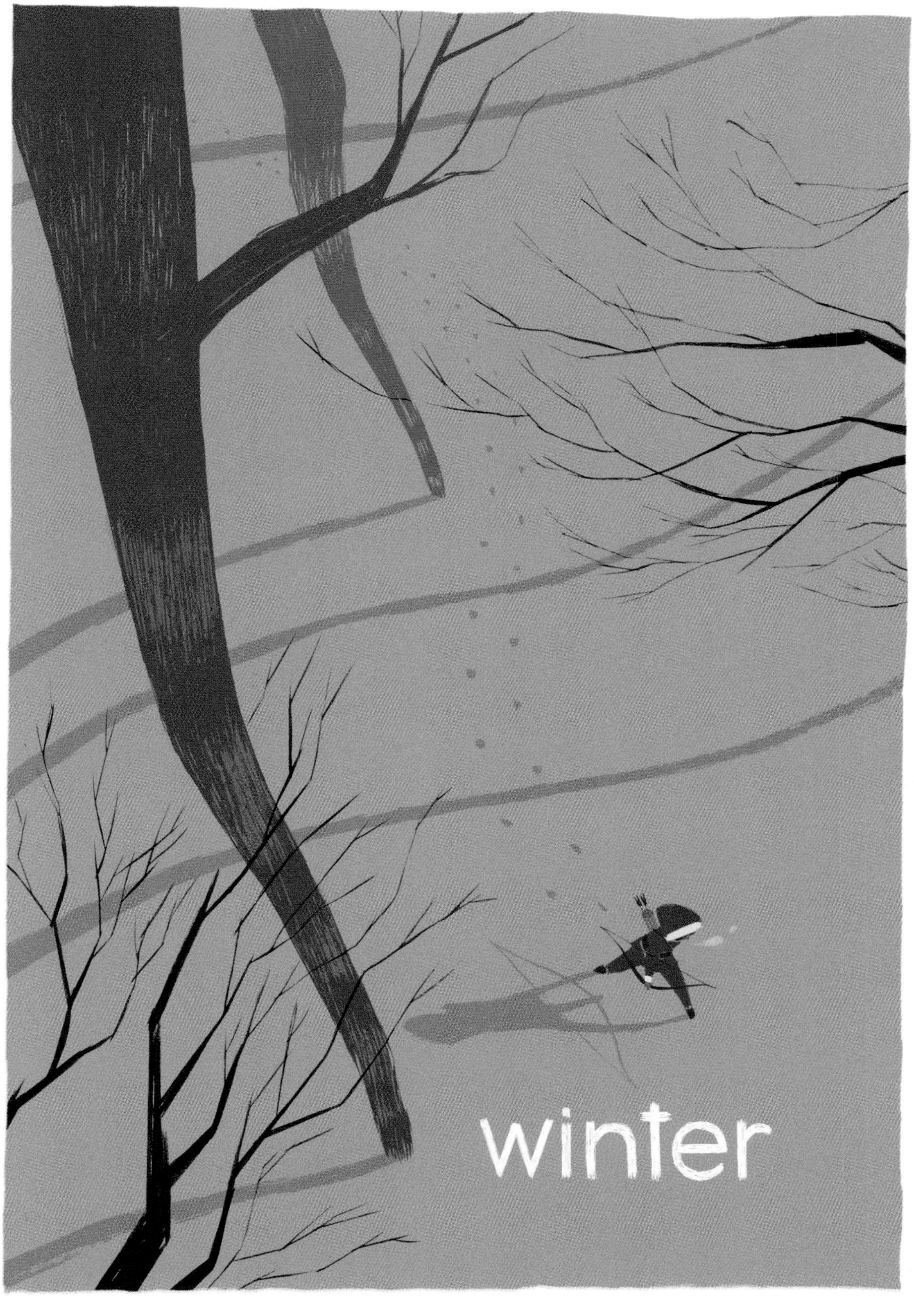
winter

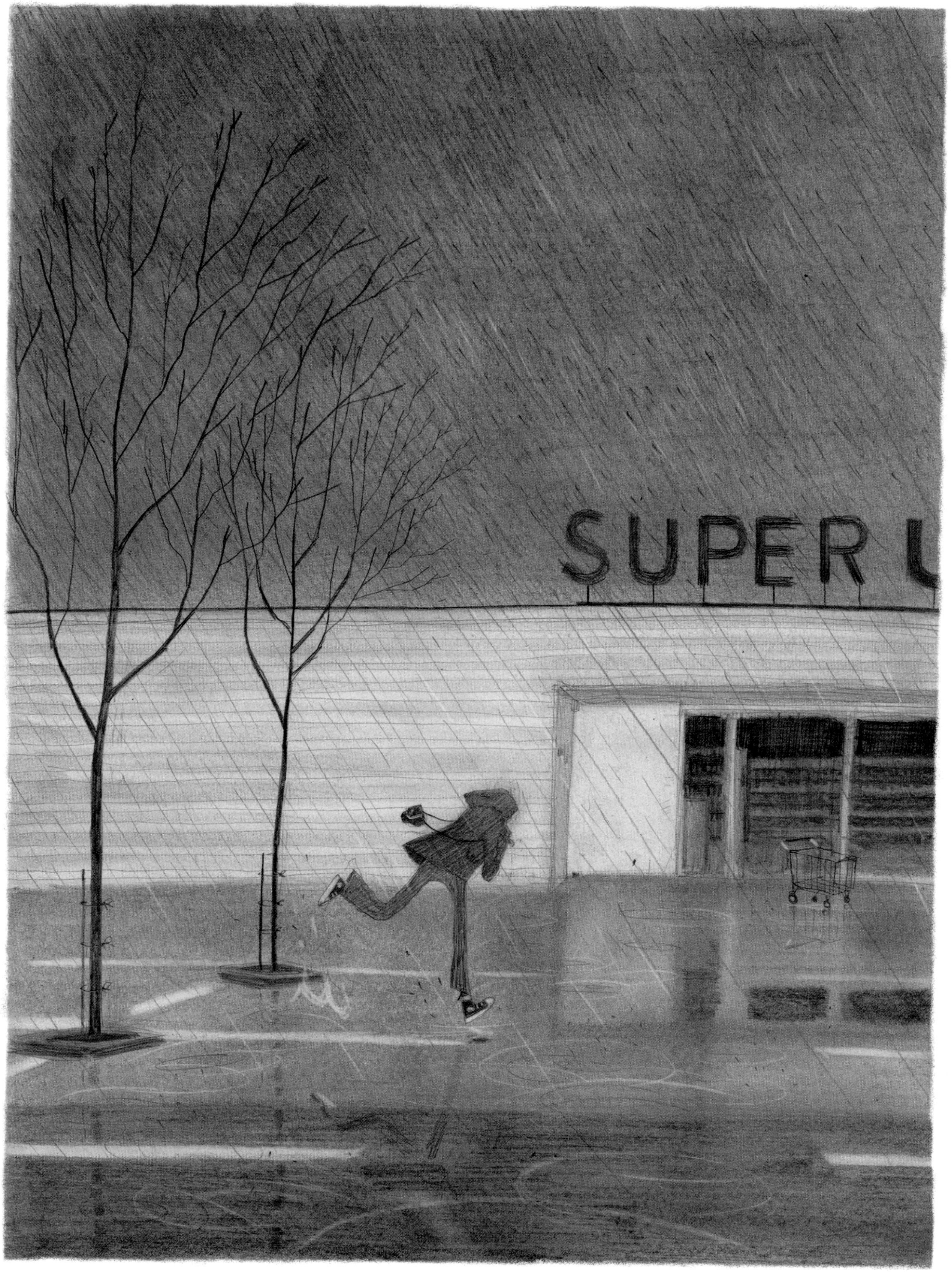
SUPER U

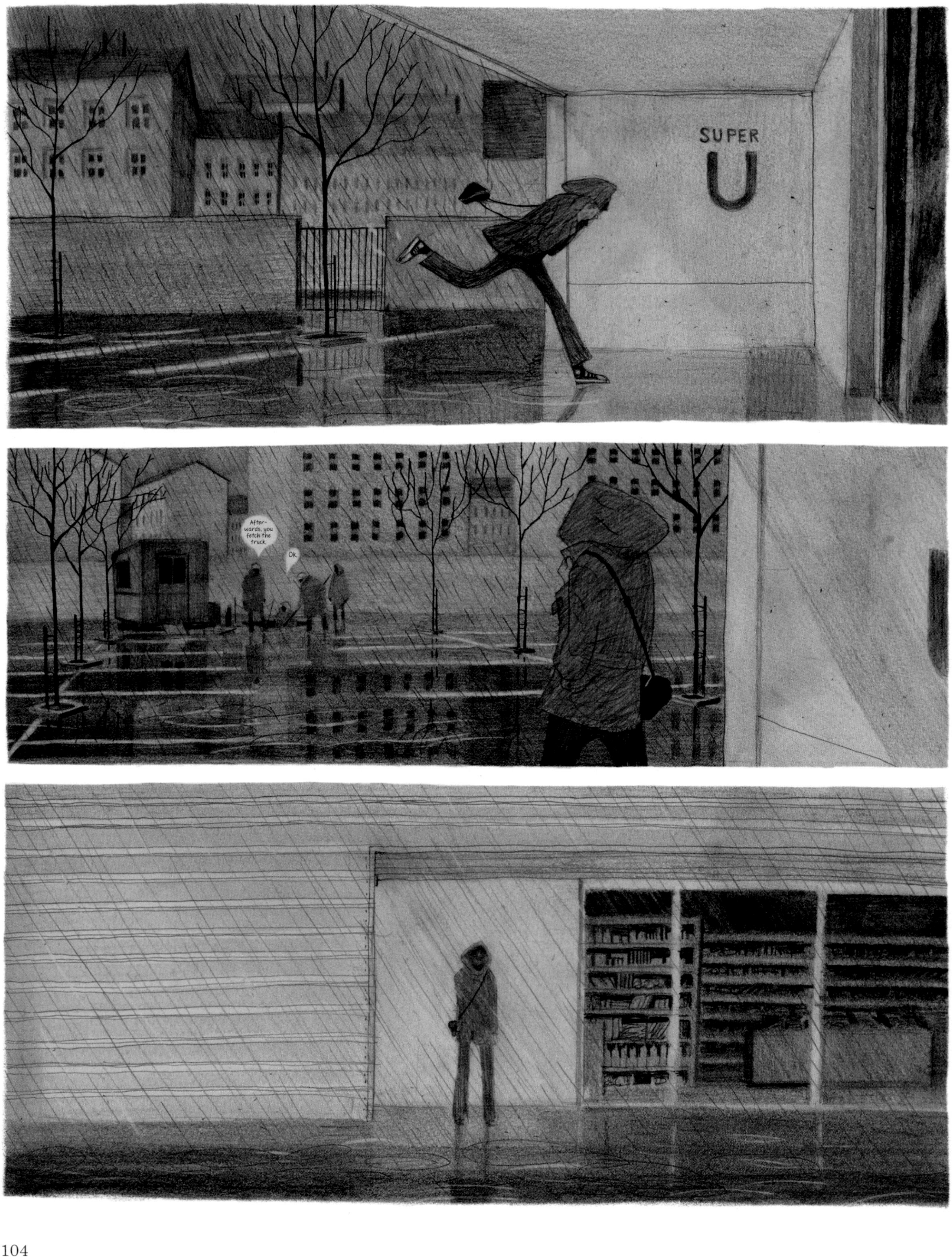
SUPER U
After-wards, you fetch the truck.
Ok.

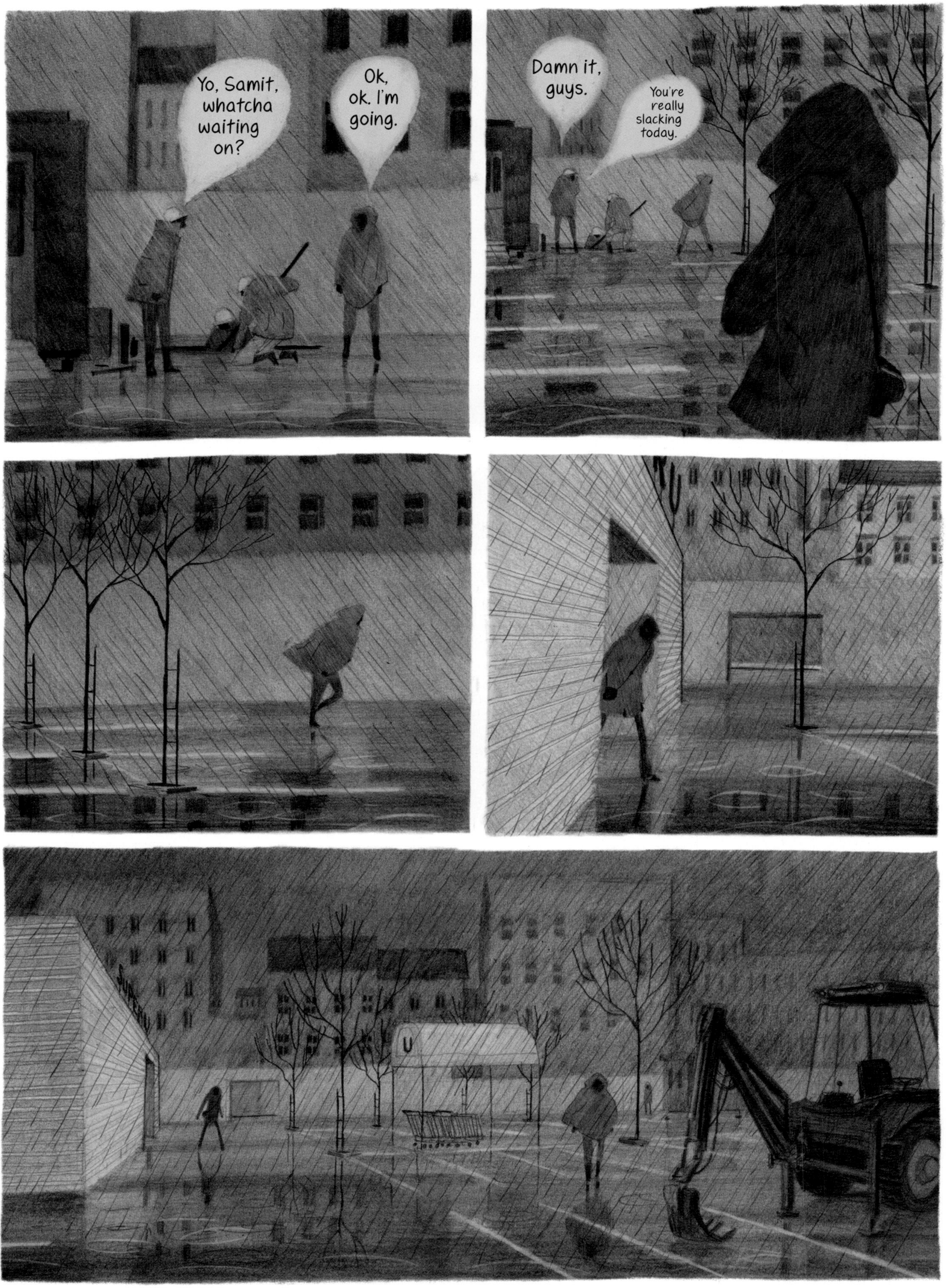
Yo, Samit, whatcha waiting on?
Ok, ok. I'm going.
Damn it, guys.
You're really slacking today.

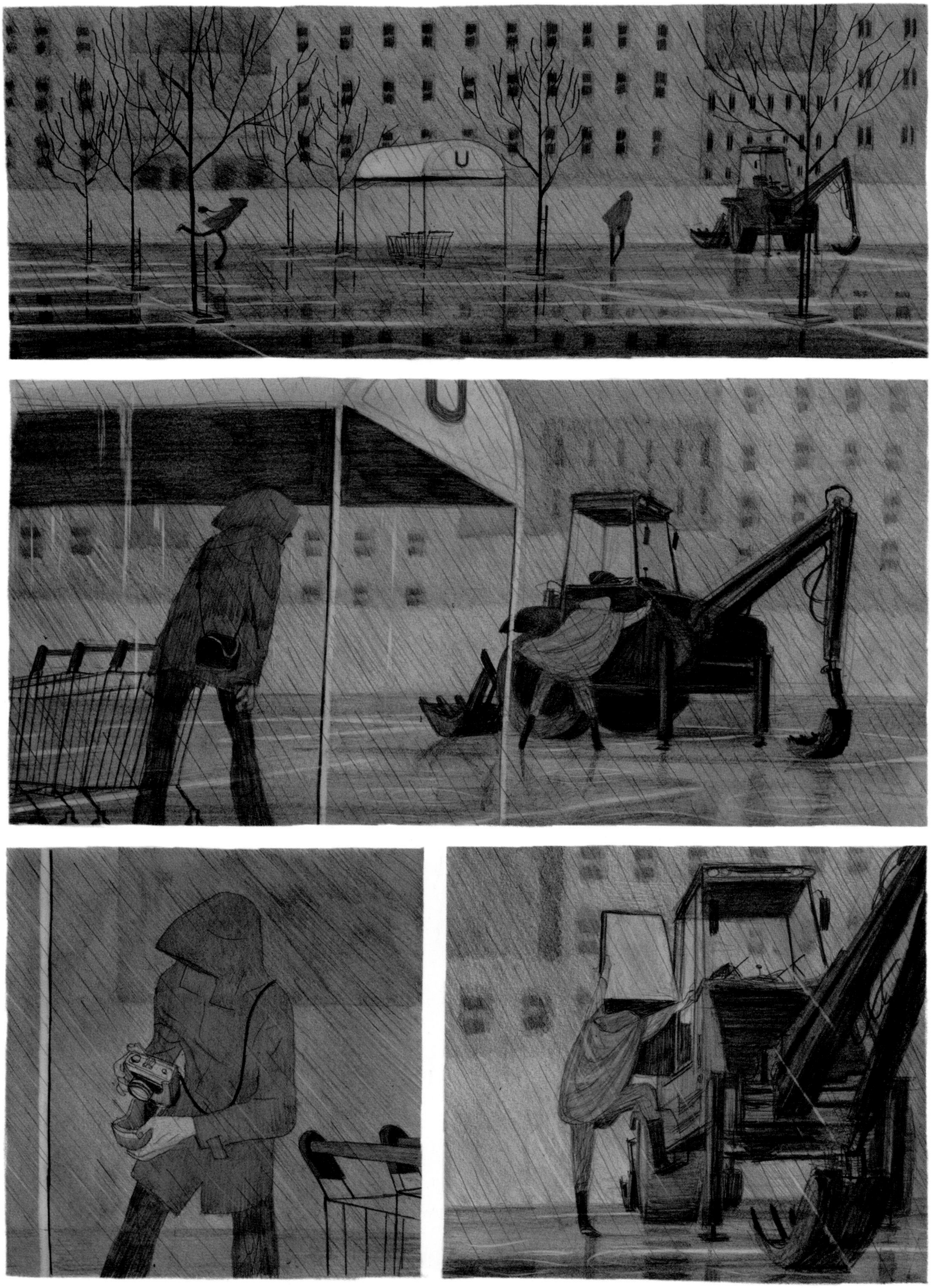
U

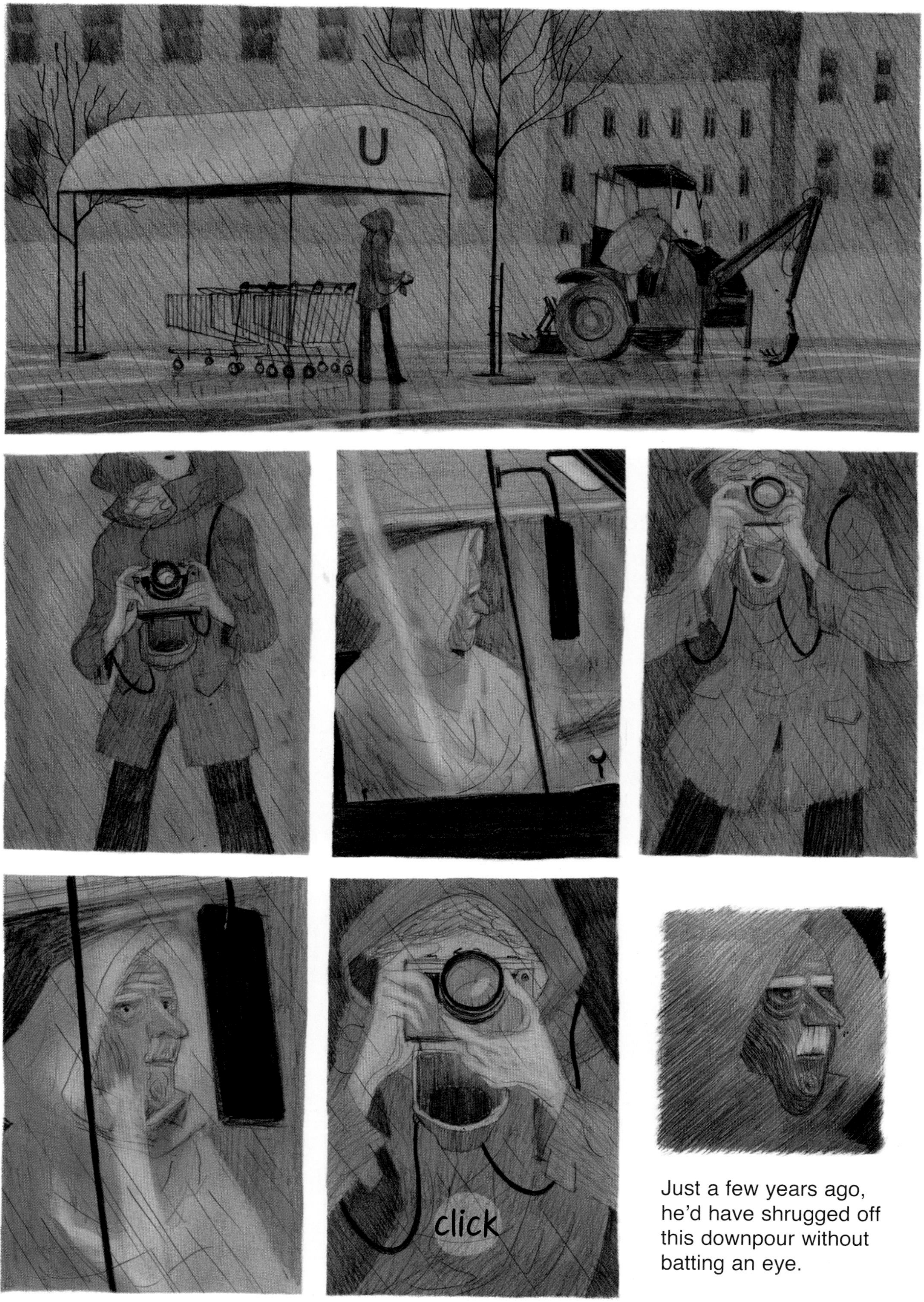
U
click
Just a few years ago, he'd have shrugged off this downpour without batting an eye.

...gallantly leapt over the rivulets and crossed the puddles of deep water to reach his machine without even trying to avoid them.

Things were different now.

The fifty yards to cross to reach the backhoe had seemed like a painful ordeal to him...

...during which the vital need to find shelter had supplanted the idea itself of a job to be done this afternoon.

His body slowly relaxes, swept through with that animal relief, that wave of thick, slightly nauseating warmth, which tells you everything's all right. The sun will rise, you've survived once again. Everyone needs that reassurance, even when the battles won are miniscule.

He's really starting to feel too old for all this. Outside, the supermarket parking lot has dissolved, once and for all swallowed up by the rain. The windows covered with condensation are now nothing but flat, gray, uniform screens of light, the portholes of a submarine gone adrift. For a short instant, they offer to him the panorama of a vast, bottomless ocean. It would be a lovely trip to cross through those membranes and slip into the water, to melt into its reassuring neutrality, no fuss, without wishes or intentions.

Ten thousand little hammers of rain drum their muffled music and remind him where he is.

Three more weeks on this job.

It seems the company has gotten the structural work subcontract for building an airport out east. Garcia told him about it yesterday. They'll need him, they need an experienced machine operator. He doesn't really want one final construction job on the other side of France, a few months before retirement, with his daughter having her baby in March. But in any event, he has no choice. Garcia will have been a pain in his ass right to the end.

At least there's the travel allotment. There's always that, what with the baby coming. His torpor fades a little, his body is waking up. He mechanically massages the aching palms of his hands while looking into the rearview mirror. The same face as before, a little older each time, that's all. Both of them have known each other for a long time, and yet, each new encounter is a surprise. For a thousandth of a second, he didn't recognize that man with the soaked hood falling over his forehead, a brief feeling of strangeness, a dissonance between that image in the mirror and what he knows of himself.

For fifty-eight years now, from inside his body, as fragile and modest as he perceives his own existence, he sees the world unfolding around him, to the point of regularly letting himself be deceived by the illusion of being very precisely placed in its center.

If it's that way for each individual, our perception of others will never reveal to us who and what they are. No more than the reflection of himself seen in the rearview mirror says who or what he is.

We are permanently inaccessible to one another.

Someone's shouting and banging on the window.

Garcia.

You'd best get your ass moving to finish this damned hole.

He starts the engine. He'd have liked to have hung onto the ideas in his mind, to talk about them with his daughter that evening when he goes to see her. Garcia keeps shouting his head off, yes, without a doubt, he'll have to remember to talk to her about it, the machine comes to life, the articulated arm slowly detaches itself from the earth, there was something to understand, Garcia heads off to give hell to someone else, but what was it really about, the rain seems like it's settling down, the bucket digs easily into the soil, he'll have finished the hole by this evening, no problem, the rain will just have to let up a little.

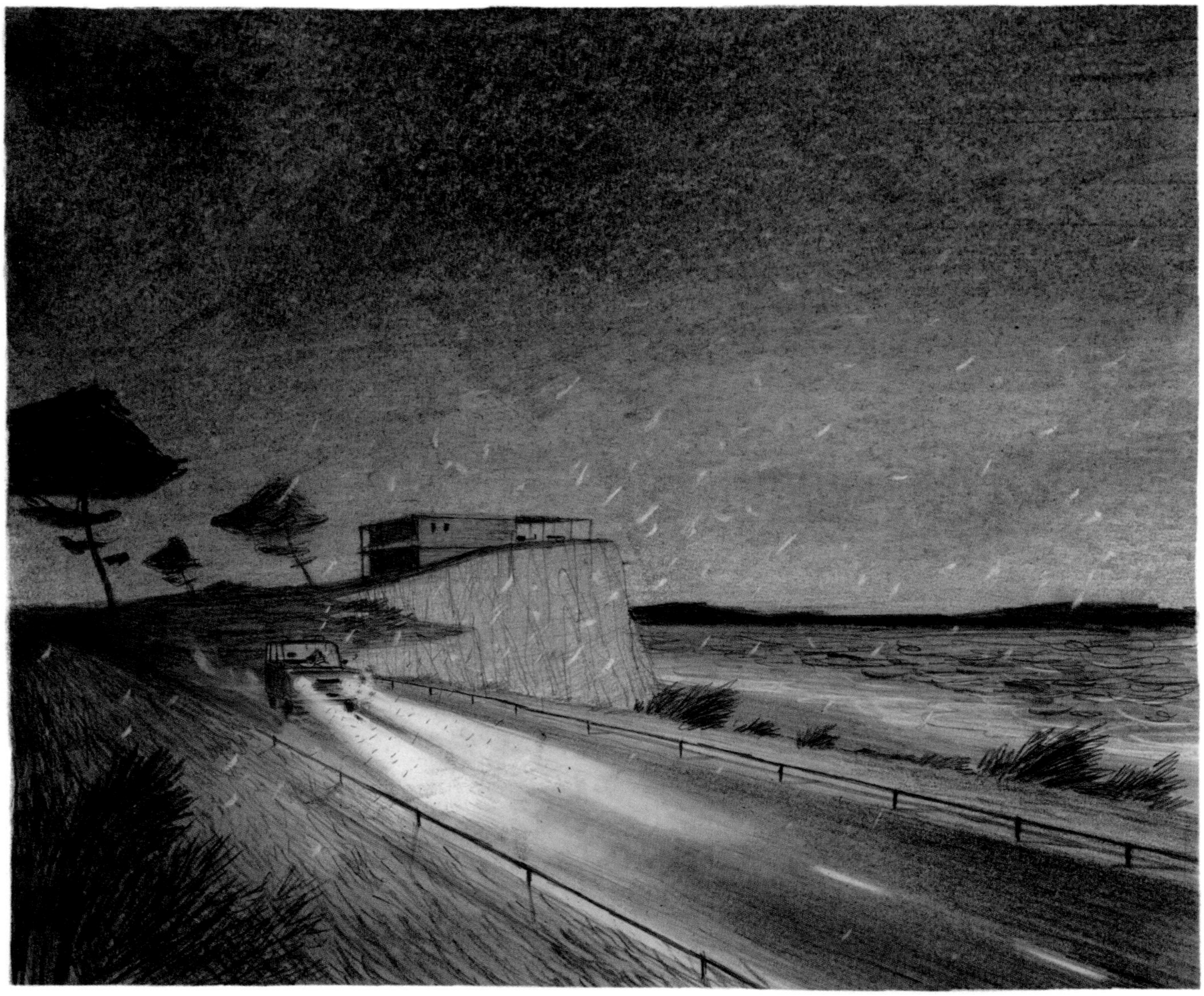

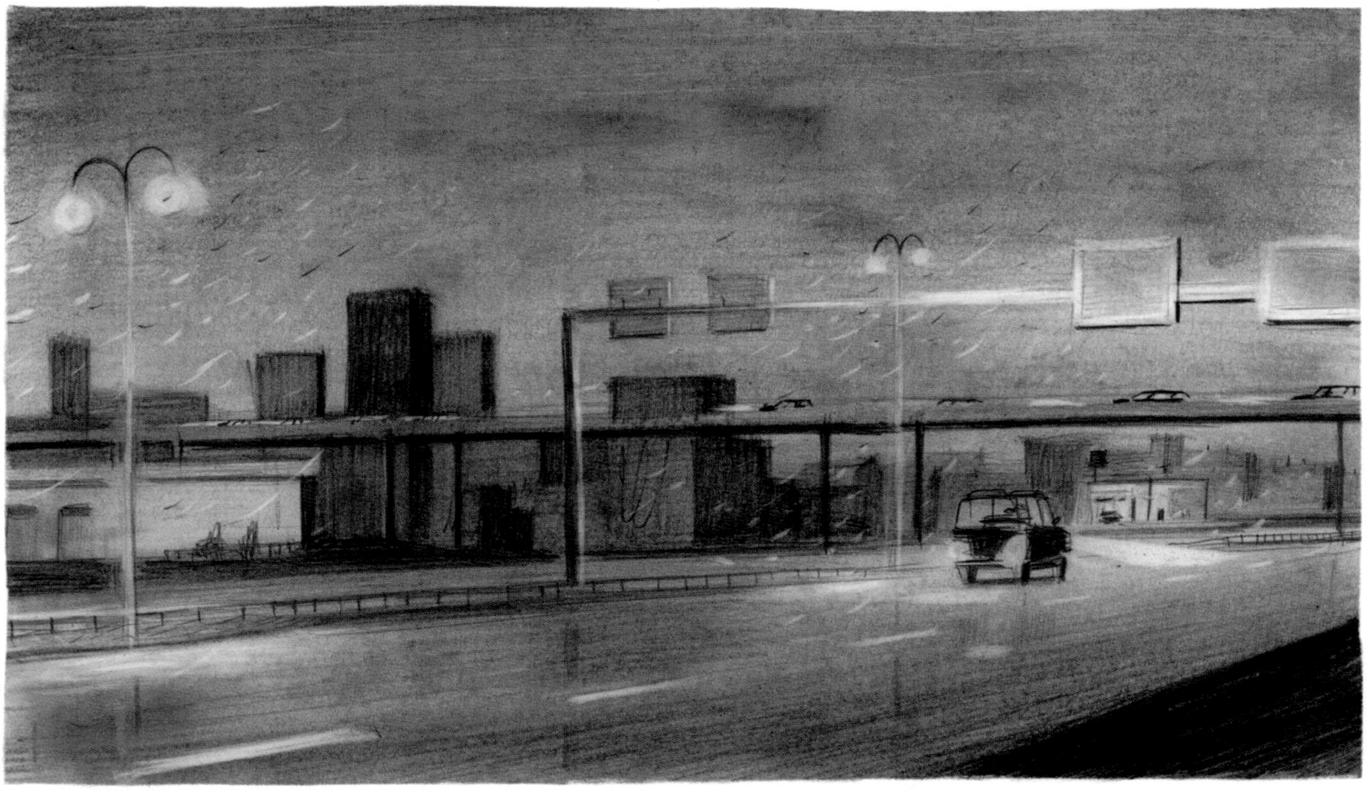

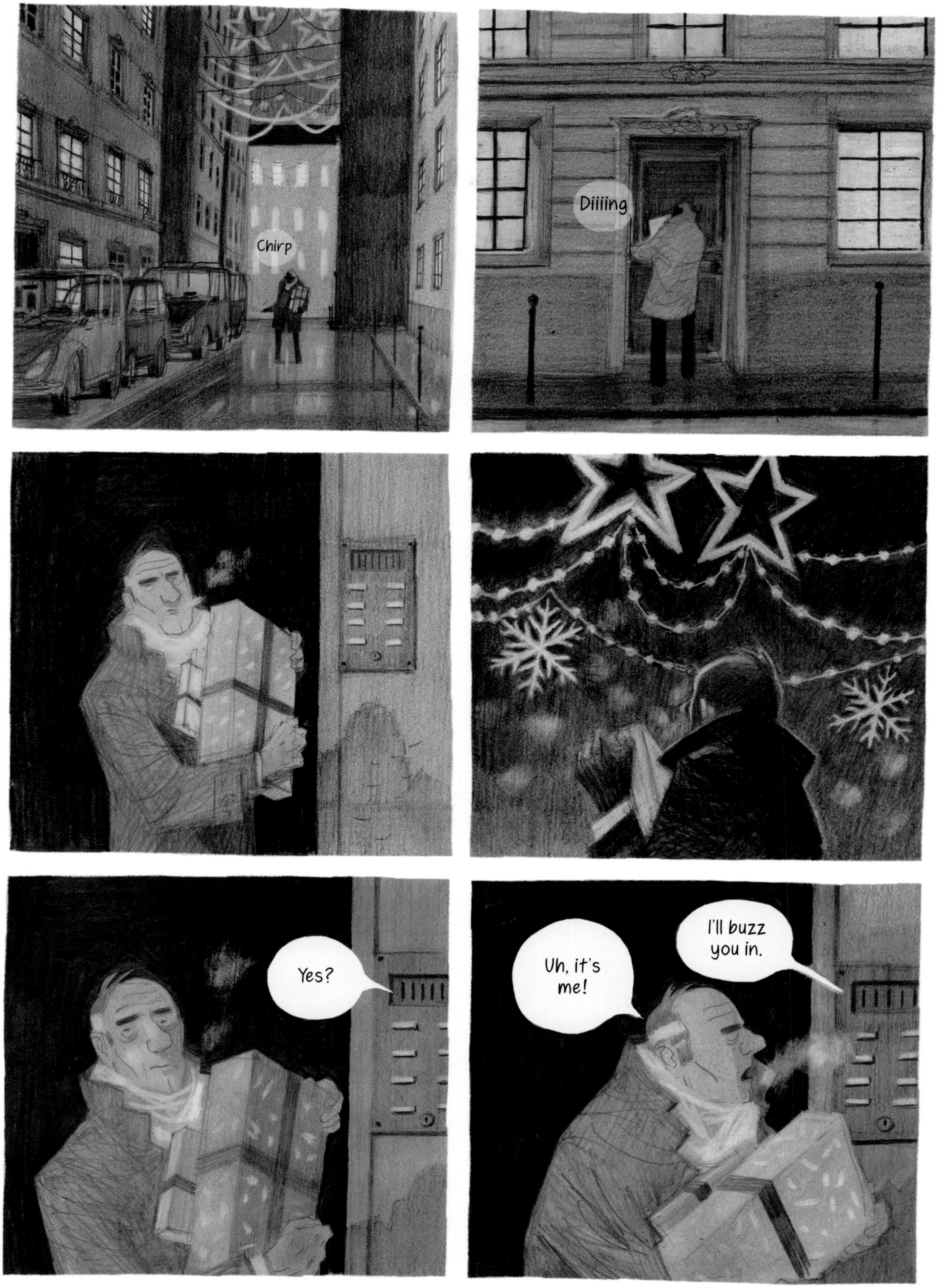
Chirp
Diiiing
Yes?
Uh, it's me!
I'll buzz you in.

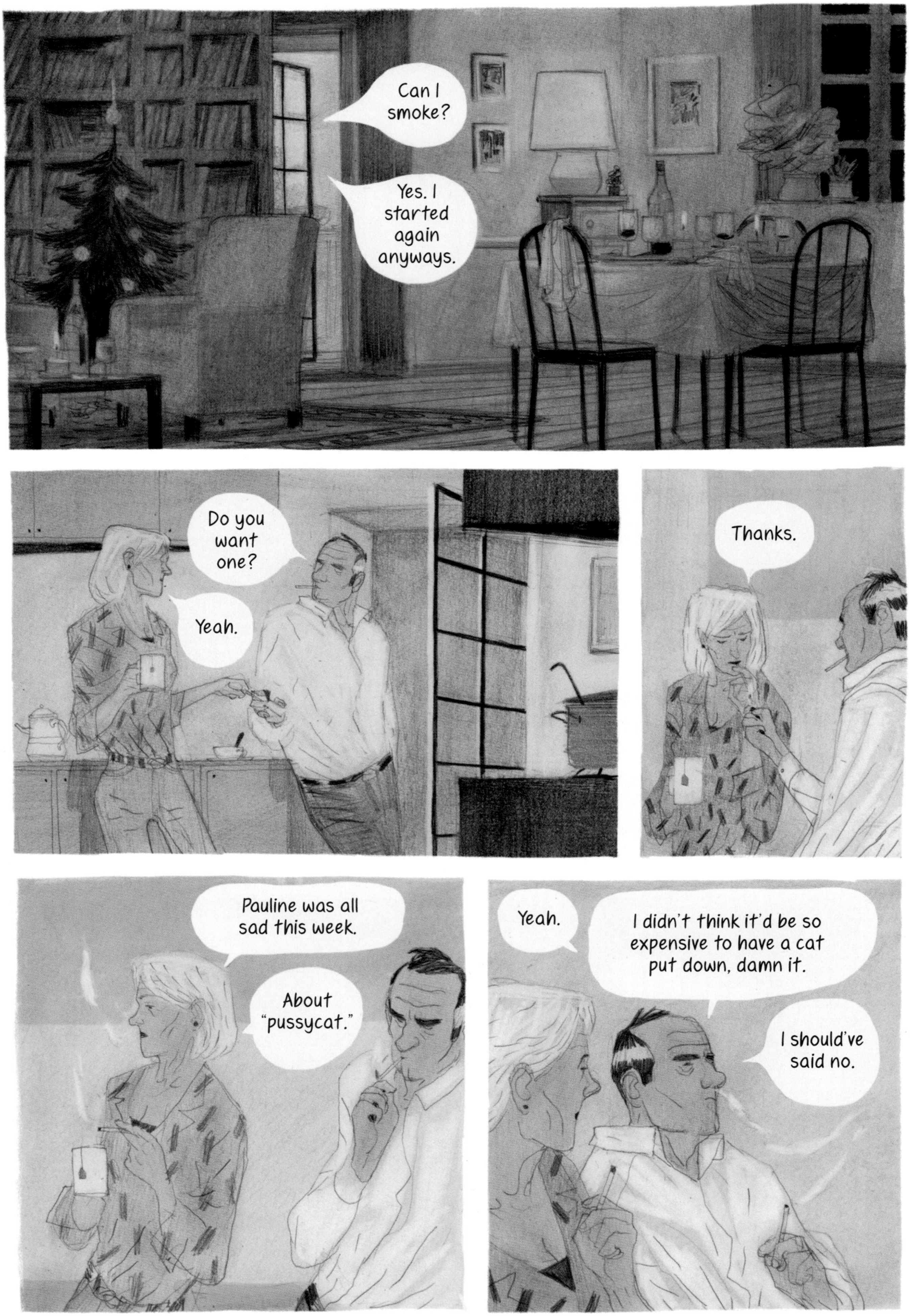
Can I smoke?
Yes. I started again anyways.
Do you want one?
Yeah.
Thanks.
Pauline was all sad this week.
About "pussycat."
Yeah.
I didn't think it'd be so expensive to have a cat put down, damn it.
I should've said no.

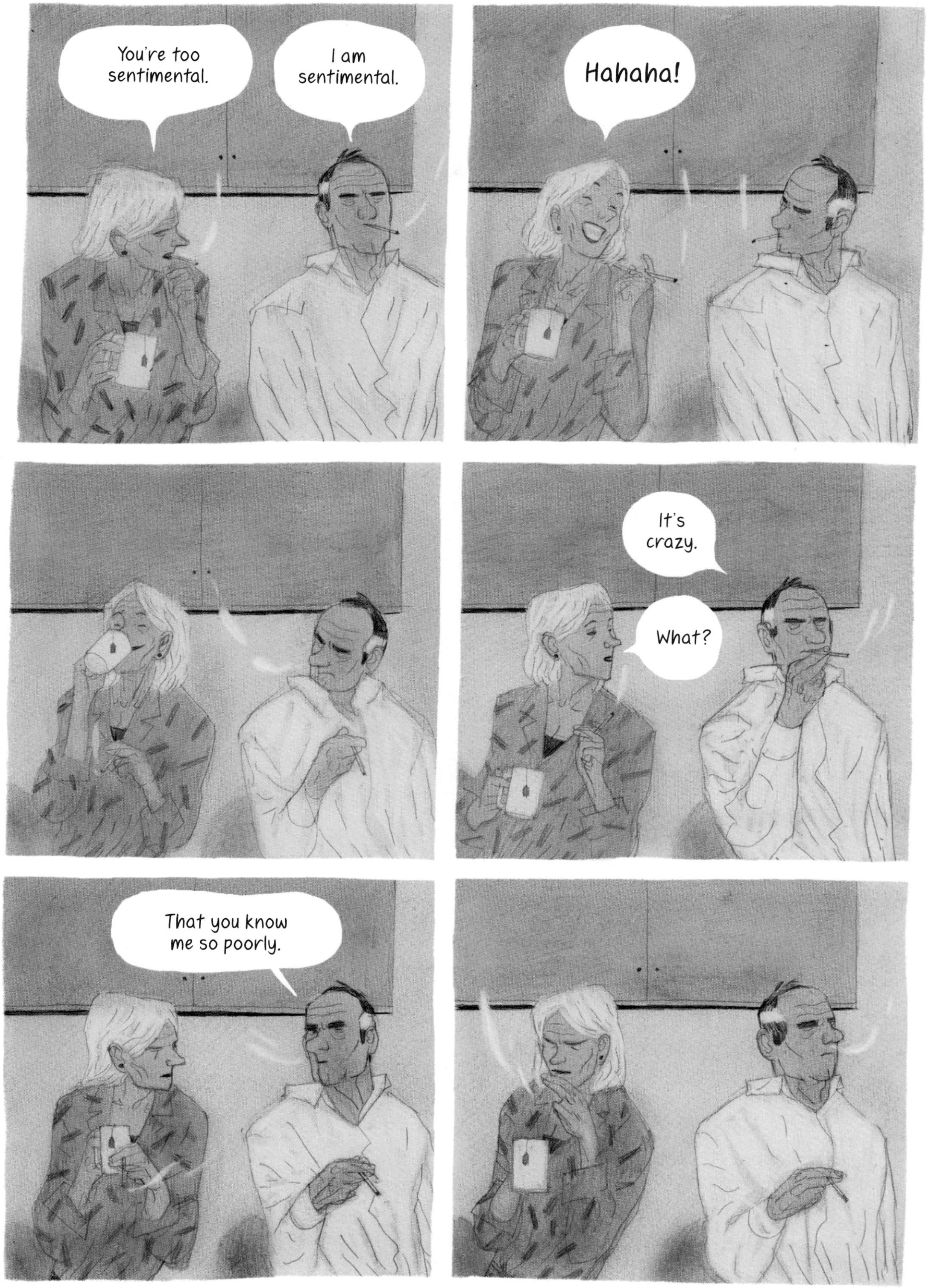
You're too sentimental.
I am sentimental.
Hahaha!
It's crazy.
What?
That you know me so poorly.

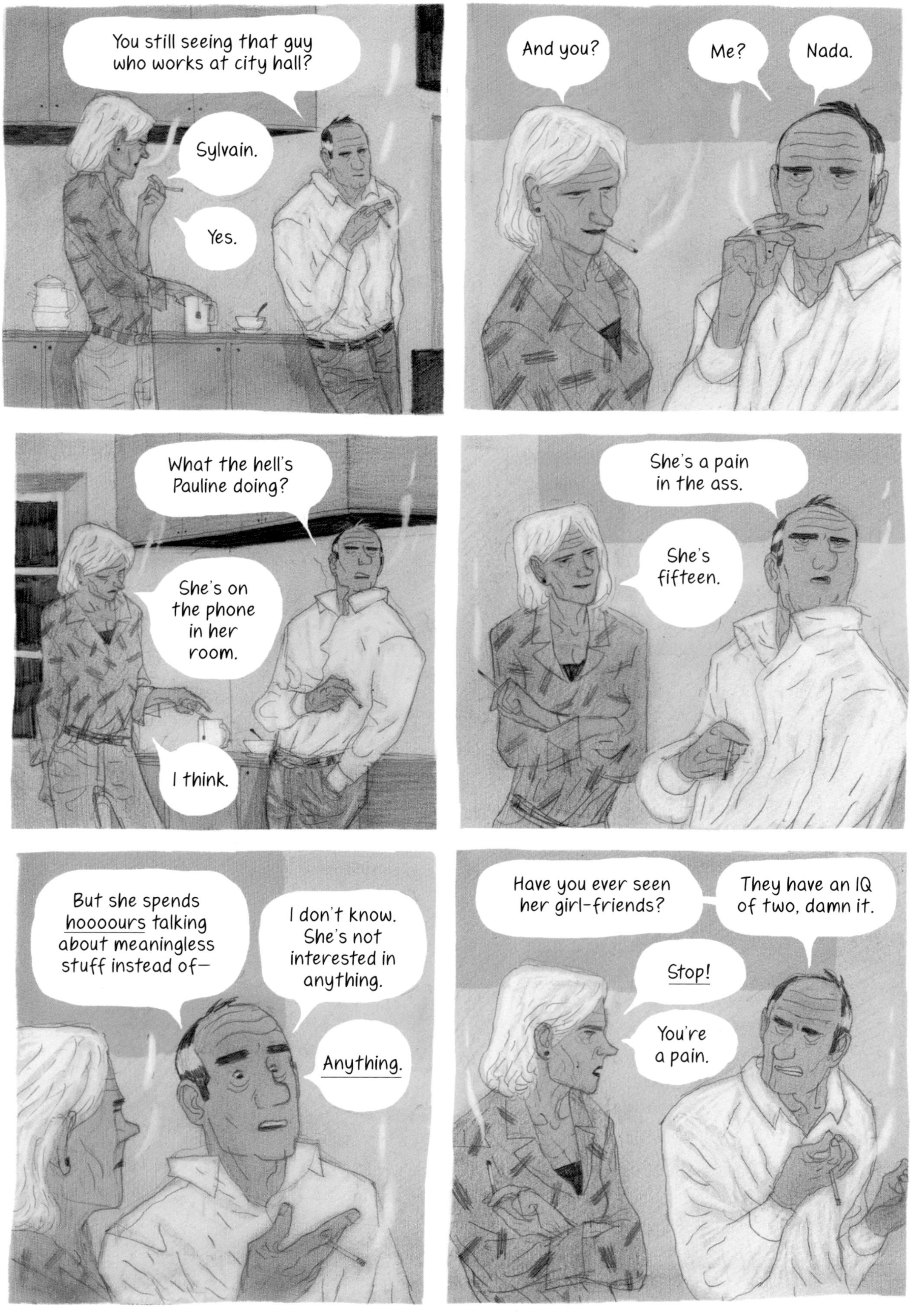
You still seeing that guy who works at city hall?
Sylvain.
Yes.
And you?
Me?
Nada.
What the hell's Pauline doing?
She's on the phone in her room.
I think.
She's a pain in the ass.
She's fifteen.
But she spends hooooours talking about meaningless stuff instead of—
I don't know. She's not interested in anything.
Anything.
Have you ever seen her girl-friends?
They have an IQ of two, damn it.
Stop!
You're a pain.

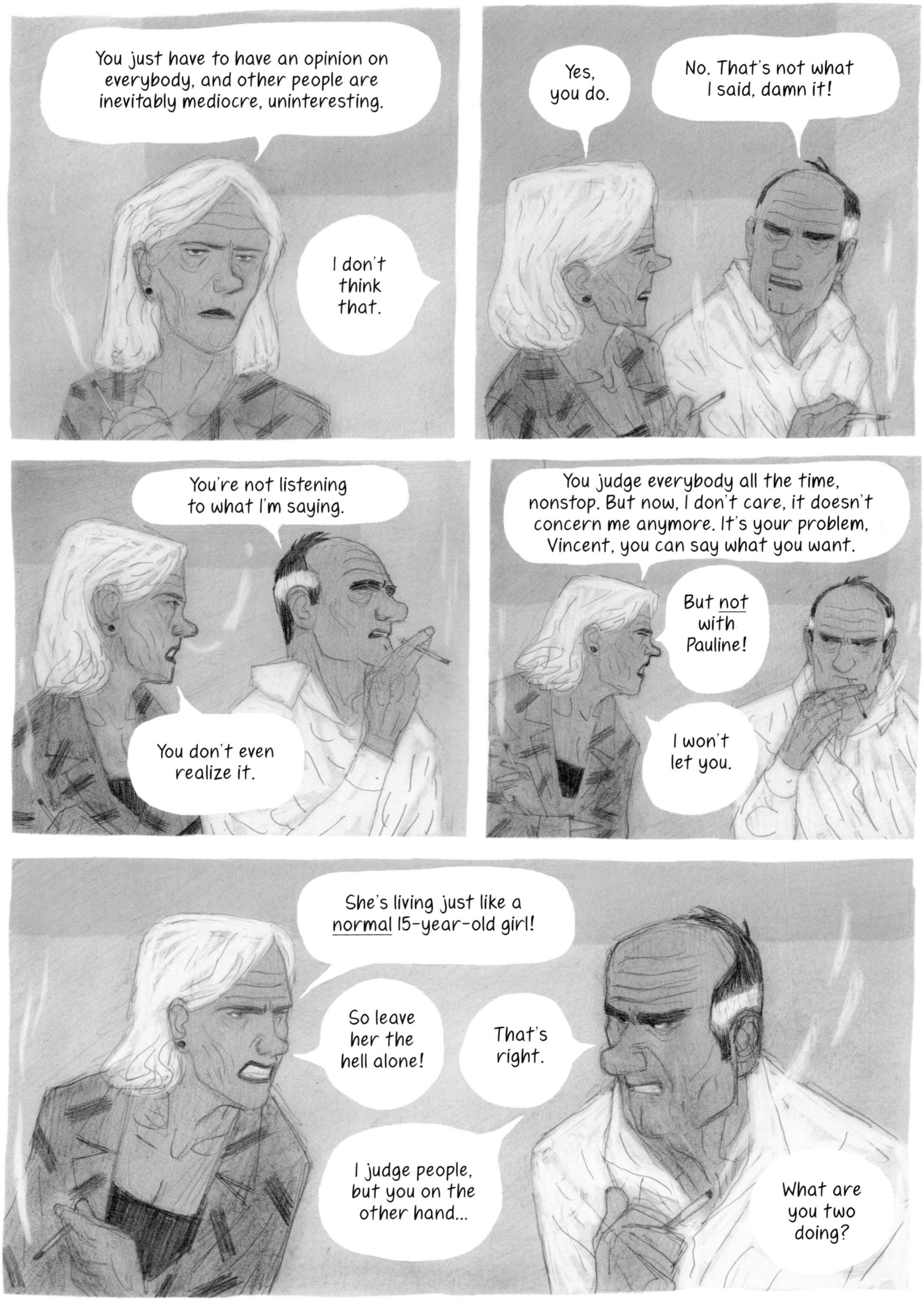
You just have to have an opinion on everybody, and other people are inevitably mediocre, uninteresting.
I don't think that.
Yes, you do.
No. That's not what I said, damn it!
You're not listening to what I'm saying.
You don't even realize it.
You judge everybody all the time, nonstop. But now, I don't care, it doesn't concern me anymore. It's your problem, Vincent, you can say what you want.
But not with Pauline!
I won't let you.
She's living just like a normal 15-year-old girl!
So leave her the hell alone!
That's right.
I judge people, but you on the other hand...
What are you two doing?

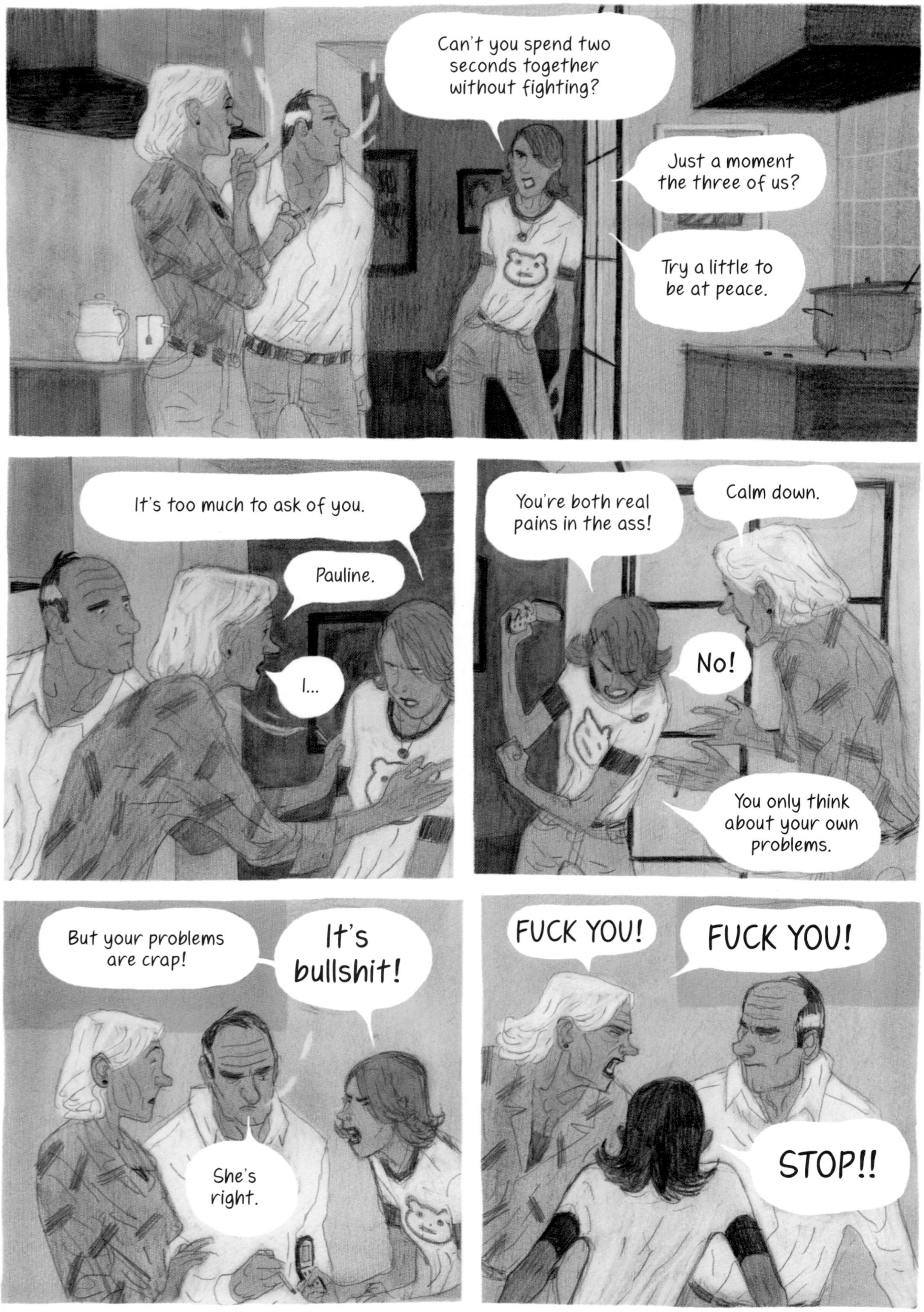
Can't you spend two seconds together without fighting?
Just a moment the three of us?
Try a little to be at peace.
It's too much to ask of you.
Pauline.
I...
You're both real pains in the ass!
Calm down.
No!
You only think about your own problems.
But your problems are crap!
It's bullshit!
She's right.
FUCK YOU!
FUCK YOU!
STOP!!

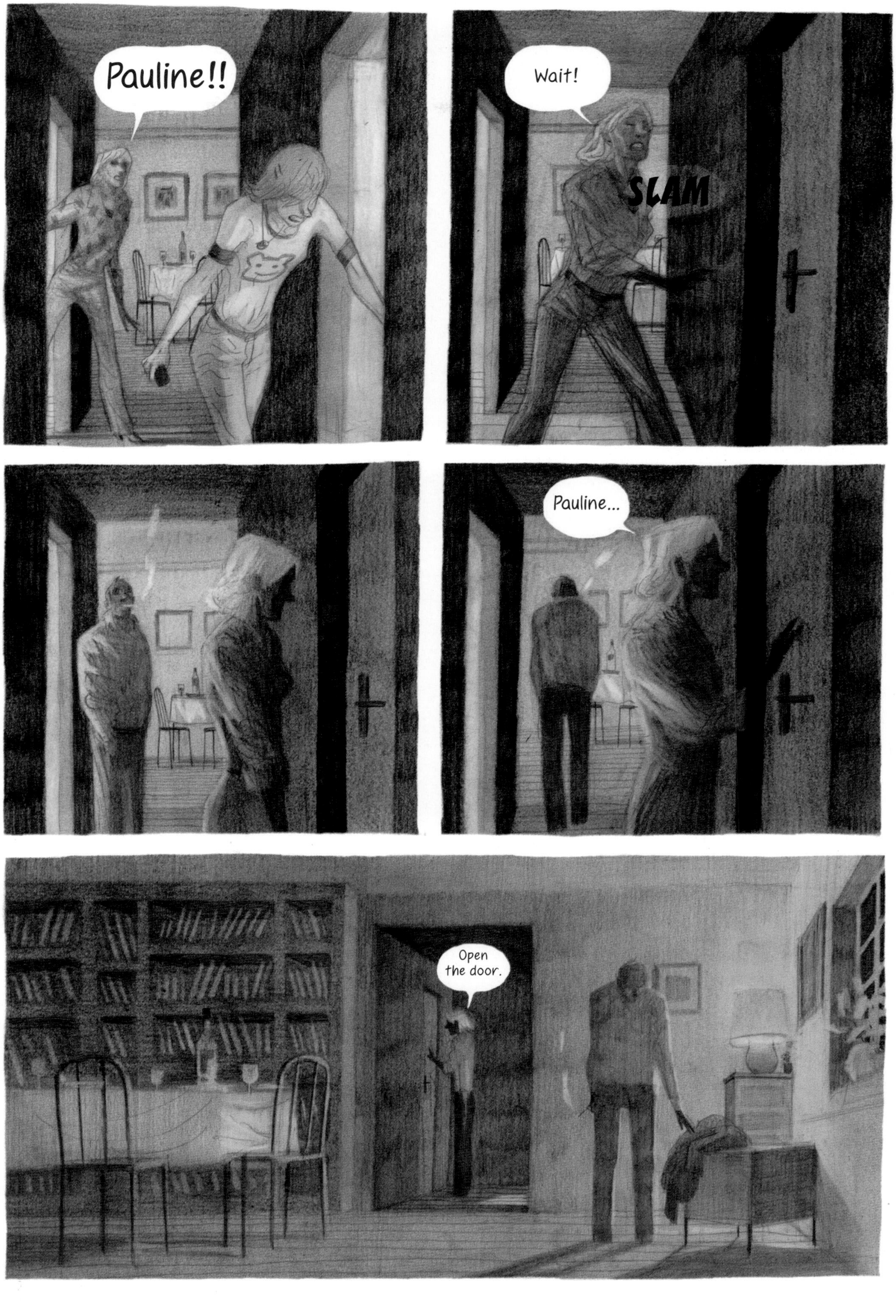
Pauline!!
Wait!
SLAM
Pauline...
Open the door.

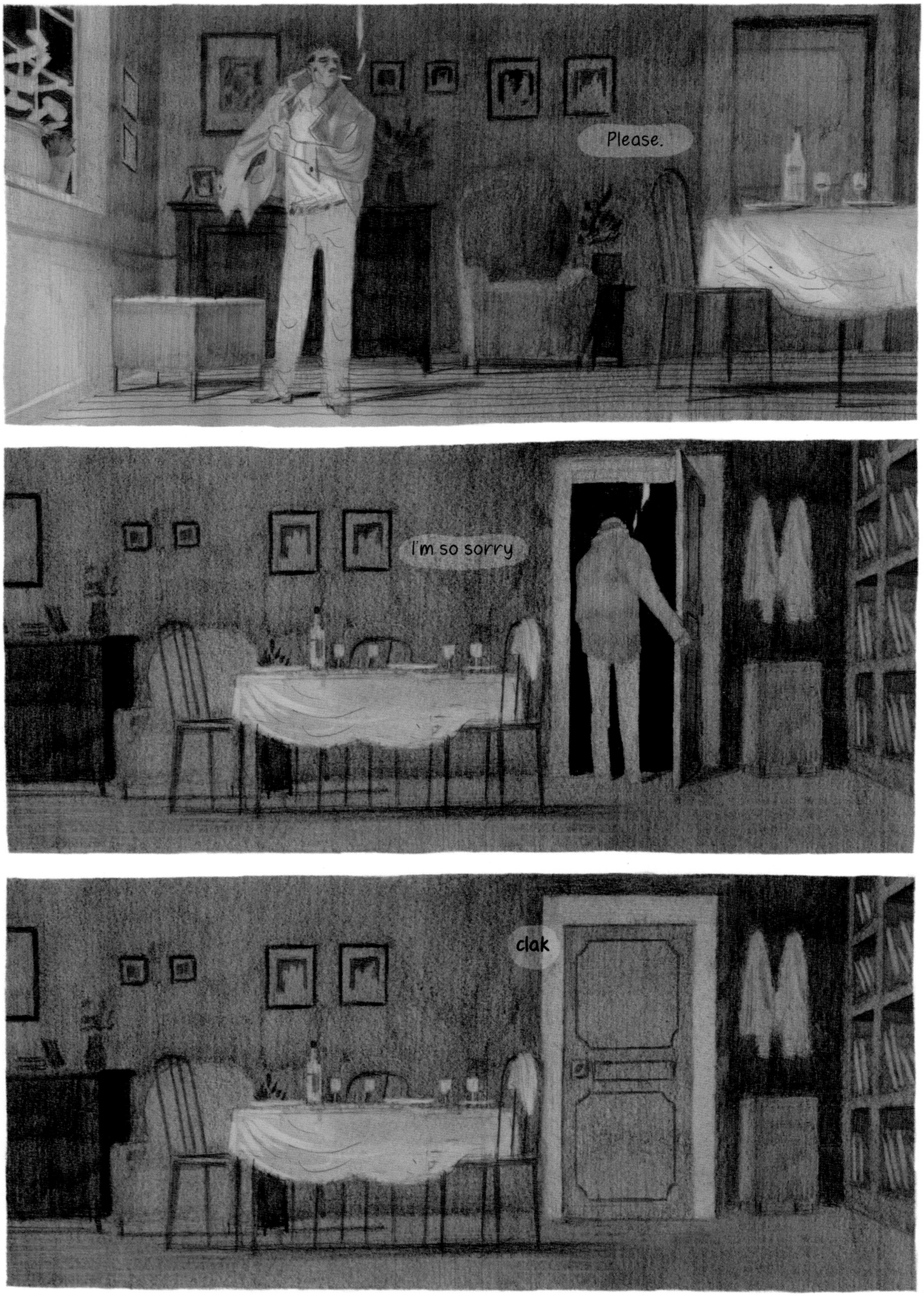
Please.
I'm so sorry
clak

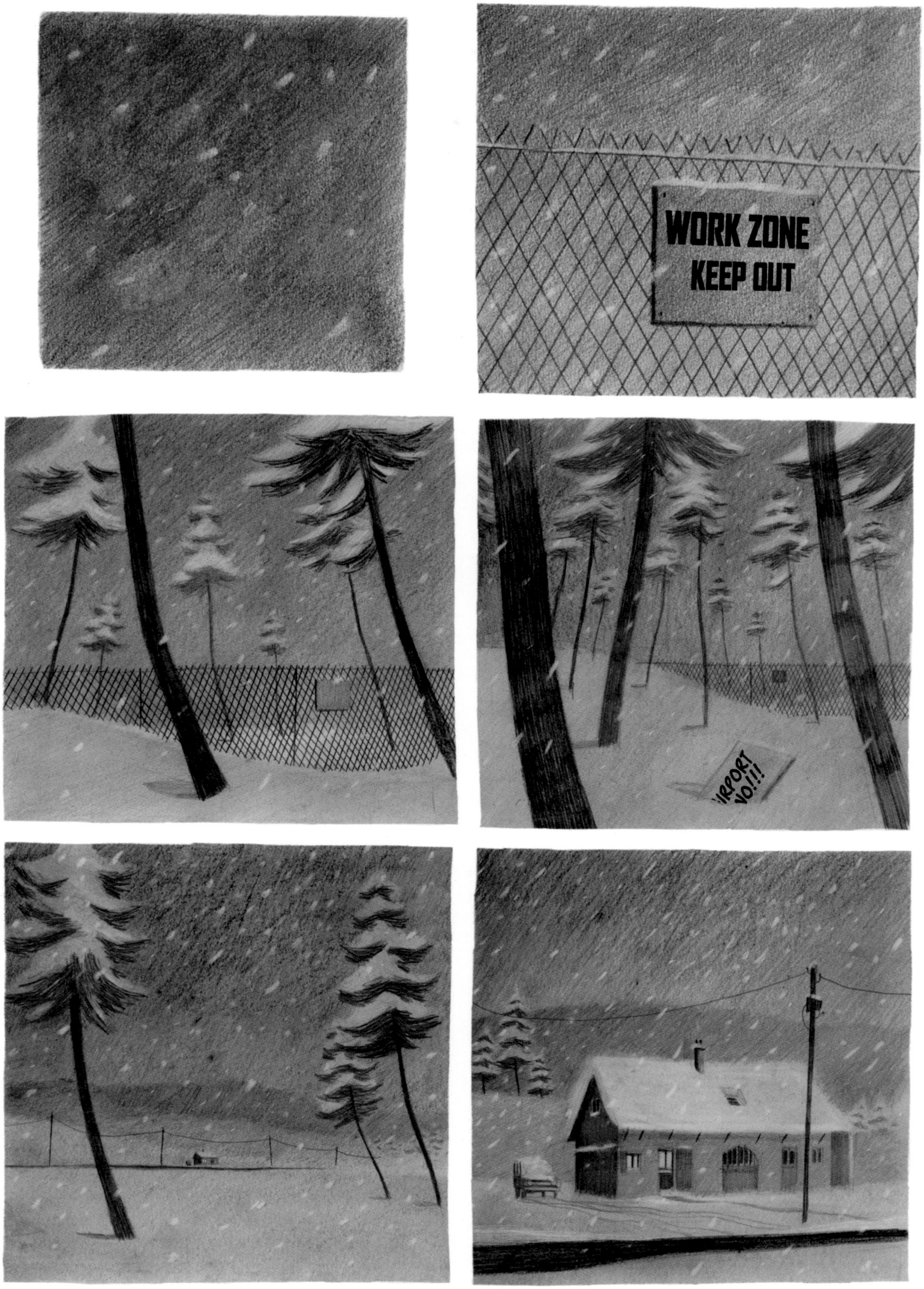
WORK ZONE
KEEP OUT

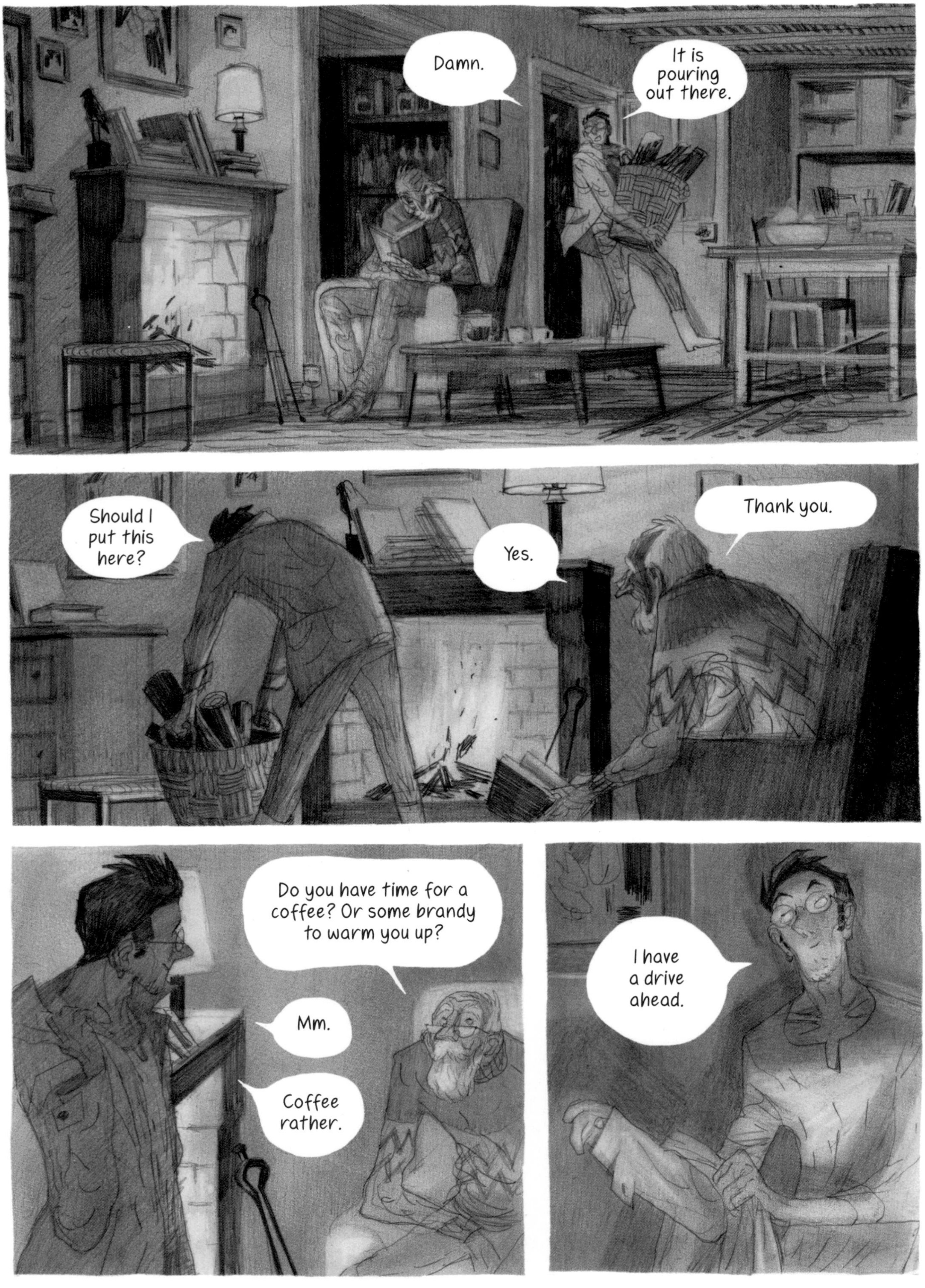
Damn.
It is pouring out there.
Should I put this here?
Yes.
Thank you.
Do you have time for a coffee? Or some brandy to warm you up?
Mm.
Coffee rather.
I have a drive ahead.

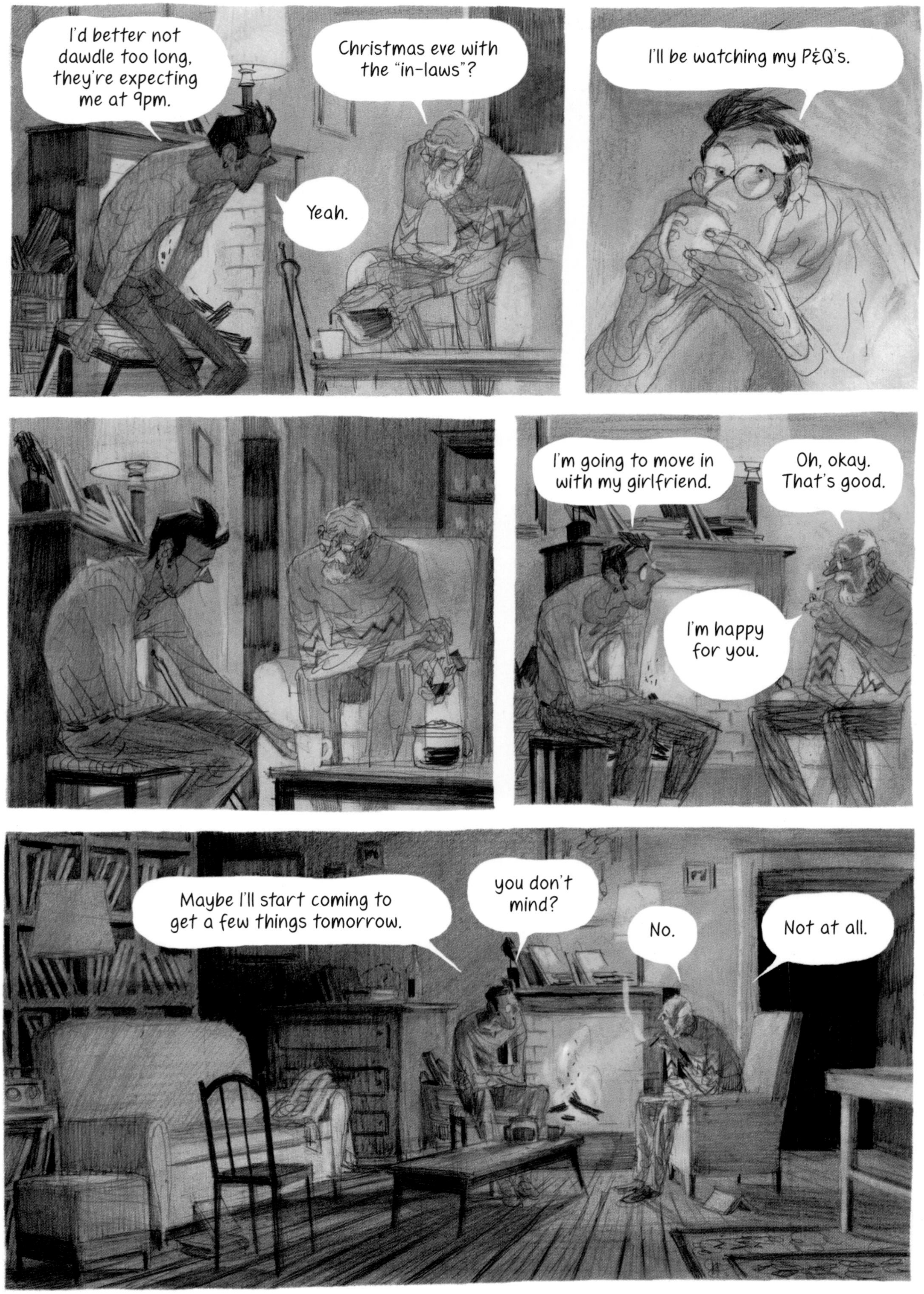
I'd better not dawdle too long, they're expecting me at 9pm.
Christmas eve with the "in-laws"?
Yeah.
I'll be watching my P&Q's.
I'm going to move in with my girlfriend.
Oh, okay. That's good.
I'm happy for you.
Maybe I'll start coming to get a few things tomorrow.
you don't mind?
No.
Not at all.

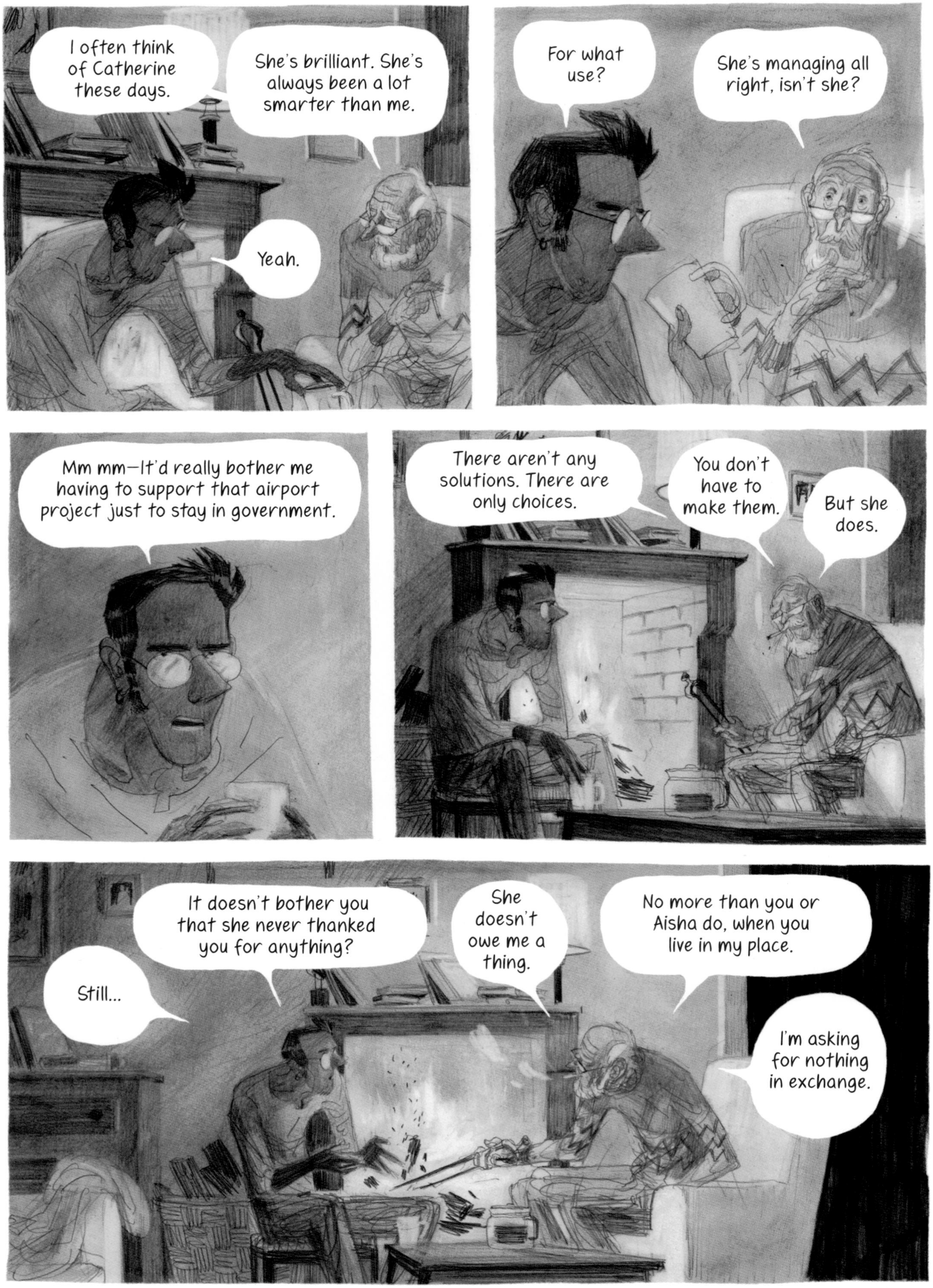
I often think of Catherine these days.
She's brilliant. She's always been a lot smarter than me.
Yeah.
For what use?
She's managing all right, isn't she?
Mm mm—It'd really bother me having to support that airport project just to stay in government.
There aren't any solutions. There are only choices.
You don't have to make them.
But she does.
It doesn't bother you that she never thanked you for anything?
Still...
She doesn't owe me a thing.
No more than you or Aisha do, when you live in my place.
I'm asking for nothing in exchange.

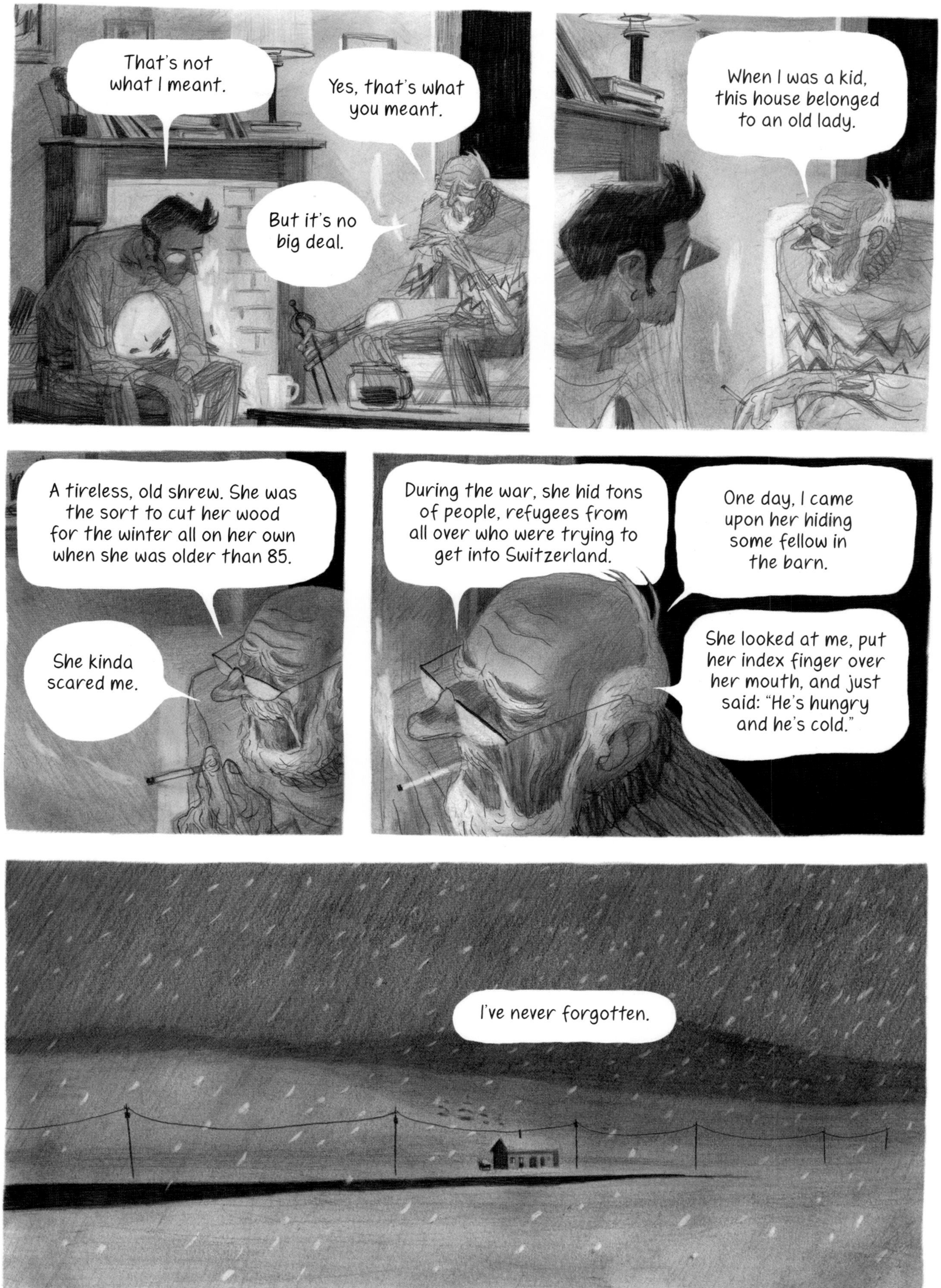
That's not what I meant.
Yes, that's what you meant.
But it's no big deal.
When I was a kid, this house belonged to an old lady.
A tireless, old shrew. She was the sort to cut her wood for the winter all on her own when she was older than 85.
She kinda scared me.
During the war, she hid tons of people, refugees from all over who were trying to get into Switzerland.
One day, I came upon her hiding some fellow in the barn.
She looked at me, put her index finger over her mouth, and just said: "He's hungry and he's cold."
I've never forgotten.

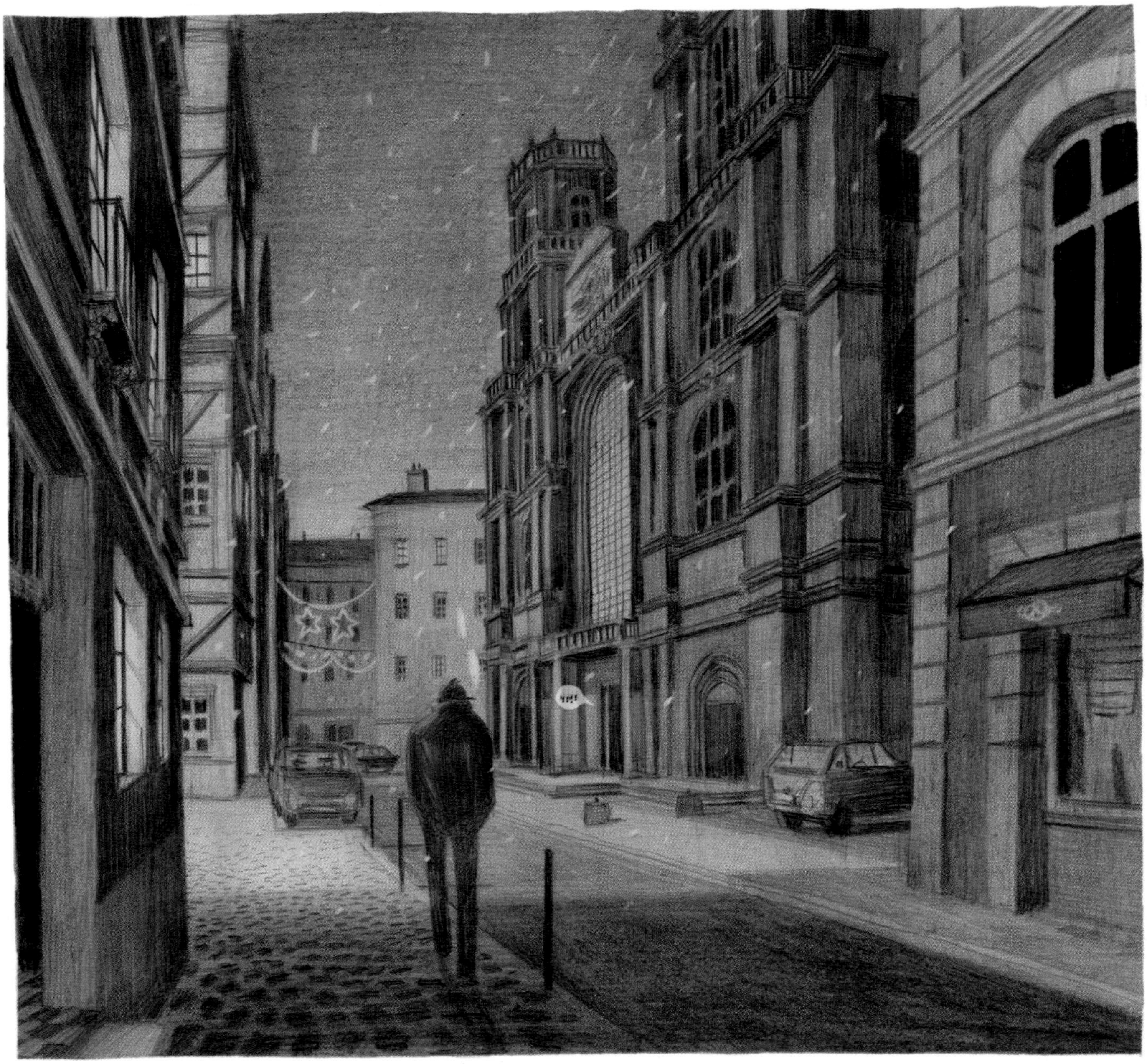

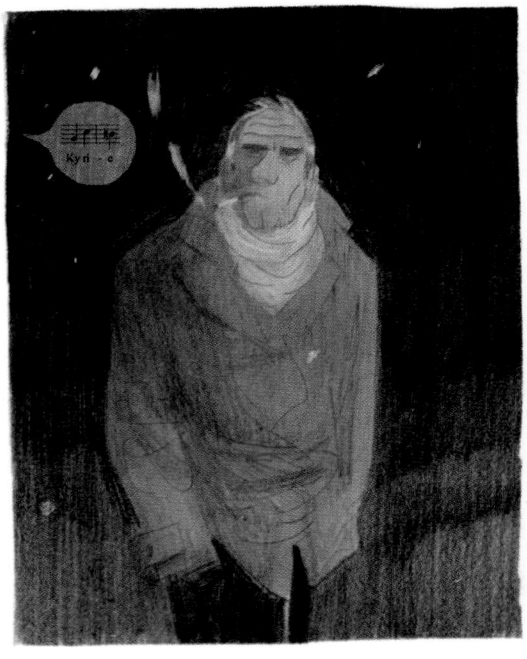
Kyri - e

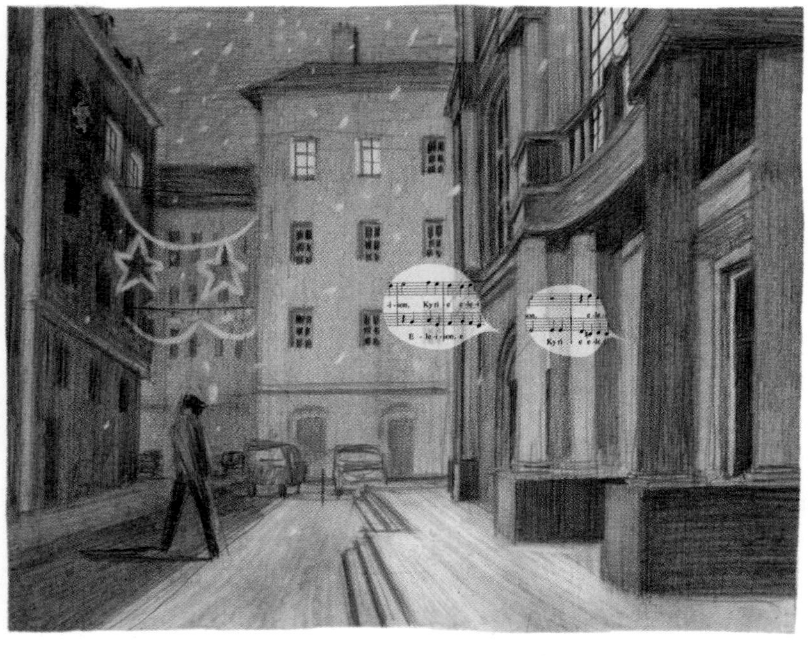
-i - son, Kyri - e e - le -
E - le - i - son, e
son. e - le -
Kyri e e - le

It's closed.
What do you mean "closed"? It's Midnight Mass!
Ah... maybe.
Otherwise, go pray at home, God is everywhere!
Or so they say...

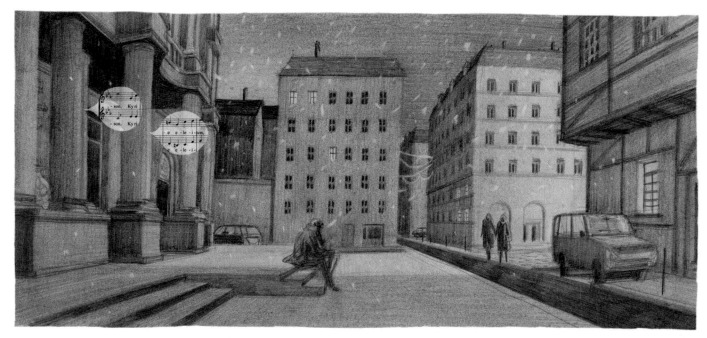

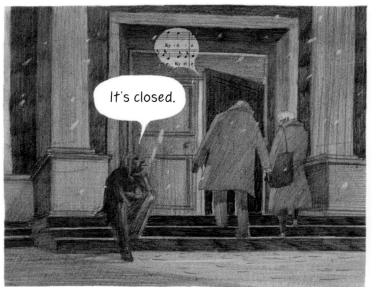

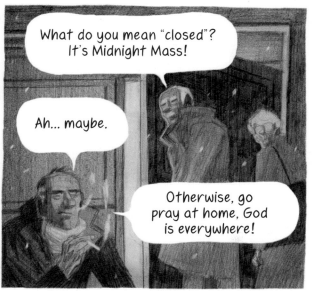

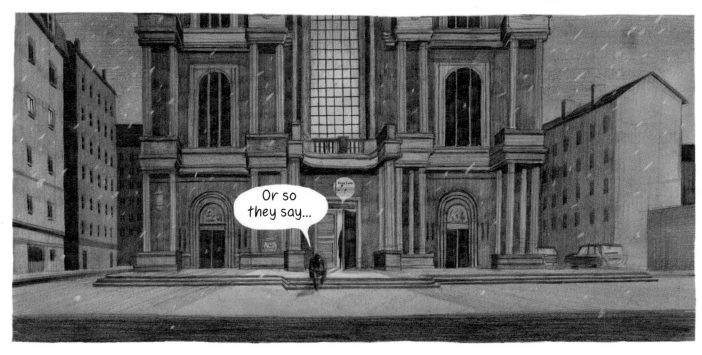

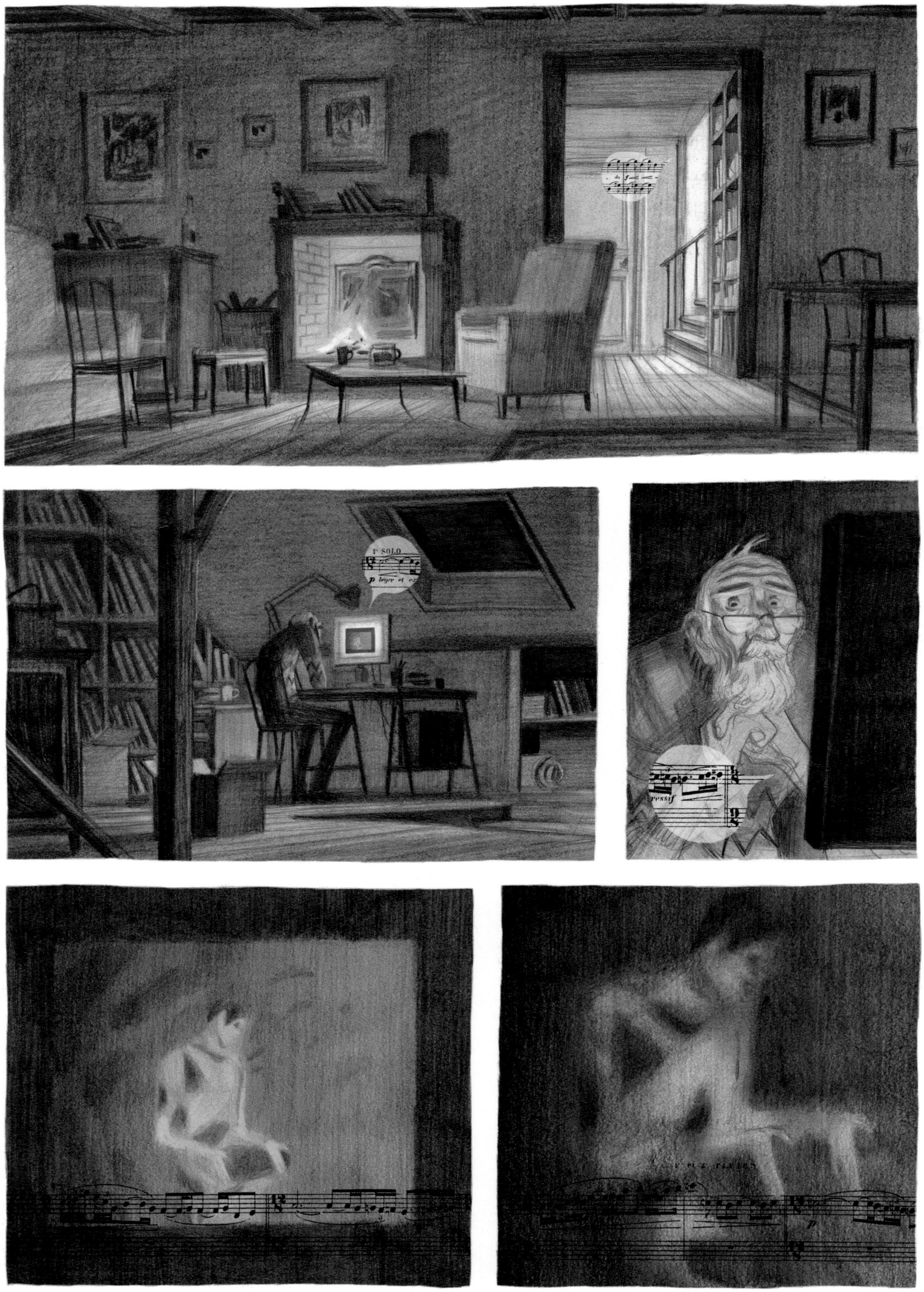
1er SOLO
p léger et
ressif

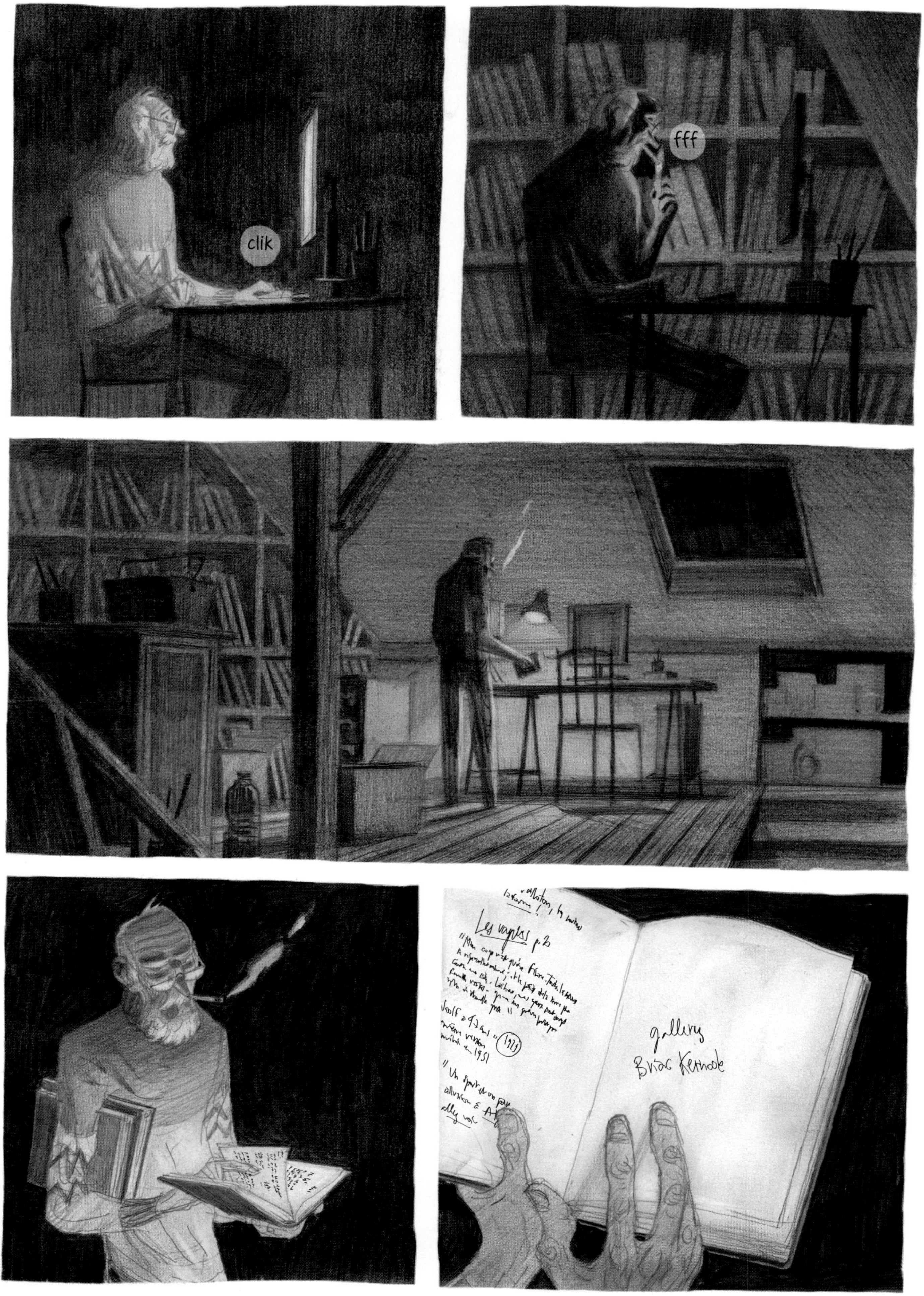
clik
fff

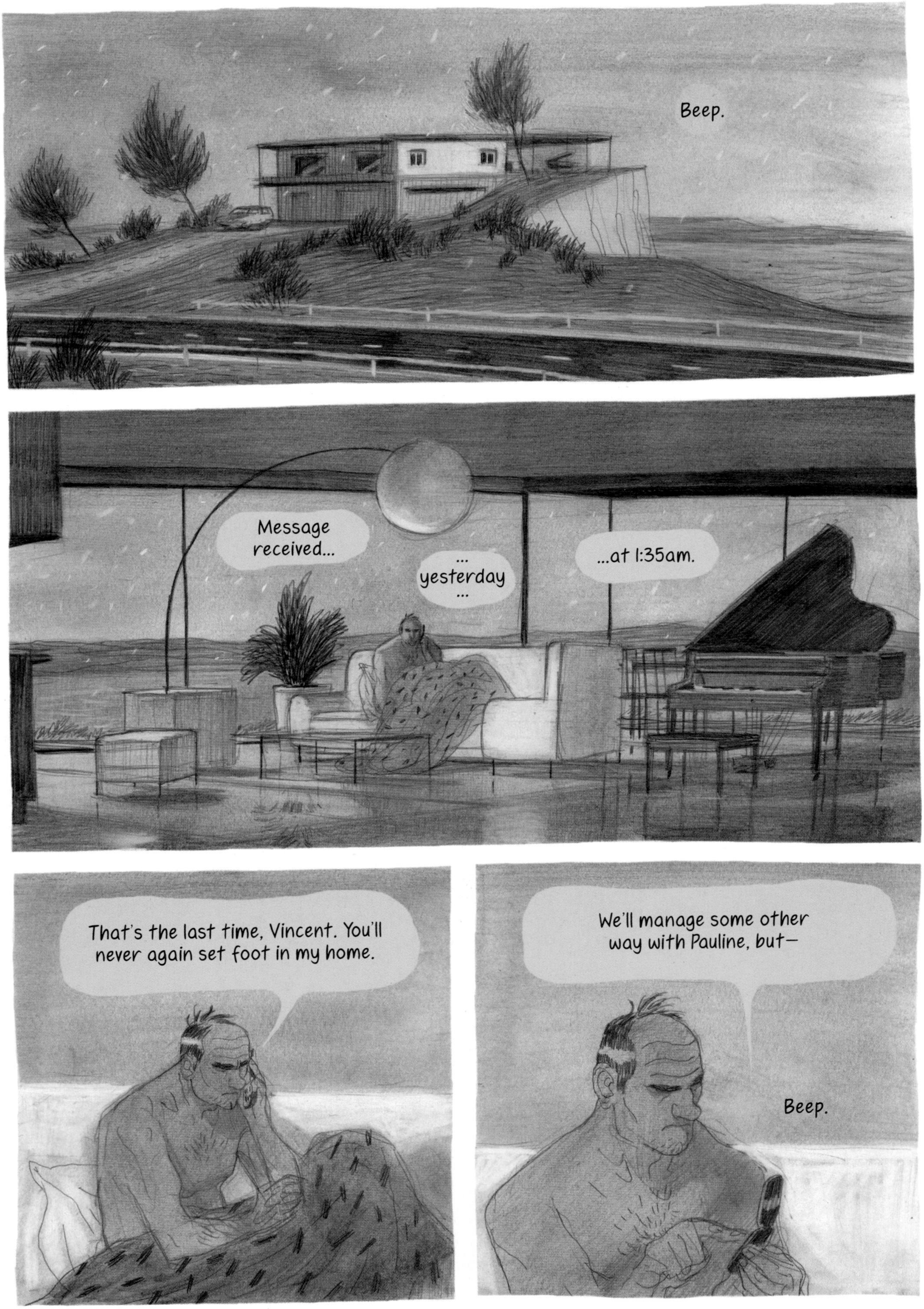
Beep.
Message received...
... yesterday ...
...at 1:35am.
That's the last time, Vincent. You'll never again set foot in my home.
We'll manage some other way with Pauline, but—
Beep.

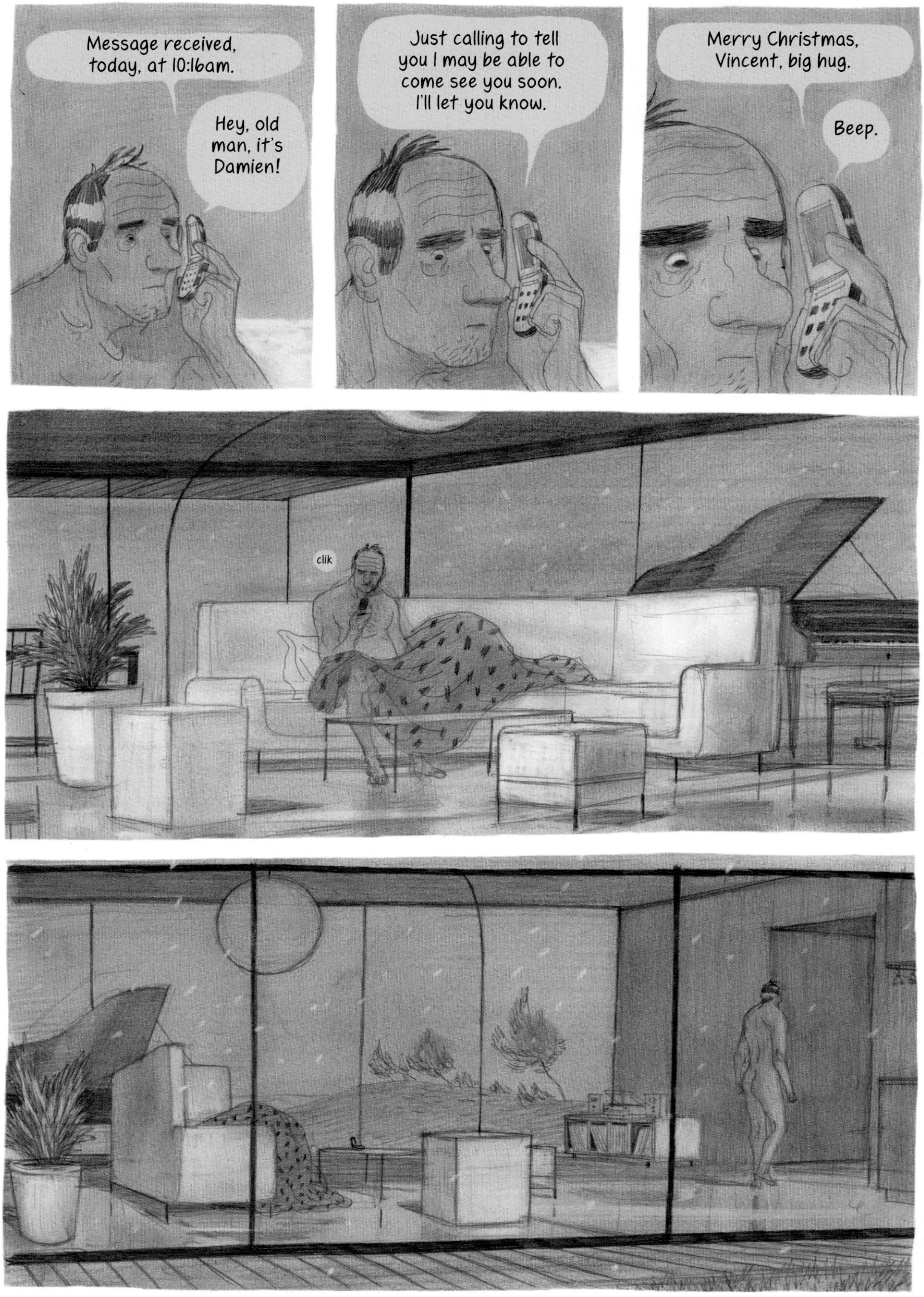
Message received, today, at 10:16am.
Hey, old man, it's Damien!
Just calling to tell you I may be able to come see you soon. I'll let you know.
Merry Christmas, Vincent, big hug.
Beep.
clik

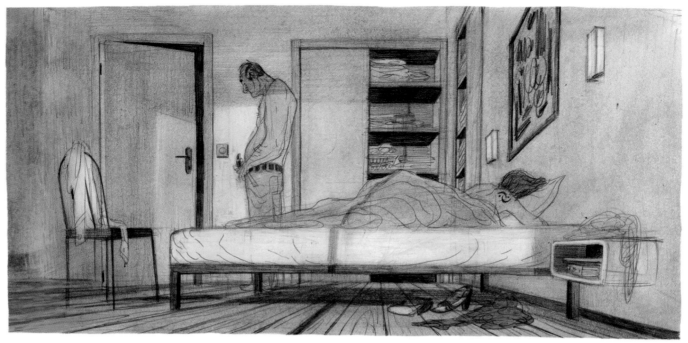

It's noon.

You'd better get going.

Huh...

What?

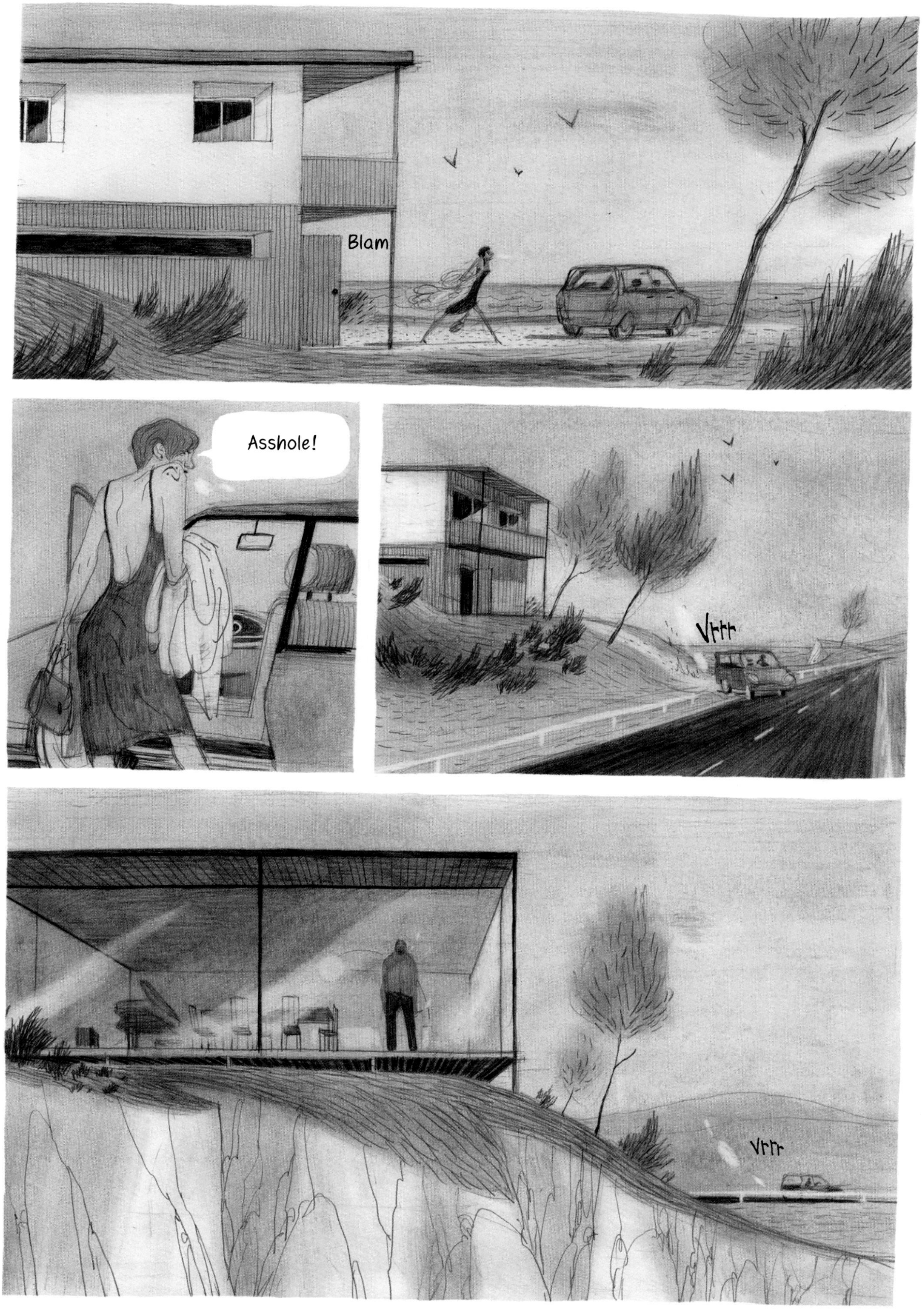
Blam
Asshole!
Vrrr
Vrrr

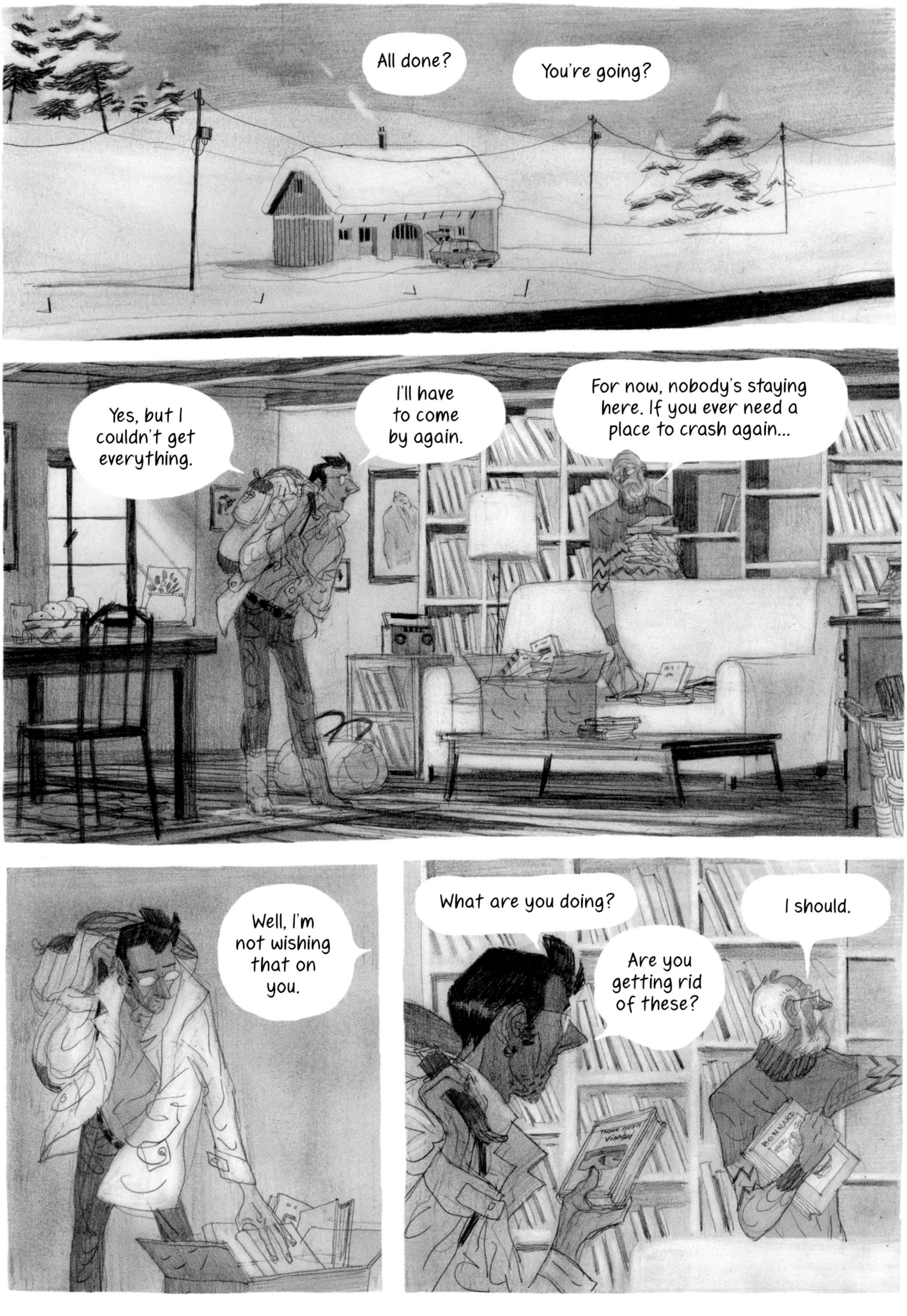
All done?
You're going?
Yes, but I couldn't get everything.
I'll have to come by again.
For now, nobody's staying here. If you ever need a place to crash again...
Well, I'm not wishing that on you.
What are you doing?
Are you getting rid of these?
I should.

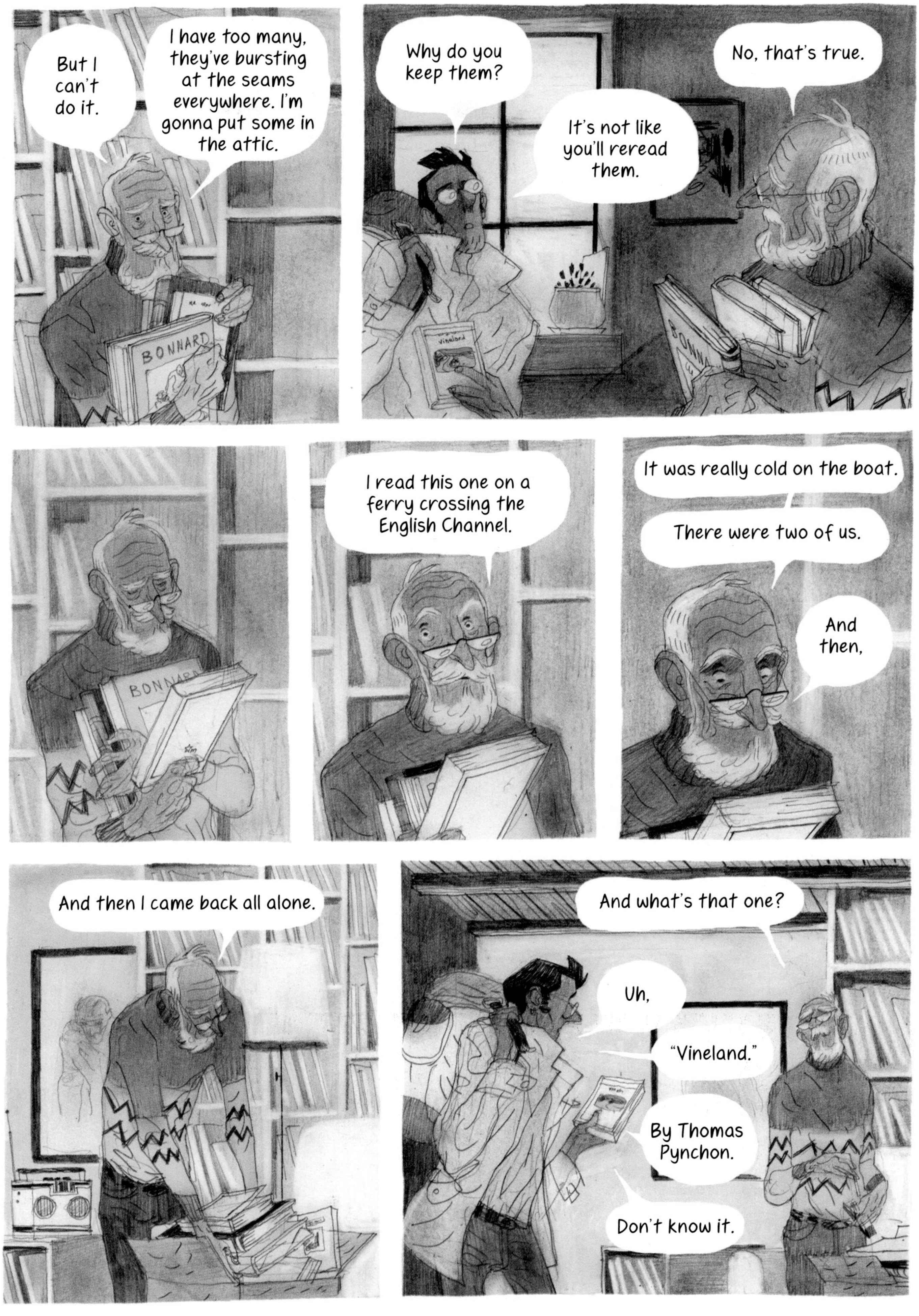
But I can't do it.
I have too many, they've bursting at the seams everywhere. I'm gonna put some in the attic.
Why do you keep them?
It's not like you'll reread them.
No, that's true.
I read this one on a ferry crossing the English Channel.
It was really cold on the boat.
There were two of us.
And then,
And then I came back all alone.
And what's that one?
Uh,
"Vineland."
By Thomas Pynchon.
Don't know it.

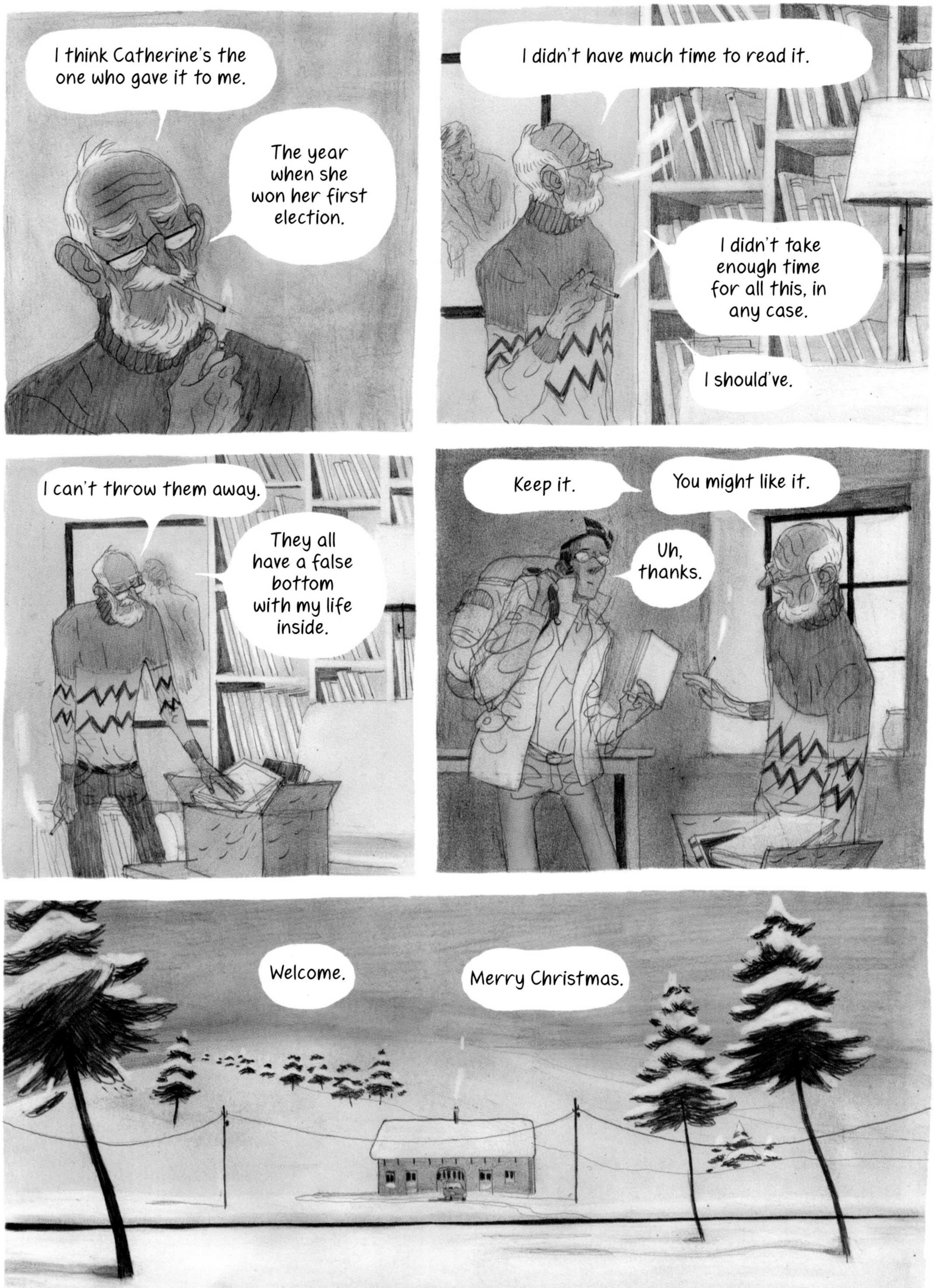
I think Catherine's the one who gave it to me.
The year when she won her first election.
I didn't have much time to read it.
I didn't take enough time for all this, in any case.
I should've.
I can't throw them away.
They all have a false bottom with my life inside.
Keep it.
You might like it.
Uh, thanks.
Welcome.
Merry Christmas.

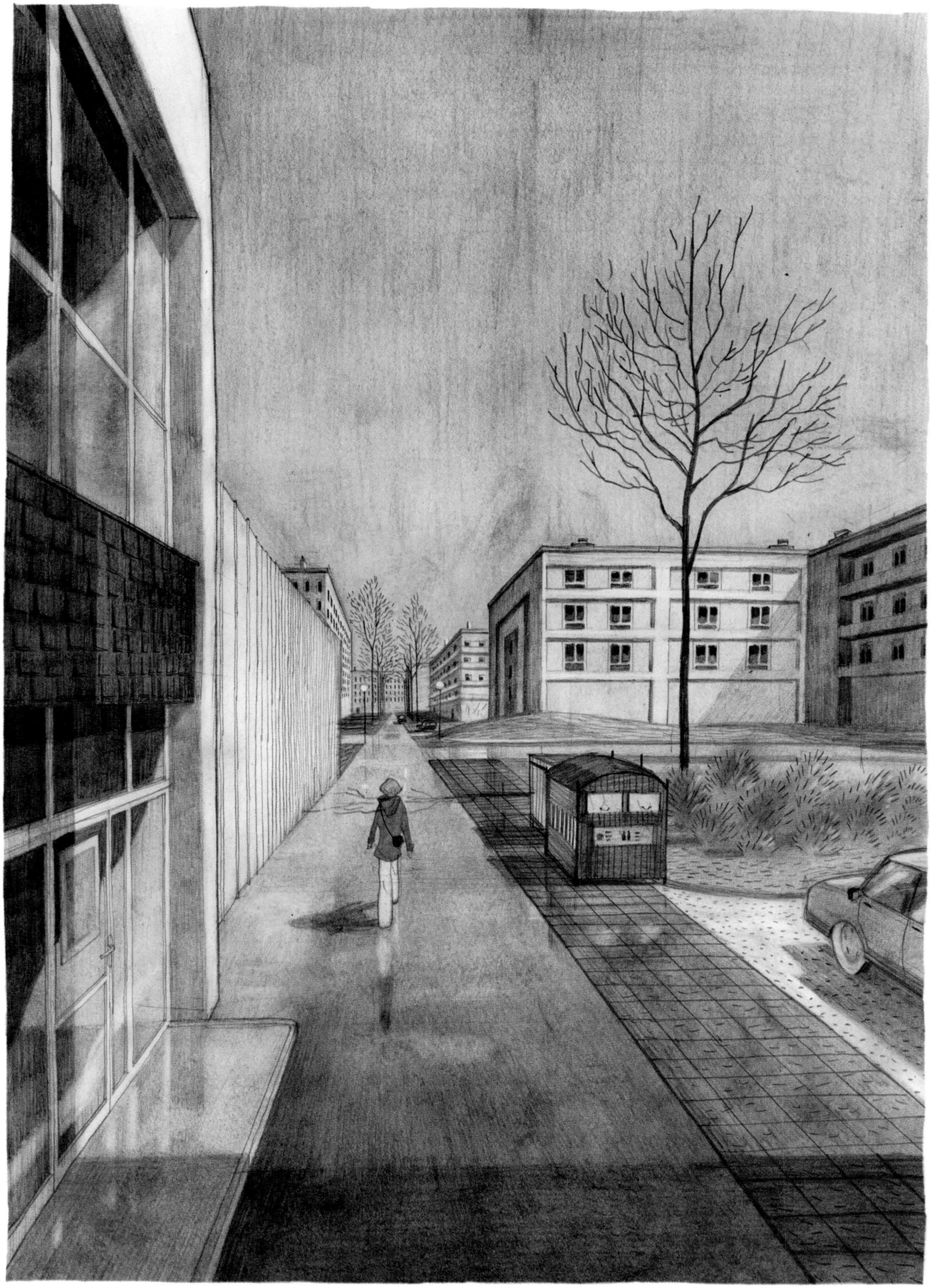

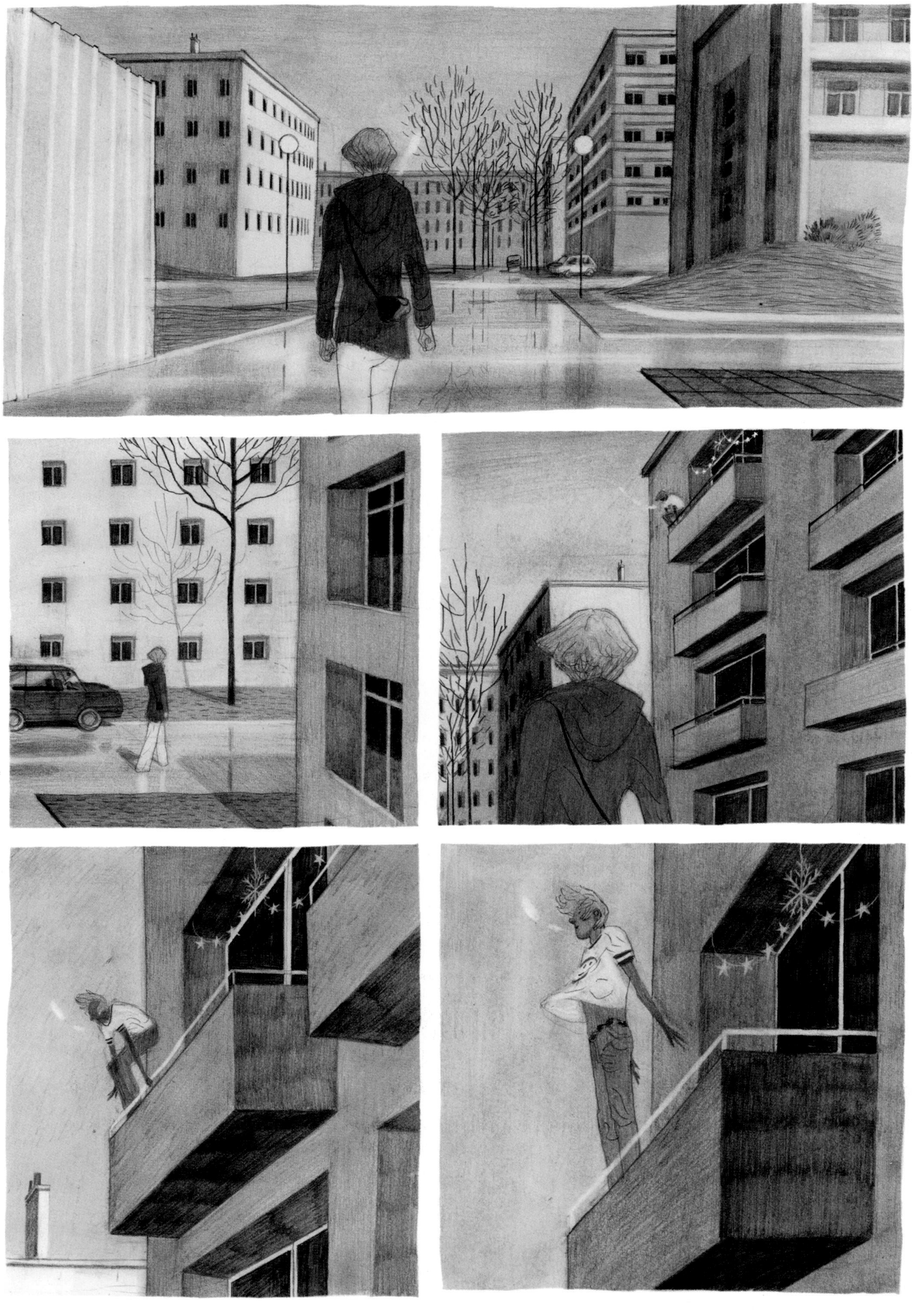

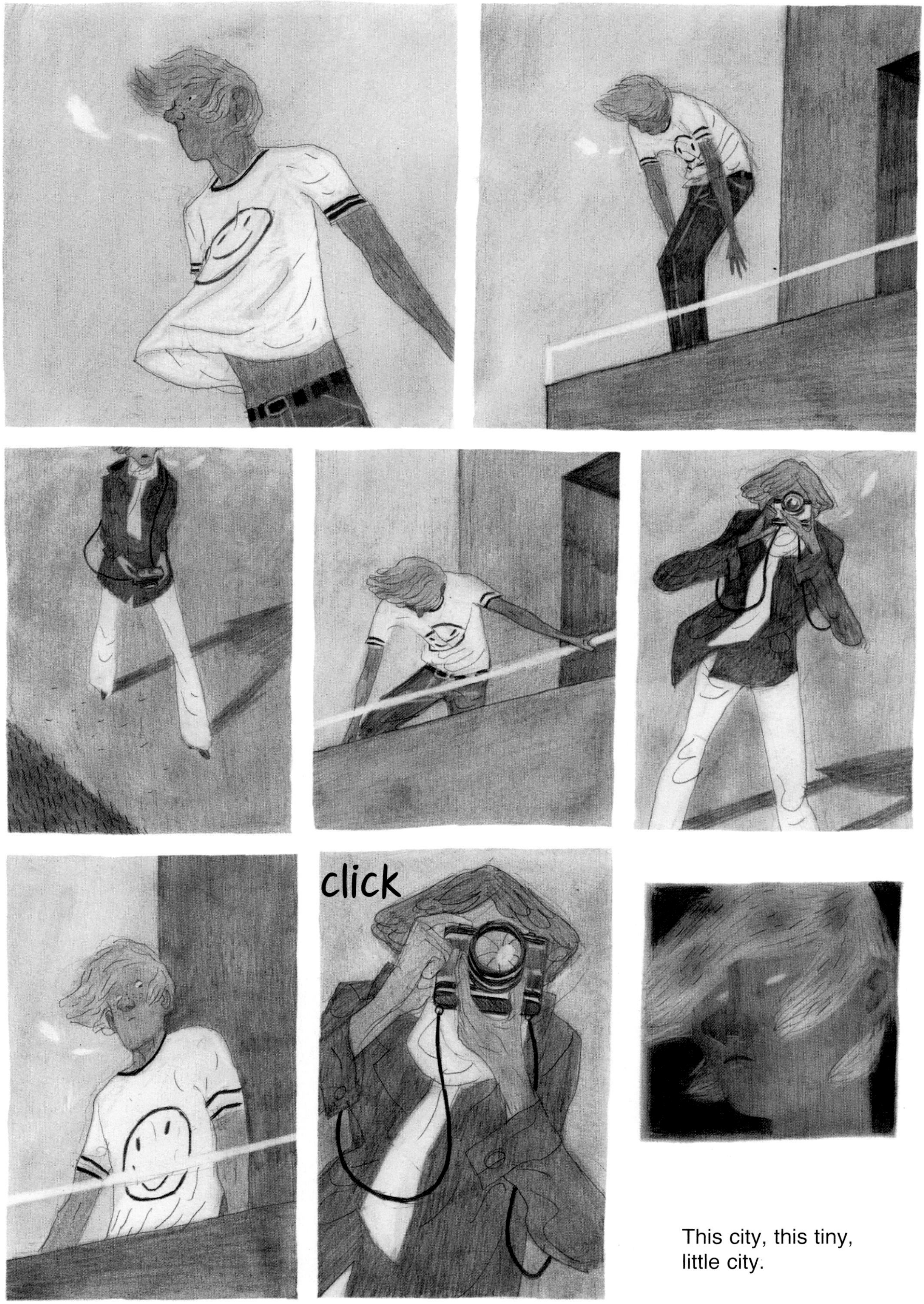
click
This city, this tiny,
little city.

Sometimes, he feels like he can stand up, look straight ahead, and take it all into his arms.

Then he could lift it, gently shrink it to his own size.

  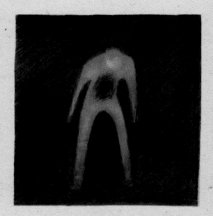

Know each of its lanes, its passersby, its cars going by briskly rolling along.

He'd understand where they were going, he'd share their secrets, he'd know where to go, too.

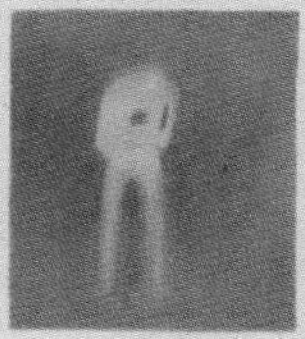

He'd be in his proper place.
But it never lasts.
A soon as the wind turns, hearing his mother's voice on the stairs, from a glance in the Monday morning bus, or even from the sounds of his steps in the street, he feels himself becoming miniscule again. His body then appears to him as it is, crumbly, like sand cliffs. They collapse silently at the slightest misstep, leaving room for that familiar void of which he's made, which he coils around, for lack of a better alternative.

Every day, between noon and two o'clock, he sits near them on a bench, in front of the high school gymnasium, like a heavy, little boy, embarrassed by the thick folds of his gut, his overly short tee-shirt pulling out of his winter pants sticking to his thighs. He remains immobile, for fear that they'll notice him. But their looks are turned elsewhere, towards their own arabesques. Each grain of light animates them, unfurling with a purpose. Their arms make perfect circles. They're already the masters of a world built for them. They laugh, they have parties.

He went there once, keeping to the garden. Further down the alley, muffled beats came through the garden door behind which the world of the living was dancing. She was outside, too. Sitting in the shadow, on a low wall, four or five yards away from him. He didn't know how to cross so wide a gulf. She was looking straight ahead. Yet, he was sure, yes, almost sure that that fixed gaze had been addressed to him. They remained like that for a long moment. And then she got up. The door opened. Music invaded the entire space. For a short instant, the garden became white and hard like a stone, and the door closed behind her. Nothing but the night and the beats remained. He left. On his return trip, the immobility of the streets made him think of tidy bedrooms, always ready to welcome you, but where no one has slept in a long time.

Sometimes, the puddles of water in front of the florist's on the square, the gravel crunching under his feet, or the heads bobbing gently on the morning bus, all seemed to be saying something. It's as though the air is charged with a melody that he can't manage to hum. He often tries, then gives up. It's no use, no use at all.

With the money from his birthday, he'd have enough to catch the train for anywhere. He'd just have to leave a note on the kitchen table for his parents. It's a soothing idea. A small fire of twigs he sometimes lights to keep himself warm.

The hours are centuries, they don't lead anywhere. He'd have to disappear to no longer feel that void. It's just too long, a life like that.

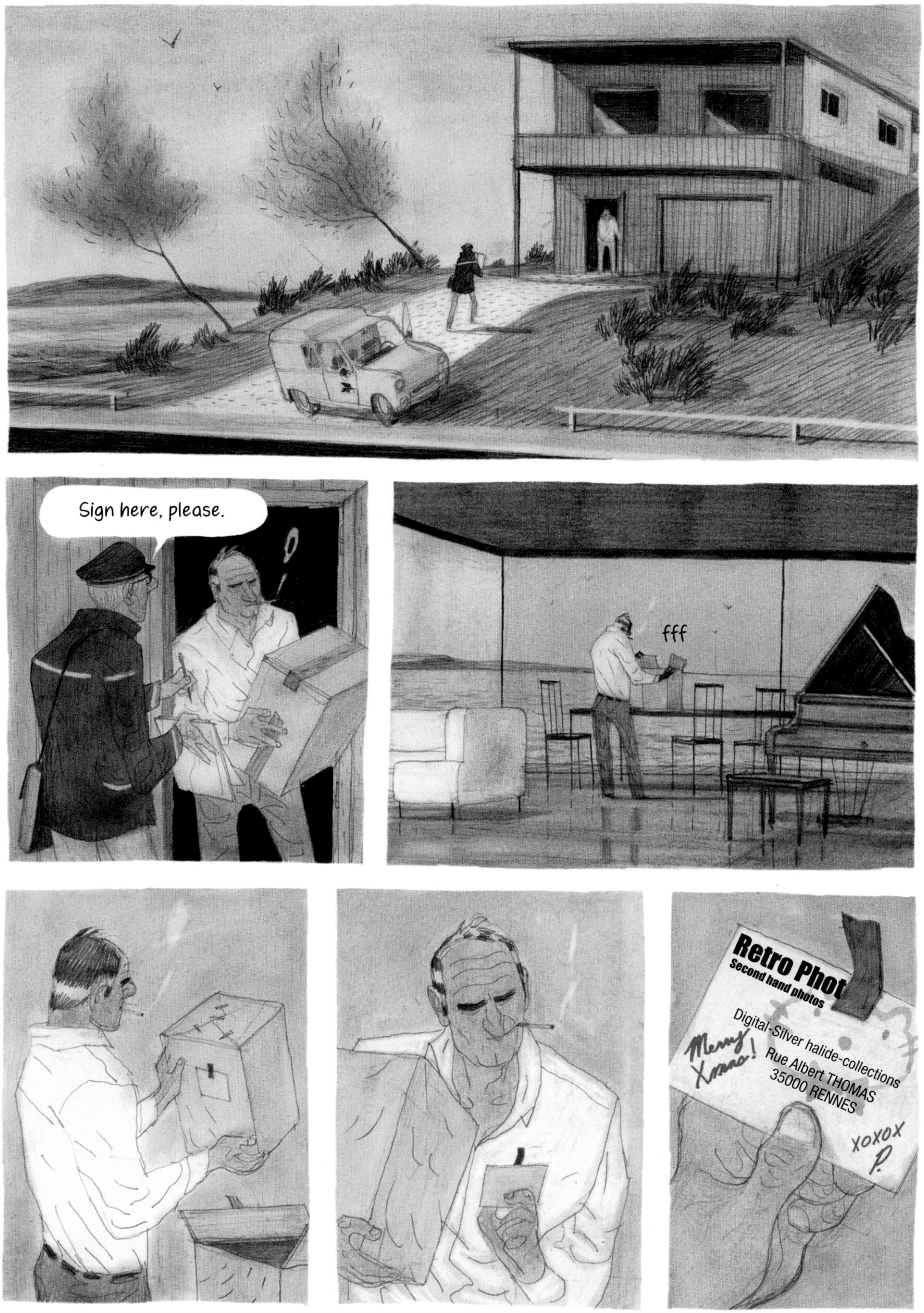
Sign here, please.
fff
Retro Phot
Second hand photos
Digital-Silver halide-collections
Rue Albert THOMAS
35000 RENNES
Merry Xmas!
XOXOX
P.

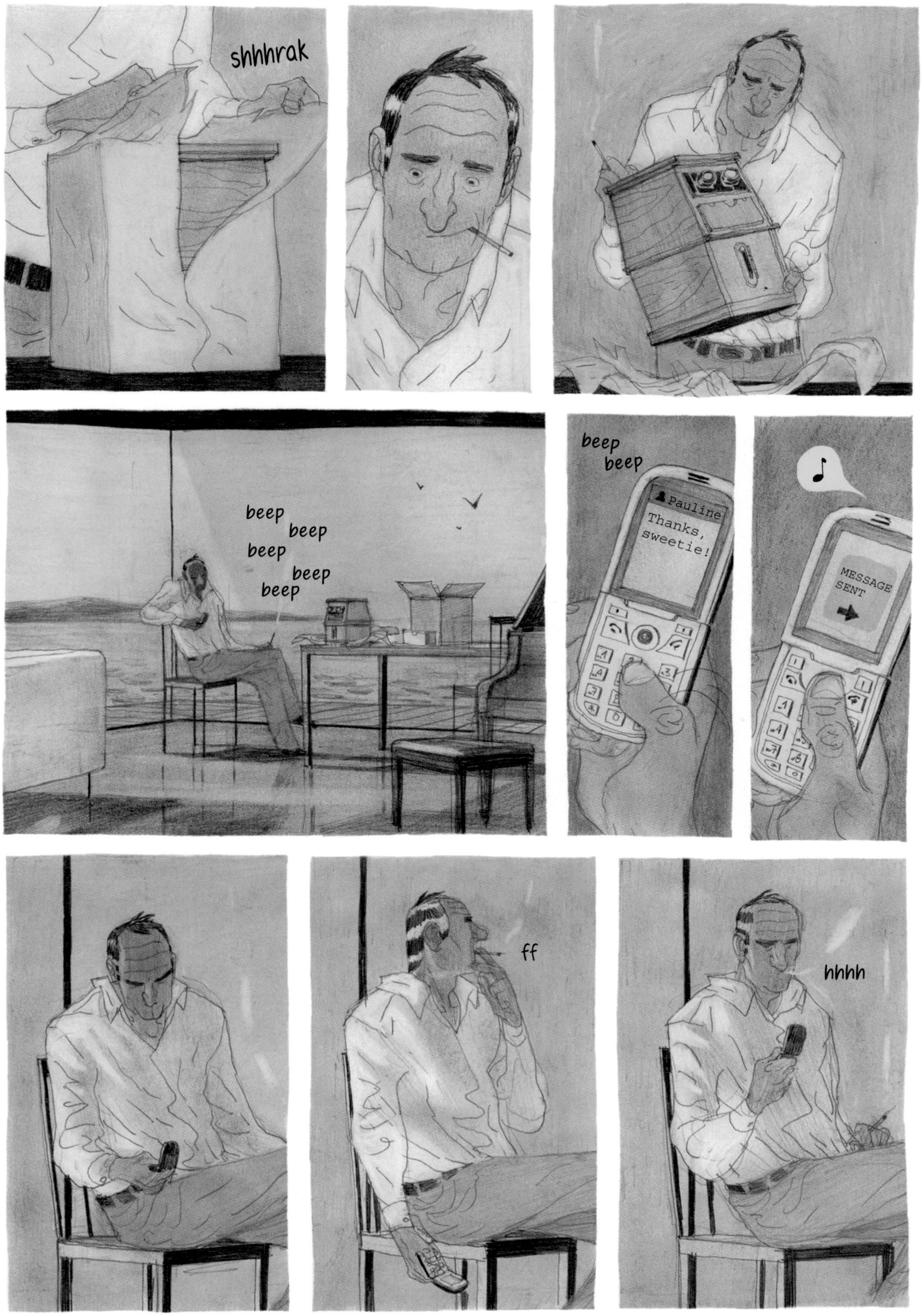
shhhrak
beep beep beep beep beep
beep beep
Pauline
Thanks, sweetie!
MESSAGE SENT
ff
hhhh

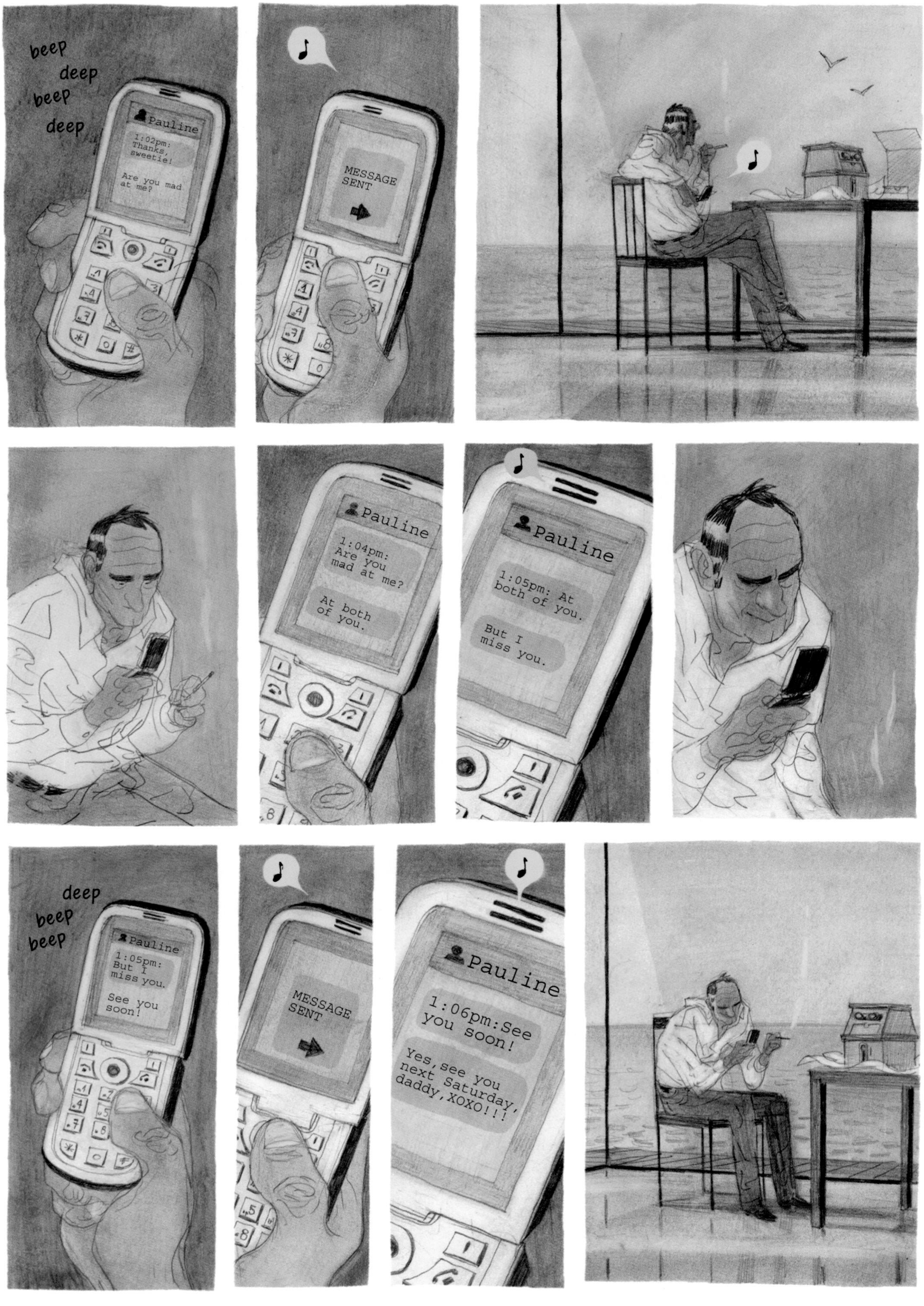
beep
deep
beep
deep
Pauline
1:02pm: Thanks, sweetie!
Are you mad at me?
MESSAGE SENT
Pauline
1:04pm: Are you mad at me?
At both of you.
Pauline
1:05pm: At both of you.
But I miss you.
deep
beep
beep
Pauline
1:05pm: But I miss you.
See you soon!
MESSAGE SENT
Pauline
1:06pm: See you soon!
Yes, see you next Saturday, daddy, XOXO!!!

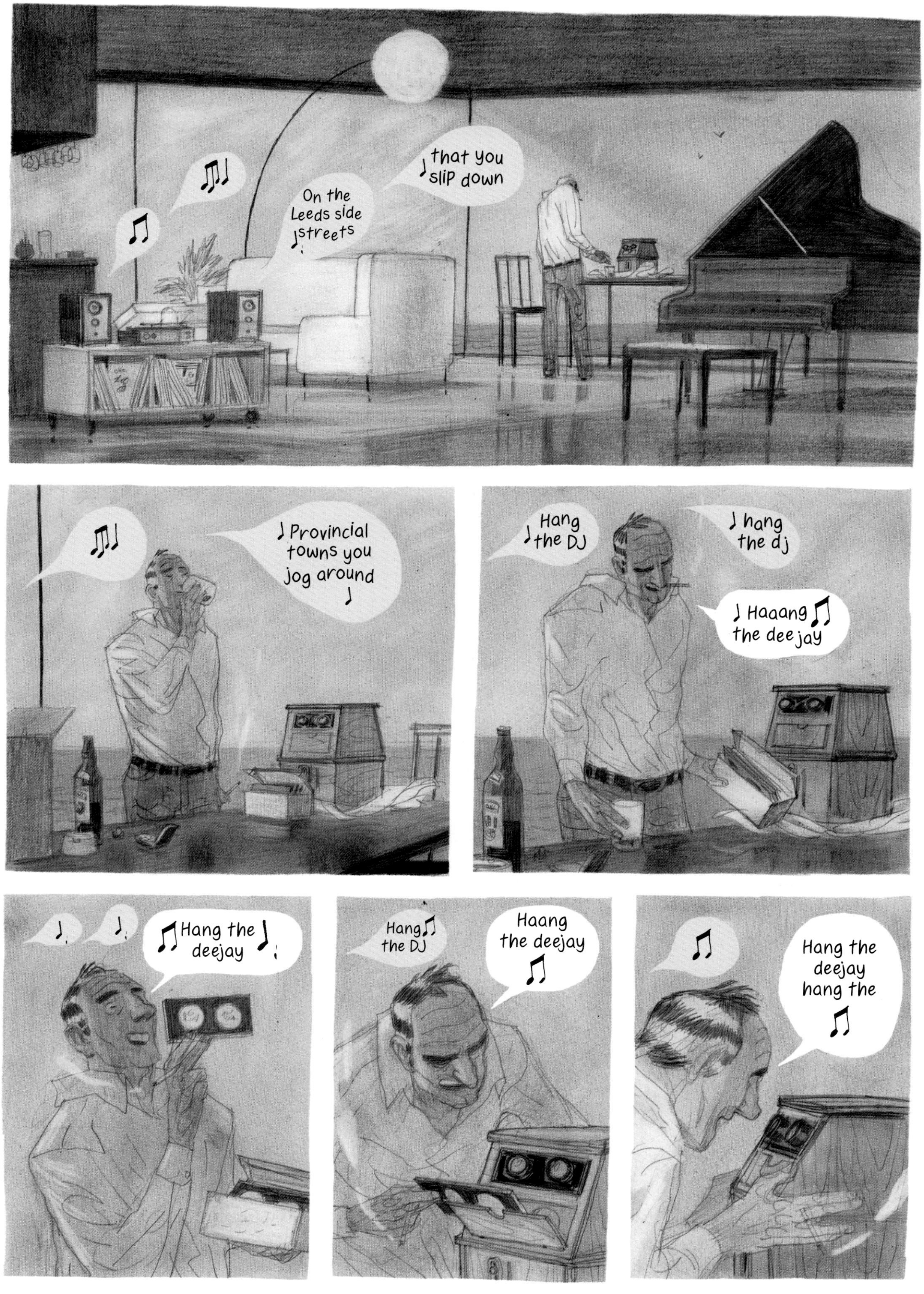
On the Leeds side streets
that you slip down
Provincial towns you jog around
Hang the DJ
hang the dj
Haaang the deejay
Hang the deejay
Hang the DJ
Haaang the deejay
Hang the deejay hang the

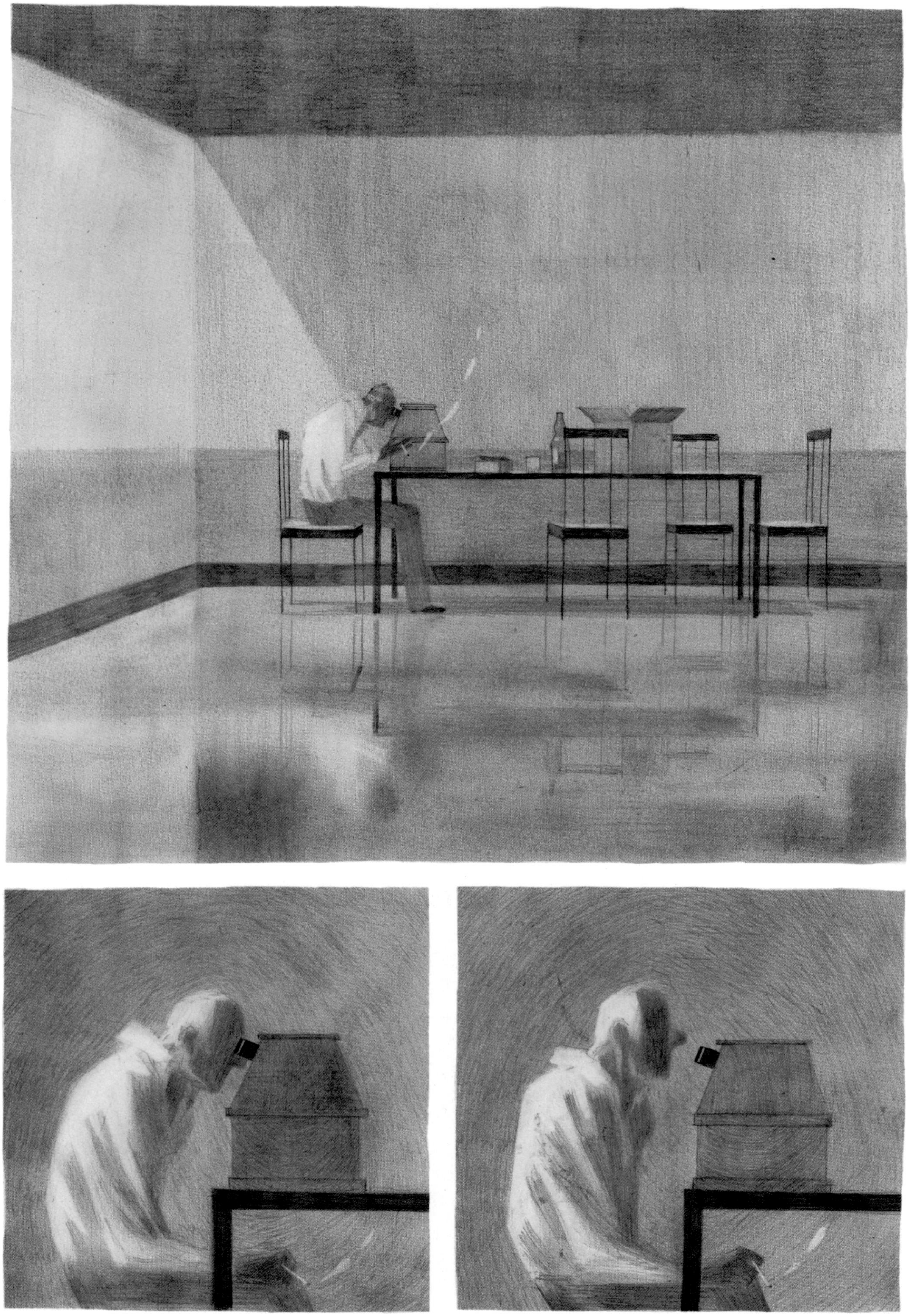

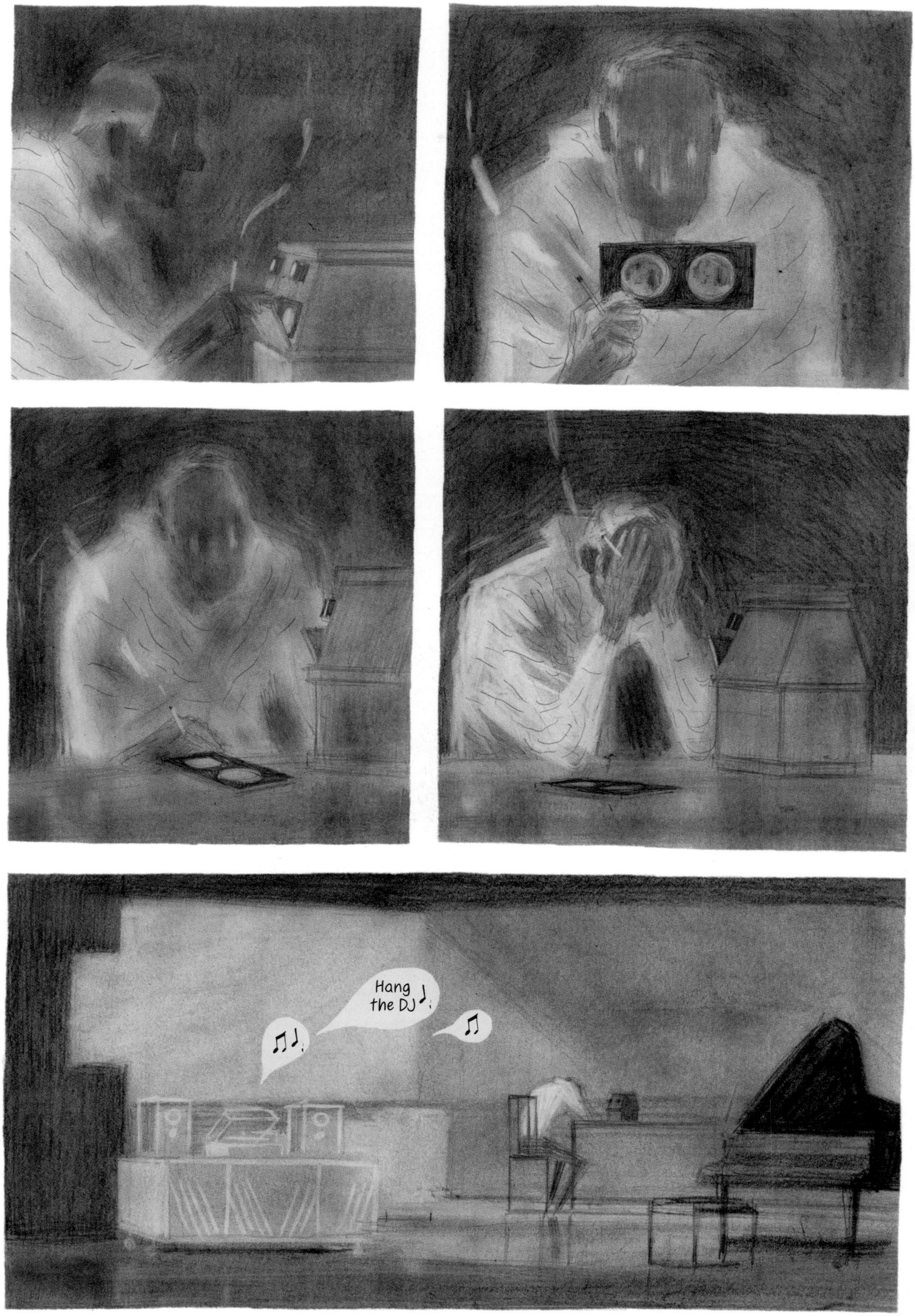
Hang the DJ

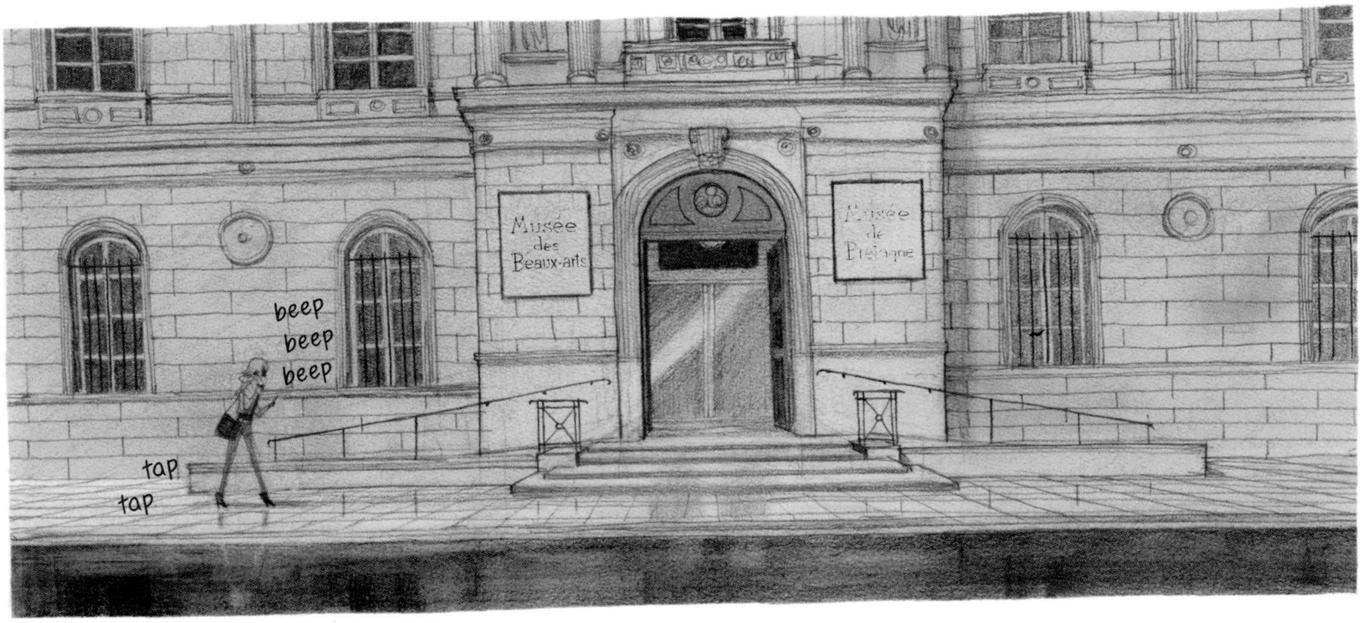
Musée des Beaux-arts
beep
beep
beep
tap
tap

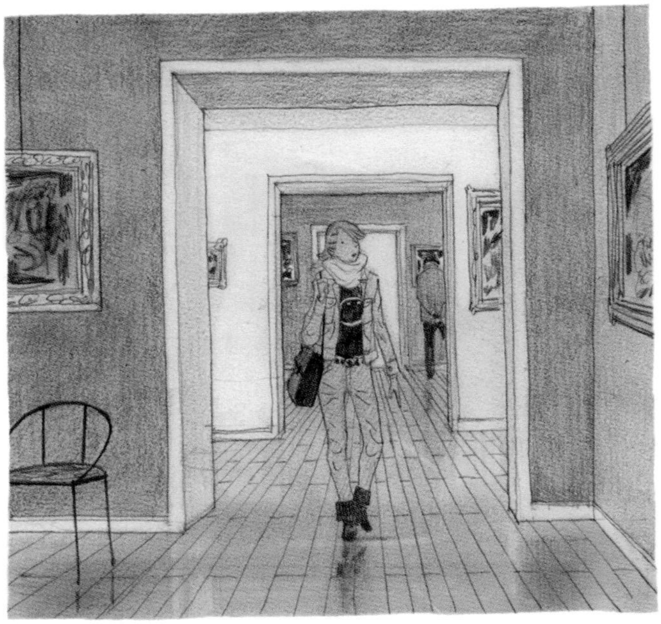

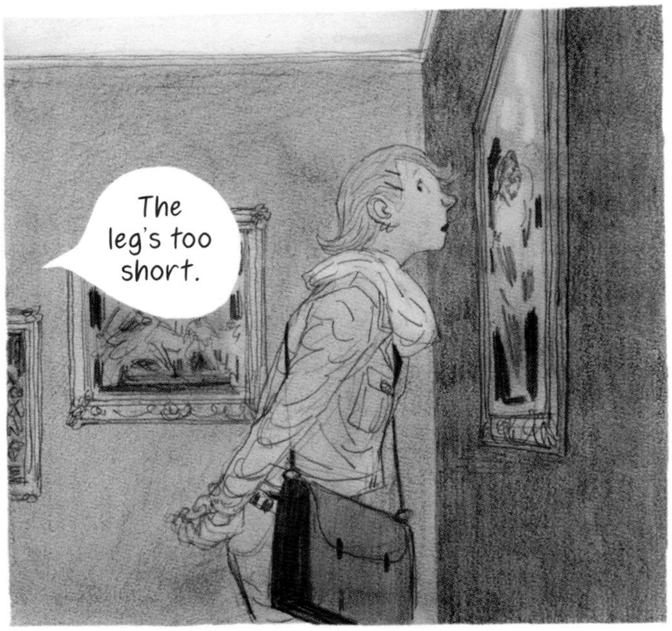
The leg's too short.

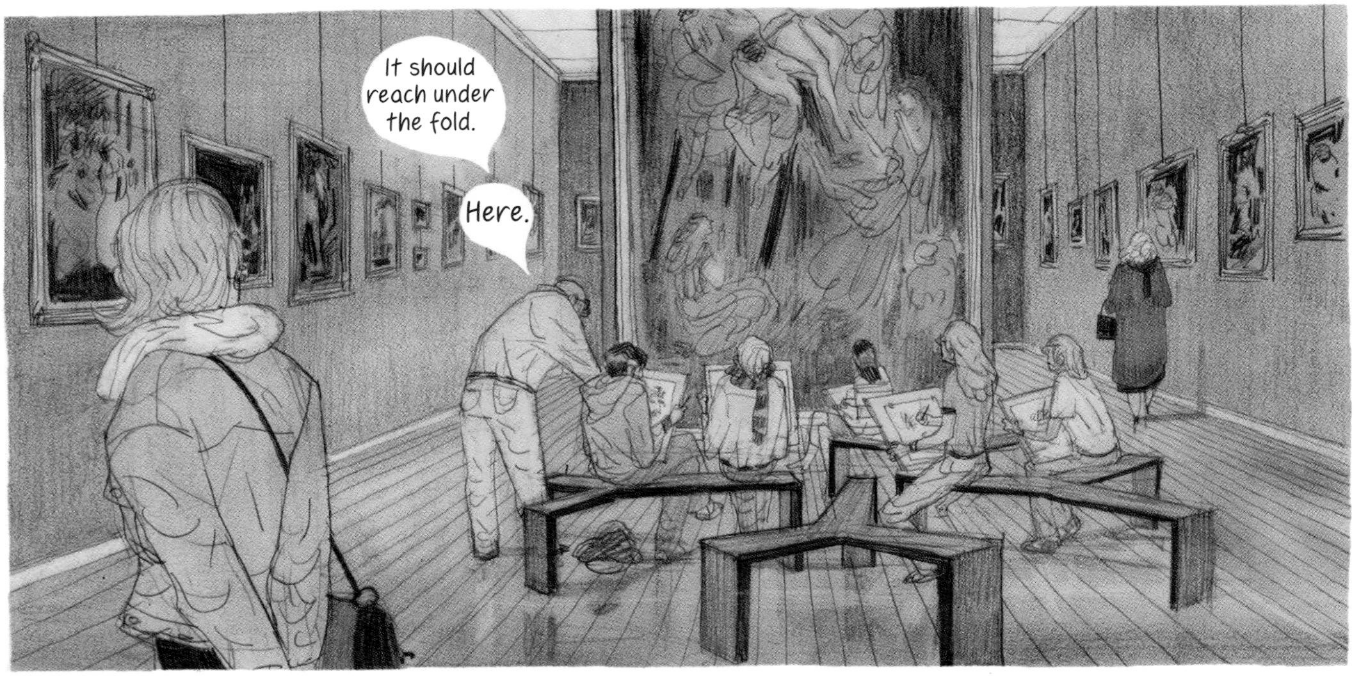
It should reach under the fold.
Here.

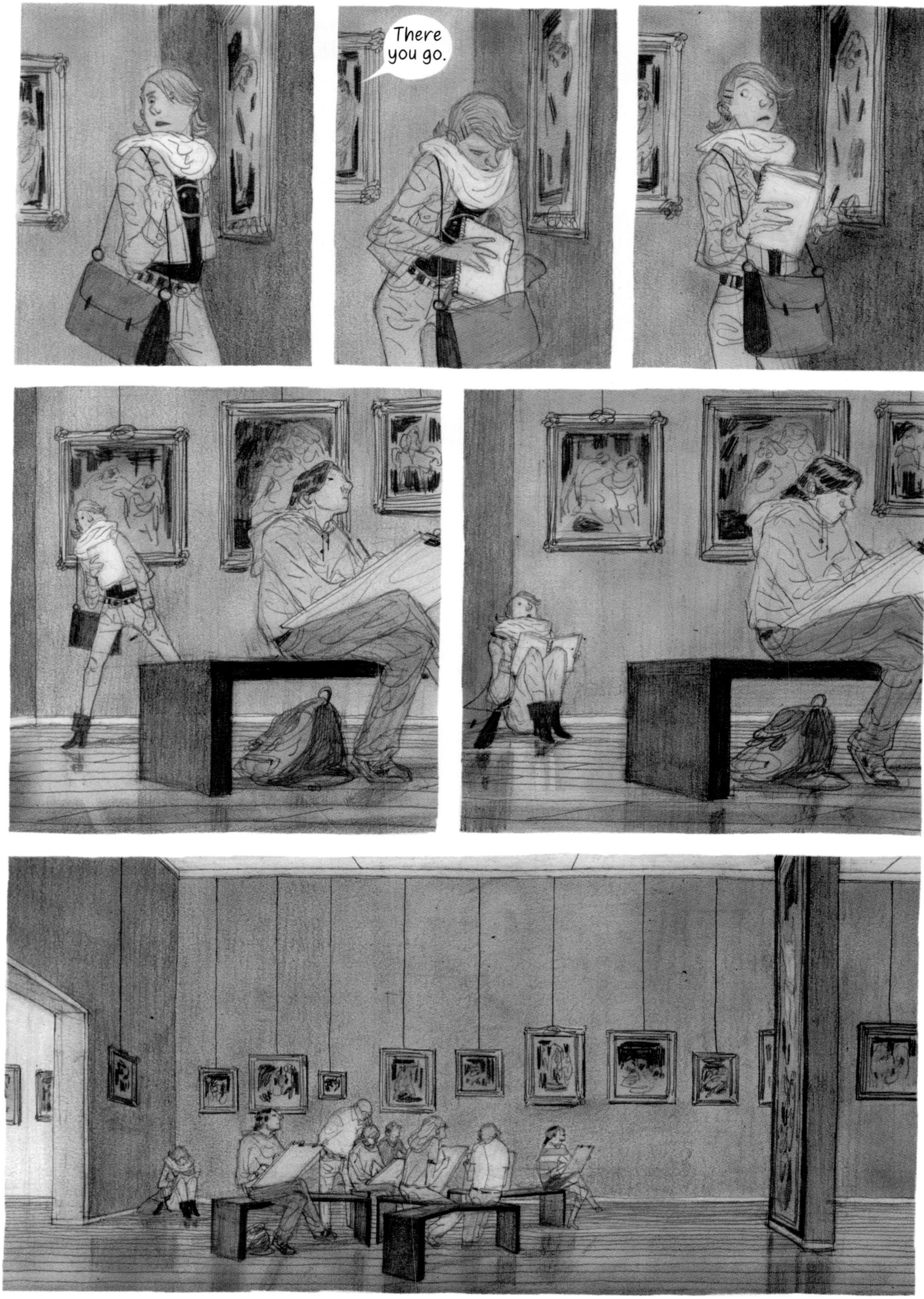
There you go.

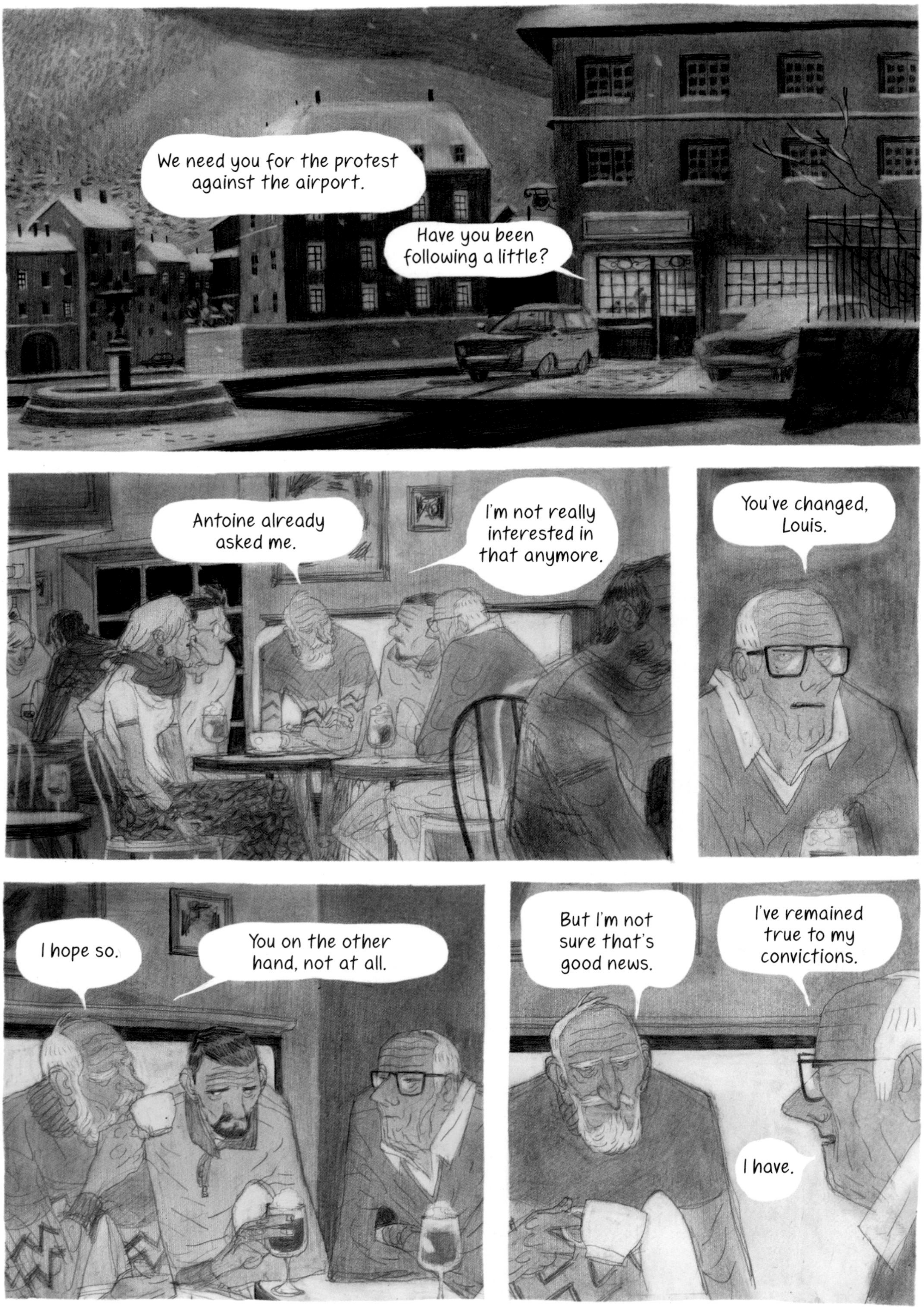
We need you for the protest against the airport.
Have you been following a little?
Antoine already asked me.
I'm not really interested in that anymore.
You've changed, Louis.
I hope so.
You on the other hand, not at all.
But I'm not sure that's good news.
I've remained true to my convictions.
I have.

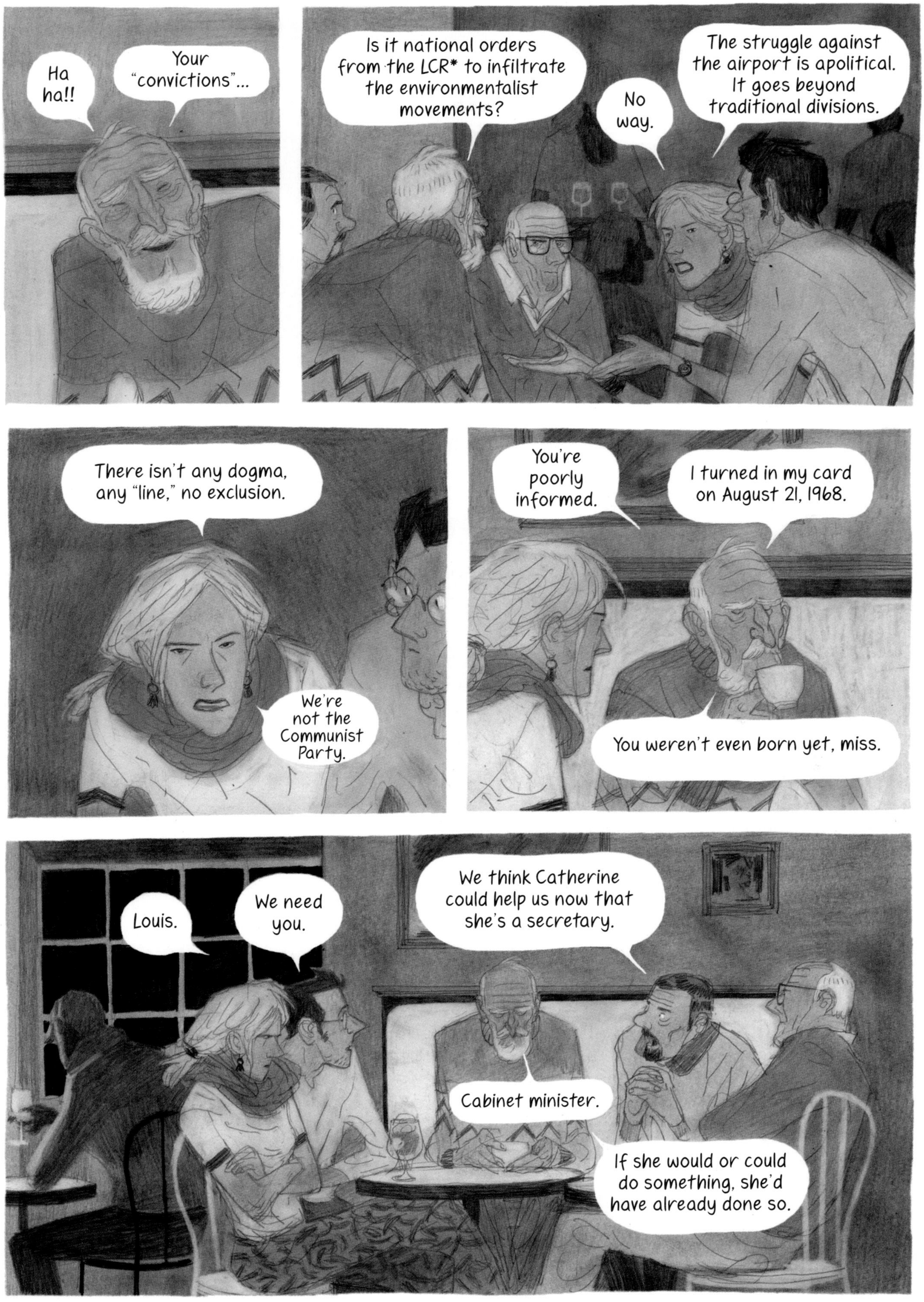
Ha ha!!
Your "convictions"...
Is it national orders from the LCR* to infiltrate the environmentalist movements?
No way.
The struggle against the airport is apolitical. It goes beyond traditional divisions.
There isn't any dogma, any "line," no exclusion.
We're not the Communist Party.
You're poorly informed.
I turned in my card on August 21, 1968.
You weren't even born yet, miss.
Louis.
We need you.
We think Catherine could help us now that she's a secretary.
Cabinet minister.
If she would or could do something, she'd have already done so.

*Ligue communiste révolutionnaire, or Revolutionary Communist League

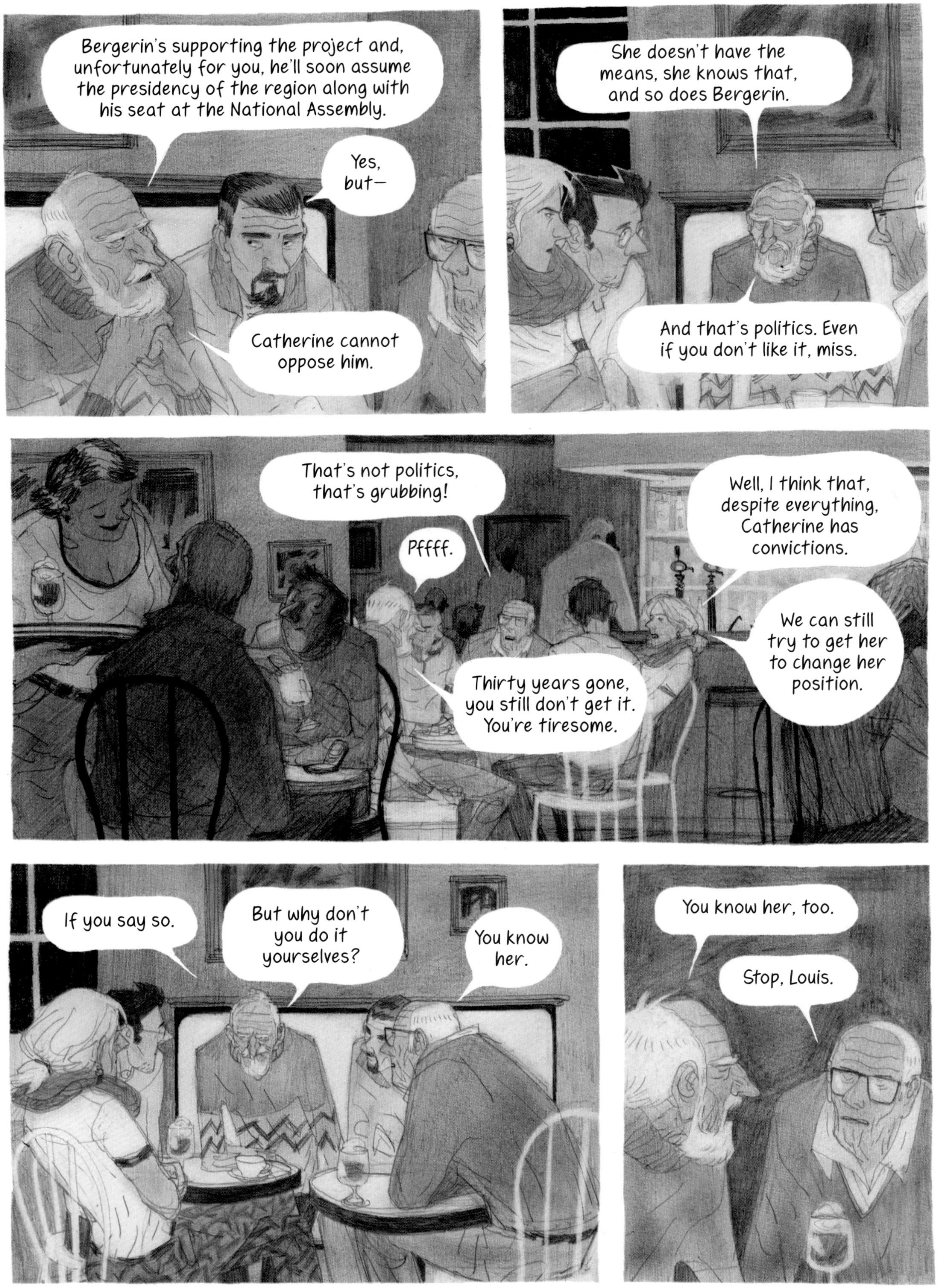
Bergerin's supporting the project and, unfortunately for you, he'll soon assume the presidency of the region along with his seat at the National Assembly.
Yes, but—
Catherine cannot oppose him.
She doesn't have the means, she knows that, and so does Bergerin.
And that's politics. Even if you don't like it, miss.
That's not politics, that's grubbing!
Pffff.
Well, I think that, despite everything, Catherine has convictions.
We can still try to get her to change her position.
Thirty years gone, you still don't get it. You're tiresome.
If you say so.
But why don't you do it yourselves?
You know her.
You know her, too.
Stop, Louis.

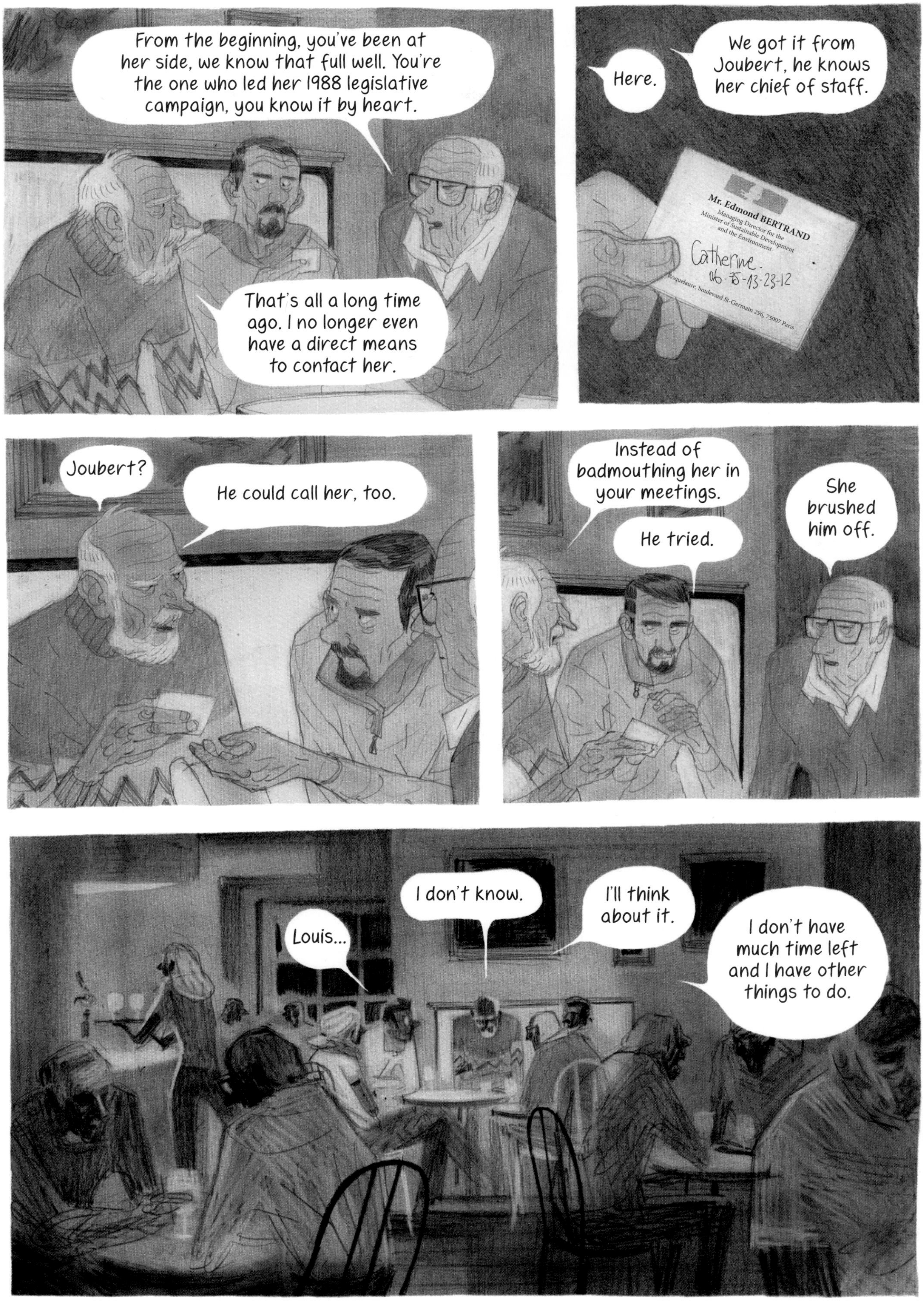
From the beginning, you've been at her side, we know that full well. You're the one who led her 1988 legislative campaign, you know it by heart.
That's all a long time ago. I no longer even have a direct means to contact her.
Here.
We got it from Joubert, he knows her chief of staff.
Mr. Edmond BERTRAND
Managing Director for the Minister of Sustainable Development and the Environment
Catherine.
06-75-13-23-12
Roquelaure, boulevard St-Germain 296, 75007 Paris
Joubert?
He could call her, too.
Instead of badmouthing her in your meetings.
He tried.
She brushed him off.
Louis...
I don't know.
I'll think about it.
I don't have much time left and I have other things to do.

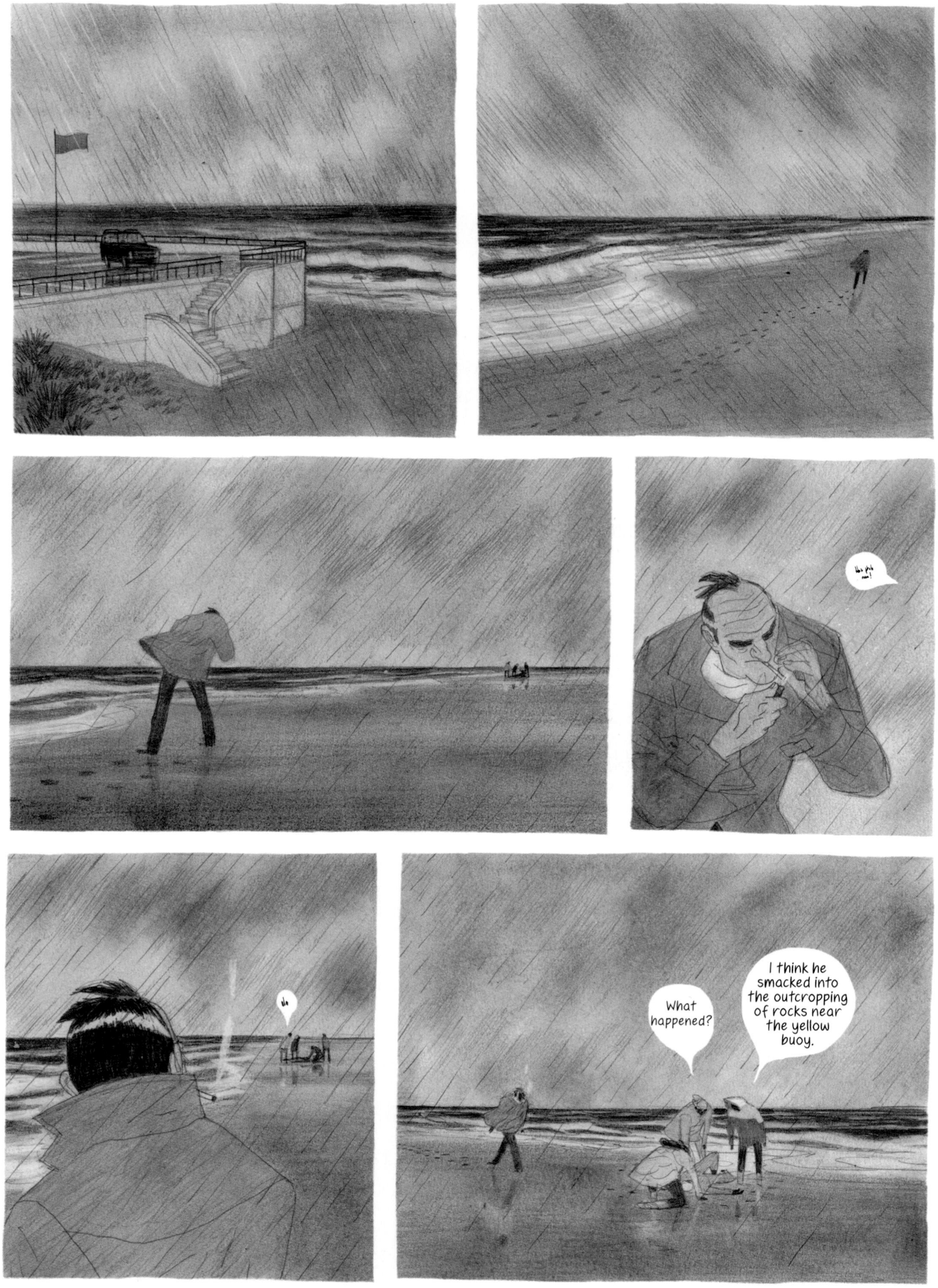
What happened?
I think he smacked into the outcropping of rocks near the yellow buoy.

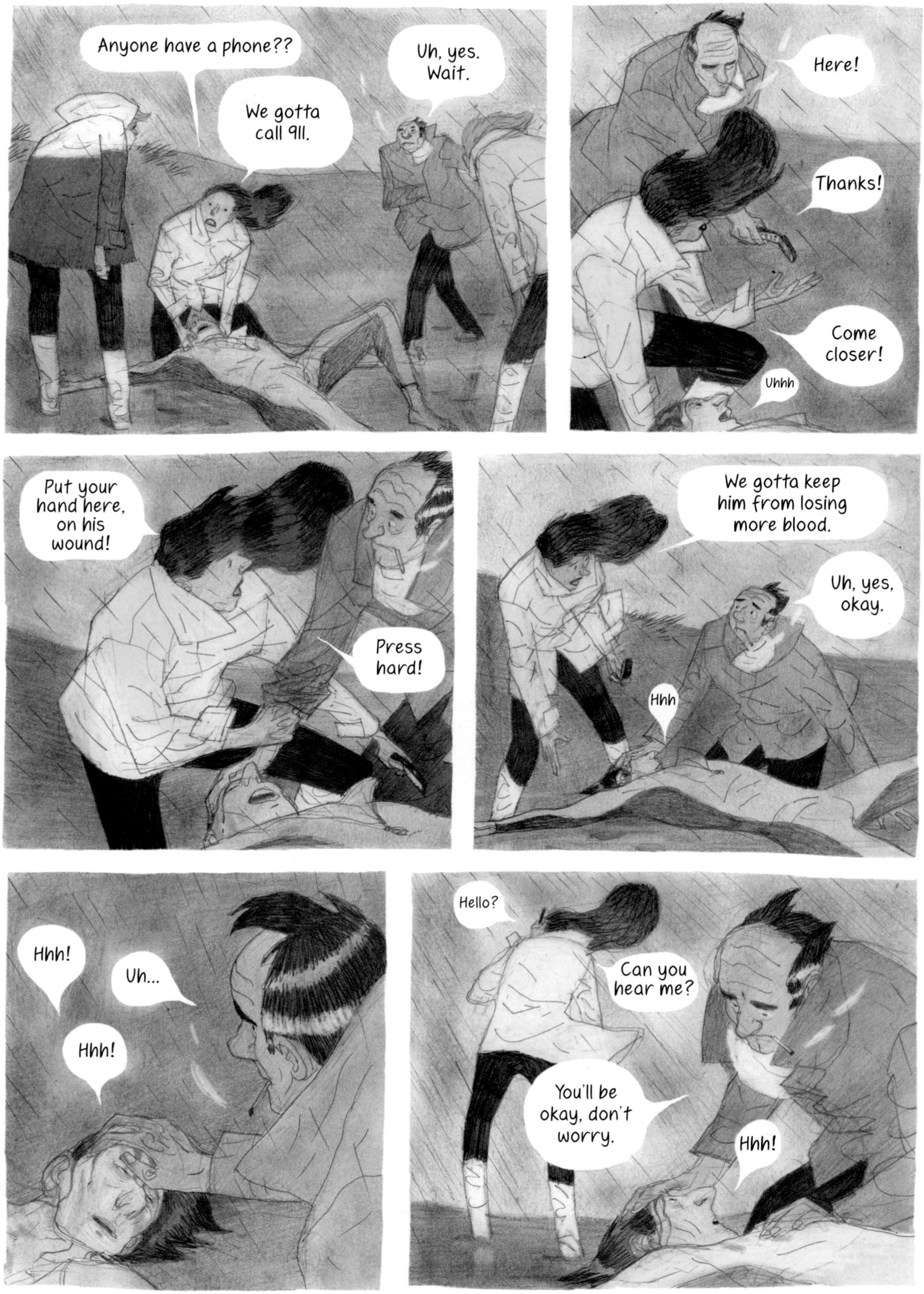
Anyone have a phone??
We gotta call 911.
Uh, yes. Wait.
Here!
Thanks!
Come closer!
Uhhh
Put your hand here, on his wound!
Press hard!
We gotta keep him from losing more blood.
Uh, yes, okay.
Hhh
Hhh!
Uh...
Hhh!
Hello?
Can you hear me?
You'll be okay, don't worry.
Hhh!

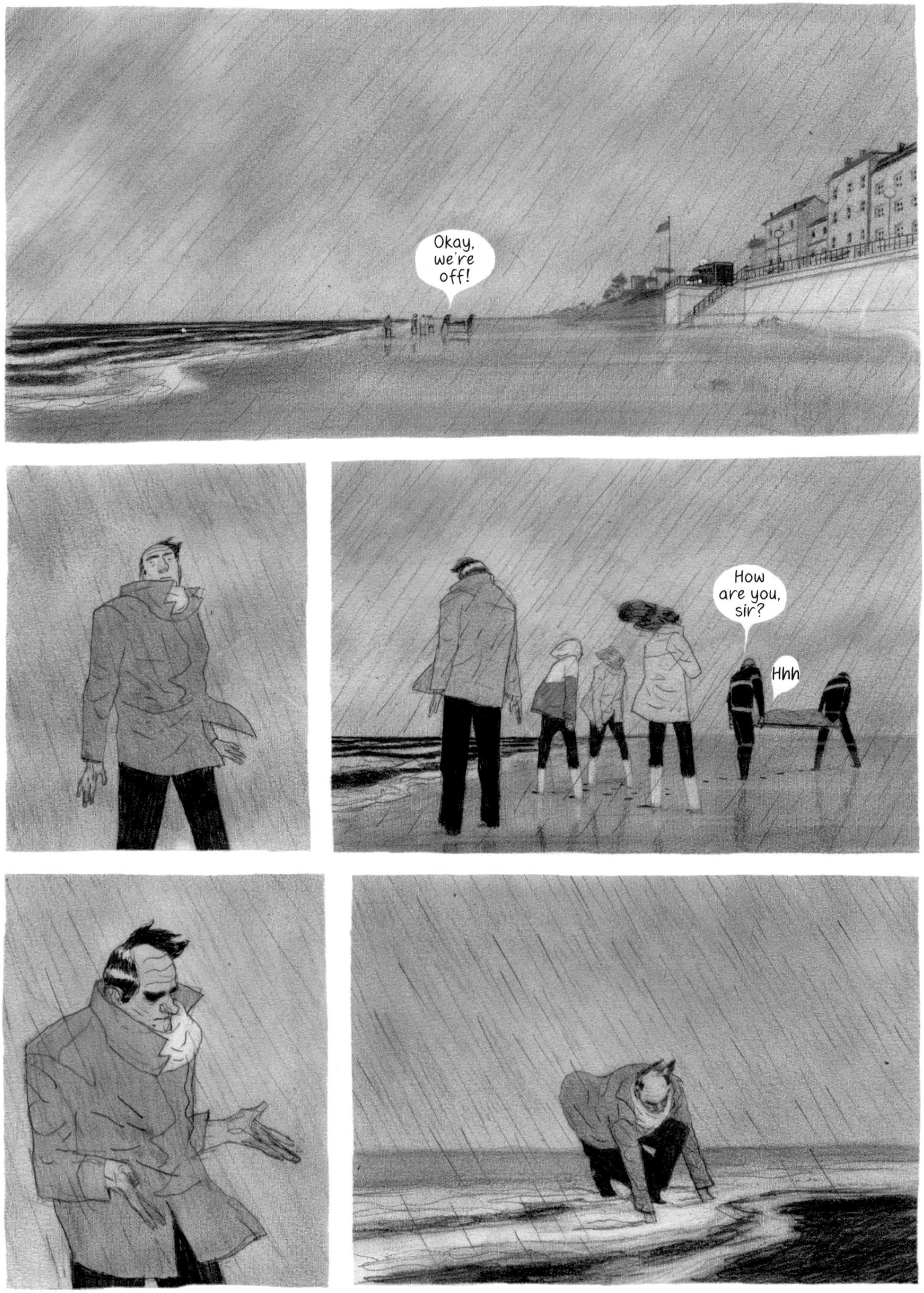
Okay, we're off!
How are you, sir?
Hhh

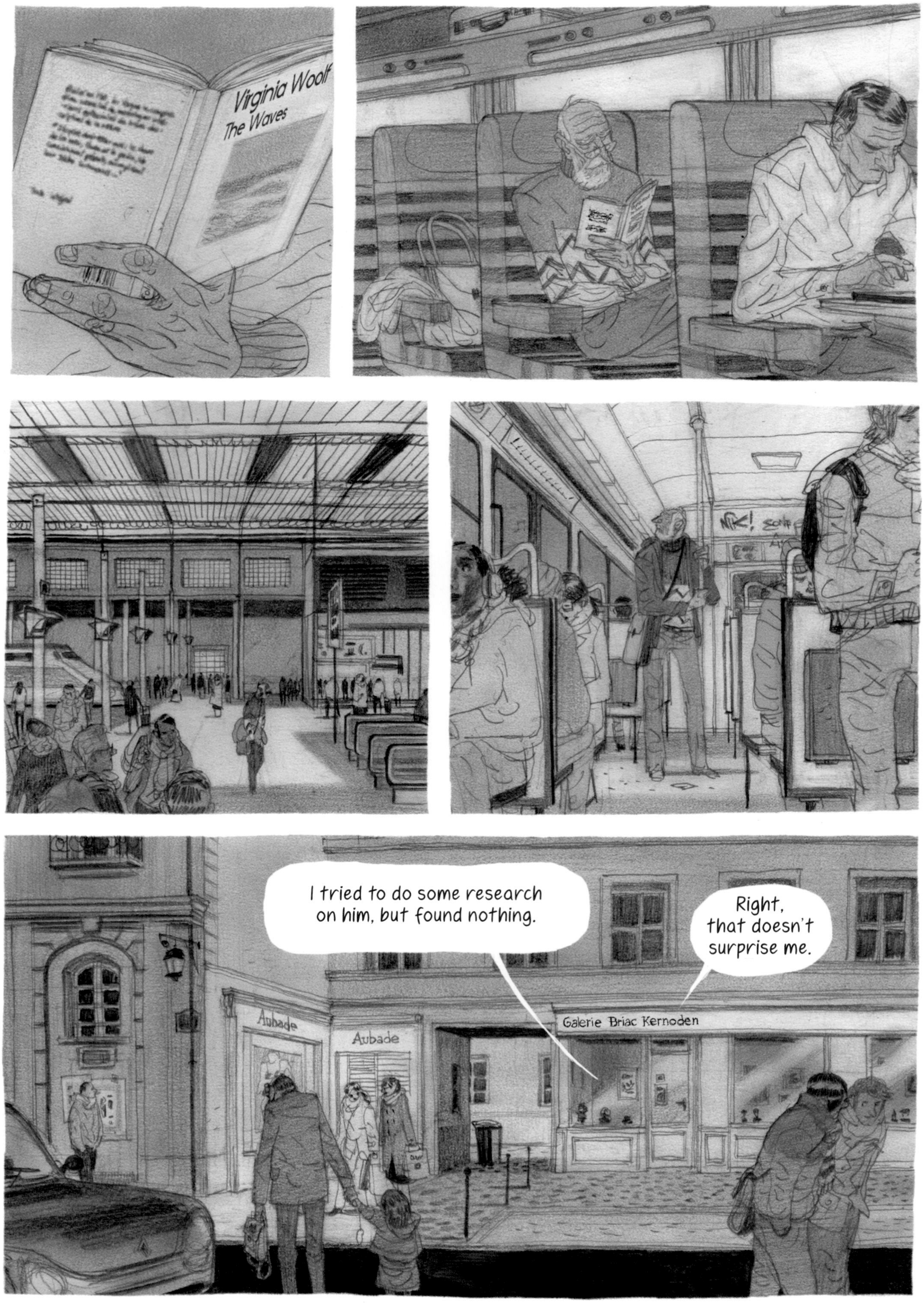
Virginia Woolf
The Waves
Aubade
Aubade
Galerie Briac Kernoden
I tried to do some research on him, but found nothing.
Right, that doesn't surprise me.

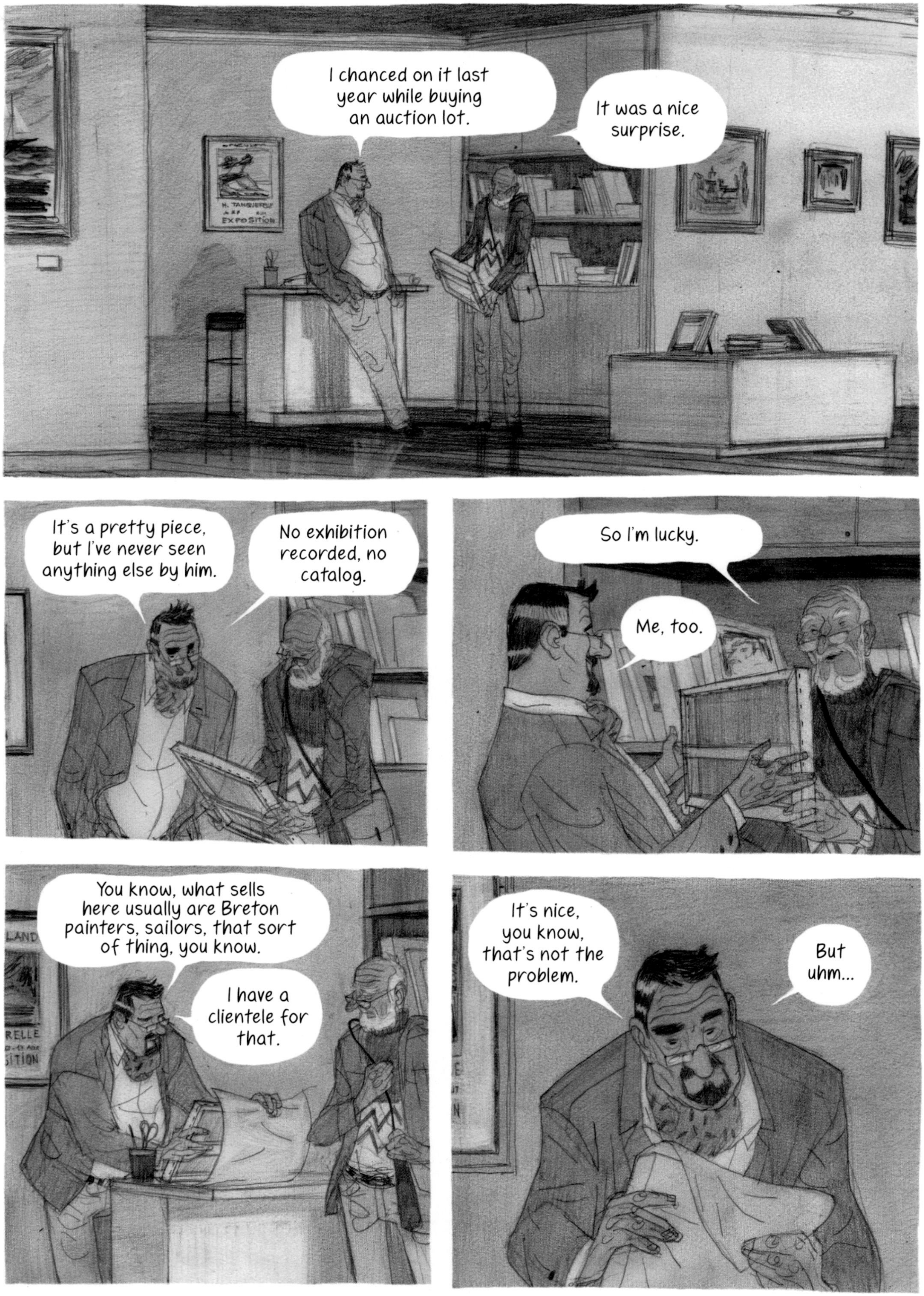
I chanced on it last year while buying an auction lot.
It was a nice surprise.
H. TANGUERUF
EXPOSITION
It's a pretty piece, but I've never seen anything else by him.
No exhibition recorded, no catalog.
So I'm lucky.
Me, too.
You know, what sells here usually are Breton painters, sailors, that sort of thing, you know.
I have a clientele for that.
It's nice, you know, that's not the problem.
But uhm...

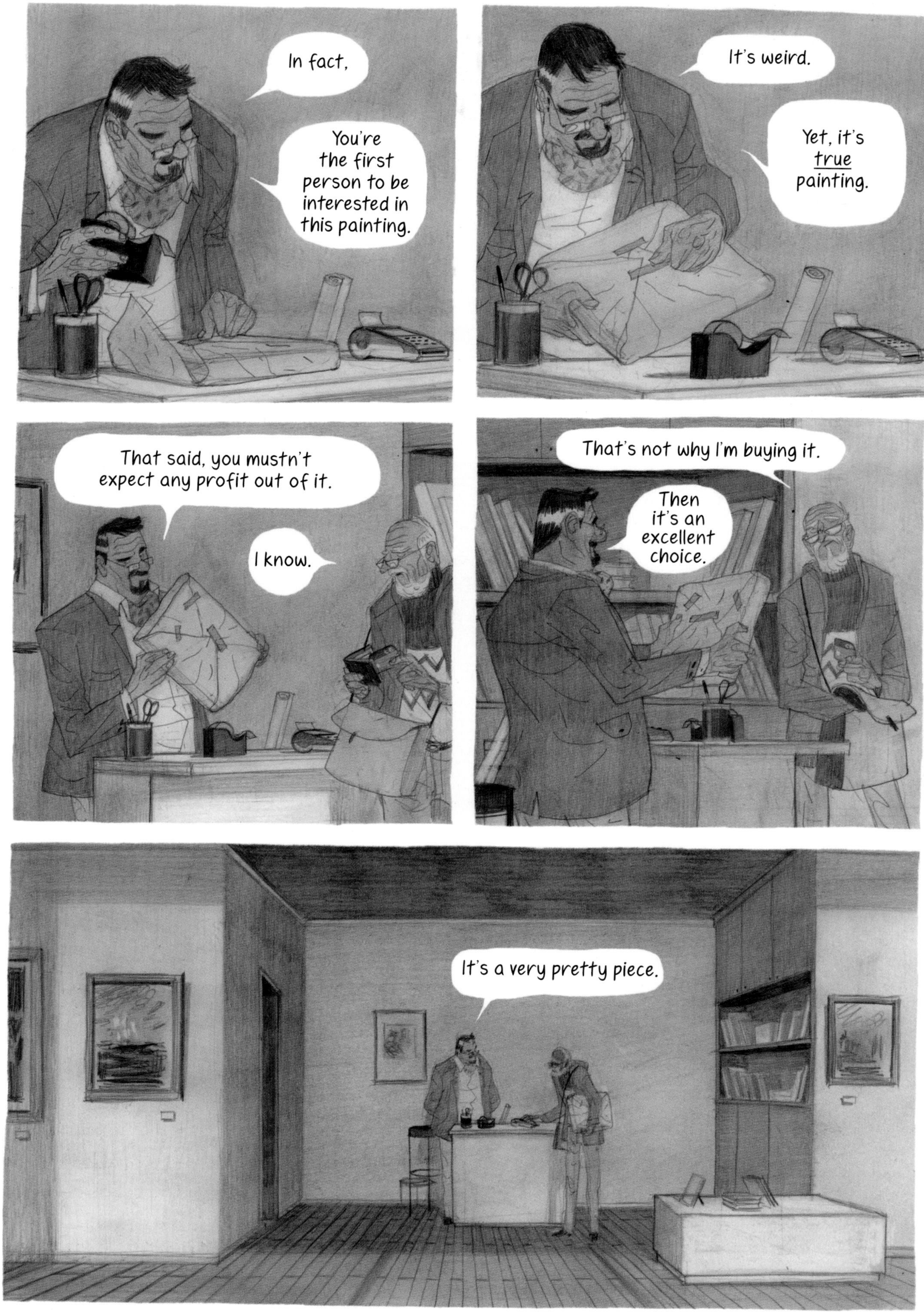
In fact,
You're the first person to be interested in this painting.
It's weird.
Yet, it's true painting.
That said, you mustn't expect any profit out of it.
I know.
That's not why I'm buying it.
Then it's an excellent choice.
It's a very pretty piece.

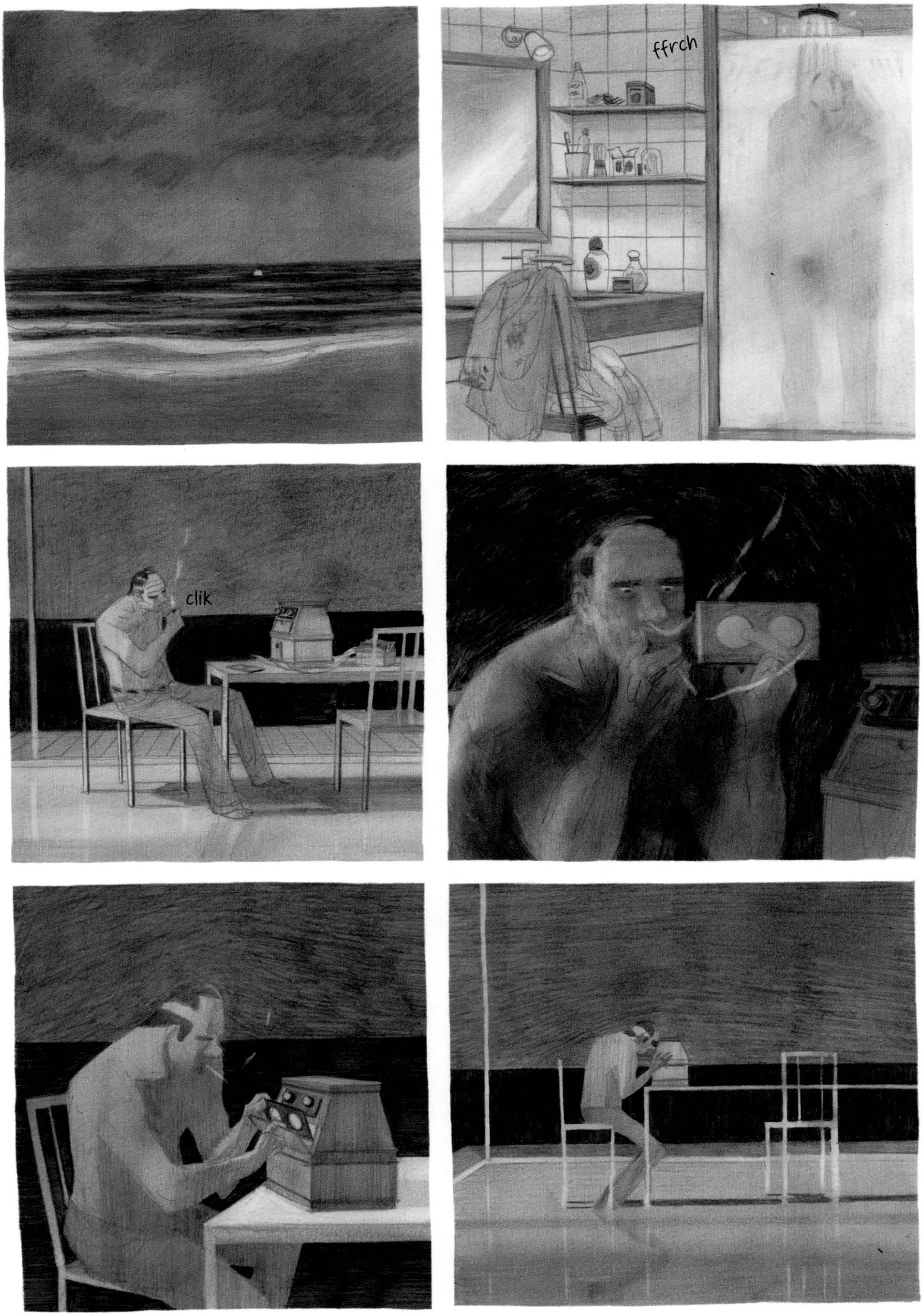
ffrch
clik

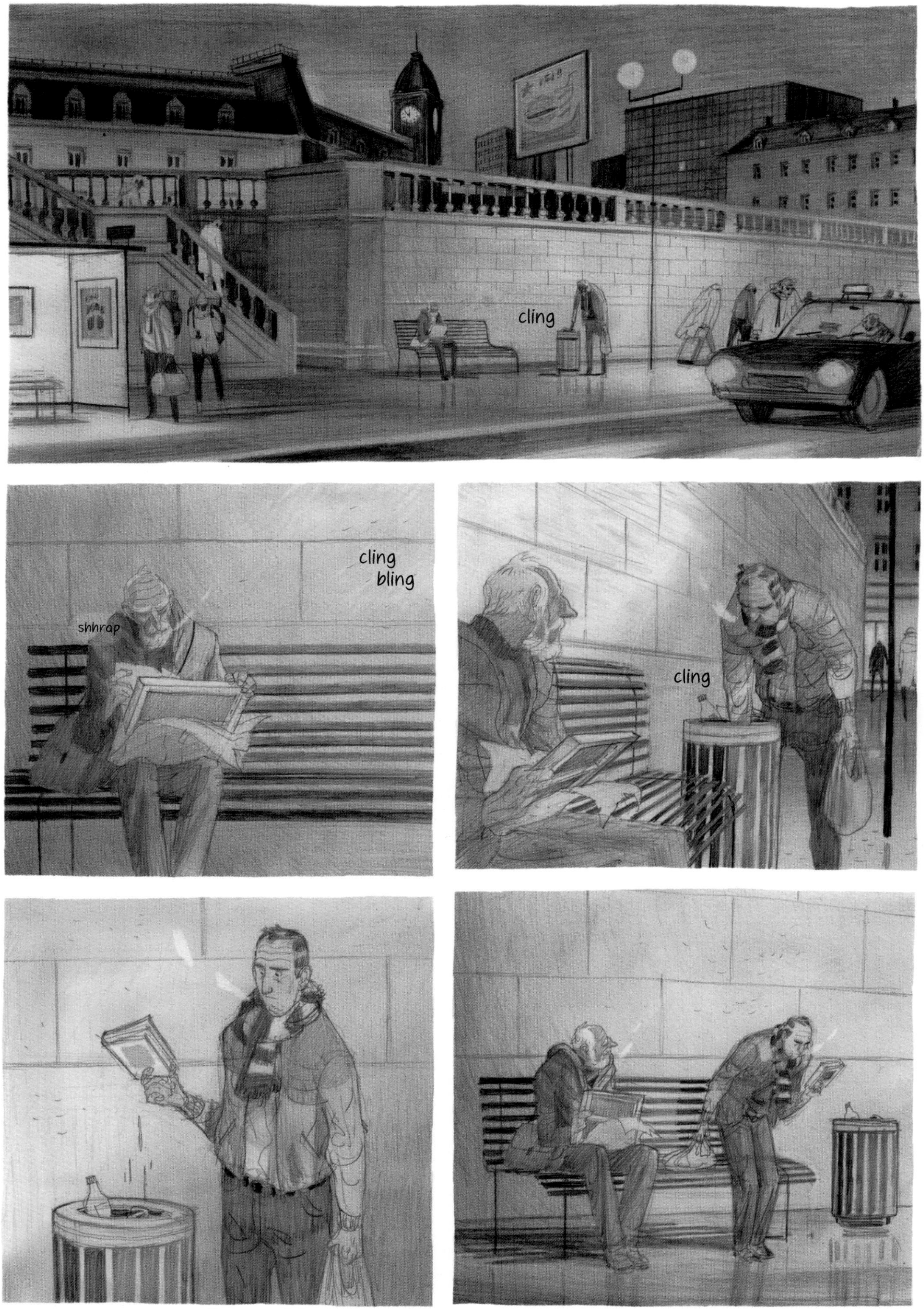
cling
cling
bling
shhrap
cling

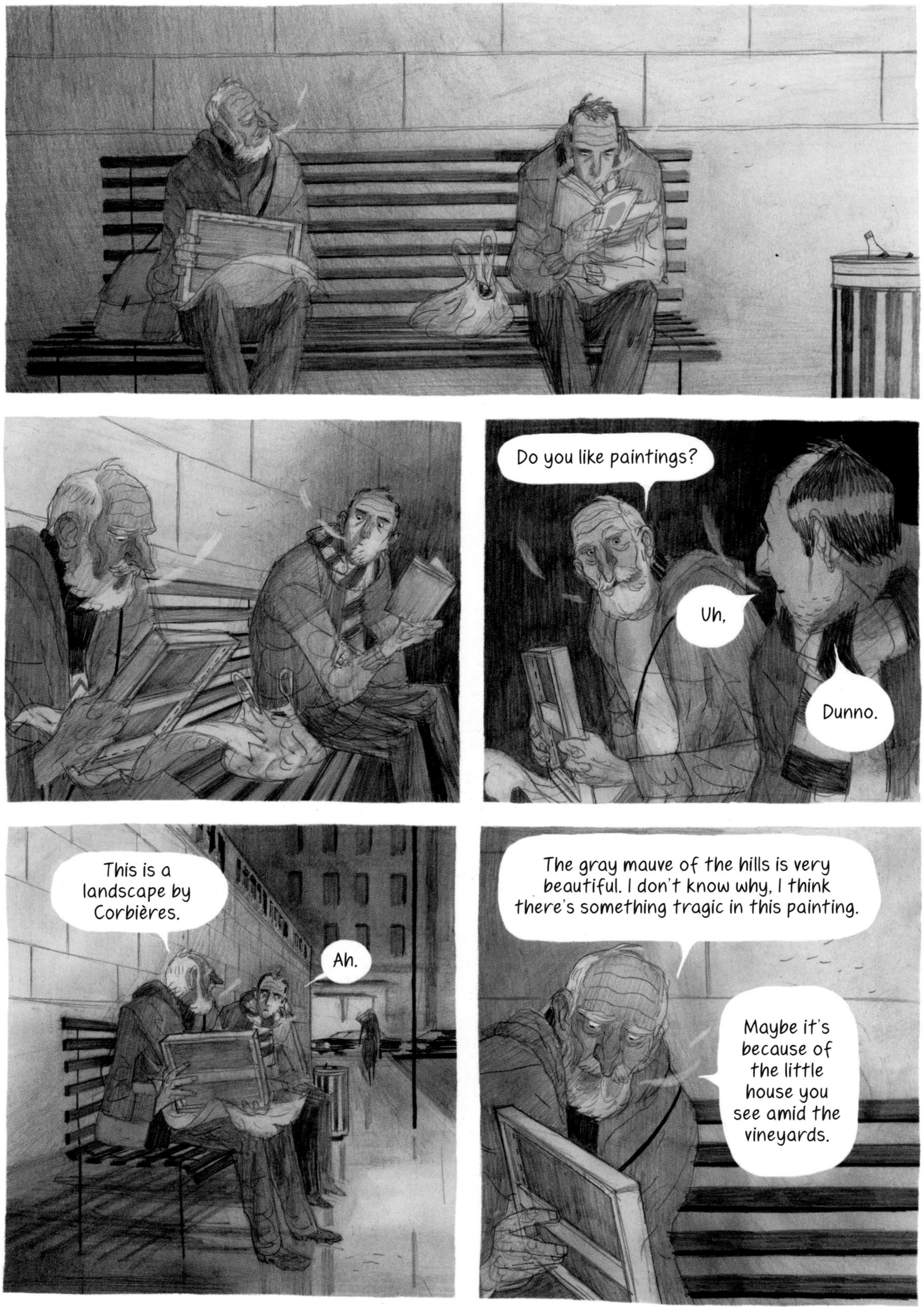
Do you like paintings?
Uh,
Dunno.
This is a landscape by Corbières.
Ah.
The gray mauve of the hills is very beautiful. I don't know why, I think there's something tragic in this painting.
Maybe it's because of the little house you see amid the vineyards.

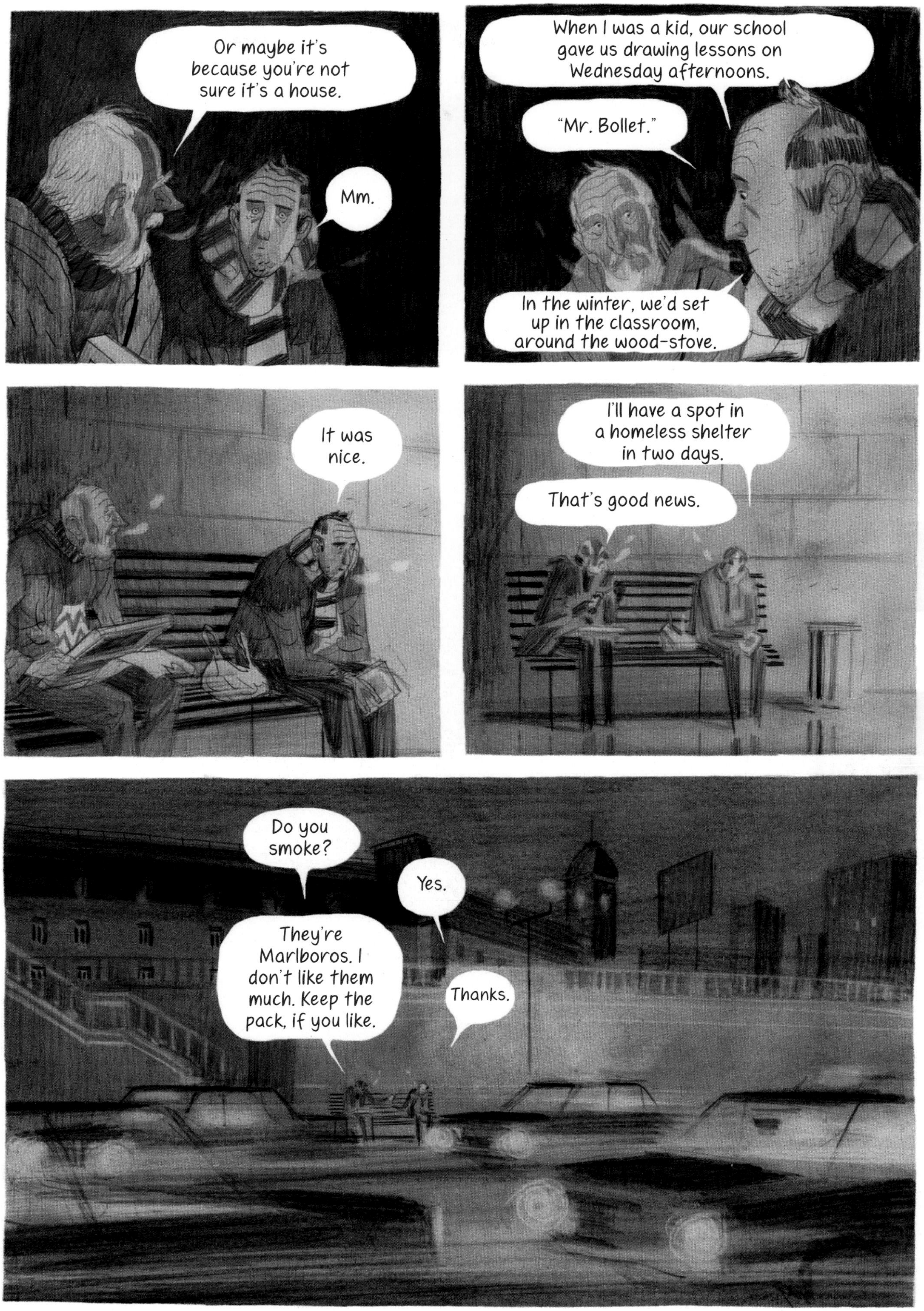
Or maybe it's because you're not sure it's a house.
Mm.
When I was a kid, our school gave us drawing lessons on Wednesday afternoons.
"Mr. Bollet."
In the winter, we'd set up in the classroom, around the wood-stove.
It was nice.
I'll have a spot in a homeless shelter in two days.
That's good news.
Do you smoke?
Yes.
They're Marlboros. I don't like them much. Keep the pack, if you like.
Thanks.

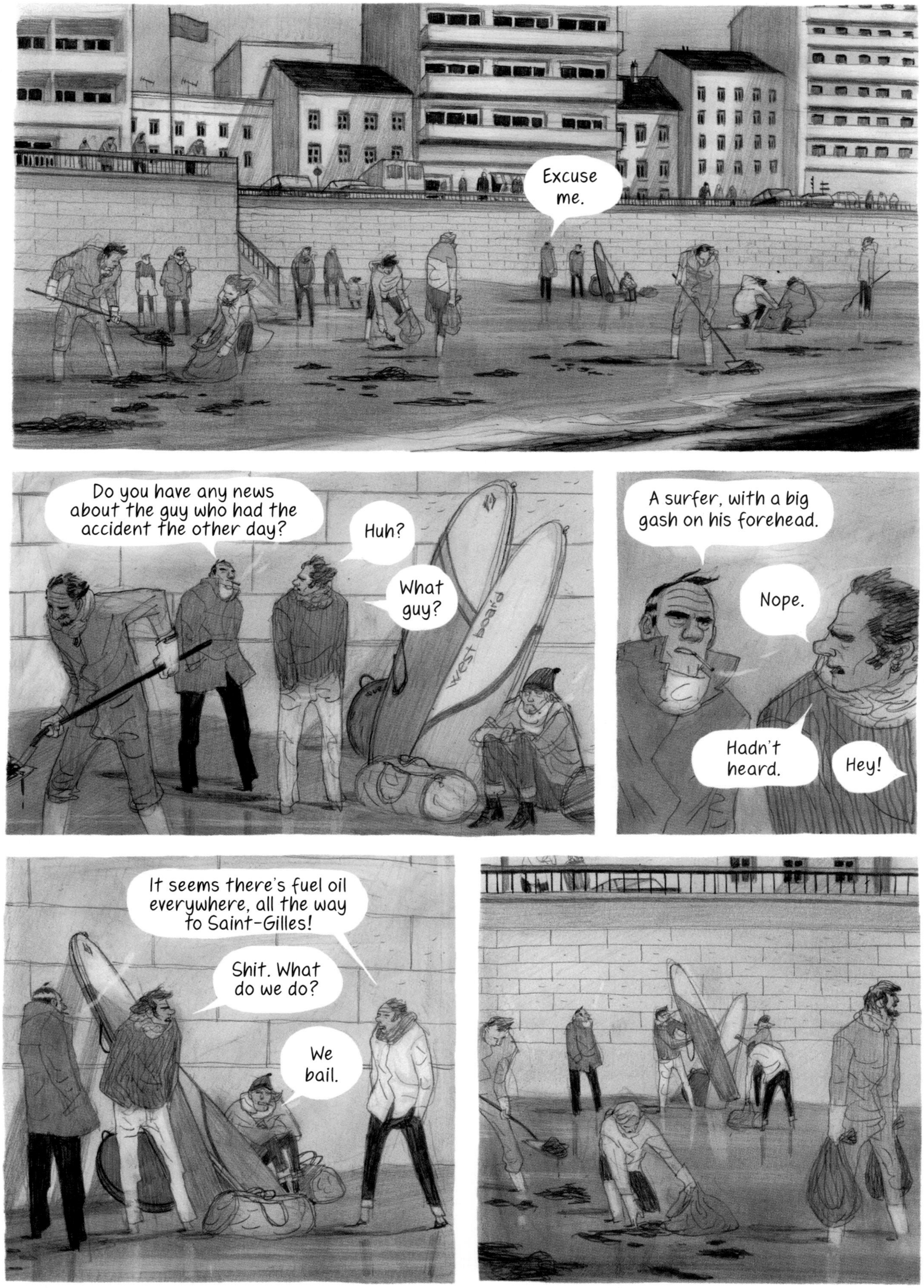
Excuse me.
Do you have any news about the guy who had the accident the other day?
Huh?
What guy?
A surfer, with a big gash on his forehead.
Nope.
Hadn't heard.
Hey!
It seems there's fuel oil everywhere, all the way to Saint-Gilles!
Shit. What do we do?
We bail.
west board

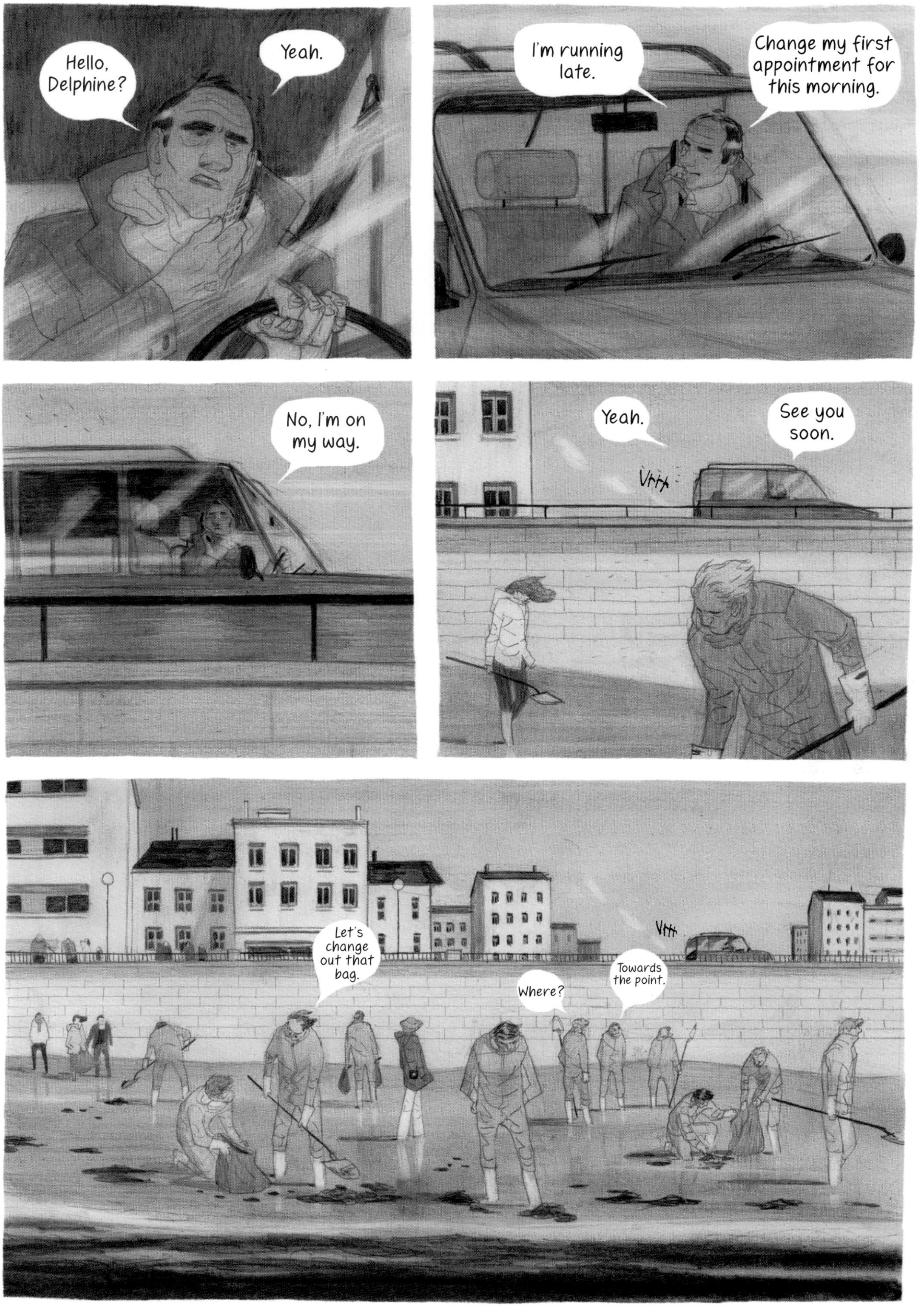
Hello, Delphine?
Yeah.
I'm running late.
Change my first appointment for this morning.
No, I'm on my way.
Yeah.
See you soon.
Vrrr
Vrrr
Let's change out that bag.
Where?
Towards the point.

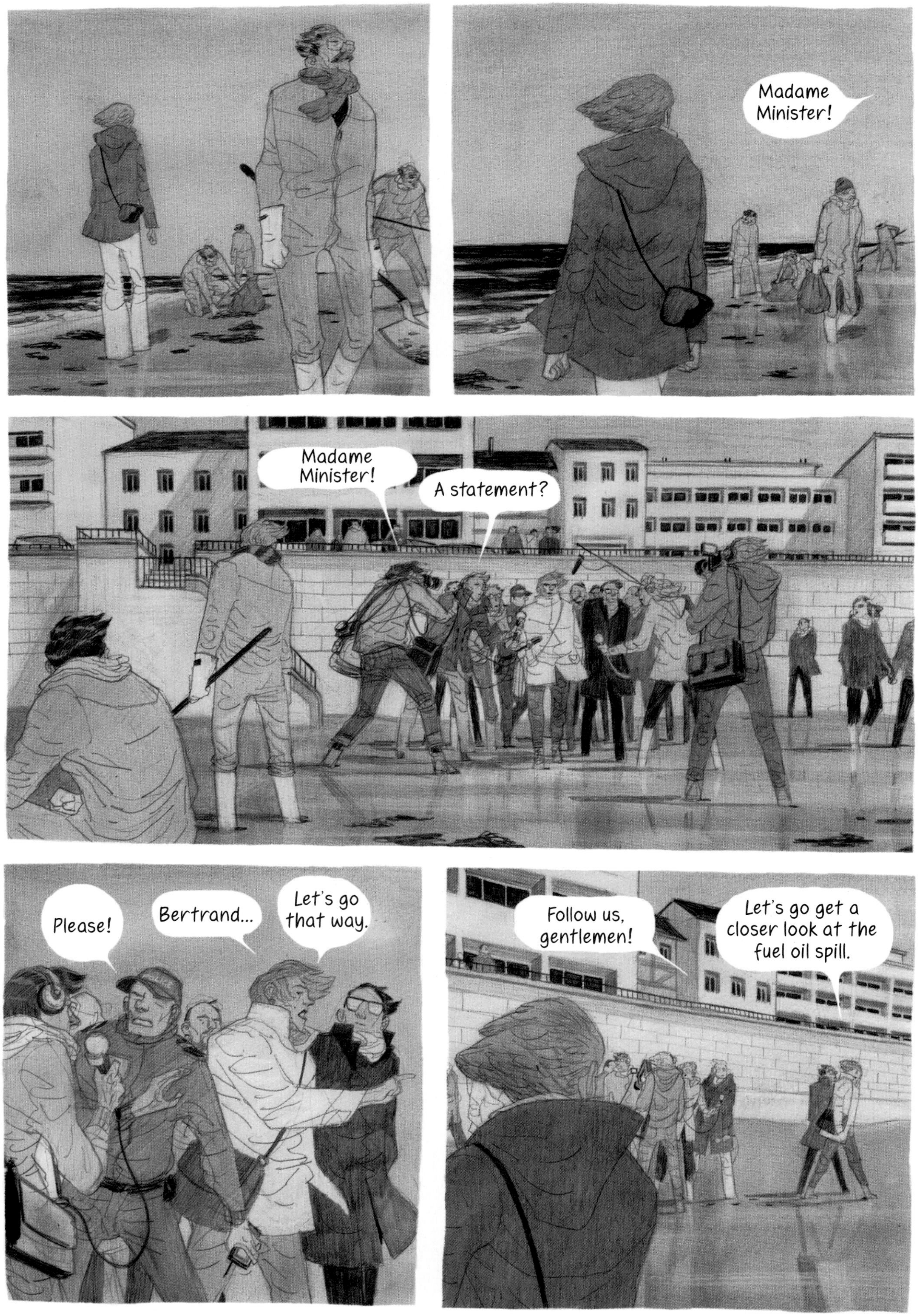
Madame Minister!
Madame Minister!
A statement?
Please!
Bertrand...
Let's go that way.
Follow us, gentlemen!
Let's go get a closer look at the fuel oil spill.

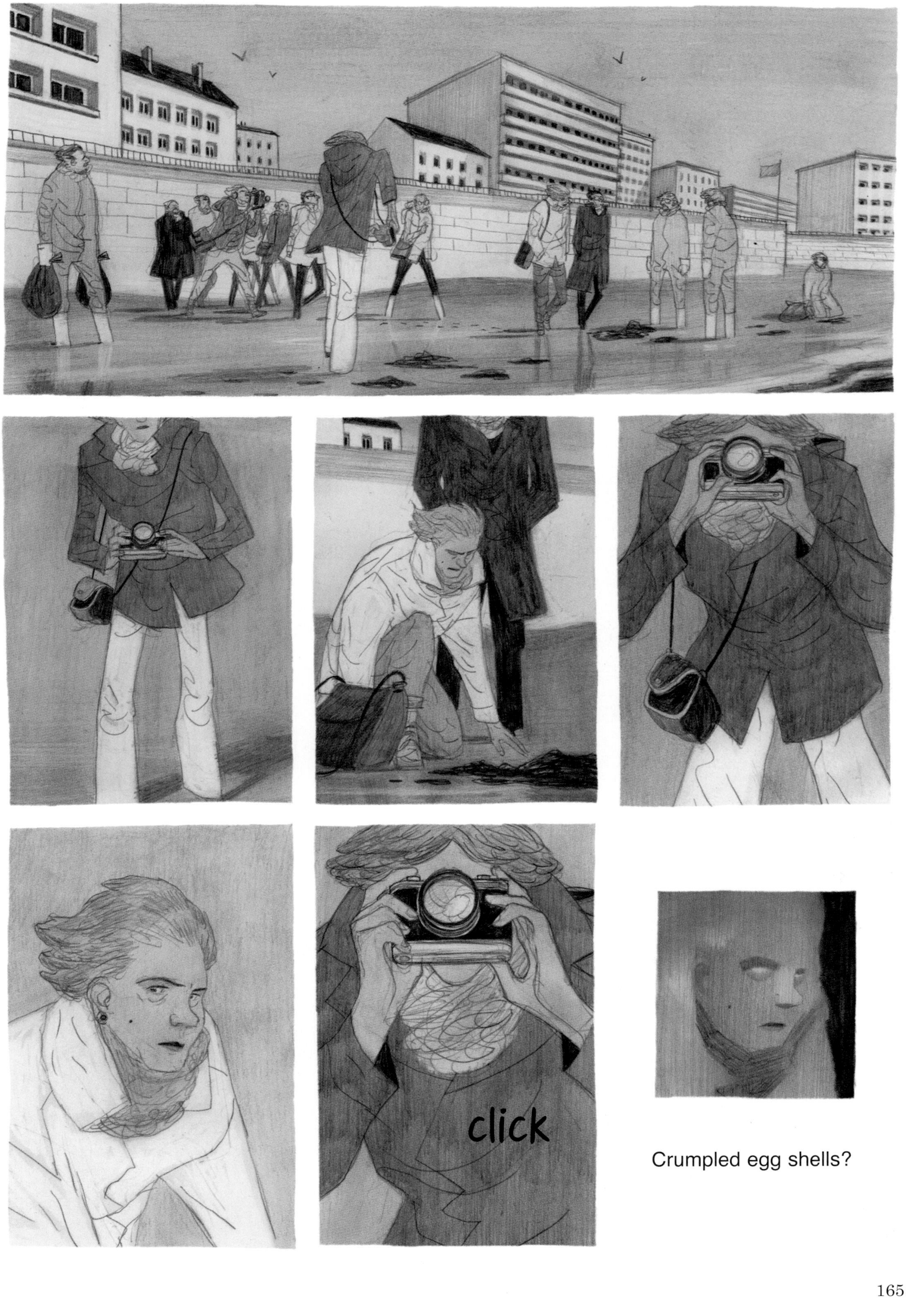
click
Crumpled egg shells?

No, that's not it exactly.

  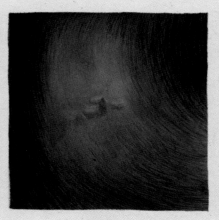

She'd need quiet, and for everyone to be still for a moment. Bertrand, the reporters, the mayor and his aides.

To be able to close her eyes and better hear the cracking of the shells under her feet.

But that's impossible, of course.

She slows down her pace, all the same, one foot in front of the other, slowly, to force them to do likewise. Gaining a few seconds and perhaps managing to understand why this noise is familiar to her.

The little, fluorescent cap worn by that volunteer, when they arrived on the beach.
The rustling of the mother-of-pearl under the big Patauga boots Bertrand had loaned her to walk on the beach.
Her leather bag, bulging with her high heels, hitting against her hips.

Bertrand squeezes her arm, he no doubt wants to tell her something, but her attention is elsewhere, occupied despite herself in finding in her memory a leather bag, a cap, and little, white shells.
A slight drowsiness gently envelops her.
Bertrand's voice whispers incomprehensible words in her ear, and suddenly the "Treige de la Cordière" comes to mind, along with the numbness of winter mornings in that alley leading to school, with Mathilde, their over-the-shoulder bags filled with notebooks, books, and lunch, the silhouette of their hooded coats in the middle of the valley, midnight blue paper cut out over a white background, the muffled squeak of the snow under their boots, the regular noise of their steps... the signs of a joyful day.
Mrs. Camelin had immediately noticed her immense appetite. From the very first day, and for those five years In the Pontets school, she'd busied herself in satisfying that all-consuming curiosity.

The shells, Mrs. Camelin, the hard-to-find words to thank her, the flakes on their hooded coats. She barely hears the reporter's question. Bertrand gives her a worried look. She answers, despite everything, thinking about little steps in the snow.

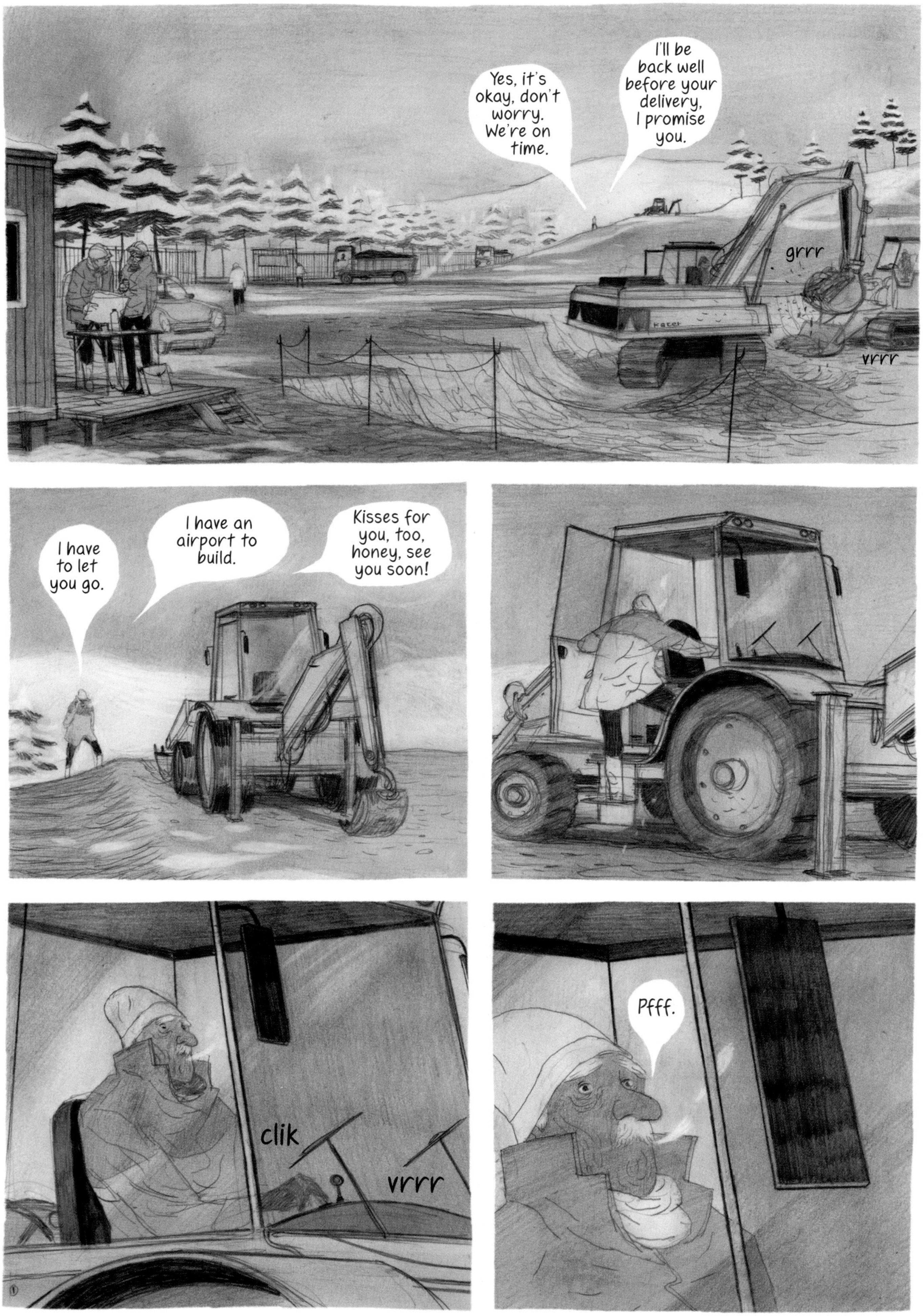
Yes, it's okay, don't worry. We're on time.
I'll be back well before your delivery, I promise you.
grrr
vrrr
I have to let you go.
I have an airport to build.
Kisses for you, too, honey, see you soon!
clik
vrrr
Pfff.

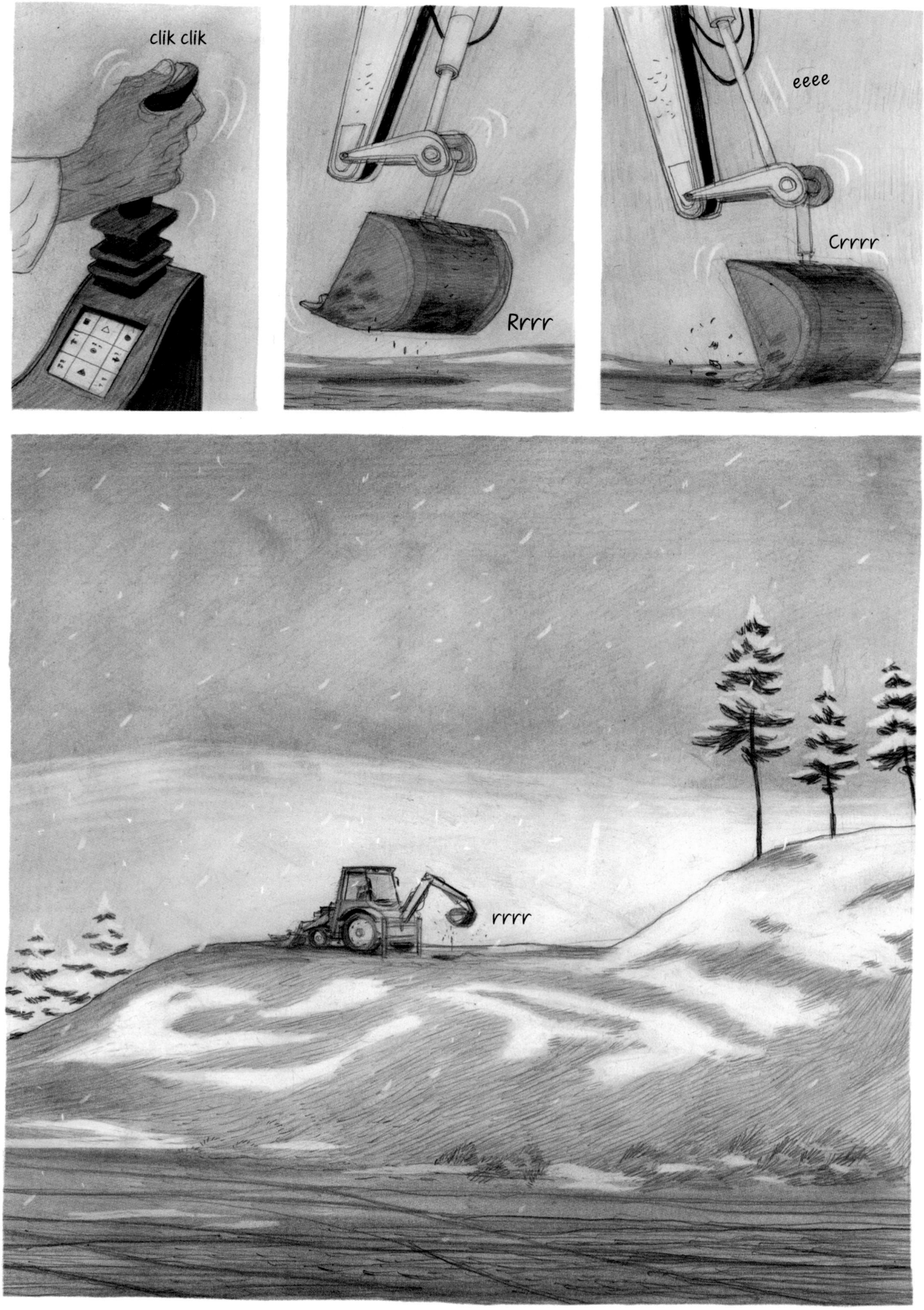
clik clik
Rrrr
eeee
Crrrr
rrrr

In the distance, way up top,
just before the ocean, I see
dark trees, almost flattened.

Stone pines, maybe?

I'm taking small steps forward, the wind and rain are in my face, my hood is buffeting my ears, but I keep on going. The path is a soup of soft earth, blue flint, and bits of plants. You have to go for it, with great strides or small steps, it doesn't matter, as long as you go.

If I hadn't chanced upon those pictures of Fred, I'd have stayed inside. I was sorting the negatives from the last two months to try to make a selection, to start to choose the prints. The photo packet was in an old file, I'd forgotten it.

At first, it's cold, my body is heavy, dull, useless, withdrawn into itself. It's not accepting this effort, rain, mud, smell of moss and rotten wood, all this water streaming down my face, down my neck, over my mouth, mixed with sweat. Little by little, under these repeated assaults, the airtight bulkheads between my inside and out give way one by one. My body resigns itself. It accepts everything conspiring against it. My legs come to life, hesitating no longer. One foot in front of the other, my breath feeding the machine, unconsciously, in rhythm. The water passes over me in an unbroken flow. Water, clear, above, below, everywhere, through me. Blue. Mineral. Nothing hurts now, nothing exists any longer. No one left to battle, convince or seduce. I should run like this for my whole life. It wouldn't be so absurd, after all. But in less than thirty minutes, I'll be home again, I'll be exhausted, and it'll stop. I should train, persevere, get organized, do an exercise program, stop smoking.
I just don't want to.

What did he say to me?

I turn around while jogging, with a detached air. There you have it, as soon as there's someone else, it all collapses, the show starts again, I can't keep myself from pretending. "What did you say, I couldn't hear?'
I'm speaking too loudly because of the wind. My voice sounds fake, I don't recognize it.

He looks at me without answering and gestures with his chin towards a spaniel emerging from a thicket. By the time I understood he was calling his dog, I was already running towards him. I don't stop. I pass silently in front of them and move away in small strides. As though that brutal change of direction had been intentional all along. Pretending, once again.

Everything has become heavy and useless again, my legs don't want to go on, I feel ridiculous. All the same, I try to keep going till the highway, but I already know I'll walk the last mile. The photos of Fred date from a few months before our final exams in college. I thought they were lost. For years, I often thought of that night when that totally drunk imbecile got into the back seat of a car driven by another completely drunk imbecile. You need time to understand that it's just that clear and final. On, off. Alive, dead. The girls who'd fall into his arms, his casualness, the hand which, despite himself, he'd put in front of his mouth whenever he'd burst into laughter, to hide his teeth which he disliked. I missed it all terribly. During the mass, the priest had uttered mechanical words, fabricated from compassion found in books. He knew no more than we did. He'd never lost a son, a friend, he seemed to believe that some really could die at the age of twenty-one. It was conceivable, very sad no doubt, yes, he understood our pain, but we would find comfort in prayer, humility, and contemplation. I'm still mad at myself for not screaming at him to shut up forever. Our gazes crossed, I put all the hatred I had in it, until he lowered his eyes.

I'm done, I can't go on, forget it. I stop in the middle of the moor, bending over to catch my breath. The road's still a ten-minute walk away. I'm mad at myself for speaking to that guy. I feel so ridiculous for hoping for his attention, for his words to be meant for me. I gotta learn to give up on that, to rid myself of that expectation. Otherwise, I'll lose myself.

I went to see the patches of fuel oil on the beach at Carré, it's all everybody's been talking about since the day before yesterday. There was that government woman that everybody loves to hate, I don't recall her name. I slipped into the small group of reporters buzzing about her. She seemed distracted, confused. I took a few photos. I need to give some kind of direction to all this. I should also find a little money for prints, but I don't know if it's worth the bother. I've been here for months and I feel like I haven't found anything. It's there, right in front of me, but I can't see it. I feel myopic. I'm groping along. I sense vague shapes but I don't recognize them. I try to listen to the vibration, without ever being sure I really hear it.

Perhaps it's an illusion. I'm making up a story but there's nothing to find. What sense does it make to be turning up every stone without knowing what you're looking for? It would be so comforting if it all made sense.
I'm starting to get cold. Fortunately, the house isn't very far away.

It's puzzling. Barely a few months is all it takes to completely forget your best friend's voice. It takes a little longer to not be angry anymore. Ever since I've been here alone, I feel like I'm walking around carrying dead voices. We dance round and round and they carry me along but scare me at the same time. Every day, they tell me the same story. I'm thirty-one, I feel lost, I'll have but one life, and it's slipping through my fingers like a torrent. I'd like to hold onto it, understand what I must do with it, what thirst it must quench.

Fred, Ivon, Thomas and his oversized pajamas, the gray shadow of illness on his serious, little boy's face. He looked so exhausted. We'd played all afternoon. I regret so much that little step backwards when he suggested I come into his bedroom. I'd looked at his skinny wrists, that implacable fatigue in his eyes, and I'd taken a small step backwards.

I'd like to be forgiven for my mistakes, but nobody can do that. You have to be satisfied with your own forgiveness.

I see the house now.

Its silhouette appears behind the final two hundred yards of rain I have left to go through. You never cross paths with anyone on this road, nor in the vicinity either. Out of prudence, I've nonetheless carefully avoided taking any pictures in this area. I don't want people asking me any whys or hows. I'd rather be invisible. One young guy kind of tried to flirt with me the other night at the bar. I let him do it. A little. I was in a good mood. I understood while listening to his shtick that my presence had been noticed despite my efforts. I explained to him I'm house-sitting Olivier and Sylvia's place during their absence, the little home-improvement jobs and the yard work in compensation, and it seemed to convince him. It's easier and easier to hide myself, it's gotten comfortable. I've known for a long time it's useless to try to share what you don't understand yourself.

Yesterday, I found a bottle of whisky in the little, blue kitchen cabinet. I didn't dare open it.

I really need a very hot shower right away.

And maybe a glass of whisky right afterwards.

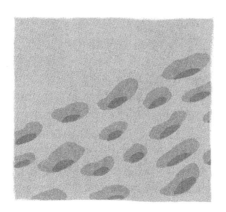

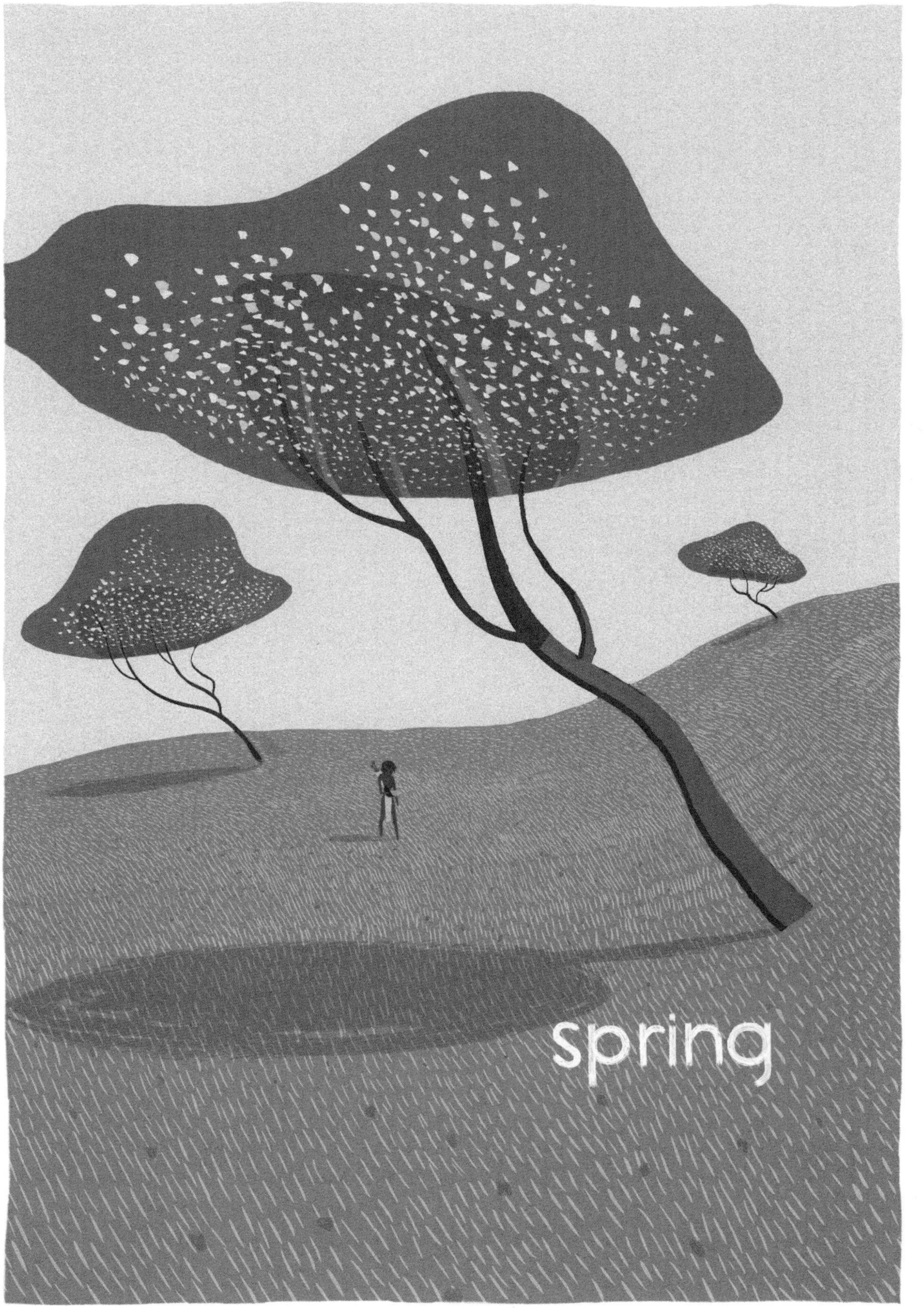
spring

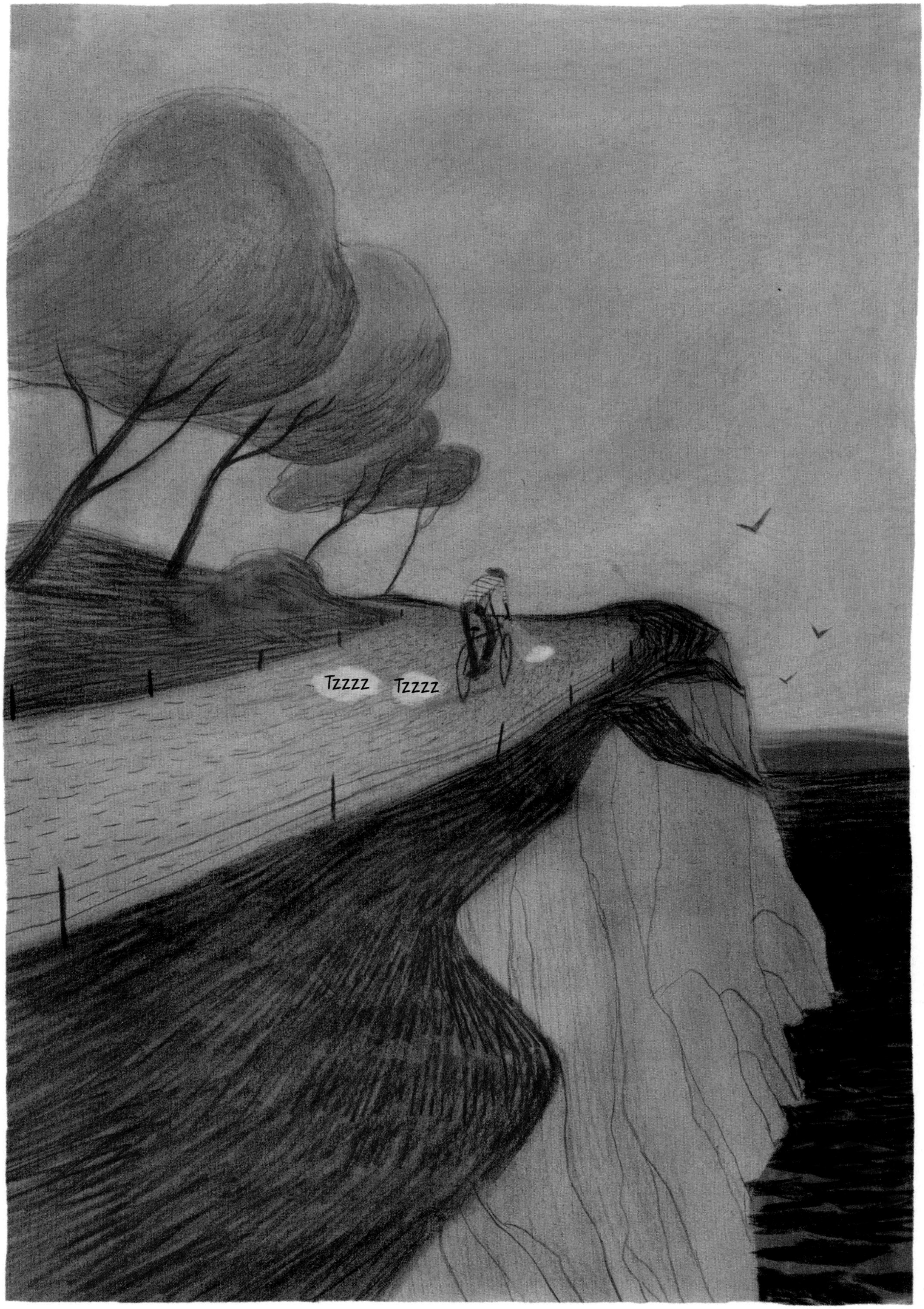
Tzzzz
Tzzzz

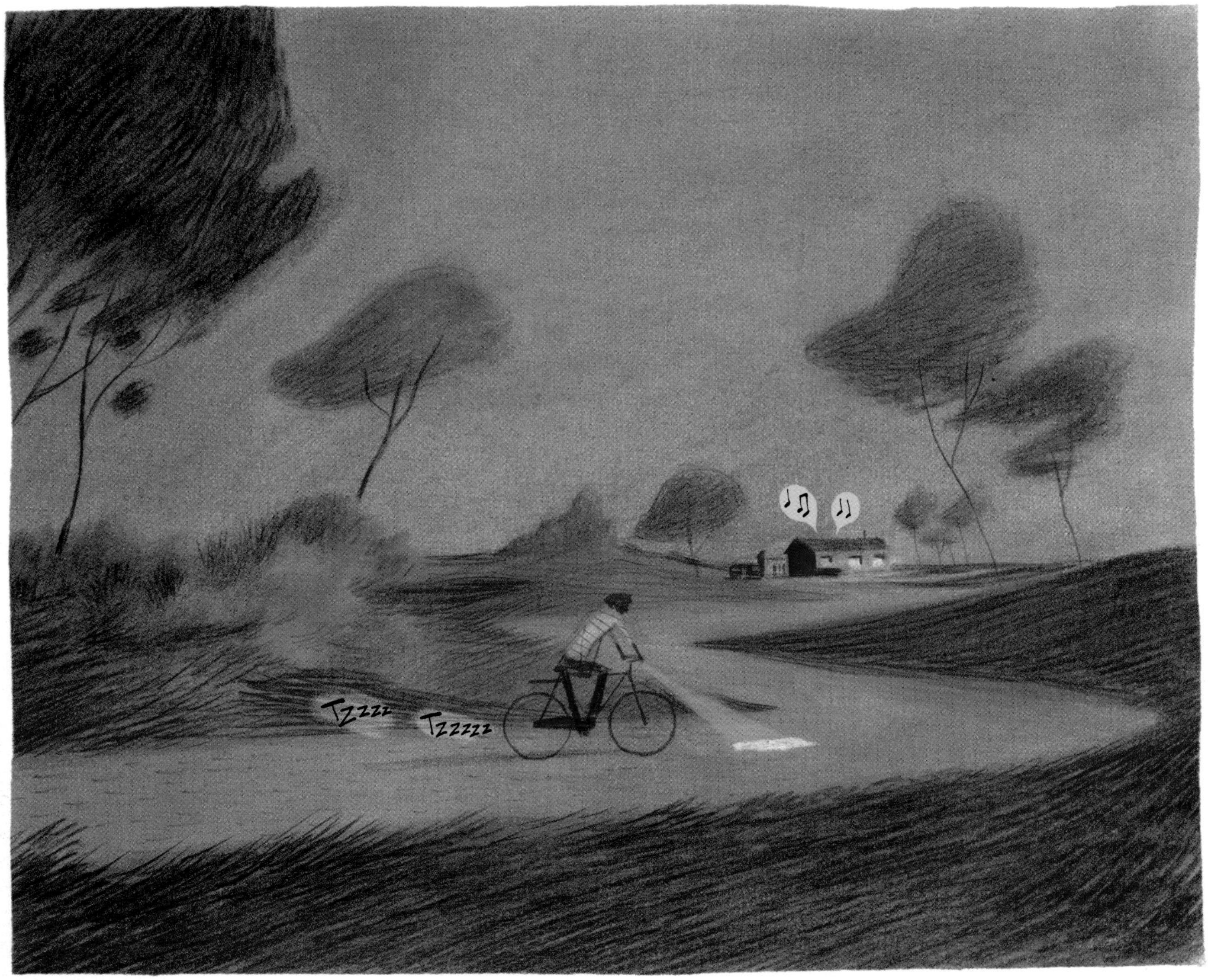
TZzzz
TZzzzz

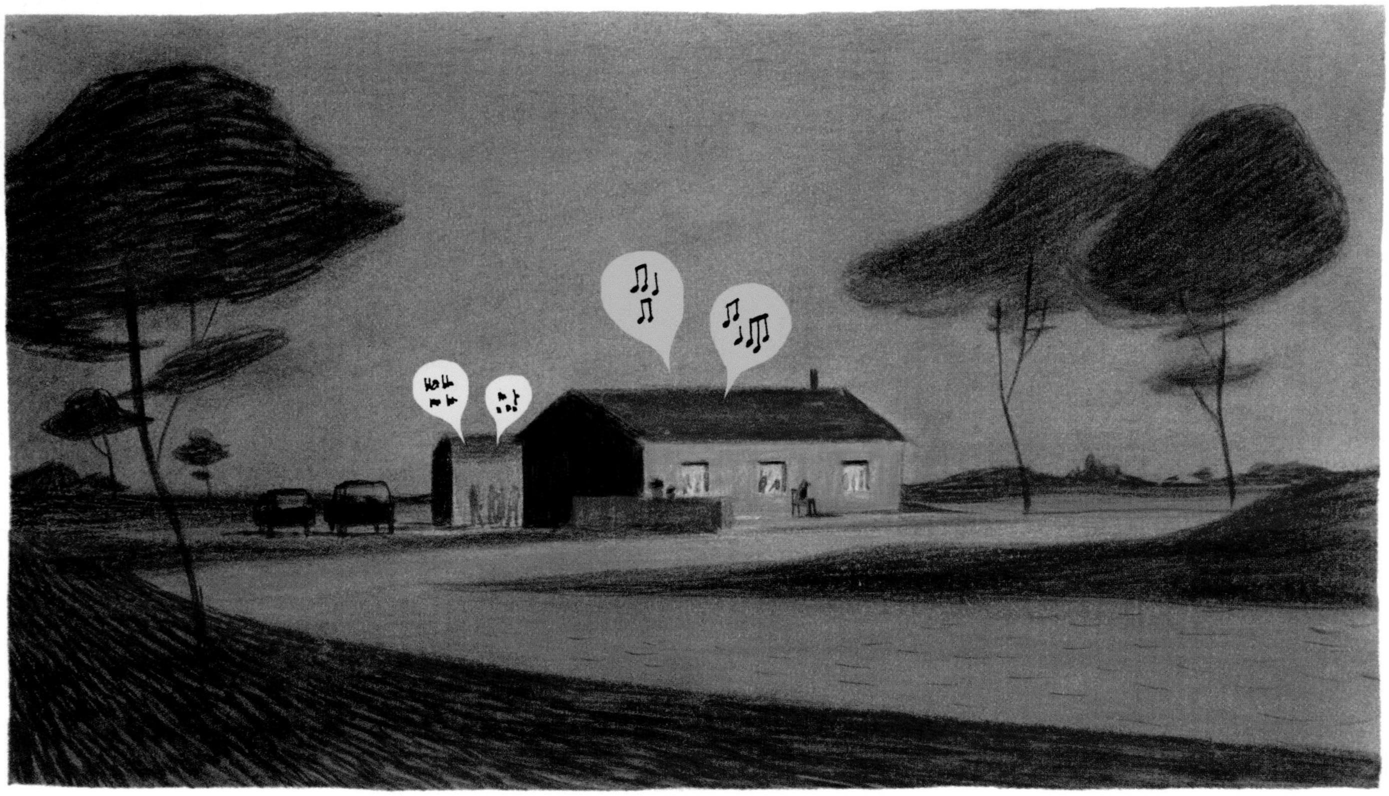

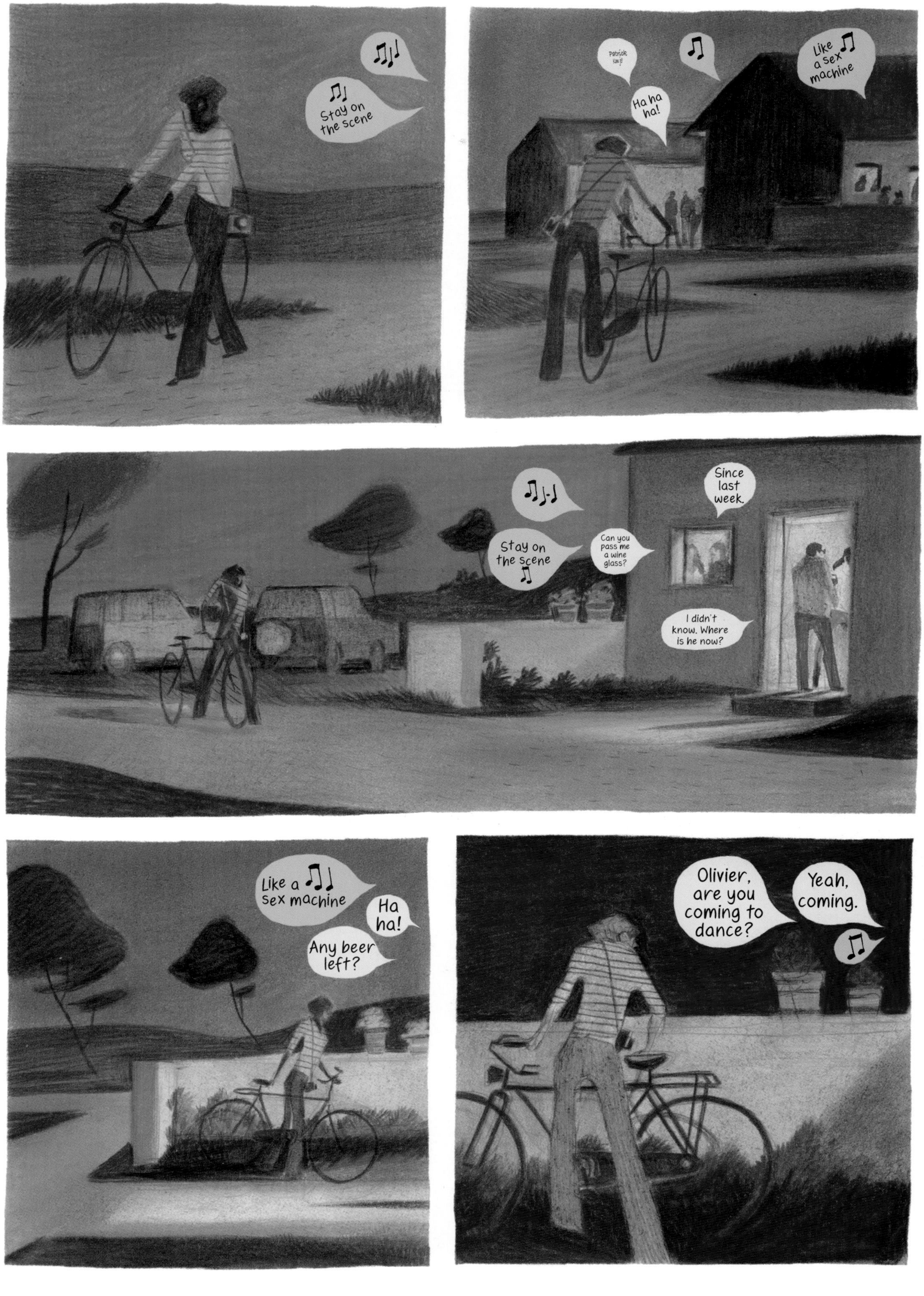

Stay on the scene
Patrick
Ha ha ha!
Like a sex machine
Since last week.
Stay on the scene
Can you pass me a wine glass?
I didn't know. Where is he now?
Like a sex machine
Ha ha!
Any beer left?
Olivier, are you coming to dance?
Yeah, coming.

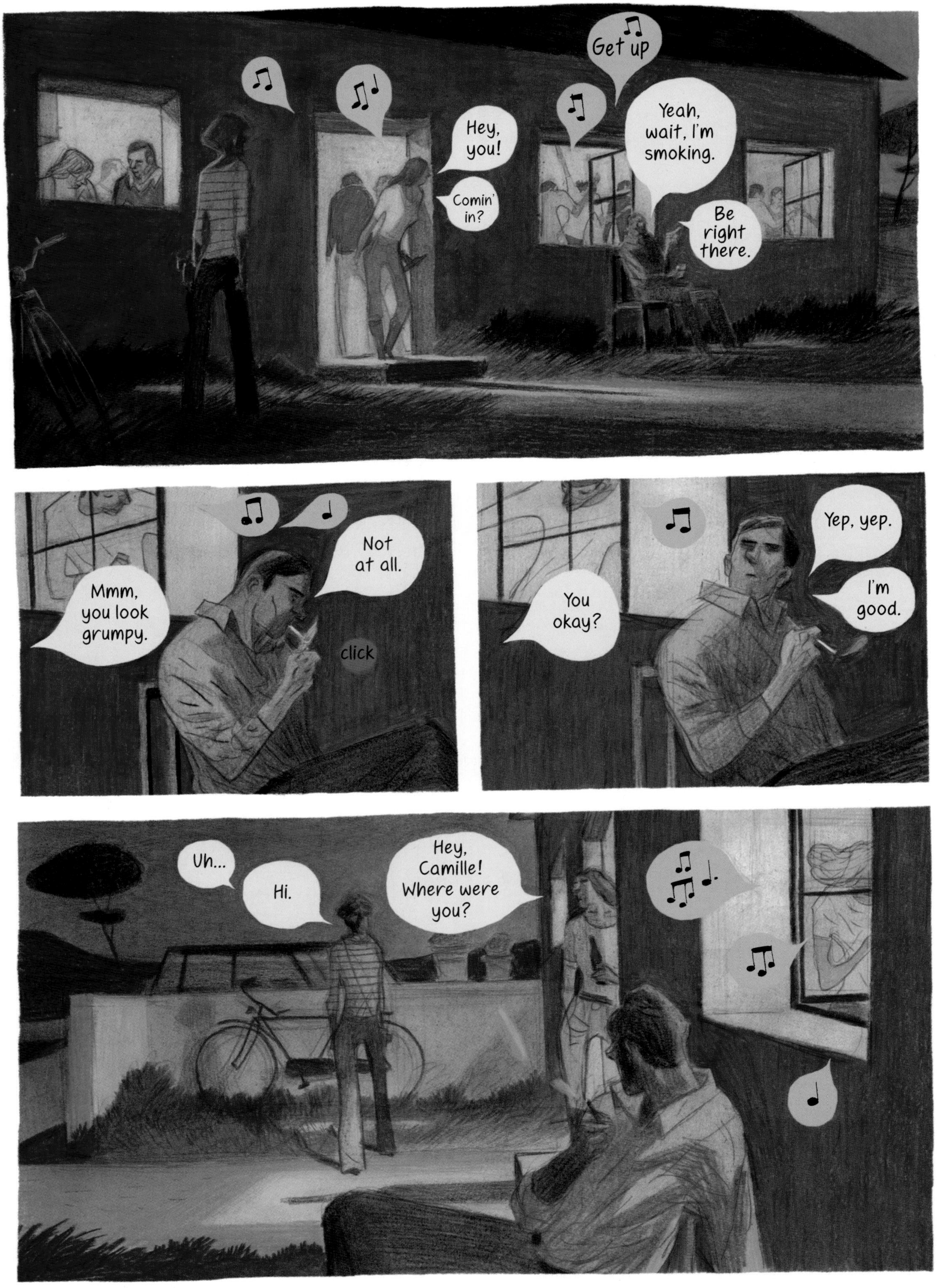
Get up
Hey, you!
Comin' in?
Yeah, wait, I'm smoking.
Be right there.
Mmm, you look grumpy.
Not at all.
click
You okay?
Yep, yep.
I'm good.
Uh...
Hi.
Hey, Camille! Where were you?

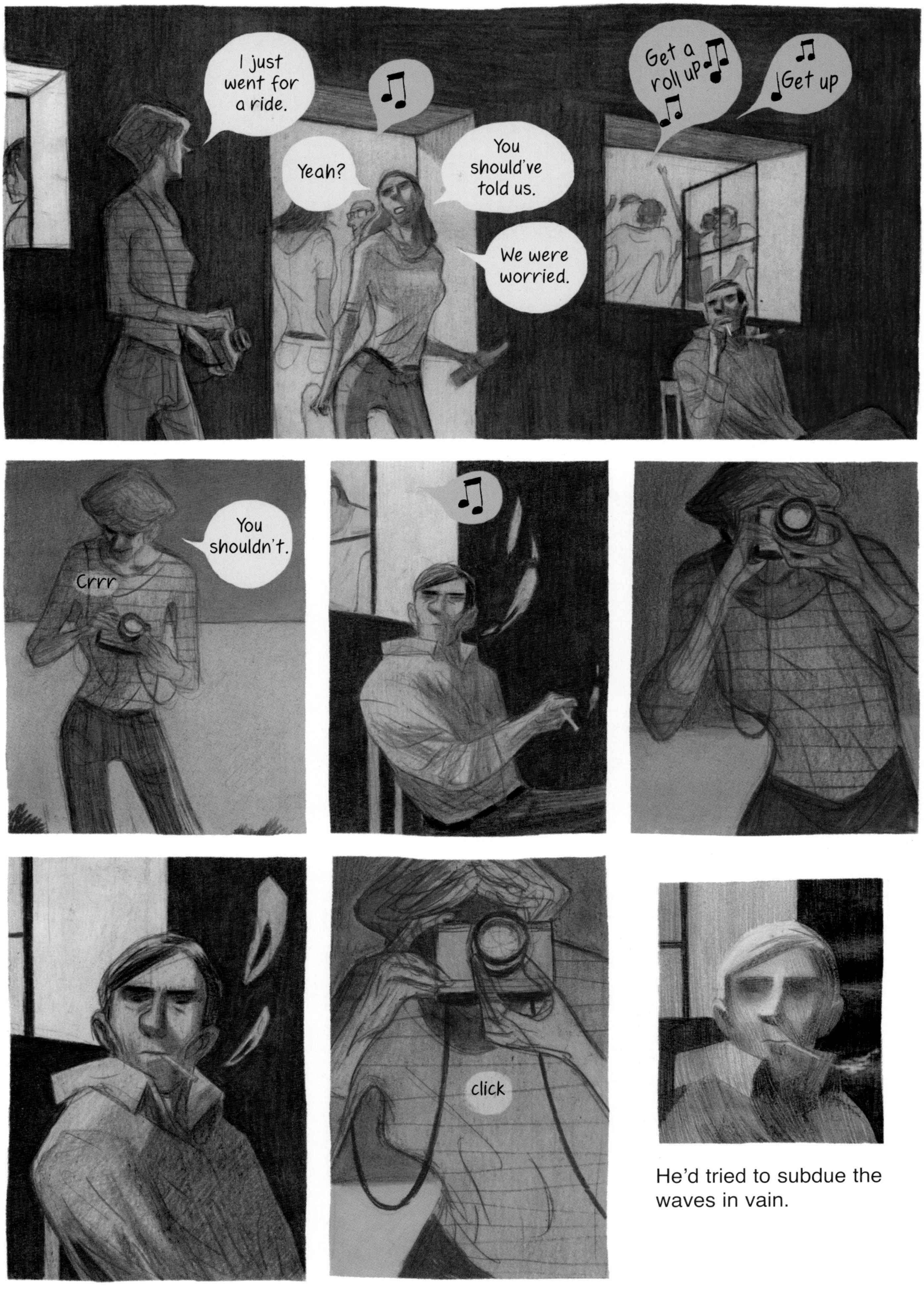
I just went for a ride.
Yeah?
♫
You should've told us.
We were worried.
Get a roll up
Get up
You shouldn't.
Crrr
♫
click

He'd tried to subdue the waves in vain.

A whirlwind of confused thoughts set out on repeated attacks to shatter against an invisible wall.

The waves grew, unstoppable.

Whenever he thought he'd finally managed to contain them for a moment, in hopes of seizing them, understanding them, they'd disappear, leaving a void behind them. A river run dry.

He'd thought something, a thousand things, but what?

Outside, space spread out before him, sky and earth merging together in the night, is sufficient comfort to finally calm this tempest.

He remembers now.

Their arrival at the train station that morning.
The ritual accolades. The habitual enthusiasms, the urges of mechanical joys, the feeling of a sad comedy where everyone, him most of all, plays their role ardently. He'd then felt the cold mask of forced smiles slipping onto his face, locked tight, cinched with leather against his skull. He'd like to have torn it off, but his hands were taken. They were shaking other hands, hugging lifeless chests, lighting cigarettes, sleights of hand. What a waste of time. The years have passed so fast, and there's this sudden fear of having lived them in vain. Why must one pretend to never feel that even greater terror that, one day, maybe tomorrow, it'll all end? Why must we hide what we are and pretend to not feel that dizziness?
He was mad at them for being satisfied with this masquerade, for not helping him to find again that momentum they'd once so strongly felt between them.
It had barely lasted a few seconds, on the train station platform. Words stifled, violently folded upon themselves like a hurricane forcibly locked away inside a mote of dust. Words reduced to one of those minuscule scars whose pain sometimes comes to life later.

Despite the party's racket, he can hear the ocean's regular song borne on the wind. He hunkers down a little to protect himself against the cold, feels the strength of his legs pressed against each other, inhales his cigarette's smoke in one breath, and keeps it inside himself, as long as possible, before letting it escape through his lips. He's inside a living body, sheltered. His fears have drifted off. They now seem so far away,

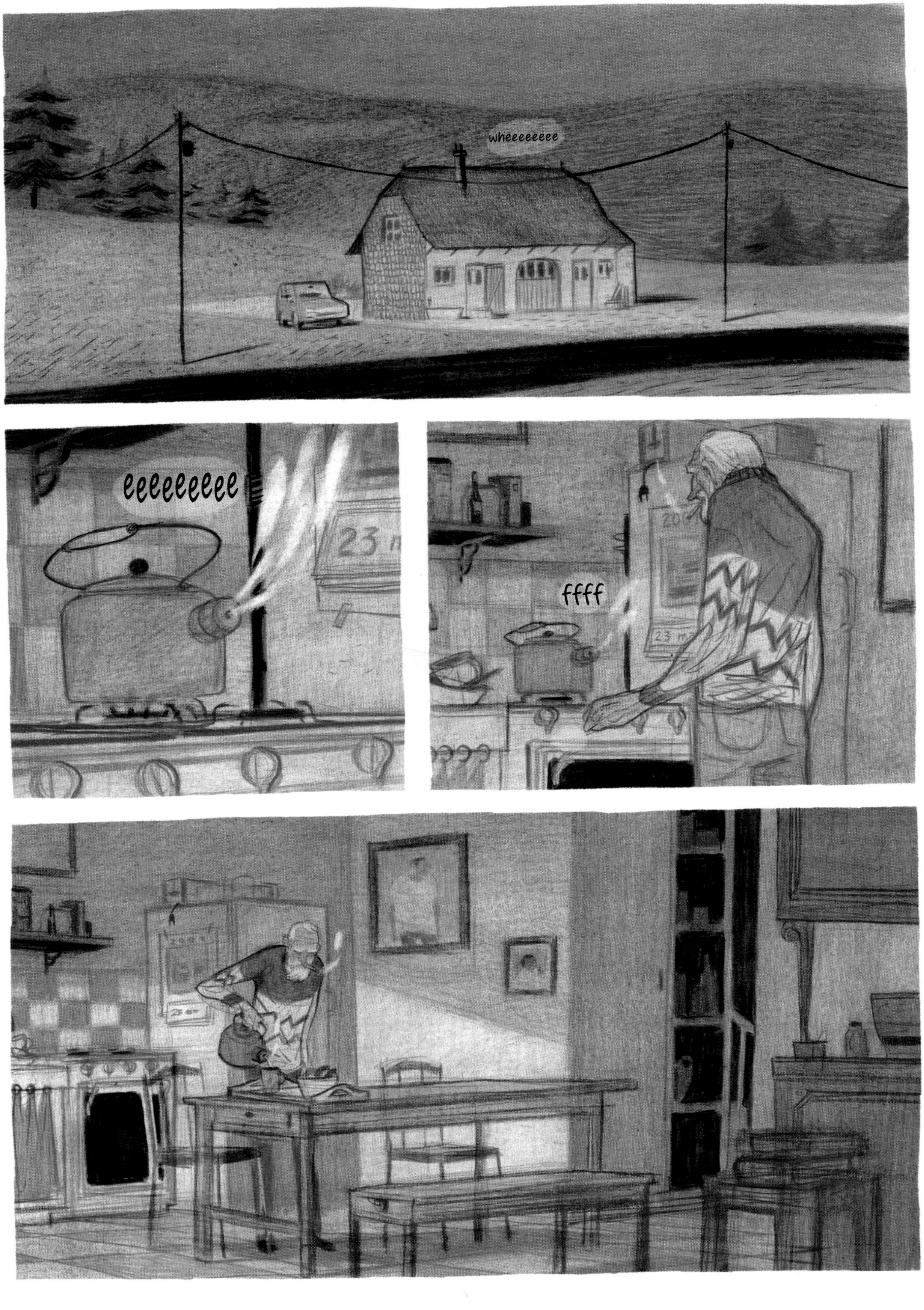
wheeeeeeee
eeeeeeeee
ffff

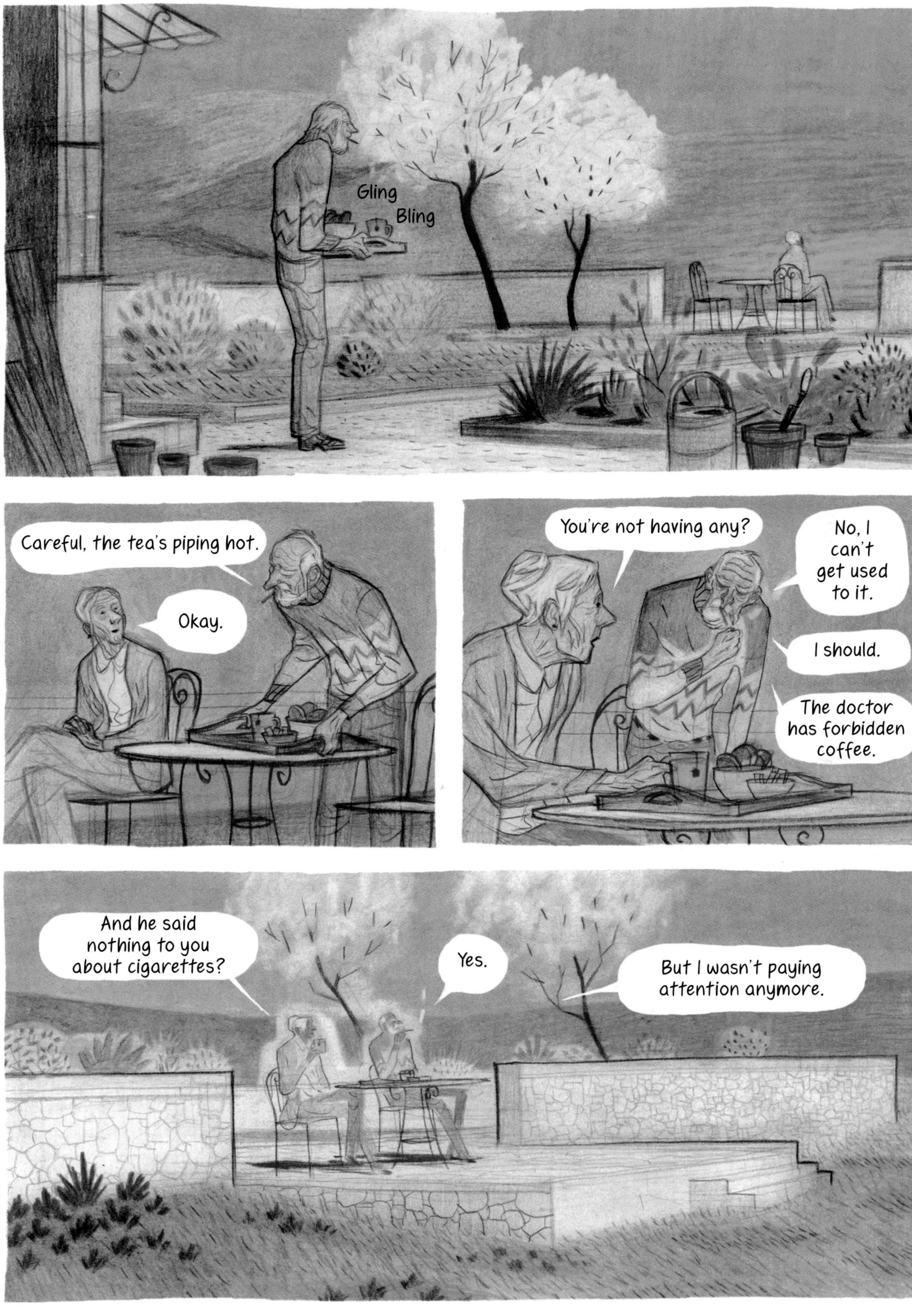
Gling
Bling
Careful, the tea's piping hot.
Okay.
You're not having any?
No, I can't get used to it.
I should.
The doctor has forbidden coffee.
And he said nothing to you about cigarettes?
Yes.
But I wasn't paying attention anymore.

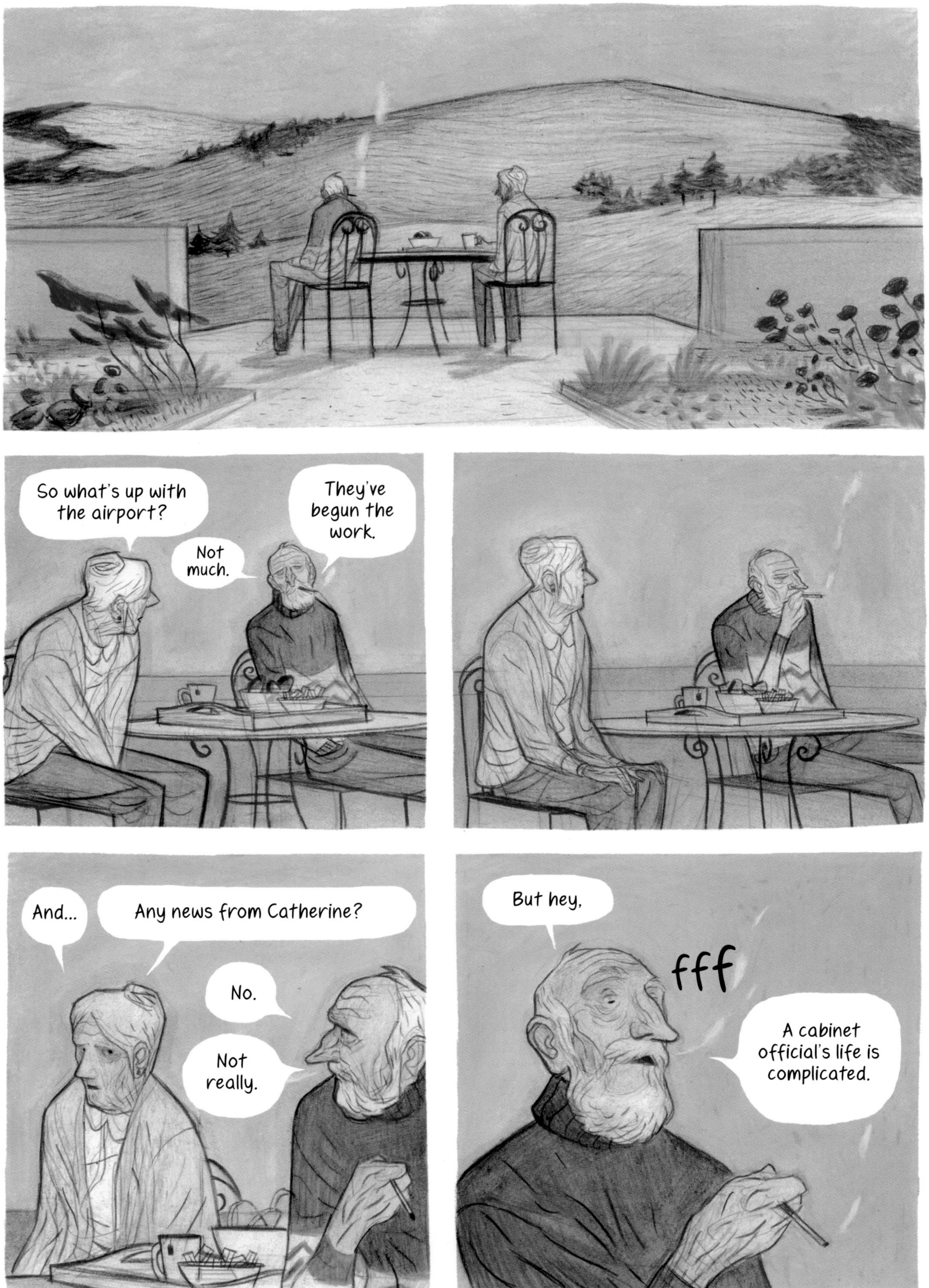
So what's up with the airport?
Not much.
They've begun the work.
And...
Any news from Catherine?
No.
Not really.
But hey,
fff
A cabinet official's life is complicated.

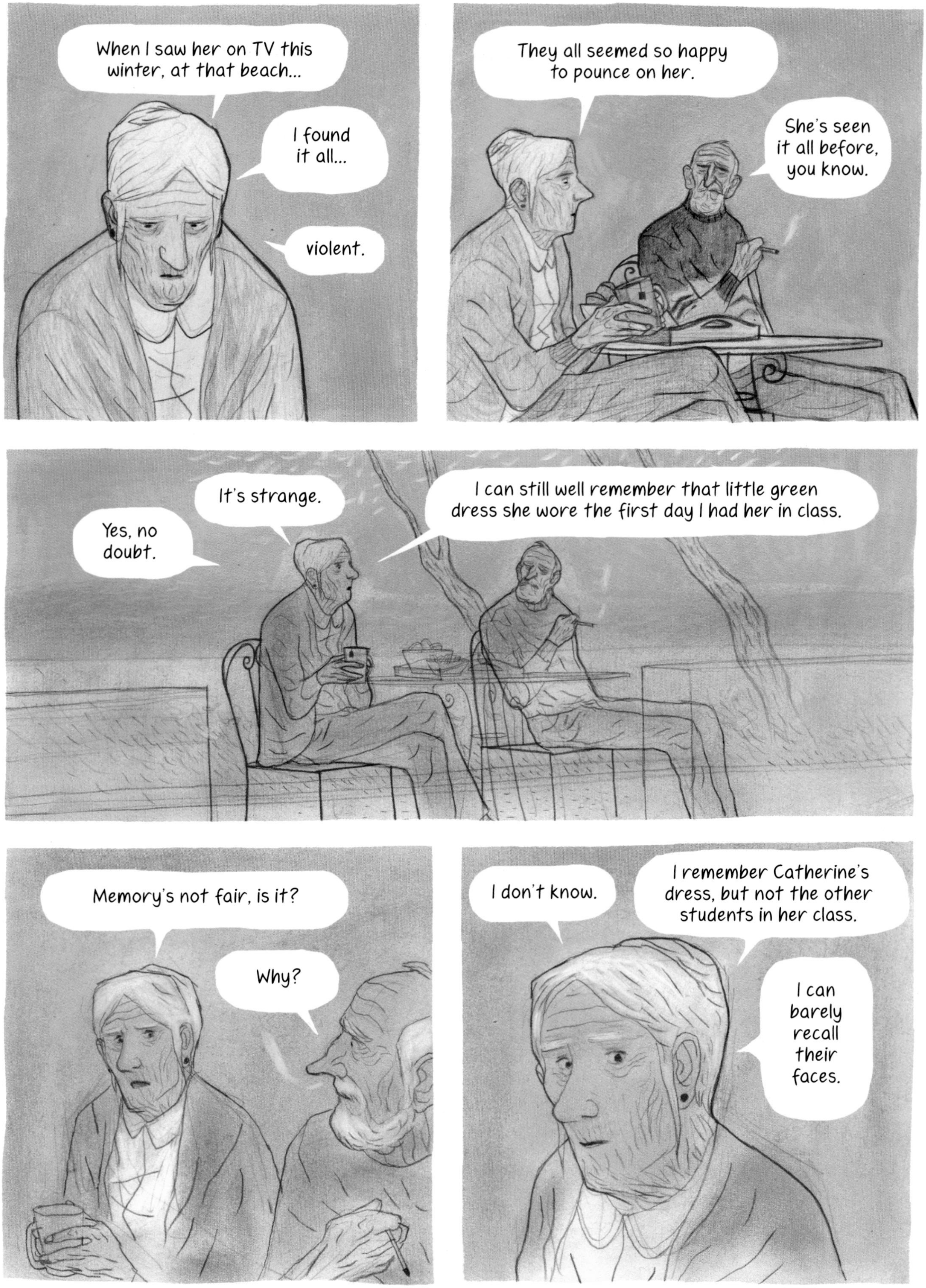
When I saw her on TV this winter, at that beach...
I found it all...
violent.
They all seemed so happy to pounce on her.
She's seen it all before, you know.
Yes, no doubt.
It's strange.
I can still well remember that little green dress she wore the first day I had her in class.
Memory's not fair, is it?
Why?
I don't know.
I remember Catherine's dress, but not the other students in her class.
I can barely recall their faces.

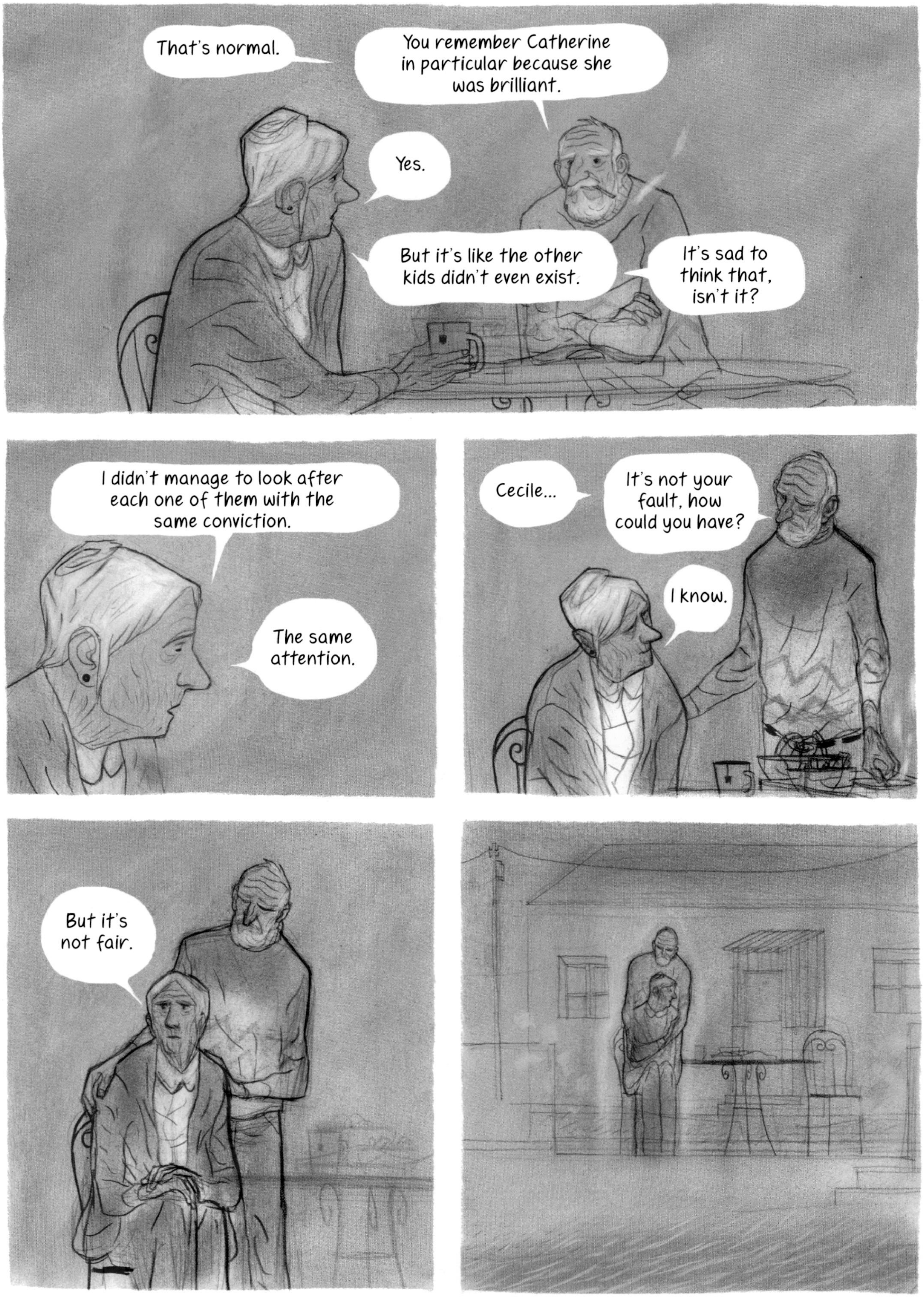
That's normal.
You remember Catherine in particular because she was brilliant.
Yes.
But it's like the other kids didn't even exist.
It's sad to think that, isn't it?
I didn't manage to look after each one of them with the same conviction.
The same attention.
Cecile...
It's not your fault, how could you have?
I know.
But it's not fair.

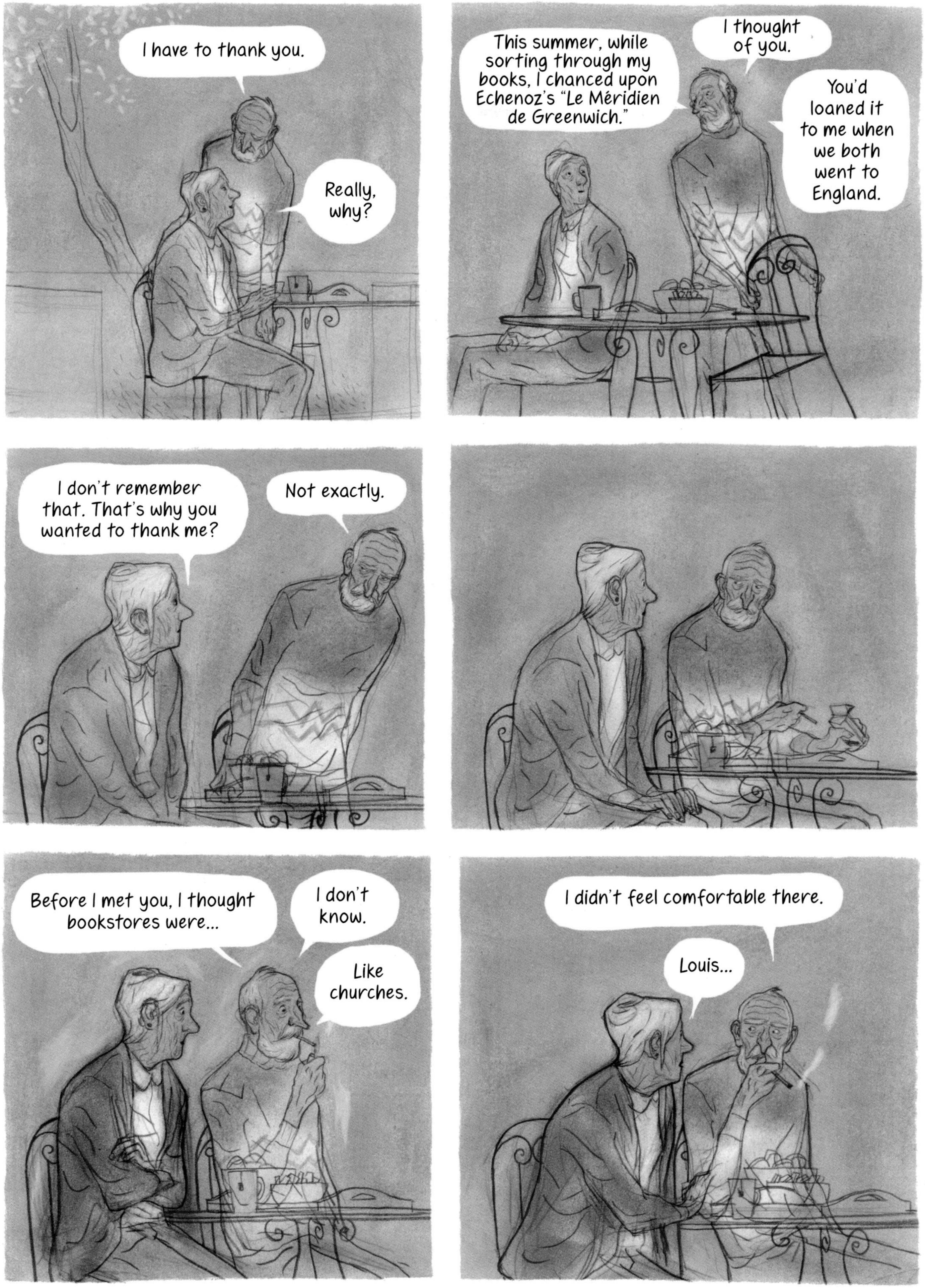
I have to thank you.
Really, why?
This summer, while sorting through my books, I chanced upon Echenoz's "Le Méridien de Greenwich."
I thought of you.
You'd loaned it to me when we both went to England.
I don't remember that. That's why you wanted to thank me?
Not exactly.
Before I met you, I thought bookstores were...
I don't know.
Like churches.
I didn't feel comfortable there.
Louis...

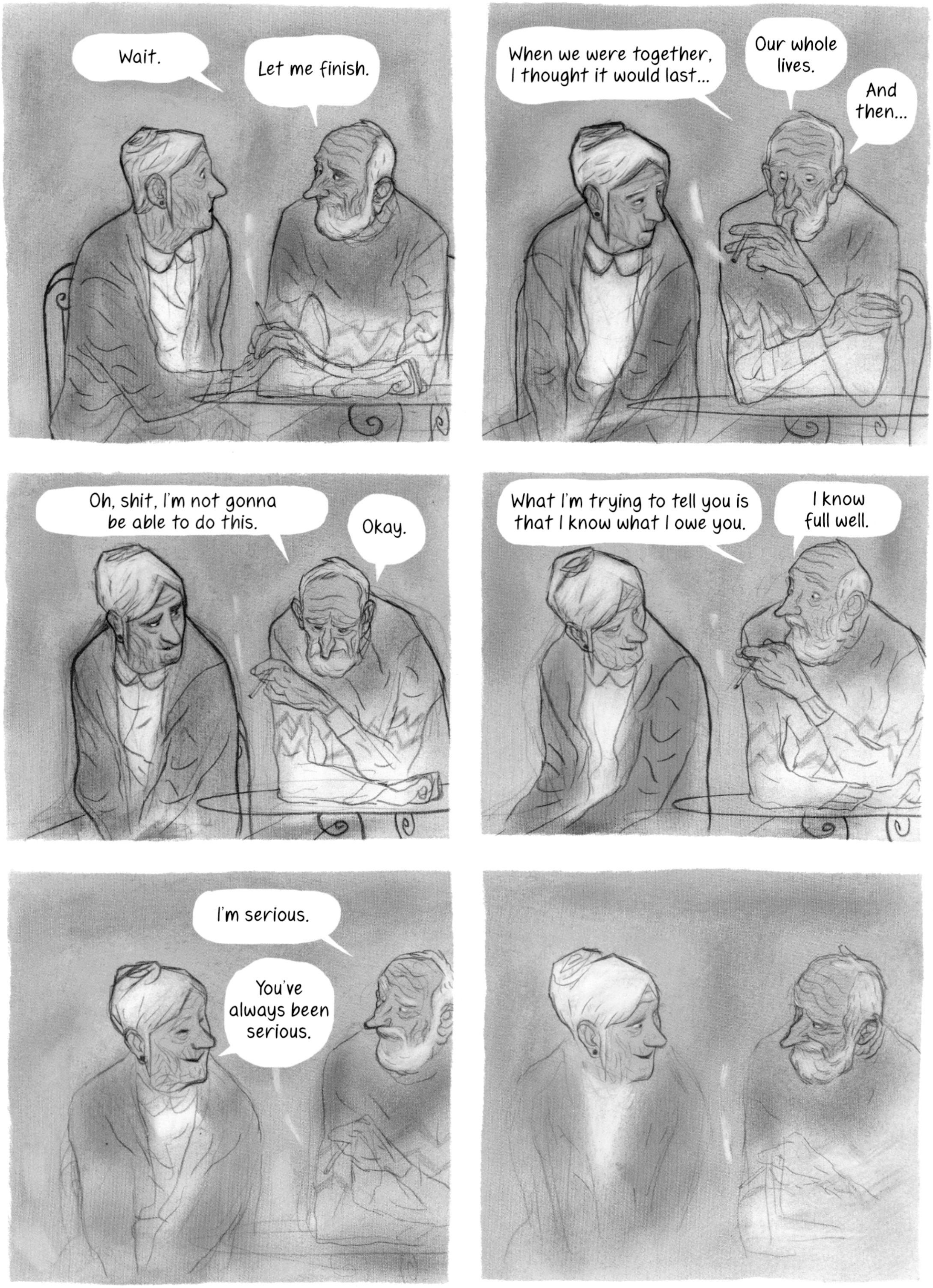
Wait.
Let me finish.
When we were together, I thought it would last...
Our whole lives.
And then...
Oh, shit, I'm not gonna be able to do this.
Okay.
What I'm trying to tell you is that I know what I owe you.
I know full well.
I'm serious.
You've always been serious.

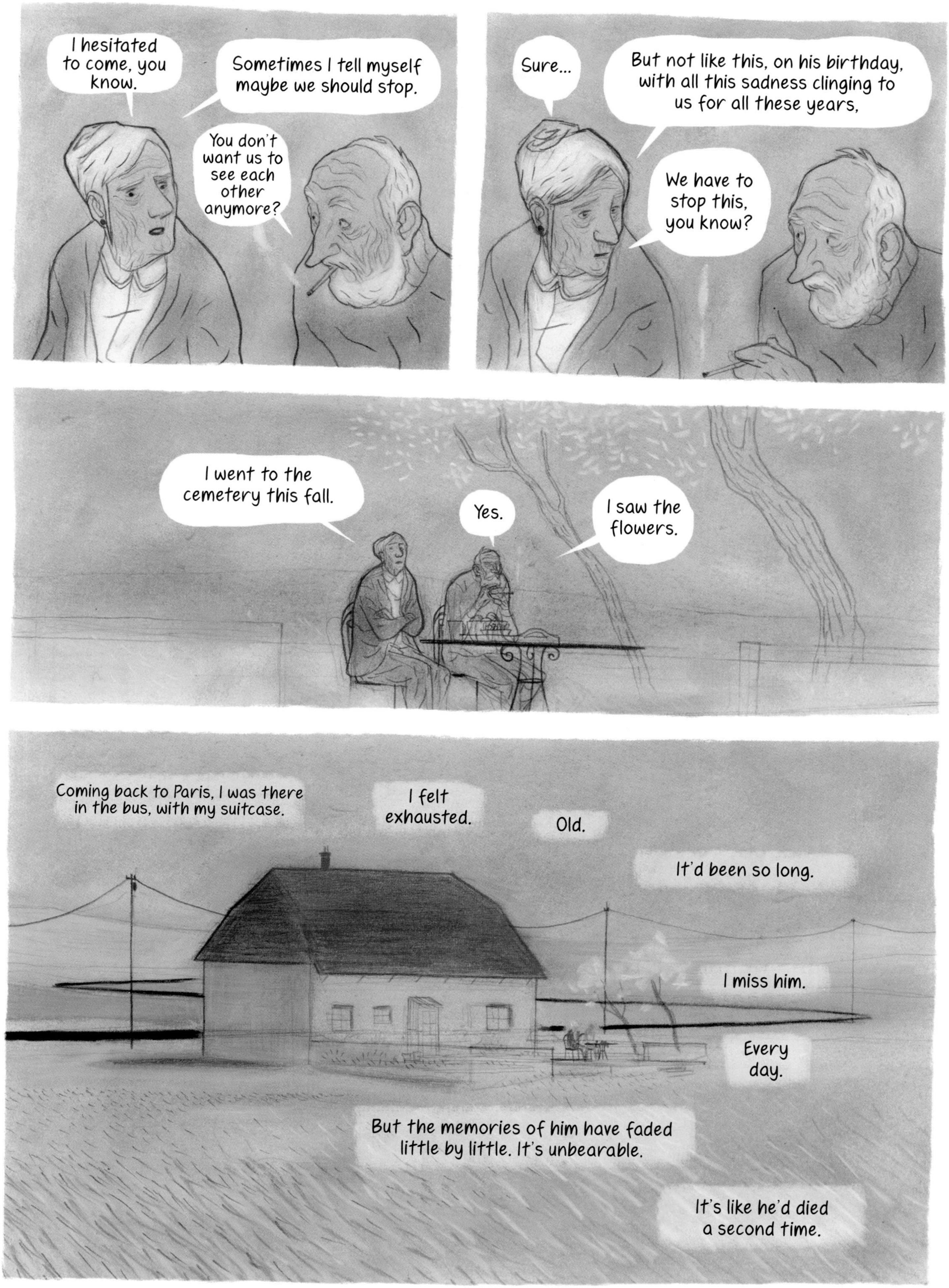
I hesitated to come, you know.
Sometimes I tell myself maybe we should stop.
You don't want us to see each other anymore?
Sure...
But not like this, on his birthday, with all this sadness clinging to us for all these years,
We have to stop this, you know?
I went to the cemetery this fall.
Yes.
I saw the flowers.
Coming back to Paris, I was there in the bus, with my suitcase.
I felt exhausted.
Old.
It'd been so long.
I miss him.
Every day.
But the memories of him have faded little by little. It's unbearable.
It's like he'd died a second time.

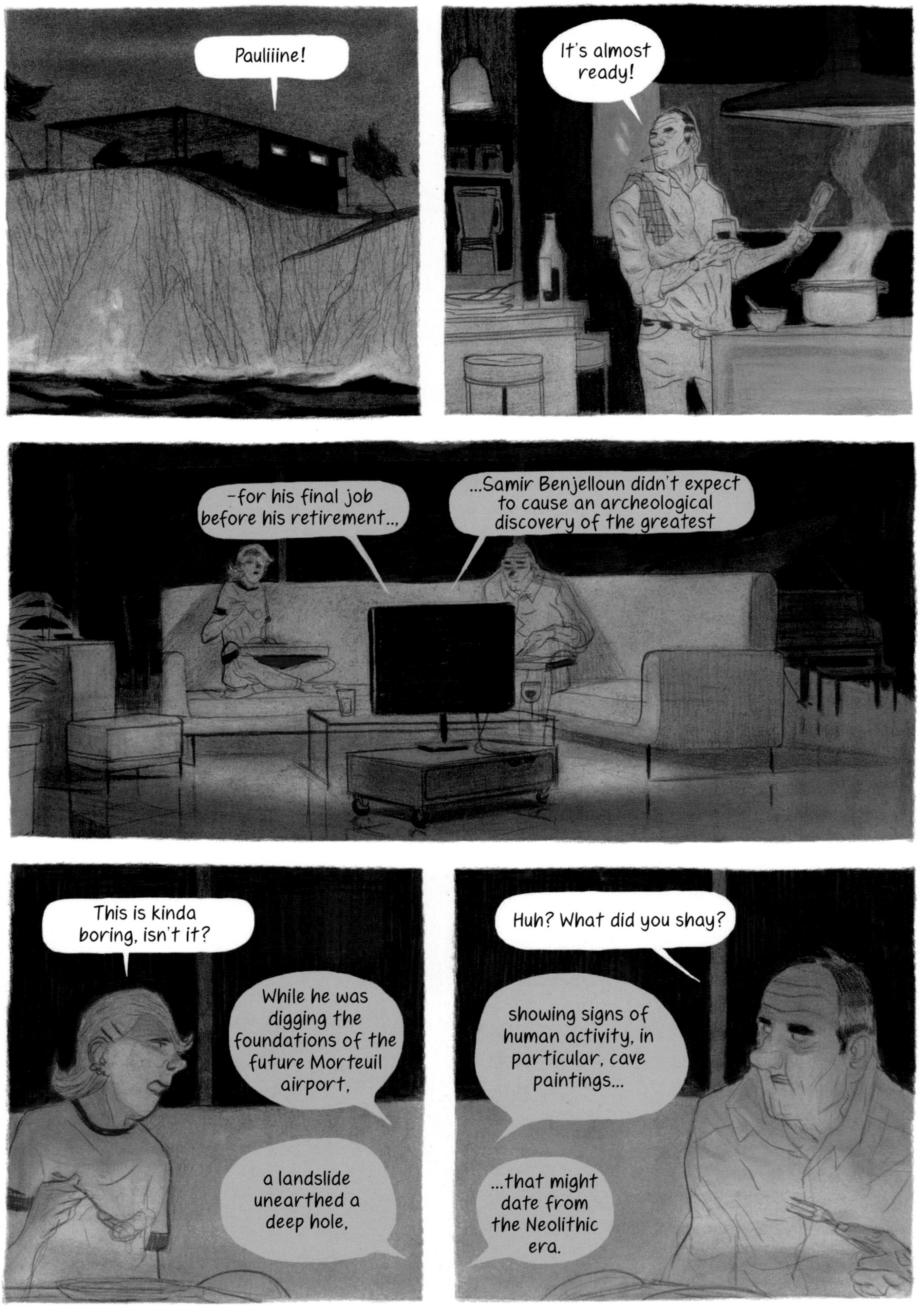
Pauliiine!
It's almost ready!
-for his final job before his retirement...,
...Samir Benjelloun didn't expect to cause an archeological discovery of the greatest
This is kinda boring, isn't it?
While he was digging the foundations of the future Morteuil airport,
a landslide unearthed a deep hole,
Huh? What did you shay?
showing signs of human activity, in particular, cave paintings...
...that might date from the Neolithic era.

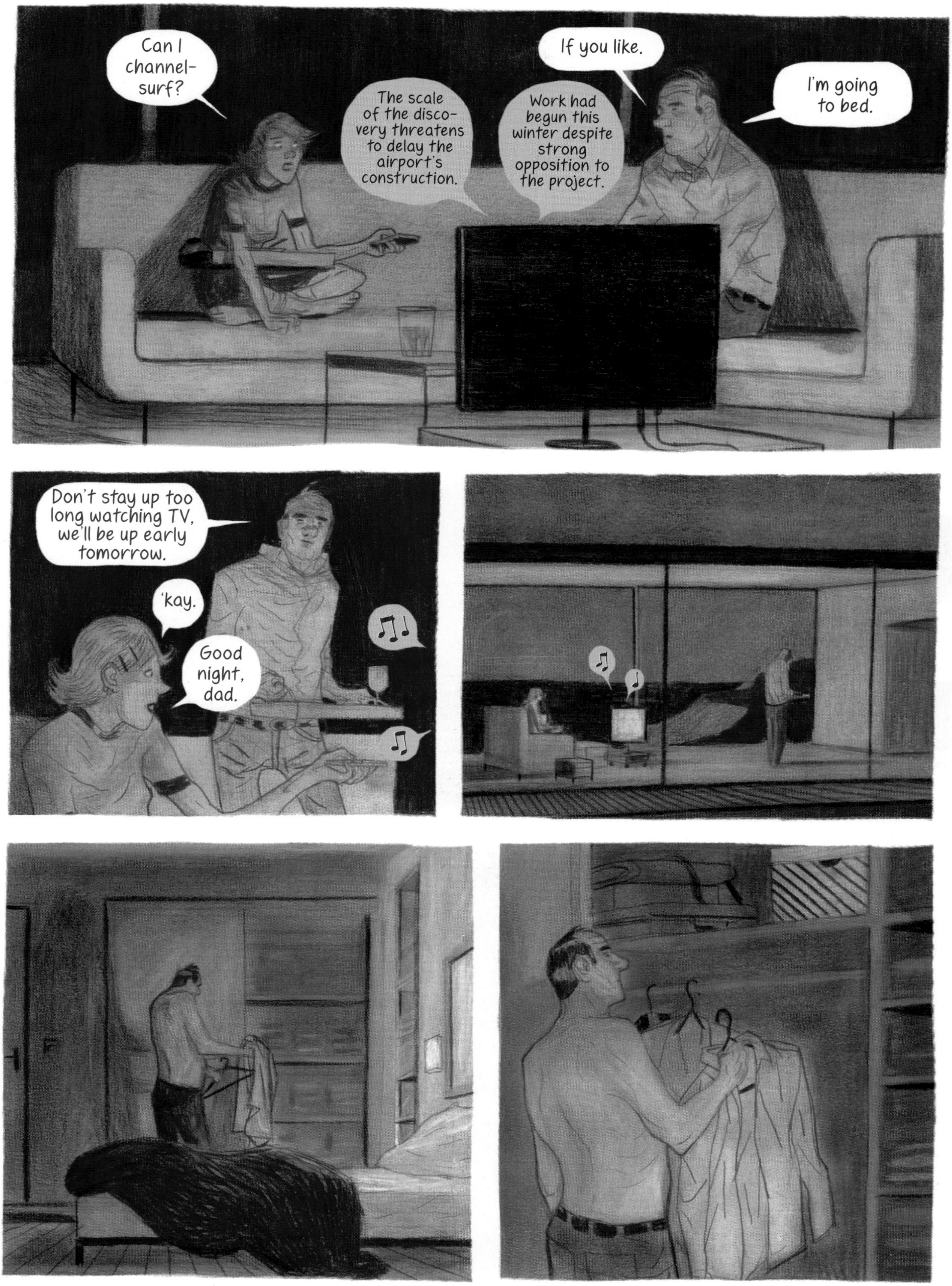

Can I channel-surf?
The scale of the discovery threatens to delay the airport's construction.
Work had begun this winter despite strong opposition to the project.
If you like.
I'm going to bed.
Don't stay up too long watching TV, we'll be up early tomorrow.
'kay.
Good night, dad.

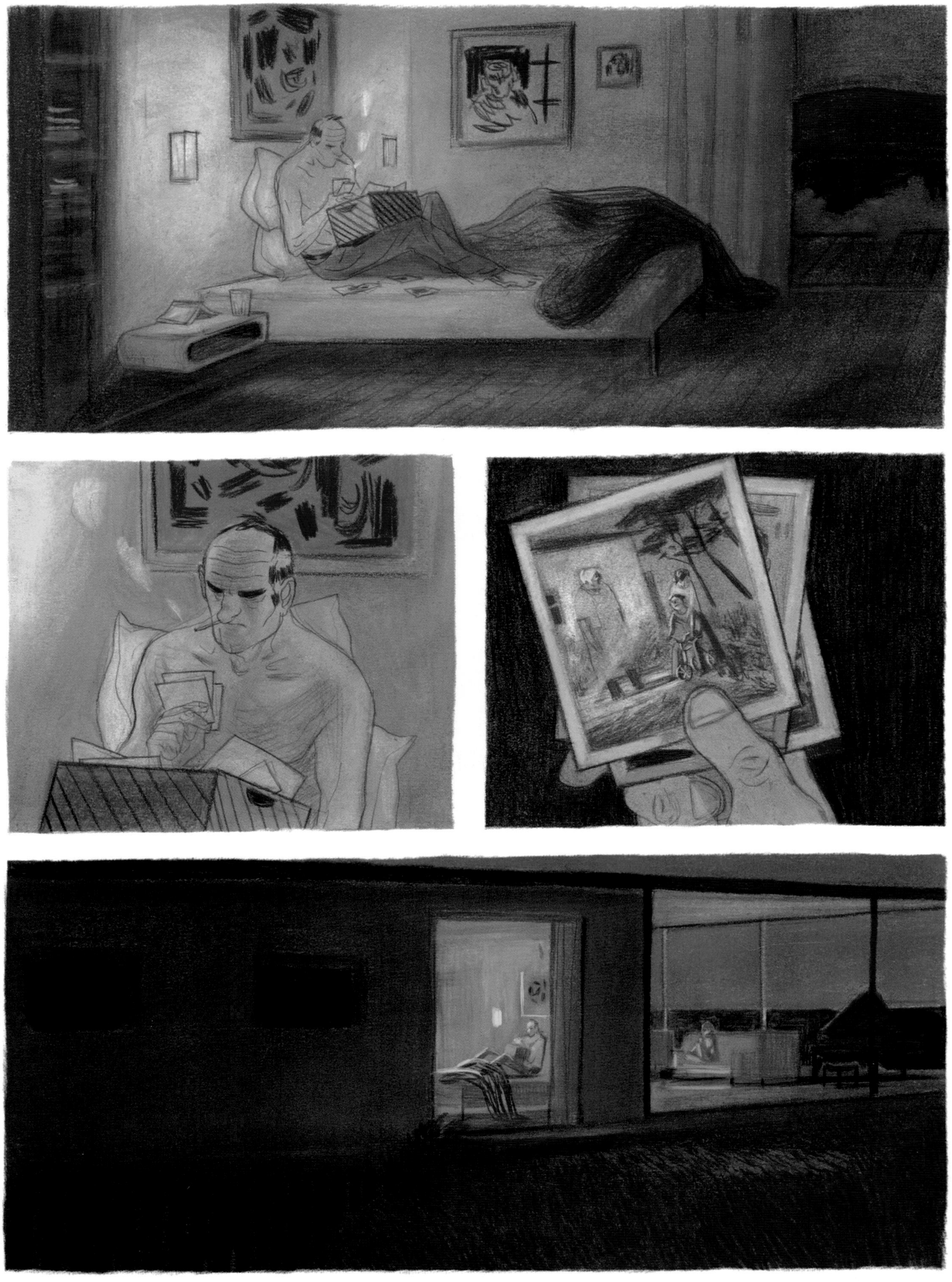

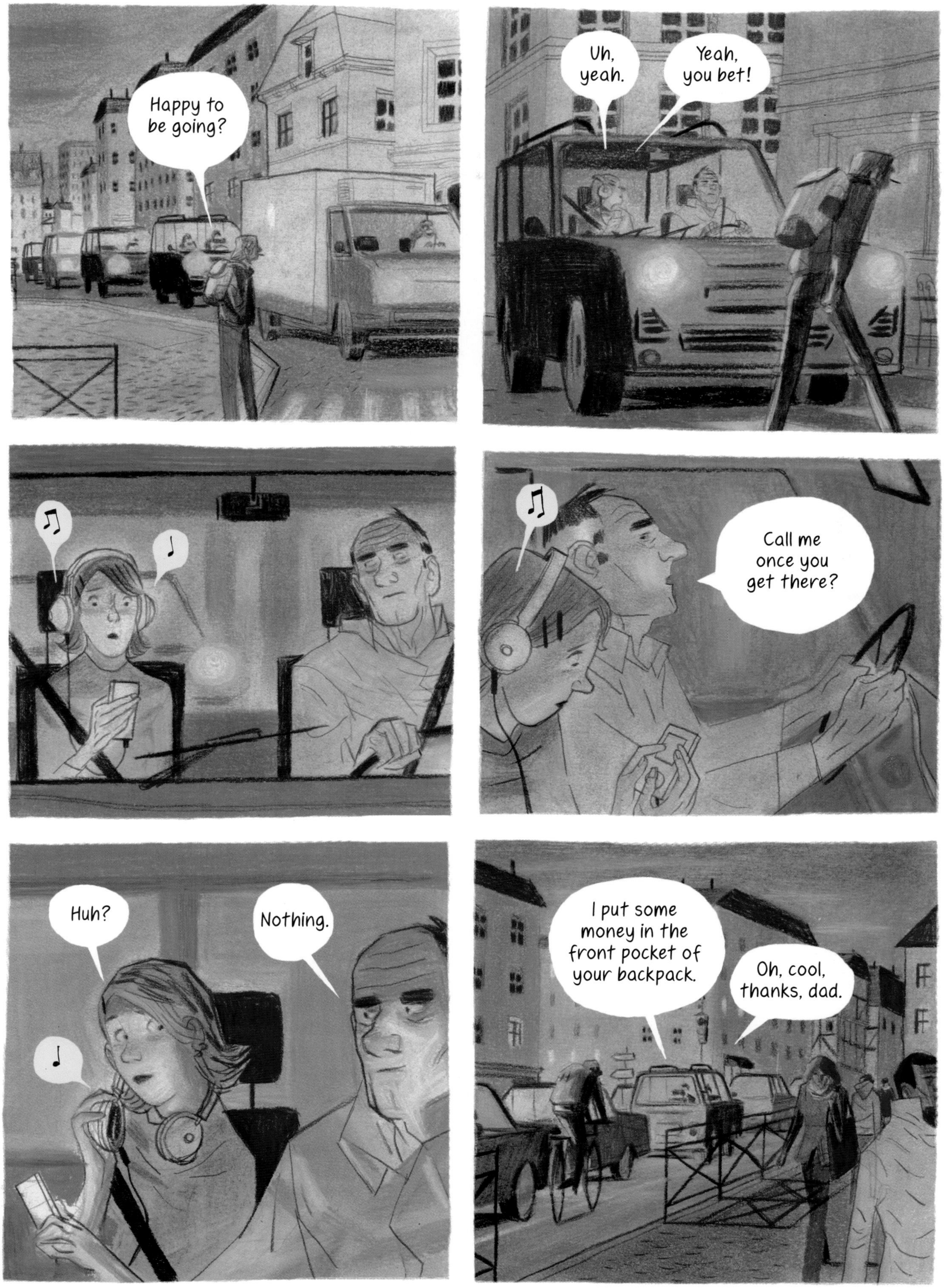
Happy to be going?
Uh, yeah.
Yeah, you bet!
♫
♩
♫
Call me once you get there?
Huh?
♩
Nothing.
I put some money in the front pocket of your backpack.
Oh, cool, thanks, dad.

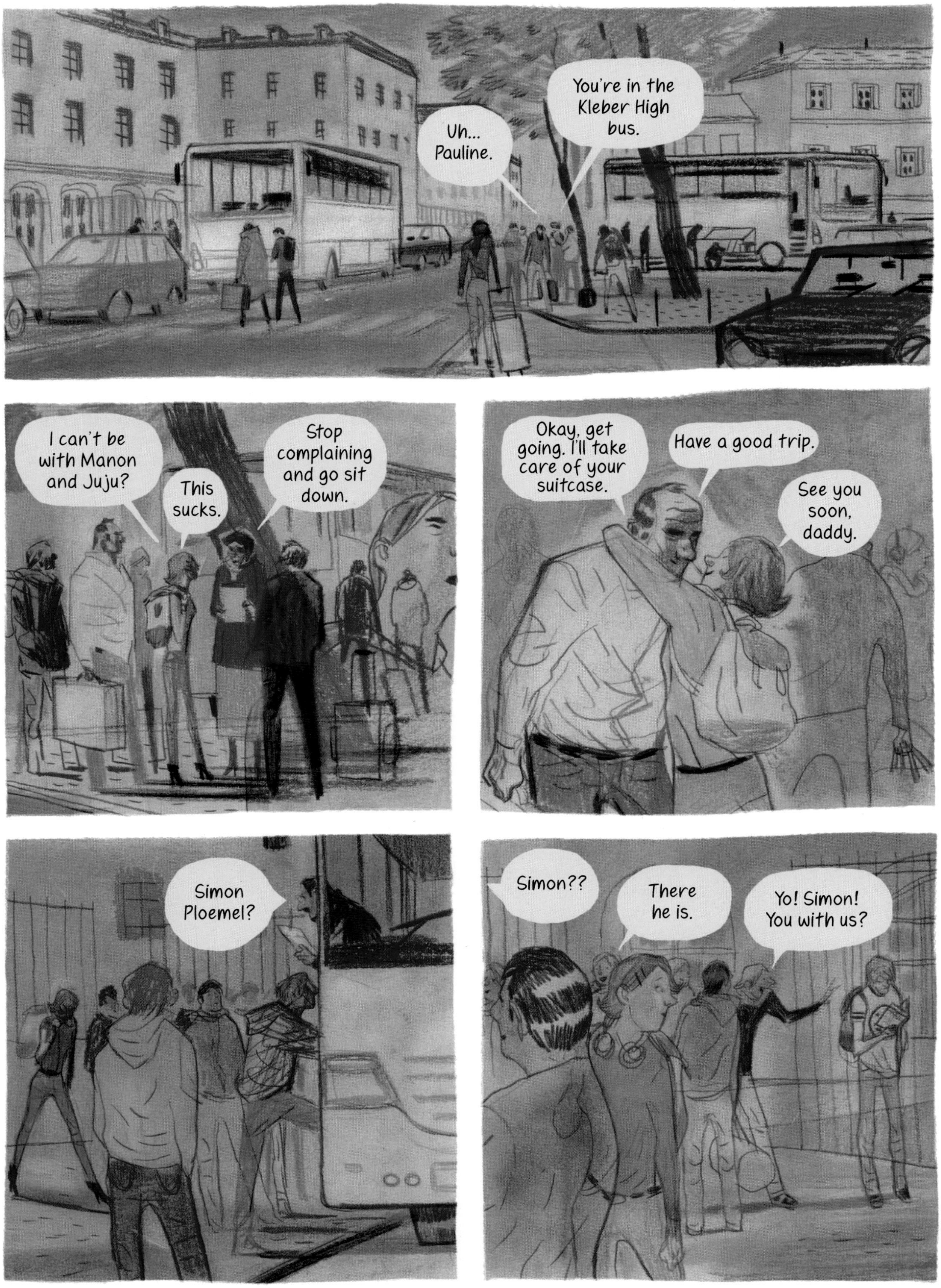
Uh... Pauline.
You're in the Kleber High bus.
I can't be with Manon and Juju?
This sucks.
Stop complaining and go sit down.
Okay, get going. I'll take care of your suitcase.
Have a good trip.
See you soon, daddy.
Simon Ploemel?
Simon??
There he is.
Yo! Simon! You with us?

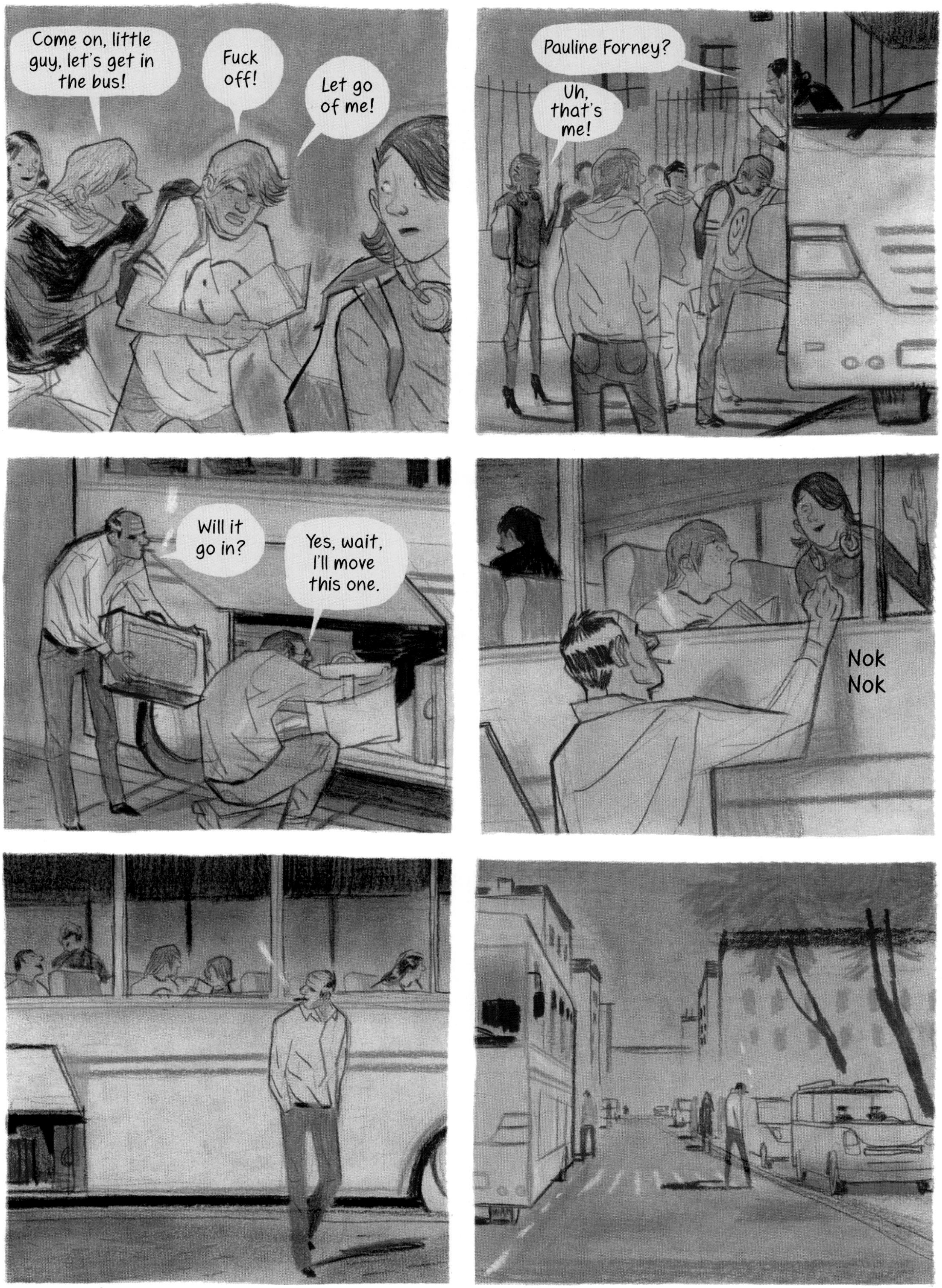
Come on, little guy, let's get in the bus!
Fuck off!
Let go of me!
Pauline Forney?
Uh, that's me!
Will it go in?
Yes, wait, I'll move this one.
Nok Nok

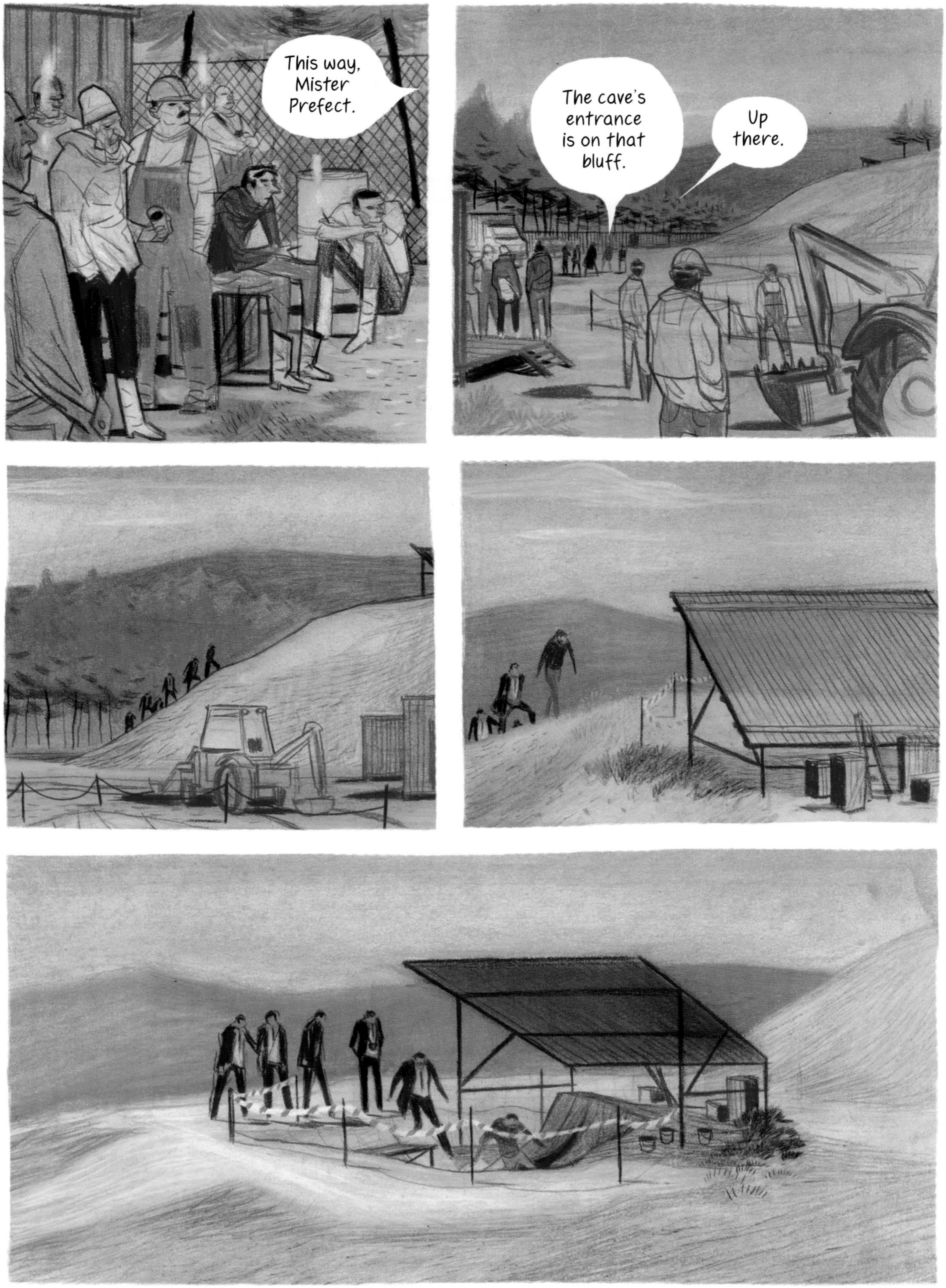
This way, Mister Prefect.
The cave's entrance is on that bluff.
Up there.

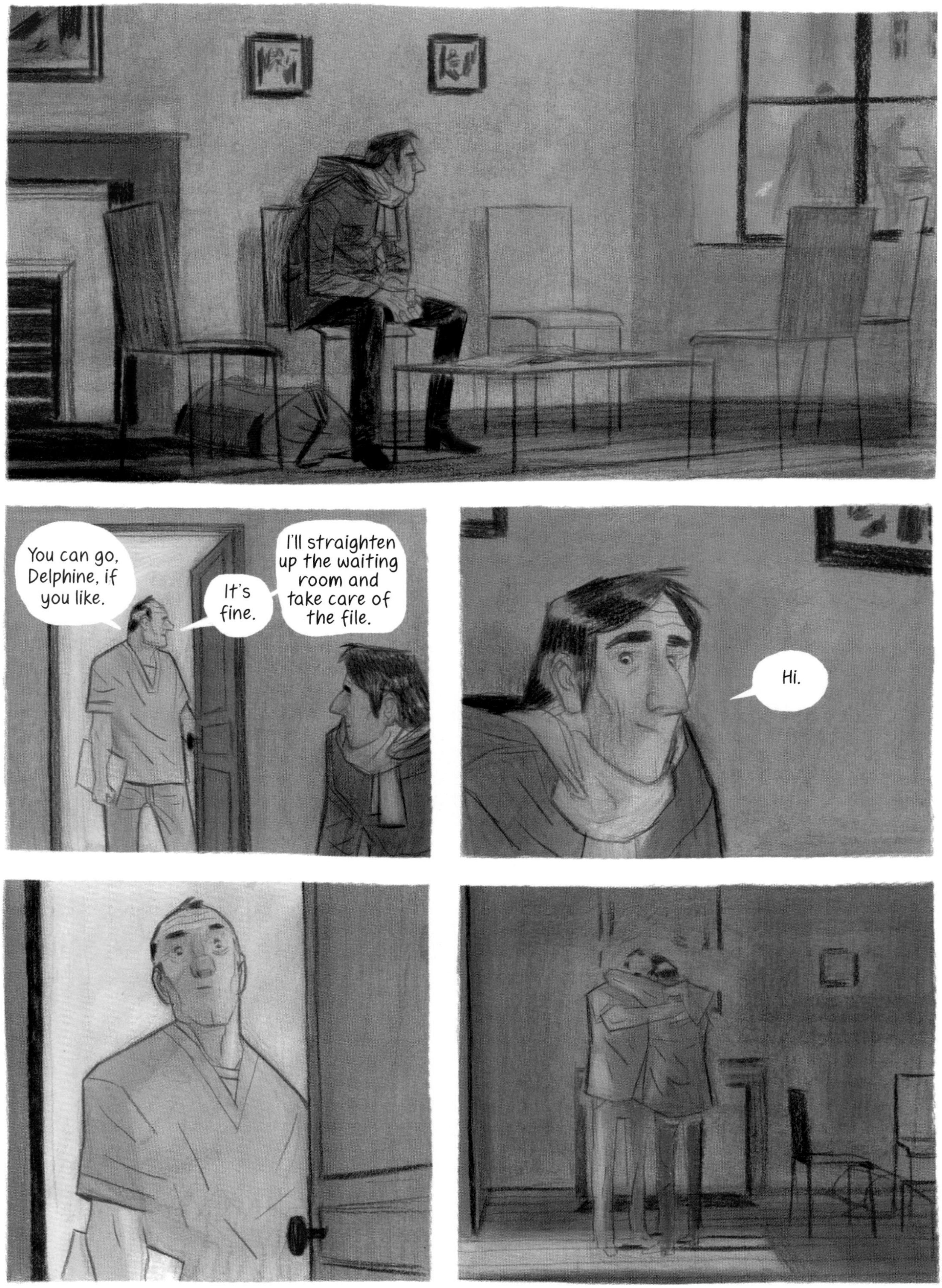
You can go, Delphine, if you like.
It's fine.
I'll straighten up the waiting room and take care of the file.
Hi.

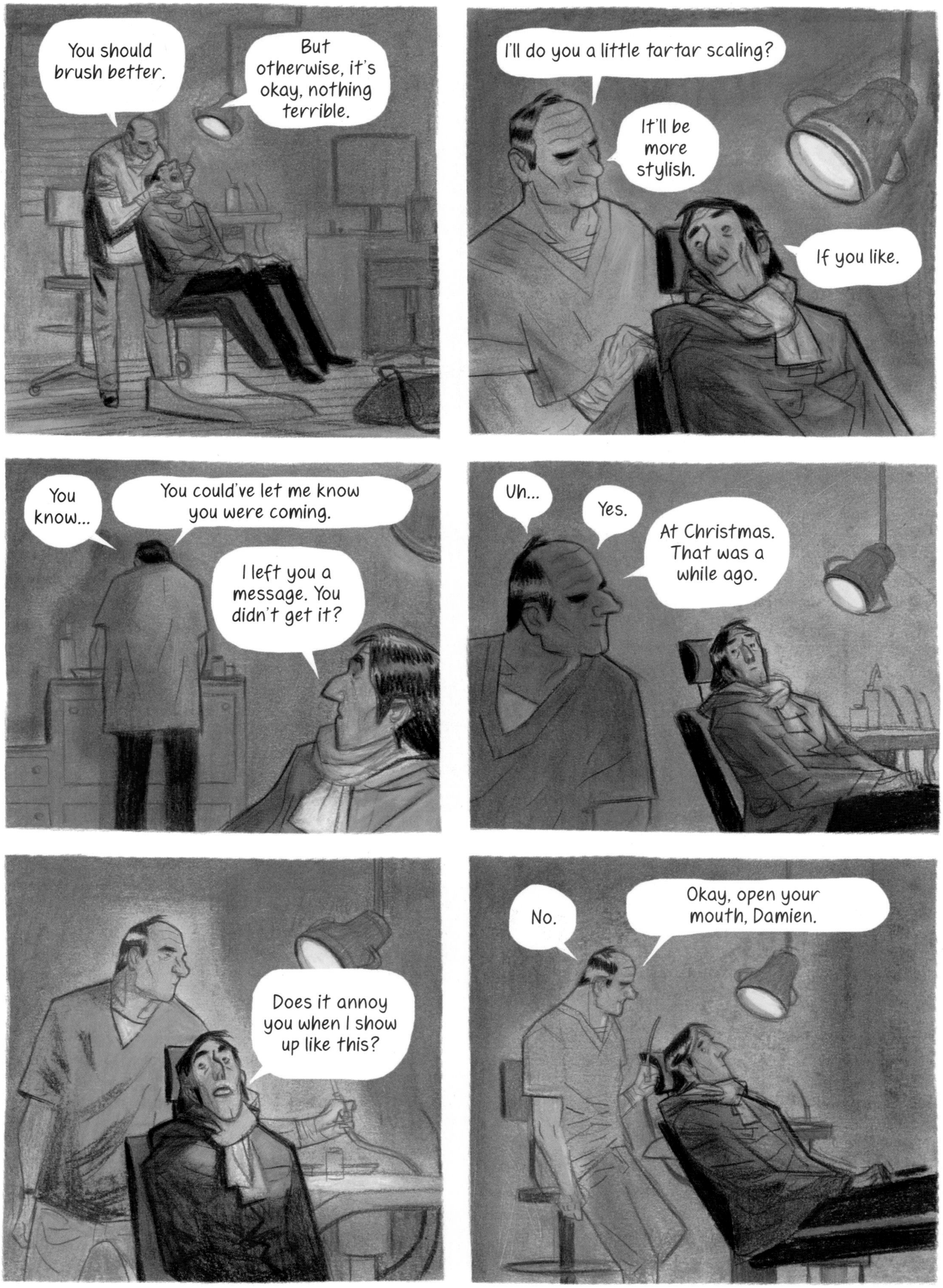
You should brush better.
But otherwise, it's okay, nothing terrible.
I'll do you a little tartar scaling?
It'll be more stylish.
If you like.
You know...
You could've let me know you were coming.
I left you a message. You didn't get it?
Uh...
Yes.
At Christmas. That was a while ago.
Does it annoy you when I show up like this?
No.
Okay, open your mouth, Damien.

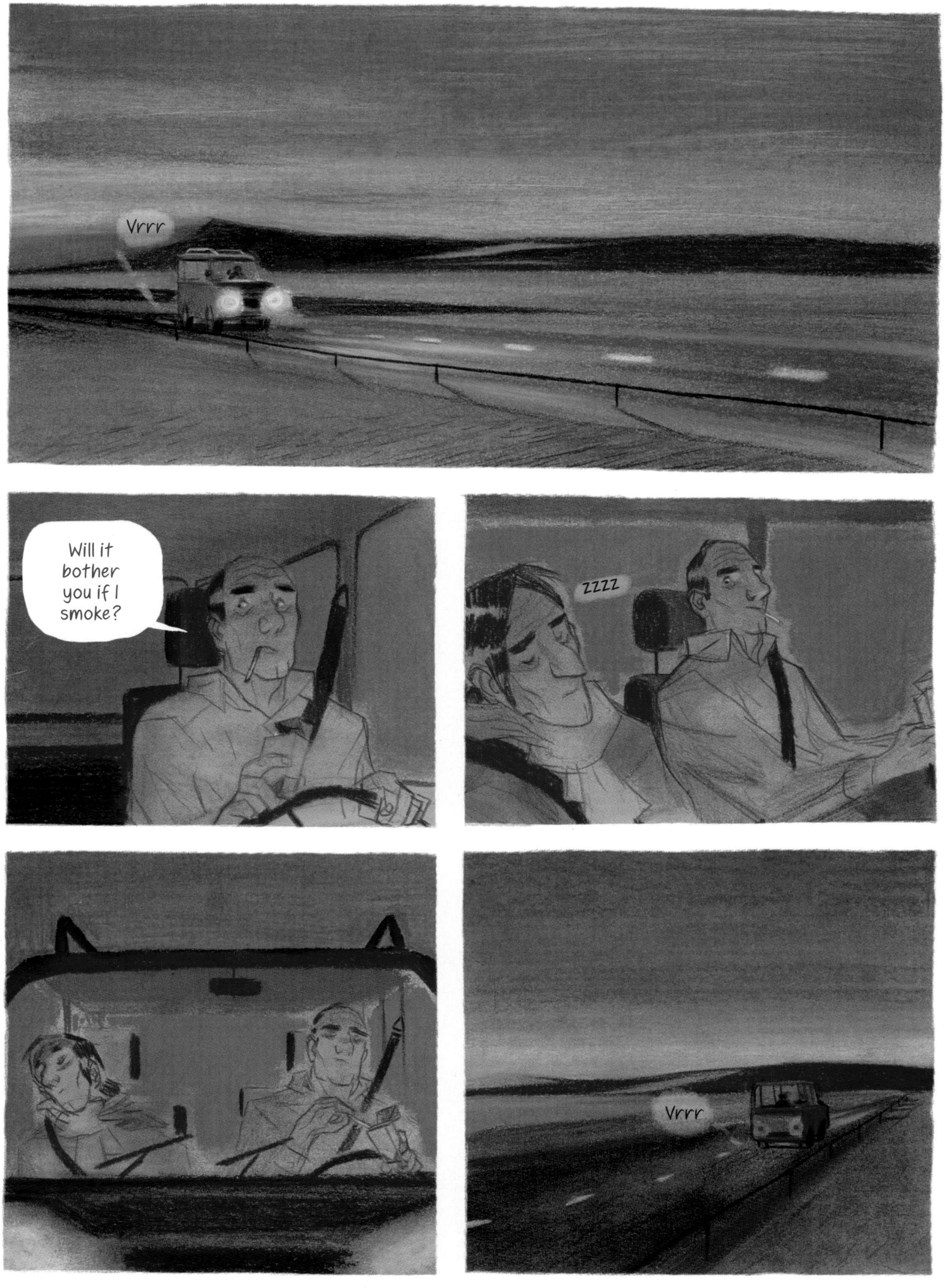
Vrrr
Will it bother you if I smoke?
ZZZZ
Vrrr

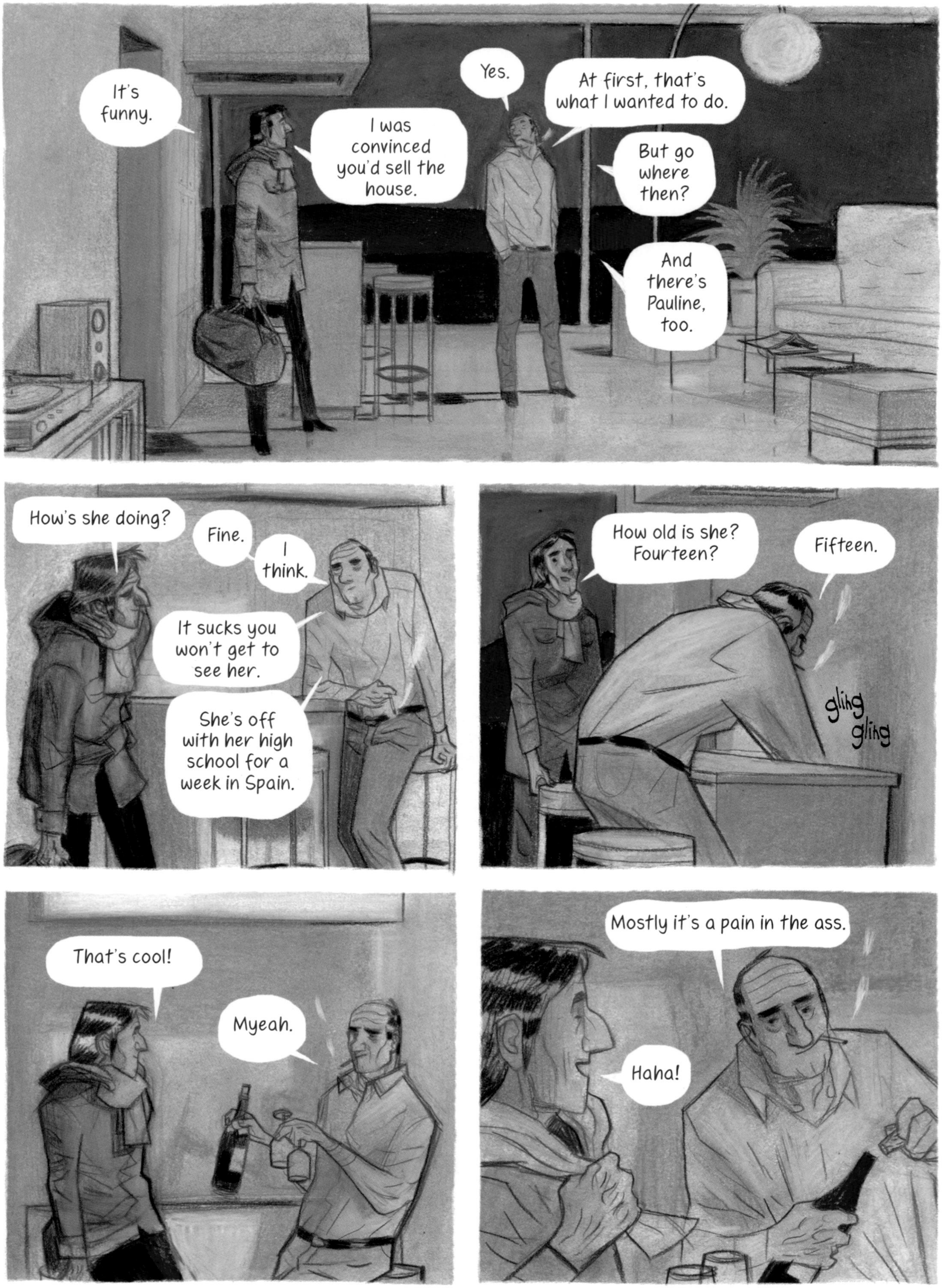
It's funny.
I was convinced you'd sell the house.
Yes.
At first, that's what I wanted to do.
But go where then?
And there's Pauline, too.
How's she doing?
Fine.
I think.
It sucks you won't get to see her.
She's off with her high school for a week in Spain.
How old is she? Fourteen?
Fifteen.
gling gling
That's cool!
Myeah.
Mostly it's a pain in the ass.
Haha!

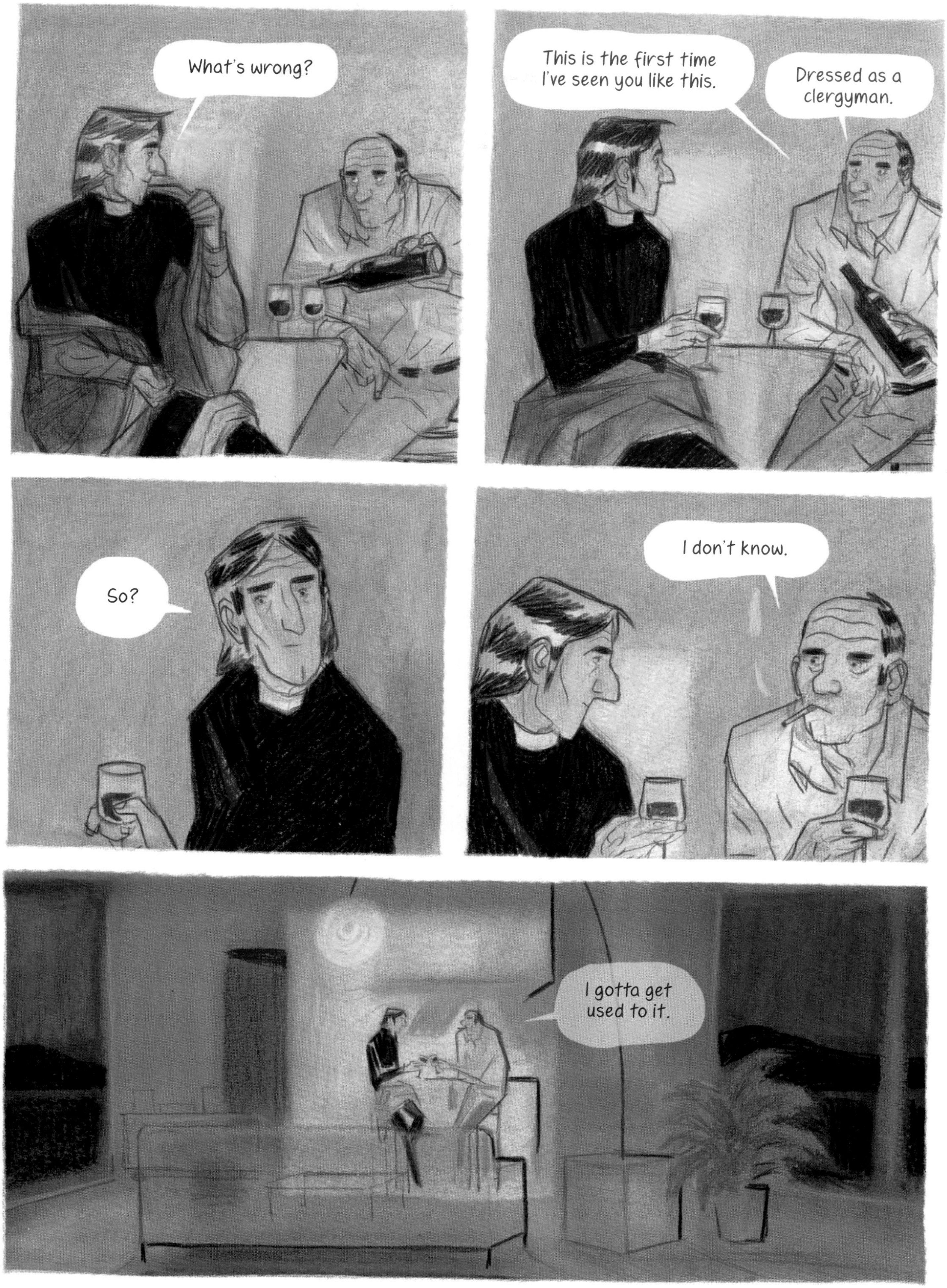
What's wrong?
This is the first time I've seen you like this.
Dressed as a clergyman.
So?
I don't know.
I gotta get used to it.

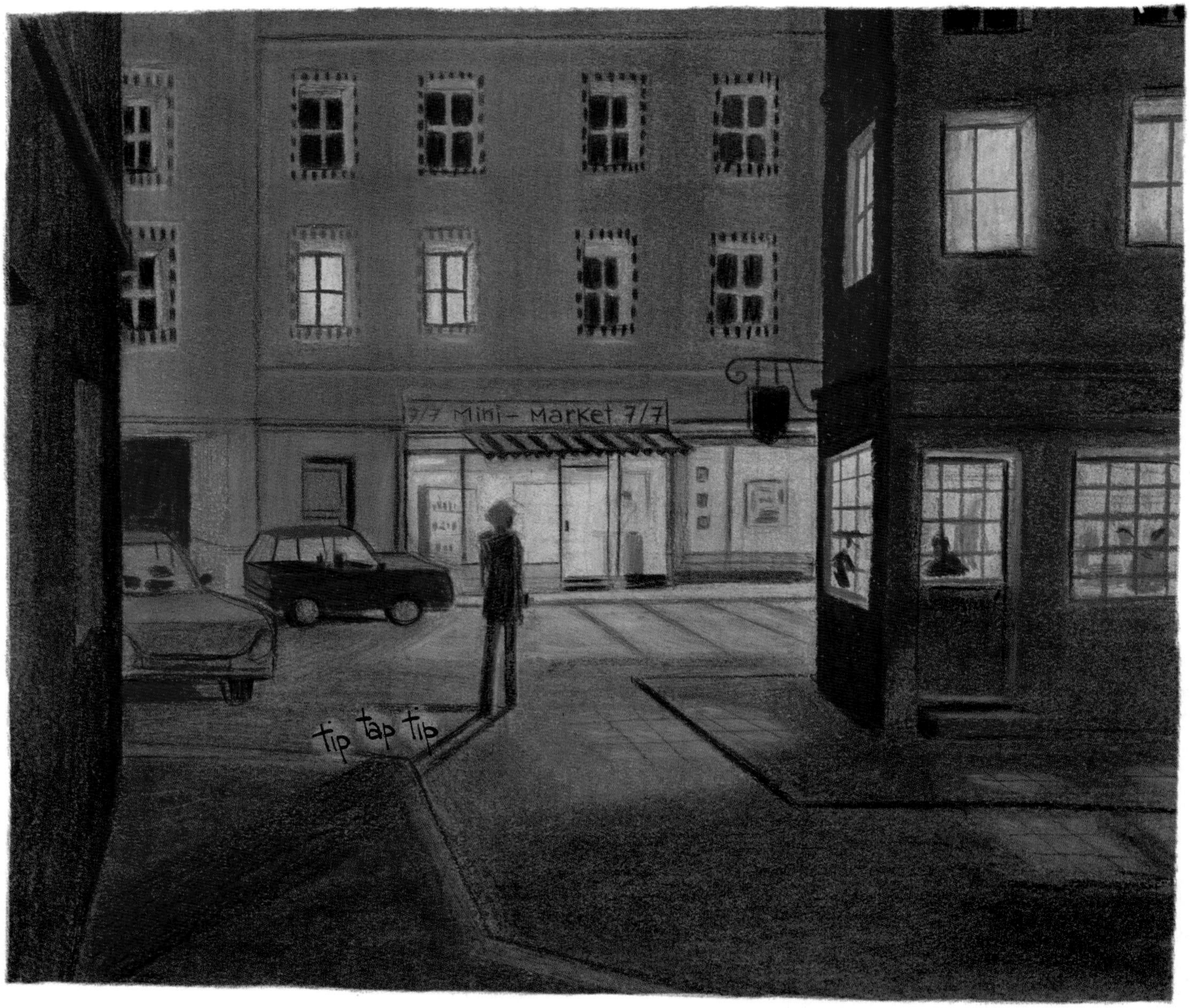
7/7 Mini- Market 7/7
tip tap tip

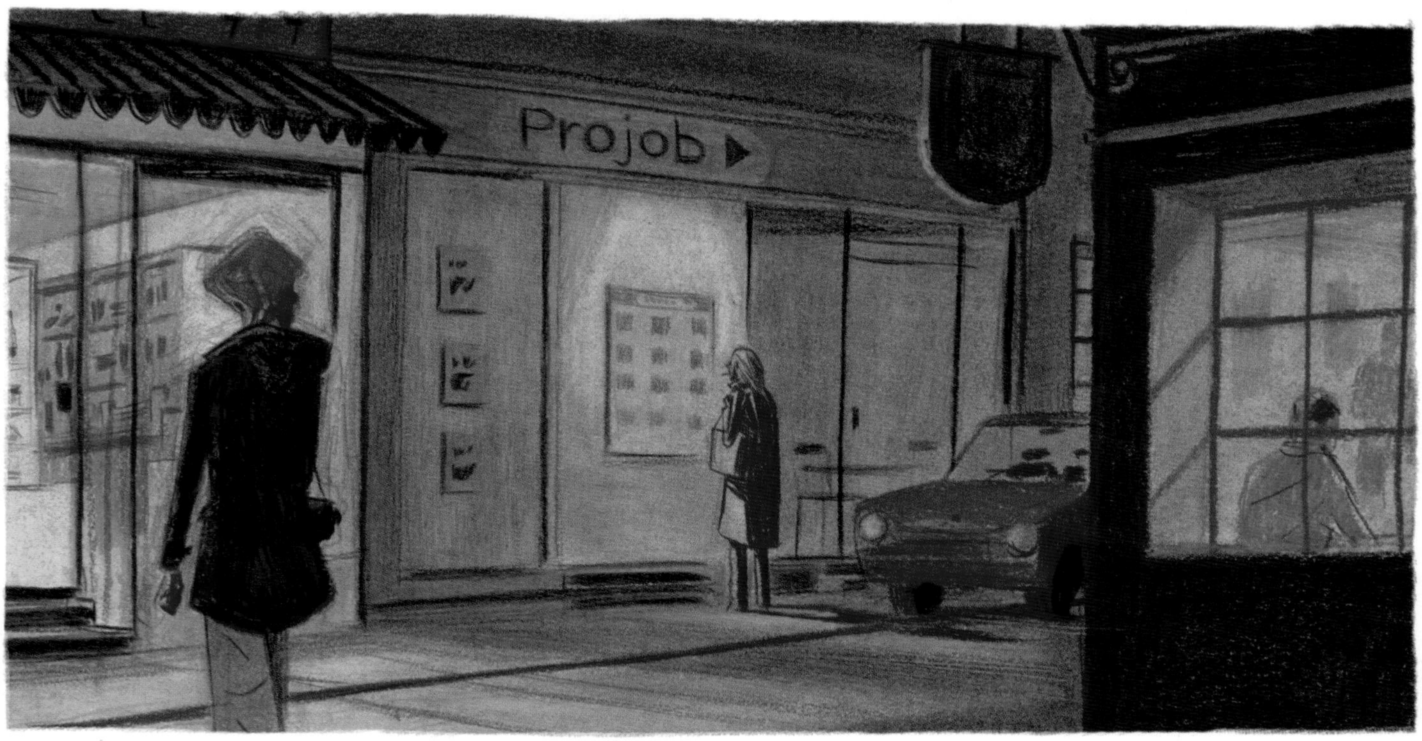
Projob ▶

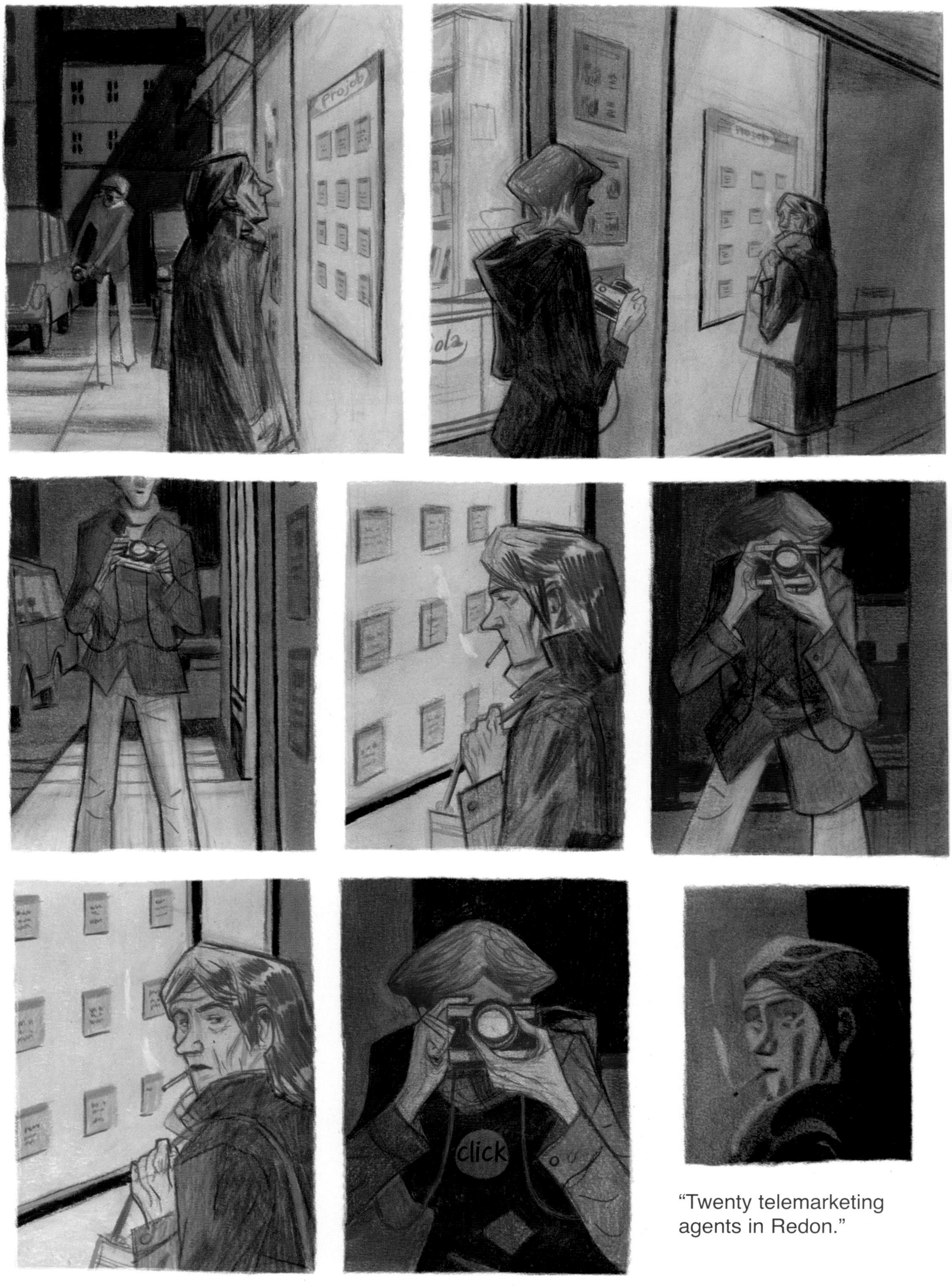
click
“Twenty telemarketing agents in Redon.”

Unfortunately she can't show she has any degree in business and/or successful experience in inside or outside sales.

In her right ear, there's a very shrill note.

Mixed with a breath of air.

 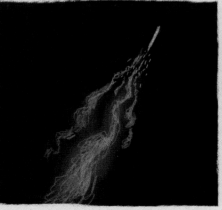 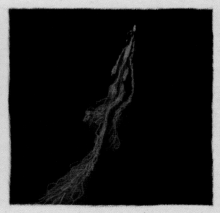

She's been suffering from this parasitic sound forever.

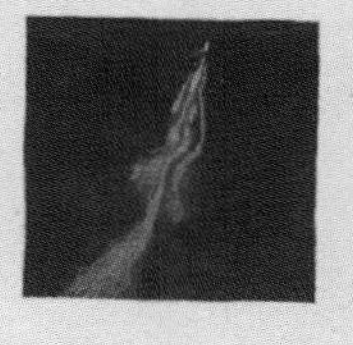

Thanks to the upright piano in Miss Chevalier's music class at the Chateaubriand Middle School, this permanent buzzing in her ear had turned out to be a B flat. Two octaves above the treble clef.

"Salesperson for a specialized franchise in ice cream sales, in the Great West region."
Nor has she come from sales training and/or had six months of experience in sales. In February, after her third temp contract, the Breizh-Bay HR director had let her hope her position "could" evolve into a permanent job. The announcement of the first layoffs a few months later had, in retrospect, completely justified that use of the conditional tense.

That morning, she went to see her father.
She's been going there at least once a week for a month and a half. In the small room of the locked area of the Regnier Hospital's adult psychiatry ward, where he'd been admitted at the beginning of spring, just after her final temp job at Breizh-Bay.
She's coming not so much to care for him as to observe as closely as possible the disorders from which he's suffering. That dissonance, that nobody besides her has ever seemed to hear, about which she was unable to speak, was finally audible, fully exposed.
She'd known about it since her childhood. You mustn't hurt his feelings or upset him. The slightest jostle could capsize him. Not only had she seen his breaches early on, but especially the immense hollow hidden behind those anodyne crevices. One day or the other, she knew, it'd all come tumbling down.
Her father, back when he still spoke, had the annoying habit of not naming objects, people, or events. "Thingamabob," "thingamajig," and "whatchamacallit" served to articulate his increasingly impoverished thought. No doubt occupied elsewhere, struggling against the fault line.

She'd cried a lot on the phone upon learning of his hospitalization. Her brother had consoled her from afar. She mustn't worry, it wouldn't last long. Their father would be out soon. But she wasn't worried. She wasn't crying over her father's illness, but the impossibility of naming it for all those years. The dissonance was finally stopping.

The B flat in her right ear is becoming ever more present. It's difficult for her to concentrate on the job ads stuck on the window. The note's going higher, like an arrow shot into the sky. Like those rockets on July 14th that clutter the whole of space, filling it with their light, attracting to themselves all the attention of the onlookers.

Nothing else existed while that rocket climbed and whose explosion you expect like the promise of relief.

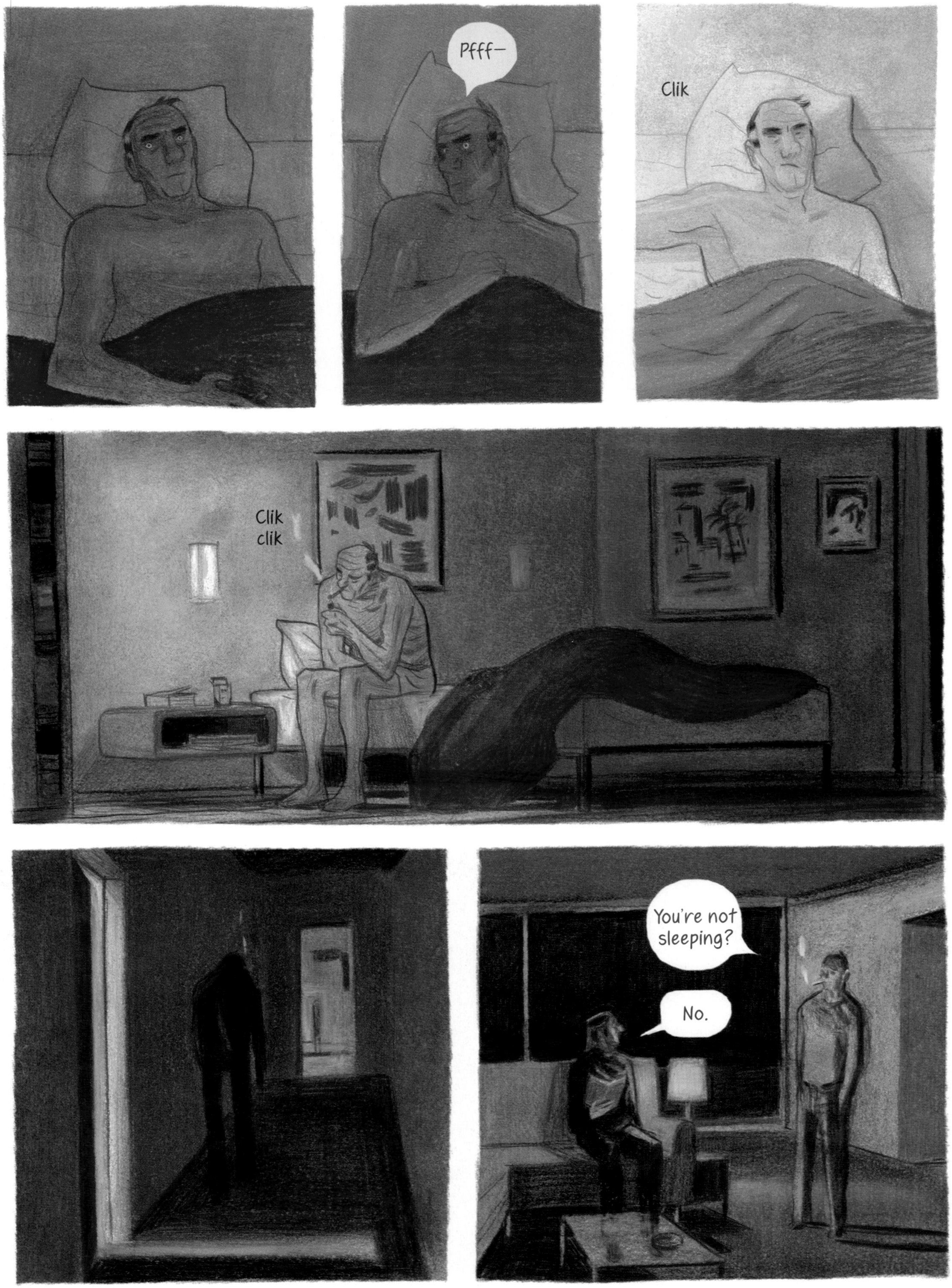
Pfff–
Clik
Clik
clik
You're not sleeping?
No.

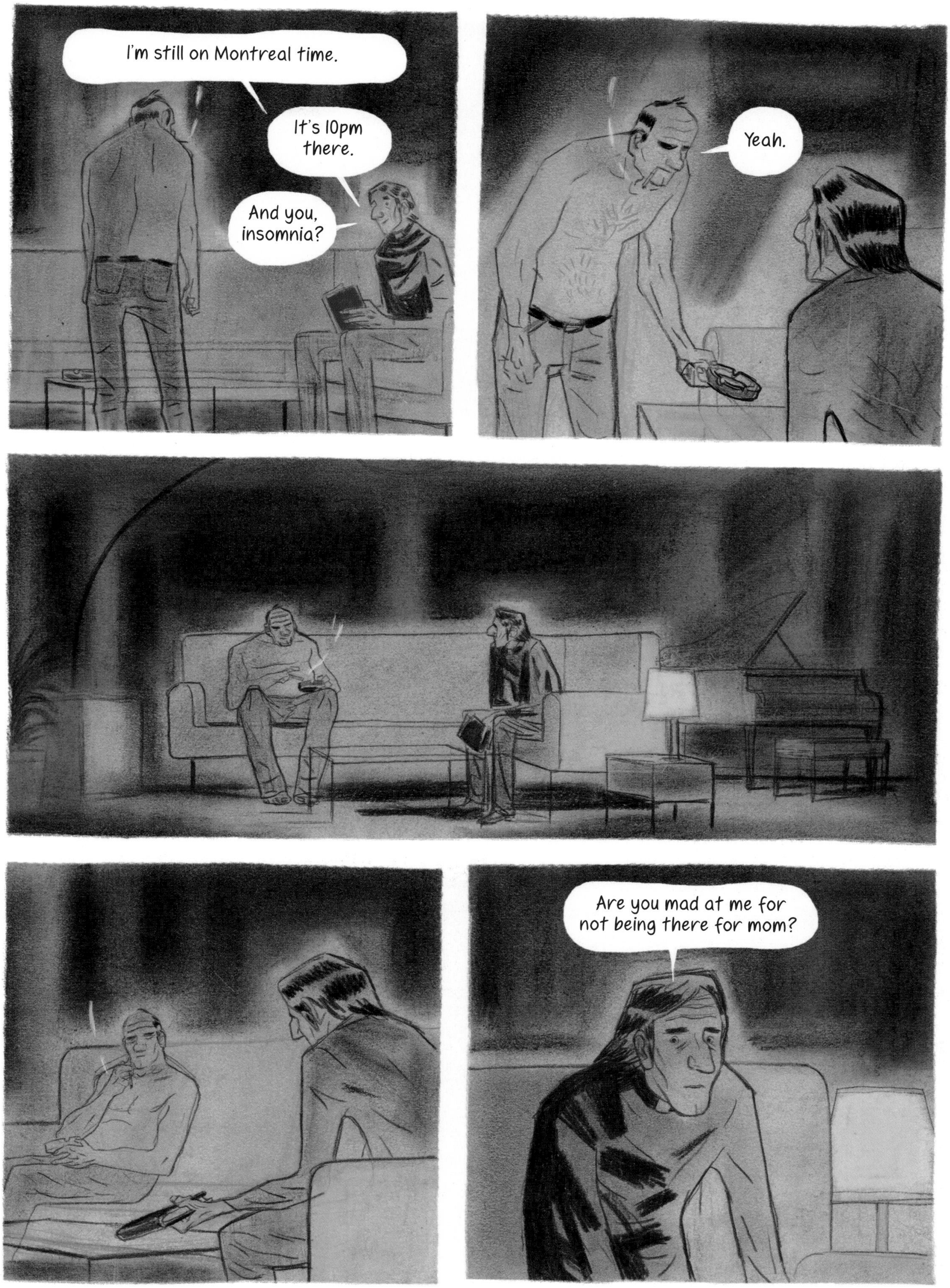
I'm still on Montreal time.
It's 10pm there.
And you, insomnia?
Yeah.
Are you mad at me for not being there for mom?

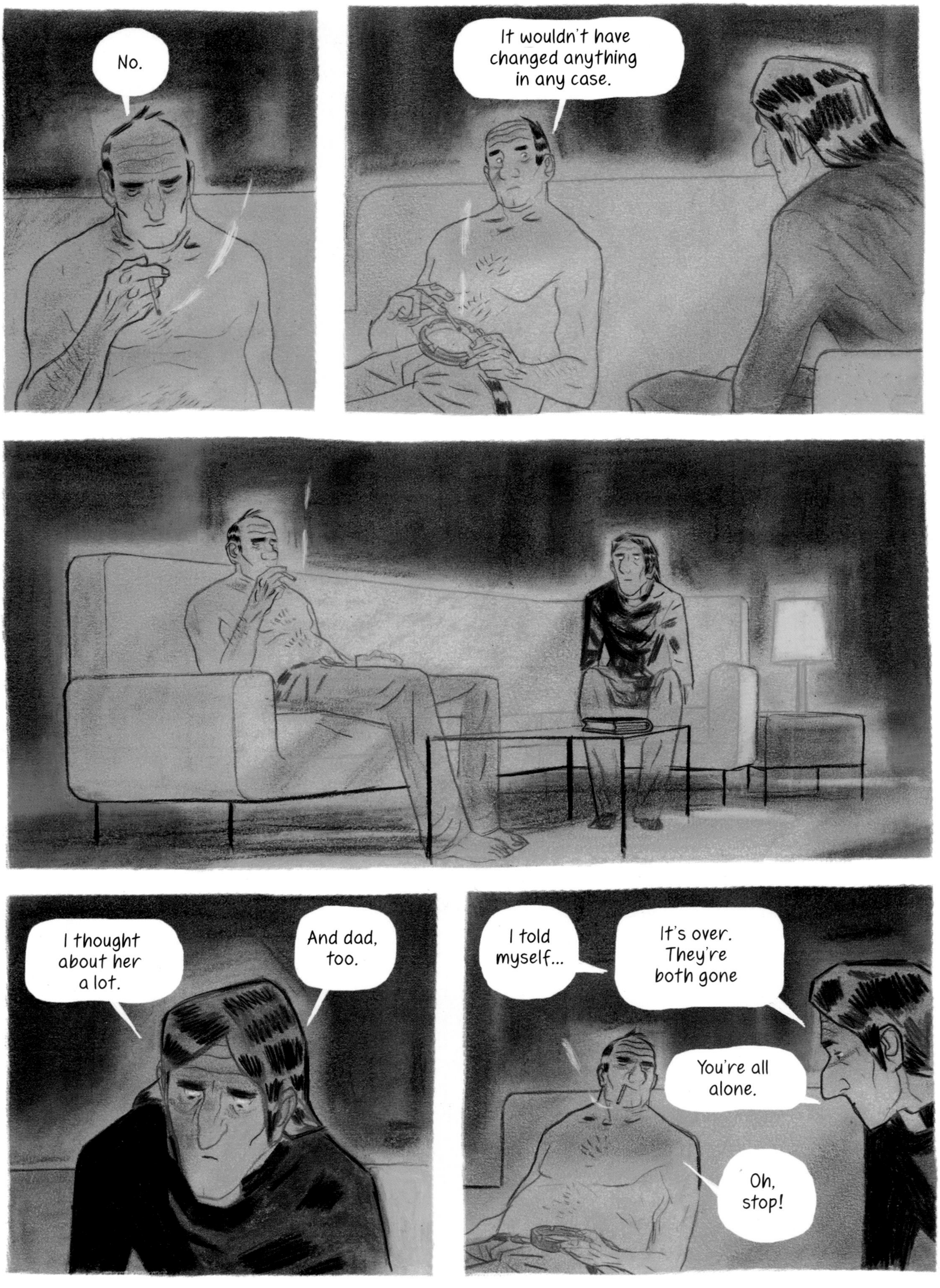
No.
It wouldn't have changed anything in any case.
I thought about her a lot.
And dad, too.
I told myself...
It's over. They're both gone
You're all alone.
Oh, stop!

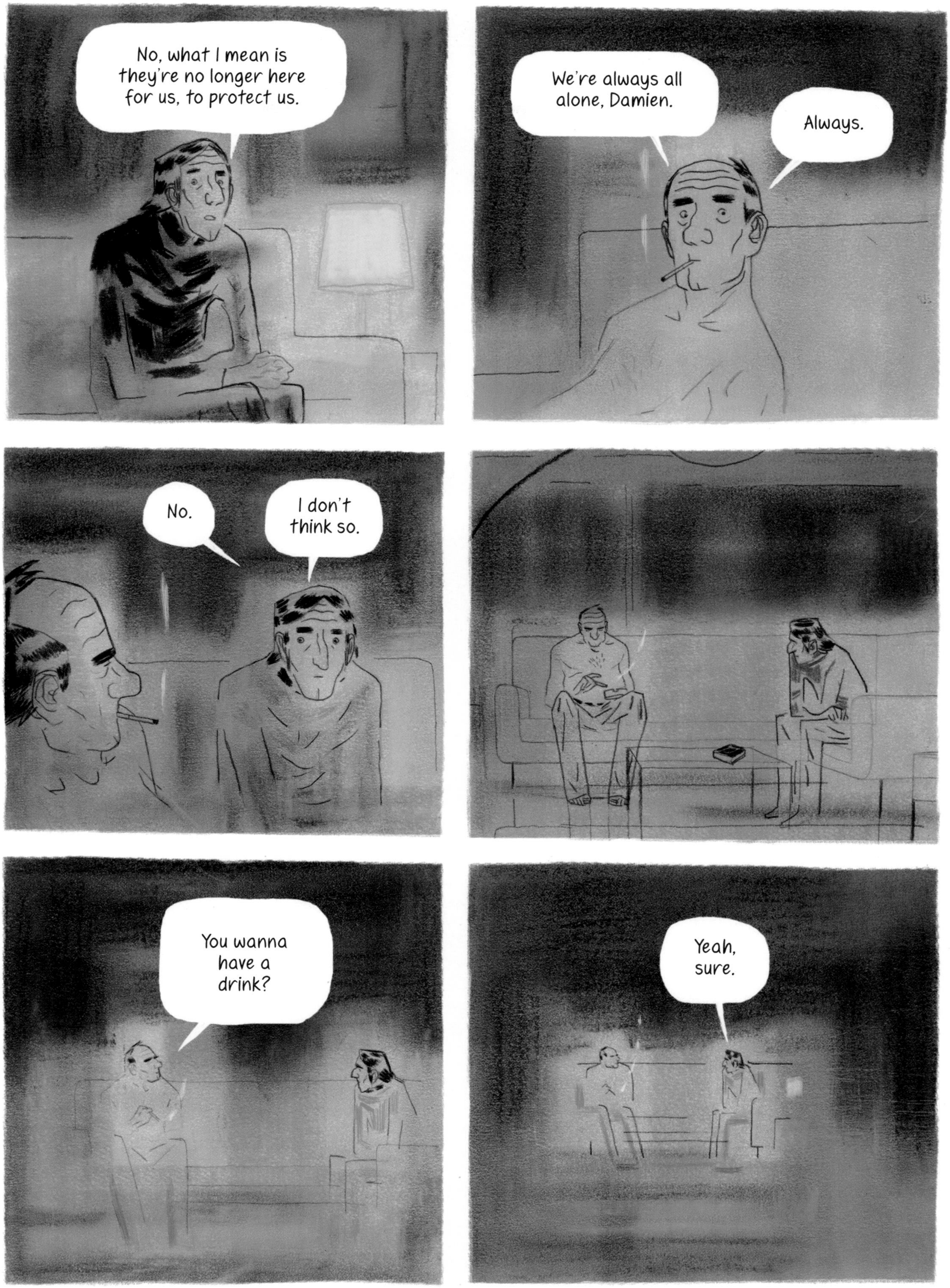
No, what I mean is they're no longer here for us, to protect us.
We're always all alone, Damien.
Always.
No.
I don't think so.
You wanna have a drink?
Yeah, sure.

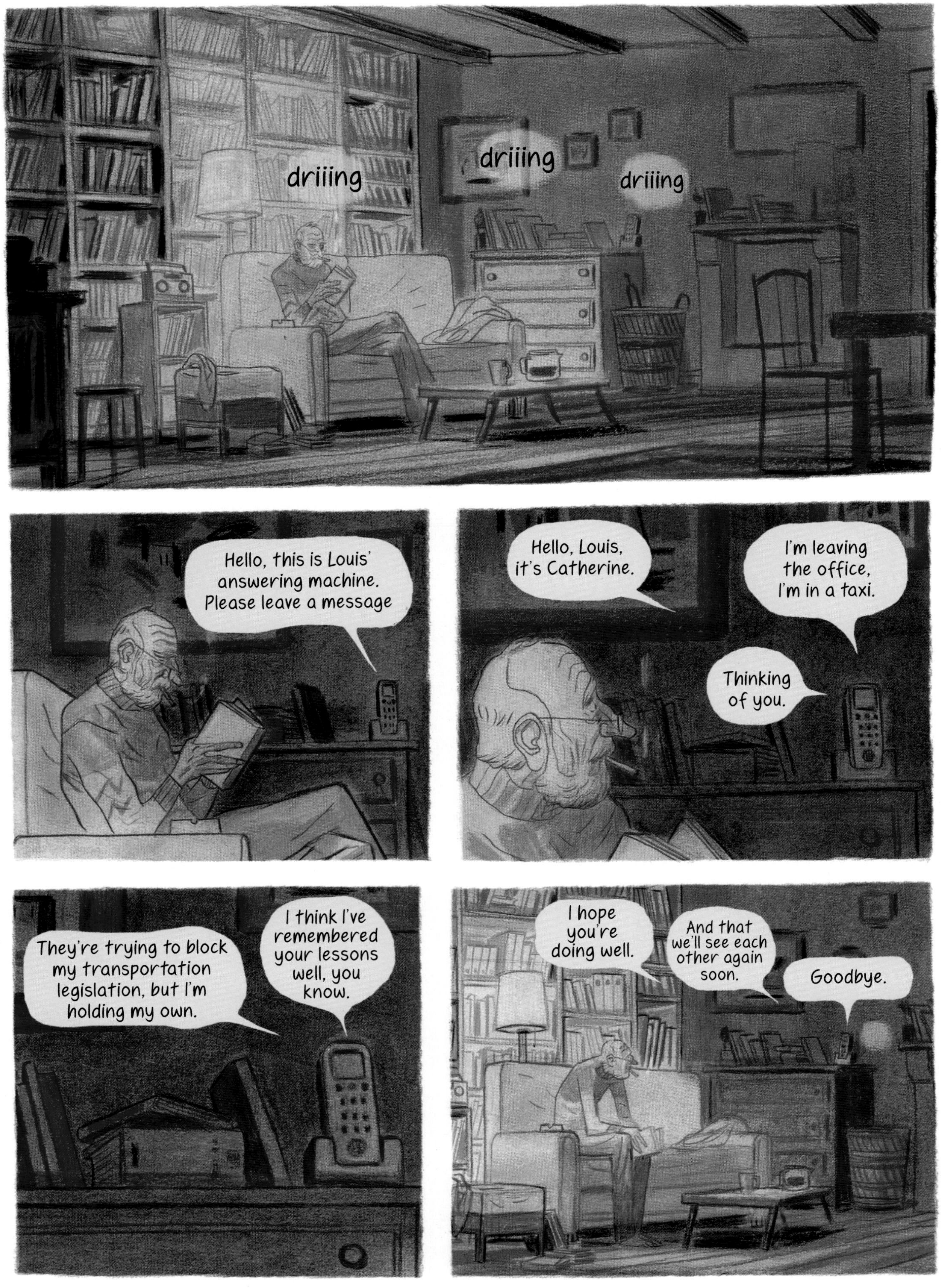
driiing
driiing
driiing
Hello, this is Louis' answering machine. Please leave a message
Hello, Louis, it's Catherine.
I'm leaving the office, I'm in a taxi.
Thinking of you.
They're trying to block my transportation legislation, but I'm holding my own.
I think I've remembered your lessons well, you know.
I hope you're doing well.
And that we'll see each other again soon.
Goodbye.

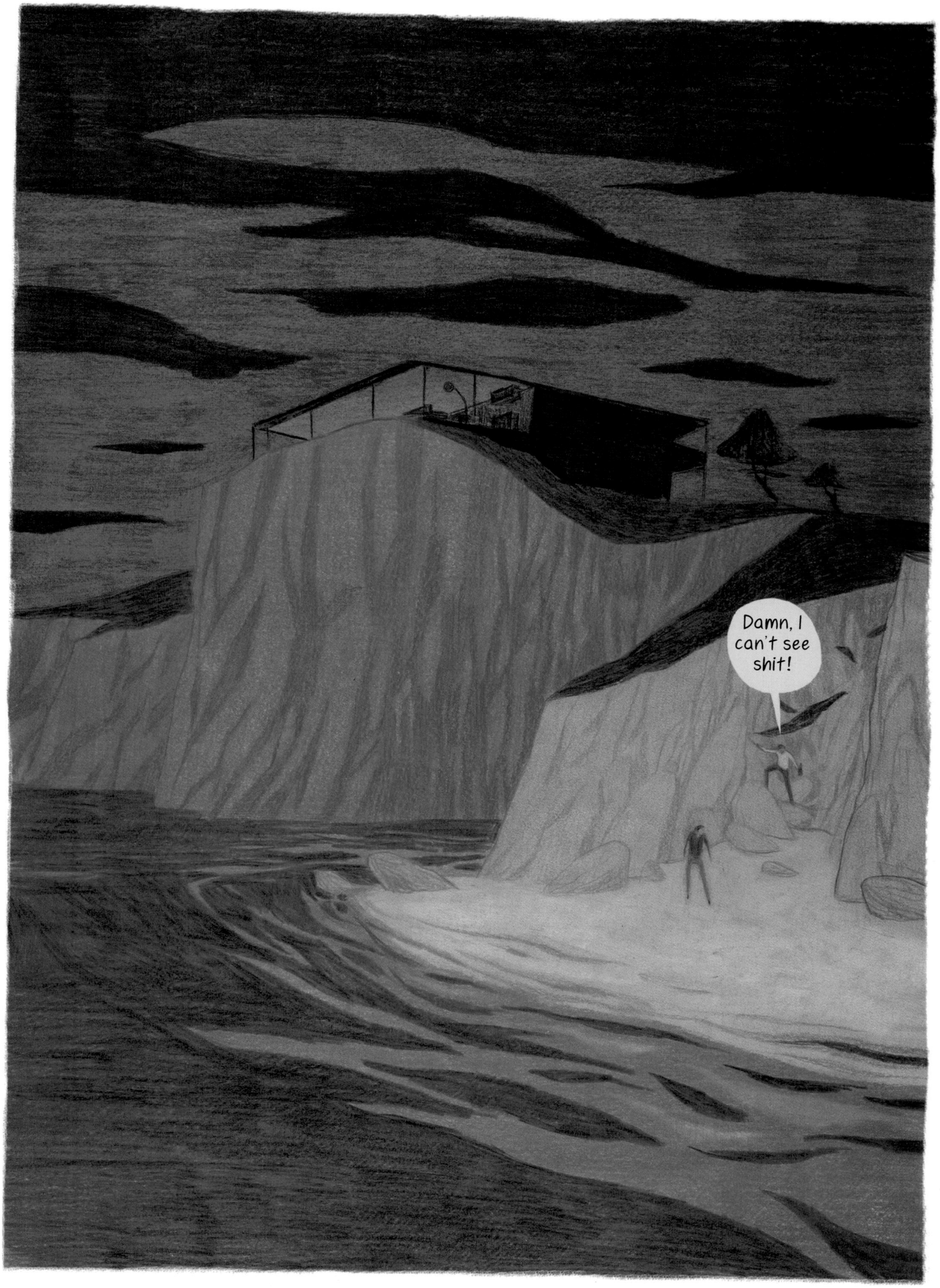
Damn, I can't see shit!

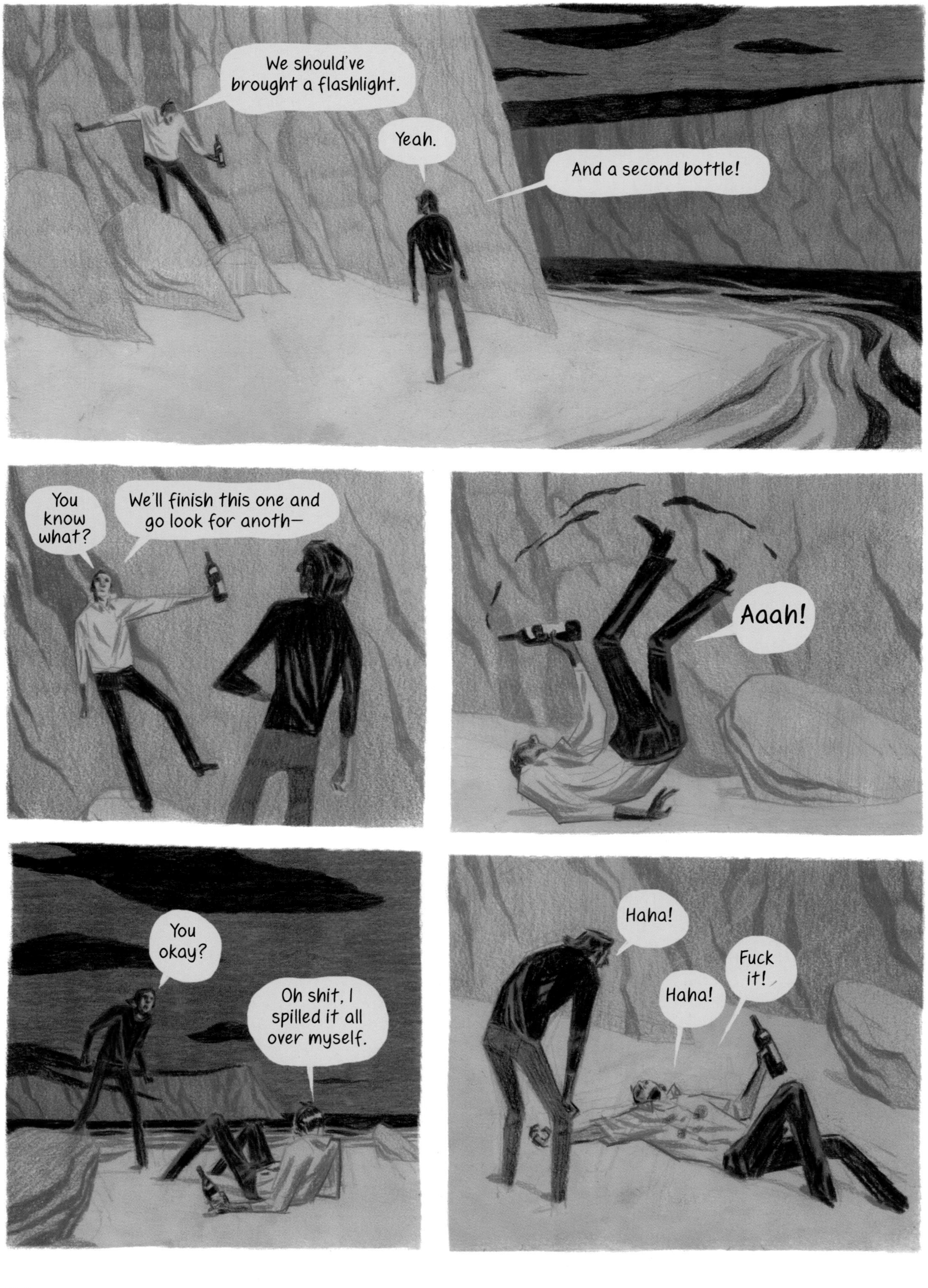
We should've brought a flashlight.
Yeah.
And a second bottle!
You know what?
We'll finish this one and go look for anoth—
Aaah!
You okay?
Oh shit, I spilled it all over myself.
Haha!
Haha!
Fuck it!

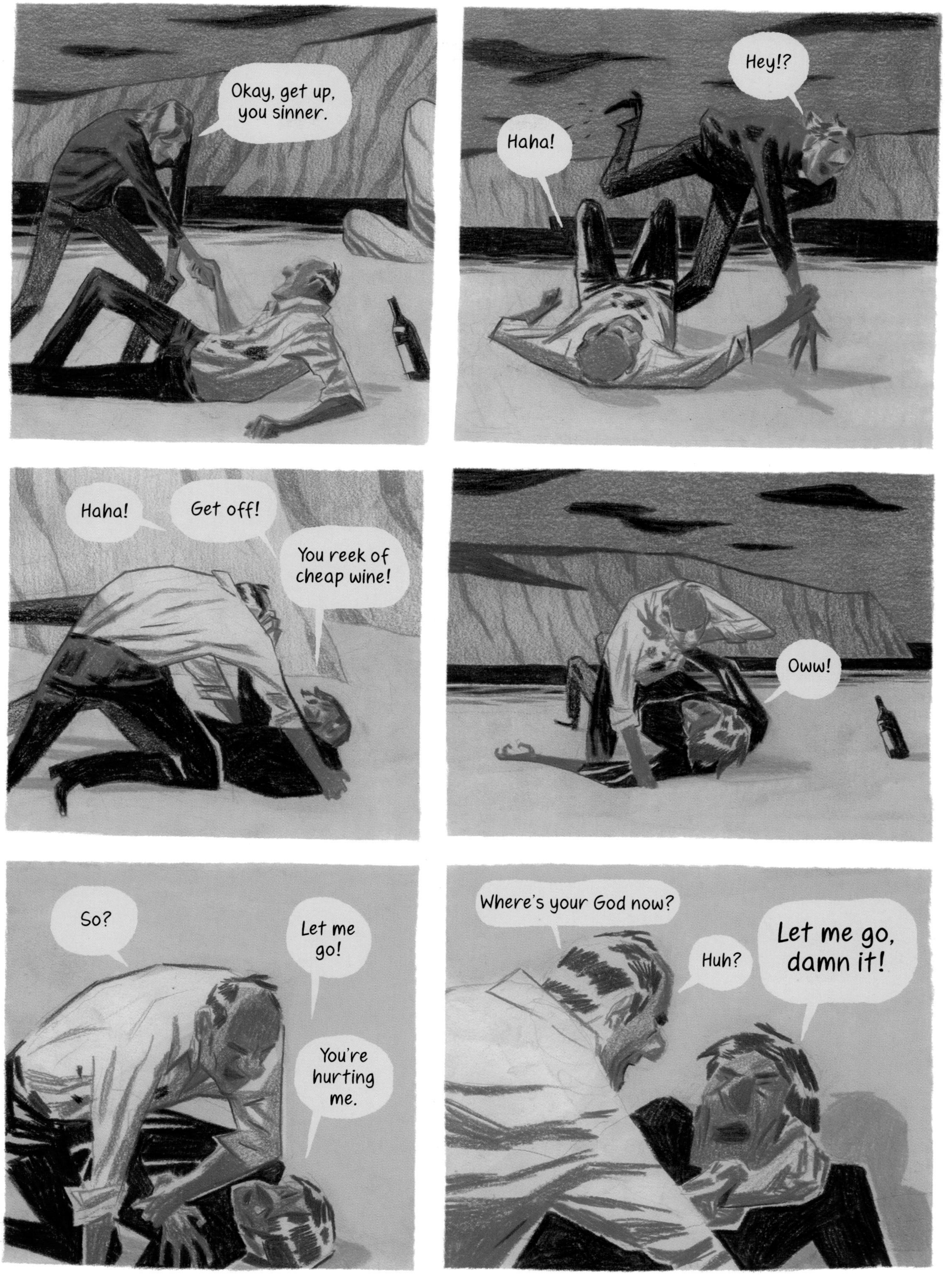
Okay, get up, you sinner.
Hey!?
Haha!
Haha!
Get off!
You reek of cheap wine!
Oww!
So?
Let me go!
You're hurting me.
Where's your God now?
Huh?
Let me go, damn it!

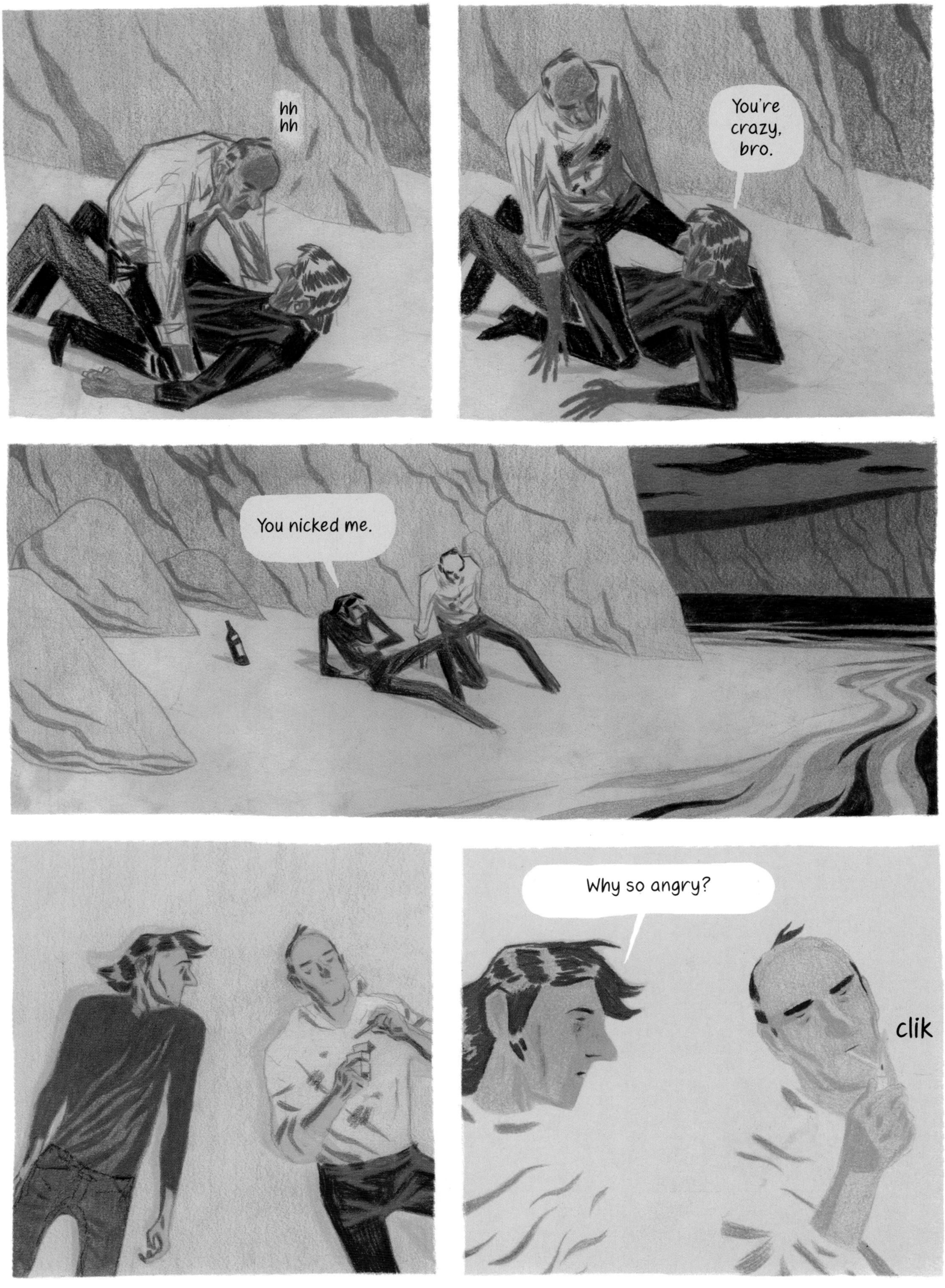
hh
hh
You're crazy, bro.
You nicked me.
Why so angry?
clik

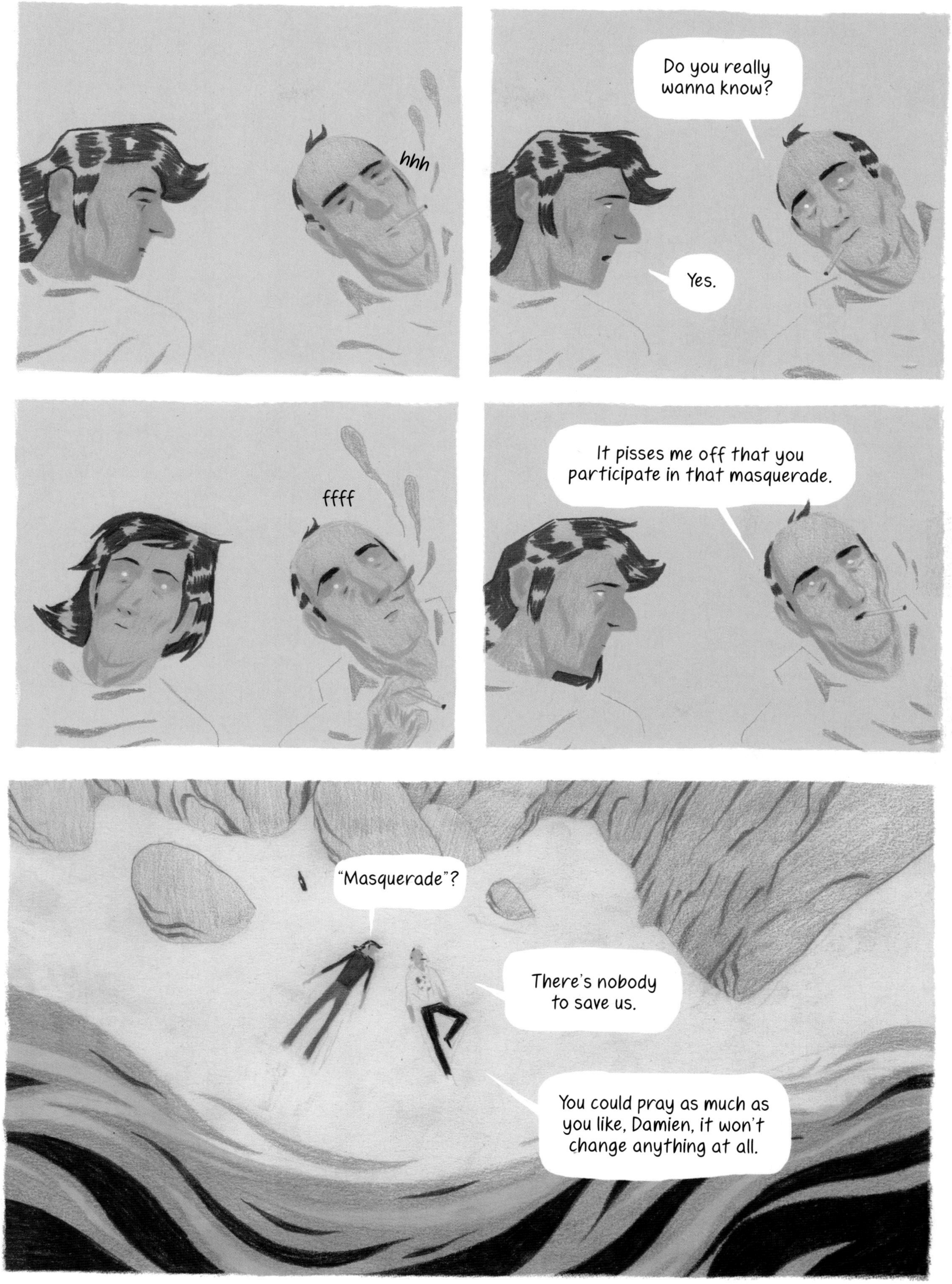
hhh
Do you really wanna know?
Yes.
ffff
It pisses me off that you participate in that masquerade.
"Masquerade"?
There's nobody to save us.
You could pray as much as you like, Damien, it won't change anything at all.

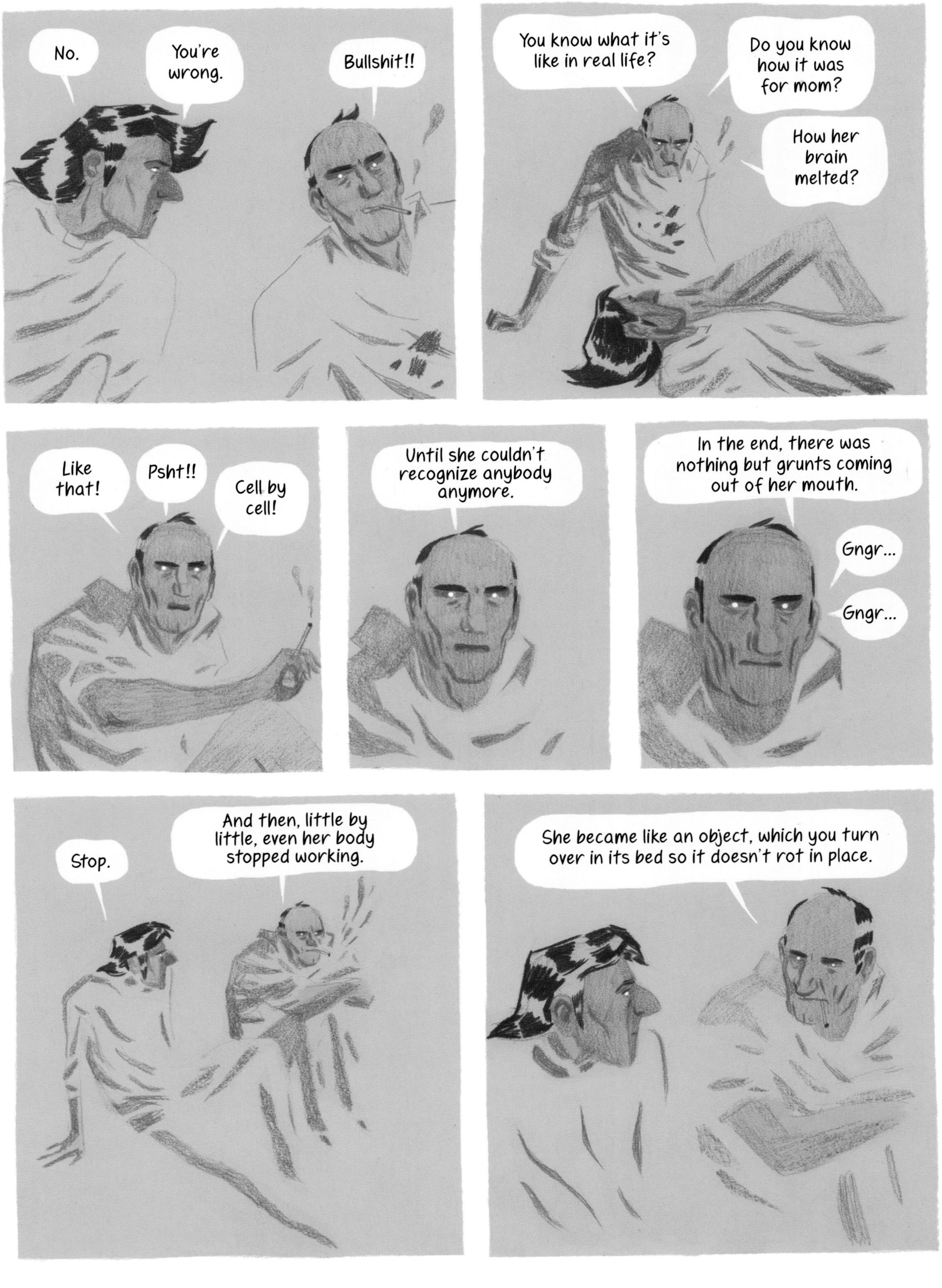
No.
You're wrong.
Bullshit!!
You know what it's like in real life?
Do you know how it was for mom?
How her brain melted?
Like that!
Psht!!
Cell by cell!
Until she couldn't recognize anybody anymore.
In the end, there was nothing but grunts coming out of her mouth.
Gngr...
Gngr...
Stop.
And then, little by little, even her body stopped working.
She became like an object, which you turn over in its bed so it doesn't rot in place.

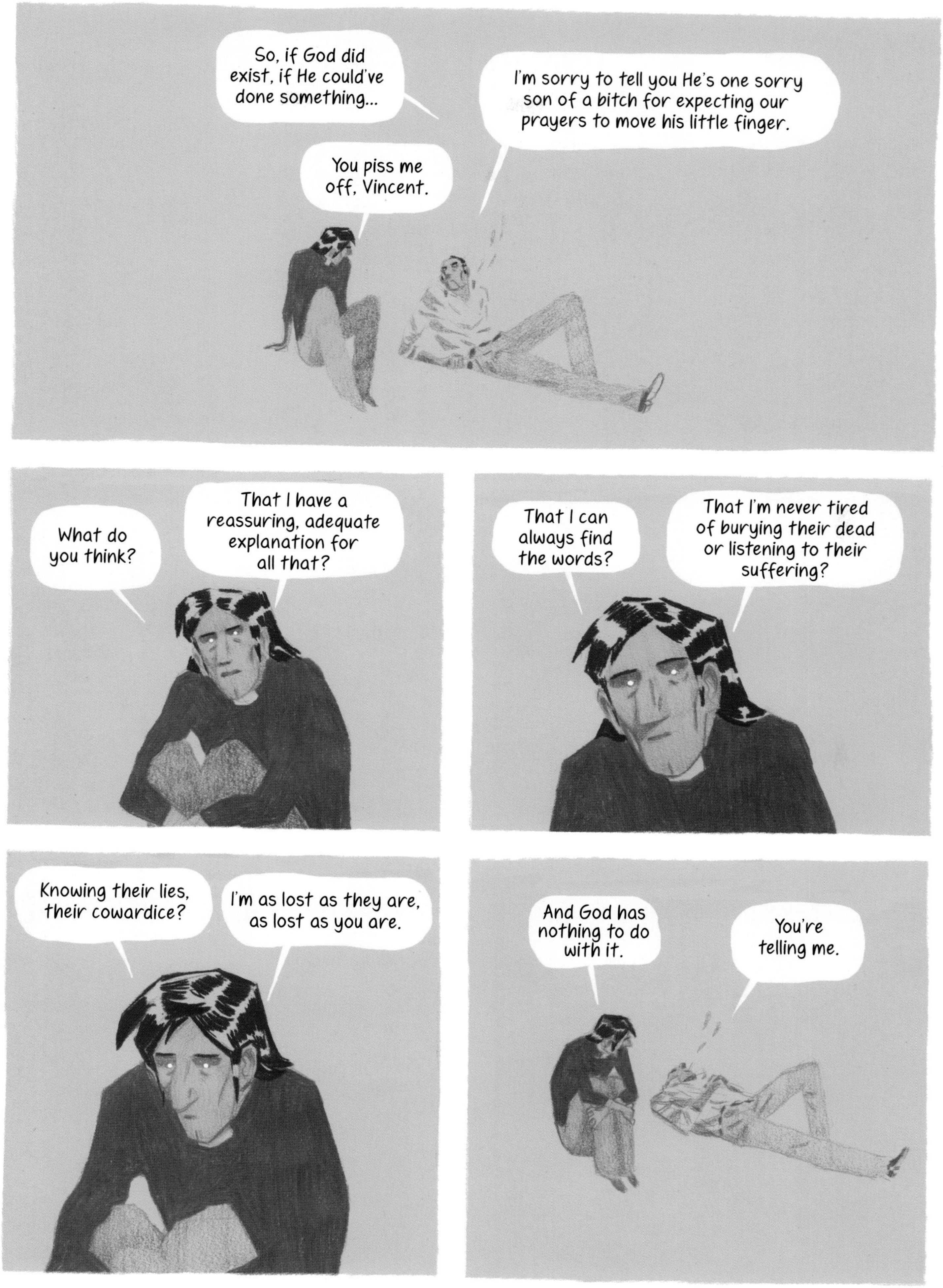
So, if God did exist, if He could've done something...
I'm sorry to tell you He's one sorry son of a bitch for expecting our prayers to move his little finger.
You piss me off, Vincent.
What do you think?
That I have a reassuring, adequate explanation for all that?
That I can always find the words?
That I'm never tired of burying their dead or listening to their suffering?
Knowing their lies, their cowardice?
I'm as lost as they are, as lost as you are.
And God has nothing to do with it.
You're telling me.

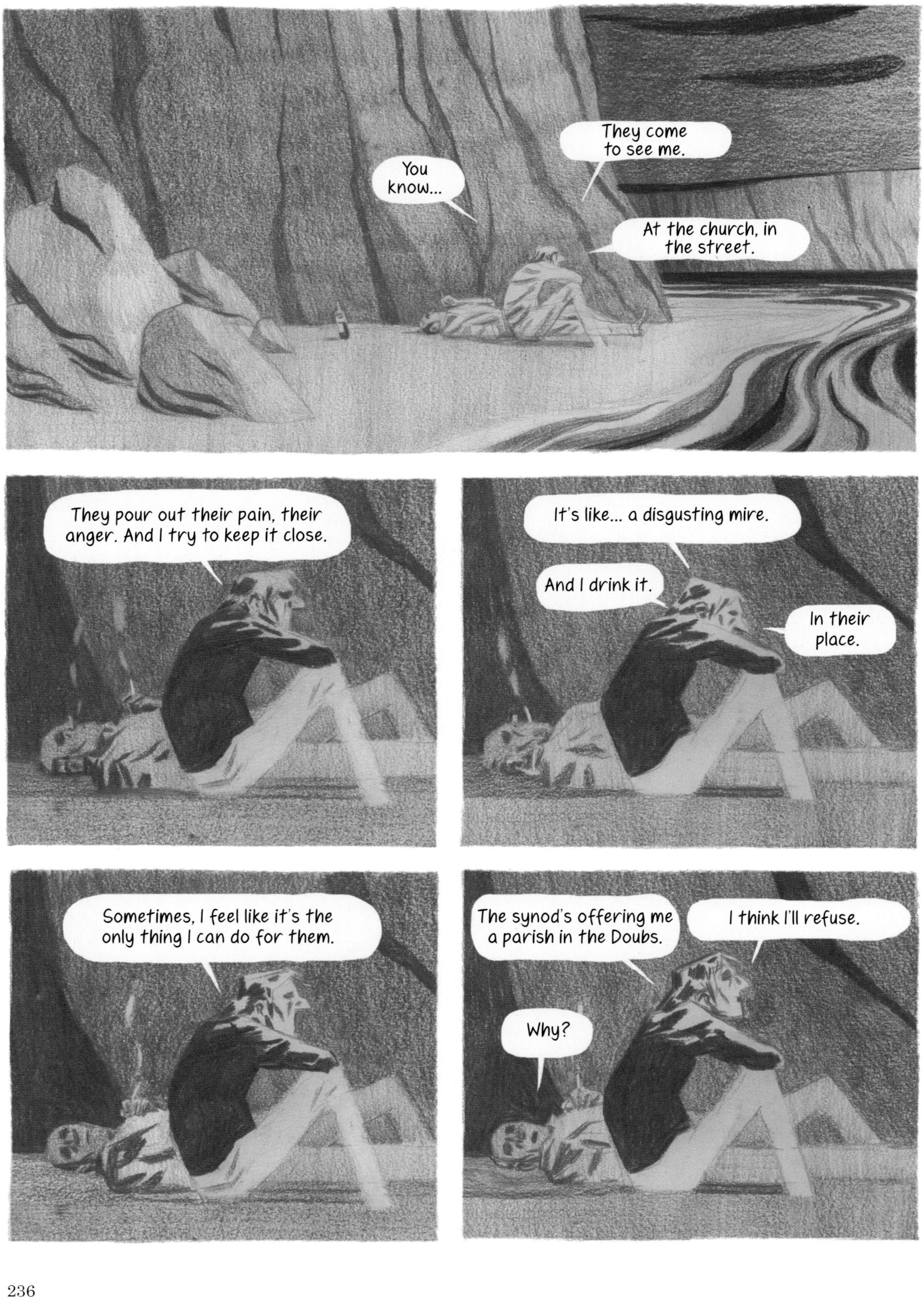

You know...
They come to see me.
At the church, in the street.
They pour out their pain, their anger. And I try to keep it close.
It's like... a disgusting mire.
And I drink it.
In their place.
Sometimes, I feel like it's the only thing I can do for them.
The synod's offering me a parish in the Doubs.
I think I'll refuse.
Why?

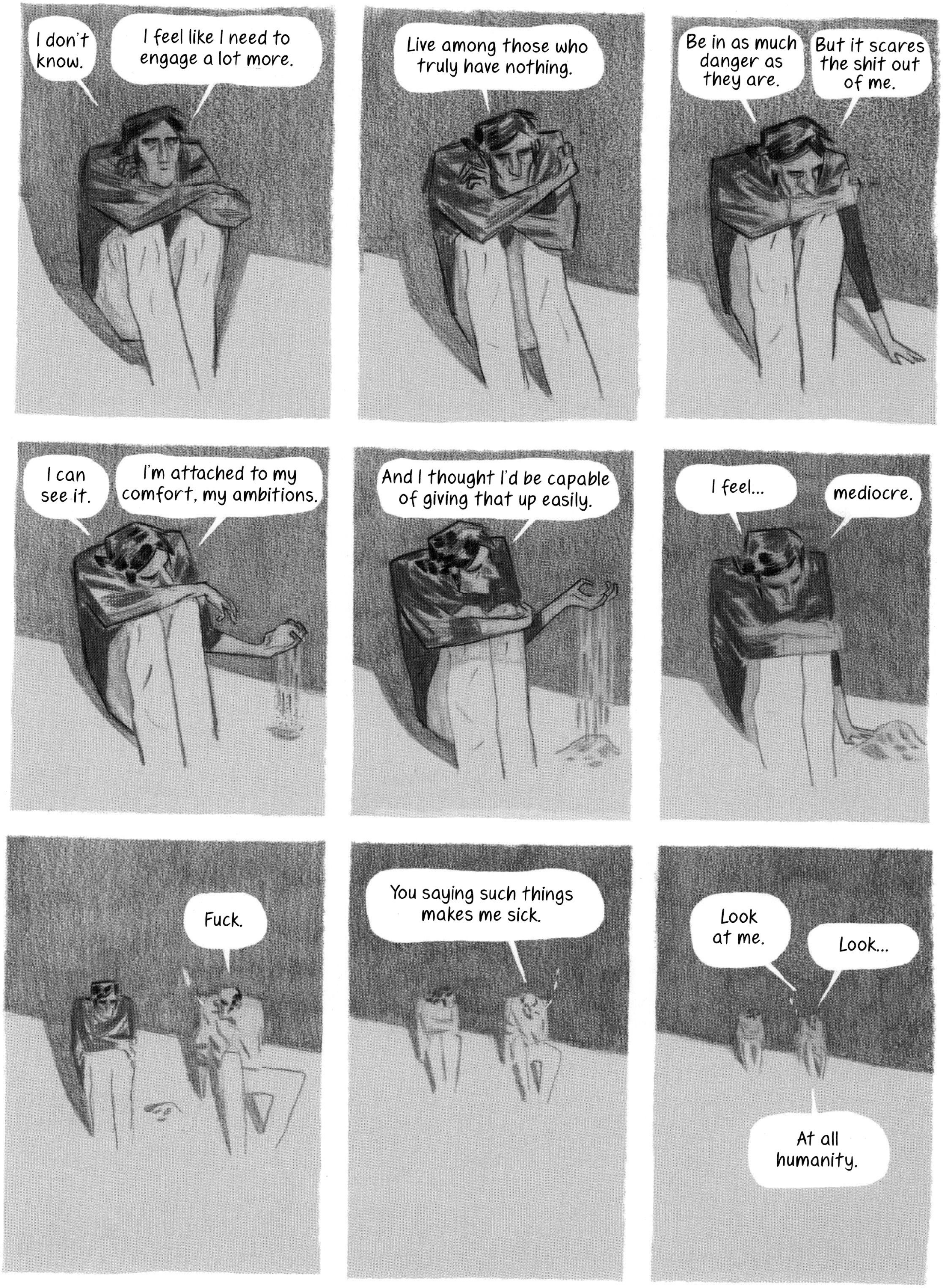
I don't know.
I feel like I need to engage a lot more.
Live among those who truly have nothing.
Be in as much danger as they are.
But it scares the shit out of me.
I can see it.
I'm attached to my comfort, my ambitions.
And I thought I'd be capable of giving that up easily.
I feel...
mediocre.
Fuck.
You saying such things makes me sick.
Look at me.
Look...
At all humanity.

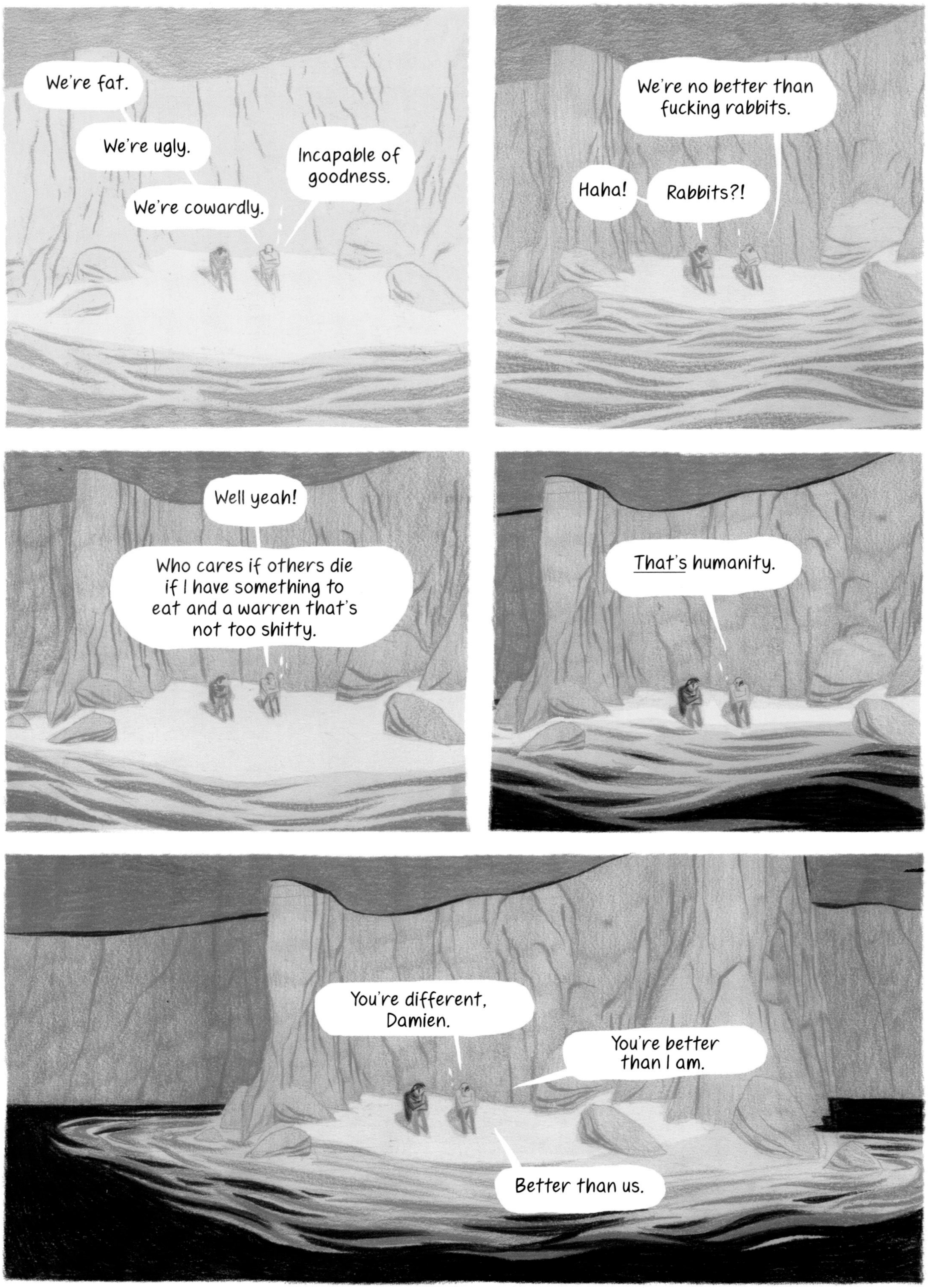
We're fat.
We're ugly.
We're cowardly.
Incapable of goodness.
We're no better than fucking rabbits.
Haha!
Rabbits?!
Well yeah!
Who cares if others die if I have something to eat and a warren that's not too shitty.
That's humanity.
You're different, Damien.
You're better than I am.
Better than us.

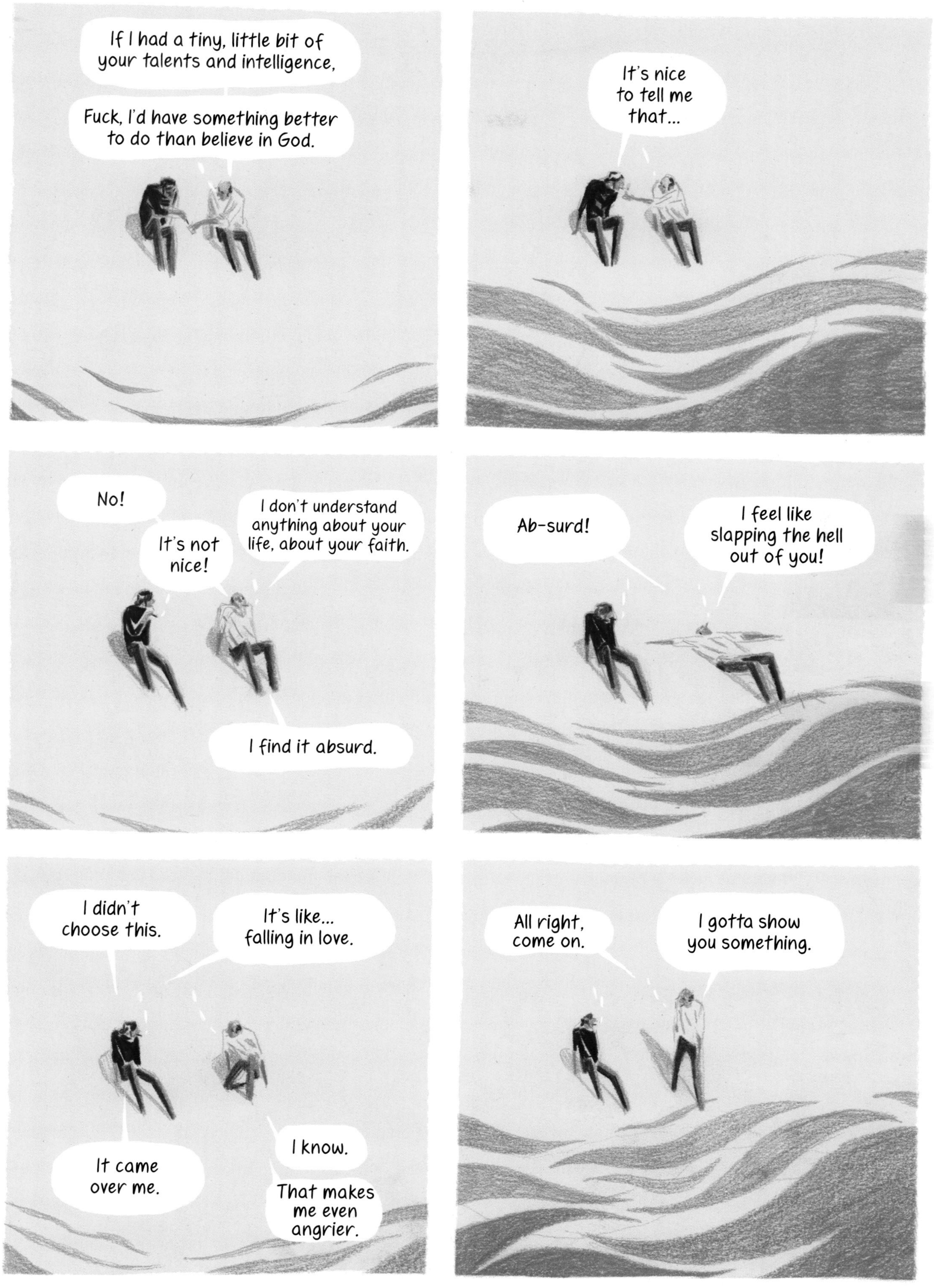
If I had a tiny, little bit of your talents and intelligence,
Fuck, I'd have something better to do than believe in God.
It's nice to tell me that...
No!
It's not nice!
I don't understand anything about your life, about your faith.
I find it absurd.
Ab-surd!
I feel like slapping the hell out of you!
I didn't choose this.
It's like... falling in love.
It came over me.
I know.
That makes me even angrier.
All right, come on.
I gotta show you something.

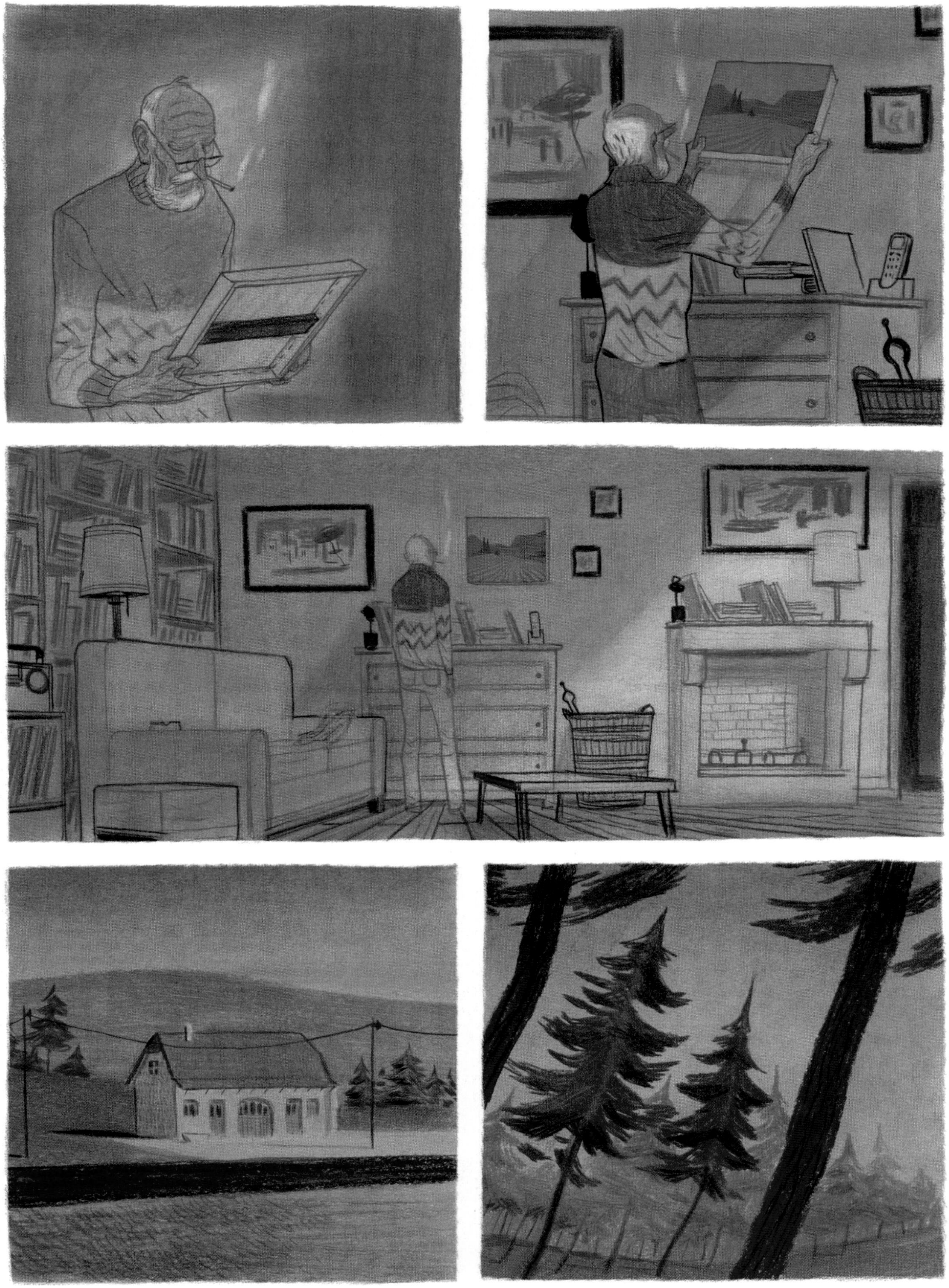

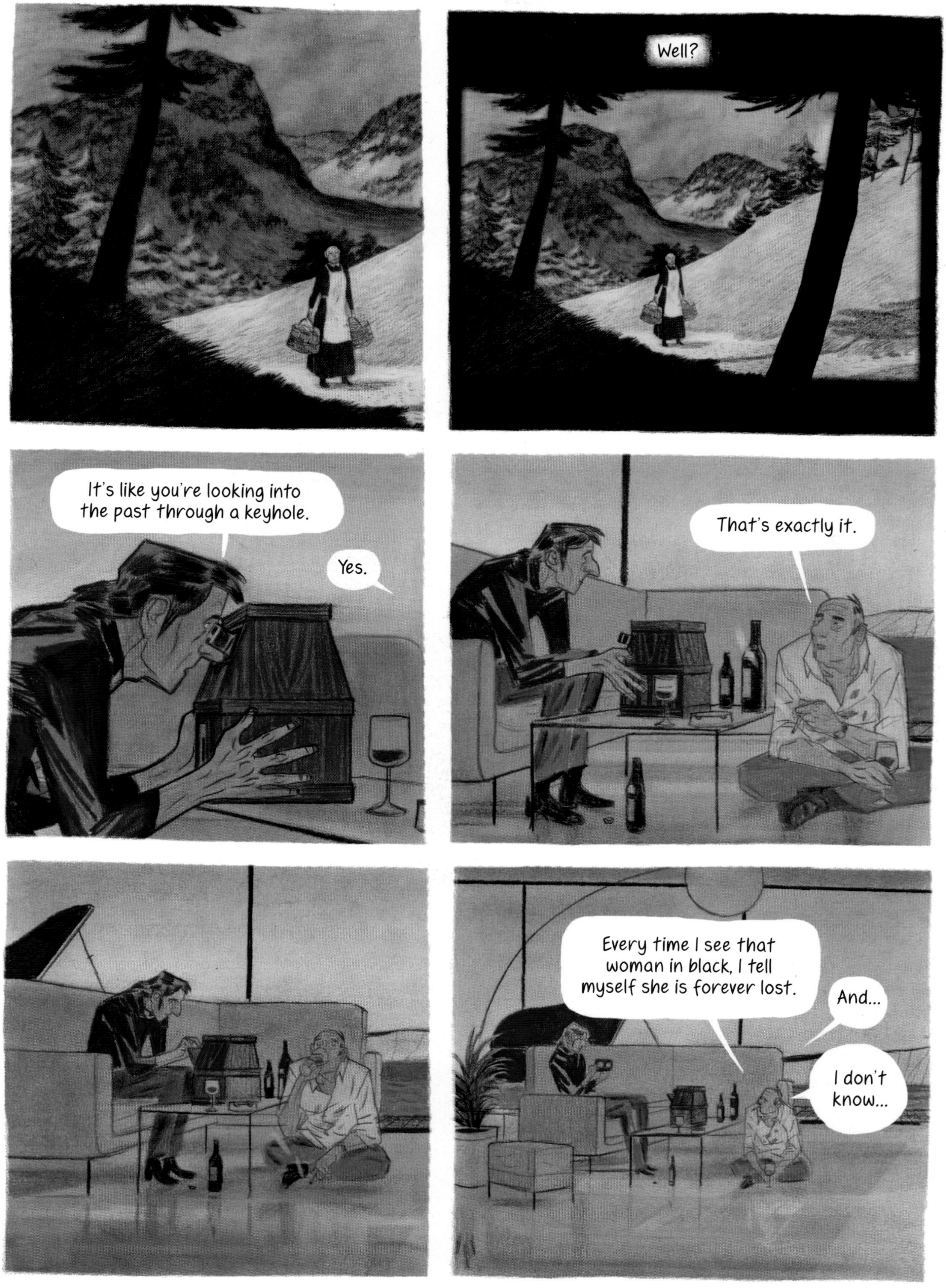
Well?
It's like you're looking into the past through a keyhole.
Yes.
That's exactly it.
Every time I see that woman in black, I tell myself she is forever lost.
And...
I don't know...

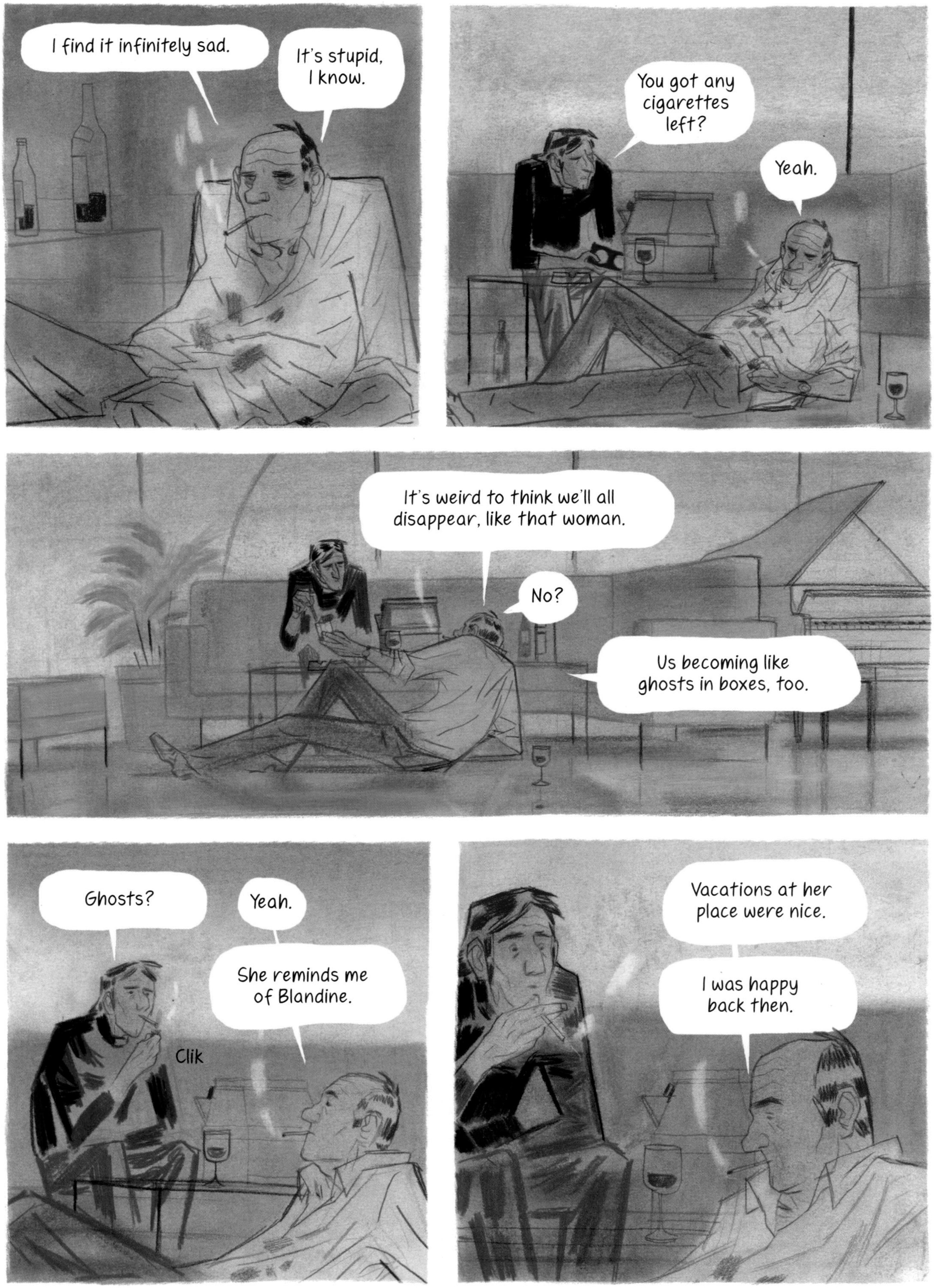
I find it infinitely sad.
It's stupid, I know.
You got any cigarettes left?
Yeah.
It's weird to think we'll all disappear, like that woman.
No?
Us becoming like ghosts in boxes, too.
Ghosts?
Yeah.
She reminds me of Blandine.
Clik
Vacations at her place were nice.
I was happy back then.

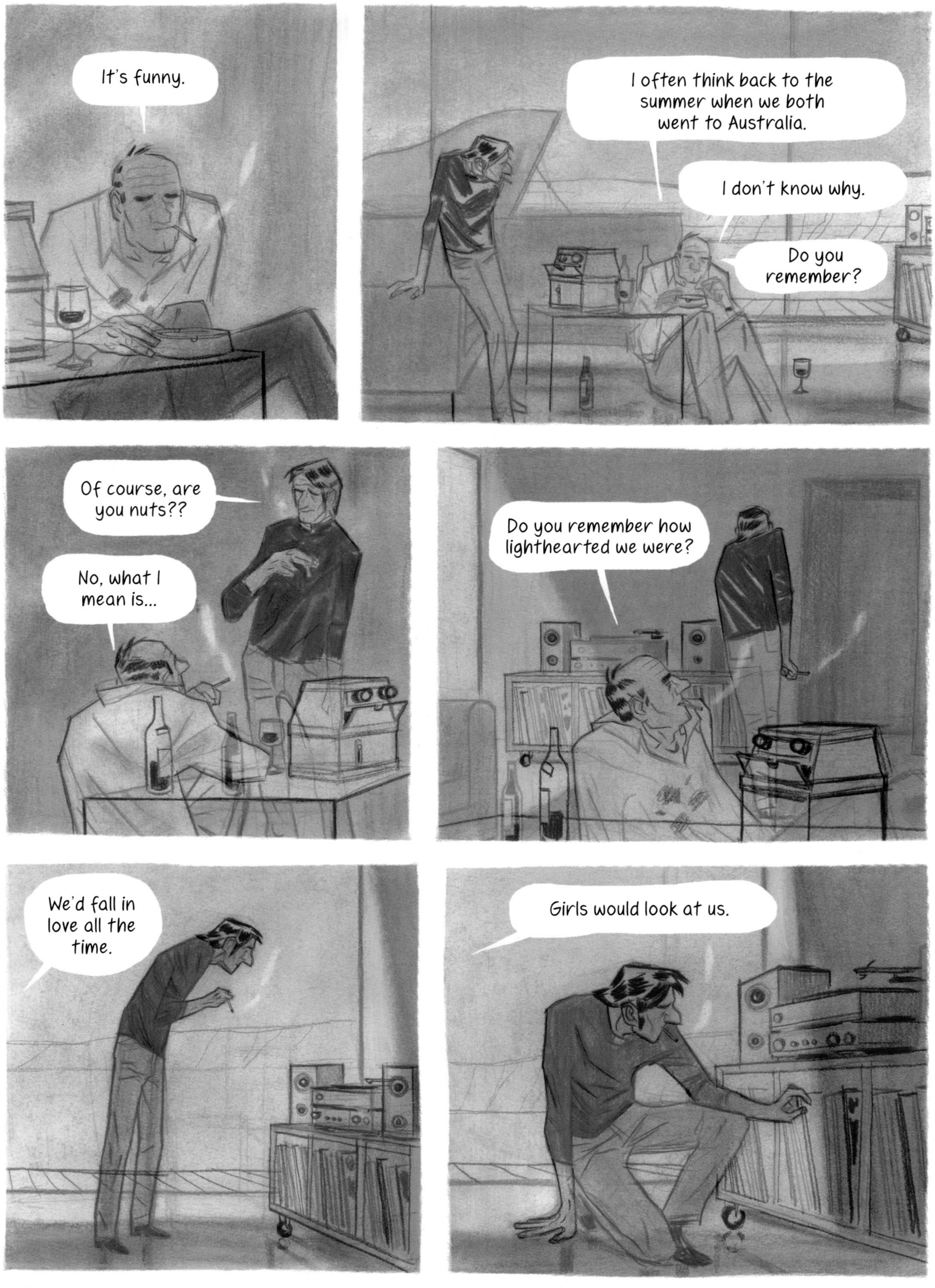
It's funny.
I often think back to the summer when we both went to Australia.
I don't know why.
Do you remember?
Of course, are you nuts??
No, what I mean is...
Do you remember how lighthearted we were?
We'd fall in love all the time.
Girls would look at us.

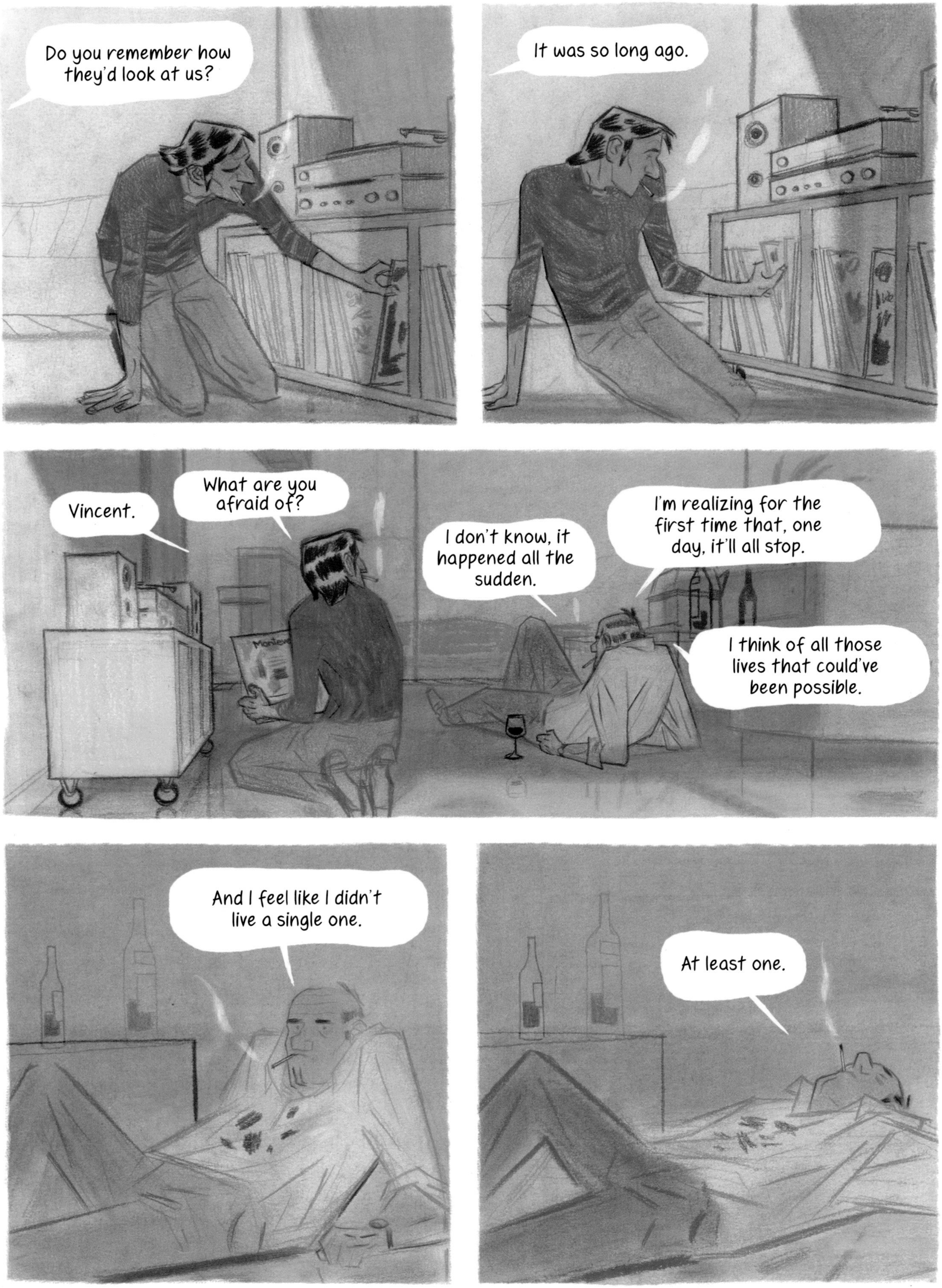
Do you remember how they'd look at us?
It was so long ago.
Vincent.
What are you afraid of?
I don't know, it happened all the sudden.
I'm realizing for the first time that, one day, it'll all stop.
I think of all those lives that could've been possible.
And I feel like I didn't live a single one.
At least one.

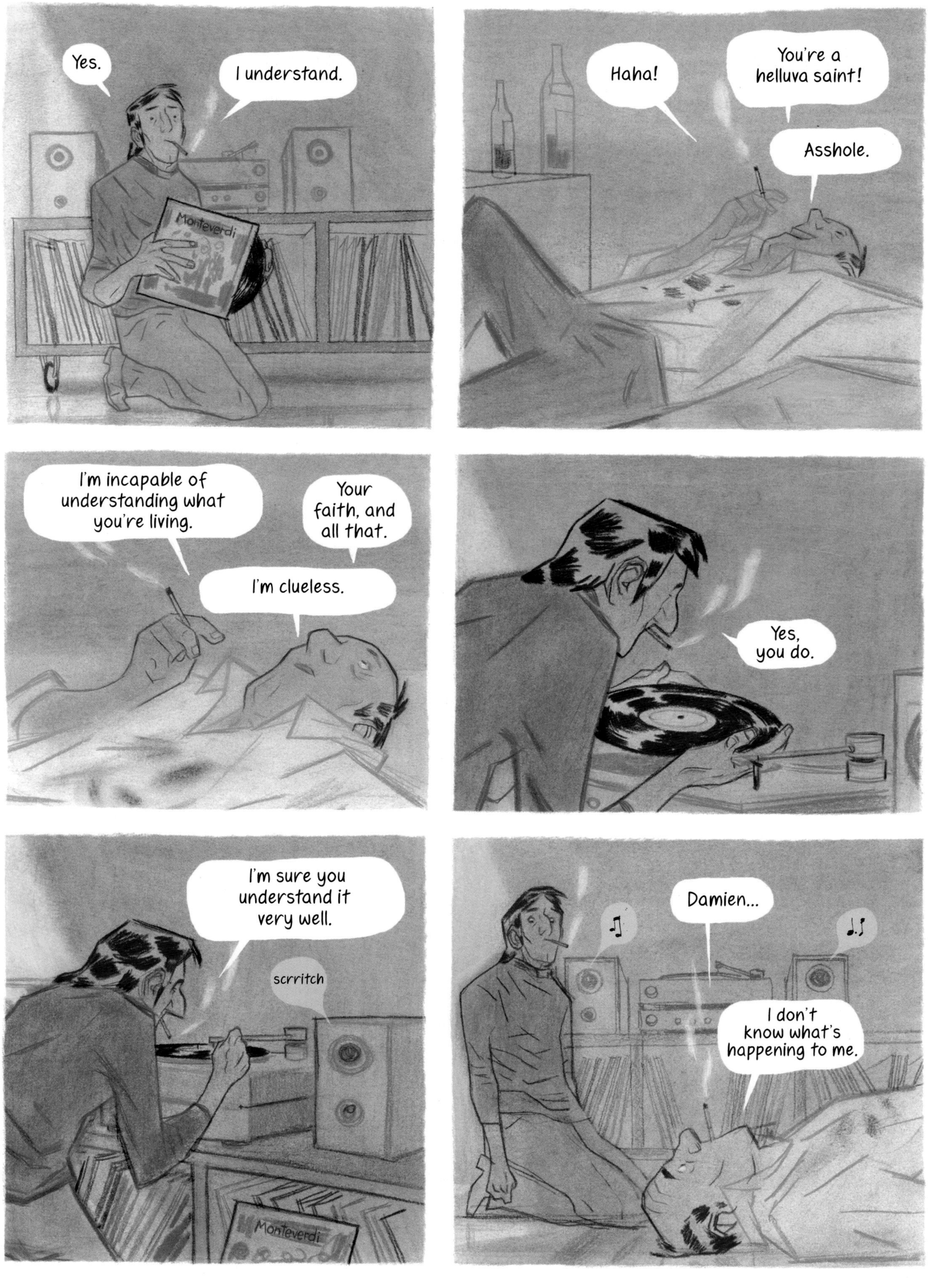
Yes.
I understand.
Monteverdi
Haha!
You're a helluva saint!
Asshole.
I'm incapable of understanding what you're living.
Your faith, and all that.
I'm clueless.
Yes, you do.
I'm sure you understand it very well.
scrritch
Monteverdi
Damien...
I don't know what's happening to me.

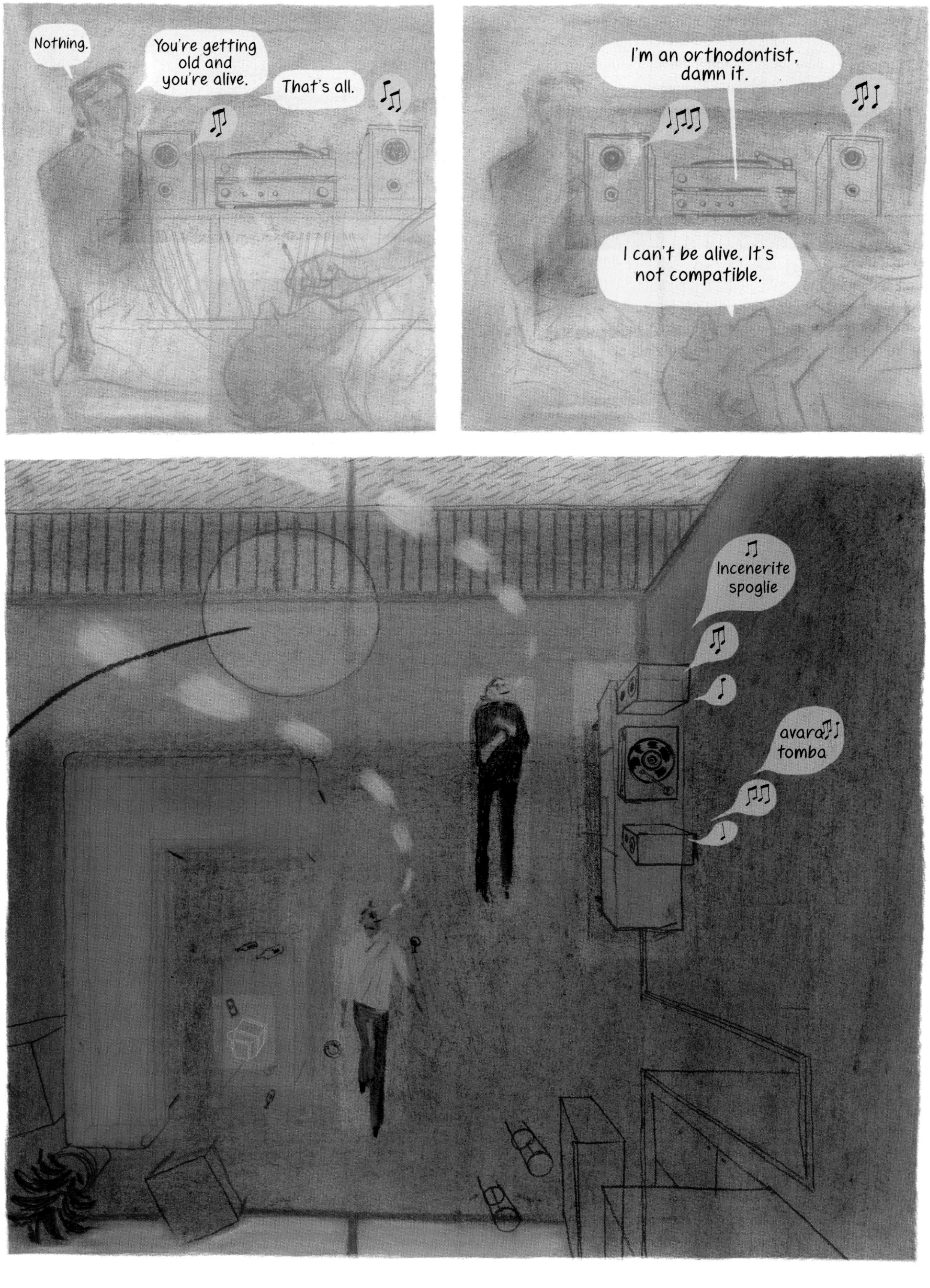
Nothing.
You're getting old and you're alive.
That's all.
I'm an orthodontist, damn it.
I can't be alive. It's not compatible.
Incenerite spoglie
avara tomba

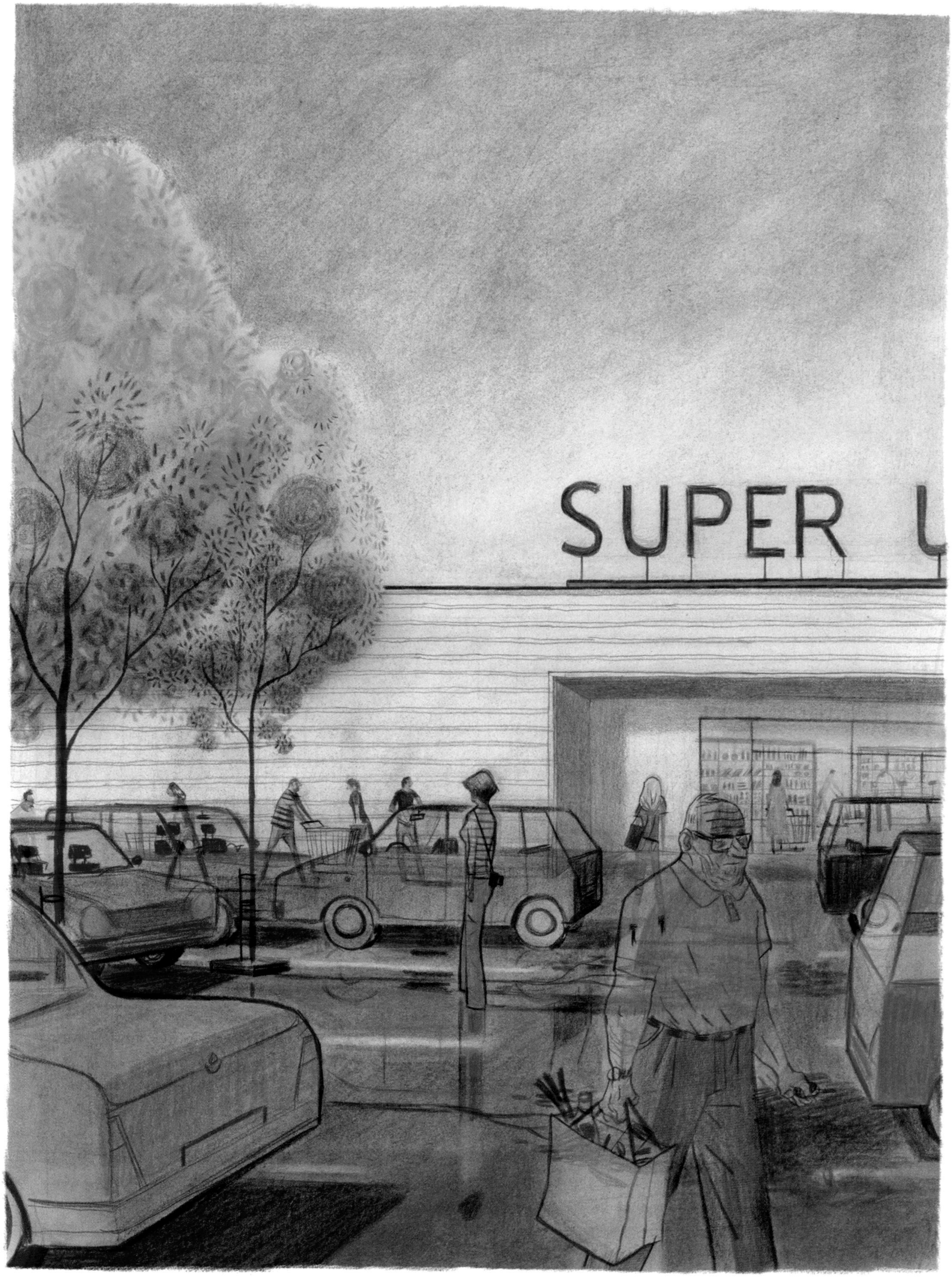
SUPER U

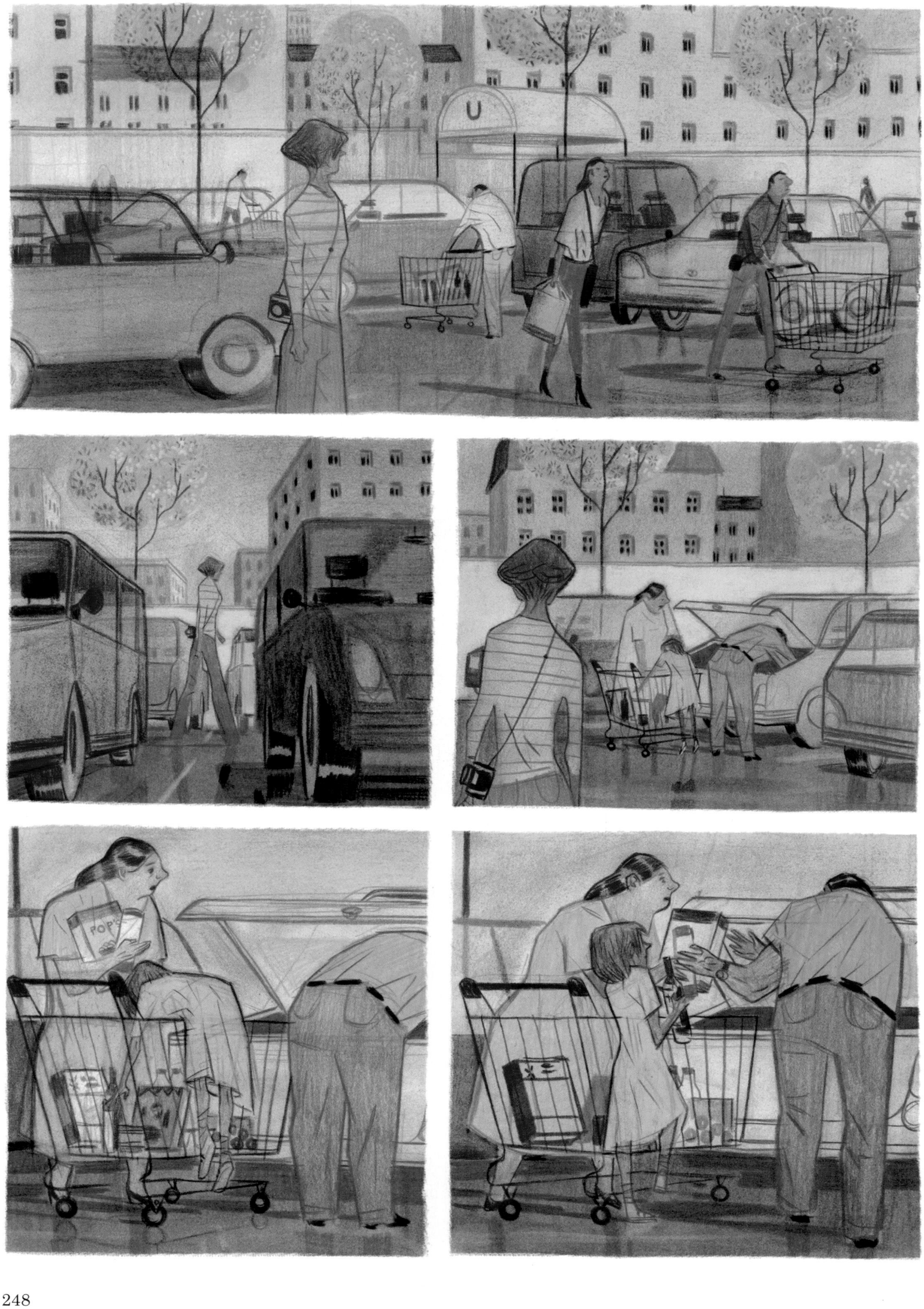
U

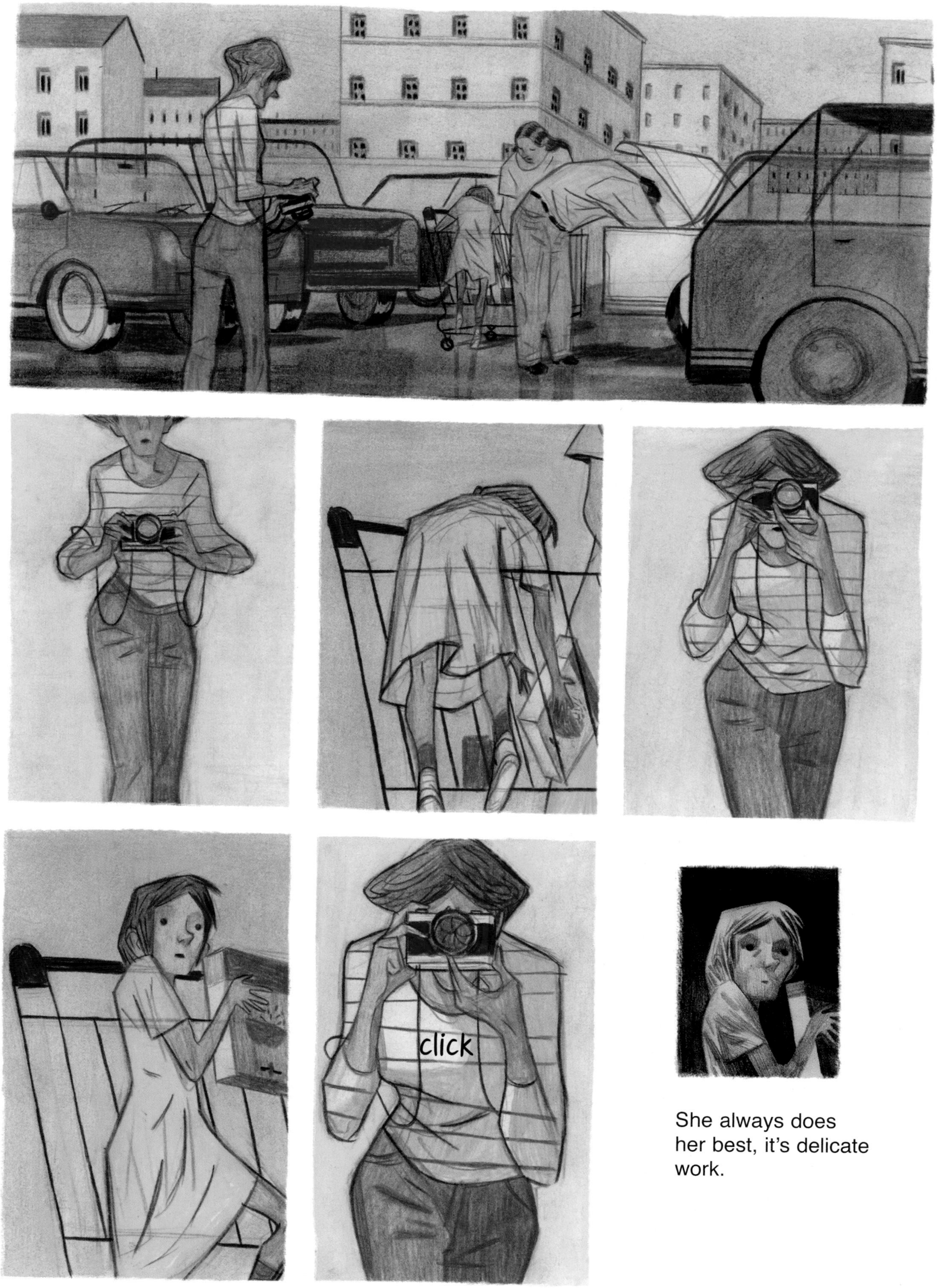
click
She always does her best, it's delicate work.

She must display their purchases in the proper order, so her father can correctly order them in the car's trunk.

Each object must find its right place.

You don't put the cheeses under the canned goods.

That's just common sense.

The glass bottles must be wedged in behind the rolls of paper towels. The dairy products set in last, in a separate bag, beside the frozen foods. It all takes a little time, but it's necessary.

They always go to the supermarket on Saturday afternoon, around 1:30pm. That lets them do the housework thoroughly then have an early lunch without having to hurry. After the meal, she wipes off the dishes like every Saturday at noon. She must begin with the glasses, with the special dish towel, then she won't leave pieces of fluff on the sides.
If it's not too late, she has time to go up to her room, while they have a coffee. Then, she quietly closes the door behind her and lies on her belly on the floor to read a few pages, enveloped in the warmth of the sunlight reflected by the wooden floor.

Sometimes, while they're waiting patiently at the register, she can't manage to suppress her need to bounce from one foot to the other. So she contains her movements, with all her might, to make them as unobtrusive as possible. She knows just how exasperating it can be to have a child who can't keep still. They're tired. Everyone's tired of shopping on Saturday afternoons after a week of work. Nobody enjoys it. But it has to be done.

Her father makes sure one last time that everything's in order and proceeds to a few, last, little adjustments.
One day, a carton of fruit juice had slid into the trunk. They'd found it behind the bottles of water.
She sits on the rear seat, the car starts up.
On the way home, like every Saturday afternoon, she feels those invisible, freezing tingles. She doesn't know what to do about them.

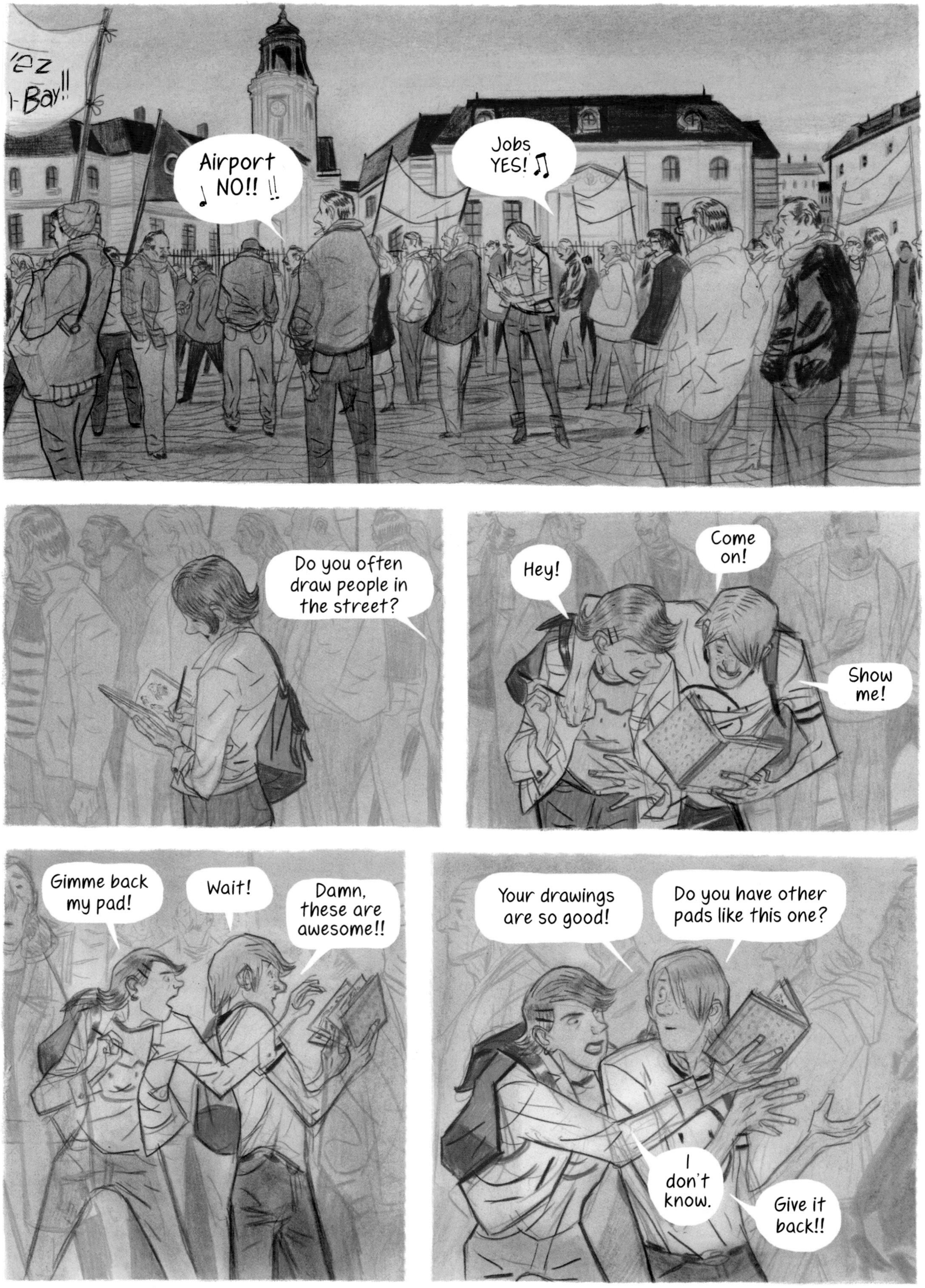
Airport NO!!
Jobs YES!
Do you often draw people in the street?
Hey!
Come on!
Show me!
Gimme back my pad!
Wait!
Damn, these are awesome!!
Your drawings are so good!
Do you have other pads like this one?
I don't know.
Give it back!!

You don't know?
You're a pain. I don't know.
I don't count 'em every month for kicks.
You fill several pads like that every month?
Yes, three or four.
I don't count.
I have a buddy who's taking evening classes at the Art School.
So what?
It's on Thursday, I think.
You should go.

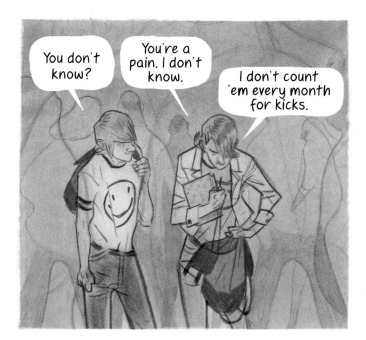

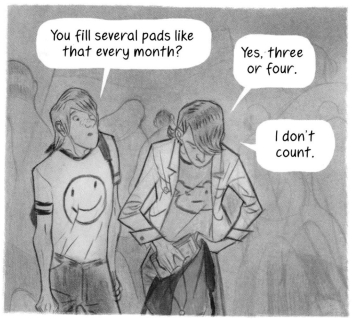

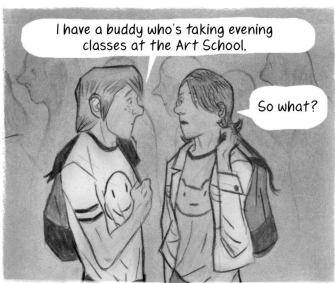

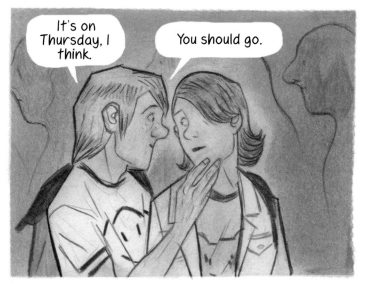

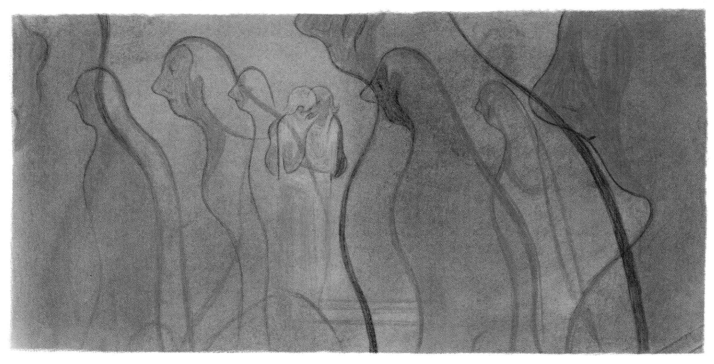

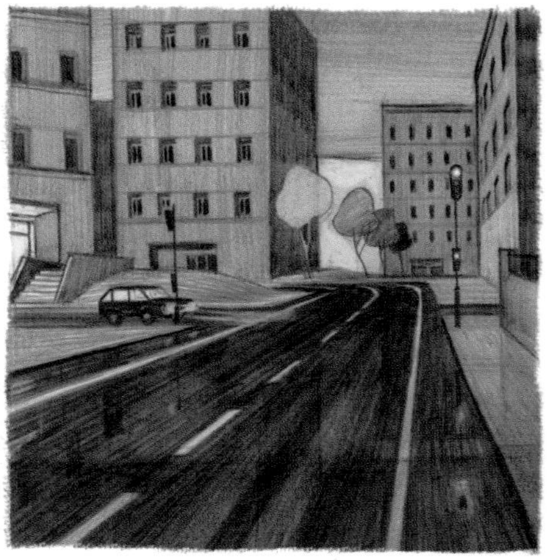

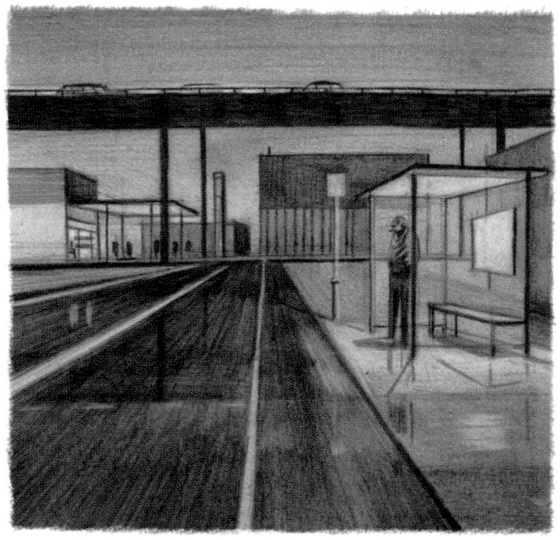

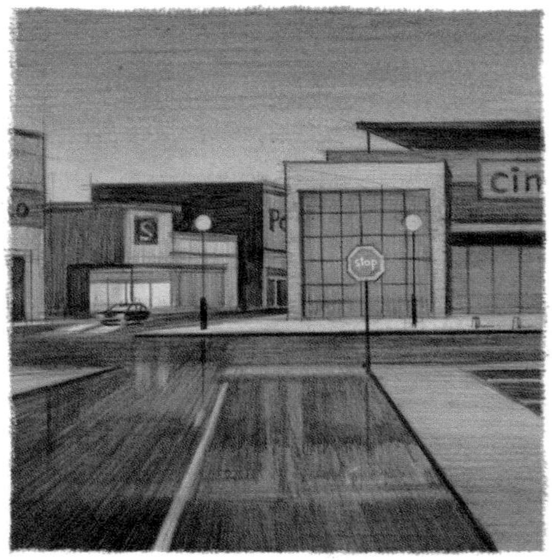
stop

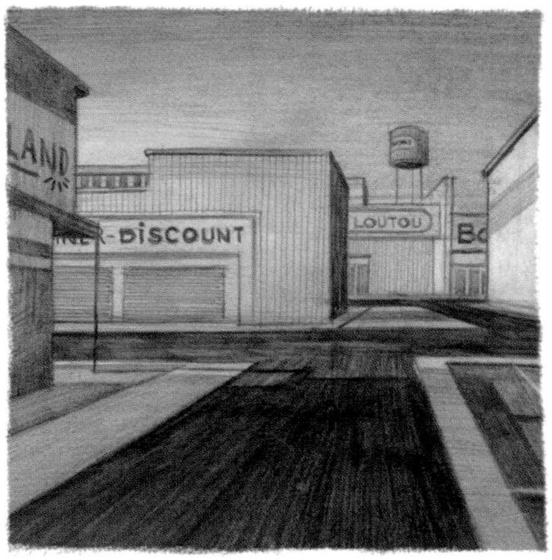
DISCOUNT
LOUTOU

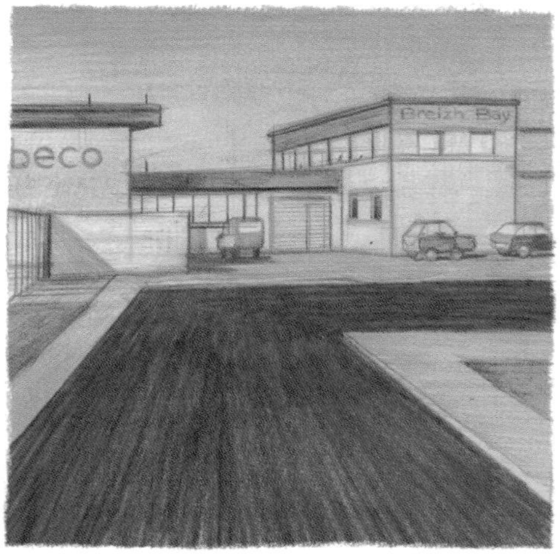
beco
Breizh Bay

I'd been speechless, paralyzed.

It'd been stupid to think I was completely safe.

Olivier had had that cheerful tone of enthusiastic, little boys. I imagined him bouncing around with excitement on the other end of the line. He was going to reassemble the entire group to join me in two weeks. We'd all have an awesome weekend together, just like old times, and we'd have cook-outs, picnics on the beach, and do some boating. The list of festivities was endless. I muttered two or three empty words, yes, really, what a marvelous idea, then hung up as quickly as possible to collapse onto the couch with a muted, familiar anguish in the depths of my guts, one long since forgotten.

The light from the bike's headlamp is dancing on the tarmac. The world seems reduced to this trembling ring of light. The dynamo's regular crackle reveals the silence surrounding me and gives it even more value.

I was unable to escape that weekend of the veterans of Rennes' School of Law. It was the price to pay for my lodging. From their arrival Friday evening till their departure for Paris on Sunday morning, the feeling of being caught in a trap pretty much never left me. But despite it all, I realized something. There was pride in that fear, the fear of being treated with that poisonous tenderness reserved for those who, as foreseen, have failed, because they reassure us. It did me good to figure out that, in reality, they no longer expected anything of me.

It's still very early.
I'm pedaling mechanically, a bit sleepily, the bitter taste of coffee in my mouth. My body will awaken soon, on the road. I feel it gradually opening up.

For Saturday night, they'd decided to organize a big party like the old days, and I'd drunk a lot, while keeping a little apart. Fred wasn't there anymore. We didn't go outside to throw up in the yard.

I was watching them, all crammed together in the living room, all as drunk as me. I'd have preferred for any of them to have died instead of him. It was really disgusting to think such a thing. I'd stumbled off to take a long bike ride, just to catch my breath a little. When I returned, everyone in the house was dancing. Olivier was sitting outside, alone, with a funny stare into space. I'd never seen him like that, unbalanced, a bit out of sorts. For the first time, he seemed neither worse nor better than me. I'd reflexively taken a picture of him. At the sound of the shutter, he'd turned his face to look at me. Once again, he was wearing the armor of his self-assured smile. At the same instant, Sylvie had come out of the house, pretending to have been concerned about my absence. I'd gone back into the house, without answering. In a quarter of a second, everyone had resumed his or her place.

I'm perfectly awake now. By joining the highway, I'd soon cross paths with the first cars. I'm savoring these last minutes of solitude, the perfect curves of my bicycle on the sinuous, little road lined with fields of beets. The fresh smell of damp earth and lush grass transports me, despite myself, far away, near to Narbonne. I'm four or five years old, lying in a bed in a strange bedroom, my eyes wide open. I'm not allowed to get up before the adults. I wait, while looking at the cracks in the ceiling. Suddenly, I hear the house's windows opening one by one. The announcement of the new day's official beginning. I jump out of my bed, open my shutters in turn, and that green smell of morning washes over me.

It barely takes me twenty minutes to reach the train station and climb aboard the 5:48am commuter train. I wedge my old Peugeot bicycle into the luggage compartment, then I sit down in a corner, at the far end of the train car, in one of the last free seats. From there, I can see the other passengers snoozing in their seats. They look like little children pressing against one another. I'd like the train to arrive in Rennes without making any noise to let them sleep a little longer. They seem so tired.
I'd not been to the sleepy house of Saint-Vincent des Corbières for years. The last time was long before my grandmother's death.

I must have been ten. The old baker had just died. He was Belgian, but the residents of Saint-Vincent liked him even so. They came in great numbers to visit his house, on the eve of his estate auction. Furniture of little worth or charm. The banal interior of a bachelor's life, if he'd not had a hundred canvases hanging on his walls. Nobody had ever seen them. The baker had painted his whole life, in secret. Everyone passed silently from one room to another. We were simultaneously visiting the home and the heart of the deceased. My grandmother stopped in front of a small canvas. I remember a small stain of color amid the vines.
She said to me: "Did you see? That's the house." She looked terribly moved. I didn't really understand why.

I'd needed some money at the end of March. After first having to give up making any prints, for lack of money, I couldn't even manage to pay for developing my film anymore. The rolls were piling up in a shoe box. It was getting difficult to remember with any precision the images that corresponded to the dates scribbled on the plastic cases. Sometimes a few words hastily added helped me to remember a little: "Rain construction site," "Supermarket parking." I was barely spending anything, but even that was too much. I'd have to have proof of residency to get my welfare check. The prospect of having to ask Olivier and Sylvie to resolve that problem had made me give up doing so. I was alone, I didn't have to explain myself to anyone, but I couldn't make use of that freedom as I would've liked. I needed to find a little money to get by on. It was an unpleasant fact. I would have liked to have not had to pay that price. Not having to hang my head in temp agencies again. To say anything so they'll choose me, me and nobody else, to go do assembly line work on electrical boxes or clean miles of hallways in offices.
But that's what I did.

Something had kept me from selling the camera and chucking it all. I hadn't managed to admit, once and for all, that these photos were of no use at all. Out of pride perhaps, once again. Or even more simply, for lack of any other possible direction.

Once there, I cross the train station to exit onto Rue de Quineleu, near the detention center. Then it's easy. I just have to slip onto the deserted boulevards, go down to the park, head along the stone wall beneath the chestnut trees, then head back up after the stadium. I take the bike path to follow the four-lane road, then I turn right at the multiplex level to enter the urban development zone. A few, scarce cars pass me by. Like me, they're going into the western part, the one with studios, warehouses, and factories.

I'd been hired in March. Instantly, I'd rediscovered the harassing fatigue of the void, the surveillance of the supervisors, the absurd work. The little hook into the notch, stretch the spring, attach it, push hard to engage the press button, one hundred and fifty times an hour, at a minimum. The time I had free outside of my work hours barely allowed me to recuperate a little from the day gone by to be able to face the next day. At the end of my contract, I'd left the inertia and torpor of this job with a light heart and enough money to resume my photography. My "assignment" had barely lasted two months, during which I'd not dared to bring my camera. I regret it now. For Isabelle and her queenly look, despite the shapeless smock on her back ruined by twenty-years of assembly line work. For Lionel, a few months shy of retirement, who still blushed whenever defective pieces were returned to him. For the man with a mustache from Monday deliveries. The faces under the neon lights, the pneumatic sighs of the machines, the odor of metal and hot grease, the sandwich machine and its little, mechanical turnstiles, the faces magnetized by the huge clock in the center workshop. It should all be shown.

I cross an enfilade of roundabouts, stores selling sports gear, carpet, wood-burning stoves, discount bedding, hardwood flooring special-ists, porches, and discount appliances. The fruit of a long, obstinate human activity devoted to creating nothing. Nightclubs sometimes pop up in these peripheral zones, between the fast food restaurants and low-cost hotel chains. Fred's accident had occurred in one of these No-Man's Lands. I see this landscape of warehouses dressed up with Christmas trees slipping past, like Fred must have seen it, slumped on the car's back seat. But maybe that night, it had been more beautiful, lively, and joyous than this one. Maybe, at the last moment, he'd lowered the back window to sober up a little. Closed his eyes to better smell the humid, morning air. Maybe he'd had a sweet moment just before.

I cross the train track, going opposite the first trucks from the incineration factory. Then I pass along the welcome area for travelers, before going over into the territory of morning workers. The sky has an intense blue that makes you think everything is still possible. Even the buildings' ugliness is lessened by it. A few lights are still on in the SOBECO offices. The "Guichard-Public Works" warehouse is already open. The Mogel factory and its blue, corrugated iron building operates without interruption, day and night. I see the entrance to the Breizh-Bay mills' parking lots, between the Pervel cannery, and the Protolec workshops. Breizh-Bay makes bay windows to order. The market isn't very big. For a very long time, there hasn't been enough work for everyone, it seems. The company had lost a major client, the subcontract for exterior joinery for an airport near Besançon or Montbéliard, somewhere in that area. The airport project had been suspended. A sluggish market, a cancelled order, the temps were let go in mid-May. Right when my "assignment" at Protolec, the factory next door, was ending. Officially, nothing serious, Breizh-Bay wasn't destabilized.

Management simply had to "adjust its staffing to this variation in production," and the departure of the temp workers met that need. After my final day of work, I'd left the factory at the beginning of the afternoon, just after the second shift's arrival. While going to fetch my bicycle from under the lean-to, I heard the first exclamations in the distance. Not paying much attention to it, I rode around the warehouse to get back to the road. The clamor was growing. In the parking lot in front of the workshops, a hundred Breizh-Bay workers were staging an impromptu protest. Men in their overalls, women in smocks, union armbands, tense faces, cigarettes smoked nervously. A few sputtering voices, the brouhaha of hushed discussions in scattered, little groups. I'd stopped without really knowing why. That's when I met Edith and her anger for the first time. I'd already crossed paths with her several times before, while arriving in the morning. But we'd been content to greet one another from afar, nothing more.

That discussion in a parking lot was unexpected. Breizh-Bay had been having difficulties for years. The cancellation of the airport project had been the knockout punch. Massive layoffs were to be feared, even if management denied it. Nobody knew what to think. I listened to Edith telling me their story. I could see on their faces houses to be paid for, car loans, bellies to fill, and shopping carts to be loaded. I stayed with them all afternoon, until they resumed their work for fear of seeing it disappear.

I pass over the speedbumps. Edith's waiting for me in front of the shop and waves to me with her hand. Behind her, a bit in the background, is a small group of workers. I recognize a few faces, those from the protest of our first encounter. They look at me a little distrustfully. I understand them. They don't know what's going to happen. Me neither. We're on an equal footing. I'm there to take photos and them, to do battle. It's an honest situation. Curiously, I feel like I'm where I belong, that hadn't happened to me in a long time. I'd really like to pull off showing them just as I see them.

They're no more pure or beautiful than anyone else. But to me it's like they're clad in a form of nobility. That of people fighting for their survival, throwing all their strength behind it. They might fall at any moment. They know it. There's beauty in that struggle to stand tall.

Every day I tell myself it's a little too late. I'll never be able to make up for those ten years wasted learning nothing, understanding nothing. I'll never be Gene Kelly, Pollock, Virginia Woolf or Chris Killip. I don't have the drive. I'm not equipped for all that. It's painful. I once thought so, a little. I'd secretly told myself that story, at the age when you can still pretend to believe in your talent, when you hope it'll build itself piece by piece in front of you. I think about all that. I ruminate again and again. I know it's useless.

I have to reduce my ego. To no longer let myself be invaded by what I am not.

Every day, I bang into the intolerable wall of my limits, but I just keep going on.

Like on a bicycle.

If I stop, I'll fall.

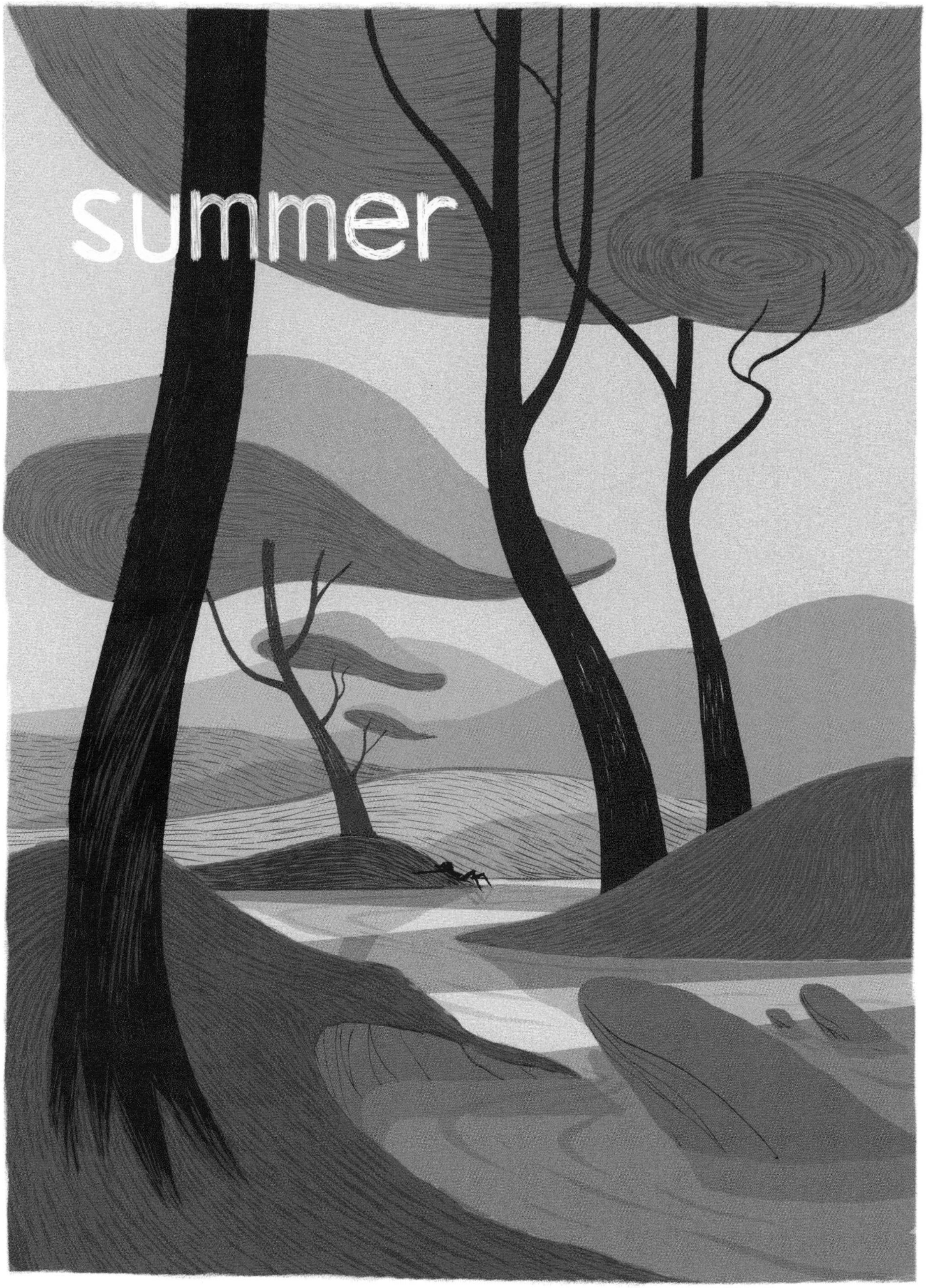
summer

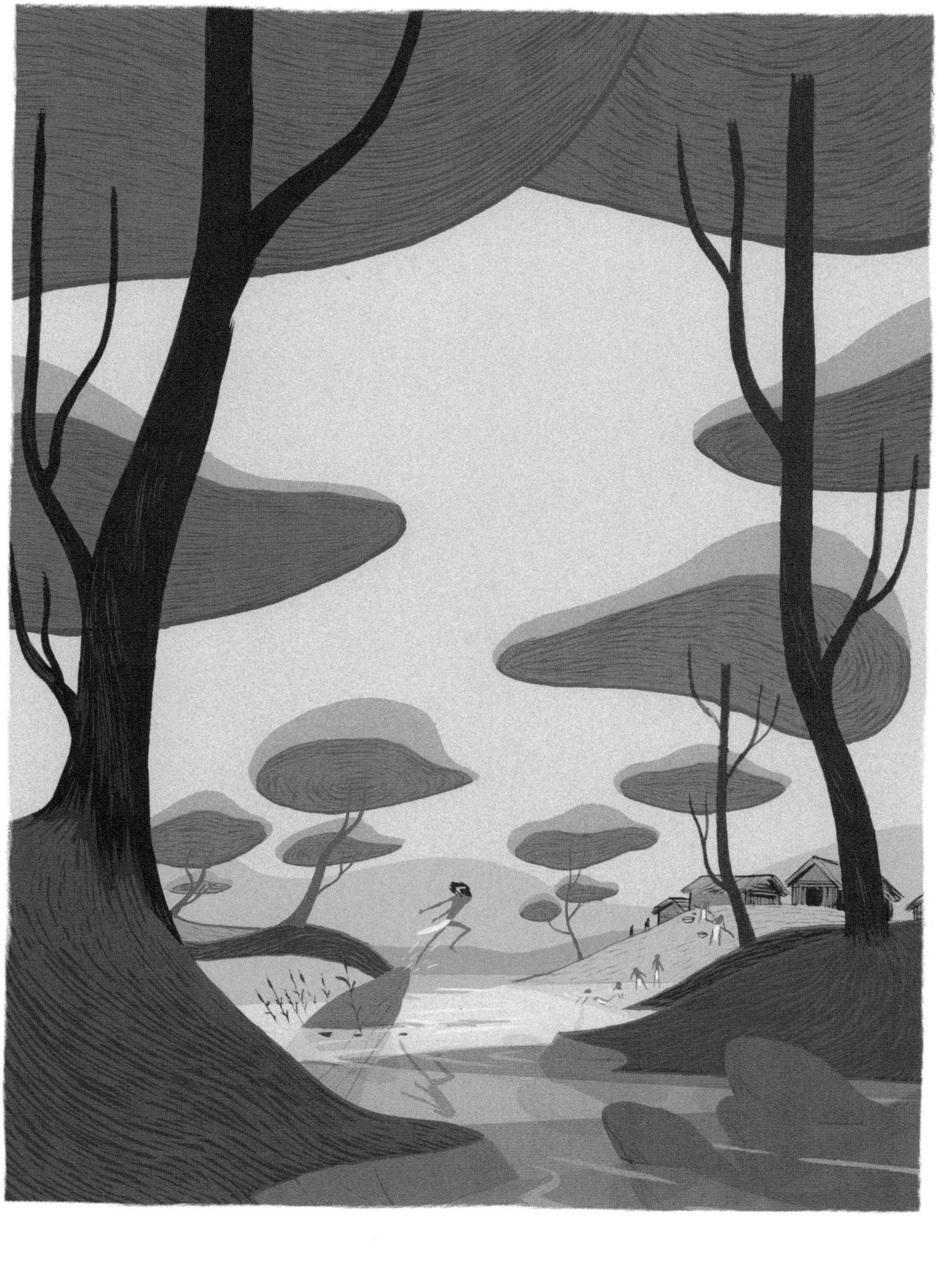

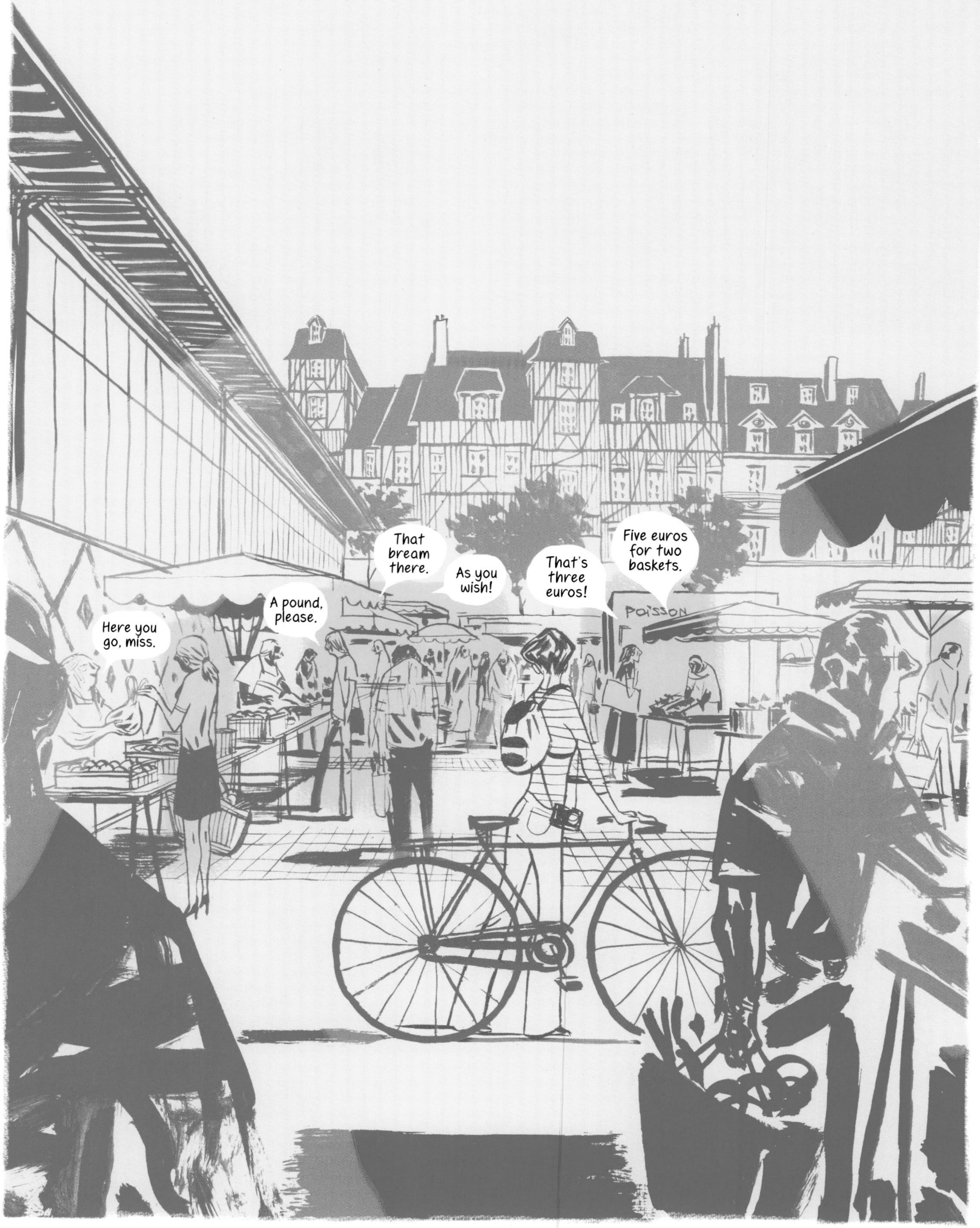
Here you go, miss.
A pound, please.
That bream there.
As you wish!
That's three euros!
Five euros for two baskets.
POISSON

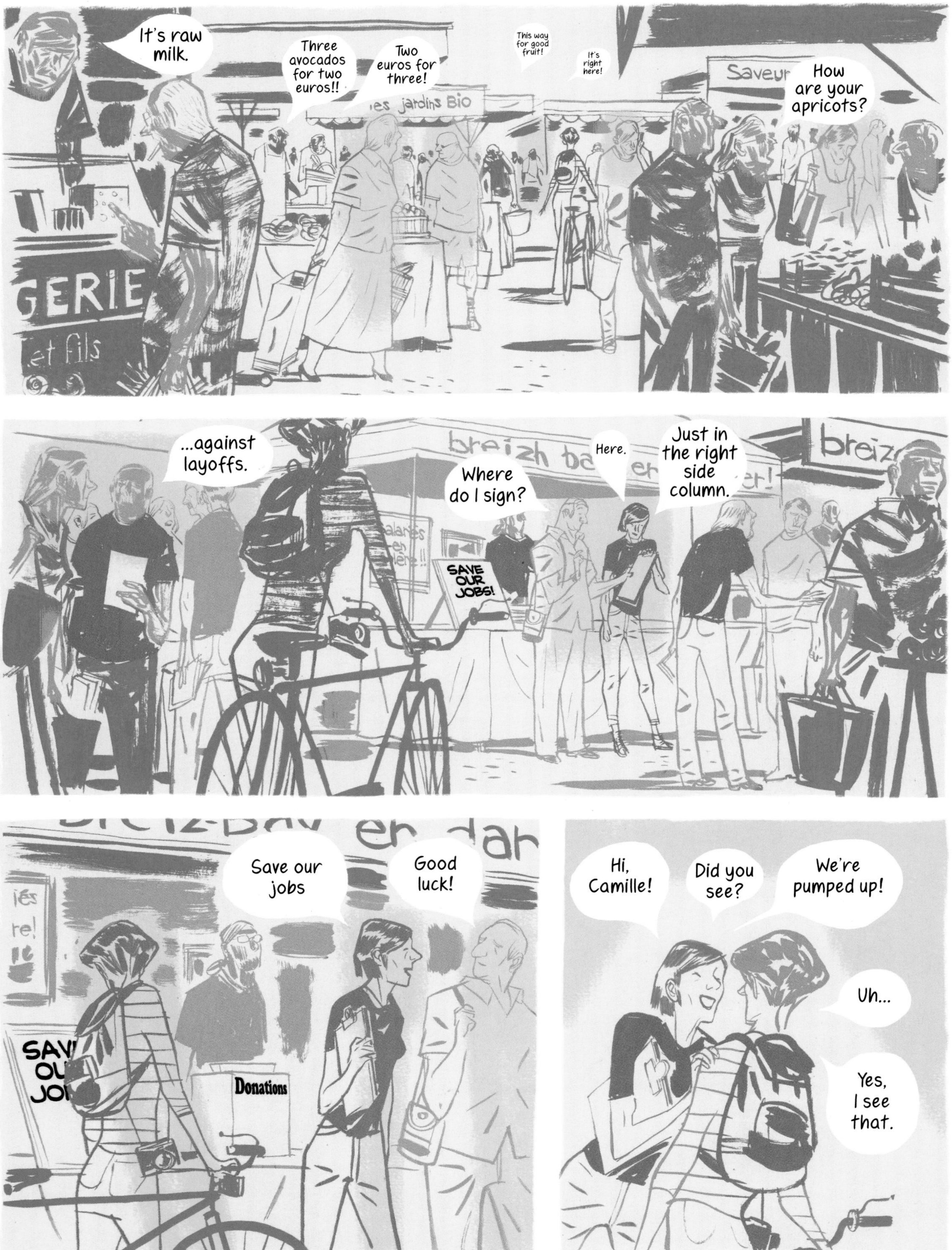

It's raw milk.
Three avocados for two euros!!
Two euros for three!
This way for good fruit!
It's right here!
How are your apricots?
GERIE
et fils
Saveur
...against layoffs.
Where do I sign?
Here.
Just in the right side column.
SAVE OUR JOBS!
Save our jobs
Good luck!
Donations
Hi, Camille!
Did you see?
We're pumped up!
Uh...
Yes, I see that.

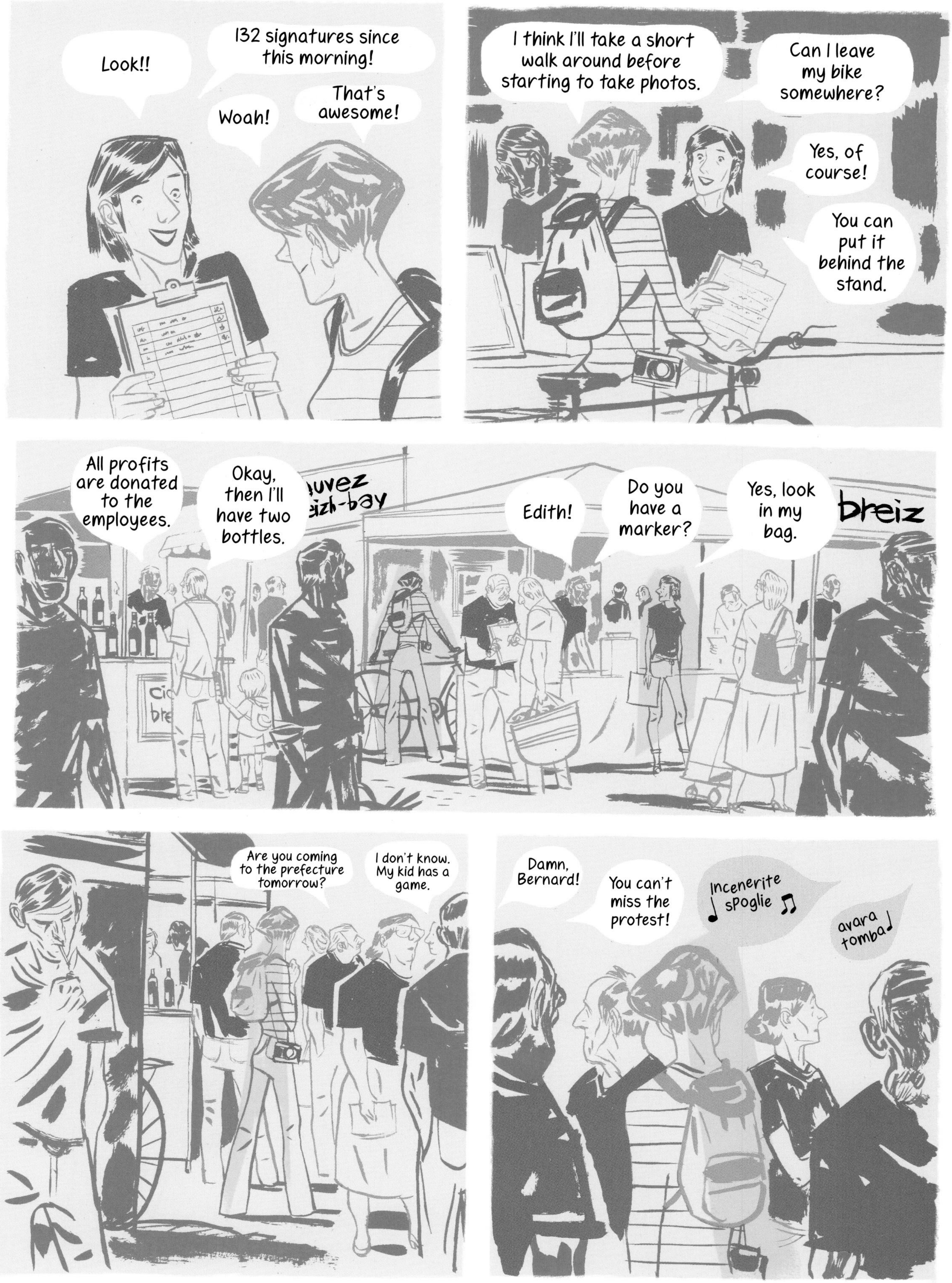
Look!!
132 signatures since this morning!
Woah!
That's awesome!
I think I'll take a short walk around before starting to take photos.
Can I leave my bike somewhere?
Yes, of course!
You can put it behind the stand.
All profits are donated to the employees.
Okay, then I'll have two bottles.
Edith!
Do you have a marker?
Yes, look in my bag.
breiz
Are you coming to the prefecture tomorrow?
I don't know. My kid has a game.
Damn, Bernard!
You can't miss the protest!
Incenerite spoglie
avara tomba

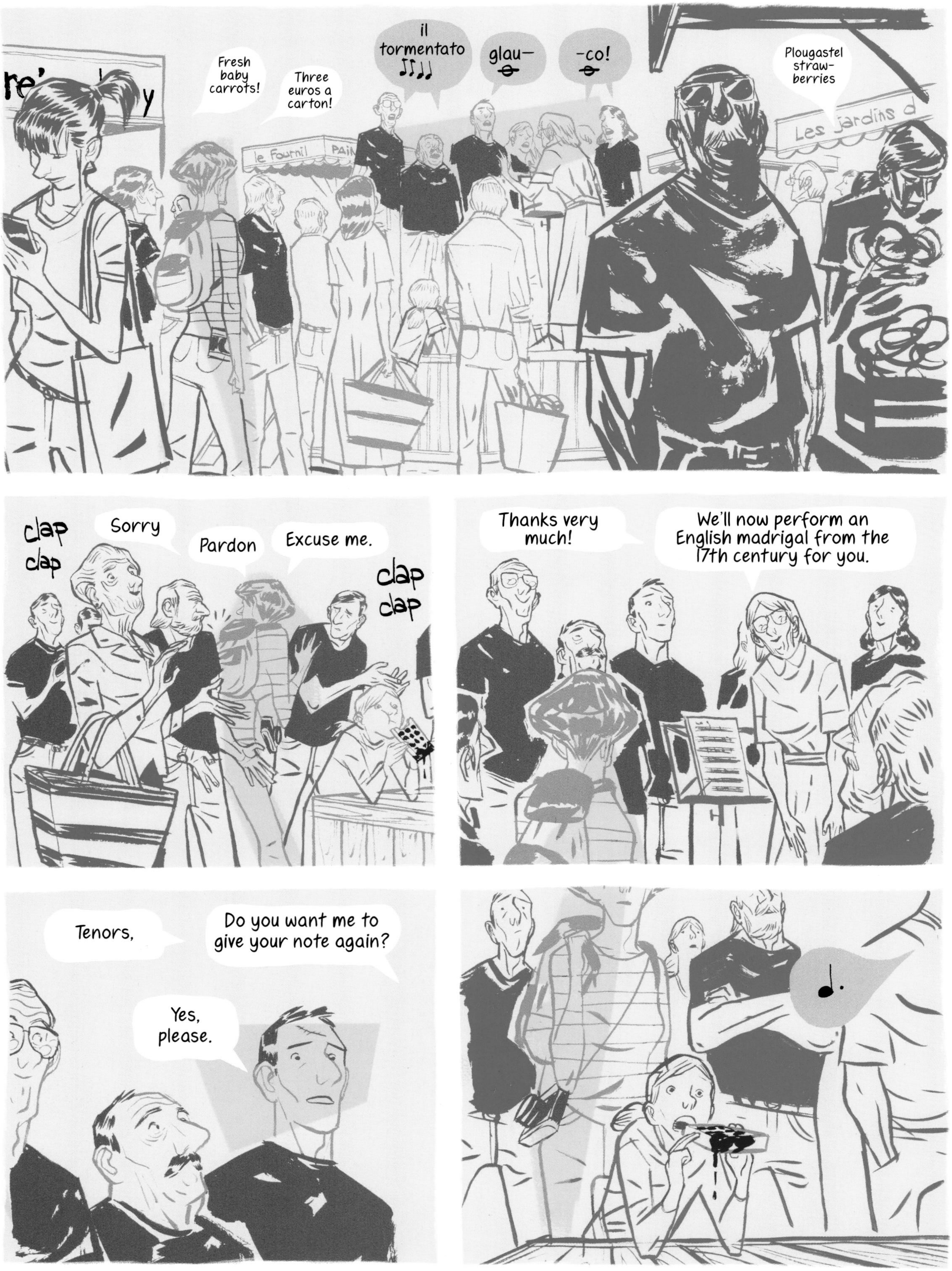
Fresh baby carrots!
Three euros a carton!
il tormentato
glau—
—co!
Plougastel straw-berries
le Fournil
PAIN
Les Jardins d
clap clap
Sorry
Pardon
Excuse me.
clap clap
Thanks very much!
We'll now perform an English madrigal from the 17th century for you.
Tenors,
Do you want me to give your note again?
Yes, please.

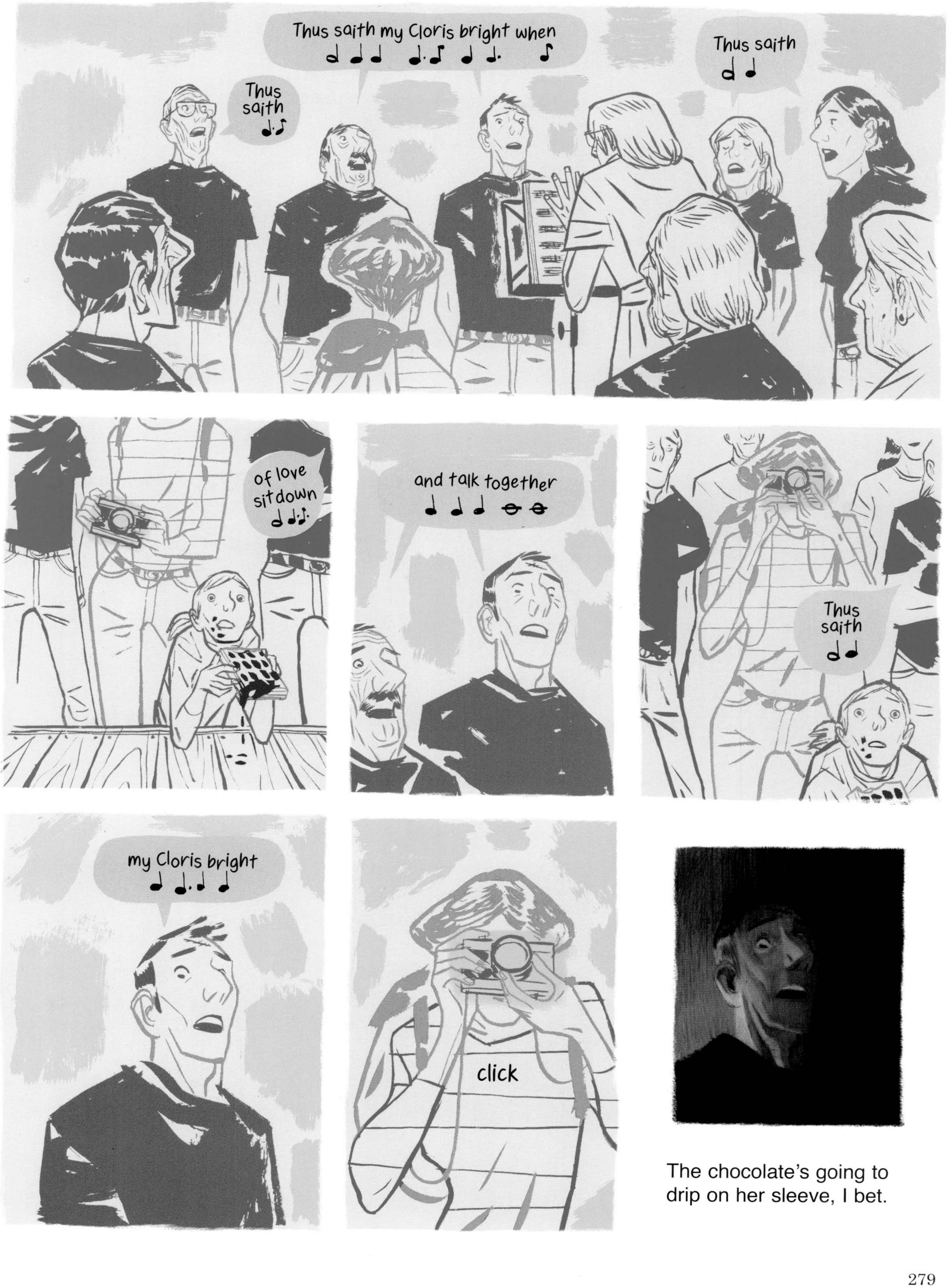
Thus saith
Thus saith my Cloris bright when
Thus saith
of love sitdown
and talk together
Thus saith
my Cloris bright
click
The chocolate's going to drip on her sleeve, I bet.

The first couplet starts out on a difficult E.

A little too high for his range.

In the front row, the little girl is gobbling down her waffle.

 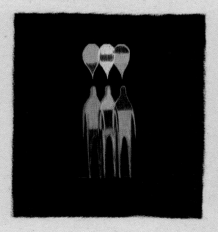 

He attacks the note with a slight delay that makes him tense despite himself.

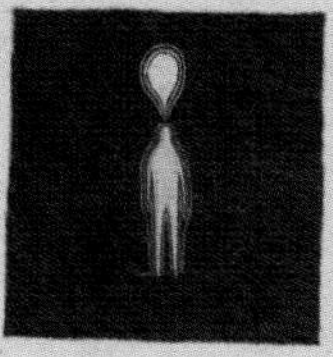

He sings distractedly, choking up.

Once a week, he goes to the Maurice Massé community center. Between the gym mats and children's drawings, they perform Renaissance songs. He hasn't missed any rehearsals, except for a few sessions this winter, after his surfing accident at the Carré beach. He'd never sung before, never dared to. But now, every Tuesday night, he has his spot in the middle of the choir. His greatest surprise was having discovered just how much his body's involvement is essential for bringing out his voice. Like an extension of himself. He sometimes manages it. Then it feels like he's entirely in the sound projected in front of him. Like a disappearance of the self.

He sneaks a glance at his score.
"John Wilbye – 1574-1638."
A man's life summed up in a few words. John Wilbye's troubles, profound joys, urges, and regrets remain forever hidden in his elegant, light music. He'll have to succeed in singing that mystery to bring him to life, but that seems entirely out of reach.
He wavers a little, perturbed by the ridiculousness of the situation. Despite the enthusiasm and motivation of the other choristers, he doesn't really see how singing John Wilbye badly can contribute in one way or another to saving jobs at the Breizh-Bay company.
In front of him, some people are eating waffles. Others are chanting slogans or buying potatoes. He's singing in public for the first time and it'd be best, no doubt, for it to never happen again.
The refrain finally starts. First, the alto, and then the soprano. He catches his breath, tries to relax despite all, prepares for the note in his mind, opens his mouth, seeks the resonance in his palate, and sings.
A G. Over the minor A of the female voices. A chord held for a 4/4 measure. His throat opens up. A column of sound crosses through him from one end to the other, just like it crosses through each of them. No one fades away, no one forgets themselves, and yet they form but a whole, the sum of their united voices. A complex sound, colored with high-pitched harmonics that surge forth and disappear, that gathers them and bears them, much higher than themselves.

A draft of air causes the t-shirts to dance in the vendors' stalls.
The little girl cries, her parents fuss at her about the chocolate.
Three guys are talking loudly in front of the refreshment stand.

It's no longer important at all.

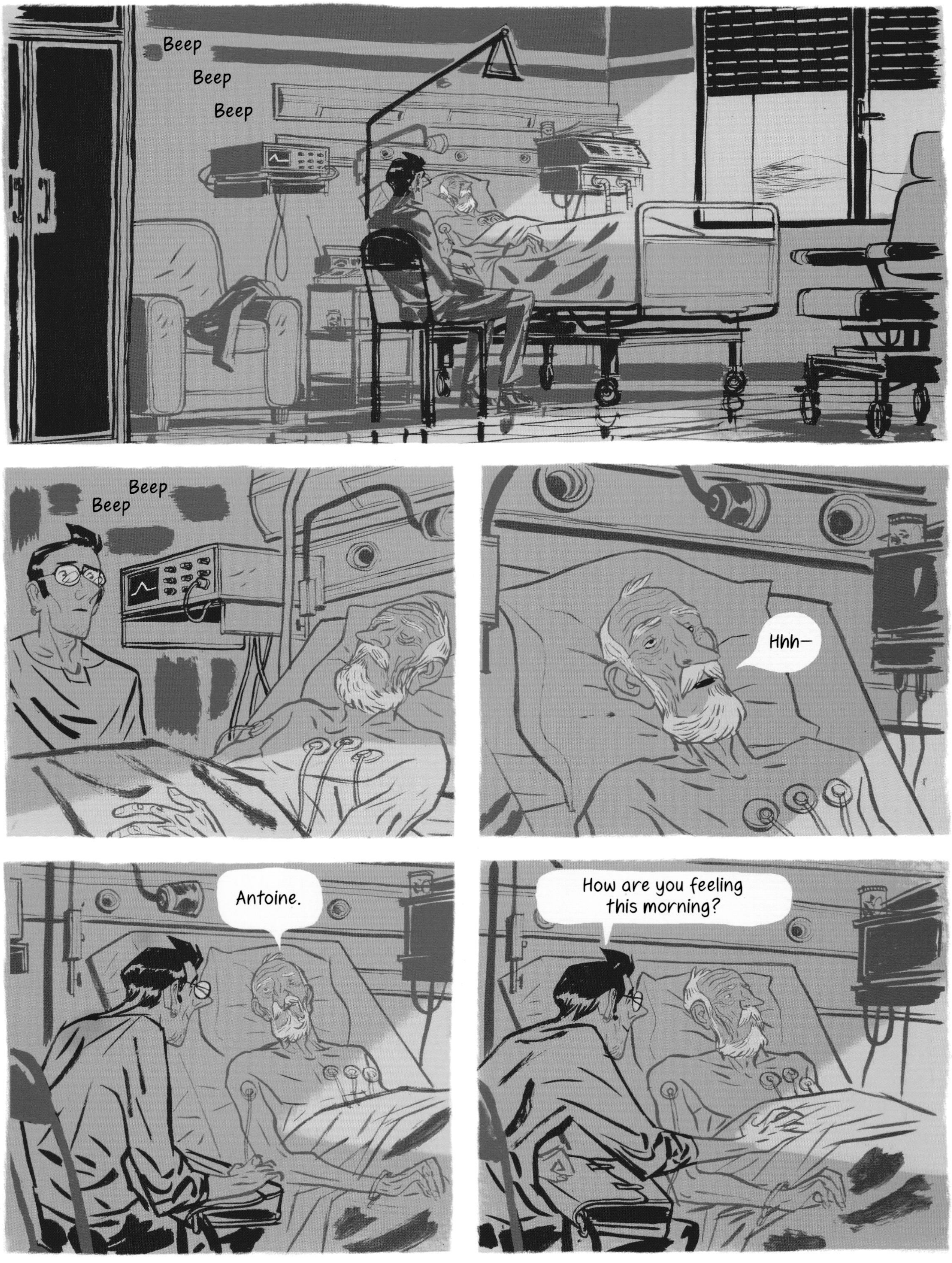
Beep
Beep
Beep
Beep
Beep
Hhh—
Antoine.
How are you feeling this morning?

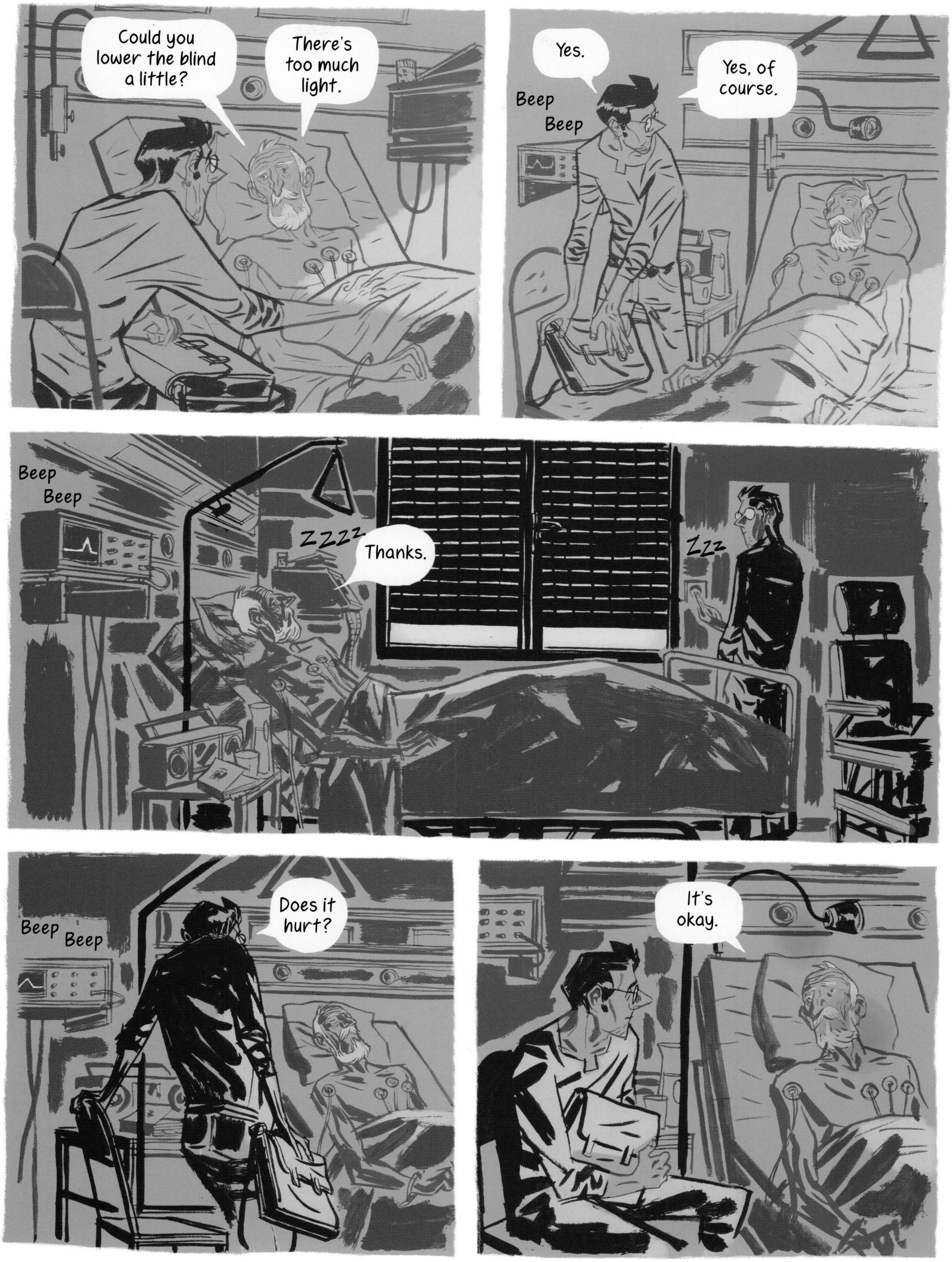
Could you lower the blind a little?
There's too much light.
Yes.
Beep
Beep
Yes, of course.
Beep
Beep
ZZZZ
Thanks.
ZZZ
Beep
Beep
Does it hurt?
It's okay.

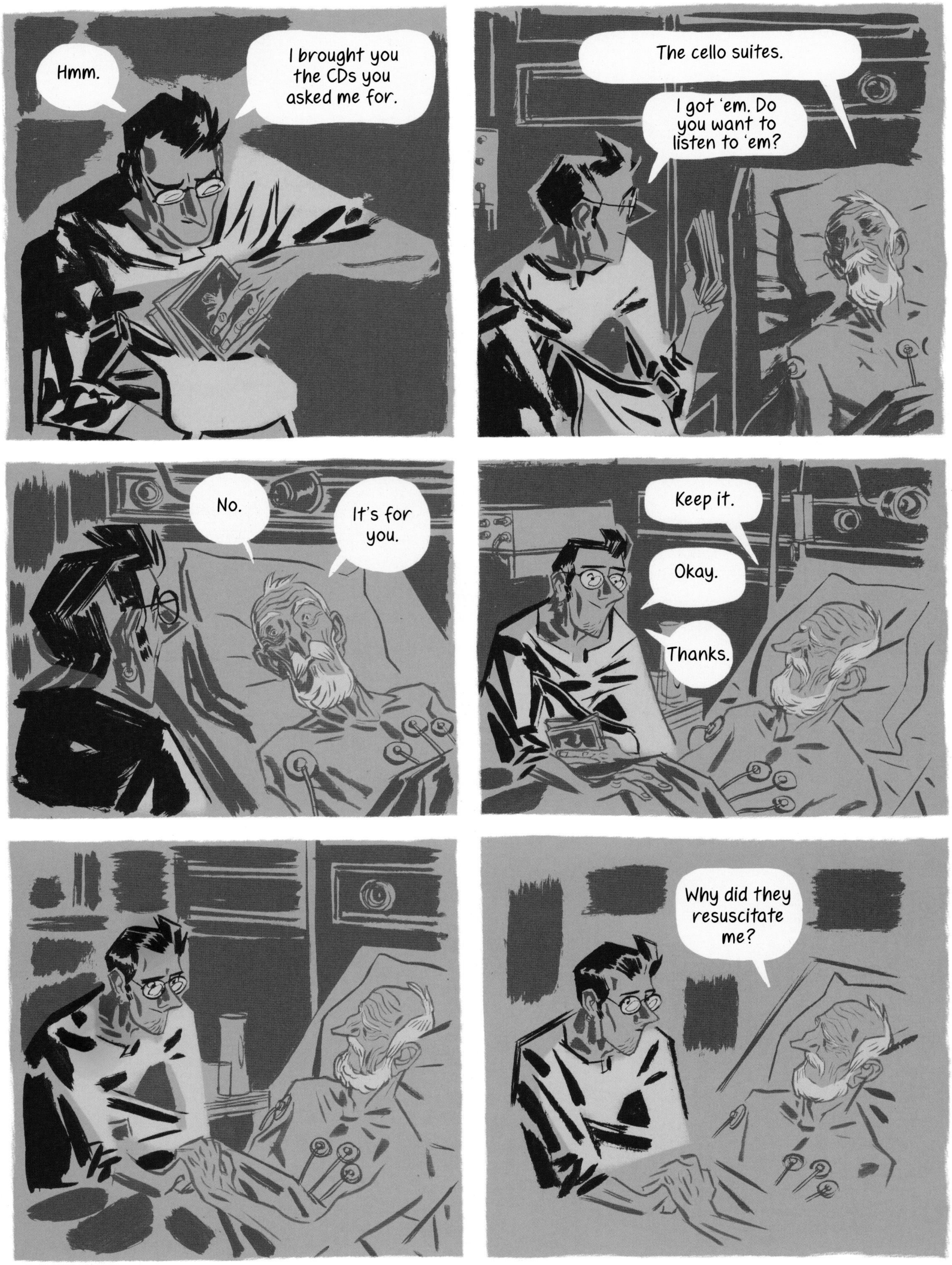
Hmm.
I brought you the CDs you asked me for.
The cello suites.
I got 'em. Do you want to listen to 'em?
No.
It's for you.
Keep it.
Okay.
Thanks.
Why did they resuscitate me?

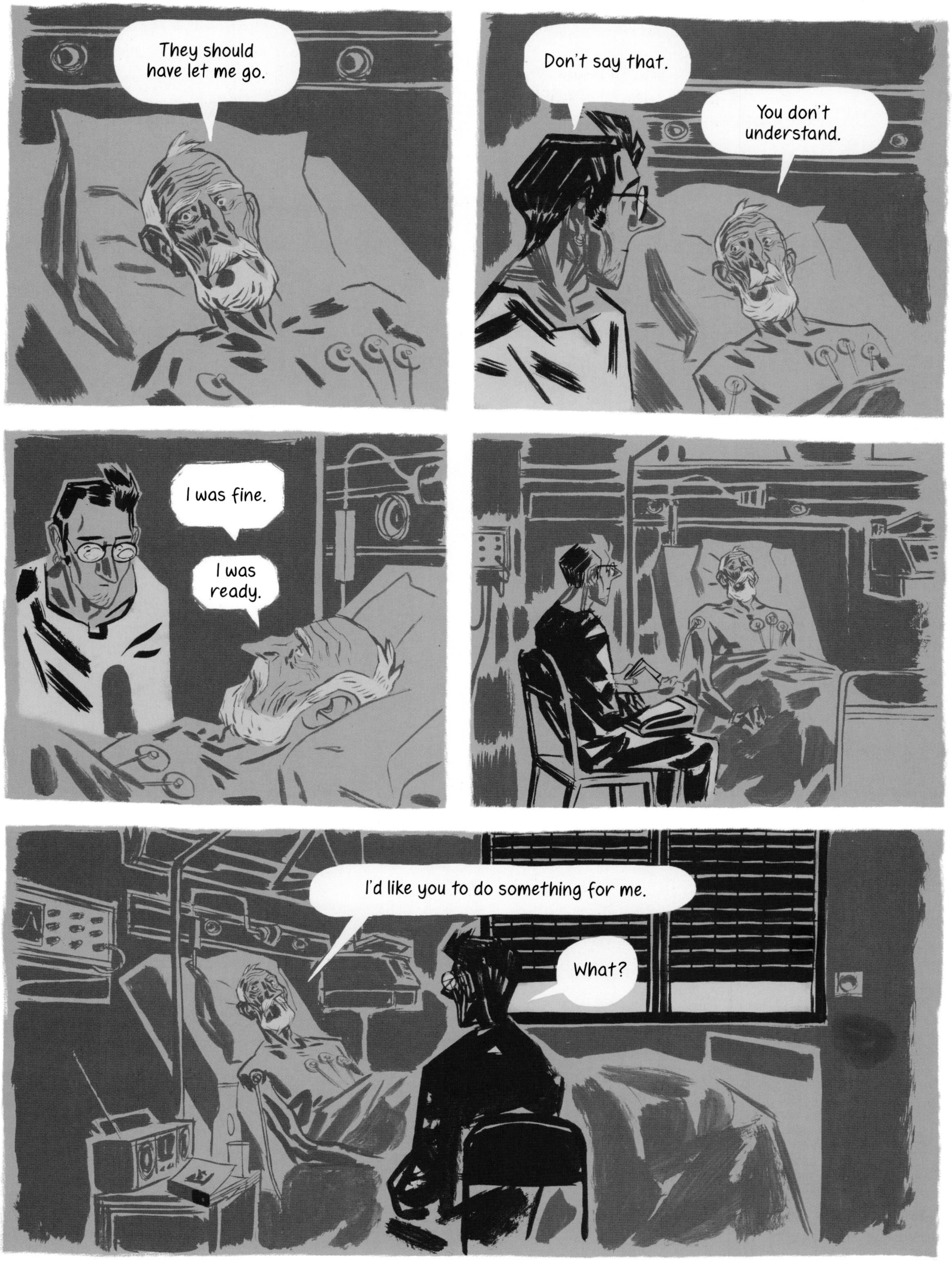
They should have let me go.
Don't say that.
You don't understand.
I was fine.
I was ready.
I'd like you to do something for me.
What?

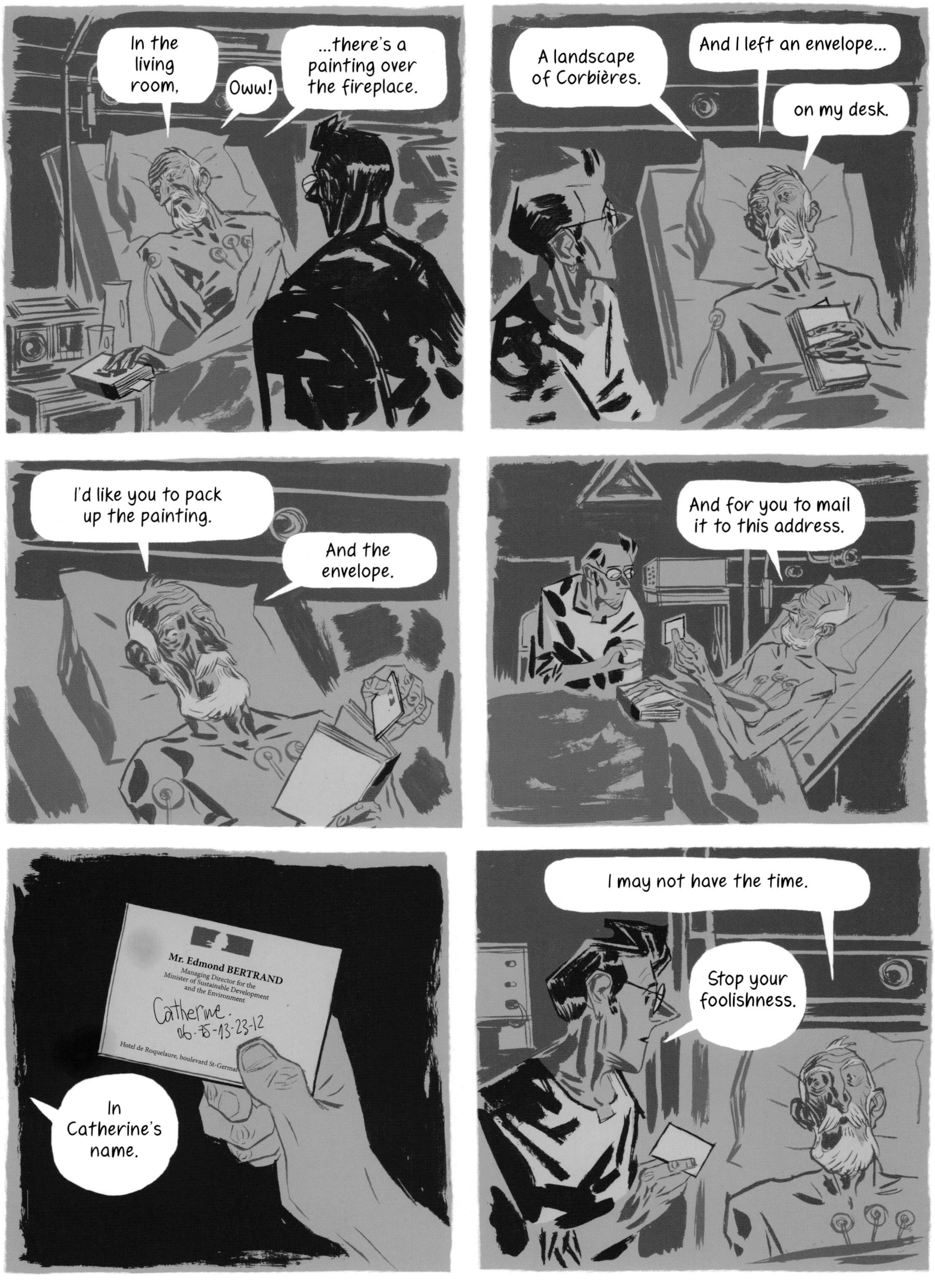
In the living room,
Oww!
...there's a painting over the fireplace.
A landscape of Corbières.
And I left an envelope...
on my desk.
I'd like you to pack up the painting.
And the envelope.
And for you to mail it to this address.
Mr. Edmond BERTRAND
Managing Director for the Minister of Sustainable Development and the Environment
Catherine.
06-75-13-23-12
Hotel de Roquelaure, boulevard St-Germa
In Catherine's name.
I may not have the time.
Stop your foolishness.

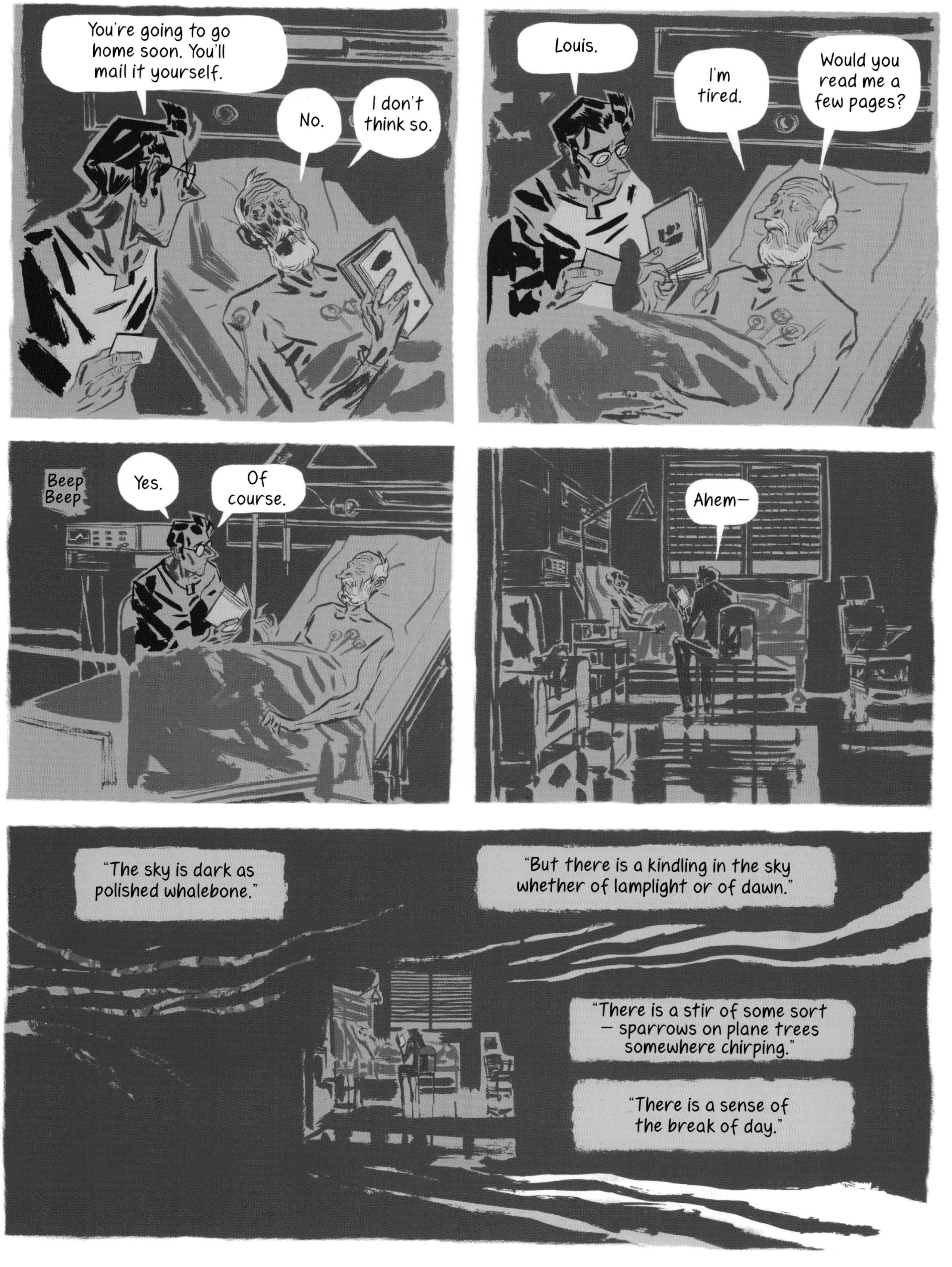
You're going to go home soon. You'll mail it yourself.
No.
I don't think so.
Louis.
I'm tired.
Would you read me a few pages?
Beep Beep
Yes.
Of course.
Ahem—
"The sky is dark as polished whalebone."
"But there is a kindling in the sky whether of lamplight or of dawn."
"There is a stir of some sort — sparrows on plane trees somewhere chirping."
"There is a sense of the break of day."

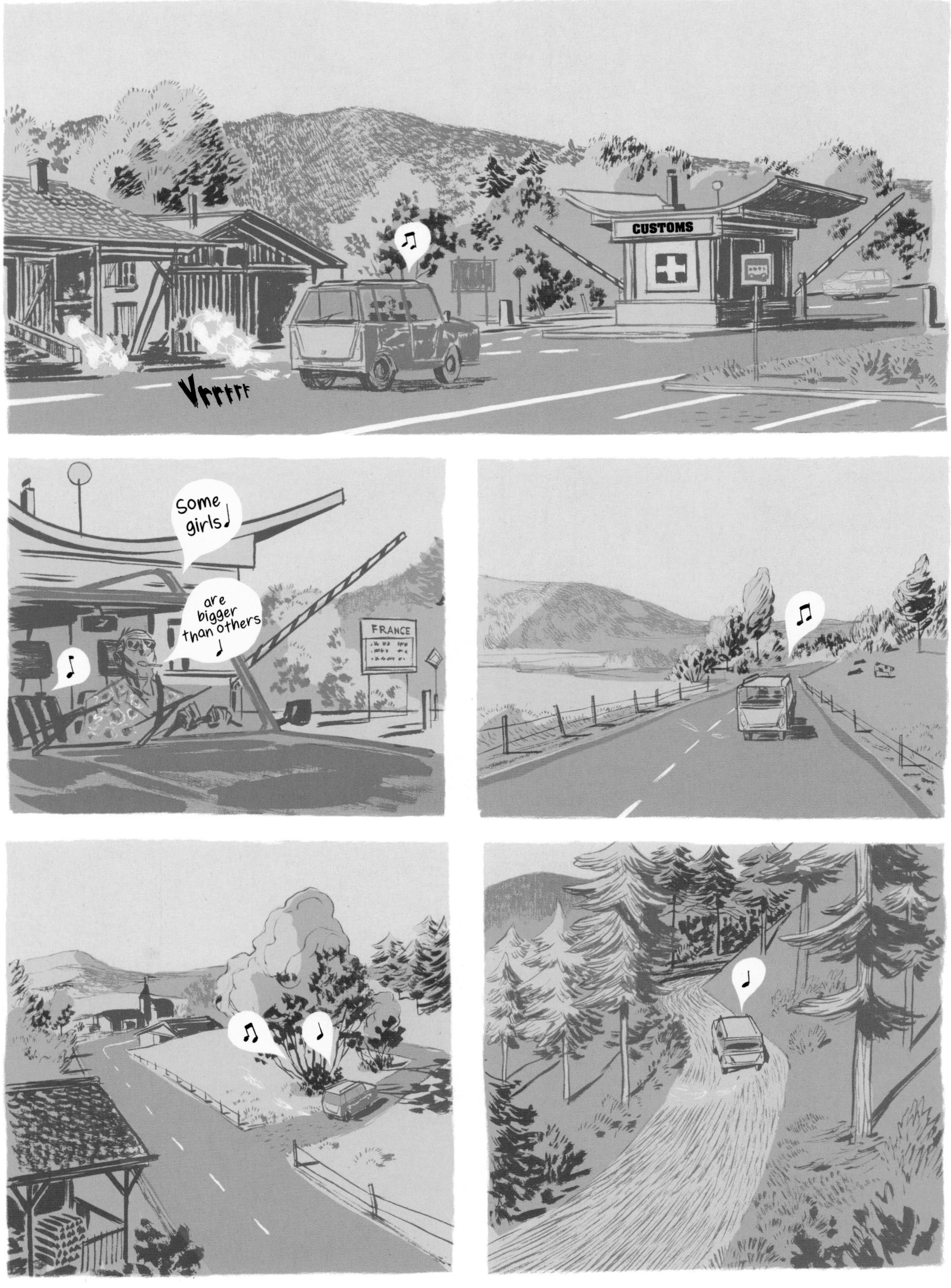
CUSTOMS
Vrrrrr
Some girls
are bigger than others
FRANCE

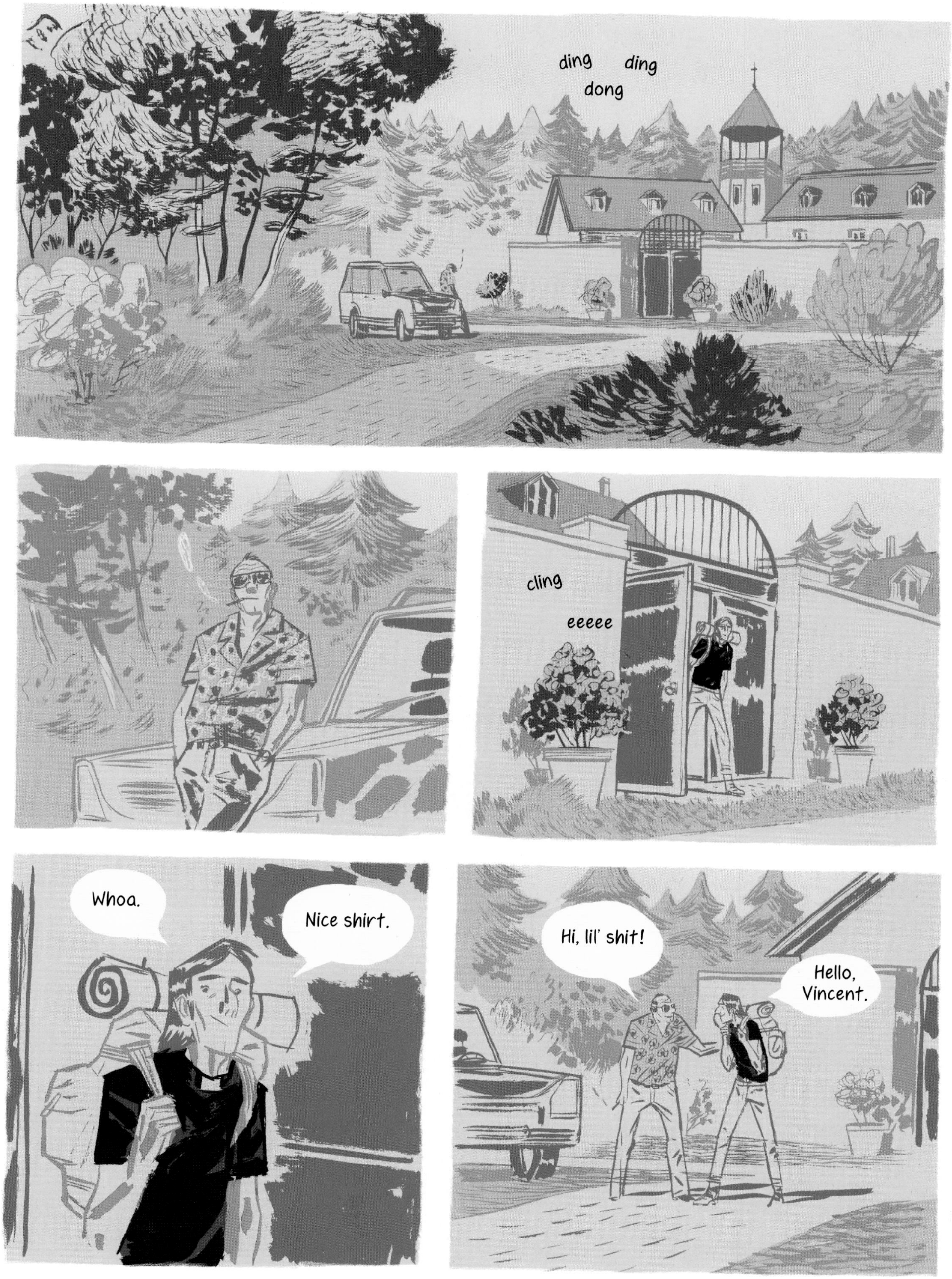
ding
dong
ding
cling
eeeee
Whoa.
Nice shirt.
Hi, lil' shit!
Hello, Vincent.

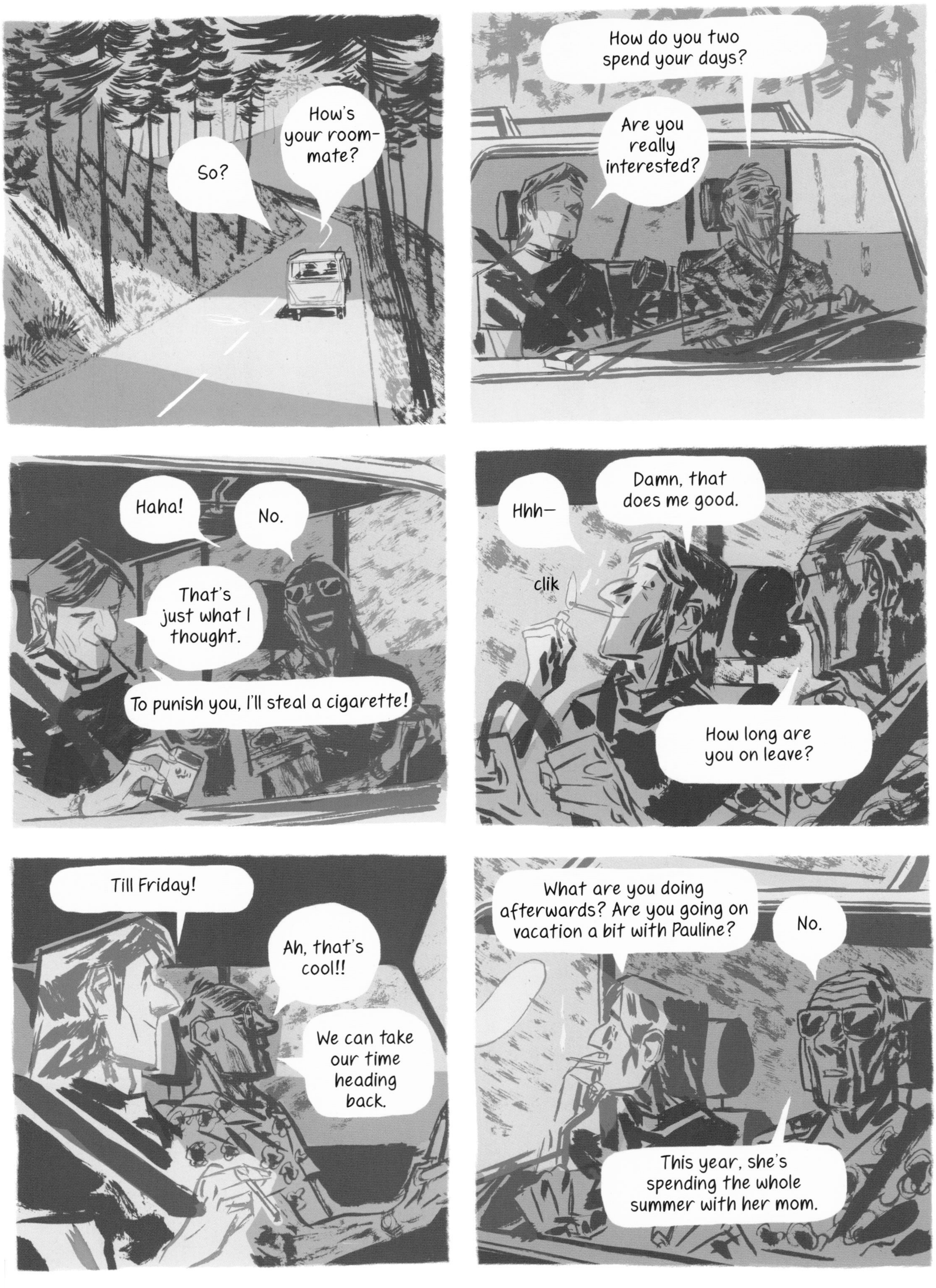
So?
How's your room-mate?
How do you two spend your days?
Are you really interested?
Haha!
No.
That's just what I thought.
To punish you, I'll steal a cigarette!
Hhh—
Damn, that does me good.
clik
How long are you on leave?
Till Friday!
Ah, that's cool!!
We can take our time heading back.
What are you doing afterwards? Are you going on vacation a bit with Pauline?
No.
This year, she's spending the whole summer with her mom.

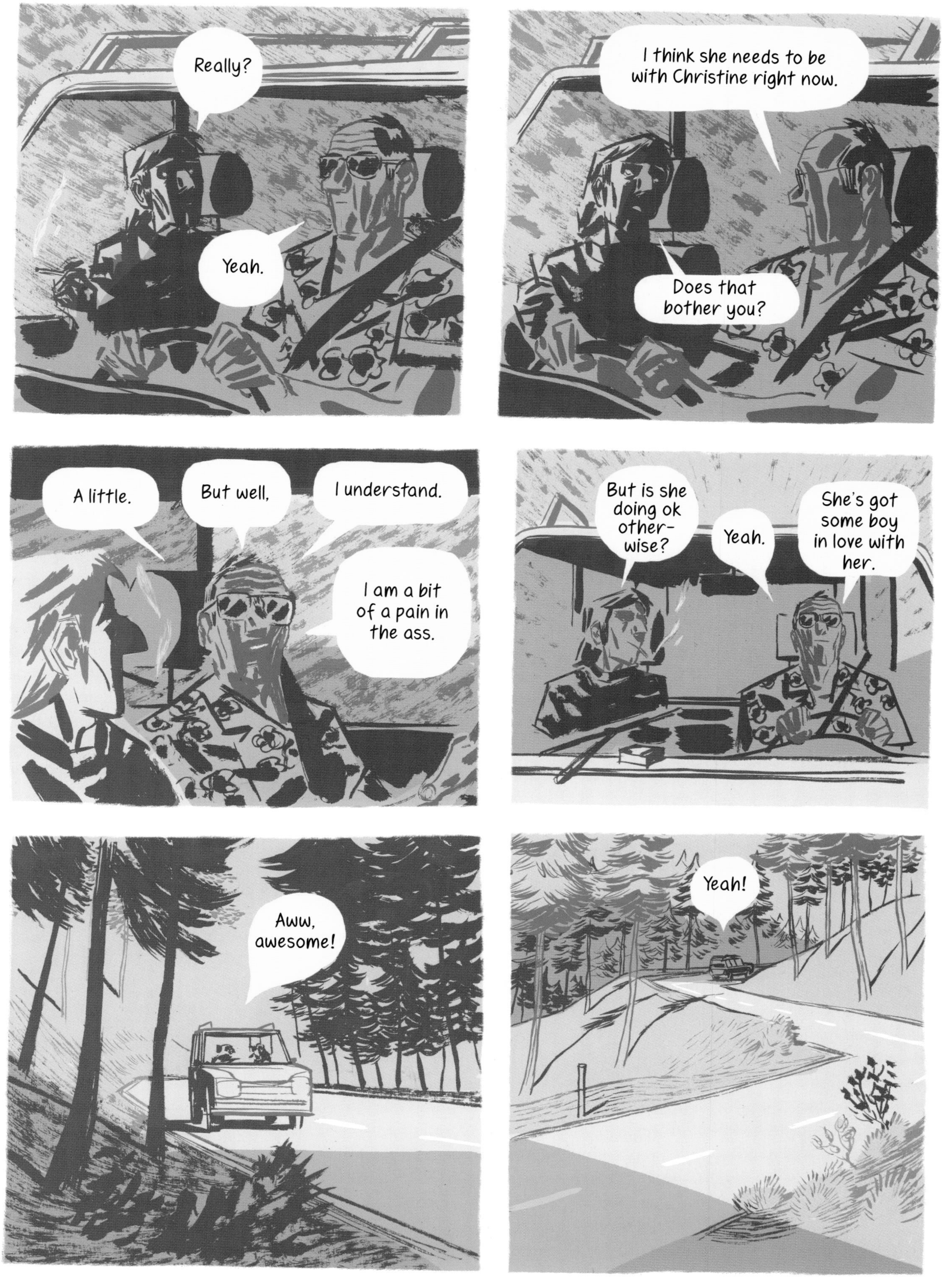
Really?
Yeah.
I think she needs to be with Christine right now.
Does that bother you?
A little.
But well,
I understand.
I am a bit of a pain in the ass.
But is she doing ok other-wise?
Yeah.
She's got some boy in love with her.
Aww, awesome!
Yeah!

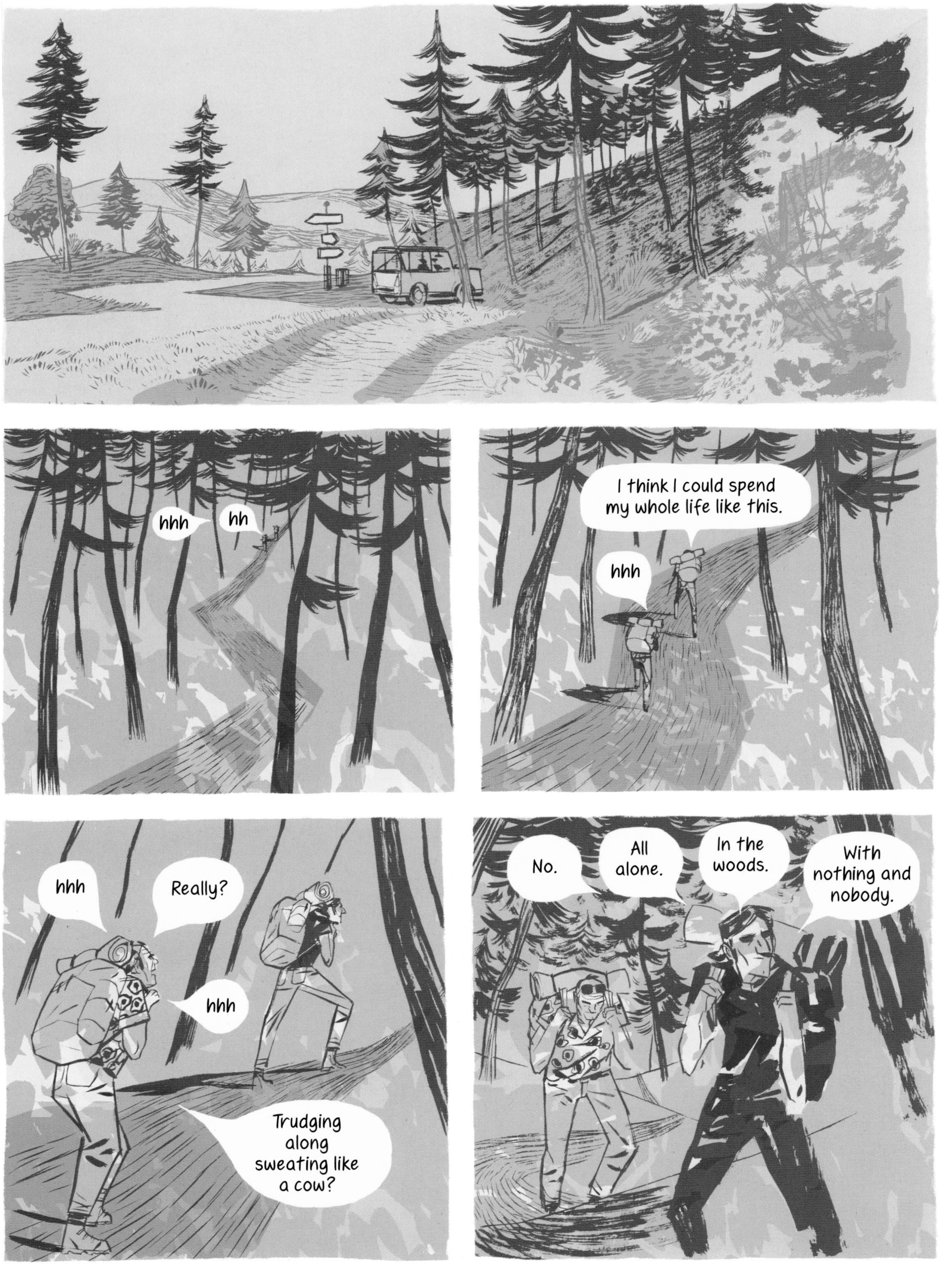
hhh
hh
I think I could spend my whole life like this.
hhh
hhh
Really?
hhh
Trudging along sweating like a cow?
No.
All alone.
In the woods.
With nothing and nobody.

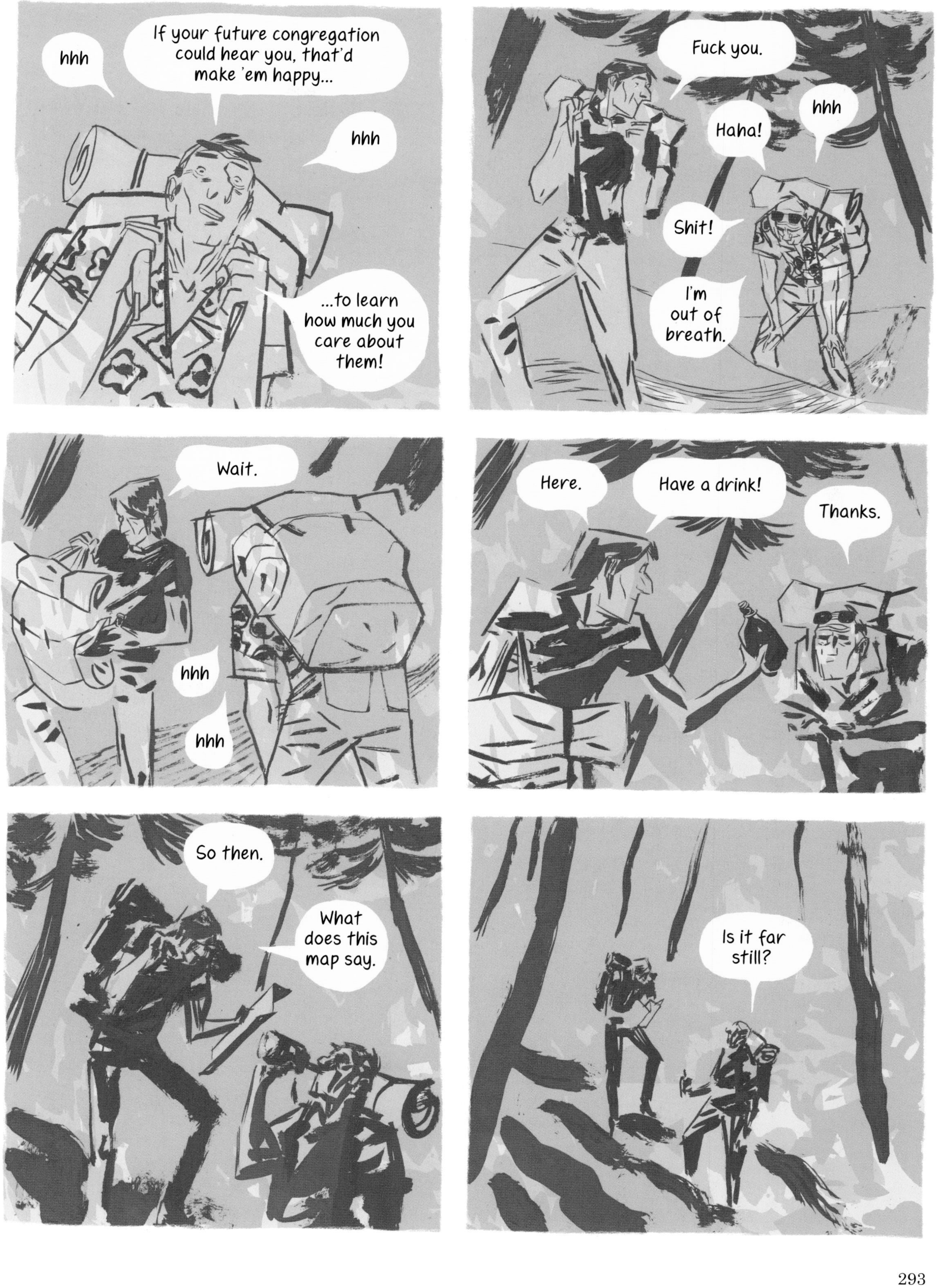
hhh
If your future congregation could hear you, that'd make 'em happy...
hhh
...to learn how much you care about them!
Fuck you.
Haha!
hhh
Shit!
I'm out of breath.
Wait.
hhh
hhh
Here.
Have a drink!
Thanks.
So then.
What does this map say.
Is it far still?

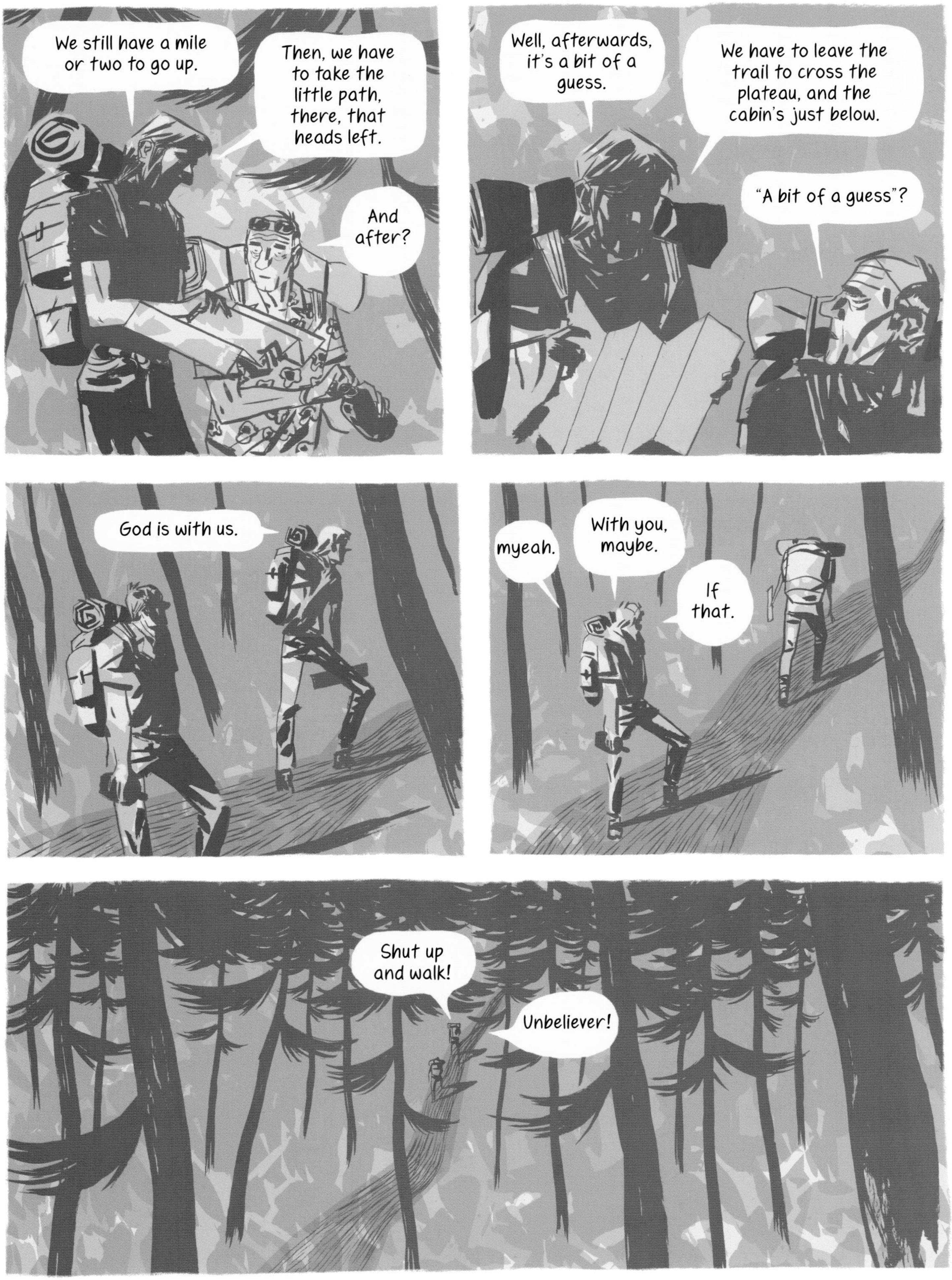
We still have a mile or two to go up.
Then, we have to take the little path, there, that heads left.
And after?
Well, afterwards, it's a bit of a guess.
We have to leave the trail to cross the plateau, and the cabin's just below.
"A bit of a guess"?
God is with us.
myeah.
With you, maybe.
If that.
Shut up and walk!
Unbeliever!

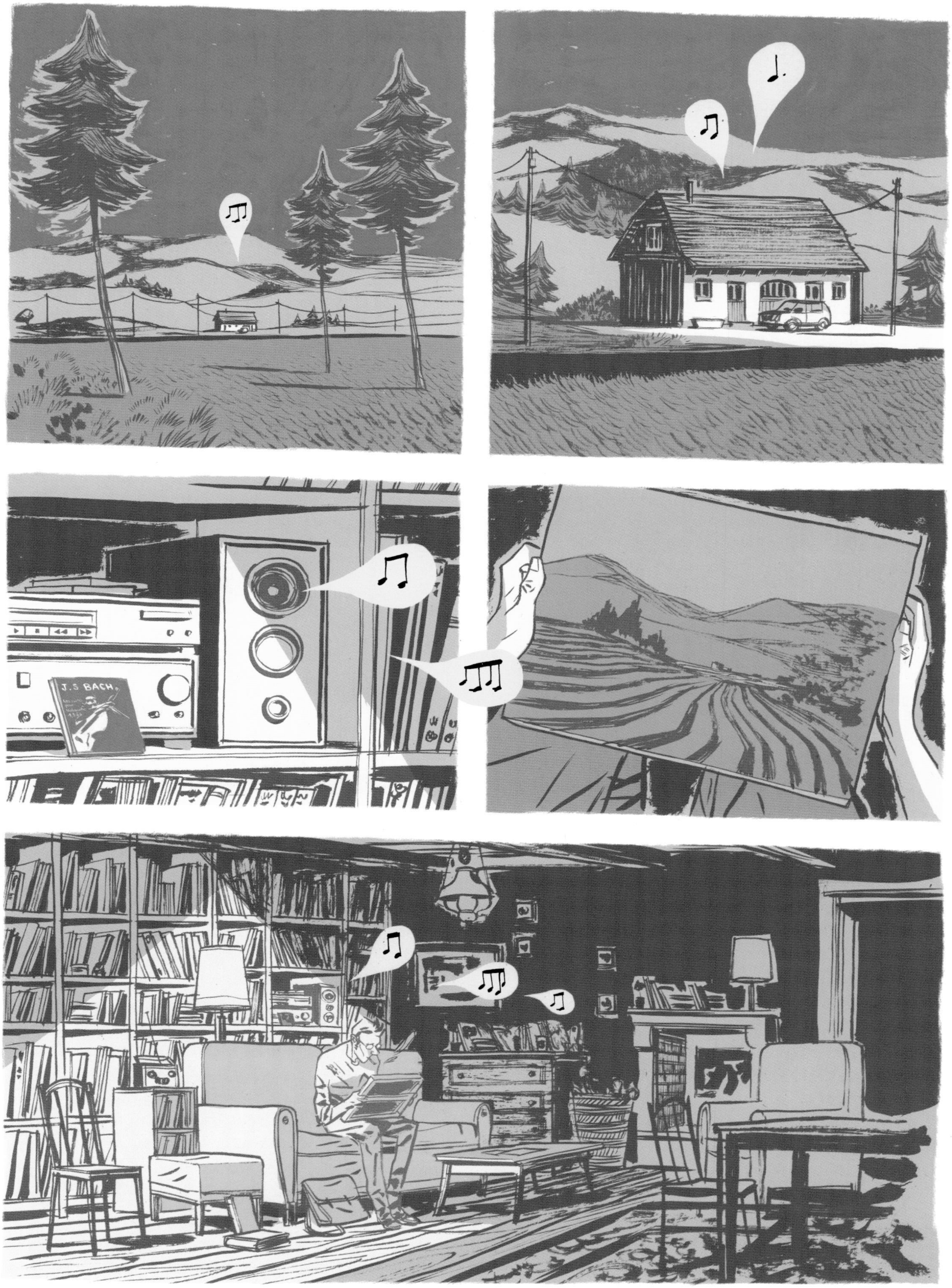
J.S BACH

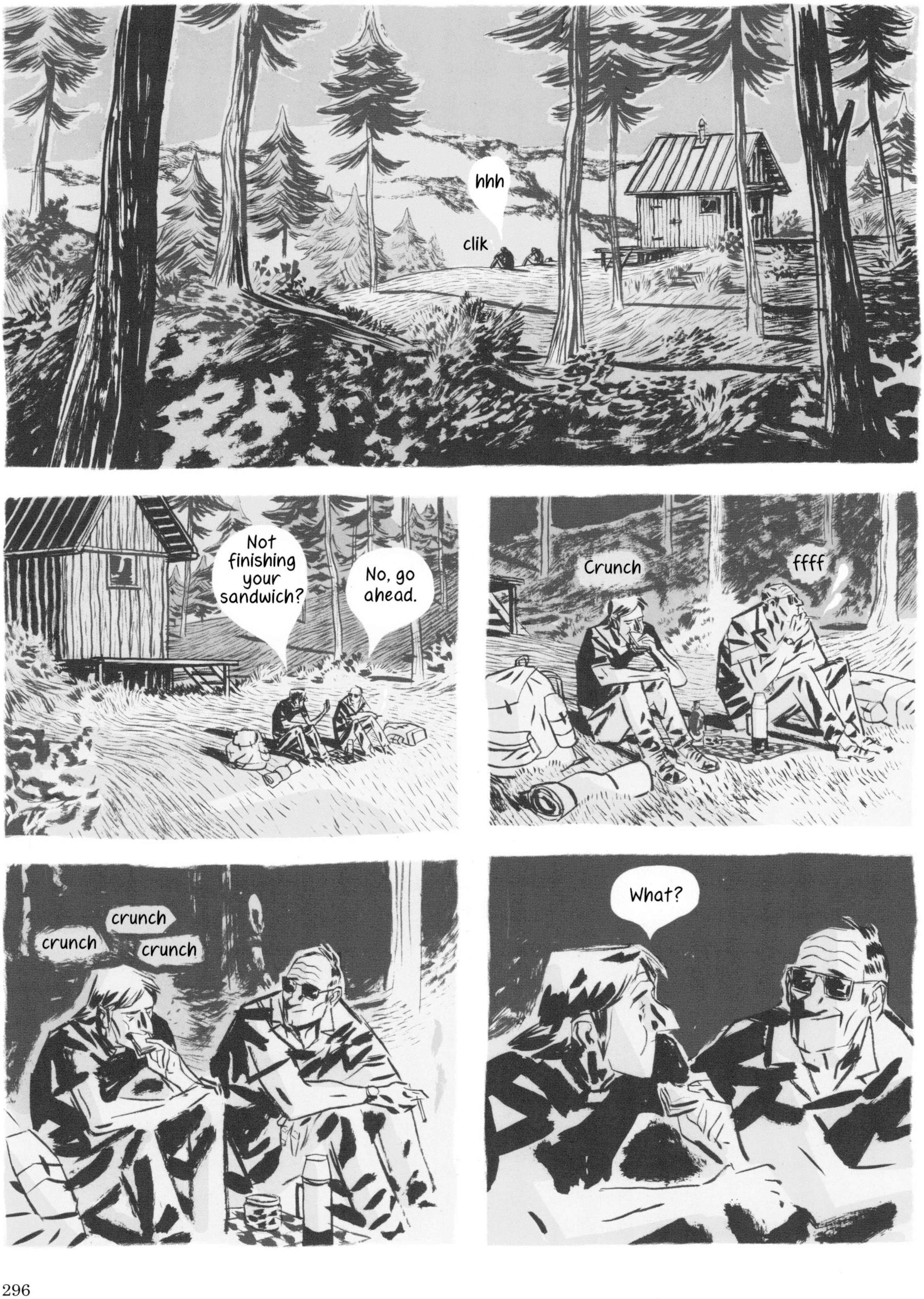
hhh
clik
Not finishing your sandwich?
No, go ahead.
Crunch
ffff
crunch
crunch
crunch
What?

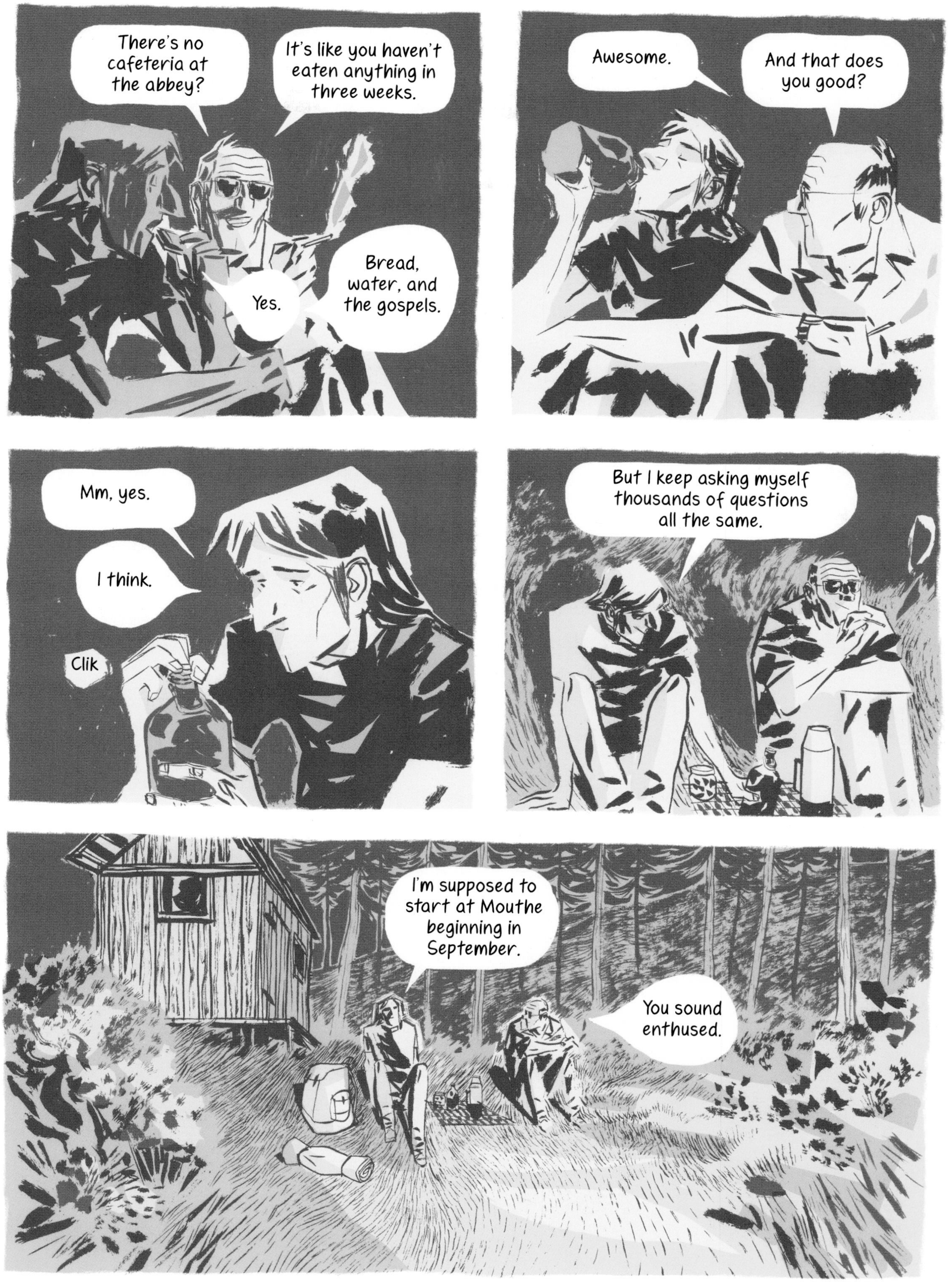
There's no cafeteria at the abbey?
It's like you haven't eaten anything in three weeks.
Yes.
Bread, water, and the gospels.
Awesome.
And that does you good?
Mm, yes.
I think.
Clik
But I keep asking myself thousands of questions all the same.
I'm supposed to start at Mouthe beginning in September.
You sound enthused.

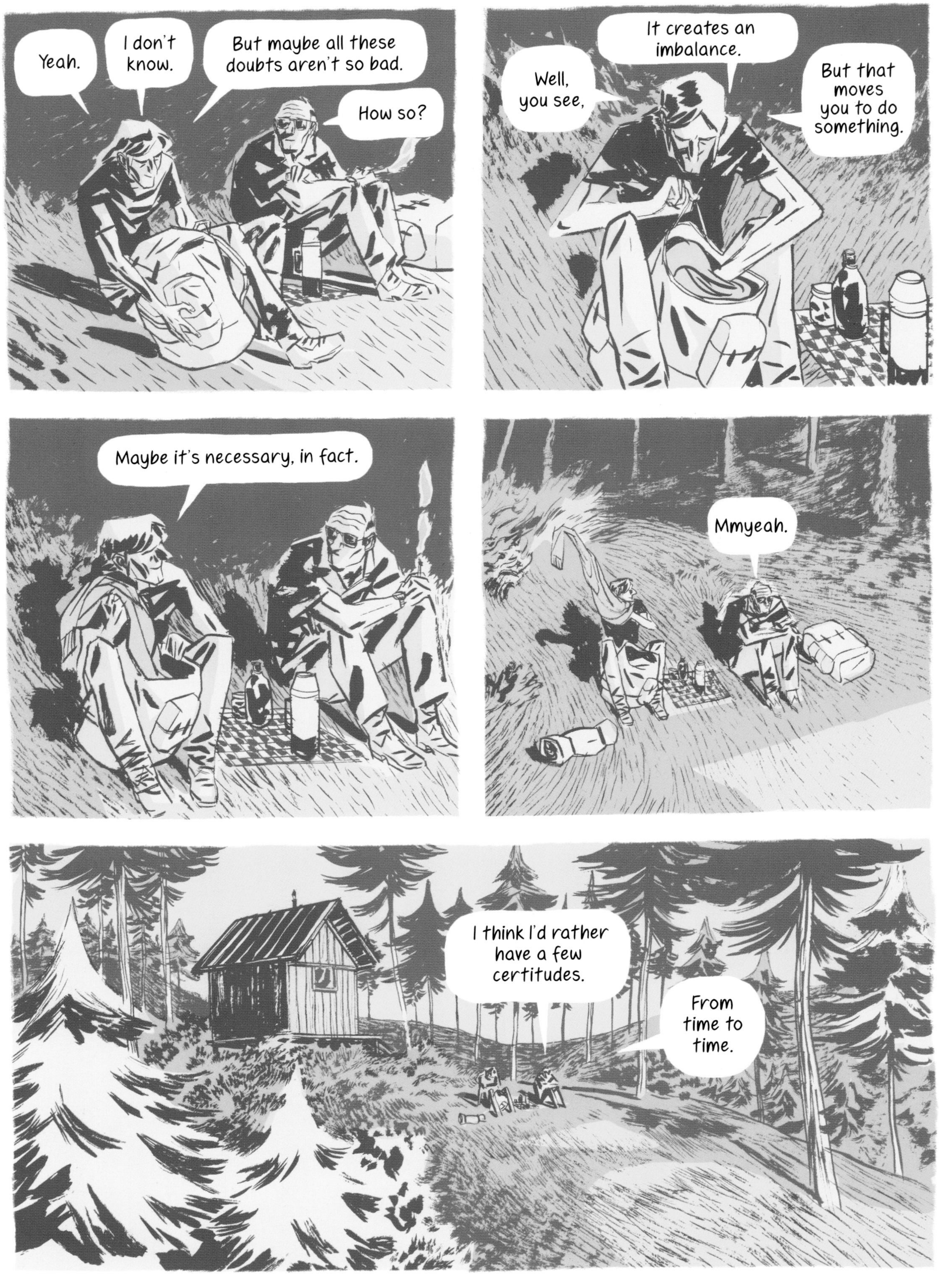
Yeah.
I don't know.
But maybe all these doubts aren't so bad.
How so?
Well, you see,
It creates an imbalance.
But that moves you to do something.
Maybe it's necessary, in fact.
Mmyeah.
I think I'd rather have a few certitudes.
From time to time.

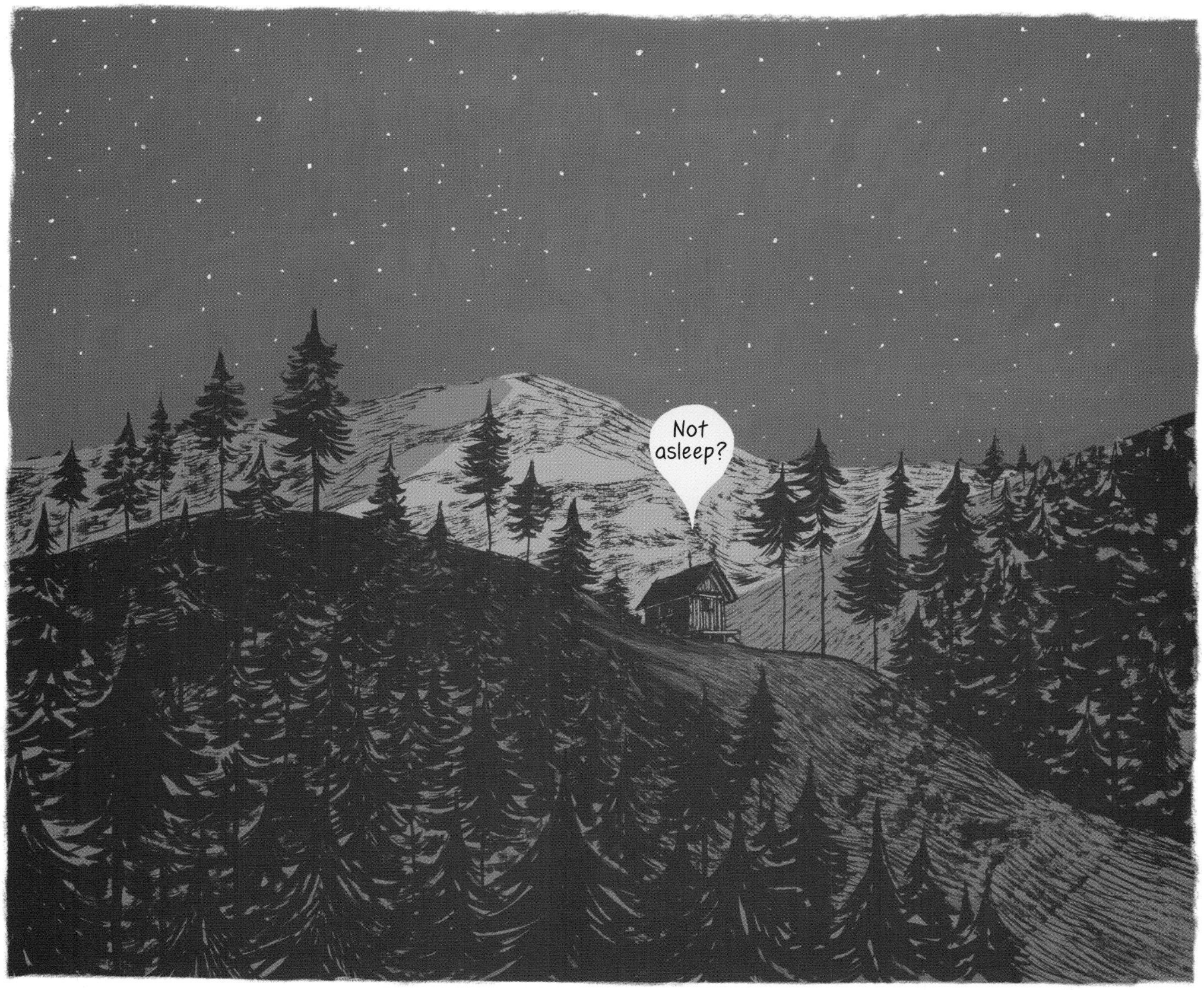
Not
asleep?

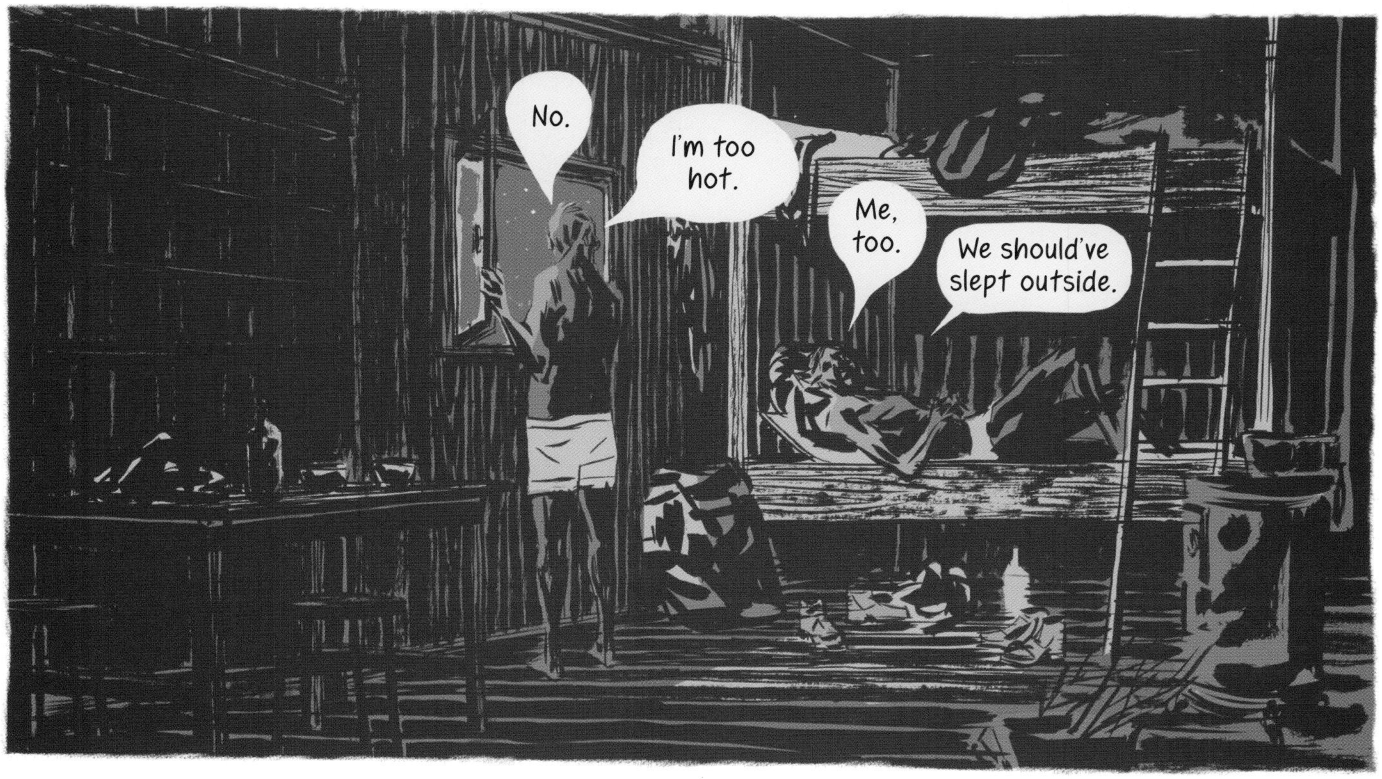
No.
I'm too
hot.
Me,
too.
We should've
slept outside.

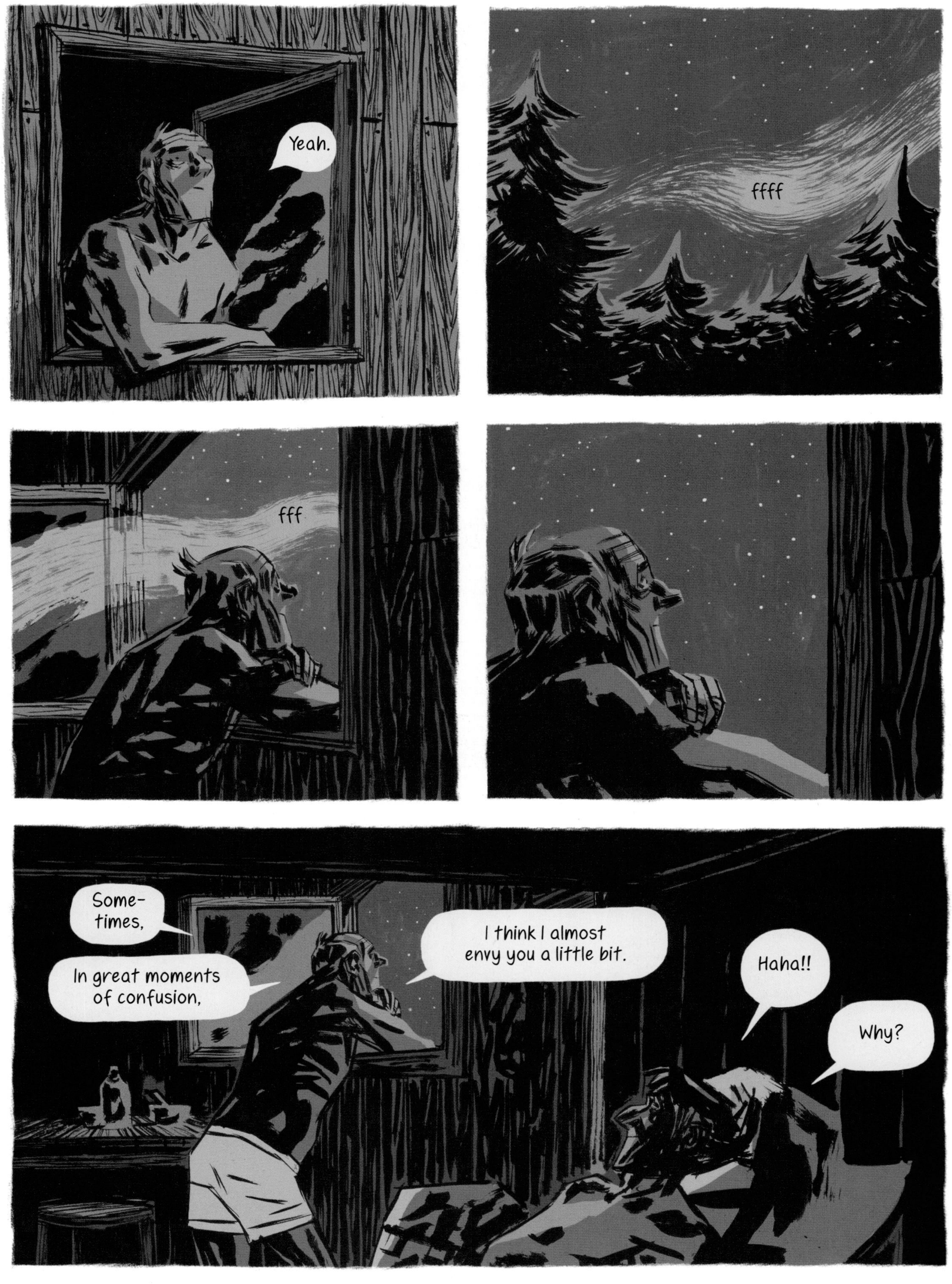
Yeah.
ffff
fff
Some-
times,
In great moments
of confusion,
I think I almost
envy you a little bit.
Haha!!
Why?

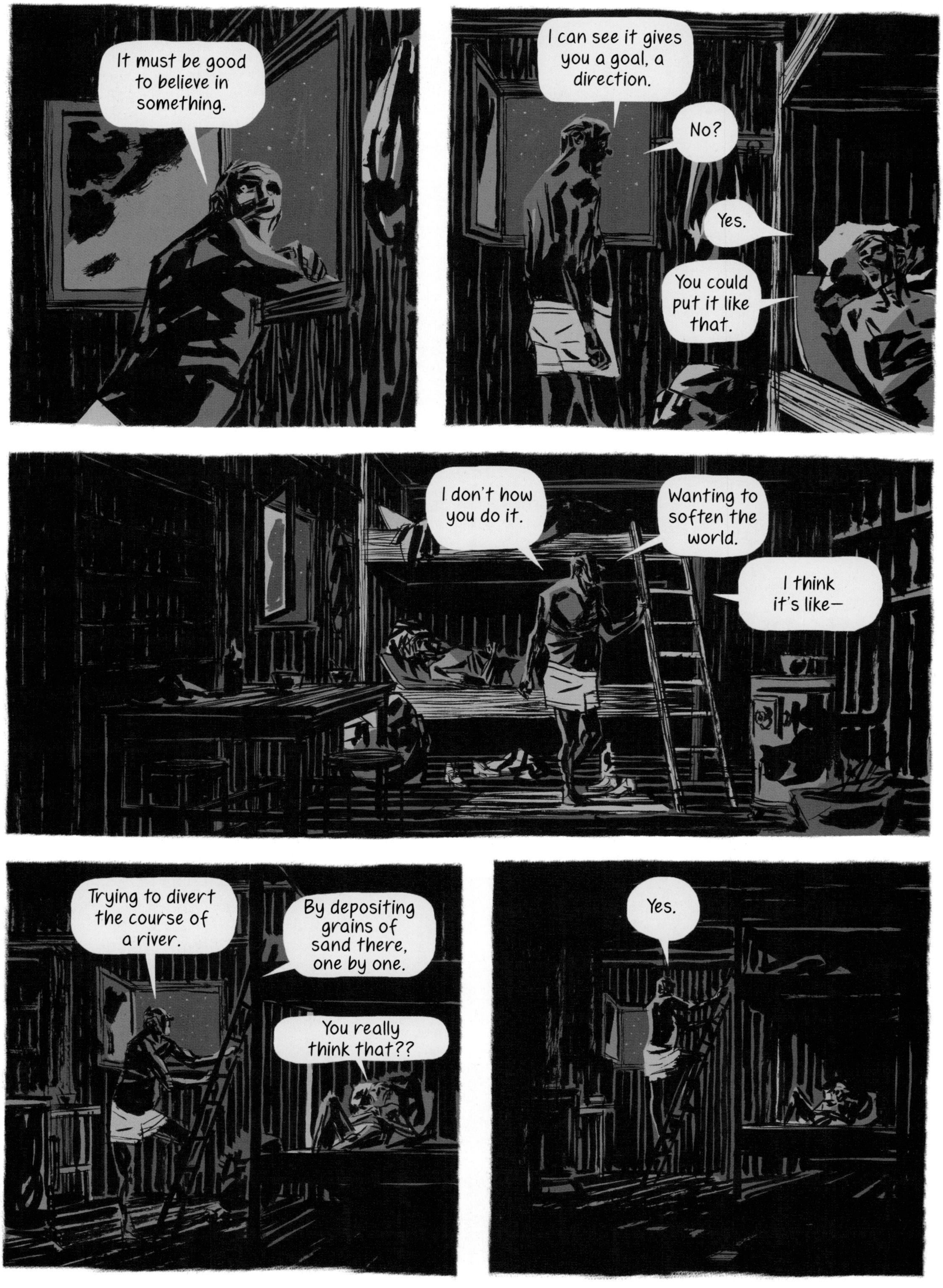
It must be good to believe in something.
I can see it gives you a goal, a direction.
No?
Yes.
You could put it like that.
I don't how you do it.
Wanting to soften the world.
I think it's like—
Trying to divert the course of a river.
By depositing grains of sand there, one by one.
You really think that??
Yes.

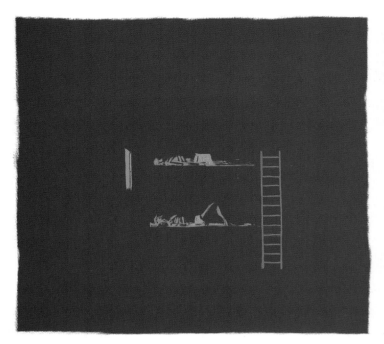

Do you know what Leonard Woolf said, the husband of Virginia?

"The world would be exactly the same if I had spent my life playing Ping-Pong."

Mmm.

If I didn't think the same thing about my own life, I'd find that funny.

Yes, it's nicely put.

But if he'd spent his life playing Ping-Pong, Virginia Woolf, no doubt, wouldn't have ever had the strength to write her novels.

That's not what would have changed the world.

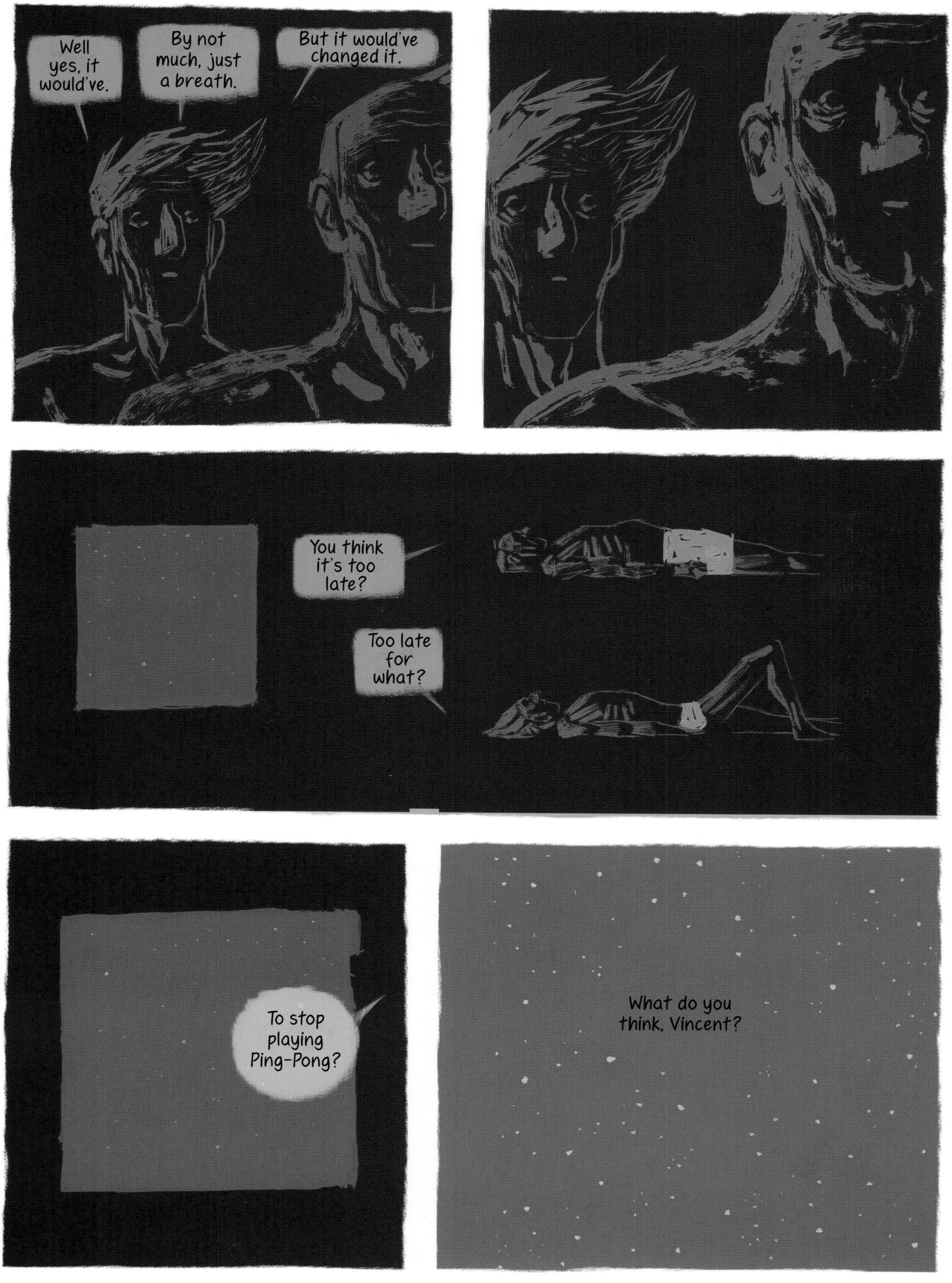
Well yes, it would've.
By not much, just a breath.
But it would've changed it.
You think it's too late?
Too late for what?
To stop playing Ping-Pong?
What do you think, Vincent?

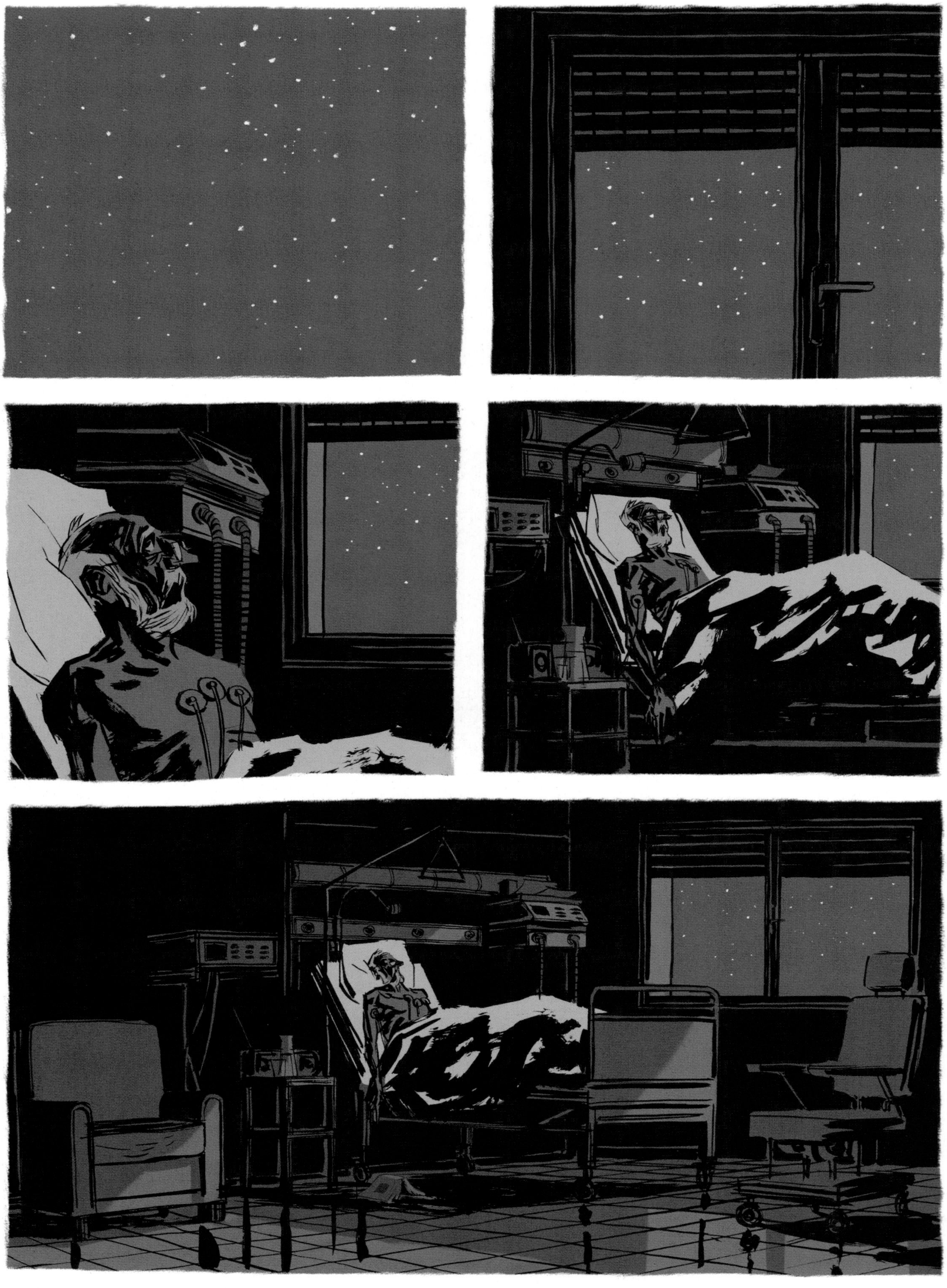

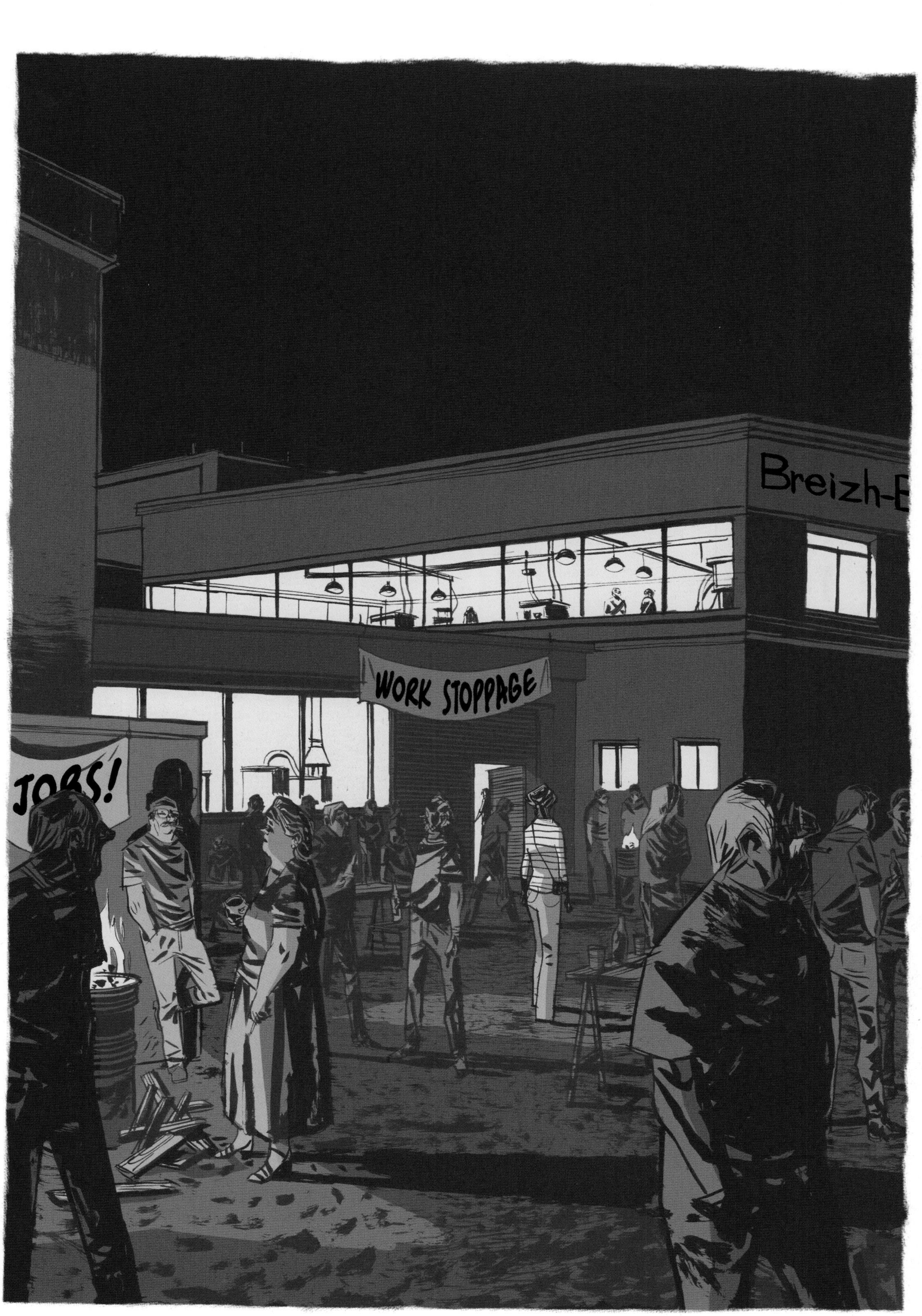
Breizh-B
WORK STOPPAGE
JOBS!

You staying here tonight?
Yeah.
I told Delphine.
I don't know.
Anybody seen the bottle-opener?
Haha!
Hey, Eric...
Aren't you on the dishwashing crew?
No way!
Pff, it's a real mess for work schedules!
Psstt, Catherine!
You wouldn't have a second pillow?
Nope.
So,
How's the press release coming along?
Here.
We're redoing the intro.

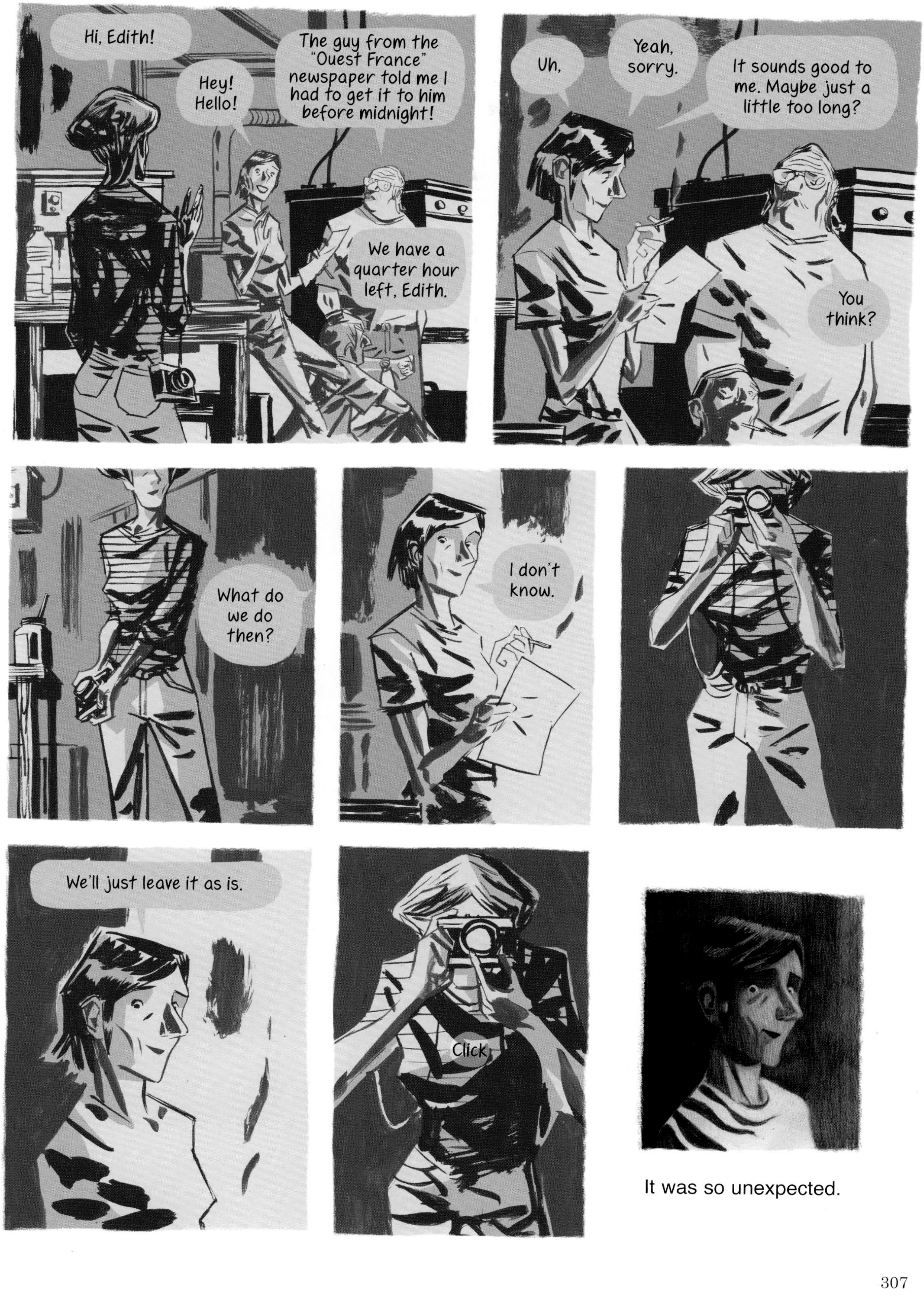
Hi, Edith!
Hey! Hello!
The guy from the "Ouest France" newspaper told me I had to get it to him before midnight!
We have a quarter hour left, Edith.
Uh,
Yeah, sorry.
It sounds good to me. Maybe just a little too long?
You think?
What do we do then?
I don't know.
We'll just leave it as is.
Click
It was so unexpected.

She remembers the sky, blue and cold.

A few muffled notes of music in the courtyard.

The kid on the fourth floor, no doubt.

The morning air, through the half-open window in the living room.

Water's cascading down in the bathroom, then stops.

The door opens quietly, and then Camille's silhouette, naked, backlit in the hallway, the tiredness of the previous nights spent at the factory, the taste of that cigarette, the enveloping radiance of the sun, the regular pulsations of the feeling of love, of sated desire. That interior composition seems to resonate through the city, the apartment block, the little, yellow and white bedroom, a balance of noise and silence.

She'd love to be able to lock away this instant, to preserve it in the herbarium of precious moments. However, she knows, it'll no doubt disappear from her memory one day.

She's loved that girl from the very first. Ever since she saw her arriving at the factory parking lot holding her bicycle with one hand. A camera swinging on her hip.

It all may lead nowhere. But this instant, this morning, seems by itself to give a little sense to her existence. As if this life were finally worth the trouble.

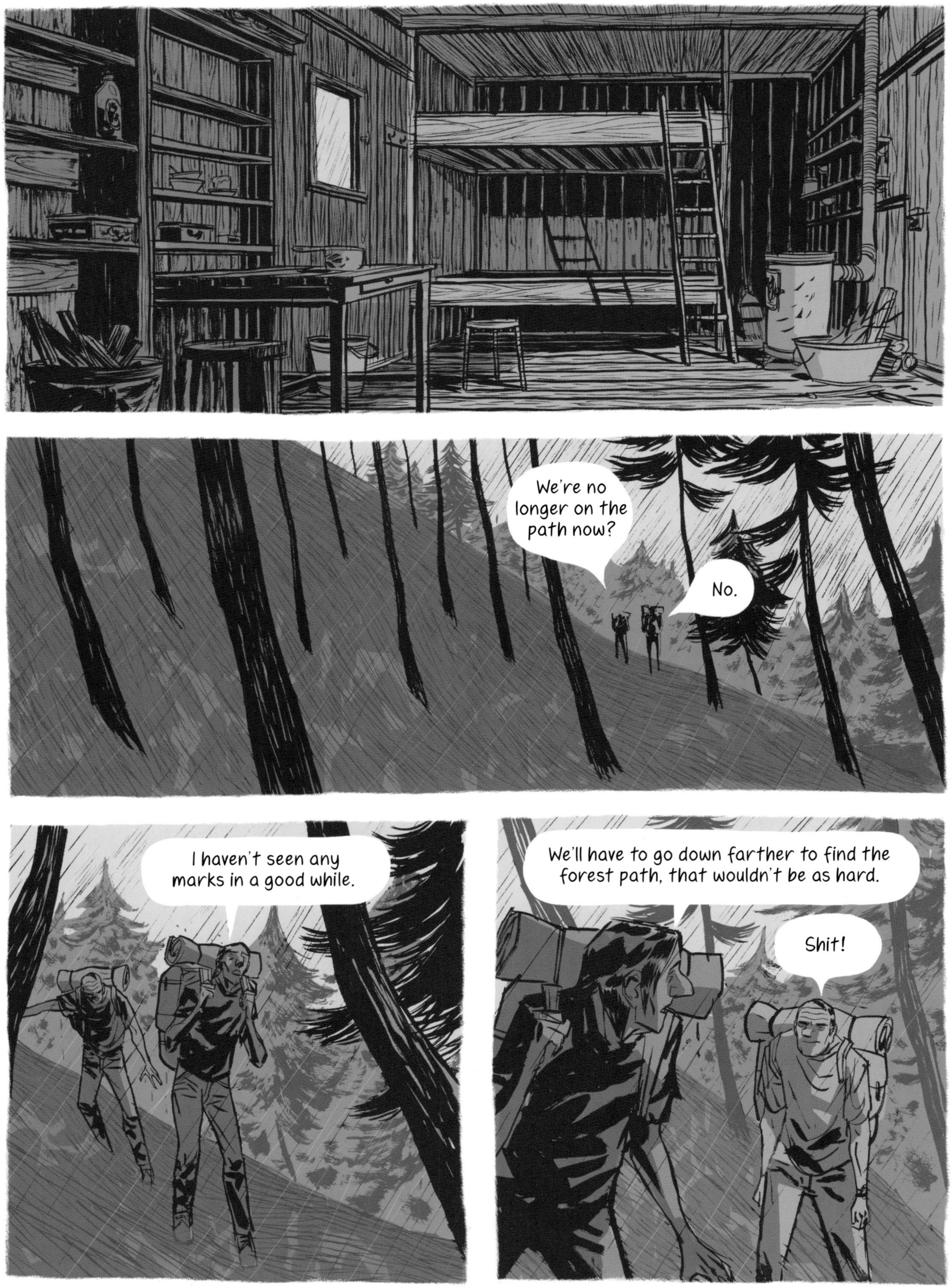
We're no longer on the path now?
No.
I haven't seen any marks in a good while.
We'll have to go down farther to find the forest path, that wouldn't be as hard.
Shit!

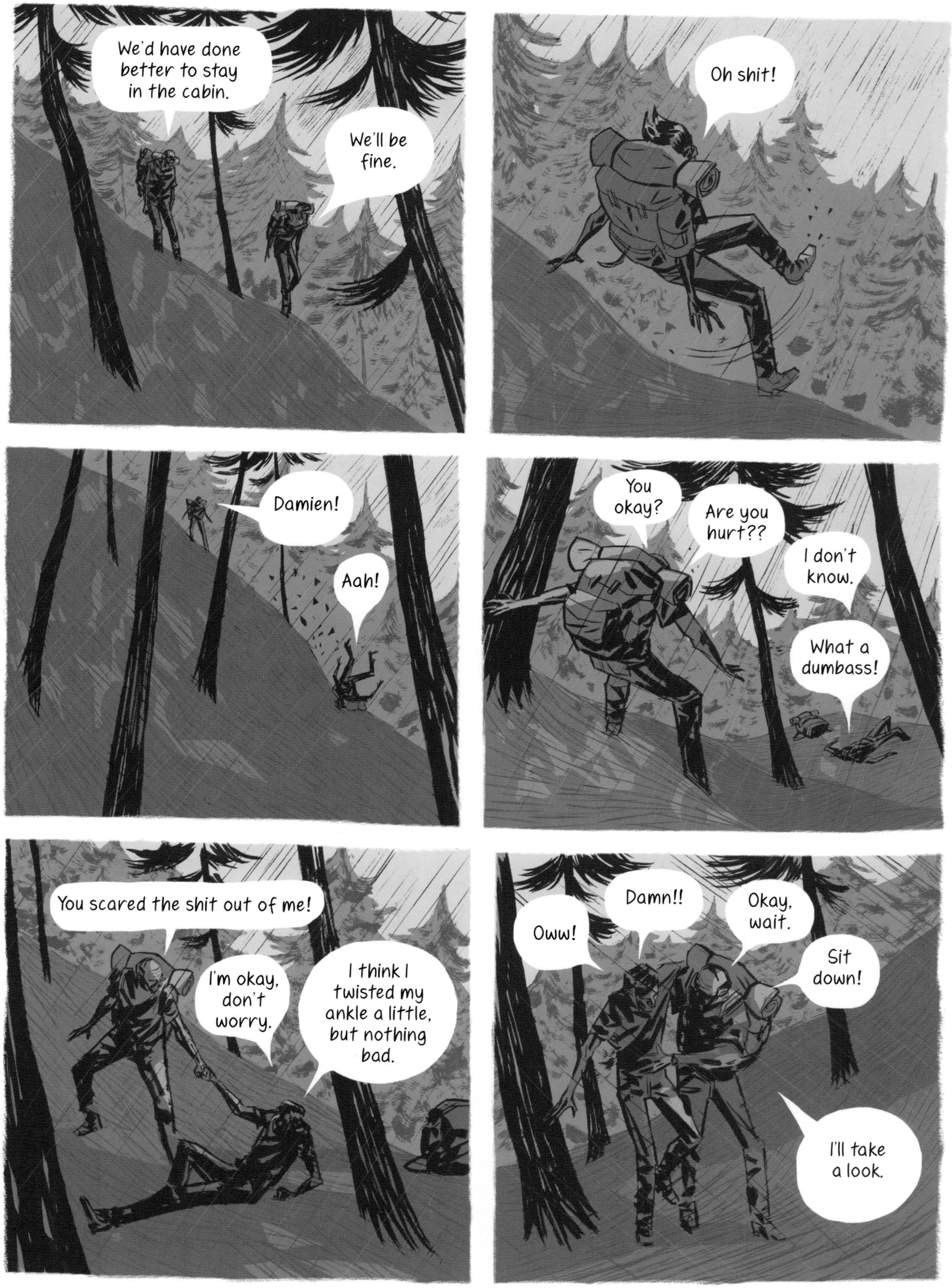
We'd have done better to stay in the cabin.
We'll be fine.
Oh shit!
Damien!
Aah!
You okay?
Are you hurt??
I don't know.
What a dumbass!
You scared the shit out of me!
I'm okay, don't worry.
I think I twisted my ankle a little, but nothing bad.
Oww!
Damn!!
Okay, wait.
Sit down!
I'll take a look.

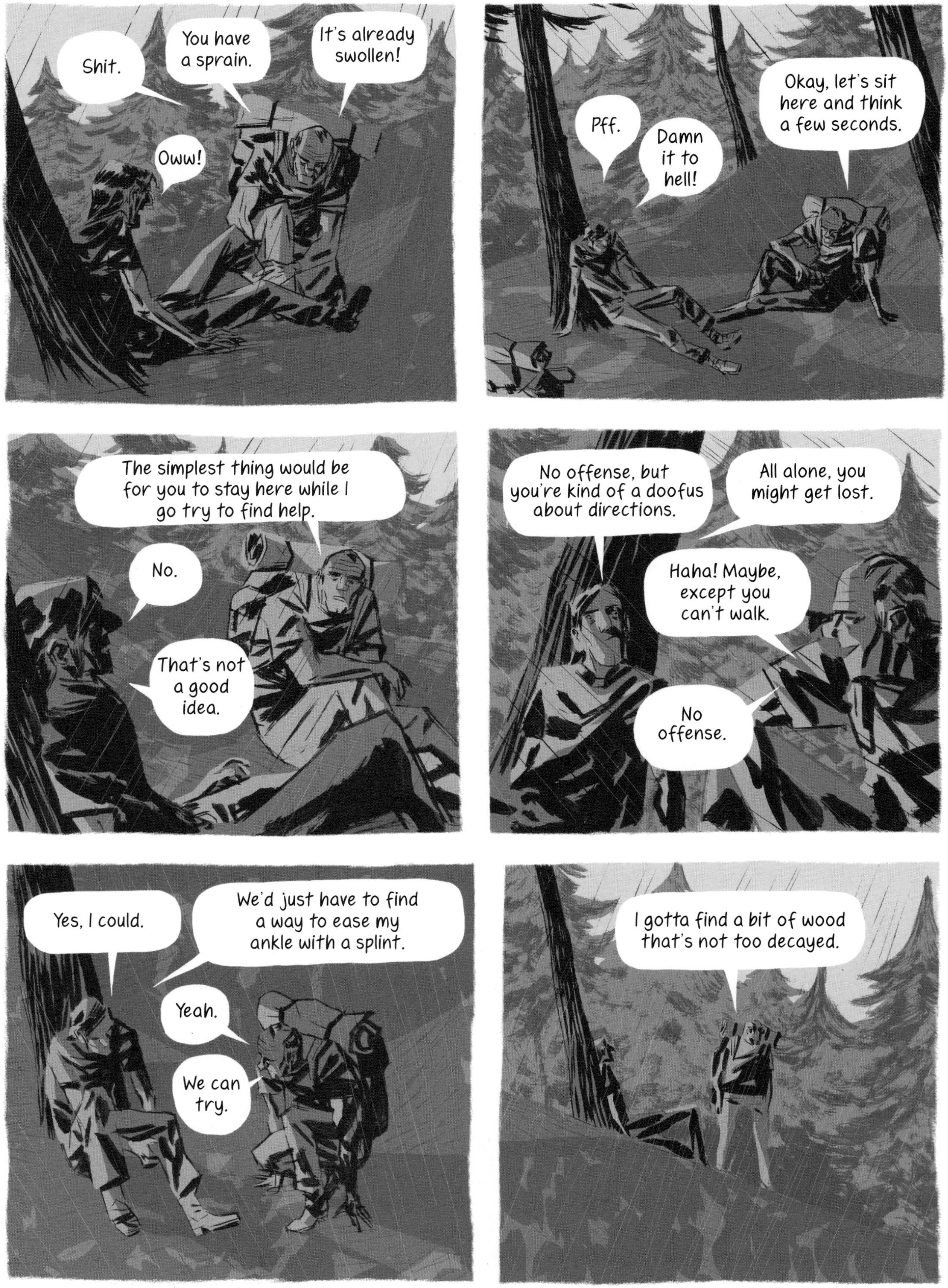
Shit.
You have a sprain.
It's already swollen!
Oww!
Pff.
Damn it to hell!
Okay, let's sit here and think a few seconds.
The simplest thing would be for you to stay here while I go try to find help.
No.
That's not a good idea.
No offense, but you're kind of a doofus about directions.
All alone, you might get lost.
Haha! Maybe, except you can't walk.
No offense.
Yes, I could.
We'd just have to find a way to ease my ankle with a splint.
Yeah.
We can try.
I gotta find a bit of wood that's not too decayed.

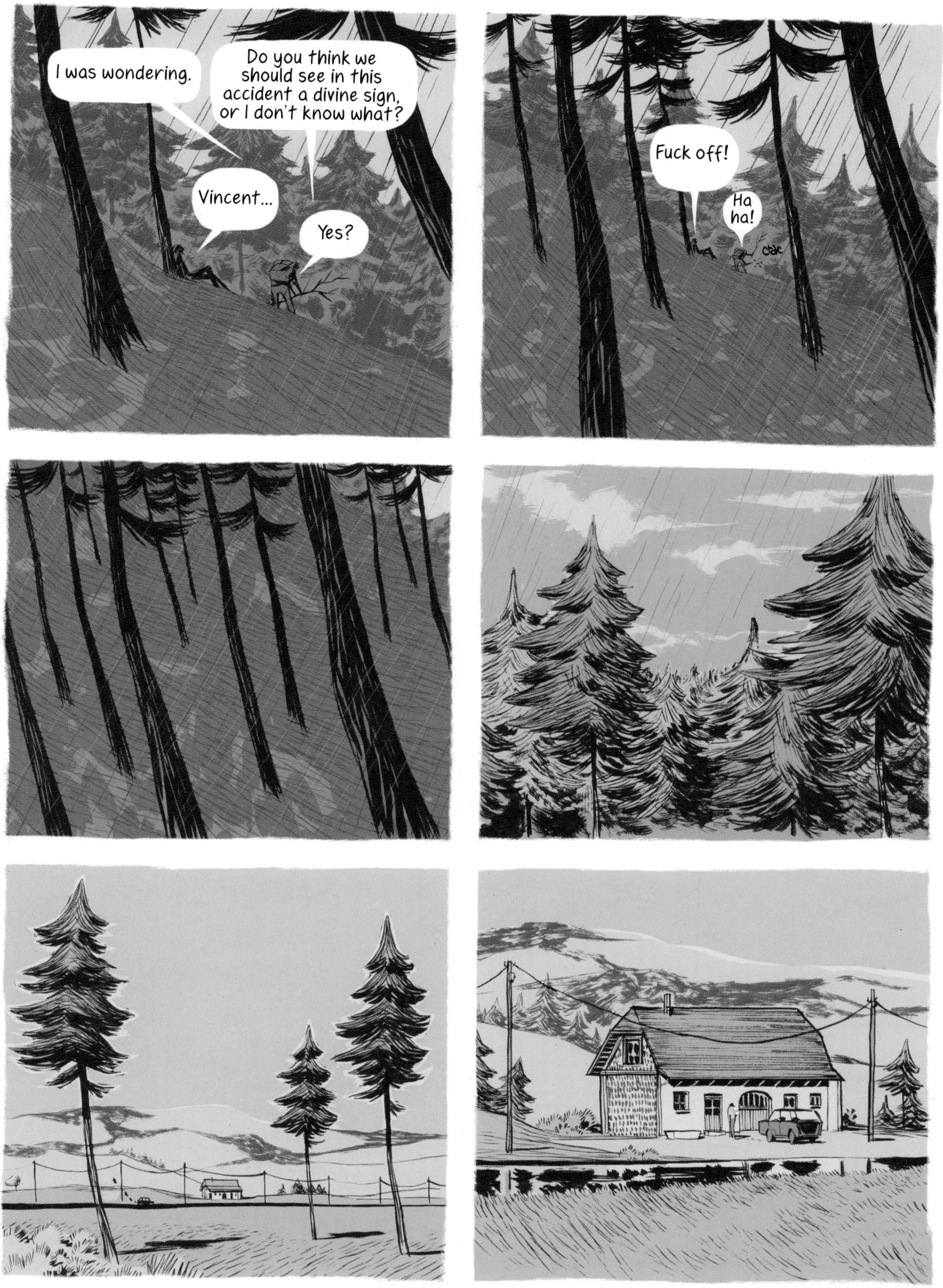
I was wondering.
Do you think we should see in this accident a divine sign, or I don't know what?
Vincent...
Yes?
Fuck off!
Ha ha!
clac

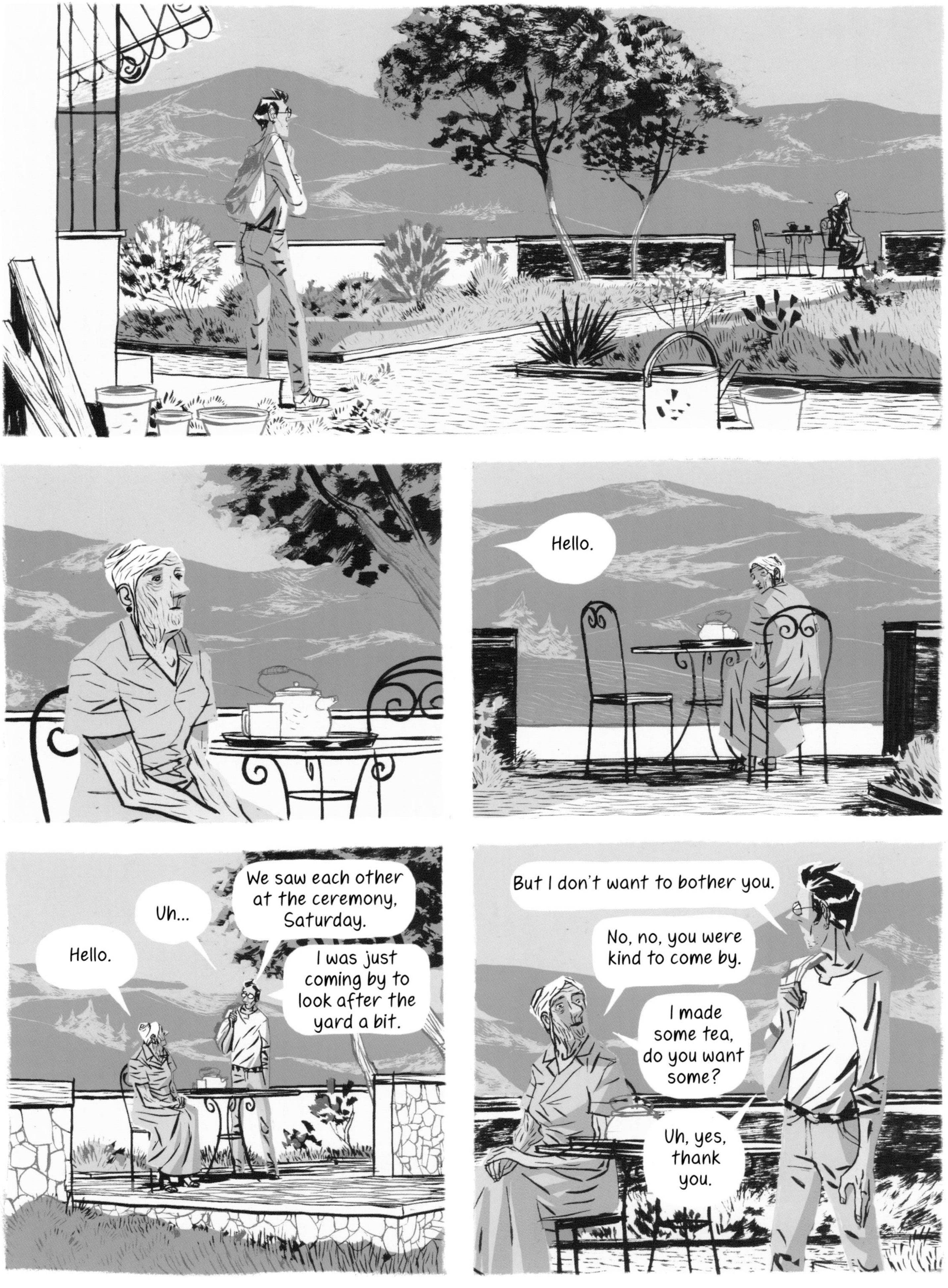
Hello.
Hello.
Uh...
We saw each other at the ceremony, Saturday.
I was just coming by to look after the yard a bit.
But I don't want to bother you.
No, no, you were kind to come by.
I made some tea, do you want some?
Uh, yes, thank you.

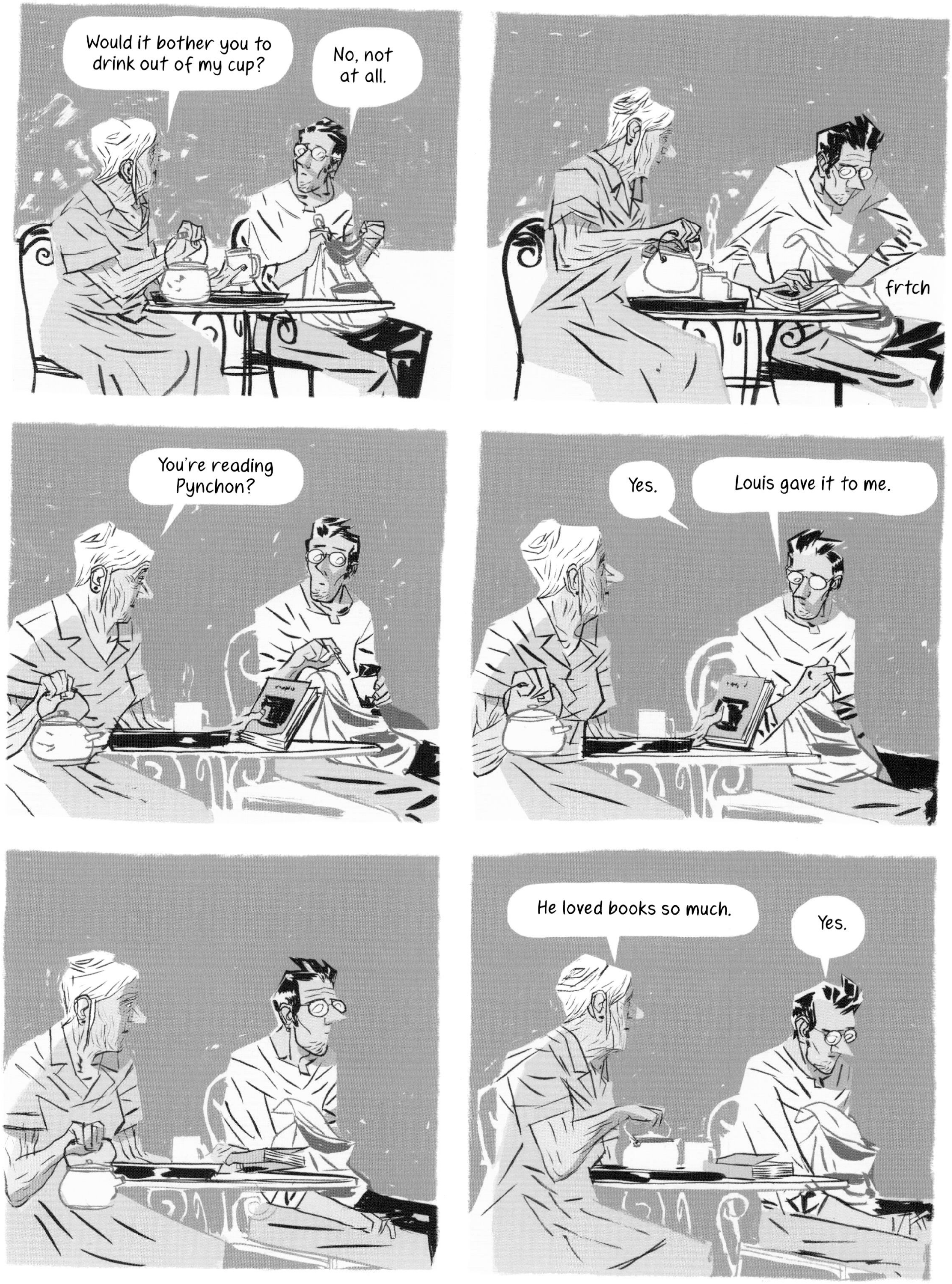
Would it bother you to drink out of my cup?
No, not at all.
frtch
You're reading Pynchon?
Yes.
Louis gave it to me.
He loved books so much.
Yes.

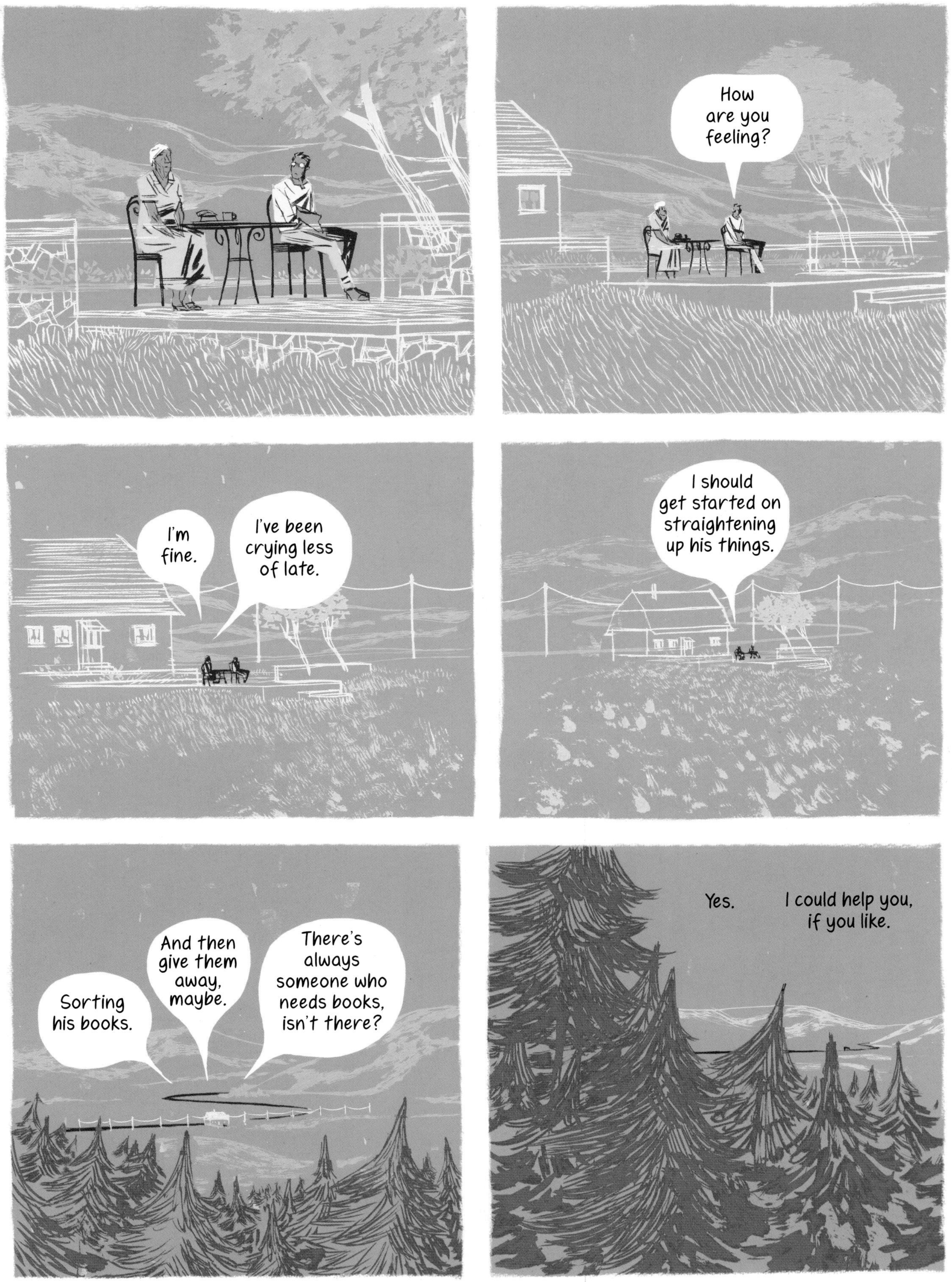
How are you feeling?
I'm fine.
I've been crying less of late.
I should get started on straightening up his things.
Sorting his books.
And then give them away, maybe.
There's always someone who needs books, isn't there?
Yes.
I could help you, if you like.

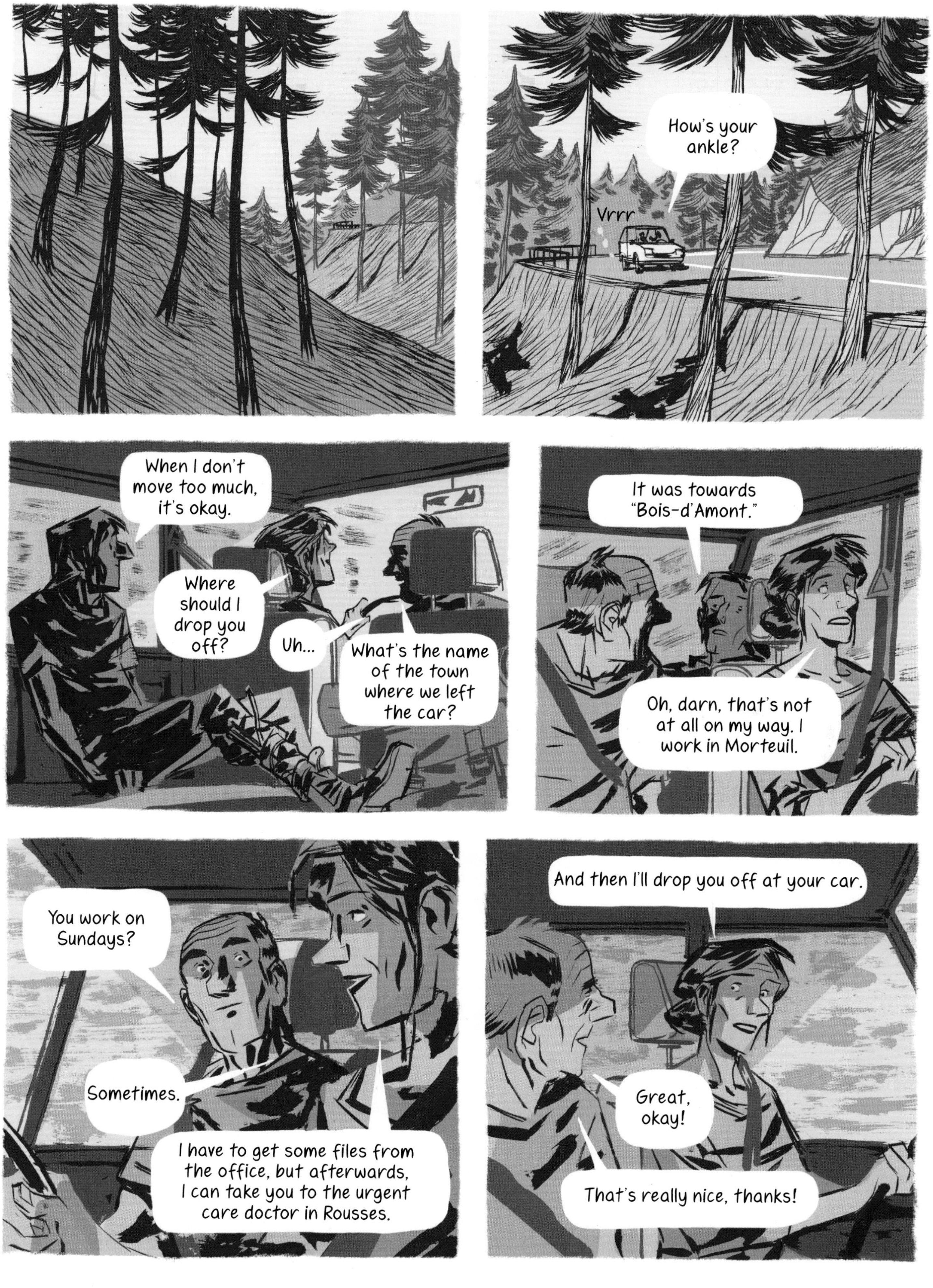
How's your ankle?
Vrrr
When I don't move too much, it's okay.
Where should I drop you off?
Uh...
What's the name of the town where we left the car?
It was towards "Bois-d'Amont."
Oh, darn, that's not at all on my way. I work in Morteuil.
You work on Sundays?
Sometimes.
I have to get some files from the office, but afterwards, I can take you to the urgent care doctor in Rousses.
And then I'll drop you off at your car.
Great, okay!
That's really nice, thanks!

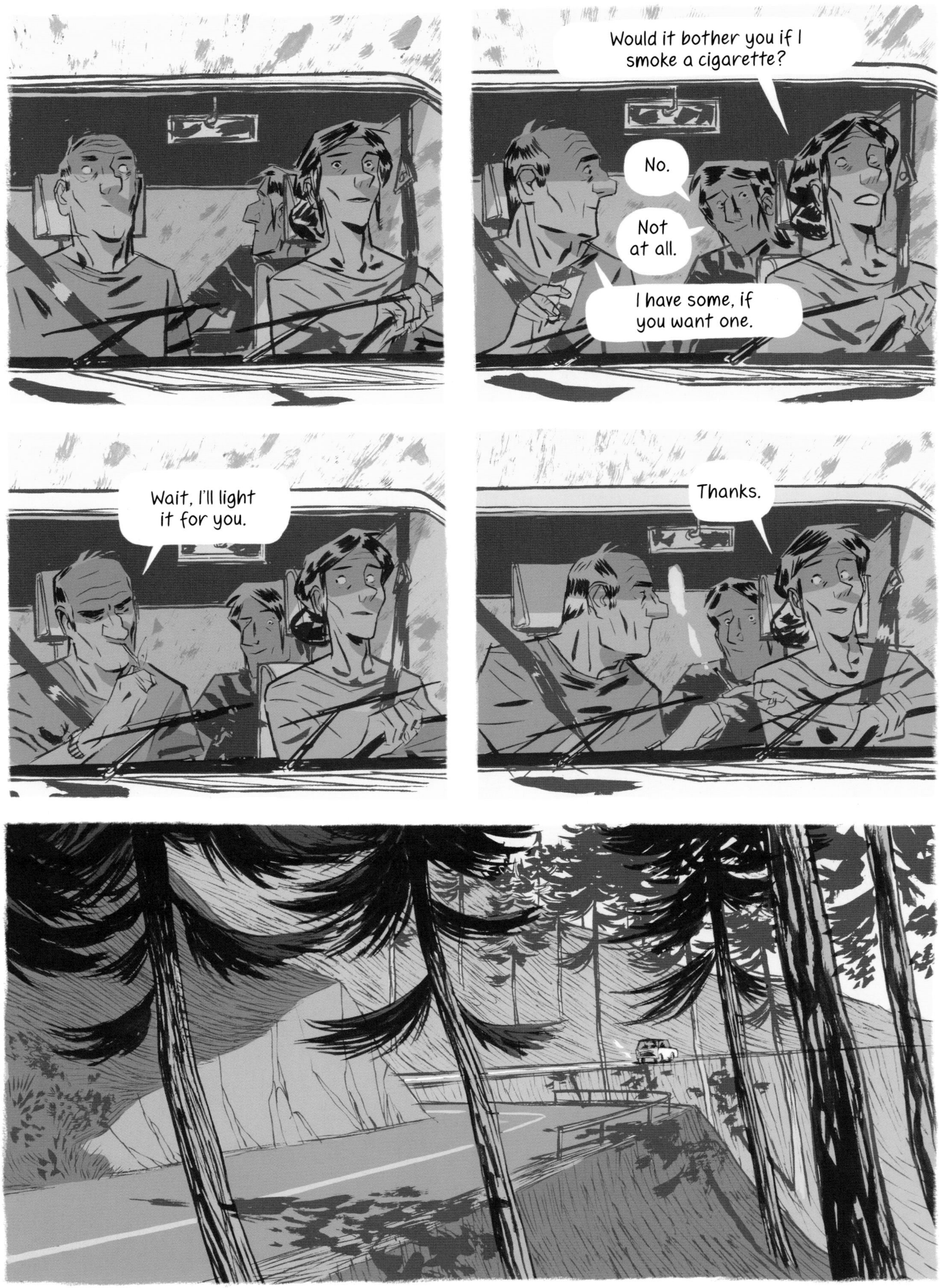
Would it bother you if I smoke a cigarette?
No.
Not at all.
I have some, if you want one.
Wait, I'll light it for you.
Thanks.

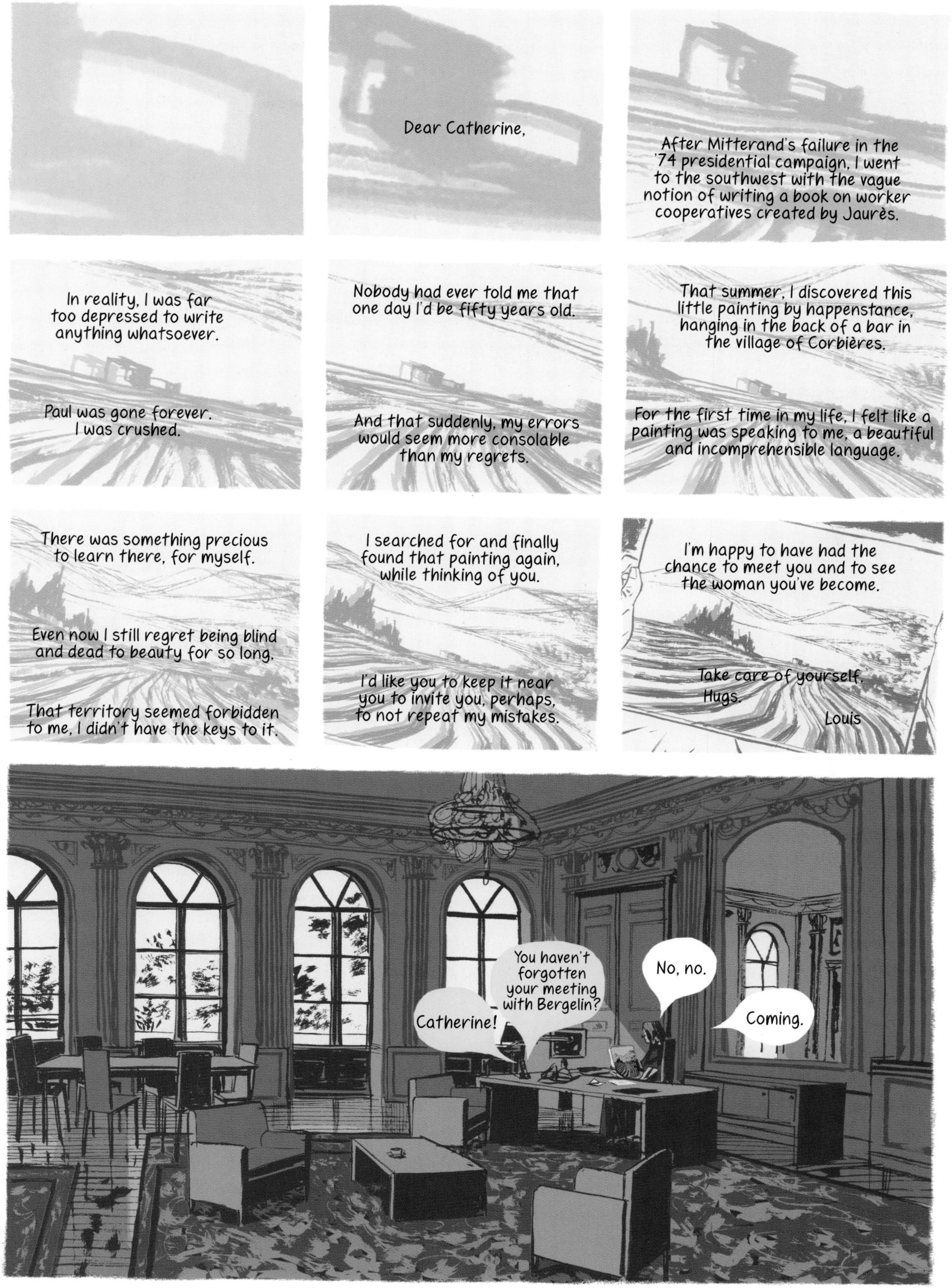
Dear Catherine,
After Mitterand's failure in the '74 presidential campaign, I went to the southwest with the vague notion of writing a book on worker cooperatives created by Jaurès.
In reality, I was far too depressed to write anything whatsoever.
Paul was gone forever. I was crushed.
Nobody had ever told me that one day I'd be fifty years old.
And that suddenly, my errors would seem more consolable than my regrets.
That summer, I discovered this little painting by happenstance, hanging in the back of a bar in the village of Corbières.
For the first time in my life, I felt like a painting was speaking to me, a beautiful and incomprehensible language.
There was something precious to learn there, for myself.
Even now I still regret being blind and dead to beauty for so long.
That territory seemed forbidden to me, I didn't have the keys to it.
I searched for and finally found that painting again, while thinking of you.
I'd like you to keep it near you to invite you, perhaps, to not repeat my mistakes.
I'm happy to have had the chance to meet you and to see the woman you've become.
Take care of yourself.
Hugs.
Louis
Catherine!
You haven't forgotten your meeting with Bergelin?
No, no.
Coming.

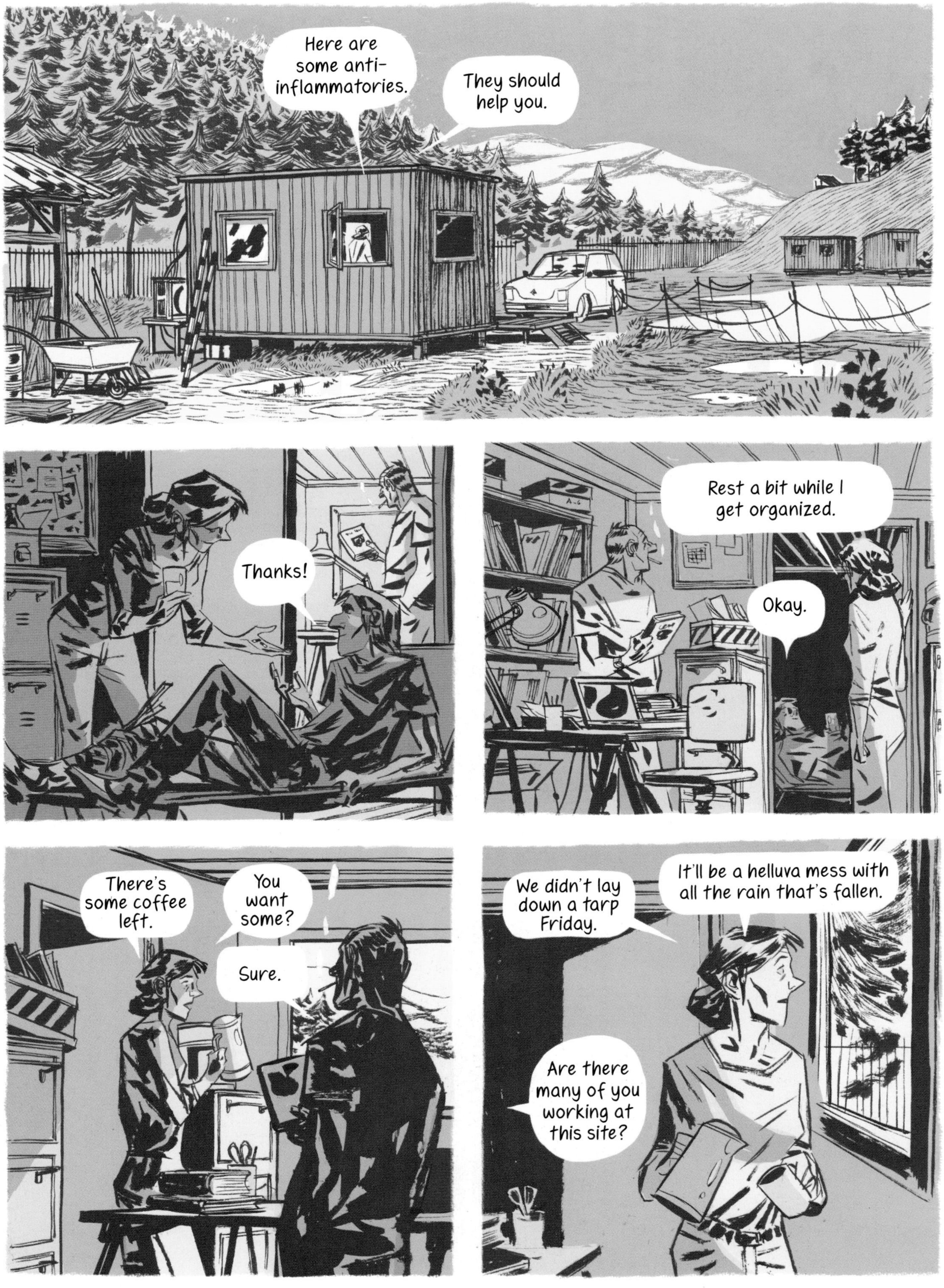
Here are some anti-inflammatories.
They should help you.
Thanks!
Rest a bit while I get organized.
Okay.
There's some coffee left.
You want some?
Sure.
We didn't lay down a tarp Friday.
It'll be a helluva mess with all the rain that's fallen.
Are there many of you working at this site?

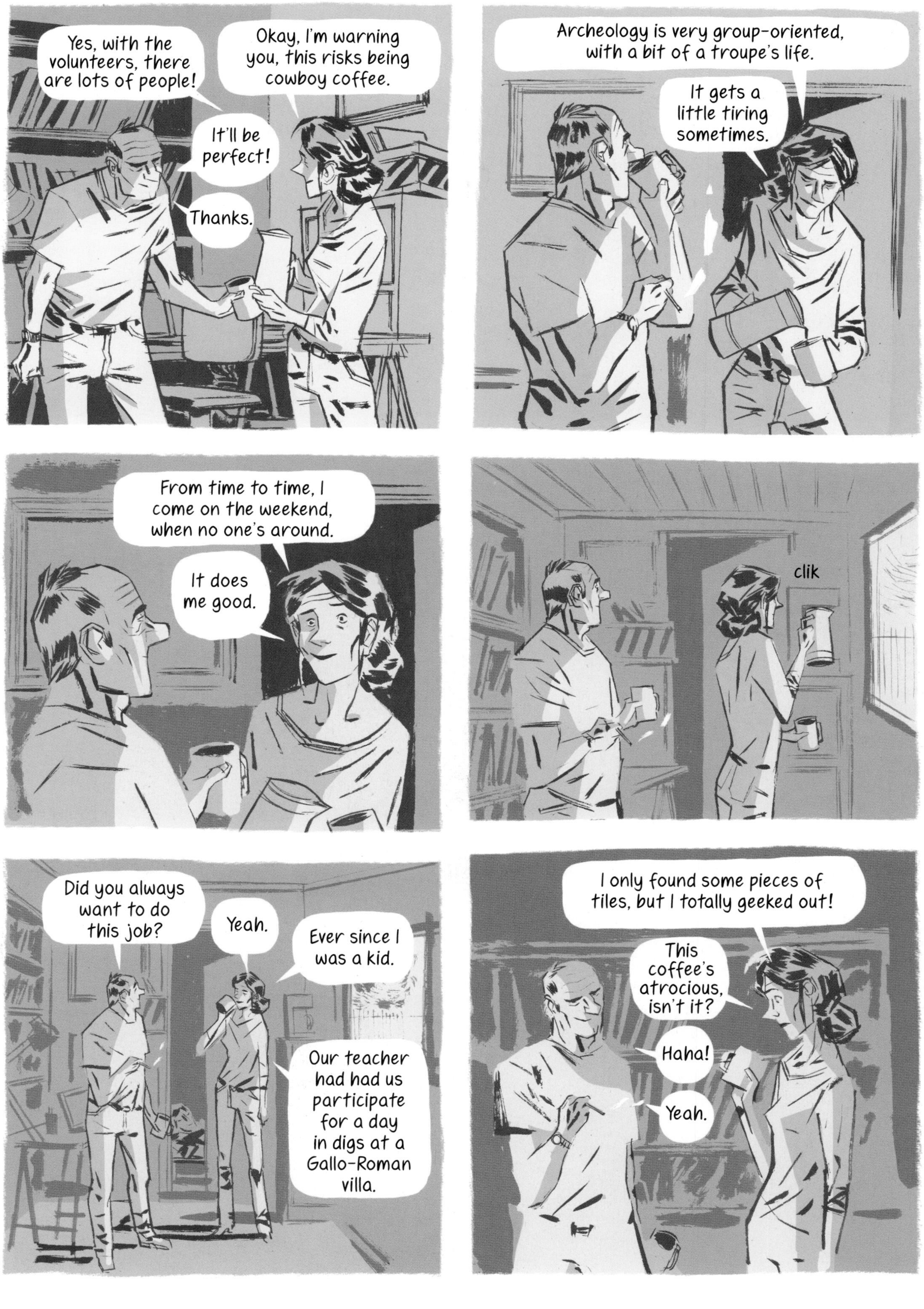
Yes, with the volunteers, there are lots of people!
Okay, I'm warning you, this risks being cowboy coffee.
It'll be perfect!
Thanks.
Archeology is very group-oriented, with a bit of a troupe's life.
It gets a little tiring sometimes.
From time to time, I come on the weekend, when no one's around.
It does me good.
clik
Did you always want to do this job?
Yeah.
Ever since I was a kid.
Our teacher had had us participate for a day in digs at a Gallo-Roman villa.
I only found some pieces of tiles, but I totally geeked out!
This coffee's atrocious, isn't it?
Haha!
Yeah.

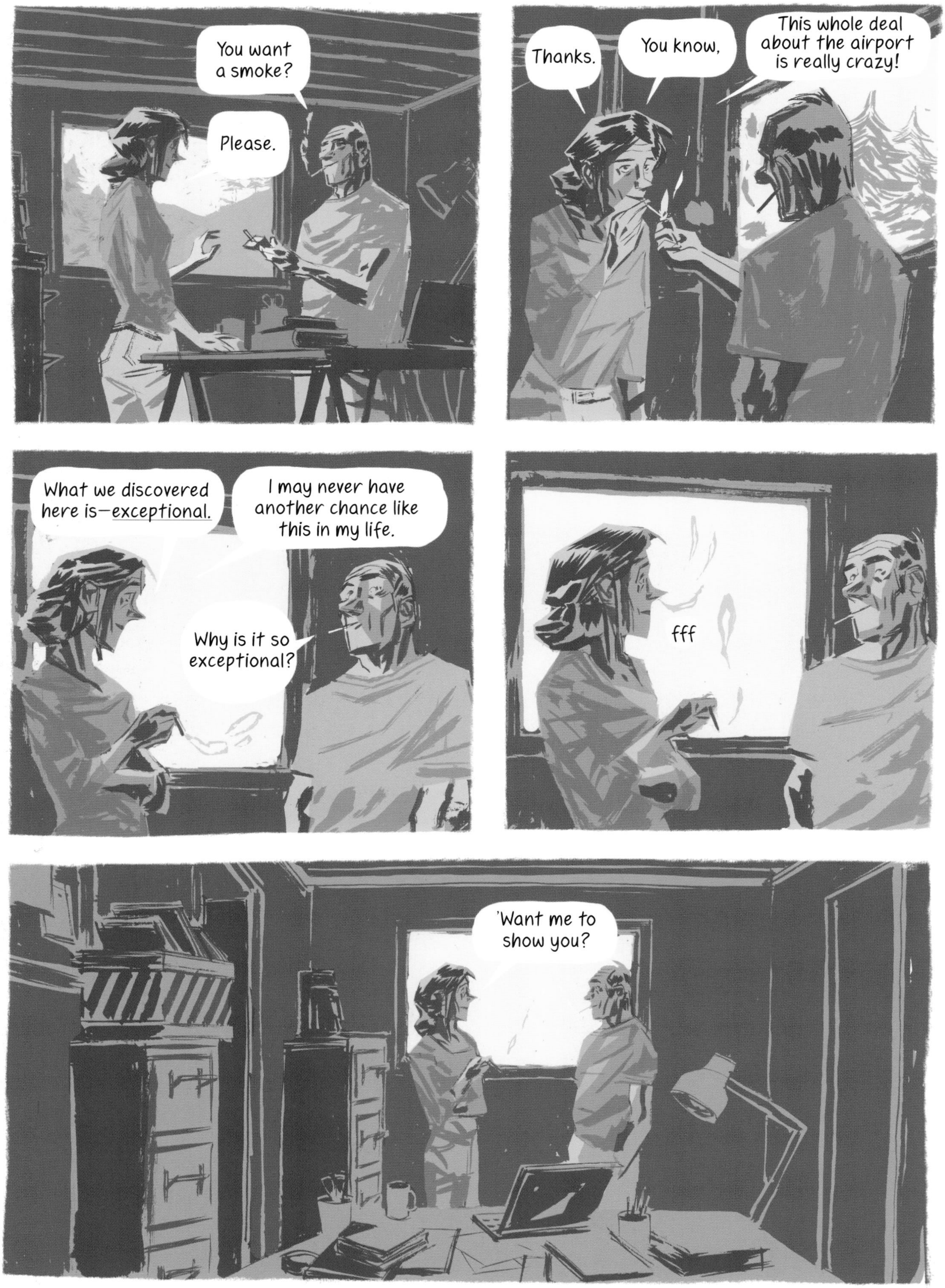
You want a smoke?
Please.
Thanks.
You know,
This whole deal about the airport is really crazy!
What we discovered here is—exceptional.
I may never have another chance like this in my life.
Why is it so exceptional?
fff
'Want me to show you?

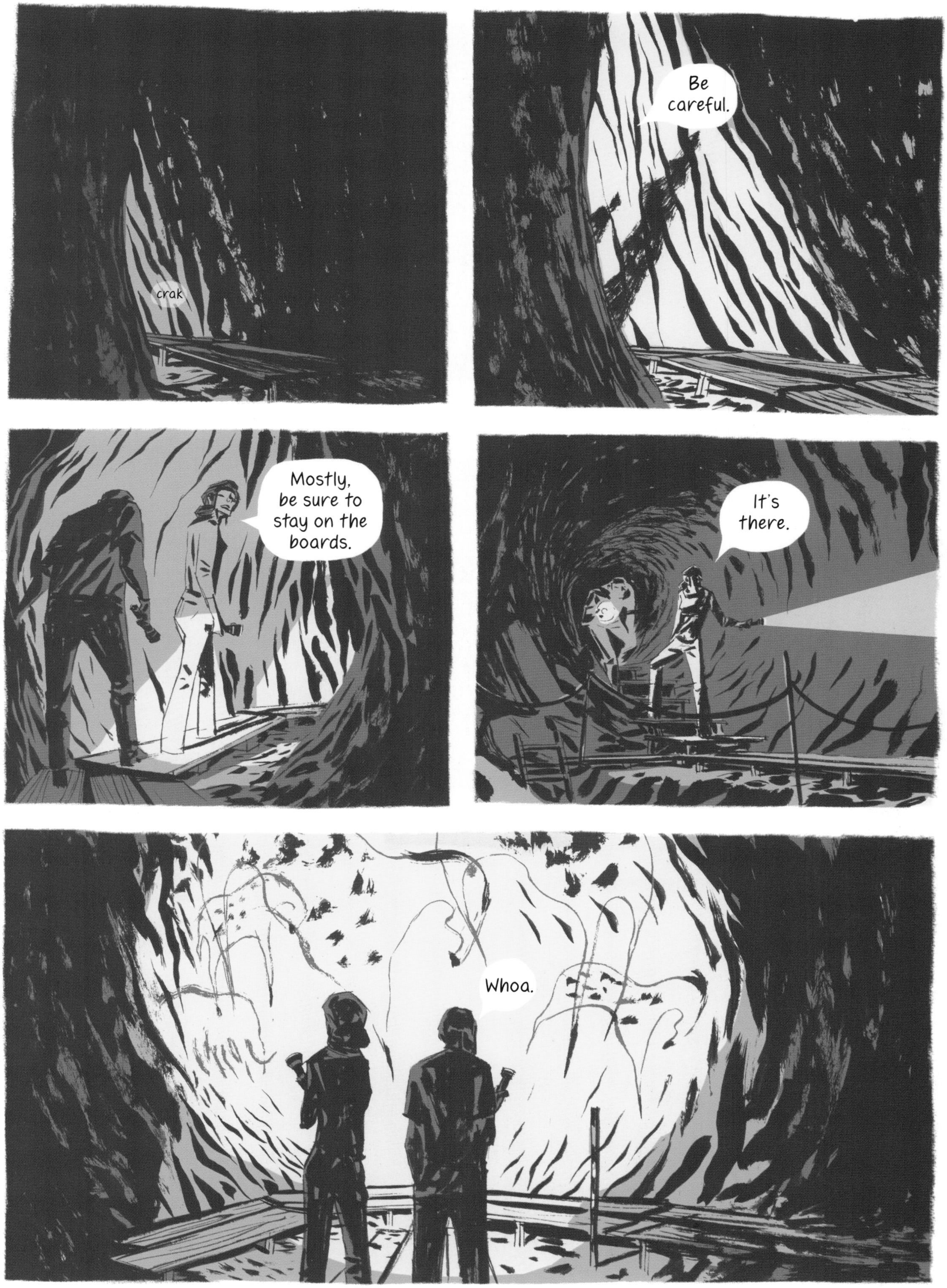
crak
Be careful.
Mostly, be sure to stay on the boards.
It's there.
Whoa.

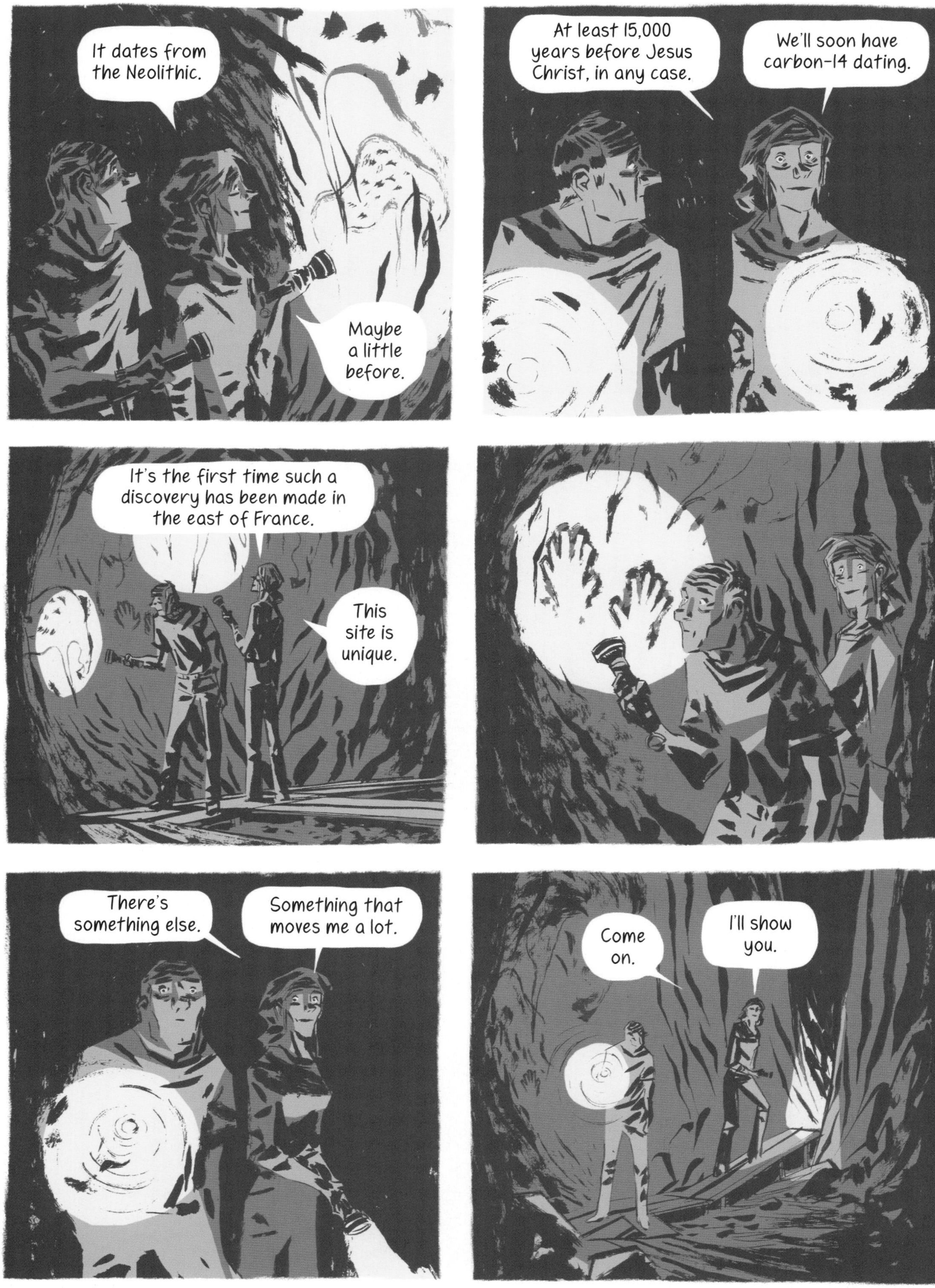
It dates from the Neolithic.
Maybe a little before.
At least 15,000 years before Jesus Christ, in any case.
We'll soon have carbon-14 dating.
It's the first time such a discovery has been made in the east of France.
This site is unique.
There's something else.
Something that moves me a lot.
Come on.
I'll show you.

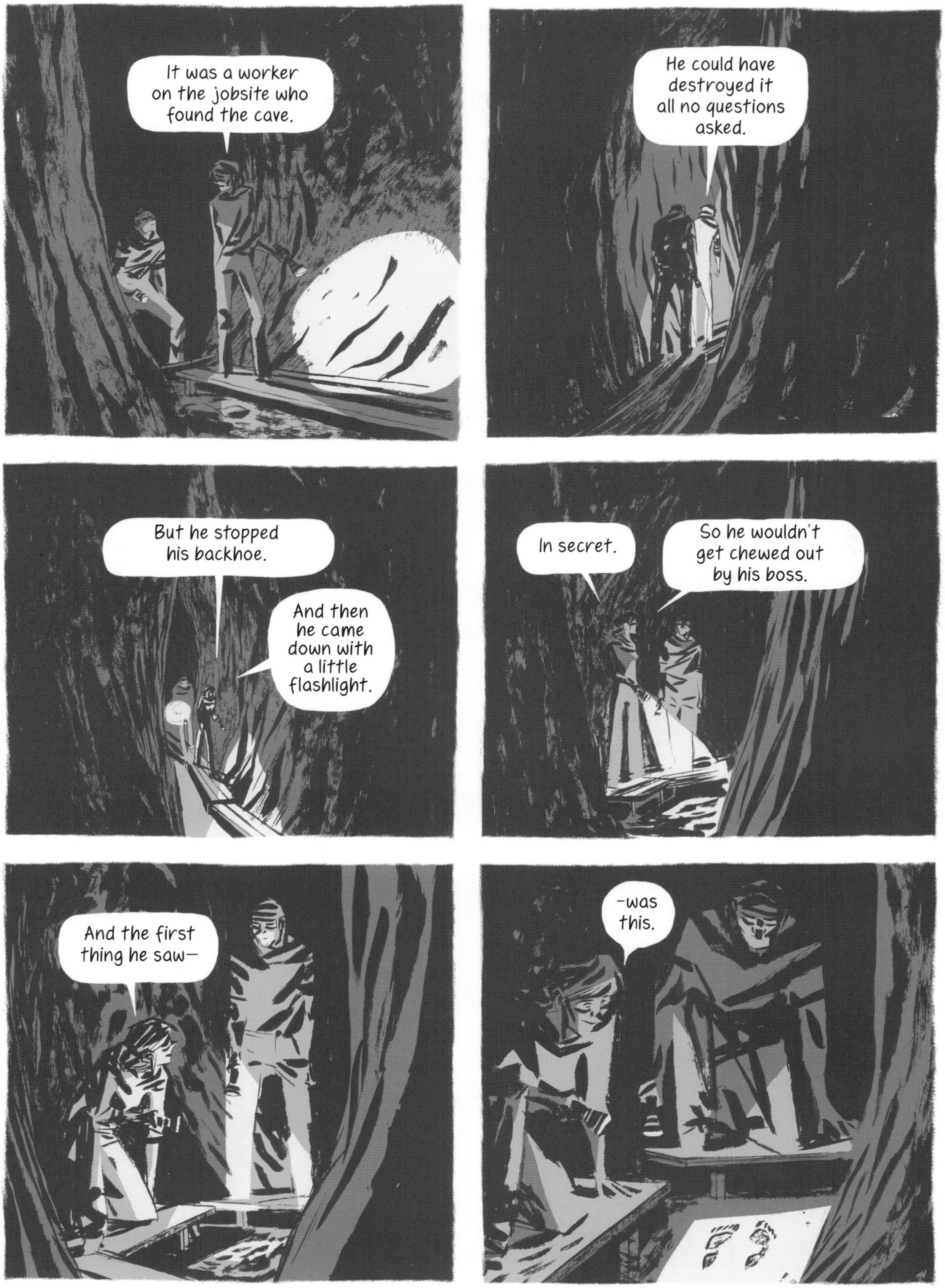
It was a worker on the jobsite who found the cave.
He could have destroyed it all no questions asked.
But he stopped his backhoe.
And then he came down with a little flashlight.
In secret.
So he wouldn't get chewed out by his boss.
And the first thing he saw—
-was this.

What's your name?
Garance.
Paul CAMELIN
5 décembre 1951
23 mars 1963
Louis CAMELIN
4 avril 1925
27 juin 2001

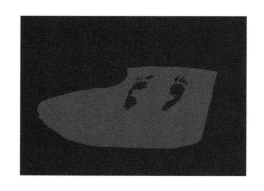

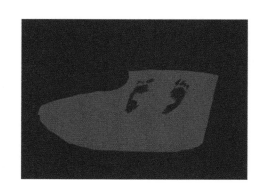

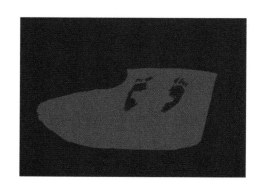

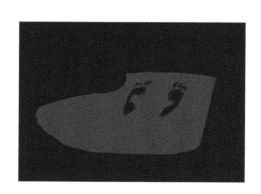

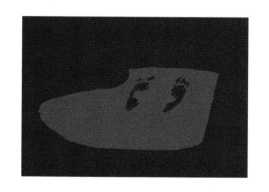

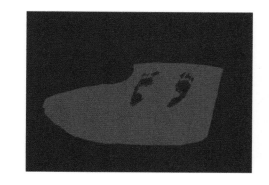

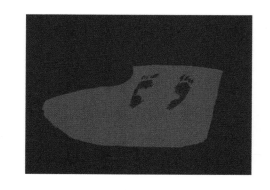

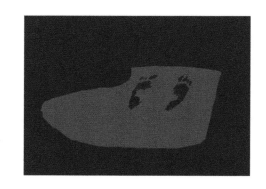

beep
deep
beep
cling!

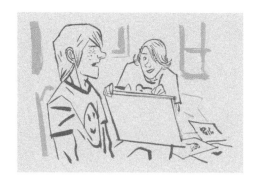

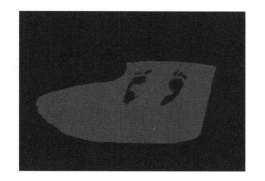

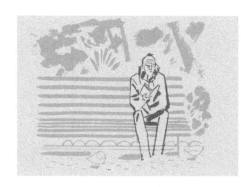

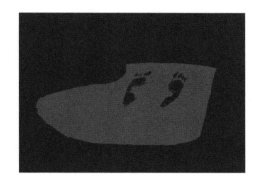

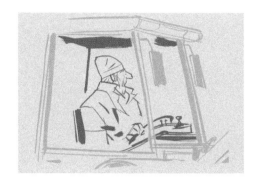

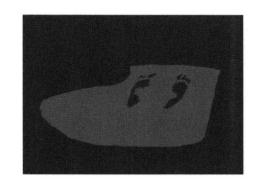

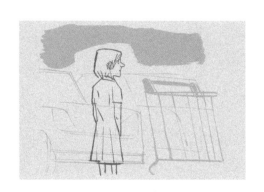

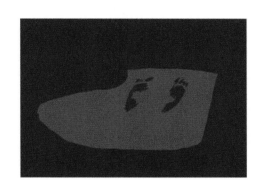

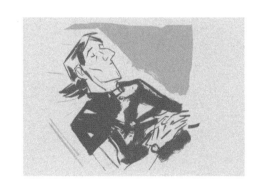

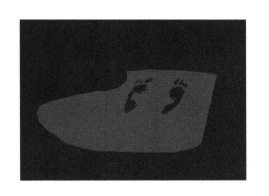

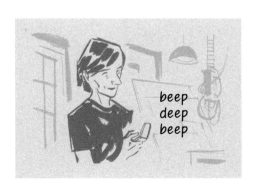

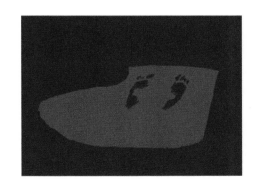

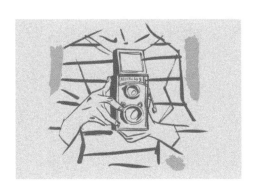

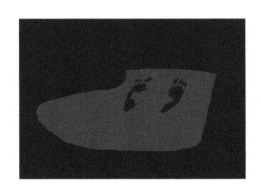

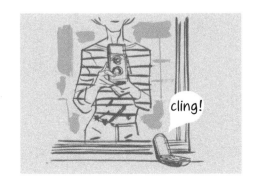

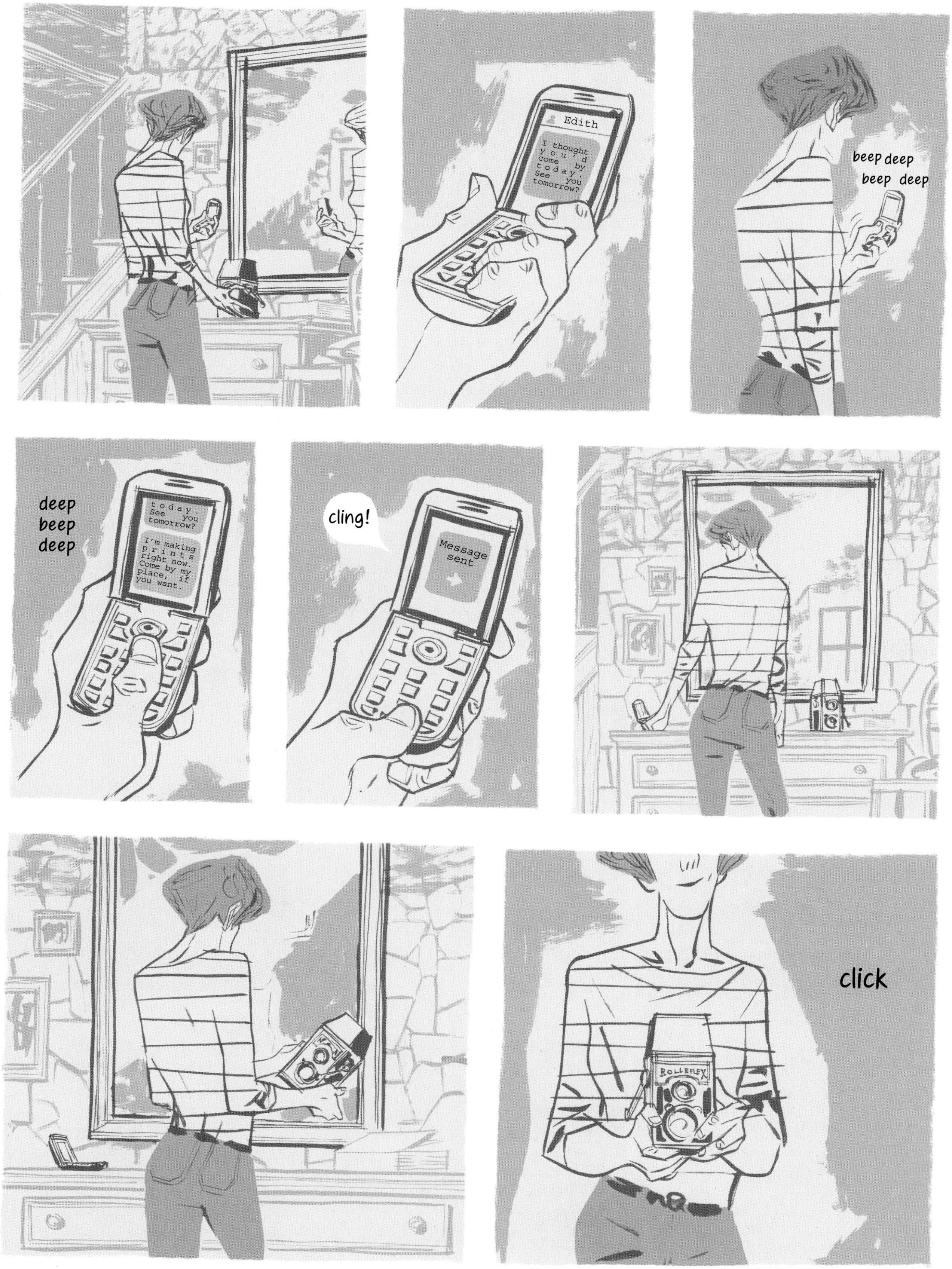
Edith
I thought you'd come by today. See you tomorrow?
beep deep
beep deep
deep
beep
deep
today. See you tomorrow?
I'm making prints right now. Come by my place, if you want.
cling!
Message sent
click

She really had promised herself.

To remain alone. To not depend on anyone. Ever. Loving is promising, promising is lying and a lot more words yet, piled one on top of the other. Like the scales of armor put on for a battle which, for the first time, she doubted was worth the bother to fight.

For three months, she'd been living on the periphery of their battles. The occupied factory. The protests in front of the prefecture. The joint union meetings. The endless nights discussing hopes and fears. She watched them. And it's no doubt the only place she can hold.
Taking pictures to try to seize that little slice of human truth, a singular one, yet which animates us all. Capturing it with precision and prudence. Quietly, at the tips of her fingers. Showing it. Giving it its due importance, that of a derisory but necessary atom among the infinity of particles in motion, all of them indispensable to one another. She didn't undertake this work for Edith, to seduce or console her. But she would've never undertaken it with this quiet resolution had nothing happened between them.

She mentally draws the improbable path she'd traveled to their meeting, to find a logic there. In vain. In fact, her defenses had no chance of holding out, because the assault was unforeseeable. It was useless to continue to pretend to struggle.
Tomorrow, in six months, a year, or a day, that urge will peter out. She's not deluding herself. But it has no importance. There's something to share, now.

She looks at the images already taken, hundreds of images.
She'll have to make a choice.
Build, advance, make a mistake, and start over. Try to make something of each of these instances preserved like a line in the earth.

A sign, a path, maybe, for someone, one day, later.

Born November 22, 1972 in Poitiers (Vienne). A big comic reader during childhood and adolescence, Cyril Pedrosa first went into scientific studies. After some trial and error, he finally studied animation design at the Gobelins, a Parisian establishment dedicated to careers in the moving image. He went on to work on Disney animated feature films such as "The Hunchback of Notre Dame" and "Hercules" where he acquired a speed of execution and a sense of movement that will later serve him well. Meeting writer David Chauvel inspired him to turn to comics. A rising star in graphic storytelling, his unique work is a product of his animation background combined with his literary influences of Borges, Marquez and Tolkien. His moving journal of going back to his family roots, "Portugal," is a bestseller. The reception for 'Equinoxes' is equally strong.

The devil is in the details.
Thanks to Philippe Ghielmetti for his invaluable and precise help in the layout of this book.
For his wise gaze, his demanding re-reads, and his unfailing support, a huge thanks to José-Louis Bocquet.
It's impossible here to describe that impetus, but without Roxanne, this book simply wouldn't exist.
Cyril Pedrosa

If you liked this you may also like from NBM Graphic Novels:

Guardians of the Louvre by Jiro Taniguchi
Feverish artist sees his favorite painters in the flesh from within the galleries of the Louvre. In the Louvre collection inviting artists to do a story around the museum.

Girl in Dior by Annie Goetzinger
Cub fashion reporter becomes leading model for Dior as he launches his house in this beautiful biography of the famous couturier.

Fires Above Hyperion by Patrick Atangan
Wry stories of the LA gay dating scene.

See previews, get exclusives and order from:
NBMPUB.COM

we have over 200 titles available
Catalog upon request
NBM Graphic Novels
160 Broadway, Suite 700, East Wing,
New York, NY 10038

This graphic novel is also available as an e-book

JIRO TANIGUCHI
GUARDIANS OF THE LOUVRE
nbm
LOUVRE éditions

Annie Goetzinger
Girl in
Dior

Fires Above Hyperion
PATRICK ATANGAN
ONE DAY I WOKE UP AND REALIZED I HAD BEEN DATING FOR TWENTY YEARS. TWENTY YEARS. IT'S HARD TO IMAGINE ANYONE WITH AS LITTLE RESOLVE AS I HAVE DOING ANYTHING FOR SO LONG.

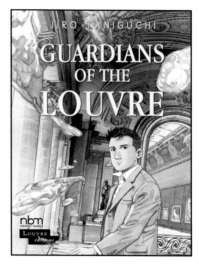